NOSTROMO

JOSEPH CONRAD was born Józef Teodor Konrad Korzeniowski in the Russian part of Poland in 1857. His parents were punished by the Russians for their Polish nationalist activities and both died while Conrad was still a child. In 1874 he left Poland for France and in 1878 began a career with the British merchant navy. He spent nearly twenty years as a sailor and did not begin writing novels until he was approaching forty. He became a British citizen in 1886 and settled permanently in England after his marriage to Jessie George in 1896.

Conrad is a writer of extreme subtlety and sophistication; works such as *Heart of Darkness*, *Lord Jim*, and *Nostromo* display technical complexities which have established Conrad as one of the first English 'Modernists'. He is also noted for the unprecedented vividness with which he communicates a pessimist's view of man's personal and social destiny in such works as *The Secret Agent*, *Under Western Eyes*, and *Victory*. Despite the immediate critical recognition that they received in his life-time Conrad's major novels did not sell, and he lived in relative poverty until the commercial success of *Chance* (1913) secured for him a wider public and an assured income. In 1923 he visited America, with great acclaim, and he was offered a knighthood (which he declined) shortly before his death in 1924. Since then his reputation has steadily grown and he is now seen as a writer who revolutionized the English novel and was arguably the most important single innovator of the twentieth century.

KEITH CARABINE was born in Manchester and educated at Leeds and Yale. He teaches English and American Literature at the University of Kent at Canterbury and has published articles on Sherwood Anderson, Hemingway, Hawthorne, Wright Morris, Conrad, and Dickens.

THE WORLD'S CLASSICS

JOSEPH CONRAD

Nostromo

A Tale of the Seaboard

Edited with an introduction by
KEITH CARABINE

Oxford   New York
OXFORD UNIVERSITY PRESS

Oxford University Press, Walton Street, Oxford OX2 6DP

Oxford New York

Athens Auckland Bangkok Bombay
Calcutta Cape Town Dar es Salaam Delhi
Florence Hong Kong Istanbul Karachi
Kuala Lumpur Madras Madrid Melbourne
Mexico City Nairobi Paris Singapore
Taipei Tokyo Toronto

and associated companies in
Berlin Ibadan

Oxford is a trade mark of Oxford University Press

Introduction, Notes, Glossary © Keith Carabine 1984
Bibliography, Chronology © John Batchelor 1983
Updated Bibliography © John Batchelor 1995

This edition first published 1984 as a World's Classics paperback

British Library Cataloguing in Publication Data

Data available

Library of Congress Cataloging in Publication Data
Conrad Joseph, 1857-1924.
Nostromo: a tale of the seaboard.
(The World's classics)
Bibliography: p.
I. Carabine, Keith. II. Title. III. Series.
PR6005.04N578 1984 823'.912 83 23742
ISBN 0-19-281624-1

9 10 8

Printed in Great Britain by
BPC Paperbacks Ltd.
Aylesbury, Bucks

CONTENTS

To
John Galsworthy

INTRODUCTION

1

On 12 December 1902 shortly after his forty-fifth birthday, Conrad lamented: 'I doubt if greatness can be attained now in imaginative prosework. When it comes it will be in a new form; in a form for which we are not ripe yet.'[1] Two weeks later, beset as ever by debts, depression, and gout, haunted by the sense that 'there was nothing in the world to write about', Conrad began *Nostromo*, hoping it would prove a 'silly and saleable' novella of some 35–40,000 words which would take only a month to write and would make a quick profit of £150.[2] Twenty months and 189,000 words later, he finished *Nostromo*, one of the finest 'imaginative proseworks' in the language; and one whose 'new form'—characterized by dazzling shifts of chronology and perspective—continues to puzzle and to enchant his readers.

Such high claims for *Nostromo*'s greatness demand willy-nilly a threefold demonstration: firstly, that the novel's massive tensile design reflects and embodies the solicitude, humanity, and profundity of Conrad's vision of mankind's affairs—and therefore of the artist's task—and responds to and encompasses the sheer scope and variety of his created world; secondly, that his intricate narrative tactics are neither wilful nor adventitious, but rather spring from his determination to effect a strong grasp upon our sensibilities by directly inviting us to collaborate with the processes of his fiction making. To appreciate the sheer *enterprise* of the novel will lay the groundwork for my third concern, which is a sympathetic

[1] G. Jean-Aubry, *Joseph Conrad: Life and Letters I* (London, Heinemann, 1927), p. 308. Henceforward *LLI* or *LLII*.
[2] Quoted by Fred R. Karl, *Joseph Conrad: The Three Lives* (New York, Farrar, Straus and Giroux), p. 540. Henceforward *TL*.

reappraisal of the novel's most criticized aspect, namely Nostromo's role and fate.

The most compelling and succinct of Conrad's many statements about the interdependence of the artist's and of mankind's concerns is contained in a letter he wrote to the *New York Times* on 2 August 1901:[3]

The only legitimate basis of creative work lies in the courageous recognition of all irreconcilable antagonisms that make our life so enigmatic, so burdensome, so fascinating, so dangerous, so full of hope. They exist! And this is the only fundamental truth of fiction. Its recognition must be critical in its nature, inasmuch that in its character it may be joyous; it may be sad; it may be angry with revolt or submissive in resignation . . . whatever light he (the writer) flashes on it, the fundamental truth remains; and it is only in its verve that the barren struggle of contradictions assumes the dignity of moral strife—going on ceaselessly to a mysterious end. . .

All Conrad's major fictions present and analyse such oppositions: solidarity and isolation, moral corruption and redemption, 'treasure and love' (566), individual heroism and human contingency, fidelity and betrayal, and a commitment to basic truths aligned with a recognition of their actual relativity. His recognition of the 'ceaseless. . .struggle of contradictions' springs from an inclusive vision of man's fate; and because for Conrad, as for Flaubert, 'the *whole* of the truth lies in the presentation', his vision sponsors a search for the correlative form.[4] During the writing of *Nostromo* Conrad admonished H. G. Wells for his 'exclusiveness' of intellect and feeling, because his 'sincerity' was served 'at the expense of truth'. With his aims in *Nostromo* clearly in mind, Conrad argues that the creative artist must cast 'a wide, a generous net, where there would be room for everybody; where indeed every sort of a fish would be welcome, appreciated and made use of'.[5]

[3] *TL*, p. 460.   [4] *LLI*, p. 280.   [5] *LLI*, p. 328.

Nostromo is in all respects the widest and most generous net he ever designed. We watch in wonder as he
magisterially describes the topography, climate, and sustaining superstitions of Costaguana before he presents,
through the activities, conflicts, and perspectives of a host
of characters and pressure groups, its domestic, political,
economic and cultural history over a period of some fifty
years. The novel is both an analysis and a prophecy of the
issues and conflicts which have dominated Third World
countries. It examines the attempt to graft Western
capitalist enterprise, cultural norms, and political institutions, upon the stock of a peasant, superstitious, economically underdeveloped country, recently emerging out of
Spanish colonial rule, and governed by a series of 'pronunciamentos' which have rendered the country chronically
unstable.

The bond and main source of the political, economic, and
cultural conflicts in Costaguana is, of course, the silver,
which Conrad describes as 'the pivot of the moral and
material events, affecting the lives of everyone in the
tale'.[6] The mine provides the 'generous net' which enables
Conrad to appreciate and use 'every sort of fish' and to
canvass (seemingly) every conceivable perspective and
position: whether the cravenness and greed of a Sotillo, or
'the confidence and belief' of the native miners; the
pusillanimity of a Hirsch, or the genial bravery of General
Barrios; the vanity and folly of a Pedrito Montero, or the
'luck' of young Scarfe; whether the varieties of idealism
embodied and explored in Giorgio Viola, Nostromo, the
Goulds, Holroyd, Antonia, Don José Avellanos and Father
Corbelàn, or the varieties of scepticism in Decoud,
Monygham, and Father Roman.

The 'incorruptible' treasure as in folklore tests the cor-
ruptible characters of men and nations. It is, as Captain

[6] *LLII*, p. 296.

Mitchell remarks with unconscious wisdom, 'a great force for good and evil', requiring for its successful operation the conflicting passions, beliefs, appetites and activities of men. As both the chief power in Costaguana and the novel's central metaphor the silver works as the nexus of 'a struggle of contradictions' which work thematically and formally. Thus the mine inspires in Gould (and Don José Avellanos and the Ribierists) a vision of reconciliation of 'law, good faith, order, security' which will replace 'lawlessness and disorder', because the security 'material interests' demand if they are to be established 'must be shared with oppressed people' (84). The credulous and outraged populace, however, loathe the foreigners who develop Costaguana, and readily support the Monterists who lead 'a military revolt in the name of national honour' (145). For Gould 'a better justice will come afterwards', but for his wife 'the wealthy and enterprising men' who backed the mine 'don't seem to have understood anything they have seen here' (70). 'The Treasure House of the World' underpins the economic, political, and military feasibility of the Occidental Republic's separation from Costaguana. Yet, as we realize, the very success of the development of material interests breeds a hybrid opposition (common throughout Latin America today), of socialists, trade unionists, the Catholic Church and refugees from previous revolutions. All groups in their different ways are set at odds by the status of the mine as an 'Imperium in imperio' and by the Manifest Destiny of United States imperialism so confidently predicted by Holroyd: 'We shall be giving the word for everything: industry, trade, law, journalism, art, politics and religion' (77). 'The popular Archbishop of Sulaco', a convinced nationalist and brave defender of the Catholic faith, speaks for an 'antagonism' which will never be reconciled when he warns: 'beware ... lest the people, prevented from their aspirations, should rise and claim their share of the wealth and their share of the power' (510). Dr Monygham accepts the Archbishop's militant prophecy but is far less sanguine as to the results because:

'There is no peace . . . in the development of material interests. They have their law and their justice. But it is founded on expediency, and is inhuman; . . . the time approaches when all that the Gould Concession stands for shall weigh as heavily upon the people as the barbarism, cruelty, and misrule of a few years back.' (511)

What is the reader to make of such widely different responses to the silver and such opposing estimates of its political and social power? If you believe Dr Monygham you will agree with Albert Guerard Jr, that 'the conflicts induced by capitalist exploitation outweigh the benefits accrued'.[7] Yet the forces of progress have won; and as Robert Penn Warren claims 'we must admit that the society at the end of the book is preferable to that of the beginning'.[8] One could easily draw on the novel to support the views of either of these two fine representative critics. On the one hand we can turn to Mrs Gould's heartbroken recognition: 'There was something inherent in the necessities of successful action which carried with it the moral degradation of the idea' (521) and we can effortlessly point to the ironies of success in *Nostromo*. For example Don José advocates federalism yet gives his blessing to separation, and Mrs Gould initially shares her husband's vision of the efficacy of material interests, yet 'in the grip of a merciless nightmare', when she stammers out 'Material interests', she reminds us of *Heart of Darkness* and Kurtz's 'The horror! The horror!' On the other hand the

[7] A. J. Guerard, *Conrad the Novelist* (Cambridge, Harvard University Press, 1958), p. 198.
[8] Robert Penn Warren, '"The Great Mirage": Conrad and Nostromo', *Selected Essays* (New York, Random House, 1958), p. 50.

narrator assures us that Sulaco after secession grows 'rich swiftly' and 'experiences a second youth, like a new life'; and Captain Mitchell blandly assures us, as we participate in his tour of a modern and prosperous Sulaco, that 'a New Era' has dawned (477) and that Decoud's vision of secession is 'a glorious success' (489).

As such quick forays into the novel demonstrate, Conrad's 'fundamental truth' invites and sustains opposing views which are 'irreconcilable'. The reader is obliged to *criticize* all the characters' viewpoints: no one position provides a stable point of reference from which the others can be judged. Rather we chart an abundance of recognitions which play off each other, ranging from, say, the 'opera bouffe' of Decoud; the measureless pity of Antonia who exclaims, unforgettably, 'Forgive us our misery' (361); the sardonic appraisal of human behaviour by Dr Monygham; the open-eyed resignation of Mrs Gould and 'the angry revolt' of Nostromo. The mine is to *Nostromo* what the ivory is to *Heart of Darkness* or Chancery to *Bleak House* or the whale to *Moby Dick* or the law to *The Castle*: as all the characters respond to its power and fall under its influence, as they use and interpret it, they wittingly or unwittingly disclose their deepest needs and purposes whether spiritual, emotional, material or political.

2

Range of character, breadth of canvas and mighty themes do not guarantee mighty books. *Nostromo* is a great novel because Conrad's political intelligence and prescience are (as he remarked in a late letter which reviewed his whole career) inseparable from 'my unconventional grouping and perspective . . . wherein all my "art" consists . . . It is fluid depending on grouping (sequence), which shifts, and on the changing lights giving varied effects of perspective'.[9]

Because Conrad's 'illuminating imagination'[10] permeates and controls every aspect of *Nostromo* it is possible to examine his handling of any one of his motifs (such as Higuerota, Mrs Gould's water-colour, or the portrait of Garibaldi), or any one of his minor characters, or any single time shift or switch of perspective, in order to demonstrate that his obliquities of narration are considered `and revealing. Several years ago a student challenged such a contention by pointing to Conrad's 'perverse' presentation of Don Vincente Ribiera whose puzzling appearances in the first two-fifths of the novel seem deliberately designed to ensure that our initial relation to the narrative is analogous to that of Captain Mitchell's 'privileged passenger' who is 'stunned . . . mentally by a sudden surfeit of sights, sounds, names, facts and complicated information imperfectly apprehended' (486–7).

I have therefore deliberately chosen to analyse Conrad's presentation of Ribiera as a representative case to demonstrate the novel's wonderful fusion of form and vision. For the sake of brevity my account treats only five of Ribiera's fleeting appearances in the novel and leaves extensive cross-reference to the reader.[11] Five of our seven encounters with him are interwoven variations upon two opposing images: his ignominious flight on the mule which persuades Decoud to push his plan for the secession of the Occidental Republic from the rest of Costaguana (the main action of the novel), and his appearance eighteen months *before* his flight when, as President of Costaguana, he

[9] *LLII*, p. 317.

[10] Edward Garnett, ed., *Letters from Joseph Conrad 1895–1924* (Indianapolis, Hobbs-Merrill, 1928), p. 172.

[11] The omitted appearances are his fifth (144–5) and his seventh (244–6).

oversees 'the turning of the first sod of the Sulaco National Railway' (35). On the first occasion his fate is tied to Nostromo who rescues him from the revolutionary mob (11–13, 129–31, 224–6), on the second Ribiera is the native embodiment of the hopes for the development of 'material interests' in Costaguana (34–9, 116–20).

Our first view of Ribiera is filtered through the complacent voice of 'Fussy Joe', Captain Mitchell, who manifests an Anglo-Saxon, Tory disdain for Latin American revolutionary politics:

Poor Señor Ribiera . . . had come pelting eighty miles over the mountain tracks after the lost battle of Socorro, in the hope of out-distancing the fatal news—which, of course, he could not manage to do on a lame mule. The animal, moreover, expired under him at the end of the Alameda, where the military band plays sometimes in the evenings between the revolutions. 'Sir,' Captain Mitchell would pursue . . . 'the ill-timed end of that mule attracted attention to the unfortunate rider.' (11)

Mitchell's voice is heard through a blend of direct speech and of a free indirect style. This tactic enables Conrad to write as if from *within* the prejudices and idiom of the character ('rascally mob', 'worst kind of nigger', 'thieves and murderers') and, simultaneously, allows him to place the plain voice of the character, because we are constantly aware that the voice of the author (to continue the figure) provides counterpoint and descant. He intrudes nuances and tones of which the character is unaware. Thus Mitchell's portentous gravity (unconsciously) records a moment of high farce: only the dying mule draws the attention of the deserters to the Dictator they have served and now execrate. (Mitchell is crucial to the design of *Nostromo* because he allows Conrad to release a mass of exposition economically. Both his claims to a 'profound knowledge of men and things in the country' (11) and his belief that history and narrative constitute a linear succession of public events and spectacular human deeds are systematically subverted by Conrad.)

We next meet Ribiera twenty pages later, and eighteen months before his defeat, when as President of Costaguana he celebrates the 'Progressive and patriotic undertaking' of the National Sulaco Railway (34). We now view him through the massively assured vision of Sir John Smith, the English railway magnate: 'After all he was their own creature—that Don Vincente. He was the embodied triumph of the best elements in the State. These were facts . . . ' (38). Conrad's radical disjunction of chronology critically places Sir John's urbane belief in such 'facts'. We register, as he *cannot*, the distinctly uncertain relationship between faith and action; particularly when 'the best elements of the state' are involved.

The third mention of Ribiera occurs sixty pages on and relates to the same moment: this time, however, it is filtered through the sympathetic consciousness of Mrs Gould. Chapter 8 begins with a typically deadpan, two-pronged prolepsis (anticipating the political situation at the very end of the novel) which assures us that 'material interests' finally triumphed in Sulaco and also sponsored 'quite serious, organised labour troubles' (95); and thus confirms our sense of the contradictions inherent in material success. Mrs Gould listens to Ribiera's hopes for 'a period of peace and material prosperity' for their unhappy country. She observes 'the short body obese to the point of infirmity' and thinks 'that this man of delicate and melancholy mind, physically almost a cripple, coming out of his retirement into a dangerous strife at the call of his fellows, had the right to speak with the authority of his self-sacrifice . . . this first civilian Chief of the State Costaguana' (119). Mrs Gould's kind assessment of Ribiera realigns some of our impressions and reinforces others. On the one hand we are persuaded to admire Ribiera's fidelity and his earned authority (as opposed to the assumed superiority of Mitchell and the presumptive authority of Sir John); and on the other Conrad cannily releases details ('obese to the point of infirmity') which invite our pity for Ribiera's suffering *and* re-echo the note of farce, as we understand why the poor mule limped and finally expired.

Our fourth encounter with Ribiera at the close of Part I involves a double switch of viewpoint and chronology. Nostromo's splendid public tableau with the Morenita occurs on the same day as the inauguration of the railway, and the former is described omnisciently before we move to Captain Mitchell's thoughts about the latter as another 'historic occasion' (130). Conrad then uses Captain Mitchell both to review Ribiera's downfall and, via a dramatic prolepsis (entirely characteristic of the novel's procedures), to carry us to the end of the novel—to learn that Nostromo becomes involved in 'a fatality' and 'has never been the same man since' (131). Conrad's sensational shifts whet our curiosity and baffle us by releasing information we cannot, yet, understand; and they demonstrate that Mitchell's belief that men *make* 'history' is extremely debatable in a world where human fortunes are so unpredictable.

Ribiera's sixth brief mention is in the context of Decoud's Parisian life before he learns of the former's downfall:

Of his own country he used to say to his French associates:
—Imagine an atmosphere of opera-bouffe in which all the comic business . . . is done in dead earnest . . . No man of ordinary intelligence can take part in the intrigues of *une farce macabre* . . .

And he would explain with railing verve what Don Vincente Ribiera stood for—a mournful little man oppressed by his own good intentions . . . (152–3)

The novel is not short of moments of macabre farce and 'railing verve' as the suspended corpse of Hirsch, and Conrad's lampoon of Sotillo and Gamacho, testify: but Mrs

Gould's assessment of Ribiera's 'dead earnest' commit-ent and activity (and we might add those of Gould, Don José, Father Corbelàn and Antonia) ensures that we recognize that Decoud's sardonic appraisal of the value of political and human activity is self-indulgent and partial. Decoud in fact soon changes his mind. He is confronted in Costaguana by 'the absolute change of atmosphere': 'He was moved in spite of himself by that note of passion and sorrow unknown on the more refined stage of European politics' (156). Decoud's unawareness, hitherto, of this note, which has been part of the reader's experience throughout the narrative, allows us, immediately, to *criticize* his cynicism.

Conrad's presentation of Ribiera is astonishingly econo-mical and iridescent. As fugitive and President he is a minor figure who flits through a mere twenty-five pages of narrative—as opposed to (say) the forty pages Conrad devotes to Decoud and Nostromo in the lighter, or the thirty leisurely pages which chart the conversation be-tween Nostromo and Dr Monygham in the empty Custom House. Conrad's presentation, however, enables us to appreciate both the 'irreconcilable antagonisms that make our life' and the 'unconventional grouping and perspective . . . wherein all my "art" consists'.

Ford Madox Ford said that he and Conrad 'agreed that the one quality that gave interest to Art was the quality of surprise'.[12] We should not confuse 'surprise' with either the 'twists' of an O. Henry short story or with the clever revelations of a detective story, or again with the strange and exciting adventures of a romance: as we have seen, we learn about Ribiera's sorry fate before we encounter the events that gave rise to it. Furthermore Conrad deliber-ately resists the 'surprises' associated with grand climaxes when, in Part III, Chapter 10, we are transported some

[12] F. M. Ford, *Joseph Conrad: A Personal Remembrance* (London, Duckworth, 1924), p. 189.

ten years ahead, and potentially exciting 'historical events', such as Don Pépé marching on the town at the head of the mineworkers and Dr Monygham's last minute reprieve from hanging, have become 'the more or less stereotyped relation' (473) of an old·man's gossip. Rather, as we have seen, Conrad's 'surprise' is produced by a series of juxtapositions and contrasts which involve subtle shifts of voice, viewpoint, and time, often within the same paragraph, deliberately subjecting the reader to a vertiginous process which simultaneously shakes our perceptions, disrupts our attempts to construct a stable linear narrative, and ensures, as Conrad desires, that 'the reader collaborates with the author'.[13] Our collaboration is necessary if we are to reconstruct the history of Costaguana; but more importantly our constant state of surprise means that we are obliged both to strive to understand, and to re-enact the fate of his characters caught in 'the bitter necessities of the time'. Like all of us his characters need to believe that their activities generate meaning and pattern in a world where time and materials are shaped by men. As we struggle to trace, and are made to feel, the conflicting pressures, needs, forces and motives which constitute any single event, and which ensure the breakdown of any stable relationship between word and experience, idea and actions, ends and means, so we are persuaded to undergo all 'the irreconcilable antagonisms' which render (say) Nostromo 'angry with revolt' and which 'insidiously' corrupt Gould's judgement. To collaborate with Conrad, therefore, is actively to engage with the 'truth' of the author's own restless 'verve'. He pursues an ironic method, which generates, and springs from, a dual perspective of pity and scorn. He recognizes that 'the irreconcilable antagonisms' he confronts and negotiates in his art render any stabilizing

[13] *LLI*, p. 304.

reconciliation or perspective impossible: impossible no matter how deeply he craves them, and no matter how passionately his characters believe in them.

3

To concentrate on Nostromo's role and fate is to recognize that Conrad's overriding preoccupation, as in all his major fictions, is with personal identity—phrased memorably by Stein in *Lord Jim* as the issue of 'how to be!' In the world of Costaguana, as in his native Poland, the London of *The Secret Agent* and the Russia of *Under Western Eyes*, 'the psychology of individuals even in the most extreme instances, reflects the general effects of the fears and hopes of the time'.[14] As Conrad tells us in his 'Author's Note' the issue of personal identity demands an examination of the relationship between 'the secret purposes' of his characters' 'hearts revealed in the bitter necessities' of Costaguana (xliv). *Nostromo* is a remarkable complex of personal stories which explores how the characters seek to relate their self conceptions to the competing claims of 'treasure and love'. Thus the stories of the Goulds, Decoud, Dr Monygham and Nostromo, in their different ways, illustrate a split between private being and public role.

Nostromo, unlike the other major figures, does not possess a 'secret' life, a private identity, until he is reborn into the world of consciousness on Azuera (414). Before this moment his *raison d'être* is vanity and prestige. A man of pure action, Nostromo to Decoud's amazement 'does not seem to make any difference between speaking and thinking' (246). He is incapable of distinguishing between his self and the world. It is therefore fitting that until he tastes 'the dust and ashes of the fruit of life' (416)

---

[14] 'Autocracy and War' (1905), *Notes on Life and Letters* (London, Dent, 1921), p. 113.

we only view him (unlike the major figures, but like Ribiera) *externally* through the narrator's description of his actions and gestures; through a series of ascriptions—'the lordly Capataz de Cargadores, the indispensable man, the tried and trusty Nostromo, the Mediterranean sailor' (130)—and through the viewpoints of the various characters and groups who comment on his activity.

The conflicting viewpoints on Nostromo, as with Ribiera, alert us to the ambiguous political implications of his status. He is oblivious to Mrs Viola's taunts that his personal prestige is actually based upon 'a silly name' given 'in exchange for your soul and body' (256). Appropriately, on Azuera Nostromo rehearses the public ascriptions and activities, 'the facts', which hitherto have constituted his selfhood, and thinks they constitute a *political* consciousness of 'his betrayed individuality'. Deprived however of 'certain simple realities such as . . . the adulation of men', and unable to recognize that 'men' will be 'used as they are' (177), Nostromo truly represents 'the popular mind' because he superstitiously resorts to rudimentary notions of 'power, punishment, pardon' (420). Thus he understands his decision to 'grow rich very slowly' (503) as a political act of 'revenge' upon the rich and as a dark 'bargain' with the fates. The former we realize is a self-deception because the 'facts' of his political account subserve his wounded vanity; the latter involves the false premise that his pride and courage will enable him 'to pay' the price of 'a soul lost' (Mrs Viola) and 'a vanished life' (Decoud). The terrible consequences of his primitive, vain decisions are charted in the last three chapters of the novel.

4

Few readers have been prepared to defend the ending of *Nostromo*, the reactions of two of Conrad's closest friends

being entirely typical. Cunninghame Graham thought the
book was 'wonderful' but 'the last chapters are a mistake'.
Edward Garnett agreed: 'we regret that the last two
chapters describing Nostromo's death are included in the
novel. Their touch of melodrama does violence to the
covering stillness of the close.'[15] Though the ending may
be mistaken, it has not been given its due. In the 'good
fortnight's work' left between the completion of the serial
and the finishing of the novel Conrad recast and greatly
amplified the extremely perfunctory termination of the
serial.[16] 'The technical intention' behind his revised
'presentation' of Nostromo anticipates The Secret Agent,
which Conrad described as 'a new departure in genre . . . a
sustained ironical treatment of a melodramatic subject'.[17]
Conrad therefore deliberately sacrifices the massive scale
and brilliant shifts of chronology and perspective for a
linear, stark narrative which allows him to heighten and
complicate Nostromo's response to his 'possession by the
silver' and also allows him to rehearse his central theme of
personal identity in a key which matches and embodies
Nostromo's new relationship to his world.

Central to Conrad's reworking is Nostromo's totemistic
faith in the manifold powers of the treasure. It contains
'the secret of his safety, of his magnificence'. It enables
him to control 'the future' and to place himself beyond
'every possible betrayal from rich and poor alike', beyond
human defeat and social or divine retribution (526–7). He
wishes in other words to surmount the 'irreconcilable
antagonisms' which characterize all our lives and particularly those caught up in 'the bitter necessities' of Costaguana. But of course, Nostromo's activity involves an
inescapable paradox: he is both 'master' of and 'slave' to,

[15] Quoted by C. T. Watts, Joseph Conrad's Letters to Cunninghame
Graham (Cambridge U.P., 1969), p. 159. Henceforward 'Watts'.
[16] TL, p. 566.
[17] Watts, p. 169.

the treasure. Thus he internalizes the very contradictions he wishes to eschew. Ever conscious of the split between thought and speech, between private resolve and public performance, of inner corruption and outward magnificence, he seeks vainly to conquer both 'treasure and love'.

His feeling of 'fearful . . . subjection' amplifies Mrs Gould's foreboding, 'of an unlucky sleeper, lying passive in the grip of a merciless nightmare', possessed by the knowledge of the power for 'good and evil' of 'Material interests' (522). The human cost of his divided self produces a front of 'severity' to his fellows and a secrecy and unapproachability worthy of Gould himself. But unlike Gould who is 'perfect' while he feels no inner division, Nostromo endures his inner degradation even at the zenith of his public 'magnificence'.

The most ambitious aspect of Conrad's reworking of the serial is his insistence that Nostromo, like Macbeth, enlists his finest qualities in the desperate service of 'a bargain' with the forces of evil in exchange for terrestrial power and command over the future. As Mrs Gould's qualities of compassion, tact, and generosity enable her to endure an 'immense desolation' so Nostromo's 'corrupt courage' enables him to endure a daymare of possession which destroys his 'peace'. It is one of Conrad's most measured ironies that his protagonist, who once failed to see the betrayal of his personality implicit in his nickname ('nostro uomo', 'our man'), reverts to his 'rightful name' of 'Captain Fidanza' when he decides to betray the rich and initiates a systematic betrayal, which he cannot control, of all who revere him: whether 'the orphan children of the widow of the Cargador' who regard him as an earthly divinity, the 'good comrades' of the lodge who assemble 'in his honour', or the Viola family whose children he is pledged to save. Thus Nostromo's desire to escape the contingencies man is heir to corrupts all his relationships, personal, political, and romantic, and ensures his final destruction.

Through Nostromo's relationship to the Viola sisters Conrad dramatizes the fact that the claims of the treasure render love impossible—a truth that Gould in his 'perfection' cannot see, his wife cannot avoid, and Nostromo cannot accept. Conrad's 'ironic treatment' of a 'melodramatic subject' is most clearly seen in the love triangle. Linda's love for Nostromo is deliberately histrionic: '"The world belongs to you, and you let me live in it"' (532). In the days when 'the dreaded Capataz de Cargadores' was 'magnificent and carelessly public in his amours' (129), Linda's tribute would have been a splendidly apt response. Now, however, her passionate testimony is not the culminating tribute to her lover's greatness, nor the final boon reserved for heroes of romances; rather, ironically, it is 'torturing' to Captain Fidanza, because she is a living threat to his precariously endured 'magnificence'.

Nostromo's love for Giselle is founded, and founders on, paradox. Unlike Linda, Giselle could love a 'thief' and therefore she promises to 'allay his fears as to the future' (525); but his irresistible response to her 'tranquil and fatal power' is 'a frightful danger' precisely because she threatens his hold over the future. Giselle is a siren;[18] thus his love for her anticipates his death, and exposes his profoundly mistaken belief that he can avoid 'the struggle of contradictions' that 'make' his life.

It is in this context that his picturesque dream of the future must be understood:

He would cherish her, he said, in a splendour as great as Doña Emilia's . . . He had kept the treasure for purposes of revenge; but now he cared nothing for it. He cared only for her. He would put her beauty in . . . a white palace above a blue sea. He would keep here there like a jewel in a casket. (541)

Such moments strongly suggest that Conrad's idea of

[18] Compare my note to p. 535.

treating 'a melodramatic subject' ironically is indeed a fit response to, and vehicle for, Nostromo's primitive temperament. In contrast to Mrs Gould's mature realization that 'for life to be large and full, it must contain the care of the past and of the future in every passing moment of the present' (520–1), the 'full self-knowledge' of Nostromo is truly rudimentary. Like Pedro Montero's reading of historical literature, Nostromo's dearly gained consciousness only fills 'his head with absurd visions' (387) which invite catastrophe. The very floridity of Nostromo's dream is a measure of its impossibility. Furthermore the corruption which feeds Nostromo's fantasy of domination is revealed by the image he chooses for his adoration. The 'jewel in a casket' suggests a lifeless embodiment of his desire to avoid 'every possible betrayal', and shows that his love for her can never be as powerful as his 'ardent subjection' to the treasure. His self-deception prevents Nostromo from experiencing that love which only Dr Monygham knows: 'the inexhaustible treasure of his devotion drawn upon in the secret of his heart like a store of unlawful wealth' (504). Love alone in Conrad's world is truly inexhaustible.

The novel ends with Dr Monygham's monitoring of Linda's wild, faithful cry: 'I cannot understand. But I shall never forget thee. Never!' (566). 'It is impossible to know anything', Conrad once wrote to Cunninghame Graham, 'though it is possible to believe a thing or two.'[19] Conrad's characters, like Linda, usually choose to believe the stories they tell themselves, the legends they create and the conciliations they erect. Linda's 'true cry of undying passion' reminds us of the high severity of Antonia and her 'invincible resolution' that it was 'from the first poor Martin's intention' (509) that Costaguana eventually be annexed to the Occidental Republic. Both Linda and Antonia misjudge their loved ones. But Con-

---

[19] Watts, p. 45.

rad's irony does not corrode either their faith or their love. Mrs Gould's bitter insight, that 'inherent in the necessities of successful action' is 'the moral degradation of the idea', does not repudiate her husband's recognition that 'A man must work to some end' (71). Ideals, means, and ends may have no logical, sensible relation in Conrad's world, but men must live and suffer hoping that they can be made to have.

Without the varieties of faith in the 'better justice' of the future expressed so differently by (say) Antonia, Gould, Don José, Giorgio Viola, Holroyd, Hernandez, and even Señor Fuentes—'The poor were going to be made rich now. That was very good' (396)—and without the capacity for fidelity and love of Linda and Dr Monygham, and without the sympathetic imagination of Mrs Gould, the world would indeed overwhelm us. Linda's 'one great cry' is to Dr Monygham 'the most sinister of all', not only because she worships a false 'genius' (the common fate of all who respond to the treasure's power), but also because there is, as his own story shows, 'something sinister in the power of love that, like faith, can move mountains and order cruel sacrifices'.[20] Better, however, Linda's belief in Nostromo's impossible 'conquest of treasure and love'; better the aspirations of mankind defeated by, even unaware of, 'the irreconcilable antagonisms that make our life', than the faithlessness of Decoud who, losing 'all belief in the reality of his actions past and to come', barrenly surrenders his body to 'the glittering surface' of the waters of the Placid Gulf, and is 'swallowed up in the immense indifference of things' (501).

The Chronology of Nostromo

The reader of Nostromo, as we have seen, is obliged to reconstruct the history of Costaguana and the events of

---

[20] Romance (1903; Dent Uniform Edition, 1923), p. 392.

May which lead to the secession of Sulaco; yet simultaneously Conrad seems determined to frustrate our hopes of either a linear narrative or a stable perspective. The following chronologies of the novel's main action and of the 'history' of Costaguana are designed to assist readers lost in the narrative labyrinths they do not claim to be foolproof; rather they are meant either to complement the reader's hard fought reconstruction or to induce a re-examination of the text itself. I include page references so we can see at a glance the great difference between any straight chronology we may glean, and the cyclical, indirect narrative mode which Conrad employs.

I begin with the response of the Sulaco community to the Monterist revolt because this crisis lasts about three weeks and provides the central action of the novel. (Part I, Chapters 2–4, the whole of Part II and all of Part III except the last three chapters.) In fact the major events of the novel, we gradually realize, take place over a four-day span. Exactly which four days is difficult to determine, but if we take Mitchell's recollection that Nostromo rode to Cayta on 'the fifth of May' (483) as our anchor date the following chronology emerges.[21]

Around 21 April: Ribiera defeated at the Battle of Socorro (212).

End of April: Determined to oppose the spreading Monterist revolt the Provincial Assembly of Sulaco send Barrios by sea to Cayta hoping to outflank the Monterist forces in southern Costaguana. One evening Decoud tells

[21] It is, perhaps, possible to take Mitchell's reference to 'Tres de Mayo coffee', drunk in remembrance of the defence of the Amarilla Club by the 'Caballeros' (479), as an 'anchor' date. If so the four-day span would begin (as in Jacques Berthoud's chronology in *Joseph Conrad: The Major Phase*, CUP, pp. 98–9) twenty-four hours earlier. My first dating of the Sulaco action coincided with Berthoud; but Cedric Watts, to whose timely advice I am indebted, argues for 5 May in *A Preface to Conrad*, (1982), pp. 158–63. Compare also H. S. Spatt (*Conradiana*, VIII, 1976, pp. 37–46).

Mrs Gould of Ribiera's defeat and outlines for the first time his plans for 'a Sulaco revolution' (213).

29 April, 5 a.m.: Silver arrives in Sulaco.

1 May: Rioting erupts; Hernandez' aid accepted.

2 May, 4 a.m.: Nostromo promises Decoud that the lightermen will support the Europeans (224). 6 a.m.–noon: President Ribiera arrives on his lame mule and is rescued from the mob by Nostromo. The combined forces of the Cargadores and the Blanco civilians ensure that Ribiera and the leading Blanco families escape by boat. Decoud helps to defend the Amarilla Club. 'Late in the afternoon' Gamacho and Fuentes opportunistically lead the mob (227). That evening we learn of a new double threat: Pedrito Montero in pursuit of Ribiera has struggled across the mountains, and Sotillo, the commanding officer of the southern port of Esmeralda, has changed sides and is approaching Sulaco by sea. The Provisional Assembly led by Don Juste Lopez plans to capitulate (234–5). Decoud, aware that Barrios's troops have arrived in Cayta (233), unveils his plan to remove the silver and to contact Barrios. Hernandez the bandit 'in a memorable last official act of the Ribierist party' is appointed a General.

3 May: In the early hours Nostromo brings Decoud to the Casa Viola where Theresa is dying. In the late afternoon the Blancos flee to Los Hatos to seek the promised protection of Hernandez (351–62). Decoud writes a letter to his sister (223–49) and later that evening he and Nostromo take the silver out into the Golfo Placido, and their lighter collides with Sotillo's transport-ship. Sotillo arrives in Sulaco just before midnight.

4 May: During the night Nostromo and Decoud bury the silver on the Great Isabel; at dawn Nostromo swims ashore. In the morning Pedrito enters Sulaco with his forces (384–94) and Sotillo occupies the harbour. Gould returns from escorting the Avellanos to Los Hatos (365) and learning of the 'deaths' of Nostromo and Decoud from

Dr Monygham decides to 'take up openly the plan of the provincial revolution' (379). In the evening Don Pépé and Father Roman discuss the safety of the mine (394–401); Gould has his interview with Pedrito (402–6) and Nostromo wakes in the old fort (411–12) and then collides with Monygham in the abandoned Custom House (425). The latter induces Nostromo to ride overland to Cayta to alert Barrios. Incidentally, the 24-hour stretch from the departure of Nostromo and Decoud with the silver to Monygham's confrontation with Nostromo occupies nearly a third of the novel (244–472) and is told more or less sequentially.

5 May: In the morning Nostromo begins his epic journey. He arrives in Cayta seven days later on 12 May (456). Decoud commits suicide on the morning of 16 May. Nostromo spends the night of the 17th on the Great Isabel. As Mitchell narrates (484ff.) Barrios attacks Sotillo's ship and rescues Monygham. Pépé leads the miners into Sulaco.

The chronology of Don José Avellanos's *The Fifty Years of Misrule* (a mischievous alternative title to the novel) cannot be 'accurately' reconstructed because Conrad studiously avoids dates of actual years, and because such details as he releases are irreconcilable. The inconsistencies grow out of Conrad's deliberate interweaving of actual historical figures and events (such as the references to Garibaldi and Bolívar and to the battles they fought) with his purely fictional characters such as Gould and Giorgio Viola. The reader who is tempted to plan the time span of the novel 'objectively' by checking the dates of (say) Garibaldi's career will discover that the fictional characters' private histories resist any attempt to construct a consistent overall chronology.[22] It must be said

[22] Ben Kimpel and T. C. Duncan Eves, 'The Geography and History in *Nostromo*' (*Modern Philology*, August, 1958, pp. 45–54) exaggerate the difficulties. Watts constructs an 'historical' chronology by taking Holroyd's reference to the Atacama Nitrate Wars as an anchor date

that the difficulties the novel presents are rarely due to such inconsistencies, since very few of them impinge, as we have seen, on the order of the major events. Again, the loose ends in *Nostromo* are surely a small price to pay for Conrad's wonderful ability to involve us in his densely textured and richly imagined world. Thus rather than rehearse the novel's inconsistencies (several of which are pointed out in the notes) I provide those historical dates which the careers of Giorgio and Gould afford and intermix them with the (undated) main events of Costaguanan history.

1821: Gould's grandfather 'fought in the cause of independence under Bolivar . . . on the battlefield of Cara-bobo' (46–7). 'In the days of Federation' which follow in-dependence—a period of indefinite length—Gould's uncle Henry (Enrique) is 'elected President of . . . Sulaco' and is executed by Guzman Bento who, 'becoming later Per-petual President' (47), rules for either 'fifteen' (115) or 'twelve years' (142). During his tyranny both Don José (137–40) and Dr Monygham (371–5) are imprisoned and tortured. From 1842 to 1846 Giorgio Viola enlists 'in the navy of Montevideo . . . under the command of Garibaldi' (29) at least 'forty years' (30) before Ribiera stumbles into Sulaco on his lame mule. Bento's death is followed by the long turmoil of pronunciamentos during which 'the native miners . . . had risen upon their English chiefs and mur-dered them to a man' (52). 'For many years' this is the last of the San Tomé mine; then 'an ordinary Costaguanan Government—the fourth in six years' (53) cedes the mine to Gould's father. Gould is then fourteen years old. Gould

(1884) which 'makes 1890 a probable date for the main action of the novel' (*A Preface to Conrad*, p. 159). Harvey S. Spatt, using Garibaldi's career as a starting point, sets the main action of the novel in 1886. Conrad, in a letter of 1918, claimed that the main action of *Nostromo* occurred 'in the seventh decade' of the nineteenth century (*Thoth*, Syracuse University, Spring, 1969).

would seem to be in his early twenties (61) when he returns to Costaguana. A year after his marriage Holroyd visits Sulaco (67) and the Goulds spend a year at the mine supervising its reconstruction (105). Ribiera visits Sulaco to celebrate the inauguration of the railway (34–43), and we learn there have been 'two' revolutions in Mrs Gould's time (36). We gradually realize that the second, 'the five year dictatorship' of Ribiera, which is 'invested with a mandate of reform by the best elements in the state' (117), has been financed in part by the Gould Concession. 'Eighteen months' after the inauguration Ribiera retreats over the mountains and is saved from the mob by Nostromo. The last sequence of the novel (512–66) occurs over a period of two days some ten to fifteen years after the foundation of the Occidental Republic.

A Note on Conrad's Sources

The hunt for the South American sources of *Nostromo* is led by Norman Sherry (*Conrad's Western World*, 1971). An indefatigable sleuth, Sherry dwells at length on Conrad's reading of 'a number of books written about the South American continent' (147) such as G. F. Masterman's *Seven Eventful Years in Paraguay* (1869) and Edward R. Eastwick's *Venezuela* (1868). From Masterman Conrad borrowed such names as Decoud, Padre Corbelàn, General Barrios, Gould, Captain Fidanza, Mitchell, Monygham, and Don José; from Eastwick, Guzman Blanco, Antonia Ribiera, Sotillo. Conrad, as Sherry and others demonstrate, and as my own reading confirms, freely plundered his sources for 'local colour' details, for Spanish phrases and for several incidents—the most important of which are recorded in my notes to this edition. C. T. Watts (ed.), *Joseph Conrad's Letters to Cunninghame Graham* (1969) contains a shrewd assessment of Conrad's debt to his friend, and includes a valuable note on S. P. Triana, the Colombian Ambassador to Madrid and London. The latter's 'The Partition of South America', *Anglo-Saxon Review* 10 (Sept. 1901), pp. 104–15, provides an interesting slant on the world of Costaguana.

The whole issue of sources is a vexed one and, clearly, cannot be fully addressed in a note. I feel however that Sherry's enthusiasm leads him to exaggerate the importance and value of Conrad's reading. As Sherry's own discussion shows, the 'sources' he presents do *not* enable him 'to reveal the movement of Conrad's mind over his material' (5). Indeed, Sherry's central justification that 'the world of a South American republic . . . was not in any substantial way part of Conrad's experience either at the time of writing Nostromo . . . or at any other period earlier in his life' (2) begs two questions—namely Conrad's Polish origins and his response to contemporary issues. With regard to the former Conrad's essays on Polish and European politics, particularly 'Autocracy and War' (1905) and 'The Crime of Partition' (1919) in *Notes on Life and Letters* (1921) and his account of his childhood in *A Personal Record* (1912) provide a useful starting point. Najder (ed.), *Conrad's Polish Background* (1964) is invaluable, and Gustav Morf's *The Polish Heritage of Joseph Conrad* (1930) and *The Polish Shades and Ghosts of Joseph Conrad* (1976) and Adam Gillon's *The Eternal Solitary* (1960) are suggestive. *Conradiana* XII, no. 1 (1980), is devoted to 'Conrad and the Russians'. Norman Davies's *God's Playground: A History of Poland* (1982) is lively and substantial. With regard to the latter C. T. Watts in *A Preface to Conrad* (1982) claims that a reading of the magazines which published Conrad's fiction in the decade before *Nostromo*, such as *Cosmopolis*, *Blackwood's* and *The New Review*, proves that the novel 'emerges from the international news and political debate of the day with the inevitability of a battleship emerging from the clamour and bustle of a war-time shipyard' (142).

Ian Watt, *Conrad in the Nineteenth Century* (1979) and Alan Hunter, *Joseph Conrad and the Ethics of Darwinism* (1983) treat Conrad's response to contemporary issues and ideas.

NOTE ON THE SERIALIZATION AND TEXT OF NOSTROMO

Nostromo was serialized in *T. P. O'Connor's Weekly* (*TPW*) in thirty-seven instalments from 29 January to 7 October 1904. Conrad's contempt for *TPW* was such that he refused to read the proofs and even allowed the editors to compress and divide the novel as they wished. Clearly he was prepared for the serial to be a disaster and needless to say it was. The editors butchered the instalments, varying their length from 10,500 words for the first episode, 5,000 for episodes 2–16 and 31–5, a derisory 3,400 for 17–30, and finally 7,500 words for the last two, 36–7. The serial is just over 173,000 words long, the novel, published on 14 October, approximately 189,000. The novel follows the serial very closely—apart from some omissions totalling 2,500 words—until episode 25 (pp. 344–54). Thereafter Conrad's main changes are additions of some 400 words an episode until his massive amplification of the extremely perfunctory ending of the serial (see Appendix). He added 14,000 words to the last instalment alone. As Conrad's additions include many powerful reflections, and as they reveal a major re-evaluation of Nostromo's role and function, I list most of them in the notes.

The copy text of this present edition is that of J. M. Dent's *Collected Edition* (*CE*), 1947, which is a reprint of the *Uniform Edition* (1923). I have checked *CE* against the serial; the first English edition, E^1 (London and New York, Harper and Bros., 1904); the second English edition, E^2 (Dent, 1918) and the third edition, E^3 (London, William Heinemann, 1921). A check of *CE* against E^1 reveals fourteen misprints, two of which are shared with E^2 and one with E^3. E^2 and *CE* both read 'adventurers' (320, 369) instead of 'adventures'. The single misprint E^2, E^3, and *CE* (87) share is delightful—'cotton-wool tree'—instead of 'cotton-wood tree' as in E^1 (73) and *TPW* (26

Feb., 270). The most important misprint in CE is 'Material interest' (522) which reads, in E^1, E^2, and E^3, 'Material interests'. I silently correct the remaining misprints. There are very few differences between CE, E^2 and E^3. I record in the notes the single occasion when I follow the latter and the sole instance when E^1, E^3 and CE all differ.

There are over 130 emendations of E^1 in CE, E^2 and E^3, nearly two-thirds of which are very minor matters of punctuation and typography, involving for example hyphens, capital letters, and dashes. As against E^1 CE contains thirty-two changes of words and phrases, and fourteen omissions ranging from the elision of redundant words or phrases to whole paragraphs. Typical examples of the former are E^1 'wide on the bow' (416) as against CE 'broad on the bow' (490), and the elision in CE of 'outward' (70) from E^1, 'a visible appreciation of her outward appearance' (58). The three main omissions and the most interesting changes from E^1—which E^2, E^3 and CE almost always share—are recorded in the notes.

The *Nostromo* MS. in the Rosenbach Library, Philadelphia is less than half complete. Thus pp. 195–415 and 506–66 of the CE are missing. The typescript, parts of which are in the Huntingdon Library and Yale University Library, is fragmentary. According to Frederick R. Karl[1] the parts in the Yale Library include the following: Part I, Ch. 1, eight typed pages; Part II, Ch. 2, first paragraph only; Part II, Ch. 5, fifteen pages from the twelfth paragraph in the writing of Ford; Part II, Ch. 7, thirty-five typed pages of the last eighteen pages of this chapter, including five pages in Conrad's hand; Part III, Chs. 3 and 4, thirty-five typed pages; Part III, 130 pages. The Huntingdon Library contains fragments of Part III, Chs. 1–7.

---

[1] 'The Significance of the Revisions in the Early Versions of *Nostromo*', *Modern Fiction Studies*, 5 (1959), p. 130.

SELECT BIBLIOGRAPHY

Primary Works

DENT'S collected edition (1946–55) contained almost all Conrad's works except for the dramatizations and some minor items. *Congo Diary and Other Uncollected Pieces*, edited by Zdisław Najder (1978) contains the Congo notebooks, the fragment called *The Sisters*, *The Nature of a Crime* written in collaboration with Ford Madox Hueffer (later Ford Madox Ford) and other writings. Cambridge University Press is currently publishing a critical edition of the canon, starting with *The Secret Agent* and *Almayer's Folly*.

Letters

The Collected Letters of Joseph Conrad, edited by Frederick R. Karl and Laurence Davies, began appearing in 1983. Other important editions are as follows: *Joseph Conrad: Life and Letters*, by G. Jean-Aubry (1927); *Letters from Joseph Conrad, 1895–1924*, ed. Edward Garnett (1928); *Letters of Joseph Conrad to Marguerite Poradowska*, ed. and trans. John A. Gee and Paul J. Sturm (1940); *Joseph Conrad: Letters to William Blackwood and David J. Meldrum*, ed. William Blackburn (1958); *Conrad's Polish Background: Letters to and from Polish Friends*, ed. Zdisław Najder (1964); *Joseph Conrad's Letters to Cunningham Graham* (1969), ed. C. T. Watts. There are further collections edited by Richard Curle (1928), G. Jean-Aubry (1929), Rene Rapin (1966) and Dale B. J. Randall (1968).

Memoirs, biographies, and biographical studies

The most important memoirs are those by Jessie Conrad (1926 and 1935), Richard Curle (1928), and Ford Madox Ford (1924), and there are further memoirs by Borys Conrad (1970) and John Conrad (1981). Owen Knowles's chronology (1989) and Martin Ray's collection of interviews and recollections (1990) are helpful reference works. Documents related to Conrad's Polish experience and relations are collected in Zdisław Najder (ed.), *Conrad under Familial Eyes* (1983).

The most reliable and scholarly biography is Zdisław Najder's *Joseph Conrad: A Chronicle* (1983). There are critical biographies by Jocelyn Baines (1960), Bernard Meyer (a 'psychoanalytic biography', 1967), Frederick Karl (1979), and Jeffrey Meyers (1991). The most recent critical biography is John Batchelor's *The Life of Joseph Conrad: A Critical Biography* (1994). There are further recommended biographies and biographical studies by J. D. Gordan, *Joseph Conrad: The Making of a Novelist* (1941), Norman Sherry, *Conrad's Eastern World* (1966) and *Conrad's Western World* (1971), Ian Watt, *Conrad in the Nineteenth Century* (1980), Roger Tennant (1981) and Cedric Watts (1989).

Critical studies

General studies to be recommended are Douglas Hewitt, *Joseph Conrad: A Reassessment* (1952), A. J. Guerard, *Conrad the Novelist* (1958), Jacques Berthoud, *Joseph Conrad: The Major Phase* (1978), Cedric Watts, *A Preface to Conrad* (1982) and Suresh Raval, *The Art of Failure: Conrad's Fiction* (1986). The following specialist studies can also be recommended: Eloise Knapp Hay, *The Political Novels of Joseph Conrad* (1963), Andrzej Busza, *Conrad's Polish Literary Background, Antemurale,* 10 (1966), J. Hillis Miller, 'Joseph Conrad' in his *Poets of Reality* (1966), Edward Said, *Joseph Conrad and the Fiction of Autobiography* (1966), Lawrence Graver, *Conrad's Short Fiction* (1969), Bruce Johnson, *Conrad's Models of Mind* (1971), David Thorburn, *Conrad's Romanticism* (1974), Allan Hunter, *Joseph Conrad and the Ethics of Darwinism* (1983), Redmond O'Hanlon, *Joseph Conrad and Charles Darwin* (1984), Jakob Lothe, *Conrad's Narrative Method* (1989), Jeremy Hawthorn, *Joseph Conrad: Narrative Technique and Ideological Commitment* (1990), Yves Hervouet, *The French Face of Joseph Conrad* (1990), Daphna Erdinast-Vulcan, *Joseph Conrad and the Modern Temper* (1991) and Robert Hampson, *Joseph Conrad: Betrayal and Identity* (1992).

The following collections of essays may be found helpful: R. W. Stallman (ed.), *The Art of Joseph Conrad,* (1960); Norman Sherry (ed.), *Conrad: The Critical Heritage* (1973); W. Zyla and W. M. Aycock (eds.), *Joseph Conrad: Theory and World Fiction* (1974); Norman Sherry (ed.), *Joseph Conrad: A Commemoration,* (1976); Ross C. Murfin (ed.), *Conrad Revisited: Essays for the Eighties* (1985); Mario Curreli (ed.), *The Ugo Mursia Memorial Lectures* (1988); Keith Carabine (ed.), *Joseph Conrad: Critical Assessments* (1992); and Gene M. Moore (ed.), *Conrad's Cities* (1992).

There are annotated bibliographies of Conrad by Bruce E. Teets, 1971 and 1990, and a selected annotated bibliography by Owen Knowles, 1992.

There are three scholarly journals devoted to Conrad studies: *Conradiana, The Conradian* and *L'Epoque Conradienne.*

On Nostromo

From the above list the following are particularly recommended for *Nostromo*: Guerard (1958), Hay (1963), Sherry (1971), Berthoud (1978), Watts (1982), Najder (1983), Raval (1986), Lothe (1989) and Hawthorn (1990). See also F. R. Leavis, *The Great Tradition* (1948); Robert Penn Warren, 'Nostromo', *Sewanee Review,* 59, 3 (1951); Irvine Howe, *Politics and the Novel* (1957); Michael Wilding, 'The Politics of *Nostromo*', *Essays in Criticism* 16 (1966); Avrom Fleishman, *Conrad's Politics* (1967); Juliet McLauchlan, *Conrad: Nostromo* (1966); Zdisław Najder, 'Conrad and the Idea of Honor' in Zyla and Aycock (1974); Jan Verleun, *The Stone Horse* (1982); Martin Ray, 'Conrad and Decoud', *Polish Review* 29, 3 (1984); Ian Watt, *Nostromo* (1988); Cedric Watts, *Nostromo* (1990).

A CHRONOLOGY OF JOSEPH CONRAD

1857   3 December: Born Józef Teodor Konrad Korzeniowski, of Polish parents in the Ukraine.

1861   His father, poet and translator Apollo Korzeniowski, arrested for patriotic conspiracy.

1862   Conrad's parents exiled to Vologda, Russia; their son accompanies them.

1865   Death of his mother.

1869   Death of Apollo Korzeniowski in Kraków; Conrad comes under the protection of his uncle, Tadeusz Bobrowski.

1874   Leaves Poland for Marseilles to become a trainee seaman with the French merchant navy.

1876   As a 'steward' on the *Sainte-Antoine*, becomes acquainted with Dominic Cervoni (who appears in *The Mirror of the Sea* and *The Arrow of Gold* and is the source for Nostromo, and Peyrol in *The Rover*).

1877   Possibly involved in smuggling arms to the 'Carlists' (Spanish royalists) from Marseilles.

1878   March: Shoots himself in the chest in Marseilles but is not seriously injured; as a direct result of this suicide attempt his uncle clears his debts. April: Joins his first British ship, the *Mavis*, and later in the same year joins *The Skimmer of the Sea*. Would have become liable for Russian military service if he had stayed with the French merchant navy.

1886   Becomes a British citizen and passes the examination for a Master's certificate.

1887   Is injured on the *Highland Forest* and hospitalized in Singapore.

1887–8   Gets to know the Malay archipelago as an officer of the *Vidar*.

1888   Master of the *Otago*, his only command.

1889   Resigns from the *Otago*, settles briefly in London and begins to write *Almayer's Folly*. Begins a lasting friendship with Marguerite Poradowska.

1890   Works in the Belgian Congo for the Société Anonyme

pour le Commerce du Haut-Congo.

1891–3   His pleasantest experience at sea, as an officer of the *Torrens*; meets John Galsworthy, who is among the passengers and becomes a loyal friend.

1893   Autumn: Meets Jessie George.

1894   February: Death of Tadeusz Bobrowski. October: *Almayer's Folly* accepted by Unwin. Meets Edward Garnett, Unwin's reader and an influential literary friend.

1895   *Almayer's Folly* published.

1896   *An Outcast of the Islands* published. Becomes acquainted with H. G. Wells. 24 March: marriage to Jessie George. Begins work on *The Rescue*.

1897   *The Nigger of the 'Narcissus'* published. Meets Henry James and R. B. Cunninghame Graham (to be a close friend and the source for Gould in *Nostromo*).

1898   *Tales of Unrest* ('Karain', 'The Idiots', 'An Outpost of Progress', 'The Return', 'The Lagoon') published. Enters into collaboration with Ford Madox Ford (then Hueffer). Takes over from Ford the lease of a Kentish farmhouse, 'The Pent'. Friendship with Stephen Crane. Borys Conrad born.

1898–9   'Heart of Darkness' serialized in *Blackwood's*.

1899   J. B. Pinker becomes Conrad's literary agent.

1899–1900   *Lord Jim* serialized in *Blackwood's*.

1900   Stephen Crane dies. *Lord Jim* published as a book.

1901   *The Inheritors* (collaboration with Ford) published.

1902   *Youth: and Two Other Stories* ('Youth', 'Heart of Darkness', 'The End of the Tether') published.

1903   *Typhoon: And Other Stories* ('Typhoon', 'Amy Foster', 'Falk', 'Tomorrow') and *Romance* (collaboration with Ford) published.

1904   Jessie Conrad injures her knees and is partially disabled for life. *Nostromo* published.

1906   Meets Arthur Marwood, who becomes his closest friend. John Conrad born. *The Mirror of the Sea* published.

1907   The Conrads move to The Someries, Luton Hoo. *The*

Secret Agent published.

1908 *A Set of Six* ('Gaspar Ruiz', 'The Informer', 'The Brute', 'An Anarchist', 'The Duel', 'Il Conde') published.

1909 Quarrels with Ford over his contributions to *The English Review*. The Conrads move to a cottage at Aldington, near 'The Pent'.

1910 Completion of *Under Western Eyes* accompanied by a nervous breakdown; Conrad lies in bed holding 'converse with the characters' of the novel. On his recovery the Conrads move to Capel House, Orlestone.

1911 *Under Western Eyes* published.

1912 *A Personal Record* and *'Twixt Land and Sea* ('A Smile of Fortune', 'The Secret Sharer', 'Freya of the Seven Isles') published.

1913 *Chance* published.

1914 *Chance* has good sales, especially in America; the earlier work now finds a larger public. The Conrads visit Poland and are nearly trapped by the outbreak of war.

1915 *Within the Tides* ('The Planter of Malata', 'The Partner', 'The Inn of the Two Witches') and *Victory* published.

1917 *The Shadow-Line* published. Conrad begins to write Author's Notes for a collected edition of his works.

1919 *The Arrow of Gold* published. The Conrads move to Oswalds, Bishopsbourne, near Canterbury.

1920 *The Rescue* published, 24 years after it was begun.

1921 Visit to Corsica for research on *Suspense*. Conrad in poor health. *Notes on Life and Letters* published.

1923 Conrad visits America and is lionized. *The Rover* published.

1924 May: Declines the offer of a knighthood. 3 August: Dies of a heart attack at Oswalds.

1924 *The Nature of a Crime* (collaboration with Ford) published.

1925 *Tales of Hearsay* ('The Warrior's Soul', 'Prince Roman', 'The Tale', 'The Black Mate') and *Suspense* published.

1926 *Last Essays* published.

1928 *The Sisters* (fragment) published.

AUTHOR'S NOTE

"NOSTROMO" is the most anxiously meditated of the longer novels which belong to the period following upon the publication of the "Typhoon" volume of short stories.

I don't mean to say that I became then conscious of any impending change in my mentality and in my attitude towards the tasks of my writing life. And perhaps there was never any change, except in that mysterious, extraneous thing which has nothing to do with the theories of art; a subtle change in the nature of the inspiration; a phenomenon for which I can not in any way be held responsible. What, however, did cause me some concern was that after finishing the last story*of the "Typhoon" volume it seemed somehow that there was nothing more in the world to write about.

This so strangely negative but disturbing mood lasted some little time; and then, as with many of my longer stories, the first hint for "Nostromo" came to me in the shape of a vagrant anecdote completely destitute of valuable details.

As a matter of fact in 1875 or '6, when very young, in the West Indies or rather in the Gulf of Mexico, for my contacts with land were short, few, and fleeting, I heard the story of some man who was supposed to have stolen single-handed a whole lighter-full of silver, somewhere on the Tierra Firme seaboard during the troubles of a revolution.

On the face of it this was something of a feat. But I heard no details, and having no particular interest in crime qua crime I was not likely to keep that one in my my mind. And I forgot it till twenty-six or seven years afterwards I came upon the very thing in a shabby

volume picked up outside a second-hand book-shop. It
was the life story of an American seaman written by
himself with the assistance of a journalist. In the
course of his wanderings that American sailor worked
for some months on board a schooner, the master and
owner of which was the thief of whom I had heard in
my very young days. I have no doubt of that because
there could hardly have been two exploits of that peculiar kind in the same part of the world and both connected with a South American revolution.

The fellow had actually managed to steal a lighter
with silver, and this, it seems, only because he was implicitly trusted by his employers, who must have been
singularly poor judges of character. In the sailor's
story he is represented as an unmitigated rascal, a small
cheat, stupidly ferocious, morose, of mean appearance,
and altogether unworthy of the greatness this opportunity had thrust upon him. What was interesting
was that he would boast of it openly.

He used to say: "People think I make a lot of
money in this schooner of mine. But that is nothing.
I don't care for that. Now and then I go away quietly
and lift a bar of silver. I must get rich slowly—you
understand."

There was also another curious point about the man.
Once in the course of some quarrel the sailor threatened
him: "What's to prevent me reporting ashore what
you have told me about that silver?"

The cynical ruffian was not alarmed in the least. He
actually laughed. "You fool, if you dare talk like that
on shore about me you will get a knife stuck in your
back. Every man, woman, and child in that port is
my friend. And who's to prove the lighter wasn't
sunk? I didn't show you where the silver is hidden.
Did I? So you know nothing. And suppose I lied? Eh?"

Ultimately the sailor, disgusted with the sordid meanness of that impenitent thief, deserted from the schooner. The whole episode takes about three pages of his autobiography. Nothing to speak of; but as I looked them over, the curious confirmation of the few casual words heard in my early youth evoked the memories of that distant time when everything was so fresh, so surprising, so venturesome, so interesting; bits of strange coasts under the stars, shadows of hills in the sunshine, men's passions in the dusk, gossip half-forgotten, faces grown dim. . . . Perhaps, perhaps, there still was in the world something to write about. Yet I did not see anything at first in the mere story. A rascal steals a large parcel of a valuable commodity—so people say. It's either true or untrue; and in any case it has no value in itself. To invent a circumstantial account of the robbery did not appeal to me, because my talents not running that way I did not think that the game was worth the candle. It was only when it dawned upon me that the purloiner of the treasure need not necessarily be a confirmed rogue, that he could be even a man of character, an actor and possibly a victim in the changing scenes of a revolution, it was only then that I had the first vision of a twilight country which was to become the province of Sulaco, with its high shadowy Sierra and its misty Campo for mute witnesses of events flowing from the passions of men short-sighted in good and evil.

Such are in very truth the obscure origins of "Nostromo"—the book. From that moment, I suppose, it had to be. Yet even then I hesitated, as if warned by the instinct of self-preservation from venturing on a distant and toilsome journey into a land full of intrigues and revolutions. But it had to be done.

It took the best part of the years 1903-4 to do; with

many intervals of renewed hesitation, lest I should lose myself in the ever-enlarging vistas opening before me as I progressed deeper in my knowledge of the country. Often, also, when I had thought myself to a standstill over the tangled-up affairs of the Republic, I would, figuratively speaking, pack my bag, rush away from Sulaco for a change of air and write a few pages of the "Mirror of the Sea." But generally, as I've said before, my sojourn on the Continent of Latin America, famed for its hospitality, lasted for about two years. On my return I found (speaking somewhat in the style of Captain Gulliver) my family all well, my wife heartily glad to learn that the fuss was all over, and our small boy considerably grown during my absence.

My principal authority for the history of Costaguana is, of course, my venerated friend, the late Don José Avellanos, Minister to the Courts of England and Spain, etc., etc., in his impartial and eloquent "History of Fifty Years of Misrule." That work was never published— the reader will discover why—and I am in fact the only person in the world possessed of its contents. I have mastered them in not a few hours of earnest meditation, and I hope that my accuracy will be trusted. In justice to myself, and to allay the fears of prospective readers, I beg to point out that the few historical allusions are never dragged in for the sake of parading my unique erudition, but that each of them is closely related to actuality; either throwing a light on the nature of current events or affecting directly the fortunes of the people of whom I speak.

As to their own histories I have tried to set them down, Aristocracy and People, men and women, Latin and Anglo-Saxon, bandit and politician, with as cool a hand as was possible in the heat and clash of my own conflicting emotions. And after all this is also the story of their conflicts. It is for the reader to say how far they are deserving of interest in their actions and in the secret purposes of their hearts revealed in the bitter necessities of the time. I confess that, for me, that time is the time of firm friendships and unforgotten hospitalities. And in my gratitude I must mention here Mrs. Gould, "the first lady of Sulaco," whom we may safely leave to the secret devotion of Dr. Monygham, and Charles Gould, the Idealist-creator of Material Interests whom we must leave to his Mine—from which there is no escape in this world.

About Nostromo, the second of the two racially and socially contrasted men, both captured by the silver of the San Tomé Mine, I feel bound to say something more.

I did not hesitate to make that central figure an Italian. First of all the thing is perfectly credible: Italians were swarming into the Occidental Province at the time, as anybody who will read further can see; and secondly, there was no one who could stand so well by the side of Giorgio Viola the Garibaldino, the Idealist of the old, humanitarian revolutions. For myself I needed there a man of the People as free as possible from his class-conventions and all settled modes of thinking. This is not a side snarl at conventions. My reasons were not moral but artistic. Had he been an Anglo-Saxon he would have tried to get into local politics. But Nostromo does not aspire to be a leader in a personal game. He does not want to raise himself above the mass. He is content to feel himself a power —within the People.

But mainly Nostromo is what he is because I received the inspiration for him in my early days from a Mediterranean sailor. Those who have read certain pages of mine will see at once what I mean when I say that Dominic,* the padrone of the *Tremolino*, might under given circumstances have been a Nostromo. At any rate Dominic would have understood the younger man perfectly—if scornfully. He and I were engaged together in a rather absurd adventure, but the absurdity does not matter. It is a real satisfaction to think that in my very young days there must, after all, have been something in me worthy to command that man's half-bitter fidelity, his half-ironic devotion. Many of Nostromo's speeches I have heard first in Dominic's voice. His hand on the tiller and his fearless eyes roaming the horizon from within the monkish hood shadowing his face, he would utter the usual exordium of his remorseless wisdom: "Vous autres gentilshommes!" in a caustic tone that hangs on my ear yet. Like Nostromo! "You hombres finos!" Very much like Nostromo. But Dominic the Corsican nursed a certain pride of ancestry from which my Nostromo is free; for Nostromo's lineage had to be more ancient still. He is a man with the weight of countless generations behind him and no parentage to boast of. . . . Like the People.

In his firm grip on the earth he inherits, in his improvidence and generosity, in his lavishness with his gifts, in his manly vanity, in the obscure sense of his greatness and in his faithful devotion with something despairing as well as desperate in its impulses, he is a Man of the People, their very own unenvious force, disdaining to lead but ruling from within. Years afterwards, grown older as the famous Captain Fidanza, with a stake in the country, going about his many affairs followed by respectful glances in the modernized streets of Sulaco, calling on the widow of the cargador, attending the Lodge, listening in unmoved silence to anarchist speeches at the meeting, the enigmatical patron of the new revolutionary agitation, the trusted, the wealthy comrade Fidanza with the knowledge of his moral ruin locked up in his breast, he remains essentially a man of the People. In his mingled love and scorn of life and in the bewildered conviction of having been betrayed, of dying betrayed he hardly knows by what or by whom, he is still of the People, their undoubted Great Man— with a private history of his own.

One more figure of those stirring times I would like to mention: and that is Antonia Avellanos—the "beautiful Antonia." Whether she is a possible variation of Latin-American girlhood I wouldn't dare to affirm. But, for me, she *is*. Always a little in the background by the side of her father (my venerated friend) I hope she has yet relief enough to make intelligible what I am going to say. Of all the people who had seen with me the birth of the Occidental Republic, she is the only one who has kept in my memory the aspect of continued life. Antonia the Aristocrat and Nostromo the Man of the People are the artisans of the New Era, the true creators of the New State; he by his legendary and daring feat, she, like a woman, simply by the force of what she is: the only being capable of inspiring a sincere passion in the heart of a trifler.

If anything could induce me to revisit Sulaco (I should hate to see all these changes) it would be Antonia. And the true reason for that—why not be frank about it?—the true reason is that I have modelled her on my first love.* How we, a band of tallish schoolboys, the chums of her two brothers, how we used to look up to that girl just out of the schoolroom herself, as the standard-bearer of a faith to which we all were born but which she alone knew how to hold aloft with an un-flinching hope! She had perhaps more glow and less serenity in her soul than Antonia, but she was an uncompromising Puritan of patriotism with no taint of the slightest worldliness in her thoughts. I was not the only one in love with her; but it was I who had to hear oftenest her scathing criticism of my levities—very much like poor Decoud—or stand the brunt of her austere, unanswerable invective. She did not quite understand—but never mind. That afternoon when I came in, a shrinking yet defiant sinner, to say the final good-bye I received a hand-squeeze that made my heart leap and saw a tear that took my breath away. She was softened at the last as though she had suddenly perceived (we were such children still!) that I was really going away for good, going very far away—even as far as Sulaco, lying unknown, hidden from our eyes in the darkness of the Placid Gulf.

That's why I long sometimes for another glimpse of the "beautiful Antonia" (or can it be the Other?) moving in the dimness of the great cathedral, saying a short prayer at the tomb of the first and last Cardinal-Archbishop of Sulaco, standing absorbed in filial devotion before the monument of Don José Avellanos, and, with a lingering, tender, faithful glance at the medallion-memorial to Martin Decoud, going out serenely into the sunshine of the Plaza with her upright carriage and her white head; a relic of the past disregarded by men awaiting impatiently the Dawns of other New Eras, the coming of more Revolutions.

But this is the idlest of dreams; for I did understand perfectly well at the time that the moment the breath left the body of the Magnificent Capataz, the Man of the People, freed at last from the toils of love and wealth, there was nothing more for me to do in Sulaco.

J. C.

October, 1917.

'*so foul a sky
clears not
without a storm*'*

SHAKESPEARE

NOSTROMO
A TALE OF THE SEABOARD

PART FIRST

THE SILVER OF THE MINE

NOSTROMO

CHAPTER ONE

IN THE time of Spanish rule, and for many years after-wards, the town of Sulaco—the luxuriant beauty of the orange gardens bears witness to its antiquity—had never been commercially anything more important than a coasting port with a fairly large local trade in ox-hides and indigo. The clumsy deep-sea galleons of the con-querors that, needing a brisk gale to move at all, would lie becalmed, where your modern ship built on clipper lines forges ahead by the mere flapping of her sails, had been barred out of Sulaco by the prevailing calms of its vast gulf. Some harbours of the earth are made dif-ficult of access by the treachery of sunken rocks and the tempests of their shores. Sulaco had found an in-violable sanctuary from the temptations of a trading world in the solemn hush of the deep Golfo Placido as if within an enormous semi-circular and unroofed temple open to the ocean, with its walls of lofty mountains hung with the mourning draperies of cloud.

On one side of this broad curve in the straight sea-board of the Republic of Costaguana,* the last spur of the coast range forms an insignificant cape whose name is Punta Mala. From the middle of the gulf the point of the land itself is not visible at all; but the shoulder of a steep hill at the back can be made out faintly like a shadow on the sky.

On the other side, what seems to be an isolated patch

of blue mist floats lightly on the glare of the horizon. This is the peninsula of Azuera, a wild chaos of sharp rocks and stony levels cut about by vertical ravines. It lies far out to sea like a rough head of stone stretched from a green-clad coast at the end of a slender neck of sand covered with thickets of thorny scrub. Utterly waterless, for the rainfall runs off at once on all sides into the sea, it has not soil enough—it is said—to grow a single blade of grass, as if it were blighted by a curse. The poor, associating by an obscure instinct of consolation the ideas of evil and wealth, will tell you that it is deadly because of its forbidden treasures. The common folk of the neighbourhood, peons of the estancias, vaqueros of the seaboard plains, tame Indians coming miles to market with a bundle of sugar-cane or a basket of maize worth about threepence, are well aware that heaps of shining gold lie in the gloom of the deep precipices cleaving the stony levels of Azuera. Tradition has it that many adventurers of olden time had perished in the search. The story goes also that within men's memory two wandering sailors—Americanos, perhaps, but gringos of some sort for certain—talked over a gambling, good-for-nothing mozo, and the three stole a donkey to carry for them a bundle of dry sticks, a water-skin, and provisions enough to last a few days. Thus accompanied, and with revolvers at their belts, they had started to chop their way with machetes through the thorny scrub on the neck of the peninsula.

On the second evening an upright spiral of smoke (it could only have been from their camp-fire) was seen for the first time within memory of man standing up faintly upon the sky above a razor-backed ridge on the stony head. The crew of a coasting schooner, lying becalmed three miles off the shore, stared at it with amazement till dark. A negro fisherman, living in a lonely hut in a little bay near by, had seen the start and was on the lookout for some sign. He called to his wife just as the sun was about to set. They had watched the strange portent with envy, incredulity, and awe.

The impious adventurers gave no other sign. The sailors, the Indian, and the stolen burro were never seen again. As to the mozo, a Sulaco man—his wife paid for some masses, and the poor four-footed beast, being without sin, had been probably permitted to die; but the two gringos,* spectral and alive, are believed to be dwelling to this day amongst the rocks, under the fatal spell of their success. Their souls cannot tear themselves away from their bodies mounting guard over the discovered treasure. They are now rich and hungry and thirsty—a strange theory of tenacious gringo ghosts suffering in their starved and parched flesh of defiant heretics, where a Christian would have renounced and been released.

These, then, are the legendary inhabitants of Azuera guarding its forbidden wealth; and the shadow on the sky on one side with the round patch of blue haze blurring the bright skirt of the horizon on the other, mark the two outermost points of the bend which bears the name of Golfo Placido, because never a strong wind had been known to blow upon its waters.

On crossing the imaginary line drawn from Punta Mala to Azuera the ships from Europe bound to Sulaco lose at once the strong breezes of the ocean. They become the prey of capricious airs that play with them for thirty hours at a stretch sometimes. Before them the head of the calm gulf is filled on most days of the year by a great body of motionless and opaque clouds. On the rare clear mornings another shadow is cast upon the sweep of the gulf. The dawn breaks high behind the towering and serrated wall of the Cordillera,*a clear-cut

vision of dark peaks rearing their steep slopes on a lofty
pedestal of forest rising from the very edge of the shore.
Amongst them the white head of Higuerota rises
majestically upon the blue. Bare clusters of enormous
rocks sprinkle with tiny black dots the smooth dome of
snow. ·

Then, as the midday sun withdraws from the gulf
the shadow of the mountains, the clouds begin to roll
out of the lower valleys. They swathe in sombre
tatters the naked crags of precipices above the wooded
slopes, hide the peaks, smoke in stormy trails across the
snows of Higuerota. The Cordillera is gone from you
as if it had dissolved itself into great piles of grey and
black vapours that travel out slowly to seaward and
vanish into thin air all along the front before the blazing
heat of the day. The wasting edge of the cloud-bank
always strives for, but seldom wins, the middle of the
gulf. The sun—as the sailors say—is eating it up.
Unless perchance a sombre thunder-head breaks away
from the main body to career all over the gulf till it
escapes into the offing beyond Azuera, where it bursts
suddenly into flame and crashes like a sinister pirate-
ship of the air, hove-to above the horizon, engaging the
sea.

At night the body of clouds advancing higher up
the sky smothers the whole quiet gulf below with an
impenetrable darkness, in which the sound of the falling
showers can be heard beginning and ceasing abruptly—
now here, now there. Indeed, these cloudy nights are
proverbial with the seamen along the whole west coast
of a great continent. Sky, land, and sea disappear
together out of the world when the Placido—as the saying is—goes to sleep under its black poncho. The few
stars left below the seaward frown of the vault shine
feebly as into the mouth of a black cavern. In its

vastness your ship floats unseen under your feet, her sails flutter invisible above your head. The eye of God Himself—they add with grim profanity—could not find out what work a man's hand is doing in there; and you would be free to call the devil to your aid with impunity if even his malice were not defeated by such a blind darkness.

The shores on the gulf are steep-to all round; three uninhabited islets basking in the sunshine just outside the cloud veil, and opposite the entrance to the harbour of Sulaco, bear the name of "The Isabels."

There is the Great Isabel; the Little Isabel, which is round; and Hermosa, which is the smallest.

That last is no more than a foot high, and about seven paces across, a mere flat top of a grey rock which smokes like a hot cinder after a shower, and where no man would care to venture a naked sole before sunset. On the Little Isabel an old ragged palm, with a thick bulging trunk rough with spines, a very witch amongst palm trees, rustles a dismal bunch of dead leaves above the coarse sand. The Great Isabel has a spring of fresh water issuing from the overgrown side of a ravine. Resembling an emerald green wedge of land a mile long, and laid flat upon the sea, it bears two forest trees standing close together, with a wide spread of shade at the foot of their smooth trunks. A ravine extending the whole length of the island is full of bushes; and presenting a deep tangled cleft on the high side spreads itself out on the other into a shallow depression abutting on a small strip of sandy shore.

From that low end of the Great Isabel the eye plunges through an opening two miles away, as abrupt as if chopped with an axe out of the regular sweep of the coast, right into the harbour of Sulaco. It is an oblong, lake-like piece of water. On one side the short wooded spurs and valleys of the Cordillera come down at right angles to the very strand; on the other the open view of the great Sulaco plain passes into the opal mystery of great distances overhung by dry haze. The town of Sulaco itself—tops of walls, a great cupola, gleams of white miradors in a vast grove of orange trees—lies between the mountains and the plain, at some little distance from its harbour and out of the direct line of sight from the sea.

NOSTROMO

CHAPTER TWO

THE only sign of commercial activity within the harbour, visible from the beach of the Great Isabel, is the square blunt end of the wooden jetty which the Oceanic Steam Navigation Company (the O.S.N. of familiar speech) had thrown over the shallow part of the bay soon after they had resolved to make of Sulaco one of their ports of call for the Republic of Costaguana. The State possesses several harbours on its long sea-board, but except Cayta, an important place, all are either small and inconvenient inlets in an iron-bound coast—like Esmeralda, for instance, sixty miles to the south—or else mere open roadsteads exposed to the winds and fretted by the surf.

Perhaps the very atmospheric conditions which had kept away the merchant fleets of bygone ages induced the O.S.N. Company to violate the sanctuary of peace sheltering the calm existence of Sulaco. The variable airs sporting lightly with the vast semicircle of waters within the head of Azuera could not baffle the steam power of their excellent fleet. Year after year the black hulls of their ships had gone up and down the coast, in and out, past Azuera, past the Isabels, past Punta Mala—disregarding everything but the tyranny of time. Their names, the names of all mythology, became the household words of a coast that had never been ruled by the gods of Olympus. The *Juno**was known only for her comfortable cabins amidships, the *Saturn**for the geniality of her .captain and the painted and gilt luxuriousness of her saloon, whereas

the *Ganymede**was fitted out mainly for cattle transport,
and to be avoided by coastwise passengers. The
humblest Indian in the obscurest village on the coast
was familiar with the *Cerberus*,*a little black puffer without charm or living accommodation to speak of, whose
mission was to creep inshore along the wooded beaches
close to mighty ugly rocks, stopping obligingly before
every cluster of huts to collect produce, down to three-
pound parcels of indiarubber bound in a wrapper of dry
grass.

And as they seldom failed to account for the smallest
package, rarely lost a bullock, and had never drowned
a single passenger, the name of the O.S.N. stood
very high for trustworthiness. People declared that
under the Company's care their lives and property
were safer on the water than in their own houses on
shore.

The O.S.N.'s superintendent in Sulaco for the whole
Costaguana section of the service was very proud of his
Company's standing. He resumed it in a saying which
was very often on his lips, "We never make mistakes."
To the Company's officers it took the form of a severe
injunction, "We must make no mistakes. I'll have
no mistakes here, no matter what Smith may do at his
end."

Smith, on whom he had never set eyes in his life, was
the other superintendent of the service, quartered some
fifteen hundred miles away from Sulaco. "Don't talk
to me of your Smith."

Then, calming down suddenly, he would dismiss the
subject with studied negligence.

"Smith knows no more of this continent than a
baby."

"Our excellent Señor Mitchell" for the business and
official world of Sulaco; "Fussy Joe" for the com-

manders of the Company's ships, Captain Joseph Mitchell prided himself on his profound knowledge of men and things in the country—cosas de Costaguana. Amongst these last he accounted as most unfavourable to the orderly working of his Company the frequent changes of government brought about by revolutions of the military type.

The political atmosphere of the Republic was generally stormy in these days. The fugitive patriots of the defeated party had the knack of turning up again on the coast with half a steamer's load of small arms and ammunition. Such resourcefulness Captain Mitchell considered as perfectly wonderful in view of their utter destitution at the time of flight. He had observed that "they never seemed to have enough change about them to pay for their passage ticket out of the country." And he could speak with knowledge; for on a memorable occasion he had been called upon to save the life of a dictator, together with the lives of a few Sulaco officials—the political chief, the director of the customs, and the head of police—belonging to an overturned government. Poor Señor Ribiera (such was the dictator's name) had come pelting eighty miles over mountain tracks after the lost battle of Socorro, in the hope of out-distancing the fatal news—which, of course, he could not manage to do on a lame mule. The animal, moreover, expired under him at the end of the Alameda, where the military band plays sometimes in the evenings between the revolutions. "Sir," Captain Mitchell would pursue with portentous gravity, "the ill-timed end of that mule attracted attention to the unfortunate rider. His features were recognized by several deserters from the Dictatorial army amongst the rascally mob already engaged in smashing the windows of the Intendencia."

Early on the morning of that day the local authorities of Sulaco had fled for refuge to the O.S.N. Company's offices, a strong building near the shore end of the jetty, leaving the town to the mercies of a revolutionary rabble; and as the Dictator was execrated by the populace on account of the severe recruitment law his necessities had compelled him to enforce during the struggle, he stood a good chance of being torn to pieces. Providentially, Nostromo—invaluable fellow —with some Italian workmen, imported to work upon the National Central Railway, was at hand, and managed to snatch him away—for the time at least. Ultimately, Captain Mitchell succeeded in taking everybody off in his own gig to one of the Company's steamers —it was the *Minerva*²—just then, as luck would have it, entering the harbour.

He had to lower these gentlemen at the end of a rope out of a hole in the wall at the back, while the mob which, pouring out of the town, had spread itself all along the shore, howled and foamed at the foot of the building in front. He had to hurry them then the whole length of the jetty; it had been a desperate dash, neck or nothing—and again it was Nostromo, a fellow in a thousand, who, at the head, this time, of the Company's body of lightermen, held the jetty against the rushes of the rabble, thus giving the fugitives time to reach the gig lying ready for them at the other end with the Company's flag at the stern. Sticks, stones, shots flew; knives, too, were thrown. Captain Mitchell exhibited willingly the long cicatrice of a cut over his left ear and temple, made by a razor-blade fastened to a stick—a weapon, he explained, very much in favour with the "worst kind of nigger out here."

Captain Mitchell was a thick, elderly man, wearing high, pointed collars and short side-whiskers, partial to white waistcoats, and really very communicative under his air of pompous reserve.

"These gentlemen," he would say, staring with great solemnity, "had to run like rabbits, sir. I ran like a rabbit myself. Certain forms of death are—er—distasteful to a—a—er—respectable man. They would have pounded me to death, too. A crazy mob, sir, does not discriminate. Under providence we owed our preservation to my Capataz de Cargadores,* as they called him in the town, a man who, when I discovered his value, sir, was just the bos'n of an Italian ship, a big Genoese ship, one of the few European ships that ever came to Sulaco with a general cargo before the building of the National Central. He left her on account of some very respectable friends he made here, his own countrymen, but also, I suppose, to better himself. Sir, I am a pretty good judge of character. I engaged him to be the foreman of our lightermen, and caretaker of our jetty. That's all that he was. But without him Señor Ribiera would have been a dead man. This Nostromo, sir, a man absolutely above reproach, became the terror of all the thieves in the town. We were infested, infested, overrun, sir, here at that time by ladrones and matreros, thieves and murderers from the whole province. On this occasion they had been flocking into Sulaco for a week past. They had scented the end, sir. Fifty per cent. of that murdering mob were professional bandits from the Campo, sir, but there wasn't one that hadn't heard of Nostromo. As to the town leperos, sir, the sight of his black whiskers and white teeth was enough for them. They quailed before him, sir. That's what the force of character will do for you."

It could very well be said that it was Nostromo alone who saved the lives of these gentlemen. Captain Mitchell, on his part, never left them till he had seen them collapse, panting, terrified, and exasperated, but safe, on the luxuriant velvet sofas in the first-class saloon of the *Minerva*. To the very last he had been careful to address the ex-Dictator as "Your Excellency."

"Sir, I could do no other. The man was down— ghastly, livid, one mass of scratches."

The *Minerva* never let go her anchor that call. The superintendent ordered her out of the harbour at once. No cargo could be landed, of course, and the passengers for Sulaco naturally refused to go ashore. They could hear the firing and see plainly the fight going on at the edge of the water. The repulsed mob devoted its energies to an attack upon the Custom House, a dreary, unfinished-looking structure with many windows two hundred yards away from the O.S.N. Offices, and the only other building near the harbour. Captain Mitchell, after directing the commander of the *Minerva* to land "these gentlemen" in the first port of call outside Costaguana, went back in his gig to see what could be done for the protection of the Company's property. That and the property of the railway were preserved by the European residents; that is, by Captain Mitchell himself and the staff of engineers building the road, aided by the Italian and Basque workmen who rallied faithfully round their English chiefs. The Company's lightermen, too, natives of the Republic, behaved very well under their Capataz. An outcast lot of very mixed blood, mainly negroes, everlastingly at feud with the other customers of low grog shops in the town, they embraced with delight this opportunity to settle their personal scores under such favourable auspices. There was not one of them that had not, at some time or other, looked with terror at Nostromo's revolver poked very close at his face, or been otherwise daunted by

Nostromo's resolution. He was "much of a man," their Capataz was, they said, too scornful in his temper ever to utter abuse, a tireless taskmaster, and the more to be feared because of his aloofness. And behold! there he was that day, at their head, condescending to make jocular remarks to this man or the other.

Such leadership was inspiriting, and in truth all the harm the mob managed to achieve was to set fire to one —only one—stack of railway-sleepers, which, being creosoted, burned well. The main attack on the railway yards, on the O.S.N. Offices, and especially on the Custom House, whose strong room, it was well known, contained a large treasure in silver ingots, failed completely. Even the little hotel kept by old Giorgio, standing alone halfway between the harbour and the town, escaped looting and destruction, not by a miracle, but because with the safes in view they had neglected it at first, and afterwards found no leisure to stop. Nostromo, with his Cargadores, was pressing them too hard then.

CHAPTER THREE

IT MIGHT have been said that there he was only protecting his own. From the first he had been admitted to live in the intimacy of the family of the hotel-keeper who was a countryman of his. Old Giorgio Viola, a Genoese with a shaggy white leonine head—often called simply "the Garibaldino" (as Mohammedans are called after their prophet)—was, to use Captain Mitchell's own words, the "respectable married friend" by whose advice Nostromo had left his ship to try for a run of shore luck in Costaguana.

The old man, full of scorn for the populace, as your austere republican so often is, had disregarded the preliminary sounds of trouble. He went on that day as usual pottering about the "casa" in his slippers, muttering angrily to himself his contempt of the non-political nature of the riot, and shrugging his shoulders. In the end he was taken unawares by the out-rush of the rabble. It was too late then to remove his family, and, indeed, where could he have run to with the portly Signora Teresa and two little girls on that great plain? So, barricading every opening, the old man sat down sternly in the middle of the darkened *café* with an old shot-gun on his knees. His wife sat on another chair by his side, muttering pious invocations to all the saints of the calendar.

The old republican did not believe in saints, or in prayers, or in what he called "priest's religion." Liberty and Garibaldi were his divinities; put he

16

tolerated "superstition" in women, preserving in these matters a lofty and silent attitude.

His two girls, the eldest fourteen, and the other two years younger, crouched on the sanded floor, on each side of the Signora Teresa, with their heads on their mother's lap, both scared, but each in her own way, the dark-haired Linda indignant and angry, the fair Giselle, the younger, bewildered and resigned. The Patrona removed her arms, which embraced her daughters, for a moment to cross herself and wring her hands hurriedly. She moaned a little louder.

"Oh! Gian' Battista,* why art thou not here? Oh! why art thou not here?"

She was not then invoking the saint himself, but calling upon Nostromo, whose patron he was. And Giorgio, motionless on the chair by her side, would be provoked by these reproachful and distracted appeals.

"Peace, woman! Where's the sense of it? There's his duty," he murmured in the dark; and she would retort, panting—

"Eh! I have no patience. Duty! What of the woman who has been like a mother to him? I bent my knee to him this morning; don't you go out, Gian' Battista—stop in the house, Battistino—look at those two little innocent children!"

Mrs. Viola was an Italian, too, a native of Spezzia, and though considerably younger than her husband, already middle-aged. She had a handsome face, whose complexion had turned yellow because the climate of Sulaco did not suit her at all. Her voice was a rich contralto. When, with her arms folded tight under her ample bosom, she scolded the squat, thick-legged China girls handling linen, plucking fowls, pounding corn in wooden mortars amongst the mud outbuildings at the back of the house, she could bring out such an im-

passioned, vibrating, sepulchral note that the chained
watch-dog bolted into his kennel with a great rattle.
Luis, a cinnamon-coloured mulatto with a sprouting
moustache and thick, dark lips, would stop sweeping the
café with a broom of palm-leaves to let a gentle shudder
run down his spine. His languishing almond eyes
would remain closed for a long time.

This was the staff of the Casa Viola, but all these
people had fled early that morning at the first sounds
of the riot, preferring to hide on the plain rather than
trust themselves in the house; a preference for which
they were in no way to blame, since, whether true or not,
it was generally believed in the town that the Garibaldino had some money buried under the clay floor of the
kitchen. The dog, an irritable, shaggy brute, barked
violently and whined plaintively in turns at the back,
running in and out of his kennel as rage or fear prompted
him.

Bursts of great shouting rose and died away, like wild
gusts of wind on the plain round the barricaded house;
the fitful popping of shots grew louder above the yelling.
Sometimes there were intervals of unaccountable stillness outside, and nothing could have been more gaily
peaceful than the narrow bright lines of sunlight from
the cracks in the shutters, ruled straight across the
café over the disarranged chairs and tables to the wall
opposite. Old Giorgio had chosen that bare, white-
washed room for a retreat. It had only one window,
and its only door swung out upon the track of thick
dust fenced by aloe hedges between the harbour and
the town, where clumsy carts used to creak along behind
slow yokes of oxen guided by boys on horseback.

In a pause of stillness Giorgio cocked his gun. The
ominous sound wrung a low moan from the rigid figure
of the woman sitting by his side. A sudden outbreak

of defiant yelling quite near the house sank all at once to a confused murmur of growls. Somebody ran along; the loud catching of his breath was heard for an instant passing the door; there were hoarse mutters and foot-steps near the wall; a shoulder rubbed against the shutter, effacing the bright lines of sunshine pencilled across the whole breadth of the room. Signora Teresa's arms thrown about the kneeling forms of her daughters embraced them closer with a convulsive pressure.

The mob, driven away from the Custom House, had broken up into several bands, retreating across the plain in the direction of the town. The subdued crash of irregular volleys fired in the distance was answered by faint yells far away. In the intervals the single shots rang feebly, and the low, long, white building blinded in every window seemed to be the centre of a turmoil widening in a great circle about its closed-up silence. But the cautious movements and whispers of a routed party seeking a momentary shelter behind the wall made the darkness of the room, striped by threads of quiet sunlight, alight with evil, stealthy sounds. The Violas had them in their ears as though invisible ghosts hovering about their chairs had consulted in mutters as to the advisability of setting fire to this foreigner's casa.

It was trying to the nerves. Old Viola had risen slowly, gun in hand, irresolute, for he did not see how he could prevent them. Already voices could be heard talking at the back. Signora Teresa was beside herself with terror.

"Ah! the traitor! the traitor!" she mumbled, almost inaudibly. "Now we are going to be burnt; and I bent my knee to him. No! he must run at the heels of his English."

She seemed to think that Nostromo's mere presence

in the house would have made it perfectly safe. So far,
she, too, was under the spell of that reputation the Capataz de Cargadores had made for himself by the waterside, along the railway line, with the English and with
the populace of Sulaco. To his face, and even against
her husband, she invariably affected to laugh it to scorn,
sometimes good-naturedly, more often with a curious
bitterness. But then women are unreasonable in their
opinions, as Giorgio used to remark calmly on fitting
occasions. On this occasion, with his gun held at
ready before him, he stooped down to his wife's head,
and, keeping his eyes steadfastly on the barricaded
door, he breathed out into her ear that Nostromo would
have been powerless to help. What could two men
shut up in a house do against twenty or more bent upon
setting fire to the roof? Gian' Battista was thinking of
the casa all the time, he was sure.

"He think of the casa! He'" gasped Signora Viola,
crazily. She struck her breast with her open hands.
"I know him. He thinks of nobody but himself.'

A discharge of firearms near by made her throw her
head back and close her eyes. Old Giorgio set his
teeth hard under his white moustache, and his eyes began to roll fiercely. Several bullets struck the end of
the wall together; pieces of plaster could be heard
falling outside; a voice screamed "Here they come!"
and after a moment of uneasy silence there was a rush
of running feet along the front.

Then the tension of old Giorgio's attitude relaxed,
and a smile of contemptuous relief came upon his lips
of an old fighter with a leonine face. These were not a
people striving for justice, but thieves. Even to defend his life against them was a sort of degradation for
a man who had been one of Garibaldi's immortal
thousand in the conquest of Sicily.* He had an im

mense scorn for this outbreak of scoundrels and leperos, who did not know the meaning of the word "liberty."

He grounded his old gun, and, turning his head, glanced at the coloured lithograph of Garibaldi in a black frame on the white wall; a thread of strong sunshine cut it perpendicularly. His eyes, accustomed to the luminous twilight, made out the high colouring of the face, the red of the shirt, the outlines of the square shoulders, the black patch of the Bersagliere hat with cock's feathers curling over the crown. An immortal hero! This was your liberty; it gave you not only life, but immortality as well!

For that one man his fanaticism had suffered no diminution. In the moment of relief from the apprehension of the greatest danger, perhaps, his family had been exposed to in all their wanderings, he had turned to the picture of his old chief, first and only, then laid his hand on his wife's shoulder.

The children kneeling on the floor had not moved. Signora Teresa opened her eyes a little, as though he had awakened her from a very deep and dreamless slumber. Before he had time in his deliberate way to say a reassuring word she jumped up, with the children clinging to her, one on each side, gasped for breath, and let out a hoarse shriek.

It was simultaneous with the bang of a violent blow struck on the outside of the shutter. They could hear suddenly the snorting of a horse, the restive tramping of hoofs on the narrow, hard path in front of the house; the toe of a boot struck at the shutter again; a spur jingled at every blow, and an excited voice shouted, "Hola! hola, in there!"

CHAPTER FOUR

ALL the morning Nostromo had kept his eye from afar on the Casa Viola, even in the thick of the hottest scrimmage near the Custom House. "If I see smoke rising over there," he thought to himself, "they are lost." Directly the mob had broken he pressed with a small band of Italian workmen in that direction, which, indeed, was the shortest line towards the town. That part of the rabble he was pursuing seemed to think of making a stand under the house; a volley fired by his followers from behind an aloe hedge made the rascals fly. In a gap chopped out for the rails of the harbour branch line Nostromo appeared, mounted on his silver-grey mare. He shouted, sent after them one shot from his revolver, and galloped up to the *café* window. He had an idea that old Giorgio would choose that part of the house for a refuge.

His voice had penetrated to them, sounding breathlessly hurried: "Hola! Vecchio! O, Vecchio! Is it all well with you in there?"

"You see——" murmured old Viola to his wife.

Signora Teresa was silent now. Outside Nostromo laughed.

"I can hear the padrona is not dead."

"You have done your best to kill me with fear," cried Signora Teresa. She wanted to say something more, but her voice failed her.

Linda raised her eyes to her face for a moment, but old Giorgio shouted apologetically—

"She is a little upset."

22

Outside Nostromo shouted back with another laugh—

"She cannot upset me."

Signora Teresa found her voice.

"It is what I say. You have no heart—and you have no conscience, Gian' Battista——"

They heard him wheel his horse away from the shutters. The party he led were babbling excitedly in Italian and Spanish, inciting each other to the pursuit. He put himself at their head, crying, "Avanti!"

"He has not stopped very long with us. There is no praise from strangers to be got here," Signora Teresa said, tragically. "Avanti! Yes! That is all he cares for. To be first somewhere—somehow—to be first with these English. They will be showing him to everybody. 'This is our Nostromo!'" She laughed ominously. "What a name! What is that? Nostromo? He would take a name that is properly no word from them."

Meantime Giorgio, with tranquil movements, had been unfastening the door; the flood of light fell on Signora Teresa, with her two girls gathered to her side, a picturesque woman in a pose of maternal exaltation. Behind her the wall was dazzlingly white, and the crude colours of the Garibaldi lithograph paled in the sunshine.

Old Viola, at the door, moved his arm upwards as if referring all his quick, fleeting thoughts to the picture of his old chief on the wall. Even when he was cooking for the "Signori Inglesi"—the engineers (he was a famous cook, though the kitchen was a dark place)—he was, as it were, under the eye of the great man who had led him in a glorious struggle where, under the walls of Gaeta, tyranny would have expired for ever had it not been for that accursed Piedmontese race of kings and ministers. When sometimes a frying-pan caught fire during a delicate operation with some shredded onions, and the old man was seen backing out of the doorway, swearing and coughing violently in an acrid cloud of smoke, the name of Cavour*—the arch intriguer sold to kings and tyrants—could be heard involved in imprecations against the China girls, cooking in general, and the brute of a country where he was reduced to live for the love of liberty that traitor had strangled.

Then Signora Teresa, all in black, issuing from another door, advanced, portly and anxious, inclining her fine, black-browed head, opening her arms, and crying in a profound tone—

"Giorgio! thou passionate man! Misericordia Divina! In the sun like this! He will make himself ill."

At her feet the hens made off in all directions, with immense strides; if there were any engineers from up the line staying in Sulaco, a young English face or two would appear at the billiard-room occupying one end of the house; but at the other end, in the *café*, Luis, the mulatto, took good care not to show himself. The Indian girls, with hair like flowing black manes, and dressed only in a shift and short petticoat, stared dully from under the square-cut fringes on their foreheads; the noisy frizzling of fat had stopped, the fumes floated upwards in sunshine, a strong smell of burnt onions hung in the drowsy heat, enveloping the house; and the eye lost itself in a vast flat expanse of grass to the west, as if the plain between the Sierra overtopping Sulaco and the coast range away there towards Esmeralda had been as big as half the world.

Signora Teresa, after an impressive pause, remonstrated—

"Eh, Giorgio! Leave Cavour alone and take care of

yourself now we are lost in this country all alone
with the two children, because you cannot live under a
king."

And while she looked at him she would sometimes put
her hand hastily to her side with a short twitch of her
fine lips and a knitting of her black, straight eyebrows
like a flicker of angry pain or an angry thought on her
handsome, regular features.

It was pain; she suppressed the twinge.   It had come
to her first a few years after they had left Italy to emi-
grate to America and settle at last in Sulaco after
wandering from town to town, trying shopkeeping in a
small way here and there; and once an organized enterprise of fishing—in Maldonado—for Giorgio, like the
great Garibaldi, had been a sailor in his time.

Sometimes she had no patience with pain.   For years
its gnawing had been part of the landscape embracing
the glitter of the harbour under the wooded spurs of the
range; and the sunshine itself was heavy and dull—
heavy with pain—not like the sunshine of her girlhood,
in which middle-aged Giorgio had wooed her gravely
and passionately on the shores of the gulf of Spezzia.*

"You go in at once, Giorgio," she directed.   "One
would think you do not wish to have any pity on me—
with four Signori Inglesi staying in the house."

"Va bene, va bene," Giorgio would mutter.

He obeyed.   The Signori Inglesi would require their
midday meal presently.   He had been one of the
immortal and invincible band of liberators who had
made the mercenaries of tyranny fly like chaff before a
hurricane, "un uragano terribile."*   But that was before
he was married and had children; and before tyranny
had reared its head again amongst the traitors who had
imprisoned Garibaldi, his hero.

There were three doors in the front of the house, and

each afternoon the Garibaldino could be seen at one or another of them with his big bush of white hair,* his arms folded, his legs crossed, leaning back his leonine head against the lintel, and looking up the wooded slopes of the foothills at the snowy dome of Higuerota. The front of his house threw off a black long rectangle of shade, broadening slowly over the soft ox-cart track. Through the gaps, chopped out in the oleander hedges, the harbour branch railway, laid out temporarily on the level of the plain, curved away its shining parallel ribbons on a belt of scorched and withered grass within sixty yards of the end of the house. In the evening the empty material trains of flat cars circled round the dark green grove of Sulaco, and ran, undulating slightly with white jets of steam, over the plain towards the Casa Viola, on their way to the railway yards by the harbour. The Italian drivers saluted him from the foot-plate with raised hand, while the negro brakesmen sat carelessly on the brakes, looking straight forward, with the rims of their big hats flapping in the wind. In return Giorgio would give a slight sideways jerk of the head, without unfolding his arms.

On this memorable day of the riot his arms were not folded on his chest. His hand grasped the barrel of the gun grounded on the threshold; he did not look up once at the white dome of Higuerota, whose cool purity seemed to hold itself aloof from a hot earth. His eyes examined the plain curiously. Tall trails of dust subsided here and there. In a speckless sky the sun hung clear and blinding. Knots of men ran headlong; others made a stand; and the irregular rattle of firearms came rippling to his ears in the fiery, still air. Single figures on foot raced desperately. Horsemen galloped towards each other, wheeled round together, separated at speed. Giorgio saw one fall, rider and horse disappearing as if they had galloped into a chasm, and the movements of the animated scene were like the passages of a violent game played upon the plain by dwarfs mounted and on foot, yelling with tiny throats, under the mountain that seemed a colossal embodiment of silence. Never before had Giorgio seen this bit of plain so full of active life; his gaze could not take in all its details at once; he shaded his eyes with his hand, till suddenly the thundering of many hoofs near by startled him.

A troop of horses had broken out of the fenced paddock of the Railway Company. They came on like a whirlwind, and dashed over the line snorting, kicking, squealing in a compact, piebald, tossing mob of bay, brown, grey backs, eyes staring, necks extended, nostrils red, long tails streaming. As soon as they had leaped upon the road the thick dust flew upwards from under their hoofs, and within six yards of Giorgio only a brown cloud with vague forms of necks and cruppers rolled by, making the soil tremble on its passage.

Viola coughed, turning his face away from the dust, and shaking his head slightly.

"There will be some horse-catching to be done before to-night," he muttered.

In the square of sunlight falling through the door Signora Teresa, kneeling before the chair, had bowed her head, heavy with a twisted mass of ebony hair streaked with silver, into the palm of her hands. The black lace shawl she used to drape about her face had dropped to the ground by her side. The two girls had got up, hand-in-hand, in short skirts, their loose hair falling in disorder. The younger had thrown her arm across her eyes, as if afraid to face the light. Linda, with her hand on the other's shoulder, stared fearlessly. Viola looked at his children.

The sun brought out the deep lines on his face, and, energetic in expression, it had the immobility of a carving. It was impossible to discover what he thought. Bushy grey eyebrows shaded his dark glance.

"Well! And do you not pray like your mother?"

Linda pouted, advancing her red lips, which were almost too red; but she had admirable eyes, brown, with a sparkle of gold in the irises, full of intelligence and meaning, and so clear that they seemed to throw a glow upon her thin, colourless face. There were bronze glints in the sombre clusters of her hair, and the eyelashes, long and coal black, made her complexion appear still more pale.

"Mother is going to offer up a lot of candles in the church. She always does when Nostromo has been away fighting. I shall have some to carry up to the Chapel of the Madonna in the Cathedral."

She said all this quickly, with great assurance, in an animated, penetrating voice. Then, giving her sister's shoulder a slight shake, she added—

"And she will be made to carry one, too!"

"Why made?" inquired Giorgio, gravely. "Does she not want to?"

"She is timid," said Linda, with a little burst of laughter. "People notice her fair hair as she goes along with us. They call out after her, 'Look at the Rubia! Look at the Rubiacita!' They call out in the streets. She is timid."

"And you? You are not timid—eh?" the father pronounced, slowly.

She tossed back all her dark hair.

"Nobody calls out after me."

Old Giorgio contemplated his children thoughtfully. There was two years difference between them. They had been born to him late, years after the boy had died.

Had he lived he would have been nearly as old as Gian' Battista—he whom the English called Nostromo; but as to his daughters, the severity of his temper, his advancing age, his absorption in his memories, had prevented his taking much notice of them. He loved his children, but girls belong more to the mother, and much of his affection had been expended in the worship and service of liberty.

When quite a youth he had deserted from a ship trading to La Plata, to enlist in the navy of Montevideo,* then under the command of Garibaldi. Afterwards, in the Italian legion of the Republic struggling against the encroaching tyranny of Rosas, he had taken part, on great plains, on the banks of immense rivers, in the fiercest fighting perhaps the world had ever known. He had lived amongst men who had declaimed about liberty, suffered for liberty, died for liberty, with a desperate exaltation, and with their eyes turned towards an oppressed Italy. His own enthusiasm had been fed on scenes of carnage, on the examples of lofty devotion, on the din of armed struggle, on the inflamed language of proclamations. He had never parted from the chief of his choice—the fiery apostle of independence —keeping by his side in America and in Italy till after the fatal day of Aspromonte,* when the treachery of kings, emperors, and ministers had been revealed to the world in the wounding and imprisonment of his hero—a catastrophe that had instilled into him a gloomy doubt of ever being able to understand the ways of Divine justice.

He did not deny it, however. It required patience, he would say. Though he disliked priests, and would not put his foot inside a church for anything, he believed in God. Were not the proclamations against tyrants addressed to the peoples in the name of God and liberty?

"God for men—religions for women," he muttered
sometimes. In Sicily, an Englishman who had turned
up in Palermo*after its evacuation by the army of the
king, had given him a Bible in Italian—the publication
of the British and Foreign Bible Society, bound in a
dark leather cover. In periods of political adversity,
in the pauses of silence when the revolutionists issued
no proclamations, Giorgio earned his living with the
first work that came to hand—as sailor, as dock labourer
on the quays of Genoa, once as a hand on a farm in
the hills above Spezzia—and in his spare time he
studied the thick volume. He carried it with him into
battles. Now it was his only reading, and in order not
to be deprived of it (the print was small) he had consented to accept the present of a pair of silver-mounted
spectacles from Señora Emilia Gould, the wife of
the Englishman who managed the silver mine in
the mountains three leagues from the town. She was
the only Englishwoman in Sulaco.

Giorgio Viola had a great consideration for the
English. This feeling, born on the battlefields of
Uruguay, was forty years old at the very least. Several
of them had poured their blood for the cause of freedom
in America, and the first he had ever known he remembered by the name of Samuel; he commanded a
negro company under Garibaldi, during the famous
siege of Montevideo, and died heroically with his
negroes at the fording of the Boyana. He, Giorgio, had
reached the rank of ensign—*alferez*—and cooked for the
general. Later, in Italy, he, with the rank of lieutenant,
rode with the staff and still cooked for the general. He
had cooked for him in Lombardy through the whole
campaign; on the march to Rome he had lassoed his
beef in the Campagna after the American manner; he
had been wounded in the defence of the Roman Re-

public; he was one of the four fugitives who, with the general, carried out of the woods the inanimate body of the general's wife into the farmhouse where she died, exhausted by the hardships of that terrible retreat. He had survived that disastrous time to attend his general in Palermo when the Neapolitan shells from the castle crashed upon the town. He had cooked for him on the field of Volturno* after fighting all day. And everywhere he had seen Englishmen in the front rank of the army of freedom. He respected their nation because they loved Garibaldi. Their very countesses and princesses had kissed the general's hands in London, it was said. He could well believe it; for the nation was noble, and the man was a saint. It was enough to look once at his face to see the divine force of faith in him and his great pity for all that was poor, suffering, and oppressed in this world.

The spirit of self-forgetfulness, the simple devotion to a vast humanitarian idea which inspired the thought and stress of that revolutionary time, had left its mark upon Giorgio in a sort of austere contempt for all personal advantage. This man, whom the lowest class in Sulaco suspected of having a buried hoard in his kitchen, had all his life despised money. The leaders of his youth had lived poor, had died poor. It had been a habit of his mind to disregard to-morrow. It was engendered partly by an existence of excitement, adventure, and wild warfare. But mostly it was a matter of principle. It did not resemble the carelessness of a condottiere, it was a puritanism of conduct, born of stern enthusiasm like the puritanism of religion.

This stern devotion to a cause had cast a gloom upon Giorgio's old age. It cast a gloom because the cause seemed lost. Too many kings and emperors flourished yet in the world which God had meant for the people.

He was sad because of his simplicity. Though always
ready to help his countrymen, and greatly respected by
the Italian emigrants wherever he lived (in his exile he
called it), he could not conceal from himself that they
cared nothing for the wrongs of down-trodden nations.
They listened to his tales of war readily, but seemed to
ask themselves what he had got out of it after all.
There was nothing that they could see. "We wanted
nothing, we suffered for the love of all humanity!" he
cried out furiously sometimes, and the powerful voice,
the blazing eyes, the shaking of the white mane, the
brown, sinewy hand pointing upwards as if to call
heaven to witness, impressed his hearers. After the old
man had broken off abruptly with a jerk of the head and
a movement of the arm, meaning clearly, "But what's
the good of talking to you?" they nudged each other.
There was in old Giorgio an energy of feeling, a personal
quality of conviction, something they called "terri-
bilità"—"an old lion," they used to say of him. Some
slight incident, a chance word would set him off talking
on the beach to the Italian fishermen of Maldonado, in
the little shop he kept afterwards (in Valparaiso) to his
countrymen customers; of an evening, suddenly, in the
café at one end of the Casa Viola (the other was reserved for the English engineers) to the select *clientèle* of
engine-drivers and foremen of the railway shops.

With their handsome, bronzed, lean faces, shiny
black ringlets, glistening eyes, broad-chested, bearded,
sometimes a tiny gold ring in the lobe of the ear,
the aristocracy of the railway works listened to him,
turning away from their cards or dominoes. Here
and there a fair-haired Basque studied his hand
meantime, waiting without protest. No native of
Costaguana intruded there. This was the Italian
stronghold. Even the Sulaco policemen on a night

patrol let their horses pace softly by, bending low in the saddle to glance through the window at the heads in a fog of smoke; and the drone of old Giorgio's declamatory narrative seemed to sink behind them into the plain. Only now and then the assistant of the chief of police, some broad-faced, brown little gentleman, with a great deal of Indian in him, would put in an appearance. Leaving his man outside with the horses he advanced with a confident, sly smile, and without a word up to the long trestle table. He pointed to one of the bottles on the shelf; Giorgio, thrusting his pipe into his mouth abruptly, served him in person. Nothing would be heard but the slight jingle of the spurs. His glass emptied, he would take a leisurely, scrutinizing look all round the room, go out, and ride away slowly, circling towards the town.

CHAPTER FIVE

IN THIS way only was the power of the local authorities vindicated amongst the great body of strong-limbed foreigners who dug the earth, blasted the rocks, drove the engines for the "progressive and patriotic undertaking." In these very words eighteen months before the Excellentissimo Señor don Vincente Ribiera, the Dictator of Costaguana, had described the National Central Railway in his great speech at the turning of the first sod.

He had come on purpose to Sulaco, and there was a one-o'clock dinner-party, a *convité* offered by the O.S.N. Company on board the *Juno* after the function on shore. Captain Mitchell had himself steered the cargo lighter, all draped with flags, which, in tow of the *Juno's* steam launch, took the Excellentissimo from the jetty to the ship. Everybody of note in Sulaco had been invited—the one or two foreign merchants, all the representatives of the old Spanish families then in town, the great owners of estates on the plain, grave, courteous, simple men, caballeros of pure descent, with small hands and feet, conservative, hospitable, and kind. The Occidental Province was their stronghold; their Blanco party had triumphed now; it was their President-Dictator, a Blanco of the Blancos, who sat smiling urbanely between the representatives of two friendly foreign powers. They had come with him from Sta. Marta to countenance by their presence the enterprise in which the capital of their countries was engaged.

The only lady of that company was Mrs. Gould, the

wife of Don Carlos, the administrator of the San Tomé
silver mine. The ladies of Sulaco were not advanced
enough to take part in the public life to that extent.
They had come out strongly at the great ball at the
Intendencia the evening before, but Mrs. Gould alone
had appeared, a bright spot in the group of black coats
behind the President-Dictator, on the crimson cloth-
covered stage erected under a shady tree on the shore
of the harbour, where the ceremony of turning the first
sod had taken place. She had come off in the cargo
lighter, full of notabilities, sitting under the flutter of
gay flags, in the place of honour by the side of Captain
Mitchell, who steered, and her clear dress gave the only
truly festive note to the sombre gathering in the long,
gorgeous saloon of the *Juno*.

The head of the chairman of the railway board (from
London), handsome and pale in a silvery mist of white
hair and clipped beard, hovered near her shoulder
attentive, smiling, and fatigued. The journey from
London to' Sta. Marta in mail boats and the special
carriages of the Sta. Marta coast-line (the only railway
so far) had been tolerable—even pleasant—quite tolerable. But the trip over the mountains to Sulaco was
another sort of experience, in an old diligencia over im-
passable roads skirting awful precipices.

"We have been upset twice in one day on the brink of
very deep ravines," he was telling Mrs. Gould in an
undertone. "And when we arrived here at last I don't
know what we should have done without your hospitality. What an out-of-the-way place Sulaco is!—
and for a harbour, too! Astonishing!"

"Ah, but we are very proud of it. It used to be
historically important. The highest ecclesiastical court,
for two viceroyalties, sat here in the olden time," she
instructed him with animation.

"I am impressed. I didn't mean to be disparaging.
You seem very patriotic."

"The place is lovable, if only by its situation. Perhaps you don't know what an old resident I am."

"How old, I wonder," he murmured, looking at her
with a slight smile. Mrs. Gould's appearance was
made youthful by the mobile intelligence of her face.
"We can't give you your ecclesiastical court back again;
but you shall have more steamers, a railway, a tele-
graph-cable—a future in the great world which is worth
infinitely more than any amount of ecclesiastical past.
You shall be brought in touch with something greater
than two viceroyalties. But I had no notion that a
place on a sea-coast could remain so isolated from the
world. If it had been a thousand miles inland now—most
remarkable! Has anything ever happened here for a
hundred years before to-day?"

While he talked in a slow, humorous tone, she kept
her little smile. Agreeing ironically, she assured him
that certainly not—nothing ever happened in Sulaco.
Even the revolutions, of which there had been two
in her time, had respected the repose of the place.
Their course ran in more populous southern parts
of the Republic, and the great valley of Sta. Marta,
which was like one great battlefield of the parties,
with the possession of the capital for a prize and
an outlet to another ocean. They were more advanced
over there. Here in Sulaco they heard only the echoes
of these great questions, and, of course, their official
world changed each time, coming to them over their
rampart of mountains which he himself had traversed
in an old diligencia, with such a risk to life and limb.

The chairman of the railway had been enjoying her
hospitality for several days, and he was really grateful
for it. It was only since he had left Sta. Marta that he

had utterly lost touch with the feeling of European life on the background of his exotic surroundings. In the capital he had been the guest of the Legation, and had been kept busy negotiating with the members of Don Vincente's Government—cultured men, men to whom the conditions of civilized business were not unknown.

What concerned him most at the time was the acquisition of land for the railway. In the Sta. Marta Valley, where there was already one line in existence, the people were tractable, and it was only a matter of price. A commission had been nominated to fix the values, and the difficulty resolved itself into the judicious influencing of the Commissioners. But in Sulaco—the Occidental Province for whose very development the railway was intended—there had been trouble. It had been lying for ages ensconced behind its natural barriers, repelling modern enterprise by the precipices of its mountain range, by its shallow harbour opening into the everlasting calms of a gulf full of clouds, by the benighted state of mind of the owners of its fertile territory—all these aristocratic old Spanish families, all those Don Ambrosios this and Don Fernandos that, who seemed actually to dislike and distrust the coming of the railway over their lands. It had happened that some of the surveying parties scattered all over the province had been warned off with threats of violence. In other cases outrageous pretensions as to price had been raised. But the man of railways prided himself on being equal to every emergency. Since he was met by the inimical sentiment of blind conservatism in Sulaco he would meet it by sentiment, too, before taking his stand on his right alone. The Government was bound to carry out its part of the contract with the board of the new railway company, even if it had to use force for the purpose. But he desired nothing less than an armed

disturbance in the smooth working of his plans. They
were much too vast and far-reaching, and too promising to leave a stone unturned; and so he imagined to get
the President-Dictator over there on a tour of cere-
monies and speeches, culminating in a great function
at the turning of the first sod by the harbour shore.
After all he was their own creature—that Don Vincente.
He was the embodied triumph of the best elements in
the State. These were facts, and, unless facts meant
nothing, Sir John argued to himself, such a man's influence must be real, and his personal action would
produce the conciliatory effect he required. He had
succeeded in arranging the trip with the help of a very
clever advocate, who was known in Sta. Marta as the
agent of the Gould silver mine, the biggest thing in
Sulaco, and even in the whole Republic. It was indeed
a fabulously rich mine. Its so-called agent, evidently a
man of culture and ability, seemed, without official
position, to possess an extraordinary influence in the
highest Government spheres. He was able to assure
Sir John that the President-Dictator would make the
journey. He regretted, however, in the course of the
same conversation, that General Montero insisted upon
going, too.

General Montero, whom the beginning of the struggle
had found an obscure army captain employed on the
wild eastern frontier of the State, had thrown in his lot
with the Ribiera party at a moment when special
circumstances had given that small adhesion a fortuitous importance. The fortunes of war served him
marvellously, and the victory of Rio Seco (after a day
of desperate fighting) put a seal to his success. At the
end he emerged General, Minister of War, and the
military head of the Blanco party, although there was
nothing aristocratic in his descent. Indeed, it was said

that he and his brother, orphans, had been brought up by the munificence of a famous European traveller, in whose service their father had lost his life. Another story was that their father had been nothing but a charcoal burner in the woods, and their mother a baptised Indian woman from the far interior.

However that might be, the Costaguana Press was in the habit of styling Montero's forest march from his commandancia to join the Blanco forces at the beginning of the troubles, the "most heroic military exploit of modern times." About the same time, too, his brother had turned up from Europe, where he had gone apparently as secretary to a consul. Having, however, collected a small band of outlaws, he showed some talent as guerilla chief and had been rewarded at the pacification by the post of Military Commandant of the capital.

The Minister of War, then, accompanied the Dictator. The board of the O.S.N. Company, working hand-in-hand with the railway people for the good of the Republic, had on this important occasion instructed Captain Mitchell to put the mail-boat *Juno* at the disposal of the distinguished party. Don Vincente, journeying south from Sta. Marta, had embarked at Cayta, the principal port of Costaguana, and came to Sulaco by sea. But the chairman of the railway company had courageously crossed the mountains in a ramshackle diligencia, mainly for the purpose of meeting his engineer-in-chief engaged in the final survey of the road.

For all the indifference of a man of affairs to nature, whose hostility can always be overcome by the resources of finance, he could not help being impressed by his surroundings during his halt at the surveying camp established at the highest point his railway was to reach. He spent the night there, arriving just too late to see the last dying glow of sunlight upon the snowy flank of Higuerota. Pillared masses of black basalt framed like an open portal a portion of the white field lying aslant against the west. In the transparent air of the high altitudes everything seemed very near, steeped in a clear stillness as in an imponderable liquid; and with his ear ready to catch the first sound of the expected diligencia the engineer-in-chief, at the door of a hut of rough stones, had contemplated the changing hues on the enormous side of the mountain, thinking that in this sight, as in a piece of inspired music, there could be found together the utmost delicacy of shaded expression and a stupendous magnificence of effect.

Sir John arrived too late to hear the magnificent and inaudible strain sung by the sunset amongst the high peaks of the Sierra. It had sung itself out into the breathless pause of deep dusk before, climbing down the fore wheel of the diligencia with stiff limbs, he shook hands with the engineer.

They gave him his dinner in a stone hut like a cubical boulder, with no door or windows in its two openings; a bright fire of sticks (brought on muleback from the first valley below) burning outside, sent in a wavering glare; and two candles in tin candlesticks—lighted, it was explained to him, in his honour—stood on a sort of rough camp table, at which he sat on the right hand of the chief. He knew how to be amiable; and the young men of the engineering staff, for whom the surveying of the railway track had the glamour of the first steps on the path of life, sat there, too, listening modestly, with their smooth faces tanned by the weather, and very pleased to witness so much affability in so great a man.

Afterwards, late at night, pacing to and fro outside, he had a long talk with his chief engineer. He knew him well of old. This was not the first undertaking in which their gifts, as elementally different as fire and water, had worked in conjunction. From the contact of these two personalities, who had not the same vision of the world, there was generated a power for the world's service—a subtle force that could set in motion mighty machines, men's muscles, and awaken also in human breasts an unbounded devotion to the task. Of the young fellows at the table, to whom the survey of the track was like the tracing of the path of life, more than one would be called to meet death before the work was done. But the work would be done: the force would be almost as strong as a faith. Not quite, however. In the silence of the sleeping camp upon the moonlit plateau forming the top of the pass like the floor of a vast arena surrounded by the basalt walls of precipices, two strolling figures in thick ulsters stood still, and the voice of the engineer pronounced distinctly the words—

"We can't move mountains!"

Sir John, raising his head to follow the pointing gesture, felt the full force of the words. The white Higuerota soared out of the shadows of rock and earth like a frozen bubble under the moon. All was still, till near by, behind the wall of a corral for the camp animals, built roughly of loose stones in the form of a circle, a pack mule stamped his forefoot and blew heavily twice.

The engineer-in-chief had used the phrase in answer to the chairman's tentative suggestion that the tracing of the line could, perhaps, be altered in deference to the prejudices of the Sulaco landowners. The chief engineer believed that the obstinacy of men was the lesser obstacle. Moreover, to combat that they had the great influence of Charles Gould, whereas tunnelling under Higuerota would have been a colossal undertaking.

"Ah, yes! Gould. What sort of a man is he?"

Sir John had heard much of Charles Gould in Sta.
Marta, and wanted to know more. The engineer-in-
chief assured him that the administrator of the San
Tomé silver mine had an immense influence over all
these Spanish Dons. He had also one of the best
houses in Sulaco, and the Gould hospitality was beyond all praise.

"They received me as if they had known me for
years," he said. "The little lady is kindness personified. I stayed with them for a month. He helped
me to organize the surveying parties. His practical
ownership of the San Tomé silver mine gives him a
special position. He seems to have the ear of every
provincial authority apparently, and, as I said, he can
wind all the hidalgos of the province round his little
finger. If you follow his advice the difficulties will fall
away, because he wants the railway. Of course, you
must be careful in what you say. He's English, and
besides he must be immensely wealthy. The Holroyd
house is in with him in that mine, so you may imagine——"

He interrupted himself as, from before one of the
little fires burning outside the low wall of the corral,
arose the figure of a man wrapped in a poncho up to the
neck. The saddle which he had been using for a pillow
made a dark patch on the ground against the red glow of
embers.

"I shall see Holroyd himself on my way back through
the States," said Sir John. "I've ascertained that he,
too, wants the railway."

The man who, perhaps disturbed by the proximity of
the voices, had arisen from the ground, struck a match
to light a cigarette. The flame showed a bronzed,
black-whiskered face, a pair of eyes gazing straight;

then, rearranging his wrappings, he sank full length and laid his head again on the saddle.

"That's our camp-master, whom I must send back to Sulaco now we are going to carry our survey into the Sta. Marta Valley," said the engineer. "A most useful fellow, lent me by Captain Mitchell of the O.S.N. Company. It was very good of Mitchell. Charles Gould told me I couldn't do better than take advantage of the offer. He seems to know how to rule all these muleteers and peons. We had not the slightest trouble with our people. He shall escort your diligencia right into Sulaco with some of our railway peons. The road is bad. To have him at hand may save you an upset or two. He promised me to take care of your person all the way down as if you were his father."

This camp-master was the Italian sailor whom all the Europeans in Sulaco, following Captain Mitchell's mispronunciation,* were in the habit of calling Nostromo. And indeed, taciturn and ready, he did take excellent care of his charge at the bad parts of the road, as Sir John himself acknowledged to Mrs. Gould afterwards.

CHAPTER SIX

At that time Nostromo had been already long enough in the country to raise to the highest pitch Captain Mitchell's opinion of the extraordinary value of his discovery. Clearly he was one of those invaluable subordinates whom to possess is a legitimate cause of boasting. Captain Mitchell plumed himself upon his eye for men—but he was not selfish—and in the innocence of his pride was already developing that mania for "lending you my Capataz de Cargadores" which was to bring Nostromo into personal contact, sooner or later, with every European in Sulaco, as a sort of universal factotum—a prodigy of efficiency in his own sphere of life.

"The fellow is devoted to me, body and soul!" Captain Mitchell was given to affirm; and though nobody, perhaps, could have explained why it should be so, it was impossible on a survey of their relation to throw doubt on that statement, unless, indeed, one were a bitter, eccentric character like Dr. Monygham—for instance—whose short, hopeless laugh expressed somehow an immense mistrust of mankind. Not that Dr. Monygham was a prodigal either of laughter or of words. He was bitterly taciturn when at his best. At his worst people feared the open scornfulness of his tongue. Only Mrs. Gould could keep his unbelief in men's motives within due bounds; but even to her (on an occasion not connected with Nostromo, and in a tone which for him was gentle), even to her, he had said once, "Really, it is most unreasonable to demand that a man should think of other people so much better than he is able to think of himself."

And Mrs. Gould had hastened to drop the subject. There were strange rumours of the English doctor. Years ago, in the time of Guzman Bento, he had been mixed up, it was whispered, in a conspiracy which was betrayed and, as people expressed it, drowned in blood. His hair had turned grey, his hairless, seamed face was of a brick-dust colour; the large check pattern of his flannel shirt and his old stained Panama hat were an established defiance to the conventionalities of Sulaco. Had it not been for the immaculate cleanliness of his apparel he might have been taken for one of those shiftless Europeans that are a moral eyesore to the respectability of a foreign colony in almost every exotic part of the world. The young ladies of Sulaco, adorning with clusters of pretty faces the balconies along the Street of the Constitution, when they saw him pass, with his limping gait and bowed head, a short linen jacket drawn on carelessly over the flannel check shirt, would remark to each other, "Here is the Señor doctor going to call on Doña Emilia. He has got his little coat on." The inference was true. Its deeper meaning was hidden from their simple intelligence. Moreover, they expended no store of thought on the doctor. He was old, ugly, learned—and a little "loco"—mad, if not a bit of a sorcerer, as the common people suspected him of being. The little white jacket was in reality a concession to Mrs. Gould's humanizing influence. The doctor, with his habit of sceptical, bitter speech, had no other means of showing his profound respect for the character of the woman who was known in the country as the English Señora. He presented this tribute very seriously indeed; it was no trifle for a man of his habits. Mrs. Gould felt that, too, perfectly.

She would never have thought of imposing upon him this marked show of deference.

She kept her old Spanish house (one of the finest specimens in Sulaco) open for the dispensation of the small graces of existence. She dispensed them with simplicity and charm because she was guided by an alert perception of values. She was highly gifted in the art of human intercourse which consists in delicate shades of self-forgetfulness and in the suggestion of universal comprehension. Charles Gould (the Gould family, established in Costaguana for three generations, always went to England for their education and for their wives) imagined that he had fallen in love with a girl's sound common sense like any other man, but these were not exactly the reasons why, for instance, the whole surveying camp, from the youngest of the young men to their mature chief, should have found occasion to allude to Mrs. Gould's house so frequently amongst the high peaks of the Sierra. She would have protested that she had done nothing for them, with a low laugh and a surprised widening of her grey eyes, had anybody told her how convincingly she was remembered on the edge of the snow-line above Sulaco. But directly, with a little capable air of setting her wits to work, she would have found an explanation. "Of course, it was such a surprise for these boys to find any sort of welcome here. And I suppose they are homesick. I suppose everybody must be always just a little homesick."

She was always sorry for homesick people.

Born in the country, as his father before him, spare and tall, with a flaming moustache, a neat chin, clear blue eyes, auburn hair, and a thin, fresh, red face, Charles Gould looked like a new arrival from over the sea. His grandfather had fought in the cause of

independence under Bolivar,* in that famous English
legion which on the battlefield of Carabobo*had been
saluted by the great Liberator as Saviours of his
country.   One of Charles Gould's uncles had been the
elected President of that very province of Sulaco (then
called a State) in the days of Federation, and afterwards had been put up against the wall of a church and
shot by the order of the barbarous Unionist general,
Guzman Bento.   It was the same Guzman Bento who,
becoming later Perpetual President, famed for his ruth-
less and cruel tyranny, reached his apotheosis in the
popular legend of a sanguinary land-haunting spectre
whose body had been carried off by the devil in person
from the brick mausoleum in the nave of the Church of
Assumption in Sta. Marta.   Thus, at least, the priests
explained its disappearance to the barefooted multitude that streamed in, awestruck, to gaze at the hole in
the side of the ugly box of bricks before the great altar.

Guzman Bento of cruel memory had put to death
great numbers of people besides Charles Gould's uncle;
but with a relative martyred in the cause of aristocracy,
the Sulaco Oligarchs (this was the phraseology of Guzman Bento's time; now they were called Blancos, and
had given up the federal idea), which meant the families
of pure Spanish descent, considered Charles as one of
themselves.   With such a family record, no one could
be more of a Costaguanero than Don Carlos Gould; but
his aspect was so characteristic that in the talk of
common people he was just the Inglez—the Englishman of Sulaco.   He looked more English than a casual
tourist, a sort of heretic pilgrim, however, quite unknown in Sulaco.   He looked more English than t. e
last arrived batch of young railway engineers, than
anybody out of the hunting-field pictures in the numbers of *Punch* reaching his wife's drawing-room two

months or so after date. It astonished you to hear him
talk Spanish (Castillan, as the natives say) or the
Indian dialect of the country-people so naturally. His
accent had never been English; but there was something
so indelible in all these ancestral Goulds—liberators,
explorers, coffee planters, merchants, revolutionists—
of Costaguana, that he, the only representative of the
third generation in a continent possessing its own style
of horsemanship, went on looking thoroughly English
even on horseback. This is not said of him in the
mocking spirit of the Llaneros—men of the great plains
—who think that no one in the world knows how to sit
a horse but themselves. Charles Gould, to use the
suitably lofty phrase, rode like a centaur. Riding
for him was not a special form of exercise; it was a
natural faculty, as walking straight is to all men sound
of mind and limb; but, all the same, when cantering*
beside the rutty ox-cart track to the mine he looked in
his English clothes and with his imported saddlery as
though he had come this moment to Costaguana at his
easy swift *pasotrote*, straight out of some green meadow
at the other side of the world.

His way would lie along the old Spanish road—the
Camino Real of popular speech—the only remaining
vestige of a fact and name left by that royalty old
Giorgio Viola hated, and whose very shadow had departed from the land; for the big equestrian statue of
Charles IV*at the entrance of the Alameda, towering
white against the trees, was only known to the folk
from the country and to the beggars of the town that
slept on the steps around the pedestal, as the Horse
of Stone. The other Carlos, turning off to the left
with a rapid clatter of hoofs on the disjointed pavement—Don Carlos Gould, in his English clothes, looked
as incongruous, but much more at home than the kingly

cavalier reining in his steed on the pedestal above the
sleeping leperos, with his marble arm raised towards
the marble rim of a plumed hat.

The weather-stained effigy of the mounted king, with
its vague suggestion of a saluting gesture, seemed to
present an inscrutable breast to the political changes
which had robbed it of its very name; but neither did
the other horseman, well known to the people, keen
and alive on his well-shaped, slate-coloured beast with
a white eye, wear his heart on the sleeve of his English
coat. His mind preserved its steady poise as if sheltered in the passionless stability of private and public
decencies at home in Europe. He accepted with a like
calm the shocking manner in which the Sulaco ladies
smothered their faces with pearl powder till they
looked like white plaster casts with beautiful living eyes,
the peculiar gossip of the town, and the continuous
political changes, the constant "saving of the country,"
which to his wife seemed a puerile and bloodthirsty
game of murder and rapine played with terrible earnestness by depraved children. In the early days of her
Costaguana life, the little lady used to clench her hands
with exasperation at not being able to take the public
affairs of the country as seriously as the incidental
atrocity of methods deserved. She saw in them a
comedy of naïve pretences, but hardly anything genuine
except her own appalled indignation. Charles, very
quiet and twisting his long moustaches, would decline to
discuss them at all. Once, however, he observed to
her gently—

"My dear, you seem to forget that I was born here."

These few words made her pause as if they had been
a sudden revelation. Perhaps the mere fact of being
born in the country did make a difference. She had a
great confidence in her husband; it had always been

very great. He had struck her imagination from the
first by his unsentimentalism, by that very quietude of
mind which she had erected in her thought for a sign of
perfect competency in the business of living. Don
José Avellanos, their neighbour across the street, a
statesman, a poet, a man of culture, who had represented his country at several European Courts (and
had suffered untold indignities as a state prisoner in the
time of the tyrant Guzman Bento), used to declare in
Doña Emilia's drawing-room that Carlos had all the
English qualities of character with a truly patriotic
heart.

Mrs. Gould, raising her eyes to her husband's thin,
red and tan face, could not detect the slightest quiver of
a feature at what he must have heard said of his
patriotism. Perhaps he had just dismounted on his
return from the mine; he was English enough to disregard the hottest hours of the day. Basilio, in a livery
of white linen and a red sash, had squatted for a moment
behind his heels to unstrap the heavy, blunt spurs in
the patio; and then the Señor Administrator would go
up the staircase into the gallery. Rows of plants in
pots, ranged on the balustrade between the pilasters
of the arches, screened the *corrédor**with their leaves and
flowers from the quadrangle below, whose paved space
is the true hearthstone of a South American house,
where the quiet hours of domestic life are marked by
the shifting of light and shadow on the flagstones.

Señor Avellanos was in the habit of crossing the patio
at five o'clock almost every day. Don José chose to
come over at tea-time because the English rite at Doña
Emilia's house reminded him of the time he lived in
London as Minister Plenipotentiary to the Court of
St. James. He did not like tea; and, usually, rocking
his American chair, his neat little shiny boots crossed on

the foot-rest, he would talk on and on with a sort of complacent virtuosity wonderful in a man of his age, while he held the cup in his hands for a long time. His close-cropped head was perfectly white; his eyes coal-black.

On seeing Charles Gould step into the sala he would nod provisionally and go on to the end of the oratorial period. Only then he would say—

"Carlos, my friend, you have ridden from San Tomé in the heat of the day. Always the true English activity. No? What?"

He drank up all the tea at once in one draught. This performance was invariably followed by a slight shudder and a low, involuntary "br-r-r-r," which was not covered by the hasty exclamation, "Excellent!"

Then giving up the empty cup into his young friend's hand, extended with a smile, he continued to expatiate upon the patriotic nature of the San Tomé mine for the simple pleasure of talking fluently, it seemed, while his reclining body jerked backwards and forwards in a rocking-chair of the sort exported from the United States. The ceiling of the largest drawing-room of the Casa Gould extended its white level far above his head. The loftiness dwarfed the mixture of heavy, straight-backed Spanish chairs of brown wood with leathern seats, and European furniture, low, and cushioned all over, like squat little monsters gorged to bursting with steel springs and horsehair. There were knick-knacks on little tables, mirrors let into the wall above marble consoles, square spaces of carpet under the two groups of armchairs, each presided over by a deep sofa; smaller rugs scattered all over the floor of red tiles; three windows from ceiling down to the ground, opening on a balcony, and flanked by the perpendicular folds of the dark hangings. The stateliness of ancient days lingered between the four high, smooth walls, tinted a delicate primrose-colour; and Mrs. Gould, with her little head and shining coils of hair, sitting in a cloud of muslin and lace before a slender mahogany table, resembled a fairy posed lightly before dainty philtres dispensed out of vessels of silver and porcelain.

Mrs. Gould knew the history of the San Tomé mine. Worked in the early days mostly by means of lashes on the backs of slaves, its yield had been paid for in its own weight of human bones. Whole tribes of Indians had perished in the exploitation; and then the mine was abandoned, since with this primitive method it had ceased to make a profitable return, no matter how many corpses were thrown into its maw. Then it became forgotten. It was rediscovered after the War of Independence. An English company obtained the right to work it, and found so rich a vein that neither the exactions of successive governments, nor the periodical raids of recruiting officers upon the population of paid miners they had created, could discourage their perseverance. But in the end, during the long turmoil of pronunciamentos*that followed the death of the famous Guzman Bento, the native miners, incited to revolt by the emissaries sent out from the capital, had risen upon their English chiefs and murdered them to a man. The decree of confiscation which appeared immediately afterwards in the *Diario Official*, published in Sta. Marta, began with the words: "Justly incensed at the grinding oppression of foreigners, actuated by sordid motives of gain rather than by love for a country where they come impoverished to seek their fortunes, the mining population of San Tomé, etc. . . ." and ended with the declaration: "The chief of the State has resolved to exercise to the full his power of clemency. The mine, which by every law, international, human, and divine, reverts now to the Government as national property, shall remain closed till the sword drawn for the sacred defence of liberal principles has accomplished its mission of securing the happiness of our beloved country."

And for many years this was the last of the San Tomé mine. What advantage that Government had expected from the spoliation, it is impossible to tell now. Costaguana was made with difficulty to pay a beggarly money compensation to the families of the victims, and then the matter dropped out of diplomatic despatches. But afterwards another Government bethought itself of that valuable asset. It was an ordinary Costaguana Government—the fourth in six years*—but it judged of its opportunities sanely. It remembered the San Tomé mine with· a secret conviction of its worthlessness in their own hands, but with an ingenious insight into the various uses a silver mine can be put to, apart from the sordid process of extracting the metal from under the ground. The father of Charles Gould, for a long time one of the most wealthy merchants of Costaguana, had already lost a considerable part of his fortune in forced loans to the successive Governments. He was a man of calm judgment, who never dreamed of pressing his claims; and when, suddenly, the perpetual concession of the San Tomé mine was offered to him in full settlement, his alarm became extreme. He was versed in the ways of Governments. Indeed, the intention of this affair, though no doubt deeply meditated in the closet, lay open on the surface of the document presented urgently for his signature. The third and most important clause stipulated that the concession-holder should pay at once to the Government five years' royalties on the estimated output of the mine.

Mr. Gould, senior, defended himself from this fatal

favour with many arguments and entreaties, but without success. He knew nothing of mining; he had no means to put his concession on the European market; the mine as a working concern did not exist. The buildings had been burnt down, the mining plant had been destroyed, the mining population had disappeared from the neighbourhood years and years ago; the very road had vanished under a flood of tropical vegetation as effectually as if swallowed by the sea; and the main gallery had fallen in within a hundred yards from the entrance. It was no longer an abandoned mine; it was a wild, inaccessible, and rocky gorge of the Sierra, where vestiges of charred timber, some heaps of smashed bricks, and a few shapeless pieces of rusty iron could have been found under the matted mass of thorny creepers covering the ground. Mr. Gould, senior, did not desire the perpetual possession of that desolate locality; in fact, the mere vision of it arising before his mind in the still watches of the night had the power to exasperate him into hours of hot and agitated insomnia.

It so happened, however, that the Finance Minister of the time was a man to whom, in years gone by, Mr. Gould had, unfortunately, declined to grant some small pecuniary assistance, basing his refusal on the ground that the applicant was a notorious gambler and cheat, besides being more than half suspected of a robbery with violence on a wealthy ranchero in a remote country district, where he was actually exercising the function of a judge. Now, after reaching his exalted position, that politician had proclaimed his intention to repay evil with good to Señor Gould—the poor man. He affirmed and reaffirmed this resolution in the drawing-rooms of Sta. Marta, in a soft and implacable voice, and with such malicious glances that Mr. Gould's best friends advised him earnestly to attempt no bribery

to get the matter dropped. It would have been useless.
Indeed, it would not have been a very safe proceeding.
Such was also the opinion of a stout, loud-voiced lady of
French extraction, the daughter, she said, of an officer
of high rank (*officier supérieur de l'armée*), who was
accommodated with lodgings within the walls of a
secularized convent next door to the Ministry of
Finance. That florid person, when approached on be-
half of Mr. Gould in a proper manner, and with a
suitable present, shook her head despondently. She
was good-natured, and her despondency was genuine.
She imagined she could not take money in consideration
of something she could not accomplish. The friend of
Mr. Gould, charged with the delicate mission, used to
say afterwards that she was the only honest person
closely or remotely connected with the Government
he had ever met. "No go," she had said with a cavalier,
husky intonation which was natural to her, and using
turns of expression more suitable to a child of parents
unknown than to the orphaned daughter of a general
officer. "No; it's no go. *Pas moyen, mon garçon.
C'est dommage, tout de même. Ah! zut! Je ne vole
pas mon monde. Je ne suis pas ministre—moi! Vous
pouvez emporter votre petit sac.*"*

For a moment, biting her carmine lip, she deplored
inwardly the tyranny of the rigid principles governing
the sale of her influence in high places. Then, significantly, and with a touch of impatience, "*Allez*," she
added, "*et dites bien à votre bonhomme—entendez-vous?—
qu'il faut avaler la pilule.*"*

After such a warning there was nothing for it but to
sign and pay. Mr. Gould had swallowed the pill, and
it was as though it had been compounded of some subtle
poison that acted directly on his brain. He became at
once mine-ridden, and as he was well read in light

literature it took to his mind the form of the Old Man of the Sea fastened upon his shoulders. He also began to dream of vampires. Mr. Gould exaggerated to himself the disadvantages of his new position, because he viewed it emotionally. His position in Costaguana was no worse than before. But man is a desperately conservative creature, and the extravagant novelty of this outrage upon his purse distressed his sensibilities. Everybody around him was being robbed by the grotesque and murderous bands that played their game of governments and revolutions after the death of Guzman Bento. His experience had taught him that, however short the plunder might fall of their legitimate expectations, no gang in possession of the Presidential Palace would be so incompetent as to suffer itself to be baffled by the want of a pretext. The first casual colonel of the barefooted army of scarecrows that came along was able to expose with force and precision to any mere civilian his titles to a sum of 10,000 dollars; the while his hope would be immutably fixed upon a gratuity, at any rate, of no less than a thousand. Mr. Gould knew that very well, and, armed with resignation, had waited for better times. But to be robbed under the forms of legality and business was intolerable to his imagination. Mr. Gould, the father, had one fault in his sagacious and honourable character: he attached too much importance to form. It is a failing common to mankind, whose views are tinged by prejudices. There was for him in that affair a malignancy of perverted justice which, by means of a moral shock, attacked his vigorous physique. "It will end by killing me," he used to affirm many times a day. And, in fact, since that time he began to suffer from fever, from liver pains, and mostly from a worrying inability to think of anything else. The Finance Minister could have formed no conception of the profound subtlety of his revenge. Even Mr. Gould's letters to his fourteen-year-old boy Charles, then away in England for his education, came at last to talk of practically nothing but the mine. He groaned over the injustice, the persecution, the outrage of that mine; he occupied whole pages in the exposition of the fatal consequences attaching to the possession of that mine from every point of view, with every dismal inference, with words of horror at the apparently eternal character of that curse. For the Concession had been granted to him and his descendants for ever. He implored his son never to return to Costaguana, never to claim any part of his inheritance there, because it was tainted by the infamous Concession; never to touch it, never to approach it, to forget that America existed, and pursue a mercantile career in Europe. And each letter ended with bitter self-reproaches for having stayed too long in that cavern of thieves, intriguers, and brigands.

To be told repeatedly that one's future is blighted because of the possession of a silver mine is not, at the age of fourteen, a matter of prime importance as to its main statement; but in its form it is calculated to excite a certain amount of wonder and attention. In course of time the boy, at first only puzzled by the angry jeremiads, but rather sorry for his dad, began to turn the matter over in his mind in such moments as he could spare from play and study. In about a year he had evolved from the lecture*of the letters a definite conviction that there was a silver mine in the Sulaco province of the Republic of Costaguana, where poor Uncle Harry had been shot by soldiers a great many years before. There was also connected closely with that mine a thing called the "iniquitous Gould Concession," apparently written on a paper which his father desired ardently to "tear and fling into the faces" of presidents, members of judicature, and ministers of State. And this desire persisted, though the names of these people, he noticed, seldom remained the same for a whole year together. This desire (since the thing was iniquitous) seemed quite natural to the boy, though why the affair was iniquitous he did not know. Afterwards, with advancing wisdom, he managed to clear the plain truth of the business from the fantastic intrusions of the Old Man of the Sea, vampires, and ghouls, which had lent to his father's correspondence the flavour of a gruesome Arabian Nights tale. In the end, the growing youth attained to as close an intimacy with the San Tomé mine as the old man who wrote these plaintive and enraged letters on the other side of the sea. He had been made several times already to pay heavy fines for neglecting to work the mine, he reported, besides other sums extracted from him on account of future royalties, on the ground that a man with such a valuable concession in his pocket could not refuse his financial assistance to the Government of the Republic. The last of his fortune was passing away from him against worthless receipts, he wrote, in a rage, whilst he was being pointed out as an individual who had known how to secure enormous advantages from the necessities of his country. And the young man in Europe grew more and more interested in that thing which could provoke such a tumult of words and passion.

He thought of it every day; but he thought of it without bitterness. It might have been an unfortunate affair for his poor dad, and the whole story threw a queer light upon the social and political life of Costaguana. The view he took of it was sympathetic to his father, yet calm and reflective. His personal feelings had not been outraged, and it is difficult to resent with proper and durable indignation the physical or mental anguish of another organism, even if that other organism is one's own father. By the time he was twenty Charles Gould had, in his turn, fallen under the spell of the San Tomé mine. But it was another form of enchantment, more suitable to his youth, into whose magic formula there entered hope, vigour, and self-confidence, instead of weary indignation and despair. Left after he was twenty to his own guidance (except for the severe injunction not to return to Costaguana), he had pursued his studies in Belgium and France with the idea of qualifying for a mining engineer. But this scientific aspect of his labours remained vague and imperfect in his mind. Mines had acquired for him a dramatic interest. He studied their peculiarities from a personal point of view, too, as one would study the varied characters of men. He visited them as one goes with curiosity to call upon remarkable persons. He visited mines in Germany, in Spain, in Cornwall. Abandoned workings had for him strong fascination. Their desolation appealed to him like the sight of human misery, whose causes are varied and profound. They might have been worthless, but also they might have been misunderstood. His future wife was the first, and perhaps the only person to detect this secret mood which governed the profoundly sensible, almost voiceless attitude of this man towards the world of material things. And at once her delight in him, lingering with half-open wings like those birds that cannot rise easily from a flat level, found a pinnacle from which to soar up into the skies.

They had become acquainted in Italy, where the future Mrs. Gould was staying with an old and pale aunt who, years before, had married a middle-aged,

impoverished Italian marquis. She now mourned that
man, who had known how to give up his life to the
independence and unity of his country, who had known
how to be as enthusiastic in his generosity as the youngest of those who fell for that very cause of which old
Giorgio Viola was a drifting relic, as a broken spar is
suffered to float away disregarded after a naval victory.
The Marchesa led a still, whispering existence, nun-like
in her black robes and a white band over the forehead,
in a corner of the first floor of an ancient and ruinous
palace, whose big, empty halls downstairs sheltered
under their painted ceilings the harvests, the fowls, and
even the cattle, together with the whole family of the
tenant farmer.

The two young people had met in Lucca.* After that
meeting Charles Gould visited no mines, though they
went together in a carriage, once, to see some marble
quarries, where the work resembled mining in so far
that it also was the tearing of the raw material of
treasure from the earth. Charles Gould did not open
his heart to her in any set speeches. He simply went
on acting and thinking in her sight. This is the true
method of sincerity. One of his frequent remarks
was, "I think sometimes that poor father takes a
wrong view of that San Tomé business." And they
discussed that opinion long and earnestly, as if they
could influence a mind across half the globe; but in
reality they discussed it because the sentiment of love
can enter into any subject and live ardently in remote
phrases. For this natural reason these discussions were
precious to Mrs. Gould in her engaged state. Charles
feared that Mr. Gould, senior, was wasting his strength
and making himself ill by his efforts to get rid of the
Concession. "I fancy that this is not the kind of
handling it requires," he mused aloud, as if to himself.

And when she wondered frankly that a man of character should devote his energies to plotting and intrigues, Charles would remark, with a gentle concern that understood her wonder, "You must not forget that he was born there."

She would set her quick mind to work upon that, and then make the inconsequent retort, which he accepted as perfectly sagacious, because, in fact, it was so——

"Well, and you? You were born there, too."

He knew his answer.

"That's different. I've been away ten years. Dad never had such a long spell; and it was more than thirty years ago."

She was the first person to whom he opened his lips after receiving the news of his father's death.

"It has killed him!" he said.

He had walked straight out of town with the news, straight out before him in the noonday sun on the white road, and his feet had brought him face to face with her in the hall of the ruined palazzo, a room magnificent and naked, with here and there a long strip of damask, black with damp and age, hanging down on a bare panel of the wall. It was furnished with exactly one gilt armchair, with a broken back, and an octagon columnar stand bearing a heavy marble vase ornamented with sculptured masks and garlands of flowers, and cracked from top to bottom. Charles Gould was dusty with the white dust of the road lying on his boots, on his shoulders, on his cap with two peaks. Water dripped from under it all over his face, and he grasped a thick oaken cudgel in his bare right hand.

She went very pale under the roses of her big straw hat, gloved, swinging a clear sunshade, caught just as she was going out to meet him at the bottom of the hill, where three poplars stand near the wall of a vineyard.

"It has killed him!" he repeated. "He ought to have had many years yet. We are a long-lived family."

She was too startled to say anything; he was contemplating with a penetrating and motionless stare the cracked marble urn as though he had resolved to fix its shape for ever in his memory. It was only when, turning suddenly to her, he blurted out twice, "I've come to you—— I've come straight to you——," without being able to finish his phrase, that the great pitifulness of that lonely and tormented death in Costaguana came to her with the full force of its misery. He caught hold of her hand, raised it to his lips, and at that she dropped her parasol to pat him on the cheek, murmured "Poor boy," and began to dry her eyes under the downward curve of her hat-brim, very small in her simple, white frock, almost like a lost child crying in the degraded grandeur of the noble hall, while he stood by her, again perfectly motionless in the contemplation of the marble urn.

Afterwards they went out for a long walk, which was silent till he exclaimed suddenly—

"Yes. But if he had only grappled with it in a proper way!"

And then they stopped. Everywhere there were long shadows lying on the hills, on the roads, on the enclosed fields of olive trees; the shadows of poplars, of wide chestnuts, of farm buildings, of stone walls; and in mid-air the sound of a bell, thin and alert, was like the throbbing pulse of the sunset glow. Her lips were slightly parted as though in surprise that he should not be looking at her with his usual expression. His usual expression was unconditionally approving and attentive. He was in his talks with her the most anxious and deferential of dictators, an attitude that pleased her immensely. It affirmed her power without detracting from his dignity. That slight girl, with her little feet, little hands, little face attractively overweighted by great coils of hair; with a rather large mouth, whose mere parting seemed to breathe upon you the fragrance of frankness and generosity, had the fastidious soul of an experienced woman. She was, before all things and all flatteries, careful of her pride in the object of her choice. But now he was actually not looking at her at all; and his expression was tense and irrational, as is natural in a man who elects to stare at nothing past a young girl's head.

"Well, yes. It was iniquitous. They corrupted him thoroughly, the poor old boy. Oh! why wouldn't he let me go back to him? But now I shall know how to grapple with this."

After pronouncing these words with immense assurance, he glanced down at her, and at once fell a prey to distress, incertitude, and fear.

The only thing he wanted to know now, he said, was whether she did love him enough—whether she would have the courage to go with him so far away? He put these questions to her in a voice that trembled with anxiety—for he was a determined man.

She did. She would. And immediately the future hostess of all the Europeans in Sulaco had the physical experience of the earth falling away from under her. It vanished completely, even to the very sound of the bell. When her feet touched the ground again, the bell was still ringing in the valley; she put her hands up to her hair, breathing quickly, and glanced up and down the stony lane. It was reassuringly empty. Meantime, Charles, stepping with one foot into a dry and dusty ditch, picked up the open parasol, which had bounded away from them with a martial sound of drum taps. He handed it to her soberly, a little crestfallen.

They turned back, and after she had slipped her hand on his arm, the first words he pronounced were—

"It's lucky that we shall be able to settle in a coast town. You've heard its name. It is Sulaco. I am so glad poor father did get that house. He bought a big house there years ago, in order that there should always be a Casa Gould in the principal town of what used to be called the Occidental Province. I lived there once, as a small boy, with my dear mother, for a whole year, while poor father was away in the United States on business. You shall be the new mistress of the Casa Gould."

And later, in the inhabited corner of the Palazzo above the vineyards, the marble hills, the pines and olives of Lucca, he also said—

"The name of Gould has been always highly respected in Sulaco. My uncle Harry was chief of the State for some time, and has left a great name amongst the first families. By this I mean the pure Creole families, who take no part in the miserable farce of governments. Uncle Harry was no adventurer. In Costaguana we Goulds are no adventurers. He was of the country, and he loved it, but he remained essentially an Englishman in his ideas. He made use of the political cry of his time. It was Federation. But he was no politician. He simply stood up for social order out of pure love for rational liberty and from his hate of oppression. There was no nonsense about him. He went to work in his own way because it seemed right, just as I feel I must lay hold of that mine."

In such words he talked to her because his memory was very full of the country of his childhood, his heart of his life with that girl, and his mind of the San Tomé Concession. He added that he would have to leave her for a few days to find an American, a man from San Francisco, who was still somewhere in Europe. A few months before he had made his acquaintance in an old historic German town, situated in a mining district. The American had his womankind with him, but seemed lonely while they were sketching all day long the old doorways and the turreted corners of the mediæval houses. Charles Gould had with him the inseparable companionship of the mine. The other man was interested in mining enterprises, knew something of Costaguana, and was no stranger to the name of Gould. They had talked together with some intimacy which was made possible by the difference of their ages. Charles wanted now to find that capitalist of shrewd mind and accessible character. His father's fortune in Costaguana, which he had supposed to be still considerable, seemed to have melted in the rascally crucible of revolutions. Apart from some ten thousand pounds deposited in England, there appeared to be nothing left except the house in Sulaco, a vague right of forest exploitation in a remote and savage district, and the San Tomé Concession, which had attended his poor father to the very brink of the grave.

He explained those things. It was late when they parted. She had never before given him such a fascinating vision of herself.. All the eagerness of youth for a strange life, for great distances, for a future in which there was an air of adventure, of combat—a subtle thought of redress and conquest, had filled her with an intense excitement, which she returned to the giver with a more open and exquisite display of tenderness.

He left her to walk down the hill, and directly he found himself alone he became sober. That irreparable change a death makes in the course of our daily thoughts can be felt in a vague and poignant discomfort of mind. It hurt Charles Gould to feel that never more, by no

effort of will, would he be able to think of his father in
the same way he used to think of him when the poor
man was alive. His breathing image was no longer
in his power. This consideration, closely affecting his
own identity, filled his breast with a mournful and angry
desire for action. In this his instinct was unerring.
Action is consolatory. It is the enemy of thought and
the friend of flattering illusions. Only in the conduct
of our action can we find the sense of mastery over the
Fates. For his action, the mine was obviously the only
field. It was imperative sometimes to know how to
disobey the solemn wishes of the dead. He resolved
firmly to make his disobedience as thorough (by way
of atonement) as it well could be. The mine had been
the cause of an absurd moral disaster; its working must
be made a serious and moral success. He owed it to
the dead man's memory. Such were the—properly
speaking—emotions of Charles Gould. His thoughts
ran upon the means of raising a large amount of capital
in San Francisco or elsewhere; and incidentally there
occurred to him also the general reflection that the
counsel of the departed must be an unsound guide
Not one of them could be aware beforehand what
enormous changes the death of any given individual
may produce in the very aspect of the world.

The latest phase in the history of the mine Mrs.
Gould knew from personal experience. It was in
essence the history of her married life. The mantle of
the Goulds' hereditary position in Sulaco had descended
amply upon her little person; but she would not allow
the peculiarities of the strange garment to weigh down
the vivacity of her character, which was the sign of no
mere mechanical sprightliness, but of an eager intelligence. It must not be supposed that Mrs. Gould's
mind was masculine. A woman with a masculine mind

is not a being of superior efficiency; she is simply a phenomenon of imperfect differentiation—interestingly barren and without importance. Doña Emilia's intelligence being feminine led her to achieve the conquest of Sulaco, simply by lighting the way for her unselfishness and sympathy. She could converse charmingly, but she was not talkative. The wisdom of the heart having no concern with the erection or demolition of theories any more than with the defence of prejudices, has no random words at its command. The words it pronounces have the value of acts of integrity, tolerance, and compassion. A woman's true tenderness, like the true virility of man, is expressed in action of a conquering kind. The ladies of Sulaco adored Mrs. Gould. "They still look upon me as something of a monster," Mrs. Gould had said pleasantly to one of the three gentlemen from San Francisco she had to entertain in her new Sulaco house just about a year after her marriage.

They were her first visitors from abroad, and they had come to look at the San Tomé mine. She jested most agreeably, they thought; and Charles Gould, besides knowing thoroughly what he was about, had shown himself a real hustler. These facts caused them to be well disposed towards his wife. An unmistakable enthusiasm, pointed by a slight flavour of irony, made her talk of the mine absolutely fascinating to her visitors, and provoked them to grave and indulgent smiles in which there was a good deal of deference. Perhaps had they known how much she was inspired by an idealistic view of success they would have been amazed at the state of her mind as the Spanish-American ladies had been amazed at the tireless activity of her body. She would—in her own words—have been for them "something of a monster." However, the

Goulds were in essentials a reticent couple, and their
guests departed without the suspicion of any other purpose but simple profit in the working of a silver mine.
Mrs. Gould had out her own carriage, with two white
mules, to drive them down to the harbour, whence the
Ceres was to carry them off into the Olympus of pluto-
crats. Captain Mitchell had snatched at the occasion
of leave-taking to remark to Mrs. Gould, in a low, confidential mutter, "This marks an epoch."

Mrs. Gould loved the patio of her Spanish house. A
broad flight of stone steps was overlooked silently from
a niche in the wall by a Madonna in blue robes with the
crowned child sitting on her arm. Subdued voices
ascended in the early mornings from the paved well
of the quadrangle, with the stamping of horses and
mules led out in pairs to drink at the cistern. A tangle
of slender bamboo stems drooped its narrow, blade-like
leaves over the square pool of water, and the fat coachman sat muffled up on the edge, holding lazily the ends
of halters in his hand. Barefooted servants passed to
and fro, issuing from dark, low doorways below; two
laundry girls with baskets of washed linen; the baker
with the tray of bread made for the day; Leonarda—
her own camerista—bearing high up, swung from her
hand raised above her raven black head, a bunch of
starched under-skirts dazzlingly white in the slant of
sunshine. Then the old porter would hobble in, sweeping the flagstones, and the house was ready for the day.
All the lofty rooms on three sides of the quadrangle
opened into each other and into the *corrédor*, with its
wrought-iron railings and a border of flowers, whence,
like the lady of the mediæval castle, she could witness
from above all the departures and arrivals of the Casa,
to which the sonorous arched gateway lent an air of
stately importance.

She had watched her carriage roll away with the three guests from the north. She smiled. Their three arms went up simultaneously to their three hats. Captain Mitchell, the fourth, in attendance, had already begun a pompous discourse. Then she lingered. She lingered, approaching her face to the clusters of flowers here and there as if to give time to her thoughts to catch up with her slow footsteps along the straight vista of the corridor.

A fringed Indian hammock from Aroa, gay with coloured featherwork, had been swung judiciously in a corner that caught the early sun; for the mornings are cool in Sulaco. The cluster of *flor de noche buena** blazed in great masses before the open glass doors of the reception rooms. A big green parrot, brilliant like an emerald in a cage that flashed like gold, screamed out ferociously, "Vive Costaguana!" then called twice mellifluously, "Leonarda! Leonarda!" in imitation of Mrs. Gould's voice, and suddenly took refuge in immobility and silence. Mrs. Gould reached the end of the gallery and put her head through the door of her husband's room.

Charles Gould, with one foot on a low wooden stool, was already strapping his spurs. He wanted to hurry back to the mine. Mrs. Gould, without coming in, glanced about the room. One tall, broad bookcase, with glass doors, was full of books; but in the other, without shelves, and lined with red baize, were arranged firearms: Winchester carbines, revolvers, a couple of shot-guns, and even two pairs of double-barrelled holster pistols. Between them, by itself, upon a strip of scarlet velvet, hung an old cavalry sabre, once the property of Don Enrique Gould, the hero of the Occidental Province, presented by Don José Avellanos, the hereditary friend of the family.

Otherwise, the plastered white walls were completely bare, except for a water-colour sketch of the San Tomé mountain—the work of Doña Emilia herself. In the middle of the red-tiled floor stood two long tables littered with plans and papers, a few chairs, and a glass show-case containing specimens of ore from the mine. Mrs. Gould, looking at all these things in turn, wondered aloud why the talk of these wealthy and enterprising men discussing the prospects, the working, and the safety of the mine rendered her so impatient and uneasy, whereas she could talk of the mine by the hour with her husband with unwearied interest and satisfaction.

And dropping her eyelids expressively, she added—

"What do *you* feel about it, Charley?"

Then, surprised at her husband's silence, she raised her eyes, opened wide, as pretty as pale flowers. He had done with the spurs, and, twisting his moustache with both hands, horizontally, he contemplated her from the height of his long legs with a visible appreciation of her appearance. The consciousness of being thus contemplated pleased Mrs. Gould.

"They are considerable men," he said.

"I know. But have you listened to their conversation? They don't seem to have understood anything they have seen here."

"They have seen the mine. They have understood that to some purpose," Charles Gould interjected, in defence of the visitors; and then his wife mentioned the name of the most considerable of the three. He was considerable in finance and in industry. His name was familiar to many millions of people. He was so considerable that he would never have travelled so far away from the centre of his activity if the doctors had not insisted, with veiled menaces, on his taking a long holiday.

"Mr. Holroyd's sense of religion," Mrs. Gould pursued, "was shocked and disgusted at the tawdriness of the dressed-up saints in the cathedral—the worship, he called it, of wood and tinsel. But it seemed to me that he looked upon his own God as a sort of influential partner, who gets his share of profits in the endowment of churches. That's a sort of idolatry. He told me he endowed churches every year, Charley."

"No end of them," said Mr. Gould, marvelling inwardly at the mobility of her physiognomy. "All over the country. He's famous for that sort of munificence."

"Oh, he didn't boast," Mrs. Gould declared, scrupulously. "I believe he's really a good man, but so stupid! A poor Chulo who offers a little silver arm or leg to thank his god for a cure is as rational and more touching."

"He's at the head of immense silver and iron interests," Charles Gould observed.

"Ah, yes! The religion of silver and iron. He's a very civil man, though he looked awfully solemn when he first saw the Madonna on the staircase, who's only wood and paint; but he said nothing to me. My dear Charley, I heard those men talk among themselves. Can it be that they really wish to become, for an immense consideration, drawers of water and hewers of wood to all the countries and nations of the earth?"

"A man must work to some end," Charles Gould said, vaguely.

Mrs. Gould, frowning, surveyed him from head to foot. With his riding breeches, leather leggings (an article of apparel never before seen in Costaguana), a Norfolk coat of grey flannel, and those great flaming moustaches, he suggested an officer of cavalry turned gentleman farmer. This combination was gratifying to Mrs. Gould's tastes. "How thin the poor boy is!" she thought. "He overworks himself." But there was no denying that his fine-drawn, keen red face, and his whole, long-limbed, lank person had an air of breeding and distinction. And Mrs. Gould relented.

"I only wondered what you felt," she murmured, gently.

During the last few days, as it happened, Charles Gould had been kept too busy thinking twice before he spoke to have paid much attention to the state of his feelings. But theirs was a successful match, and he had no difficulty in finding his answer.

"The best of my feelings are in your keeping, my dear," he said, lightly; and there was so much truth in that obscure phrase that he experienced towards her at the moment a great increase of gratitude and tenderness.

Mrs. Gould, however, did not seem to find this answer in the least obscure. She brightened up delicately; already he had changed his tone.

"But there are facts. The worth of the mine—as a mine—is beyond doubt. It shall make us very wealthy. The mere working of it is a matter of technical knowledge, which I have—which ten thousand other men in the world have. But its safety, its continued existence as an enterprise, giving a return to men—to strangers, comparative strangers—who invest money in it, is left altogether in my hands. I have inspired confidence in a man of wealth and position. You seem to think this perfectly natural—do you? Well, I don't know. I don't know why I have; but it is a fact. This fact makes everything possible, because without it I would never have thought of disregarding my father's wishes. I would never have disposed of the Concession as a speculator disposes of a valuable right to a company— for cash and shares, to grow rich eventually if possible, but at any rate to put some money at once in his pocket. No. Even if it had been feasible—which I doubt—I would not have done so. Poor father did not understand. He was afraid I would hang on to the ruinous thing, waiting for just some such chance, and waste my life miserably. That was the true sense of his prohibition, which we have deliberately set aside."

They were walking up and down the corridor. Her head just reached to his shoulder. His arm, extended downwards, was about her waist. His spurs jingled slightly.

"He had not seen me for ten years. He did not know me. He parted from me for my sake, and he would never let me come back. He was always talking in his letters of leaving Costaguana, of abandoning everything and making his escape. But he was too valuable a prey. They would have thrown him into one of their prisons at the first suspicion."

His spurred feet clinked slowly. He was bending over his wife as they walked. The big parrot, turning its head askew, followed their pacing figures with a round, unblinking eye.

"He was a lonely man. Ever since I was ten years old he used to talk to me as if I had been grown up. When I was in Europe he wrote to me every month. Ten, twelve pages every month of my life for ten years. And, after all, he did not know me! Just think of it— ten whole years away; the years I was growing up into a man. He could not know me. Do you think he could?"

Mrs. Gould shook her head negatively; which was just what her husband had expected from the strength of the argument. But she shook her head negatively only because she thought that no one could know her Charles —really know him for what he was but herself. The thing was obvious. It could be felt. It required no argument. And poor Mr. Gould, senior, who had died too soon to ever hear of their engagement, remained too shadowy a figure for her to be credited with knowledge of any sort whatever.

"No, he did not understand. In my view this mine could never have been a thing to sell. Never! After all his misery I simply could not have touched it for money alone," Charles Gould pursued: and she pressed her head to his shoulder approvingly.

These two young people remembered the life which had ended wretchedly just when their own lives had come together in that splendour of hopeful love, which to the most sensible minds appears like a triumph of good over all the evils of the earth. A vague idea of rehabilitation had entered the plan of their life. That it was so vague as to elude the support of argument made it only the stronger. It had presented itself to them at the instant when the woman's instinct of devotion and the man's instinct of activity receive from the strongest of illusions their most powerful impulse. The very prohibition imposed the necessity of success. It was as if they had been morally bound to make good their vigorous view of life against the unnatural error of weariness and despair. If the idea of wealth was present to them it was only so far as it was bound with that other success. Mrs. Gould, an orphan from early childhood and without fortune, brought up in an atmosphere of intellectual interests, had never considered the aspects of great wealth. They were too remote, and she had not learned that they were desirable. On the other hand, she had not known anything of absolute want. Even the very poverty of her aunt, the Marchesa, had nothing intolerable to a refined mind; it seemed in accord with a great grief: it had the austerity of a sacrifice offered to a noble ideal. Thus even the most legitimate touch of materialism was wanting in Mrs. Gould's character. The dead man of whom she thought with tenderness (because he was Charley's father) and with some impatience (because he had been weak), must be put completely in the wrong. Nothing else would do to keep their prosperity without a stain on its only real, on its immaterial side!

Charles Gould, on his part, had been obliged to keep the idea of wealth well to the fore; but he brought it forward as a means, not as an end. Unless the mine was good business it could not be touched. He had to insist on that aspect of the enterprise. It was his lever to move men who had capital. And Charles Gould believed in the mine. He knew everything that could be known of it. His faith in the mine was contagious, though it was not served by a great eloquence; but business men are frequently as sanguine and imaginative as lovers. They are affected by a personality much oftener than people would suppose; and Charles Gould, in his unshaken assurance, was absolutely convincing. Besides, it was a matter of common knowledge to the men to whom he addressed himself that mining in Costaguana was a game that could be made considerably more than worth the candle. The men of affairs knew that very well. The real difficulty in touching it was elsewhere. Against that there was an implication of calm and implacable resolution in Charles Gould's very voice. Men of affairs venture sometimes on acts that the common judgment of the world would pronounce absurd; they make their decisions on apparently impulsive and human grounds. "Very well," had said the considerable personage to whom Charles Gould on his way out through San Francisco had lucidly exposed his point of view. "Let us suppose that the mining affairs of Sulaco are taken in hand. There would then be in it: first, the house of Holroyd, which is all right; then, Mr. Charles Gould, a citizen of Costaguana, who is also all right; and, lastly, the Government of the Republic. So far this resembles the first start of the Atacama nitrate fields,* where there was a financing house, a gentleman of the name of Edwards, and—a Government; or, rather, two Governments—two South American Governments. And you know what came of it. War came of it; devastating and prolonged war came of it, Mr. Gould. However, here we possess the advantage of having only one South American Government hanging around for plunder out of the deal. It is an advantage; but then there are degrees of badness, and that Government is the Costaguana Government."

Thus spoke the considerable personage, the millionaire endower of churches on a scale befitting the greatness of his native land—the same to whom the doctors used the language of horrid and veiled menaces. He was a big-limbed, deliberate man, whose quiet burliness lent to an ample silk-faced frock-coat a superfine dignity. His hair was iron grey, his eyebrows were still black, and his massive profile was the profile of a Cæsar's head on an old Roman coin. But his parentage was German and Scotch and English, with remote strains of Danish and French blood, giving him the temperament of a Puritan and an insatiable imagination of conquest. He was completely unbending to his visitor, because of the warm introduction the visitor had brought from Europe, and because of an irrational liking for earnestness and determination wherever met, to whatever end directed.

"The Costaguana Government shall play its hand for all it's worth—and don't you forget it, Mr. Gould. Now, what is Costaguana? It is the bottomless pit of

10 per cent. loans and other fool investments. European capital had been flung into it with both hands for years. Not ours, though. We in this country know just about enough to keep indoors when it rains. We can sit and watch. Of course, some day we shall step in. We are bound to. But there's no hurry. Time itself has got to wait on the greatest country in the whole of God's Universe. We shall be giving the word for everything: industry, trade, law, journalism, art, politics, and religion, from Cape Horn clear over to Smith's Sound, and beyond, too, if anything worth taking hold of turns up at the North Pole. And then we shall have the leisure to take in hand the outlying islands and continents of the earth. We shall run the world's business whether the world likes it or not. The world can't help it—and neither can we, I guess."*

By this he meant to express his faith in destiny in words suitable to his intelligence, which was unskilled in the presentation of general ideas. His intelligence was nourished on facts; and Charles Gould, whose imagination had been permanently affected by the one great fact of a silver mine, had no objection to this theory of the world's future. If it had seemed distasteful for a moment it was because the sudden statement of such vast eventualities dwarfed almost to nothingness the actual matter in hand. · He and his plans and all the mineral wealth of the Occidental Province appeared suddenly robbed of every vestige of magnitude. The sensation was disagreeable; but Charles Gould was not dull. Already he felt that he was producing a favourable impression; the consciousness of that flattering fact helped him to a vague smile, which his big interlocutor took for a smile of discreet and admiring assent. He smiled quietly, too; and immediately Charles Gould. with that mental agility

mankind will display in defence of a cherished hope,
reflected that the very apparent insignificance of his
aim would help him to success. His personality and his
mine would be taken up because it was a matter of no
great consequence, one way or another, to a man who
referred his action to such a prodigious destiny. And
Charles Gould was not humiliated by this consideration,
because the thing remained as big as ever for him. Nobody else's vast conceptions of destiny could diminish
the aspect of his desire for the redemption of the San
Tomé mine. In comparison to the correctness of
his aim, definite in space and absolutely attainable
within a limited time, the other man appeared for an
instant as a dreamy idealist of no importance.

The great man, massive and benignant, had been
looking at him thoughtfully; when he broke the short
silence it was to remark that concessions flew about
thick in the air of Costaguana. Any simple soul that
just yearned to be taken in could bring down a concession at the first shot.

"Our consuls get their mouths stopped with them," he
continued, with a twinkle of genial scorn in his eyes.
But in a moment he became grave. "A conscientious,
upright man, that cares nothing for boodle, and keeps
clear of their intrigues, conspiracies, and factions, soon
gets his passports. See that, Mr. Gould? *Persona non
grata.** That's the reason our Government is never
properly informed. On the other hand, Europe must
be kept out of this continent, and for proper interference on our part the time is not yet ripe, I dare say.
But we here—we are not this country's Government,
neither are we simple souls. Your affair is all right.
The main question for us is whether the second partner,
and that's you, is the right sort to hold his own against
the third and unwelcome partner, which is one or

another of the high and mighty robber gangs that run the Costaguana Government. What do you think, Mr. Gould, eh?"

He bent forward to look steadily into the unflinching eyes of Charles Gould, who, remembering the large box full of his father's letters, put the accumulated scorn and bitterness of many years into the tone of his answer—

"As far as the knowledge of these men and their methods and their politics is concerned, I can answer for myself. I have been fed on that sort of knowledge since I was a boy. I am not likely to fall into mistake from excess of optimism."

"Not likely, eh? That's all right. Tact and a stiff upper lip is what you'll want; and you could bluff a little on the strength of your backing. Not too much, though. We will go with you as long as the thing runs straight. But we won't be drawn into any large trouble. This is the experiment which I am willing to make. There is some risk, and we will take it; but if you can't keep up your end, we will stand our loss, of course, and then—we'll let the thing go. This mine can wait; it has been shut up before, as you know. You must understand that under no circumstances will we consent to throw good money after bad."

Thus the great personage had spoken then, in his own private office, in a great city where other men (very considerable in the eyes of a vain populace) waited with alacrity upon a wave of his hand. And rather more than a year later, during his unexpected appearance in Sulaco, he had emphasized his uncompromising attitude with a freedom of sincerity permitted to his wealth and influence. He did this with the less reserve, perhaps, because the inspection of what had been done, and more still the way in which

successive steps had been taken, had impressed him
with the conviction that Charles Gould was perfectly
capable of keeping up his end.

"This young fellow," he thought to himself, "may
yet become a power in the land."

This thought flattered him, for hitherto the only
account of this young man he could give to his intimates
was—

"My brother-in-law met him in one of these one-
horse old German towns, near some mines, and sent
him on to me with a letter.. He's one of the Costaguana
Goulds, pure-bred Englishmen, but all born in the
country. His uncle went into politics, was the last
Provincial President of Sulaco, and got shot after a
battle. His father was a prominent business man in
Sta. Marta, tried to keep clear of their politics, and died
ruined after a lot of revolutions. And that's your
Costaguana in a nutshell."

Of course, he was too great a man to be questioned
as to his motives, even by his intimates. The outside
world was at liberty to wonder respectfully at the
hidden meaning of his actions. He was so great a man
that his lavish patronage of the "purer forms of Christianity" (which in its naïve form of church-building
amused Mrs. Gould) was looked upon by his fellow-
citizens as the manifestation of a pious and humble
spirit. But in his own circles of the financial world the
taking up of such a thing as the San Tomé mine was
regarded with respect, indeed, but rather as a subject
for discreet jocularity. It was a great man's caprice.
In the great Holroyd building (an enormous pile of
iron, glass, and blocks of stone at the corner of two
streets, cobwebbed aloft by the radiation of telegraph
wires) the heads of principal departments exchanged
humorous glances, which meant that they were not let

into the secrets of the San Tomé business. The
Costaguana mail (it was never large—one fairly heavy
envelope) was taken unopened straight into the great
man's room, and no instructions dealing with it had
ever been issued thence. The office whispered that he
answered personally—and not by dictation either, but
actually writing in his own hand, with pen and ink,
and, it was to be supposed, taking a copy in his own
private press copy-book, inaccessible to profane eyes.
Some scornful young men, insignificant pieces of minor
machinery in that eleven-storey-high workshop of great
affairs, expressed frankly their private opinion that the
great chief had done at last something silly, and was
ashamed of his folly; others, elderly and insignificant,
but full of romantic reverence for the business that had
devoured their best years, used to mutter darkly and
knowingly that this was a portentous sign; that the
Holroyd connection meant by-and-by to get hold of the
whole Republic of Costaguana, lock, stock, and barrel.
But, in fact, the hobby theory was the right one. It
interested the great man to attend personally to the
San Tomé mine; it interested him so much that he
allowed this hobby to give a direction to the first complete holiday he had taken for quite a startling number
of years. He was not running a great enterprise there;
no mere railway board or industrial corporation. He
was running a man! A success would have pleased him
very much on refreshingly novel grounds; but, on the
other side of the same feeling, it was incumbent upon
him to cast it off utterly at the first sign of failure. A
man may be thrown off. The papers had unfortunately
trumpeted all over the land his journey to Costaguana.
If he was pleased at the way Charles Gould was going
on, he infused an added grimness into his assurances of
support. Even at the very last interview, half an hour

or so before he rolled out of the patio, hat in hand, behind Mrs. Gould's white mules, he had said in Charles's room—

"You go ahead in your own way, and I shall know how to help you as long as you hold your own. But you may rest assured that in a given case we shall know how to drop you in time."

To this Charles Gould's only answer had been: "You may begin sending out the machinery as soon as you like."

And the great man had liked this imperturbable assurance. The secret of it was that to Charles Gould's mind these uncompromising terms were agreeable. Like this the mine preserved its identity, with which he had endowed it as a boy; and it remained dependent on himself alone. It was a serious affair, and he, too, took it grimly.

"Of course," he said to his wife, alluding to this last conversation with the departed guest, while they walked slowly up and down the corridor, followed by the irritated eye of the parrot—"of course, a man of that sort can take up a thing or drop it when he likes. He will suffer from no sense of defeat. He may have to give in, or he may have to die to-morrow, but the great silver and iron interests shall survive, and some day shall get hold of Costaguana along with the rest of the world."

They had stopped near the cage. The parrot, catching the sound of a word belonging to his vocabulary, was moved to interfere. Parrots are very human.

"Viva Costaguana!" he shrieked, with intense self-assertion, and, instantly ruffling up his feathers, assumed an air of puffed-up somnolence behind the glittering wires.

"And do you believe that, Charley?" Mrs. Gould

asked. "This seems to me most awful materialism, and——"

"My dear, it's nothing to me," interrupted her husband, in a reasonable tone. "I make use of what I see. What's it to me whether his talk is the voice of destiny or simply a bit of clap-trap eloquence? There's a good deal of eloquence of one sort or another produced in both Americas. The air of the New World seems favourable to the art of declamation. Have you forgotten how dear Avellanos can hold forth for hours here——?"

"Oh, but that's different," protested Mrs. Gould, almost shocked. The allusion was not to the point. Don José was a dear good man, who talked very well, and was enthusiastic about the greatness of the San Tomé mine. "How can you compare them, Charles?" she exclaimed, reproachfully "He has suffered—and yet he hopes."

The working competence of men—which she never questioned—was very surprising to Mrs. Gould, because upon so many obvious issues they showed themselves strangely muddle-headed.

Charles Gould, with a careworn calmness which secured for him at once his wife's anxious sympathy, assured her that he was not comparing. He was an American himself, after all, and perhaps he could understand both kinds of eloquence—"if it were worth while to try," he added, grimly. But he had breathed the air of England longer than any of his people had done for three generations, and really he begged to be excused. His poor father could be eloquent, too. And he asked his wife whether she remembered a passage in one of his father's last letters where Mr. Gould had expressed the conviction that "God looked wrathfully at these countries, or else He would let some ray of hope fall through a rift in the appalling darkness of intrigue, bloodshed, and crime that hung over the Queen of Continents."

Mrs. Gould had not forgotten. "You read it to me, Charley," she murmured. "It was a striking pronouncement. How deeply your father must have felt its terrible sadness!"

"He did not like to be robbed. It exasperated him," said Charles Gould. "But the image will serve well enough. What is wanted here is law, good faith, order, security. Any one can declaim about these things, but I pin my faith to material interests. Only let the material interests once get a firm footing, and they are bound to impose the conditions on which alone they can continue to exist. That's how your money-making is justified here in the face of lawlessness and disorder. It is justified because the security which it demands must be shared with an oppressed people. A better justice will come afterwards. That's your ray of hope." His arm pressed her slight form closer to his side for a moment. "And who knows whether in that sense even the San Tomé mine may not become that little rift in the darkness which poor father despaired of ever seeing?"

She glanced up at him with admiration. He was competent; he had given a vast shape to the vagueness of her unselfish ambitions.

"Charley," she said, "you are splendidly disobedient."

He left her suddenly in the *corrédor* to go and get his hat, a soft, grey sombrero, an article of national costume which combined unexpectedly well with his English get-up. He came back, a riding-whip under his arm, buttoning up a dogskin glove; his face reflected the resolute nature of his thoughts. His wife had waited for him at the head of the stairs, and before he gave her the parting kiss he finished the conversation—

"What should be perfectly clear to us," he said, "is the fact that there is no going back. Where could we begin life afresh? We are in now for all that there is in us."

He bent over her upturned face very tenderly and a little remorsefully. Charles Gould was competent because he had no illusions. The Gould Concession had to fight for life with such weapons as could be found at once in the mire of corruption that was so universal as to almost lose its significance. He was prepared to stoop for his weapons. For a moment he felt as if the silver mine, which had killed his father, had decoyed him further than he meant to go; and with the round-about logic of emotions, he felt that the worthiness of his life was bound up with success. There was no going back.

CHAPTER SEVEN

MRS. GOULD was too intelligently sympathetic not to share that feeling. It made life exciting, and she was too much of a woman not to like excitement. But it frightened her, too, a little; and when Don José Avellanos, rocking in the American chair, would go so far as to say, "Even, my dear Carlos, if you had failed; even if some untoward event were yet to destroy your work—which God forbid!—you would have deserved well of your country," Mrs. Gould would look up from the tea-table profoundly at her unmoved husband stirring the spoon in the cup as though he had not heard a word.

Not that Don José anticipated anything of the sort. He could not praise enough dear Carlos's tact and courage. His English, rock-like quality of character was his best safeguard, Don José affirmed; and, turning to Mrs. Gould, "As to you, Emilia, my soul"*—he would address her with the familiarity of his age and old friendship—"you are as true a patriot as though you had been born in our midst."

This might have been less or more than the truth. Mrs. Gould, accompanying her husband all over the province in the search for labour, had seen the land with a deeper glance than a trueborn Costaguanera could have done. In her travel-worn riding habit, her face powdered white like a plaster cast, with a further protection of a small silk mask during the heat of the day, she rode on a well-shaped, light-footed pony in the centre of a little cavalcade. Two *mozos de campo*, picturesque in great hats, with spurred bare heels, in white embroidered calzoneras, leather jackets and striped ponchos, rode ahead with carbines across their shoulders, swaying in unison to the pace of the horses. A tropilla of pack mules brought up the rear in charge of a thin brown muleteer, sitting his long-eared beast very near the tail, legs thrust far forward, the wide brim of his hat set far back, making a sort of halo for his head. An old Costaguana officer, a retired senior major of humble origin, but patronized by the first families on account of his Blanco opinions, had been recommended by Don José for commissary and organizer of that expedition. The points of his grey moustache hung far below his chin, and, riding on Mrs. Gould's left hand, he looked about with kindly eyes, pointing out the features of the country, telling the names of the little pueblos and of the estates, of the smooth-walled haciendas like long fortresses crowning the knolls above the level of the Sulaco Valley. It unrolled itself, with green young crops, plains, woodland, and gleams of water, park-like, from the blue vapour of the distant sierra to an immense quivering horizon of grass and sky, where big white clouds seemed to fall slowly into the darkness of their own shadows.

Men ploughed with wooden ploughs and yoked oxen, small on a boundless expanse, as if attacking immensity itself. The mounted figures of vaqueros galloped in the distance, and the great herds fed with all their horned heads one way, in one single wavering line as far as eye could reach across the broad *potreros*. A spreading cotton-wood tree shaded a thatched ranche by the road; the trudging files of burdened Indians taking off their hats, would lift sad, mute eyes to the cavalcade raising the dust of the crumbling *camino real* made by the hands of their enslaved forefathers. And Mrs.

Gould, with each day's journey, seemed to come nearer
to the soul of the land in the tremendous disclosure
of this interior unaffected by the slight European veneer
of the coast towns, a great land of plain and mountain
and people, suffering and mute, waiting for the future
in a pathetic immobility of patience.

She knew its sights and its hospitality, dispensed with
a sort of slumbrous dignity in those great houses presenting long, blind walls and heavy portals to the wind-
swept pastures. She was given the head of the tables,
where masters and dependants sat in a simple and
patriarchal state. The ladies of the house would talk
softly in the moonlight under the orange trees of the
courtyards, impressing upon her the sweetness of their
voices and the something mysterious in the quietude
of their lives. In the morning the gentlemen, well
mounted in braided sombreros and embroidered riding
suits, with much silver on the trappings of their horses,
would ride forth to escort the departing guests before
committing them, with grave good-byes, to the care of
God at the boundary pillars of their estates. In all
these households she could hear stories of political
outrage; friends, relatives, ruined, imprisoned, killed in
the battles of senseless civil wars, barbarously executed
in ferocious proscriptions, as though the government of
the country had been a struggle of lust between bands
of absurd devils let loose upon the land with sabres and
uniforms and grandiloquent phrases. And on all the
lips she found a weary desire for peace, the dread of
officialdom with its nightmarish parody of administration without law, without security, and without justice.

She bore a whole two months of wandering very well;
she had that power of resistance to fatigue which one
discovers here and there in some quite frail-looking
women with surprise—like a state of possession by a

remarkably stubborn spirit. Don Pépé—the old Costaguana major—after much display of solicitude for the delicate lady, had ended by conferring upon her the name of the "Never-tired Señora." Mrs. Gould was indeed becoming a Costaguanera. Having acquired in Southern Europe a knowledge of true peasantry, she was able to appreciate the great worth of the people. She saw the man under the silent, sad-eyed beast of burden. She saw them on the road carrying loads, lonely figures upon the plain, toiling under great straw hats, with their white clothing flapping about their limbs in the wind; she remembered the villages by some group of Indian women at the fountain impressed upon her memory, by the face of some young Indian girl with a melancholy and sensual profile, raising an earthenware vessel of cool water at the door of a dark hut with a wooden porch cumbered with great brown jars. The solid wooden wheels of an ox-cart, halted with its shafts in the dust, showed the strokes of the axe; and a party of charcoal carriers, with each man's load resting above his head on the top of the low mud wall, slept stretched in a row within the strip of shade.

The heavy stonework of bridges and churches left by the conquerors proclaimed the disregard of human labour, the tribute-labour of vanished nations. The power of king and church was gone, but at the sight of some heavy ruinous pile overtopping from a knoll the low mud walls of a village, Don Pépé would interrupt the tale of his campaigns to exclaim—

"Poor Costaguana! Before, it was everything for the Padres, nothing for the people; and now it is everything for these great politicos in Sta. Marta, for negroes and thieves."

Charles talked with the alcaldes, with the fiscales, with the principal people in towns, and with the caballeros on the estates. The commandantes of the districts offered him escorts—for he could show an authorization from the Sulaco political chief of the day. How much the document had cost him in gold twenty-dollar pieces was a secret between himself, a great man in the United States (who condescended to answer the Sulaco mail with his own hand), and a great man of another sort, with a dark olive complexion and shifty eyes, inhabiting then the Palace of the Intendencia in Sulaco, and who piqued himself on his culture and Europeanism generally in a rather French style because he had lived in Europe for some years—in exile, he said. However, it was pretty well known that just before this exile he had incautiously gambled away all the cash in the Custom House of a small port where a friend in power had procured for him the post of sub-collector. That youthful indiscretion had, amongst other inconveniences, obliged him to earn his living for a time as a *café* waiter in Madrid; but his talents must have been great, after all, since they had enabled him to retrieve his political fortunes so splendidly. Charles Gould, exposing his business with an imperturbable steadiness, called him Excellency.

The provincial Excellency assumed a weary superiority, tilting his chair far back near an open window in the true Costaguana manner. The military band happened to be braying operatic selections on the plaza just then, and twice he raised his hand imperatively for silence in order to listen to a favourite passage.

"Exquisite, delicious!" he murmured; while Charles Gould waited, standing by with inscrutable patience. "Lucia, Lucia di Lammermoor! I am passionate for music. It transports me. Ha! the divine—ha!—Mozart.* Si! divine . . . What is it you were saying?"

Of course, rumours had reached him already of the newcomer's intentions. Besides, he had received an official warning from Sta. Marta. His manner was intended simply to conceal his curiosity and impress his visitor. But after he had locked up something valuable in the drawer of a large writing-desk in a distant part of the room, he became very affable, and walked back to his chair smartly.

"If you intend to build villages and assemble a population near the mine, you shall require a decree of the Minister of the Interior for that," he suggested in a business-like manner.

"I have already sent a memorial," said Charles Gould, steadily, "and I reckon now confidently upon your Excellency's favourable conclusions."

The Excellency was a man of many moods. With the receipt of the money a great mellowness had descended upon his simple soul. Unexpectedly he fetched a deep sigh.

"Ah, Don Carlos! What we want is advanced men like you in the province. The lethargy—the lethargy of these aristocrats! The want of public spirit! The absence of all enterprise! I, with my profound studies in Europe, you understand——"

With one hand thrust into his swelling bosom, he rose and fell on his toes, and for ten minutes, almost without drawing breath, went on hurling himself intellectually to the assault of Charles Gould's polite silence; and when, stopping abruptly, he fell back into his chair, it was as though he had been beaten off from a fortress. To save his dignity he hastened to dismiss this silent man with a solemn inclination of the head and the words, pronounced with moody, fatigued condescension—

"You may depend upon my enlightened goodwill

as long as your conduct as a good citizen deserves
it."

He took up a paper fan and began to cool himself with
a consequential air, while Charles Gould bowed and
withdrew. Then he dropped the fan at once, and
stared with an appearance of wonder and perplexity at
the closed door for quite a long time. At last he
shrugged his shoulders as if to assure himself of his disdain. Cold, dull. No intellectuality. Red hair. A
true Englishman. He despised him.

His face darkened. What meant this unimpressed
and frigid behaviour? He was the first of the successive politicians sent out from the capital to rule the
Occidental Province whom the manner of Charles
Gould in official intercourse was to strike as offensively
independent.

Charles Gould assumed that if the appearance of
listening to deplorable balderdash must form part of the
price he had to pay for being left unmolested, the obligation of uttering balderdash personally was by no means
included in the bargain. He drew the line there. To
these provincial autocrats, before whom the peaceable
population of all classes had been accustomed to
tremble, the reserve of that English-looking engineer
caused an uneasiness which swung to and fro between
cringing and truculence. Gradually all of them discovered that, no matter what party was in power, that
man remained in most effective touch with the higher
authorities in Sta. Marta.

This was a fact, and it accounted perfectly for the
Goulds being by no means so wealthy as the engineer-in-
chief on the new railway could legitimately suppose.
Following the advice of Don José Avellanos, who was a
man of good counsel (though rendered timid by his
horrible experiences of Guzman Bento's time), Charles

Gould had kept clear of the capital; but in the current gossip of the foreign residents there he was known (with a good deal of seriousness underlying the irony) by the nickname of "King of Sulaco." An advocate of the Costaguana Bar, a man of reputed ability and good character, member of the distinguished Moraga family possessing extensive estates in the Sulaco Valley, was pointed out to strangers, with a shade of mystery and respect, as the agent of the San Tomé mine—"political, you know." He was tall, black-whiskered, and discreet. It was known that he had easy access to ministers, and that the numerous Costaguana generals were always anxious to dine at his house. Presidents granted him audience with facility. He corresponded actively with his maternal uncle, Don José Avellanos; but his letters—unless those expressing formally his dutiful affection—were seldom entrusted to the Costaguana Post Office. There the envelopes are opened, indiscriminately, with the frankness of a brazen and childish impudence characteristic of some Spanish-American Governments. But it must be noted that at about the time of the re-opening of the San Tomé mine the muleteer who had been employed by Charles Gould in his preliminary travels on the Campo added his small train of animals to the thin stream of traffic carried over the mountain passes between the Sta. Marta upland and the Valley of Sulaco. There are no travellers by that arduous and unsafe route unless under very exceptional circumstances, and the state of inland trade did not visibly require additional transport facilities; but the man seemed to find his account in it. A few packages were always found for him whenever he took the road. Very brown and wooden, in goatskin breeches with the hair outside, he sat near the tail of his own smart mule, his great hat turned against the sun, an expression of blissful vacancy on his long face, humming day after day a love-song in a plaintive key, or, without a change of expression, letting out a yell at his small tropilla in front. A round little guitar hung high up on his back; and there was a place scooped out artistically in the wood of one of his pack-saddles where a tightly rolled piece of paper could be slipped in, the wooden plug replaced, and the coarse canvas nailed on again. When in Sulaco it was his practice to smoke and doze all day long (as though he had no care in the world) on a stone bench outside the doorway of the Casa Gould and facing the windows of the Avellanos house. Years and years ago his mother had been chief laundry-woman in that family—very accomplished in the matter of clear-starching. He himself had been born on one of their haciendas. His name was Bonifacio, and Don José, crossing the street about five o'clock to call on Doña Emilia, always acknowledged his humble salute by some movement of hand or head. The porters of both houses conversed lazily with him in tones of grave intimacy. His evenings he devoted to gambling and to calls in a spirit of generous festivity upon the *peyne d'oro**girls in the more remote side-streets of the town. But he, too, was a discreet man.

CHAPTER EIGHT

THOSE of us whom business or curiosity took to Sulaco in these years before the first advent of the railway can remember the steadying effect of the San Tomé mine upon the life of that remote province. The outward appearances had not changed then as they have changed since, as I am told, with cable cars running along the streets of the Constitution, and carriage roads far into the country, to Rincon and other villages, where the foreign merchants and the Ricos generally have their modern villas, and a vast railway goods yard by the harbour, which has a quay-side, a long range of warehouses, and quite serious, organized labour troubles of its own.

Nobody had ever heard of labour troubles then. The Cargadores of the port formed, indeed, an unruly brotherhood of all sorts of scum, with a patron saint of their own. They went on strike regularly (every bull-fight day), a form of trouble that even Nostromo at the height of his prestige could never cope with efficiently; but the morning after each fiesta, before the Indian market-women had opened their mat parasols on the plaza, when the snows of Higuerota gleamed pale over the town on a yet black sky, the appearance of a phantom-like horseman mounted on a silver-grey mare solved the problem of labour without fail. His steed paced the lanes of the slums and the weed-grown enclosures within the old ramparts, between the black, lightless cluster of huts, like cow-byres, like dog-kennels. The horseman hammered with the butt of a heavy revolver at the doors of low pulperias, of obscene lean-to sheds sloping against the tumble-down piece of a noble wall, at the wooden sides of dwellings so flimsy that the sound of snores and sleepy mutters within could be heard in the pauses of the thundering clatter of his blows. He called out men's names menacingly from the saddle, once, twice. The drowsy answers—grumpy, conciliating, savage, jocular, or deprecating—came out into the silent darkness in which the horseman sat still, and presently a dark figure would flit out coughing in the still air. Sometimes a low-toned woman cried through the window-hole softly, "He's coming directly, señor," and the horseman waited silent on a motionless horse. But if perchance he had to dismount, then, after a while, from the door of that hovel or of that pulperia, with a ferocious scuffle and stifled imprecations, a cargador would fly out head first and hands abroad, to sprawl under the forelegs of the silver-grey mare, who only pricked forward her sharp little ears. She was used to that work; and the man, picking himself up, would walk away hastily from Nostromo's revolver, reeling a little along the street and snarling low curses. At sunrise Captain Mitchell, coming out anxiously in his night attire on to the wooden balcony running the whole length of the O.S.N. Company's lonely building by the shore, would see the lighters already under way, figures moving busily about the cargo cranes, perhaps hear the invaluable Nostromo, now dismounted and in the checked shirt and red sash of a Mediterranean sailor, bawling orders from the end of the jetty in a stentorian voice. A fellow in a thousand!

The material apparatus of perfected civilization which obliterates the individuality of old towns under the stereotyped conveniences of modern life had not

intruded as yet; but over the worn-out antiquity of
Sulaco, so characteristic with its stuccoed houses and
barred windows, with the great yellowy-white walls of
abandoned convents behind the rows of sombre green
cypresses, that fact—very modern in its spirit—the
San Tomé mine had already thrown its subtle influence.
It had altered, too, the outward character of the
crowds on feast days on the plaza before the open portal
of the cathedral, by the number of white ponchos with a
green stripe affected as holiday wear by the San Tomé
miners.   They had also adopted white hats with green
cord and braid—articles of good quality, which could
be obtained in the storehouse of the administration for
very little money.   A peaceable Cholo wearing these
colours (unusual in Costaguana) was somehow very
seldom beaten to within an inch of his life on a charge of
disrespect to the town police; neither ran he much risk
of being suddenly lassoed on the road by a recruiting
party of lanceros—a method of voluntary enlistment
looked upon as almost legal in the Republic.   Whole
villages were known to have volunteered for the army
in that way; but, as Don Pépé would say with a hopeless shrug to Mrs. Gould, "What would you!   Poor
people!   Pobrecitos!   Pobrecitos!   But the State must
have its soldiers."

Thus professionally spoke Don Pépé, the fighter, with
pendent moustaches, a nut-brown, lean face, and a
clean run of a cast-iron jaw, suggesting the type of a
cattle-herd horseman from the great Llanos of the
South.   "If you will listen to an old officer of Paez,*
señores," was the exordium of all his speeches in the
Aristocratic Club of Sulaco, where he was admitted on
account of his past services to the extinct cause of
Federation.   The club, dating from the days of the
proclamation of Costaguana's independence, boasted

many names of liberators amongst its first founders.
Suppressed arbitrarily innumerable times by various
Governments, with memories of proscriptions and of at
least one · wholesale massacre of its members, sadly
assembled for a banquet by the order of a zealous
military commandante (their bodies were afterwards
stripped naked and flung into the plaza out of the windows by the lowest scum of the populace), it was again
flourishing, at that period, peacefully. It extended to
strangers the large hospitality of the cool, big rooms of
its historic quarters in the front part of a house, once the
residence of a high official of the Holy Office. The two
wings, shut up, crumbled behind the nailed doors, and
what may be described as a grove of young orange trees
grown in the unpaved patio concealed the utter ruin of
the back part facing the gate. You turned in from the
street, as if entering a secluded orchard, where you came
upon the foot of a disjointed staircase, guarded by a
moss-stained effigy of some saintly bishop, mitred and
staffed, and bearing the indignity of a broken nose
meekly, with his fine stone hands crossed on his breast.
The chocolate-coloured faces of servants with mops of
black hair peeped at you from above; the click of
billiard balls came to your ears, and ascending the
steps, you would perhaps see in the first sala, very stiff
upon a straight-backed chair, in a good light, Don Pépé
moving his long moustaches as he spelt his way, at arm's
length, through an old Sta. Marta newspaper. His
horse—a stony-hearted but persevering black brute
with a hammer head—you would have seen in the
street dozing motionless under an immense saddle, with
its nose almost touching the curbstone of the sidewalk.
Don Pépé, when "down from the mountain," as the
phrase, often heard in Sulaco, went, could also be seen
in the drawing-room of the Casa Gould. He sat with

modest assurance at some distance from the tea-table. With his knees close together, and a kindly twinkle of drollery in his deep-set eyes, he would throw his small and ironic pleasantries into the current of conversation. There was in that man a sort of sane, humorous shrewdness, and a vein of genuine humanity so often found in simple old soldiers of proved courage who have seen much desperate service. Of course he knew nothing whatever of mining, but his employment was of a special kind. He was in charge of the whole population in the territory of the mine, which extended from the head of the gorge to where the cart track from the foot of the mountain enters the plain, crossing a stream over a little wooden bridge painted green—green, the colour of hope, being also the colour of the mine.

It was reported in Sulaco that up there "at the mountain" Don Pépé walked about precipitous paths, girt with a great sword and in a shabby uniform with tarnished bullion epaulettes of a senior major. Most miners being Indians, with big wild eyes, addressed him as Taita (father), as these barefooted people of Costaguana will address anybody who wears shoes; but it was Basilio, Mr. Gould's own mozo and the head servant of the Casa, who, in all good faith and from a sense of propriety, announced him once in the solemn words, "El Señor Gobernador has arrived."

Don José Avellanos, then in the drawing-room, was delighted beyond measure at the aptness of the title, with which he greeted the old major banteringly as soon as the latter's soldierly figure appeared in the doorway. Don Pépé only smiled in his long moustaches, as much as to say, "You might have found a worse name for an old soldier."

And El Señor Gobernador he had remained, with his small jokes upon his function and upon his domain,

where he affirmed with humorous exaggeration to Mrs.
Gould—

"No two stones could come together anywhere without the Gobernador hearing the click, señora."

And he would tap his ear with the tip of his forefinger
knowingly. Even when the number of the miners alone
rose to over six hundred he seemed to know each of them
individually, all the innumerable Josés, Manuels,
Ignacios, from the villages primero—segundo—or
tercero* (there were three mining villages) under his
government. He could distinguish them not only by
their flat, joyless faces, which to Mrs. Gould looked all
alike, as if run into the same ancestral mould of suffering and patience, but apparently also by the infinitely
graduated shades of reddish-brown, of blackish-brown,
of coppery-brown backs, as the two shifts, stripped to
linen drawers and leather skull-caps, mingled together
with a confusion of naked limbs, of shouldered picks,
swinging lamps, in a great shuffle of sandalled feet on
the open plateau before the entrance of the main
tunnel. It was a time of pause. The Indian boys
leaned idly against the long line of little cradle wagons
standing empty; the screeners and ore-breakers squatted on their heels smoking long cigars; the great wooden
shoots slanting over the edge of the tunnel plateau were
silent; and only the ceaseless, violent rush of water in
the open flumes could be heard, murmuring fiercely,
with the splash and rumble of revolving turbine-
wheels, and the thudding march of the stamps pounding to powder the treasure rock on the plateau below.
The heads of gangs, distinguished by brass medals
hanging on their bare breasts, marshalled their squads;
and at last the mountain would swallow one-half of the
silent crowd, while the other half would move off in long
files down the zigzag paths leading to the bottom of the

gorge. It was deep; and, far below, a thread of vegetation winding between the blazing rock faces resembled a slender green cord, in which three lumpy knots of banana patches, palm-leaf roots, and shady trees marked the Village One, Village Two, Village Three, housing the miners of the Gould Concession.

Whole families had been moving from the first towards the spot in the Higuerota range, whence the rumour of work and safety had spread over the pastoral Campo, forcing its way also, even as the waters of a high flood, into the nooks and crannies of the distant blue walls of the Sierras. Father first, in a pointed straw hat, then the mother with the bigger children, generally also a diminutive donkey, all under burdens, except the leader himself, or perhaps some grown girl, the pride of the family, stepping barefooted and straight as an arrow, with braids of raven hair, a thick, haughty profile, and no load to carry but the small guitar of the country and a pair of soft leather sandals tied together on her back. At the sight of such parties strung out on the cross trails between the pastures, or camped by the side of the royal road, travellers on horseback would remark to each other—

"More people going to the San Tomé mine. We shall see others to-morrow."

And spurring on in the dusk they would discuss th great news of the province, the news of the San Tomé mine. A rich Englishman was going to work it—and perhaps not an Englishman, *Quien sabe!* A foreigner with much money. Oh, yes, it had begun. A party of men who had been to Sulaco with a herd of black bulls for the next corrida had reported that from the porch of the posada in Rincon, only a short league from the town, the lights on the mountain were visible, twinkling above the trees. And there was a woman seen riding

a horse sideways, not in the chair seat, but upon a sort
of saddle, and a man's hat on her head. She walked
about, too, on foot up the mountain paths. A woman
engineer, it seemed she was.

"What an absurdity! Impossible, señor!"

"*Si! Si! Una Americana del Norte.*"*

"Ah, well! if your worship is informed. *Una Americana;* it need be something of that sort."

And they would laugh a little with astonishment and
scorn, keeping a wary eye on the shadows of the road,
for one is liable to meet bad men when travelling late on
the Campo.

And it was not only the men that Don Pépé knew so
well, but he seemed able, with one attentive, thoughtful
glance, to classify each woman, girl, or growing youth
of his domain. It was only the small fry that puzzled
him sometimes. He and the padre could be seen
frequently side by side, meditative and gazing across the
street of a village at a lot of sedate brown children, trying to sort them out, as it were, in low, consulting tones,
or else they would together put searching questions as
to the parentage of some small, staid urchin met
wandering, naked and grave, along the road with a
cigar in his baby mouth, and perhaps his mother's
rosary, purloined for purposes of ornamentation, hanging in a loop of beads low down on his rotund little
stomach. The spiritual and temporal pastors of the
mine flock were very good friends. With Dr. Monygham, the medical pastor, who had accepted the charge
from Mrs. Gould, and lived in the hospital building,
they were on not so intimate terms. But no one could
be on intimate terms with El Señor Doctor, who, with
his twisted shoulders, drooping head, sardonic mouth,
and side-long bitter glance, was mysterious and un-
canny. The other two authorities worked in har-

mony. Father Roman, dried-up, small, alert, wrinkled,
with big round eyes, a sharp chin, and a great snuff-
taker, was an old campaigner, too; he had shriven
many simple souls on the battlefields of the Republic,
kneeling by the dying on hillsides, in the long grass,
in the gloom of the forests, to hear the last confession
with the smell of gunpowder smoke in his nostrils, the
rattle of muskets, the hum and spatter of bullets in his
ears. And where was the harm if, at the presbytery,
they had a game with a pack of greasy cards in the
early evening, before Don Pépé went his last rounds to
see that all the watchmen of the mine—a body organized by himself—were at their posts? For that last
duty before he slept Don Pépé did actually gird his old
sword on the verandah of an unmistakable American
white frame house, which Father Roman called the
presbytery. Near by, a long, low, dark building,
steeple-roofed, like a vast barn with a wooden cross
over the gable, was the miners' chapel. There Father
Roman said Mass every day before a sombre altar-
piece representing the Resurrection, the grey slab of the
tombstone balanced on one corner, a figure soaring upwards, long-limbed and livid, in an oval of pallid light,
and a helmeted brown legionary smitten down, right
across the bituminous foreground. "This picture, my
children, *muy linda e maravillosa*,"* Father Roman would
say to some of his flock, "which you behold here through
the munificence of the wife of our Señor Administrador,
has been painted in Europe, a country of saints and
miracles, and much greater than our Costaguana."
And he would take a pinch of snuff with unction. But
when once an inquisitive spirit desired to know in what
direction this Europe was situated, whether up or down
the coast, Father Roman, to conceal his perplexity, became very reserved and severe. "No doubt it is

extremely far away. But ignorant sinners like you of
the San Tomé mine should think earnestly of everlasting punishment instead of inquiring into the
magnitude of the earth, with its countries and popula-
tions altogether beyond your understanding."

With a "Good-night, Padre;" "Good-night, Don
Pépé," the Gobernador would go off, holding up his
sabre against his side, his body bent forward, with a
long, plodding stride in the dark. The jocularity
proper to an innocent card game for a few cigars or a
bundle of yerba*was replaced at once by the stern duty
mood of an officer setting out to visit the outposts of an
encamped army. One loud blast of the whistle that
hung from his neck provoked instantly a great shrilling
of responding whistles, mingled with the barking of
dogs, that would calm down slowly at last, away up at
the head of the gorge; and in the stillness two serenos,
on guard by the bridge, would appear walking noiselessly towards him. On one side of the road a long
frame building—the store—would be closed and barricaded from end to end; facing it another white frame
house, still longer, and with a verandah—the hospital—
would have lights in the two windows of Dr. Monygham's quarters. Even the delicate foliage of a clump of
pepper trees did not stir, so breathless would be the
darkness warmed by the radiation of the over-heated
rocks. Don Pépé would stand still for a moment with
the two motionless serenos before him, and, abruptly,
high up on the sheer face of the mountain, dotted with
single torches, like drops of fire fallen from the two great
blazing clusters of lights above, the ore shoots would
begin to rattle. The great clattering, shuffling noise,
gathering speed and weight, would be caught up by the
walls of the gorge, and sent upon the plain in a growl of
thunder. The posadero in Rincon swore that on calm

nights, by listening intently, he could catch the sound in his doorway as of a storm in the mountains.

To Charles Gould's fancy it seemed that the sound must reach the uttermost limits of the province. Riding at night towards the mine, it would meet him at the edge of a little wood just beyond Rincon. There was no mistaking the growling mutter of the mountain pouring its stream of treasure under the stamps; and it came to his heart with the peculiar force of a proclamation thundered forth over the land and the marvellousness of an accomplished fact fulfilling an audacious desire. He had heard this desire. He had heard this very sound in his imagination on that far-off evening when his wife and himself, after a tortuous ride through a strip of forest, had reined in their horses near the stream, and had gazed for the first time upon the jungle-grown solitude of the gorge. The head of a palm rose here and there. In a high ravine round the corner of the San Tomé mountain (which is square like a blockhouse) the thread of a slender waterfall flashed bright and glassy through the dark green of the heavy fronds of tree-ferns. Don Pépé, in attendance, rode up, and, stretching his arm up the gorge, had declared with mock solemnity, "Behold the very paradise of snakes,* señora."

And then they had wheeled their horses and ridden back to sleep that night at Rincon. The alcalde—an old, skinny Moreno, a sergeant of Guzman Bento's time—had cleared respectfully out of his house with his three pretty daughters, to make room for the foreign señora and their worships the Caballeros. All he asked Charles Gould (whom he took for a mysterious and official person) to do for him was to remind the supreme Government—El Gobierno supremo—of a pension (amounting to about a dollar a month) to which he

believed himself entitled. It had been promised to
him, he affirmed, straightening his bent back martially,
"many years ago, for my valour in the wars with the
wild Indios when a young man, señor."

The waterfall existed no longer. The tree-ferns that
had luxuriated in its spray had dried around the dried-
up pool, and the high ravine was only a big trench half
filled up with the refuse of excavations and tailings.
The torrent, dammed up above, sent its water rushing
along the open flumes of scooped tree trunks striding on
trestle-legs to the turbines working the stamps on the
lower plateau—the *mesa grande* of the San Tomé
mountain. Only the memory of the waterfall, with its
amazing fernery, like a hanging garden above the rocks
of the gorge, was preserved in Mrs. Gould's water-
colour sketch; she had made it hastily one day from a
cleared patch in the bushes, sitting in the shade of a
roof of straw erected for her on three rough poles under
Don Pépé's direction.

Mrs. Gould had seen it all from the beginning: the
clearing of the wilderness, the making of the road, the
cutting of new paths up the cliff face of San Tomé. For
weeks together she had lived on the spot with her husband; and she was so little in Sulaco during that year
that the appearance of the Gould carriage on the
Alameda would cause a social excitement. From the
heavy family coaches full of stately señoras and black-
eyed señoritas rolling solemnly in the shaded alley white
hands were waved towards her with animation in a
flutter of greetings. Doña Emilia was "down from the
mountain."

But not for long. Doña Emilia would be gone "up to
the mountain" in a day or two, and her sleek carriage
mules would have an easy time of it for another long
spell. She had watched the erection of the first frame-

house put up on the lower mesa for an office and Don Pépé's quarters; she heard with a thrill of thankful emotion the first wagon load of ore rattle down the then only shoot; she had stood by her husband's side perfectly silent, and gone cold all over with excitement at the instant when the first battery of only fifteen stamps was put in motion for the first time. On the occasion when the fires under the first set of retorts in their shed had glowed far into the night she did not retire to rest on the rough cadre set up for her in the as yet bare frame-house till she had seen the first spungy lump of silver yielded to the hazards of the world by the dark depths of the Gould Concession; she had laid her unmercenary hands, with an eagerness that made them tremble, upon the first silver ingot turned out still warm from the mould; and by her imaginative estimate of its power she endowed that lump of metal with a justificative conception, as though it were not a mere fact, but something far-reaching and impalpable, like the true expression of an emotion or the emergence of a principle.

Don Pépé, extremely interested, too, looked over her shoulder with a smile that, making longitudinal folds on his face, caused it to resemble a leathern mask with a benignantly diabolic expression.

"Would not the muchachos of Hernandez like to get hold of this insignificant object, that looks, por Dios, very much like a piece of tin?" he remarked, jocularly.

Hernandez, the robber, had been an inoffensive, small ranchero, kidnapped with circumstances of peculiar atrocity from his home during one of the civil wars, and forced to serve in the army. There his conduct as soldier was exemplary, till, watching his chance, he killed his colonel, and managed to get clear away. With a band of deserters, who chose him for their chief, he had

taken refuge beyond the wild and waterless Bolson de
Tonoro. The haciendas paid him blackmail in cattle
and horses; extraordinary stories were told of his powers
and of his wonderful escapes from capture. He used
to ride, single-handed, into the villages and the little
towns on the Campo, driving a pack mule before him,
with two revolvers in his belt, go straight to the shop or
store, select what he wanted, and ride away unopposed
because of the terror his exploits and his audacity inspired. Poor country people he usually left alone; the
upper class were often stopped on the roads and robbed;
but any unlucky official that fell into his hands was sure
to get a severe flogging. The army officers did not like
his name to be mentioned in their presence. His
followers, mounted on stolen horses, laughed at the pursuit of the regular cavalry sent to hunt them down, and
whom they took pleasure to ambush most scientifically
in the broken ground of their own fastness. Expeditions had been fitted out; a price had been put upon his
head; even attempts had been made, treacherously of
course, to open negotiations with him, without in the
slightest way affecting the even tenor of his career. At
last, in true Costaguana fashion, the Fiscal of Tonoro,
who was ambitious of the glory of having reduced the
famous Hernandez, offered him a sum of money and a
safe conduct out of the country for the betrayal of his
band. But Hernandez evidently was not of the stuff
of which the distinguished military politicians and
conspirators of Costaguana are made. This clever but
common device (which frequently works like a charm
in putting down revolutions) failed with the chief of
vulgar Salteadores. It promised well for the Fiscal at
first, but ended very badly for the squadron of lanceros
posted (by the Fiscal's directions) in a fold of the ground
into which Hernandez had promised to lead his un-

suspecting followers. They came, indeed, at the appointed time, but creeping on their hands and knees through the bush, and only let their presence be known by a general discharge of firearms, which emptied many saddles. The troopers who escaped came riding very hard into Tonoro. It is said that their commanding officer (who, being better mounted, rode far ahead of the rest) afterwards got into a state of despairing intoxication and beat the ambitious Fiscal severely with the flat of his sabre in the presence of his wife and daughters, for bringing this disgrace upon the National Army. The highest civil official of Tonoro, falling to the ground in a swoon, was further kicked all over the body and rowelled with sharp spurs about the neck and face because of the great sensitiveness of his military colleague. This gossip of the inland Campo, so characteristic of the rulers of the country with its story of oppression, inefficiency, fatuous methods, treachery, and savage brutality, was perfectly known to Mrs. Gould. That it should be accepted with no indignant comment by people of intelligence, refinement, and character as something inherent in the nature of things was one of the symptoms of degradation that had the power to exasperate her almost to the verge of despair. Still looking at the ingot of silver, she shook her head at Don Pépé's remark—

"If it had not been for the lawless tyranny of your Government, Don Pépé, many an outlaw now with Hernandez would be living peaceably and happy by the honest work of his hands."

"Señora," cried Don Pépé, with enthusiasm, "it is true! It is as if God had given you the power to look into the very breasts of people. You have seen them working round you, Doña Emilia—meek as lambs, patient like their own burros, brave like lions. I have led them to the very muzzles of guns—I, who stand here before you, señora—in the time of Paez, who was full of generosity, and in courage only approached by the uncle of Don Carlos here, as far as I know. No wonder there are bandits in the Campo when there are none but thieves, swindlers, and sanguinary macaques to rule us in Sta. Marta. However, all the same, a bandit is a bandit, and we shall have a dozen good straight Winchesters to ride with the silver down to Sulaco."

Mrs. Gould's ride with the first silver escort to Sulaco was the closing episode of what she called "my camp life" before she had settled in her town-house permanently, as was proper and even necessary for the wife of the administrator of such an important institution as the San Tomé mine. For the San Tomé mine was to become an institution, a rallying point for everything in the province that needed order and stability to live. Security seemed to flow upon this land from the mountain-gorge. The authorities of Sulaco had learned that the San Tomé mine could make it worth their while to leave things and people alone. This was the nearest approach to the rule of common-sense and justice Charles Gould felt it possible to secure at first. In fact, the mine, with its organization, its population growing fiercely attached to their position of privileged safety, with its armoury, with its Don Pépé, with its armed body of serenos (where, it was said, many an outlaw and deserter—and even some members of Hernandez's band—had found a place), the mine was a power in the land. As a certain prominent man in Sta. Marta had exclaimed with a hollow laugh, once, when discussing the line of action taken by the Sulaco authorities at a time of political crisis—

"You call these men Government officials? They?

Never! They are officials of the mine—officials of the Concession—I tell you."

The prominent man (who was then a person in power, with a lemon-coloured face and a very short and curly, not to say woolly, head of hair) went so far in his temporary discontent as to shake his yellow fist under the nose of his interlocutor, and shriek—

"Yes! All! Silence! All! I tell you! The political Jefé, the chief of the police, the chief of the customs, the general, all, all, are the officials of that Gould."

Thereupon an intrepid but low and argumentative murmur would flow on for a space in the ministerial cabinet, and the prominent man's passion would end in a cynical shrug of the shoulders. After all, he seemed to say, what did it matter as long as the minister himself was not forgotten during his brief day of authority?* But all the same, the unofficial agent of the San Tomé mine, working for a good cause, had his moments of anxiety, which were reflected in his letters to Don José Avellanos, his maternal uncle.

"No sanguinary macaque from Sta. Marta shall set foot on that part of Costaguana which lies beyond the San Tomé bridge," Don Pépé, used to assure Mrs. Gould. "Except, of course, as an honoured guest— for our Señor Administrador is a deep politico." But to Charles Gould, in his own room, the old Major would remark with a grim and soldierly cheeriness, "We are all playing our heads at this game."

Don José Avellanos would mutter "Imperium in imperio, Emilia, my soul," with an air of profound self-satisfaction which, somehow, in a curious way, seemed to contain a queer admixture of bodily discomfort. But that, perhaps, could only be visible to the initiated.

And for the initiated it was a wonderful place, this drawing-room of the Casa Gould, with its momentary

glimpses of the master—El Señor Administrador—
older, harder, mysteriously silent, with the lines
deepened on his English, ruddy, out-of-doors complexion; flitting on his thin cavalryman's legs across the
doorways, either just "back from the mountain"
or with jingling spurs and riding-whip under his arm, on
the point of starting "for the mountain."   Then
Don Pépé, modestly martial in his chair, the llanero
who seemed somehow to have found his martial
jocularity, his knowledge of the world, and his manner
perfect for his station, in the midst of savage armed
contests with his kind; Avellanos, polished and
familiar, the diplomatist with his loquacity covering
much caution and wisdom in delicate advice, with his
manuscript of a historical work on Costaguana,
entitled "Fifty Years of Misrule," which, at present, he
thought it was not prudent (even if it were possible)
"to give to the world"; these three, and also Doña
Emilia amongst them, gracious, small, and fairy-like,
before the glittering tea-set, with one common master-
thought in their heads, with one common feeling of a
tense situation, with one ever-present aim to preserve
the inviolable character of the mine at every cost.
And there was also to be seen Captain Mitchell, a
little apart, near one of the long windows, with an air
of old-fashioned neat old bachelorhood about him,
slightly pompous, in a white waistcoat, a little disregarded and unconscious of it; utterly in the dark, and
imagining himself to be in the thick of things.   The
good man, having spent a clear thirty years of his life
on the high seas before getting what he called a "shore
billet," was astonished at the importance of transactions (other than relating to shipping) which take
place on dry land.   Almost every event out of the
usual daily course "marked an epoch" for him or else

was "history"; unless with his pomposity struggling with a discomfited droop of his rubicund, rather handsome face, set off by snow-white close hair and short whiskers, he would mutter—

"Ah, that! That, sir, was a mistake."

The reception of the first consignment of San Tomé silver for shipment to San Francisco in one of O.S.N. Co.'s mail-boats had, of course, "marked an epoch" for Captain Mitchell. The ingots packed in boxes of stiff ox-hide with plaited handles, small enough to be carried easily by two men, were brought down by the serenos of the mine walking in careful couples down the half-mile or so of steep, zigzag paths to the foot of the mountain. There they would be loaded into a string of two-wheeled carts, resembling roomy coffers with a door at the back, and harnessed tandem with two mules each, waiting under the guard of armed and mounted serenos. Don Pépé padlocked each door in succession, and at the signal of his whistle the string of carts would move off, closely surrounded by the clank of spur and carabine, with jolts and cracking of whips, with a sudden deep rumble over the boundary bridge ("into the land of thieves and sanguinary macaques," Don Pépé defined that crossing); hats bobbing in the first light of the dawn, on the heads of cloaked figures; Winchesters on hip; bridle hands protruding lean and brown from under the falling folds of the ponchos. The convoy skirting a little wood, along the mine trail, between the mud huts and low walls of Rincon, increased its pace on the *camino real*, mules urged to speed, escort galloping, Don Carlos riding alone ahead of a dust storm affording a vague vision of long ears of mules, of fluttering little green and white flags stuck upon each cart; of raised arms in a mob of sombreros with the white gleam of ranging eyes; and Don Pépé, hardly visible in the rear of that rattling dust trail, with a stiff seat and impassive face, rising and falling rhythmically on an ewe-necked silver-bitted black brute with a hammer head.

The sleepy people in the little clusters of huts, in the small ranchos near the road, recognized by the headlong sound the charge of the San Tomé silver escort towards the crumbling wall of the city on the Campo side. They came to the doors to see it dash by over ruts and stones, with a clatter and clank and cracking of whips, with the reckless rush and precise driving of a field battery hurrying into action, and the solitary English figure of the Señor Administrador riding far ahead in the lead.

In the fenced roadside paddocks loose horses galloped wildly for a while; the heavy cattle stood up breast deep in the grass, lowing mutteringly at the flying noise; a meek Indian villager would glance back once and hasten to shove his loaded little donkey bodily against a wall, out of the way of the San Tomé silver escort going to the sea; a small knot of chilly leperos under the Stone Horse of the Alameda would mutter: "Caramba!" on seeing it take a wide curve at a gallop and dart into the empty street of the Constitution; for it was con-ered the correct thing, the only proper style by the mule-drivers of the San Tomé mine to go through the waking town from end to end without a check in the speed as if chased by a devil.

The early sunshine glowed on the delicate primrose, pale pink, pale blue fronts of the big houses with all their gates shut yet, and no face behind the iron bars of the windows. In the whole sunlit range of empty balconies along the street only one white figure would be visible high up above the clear pavement—the wife of the Señor Administrador—leaning over to see the escort go by to the harbour, a mass of heavy, fair hair twisted up negligently on her little head, and a lot of lace about the neck of her muslin wrapper. With a smile to her husband's single, quick, upward glance, she would watch the whole thing stream past below her feet with an orderly uproar, till she answered by a friendly sign the salute of the galloping Don Pépé, the stiff, deferential inclination with a sweep of the hat below the knee.

The string of padlocked carts lengthened, the size of the escort grew bigger as the years went on. Every three months an increasing stream of treasure swept through the streets of Sulaco on its way to the strong room in the O.S.N. Co.'s building by the harbour, there to await shipment for the North. Increasing in volume, and of immense value also; for, as Charles Gould told his wife once with some exultation, there had never been seen anything in the world to approach the vein of the Gould Concession. For them both, each passing of the escort under the balconies of the Casa Gould was like another victory gained in the conquest of peace for Sulaco.

No doubt the initial action of Charles Gould had been helped at the beginning by a period of comparative peace which occurred just about that time; and also by the general softening of manners as compared with the epoch of civil wars whence had emerged the iron tyranny of Guzman Bento of fearful memory. In the contests that broke out at the end of his rule (which had kept peace in the country for a whole fifteen years) there was more fatuous imbecility, plenty of cruelty and suffering still, but much less of the old-time fierce and blindly ferocious political fanaticism. It was all more vile, more base, more contemptible, and infinitely more manageable in the very outspoken cynicism of motives. It was more clearly a brazen-faced scramble for a con-

stantly diminishing quantity of booty; since all enterprise had been stupidly killed in the land. Thus it
came to pass that the province of Sulaco, once the field
of cruel party vengeances, had become in a way one of
the considerable prizes of political career. The great of
the earth (in Sta. Marta) reserved the posts in the old
Occidental State to those nearest and dearest to them:
nephews, brothers, husbands of favourite sisters, bosom
friends, trusty supporters—or prominent supporters of
whom perhaps they were afraid. It was the blessed
province of great opportunities and of largest salaries;
for the San Tomé mine had its own unofficial pay list,
whose items and amounts, fixed in consultation by
Charles Gould and Señor Avellanos, were known to a
prominent business man in the United States, who for
twenty minutes or so in every month gave his undivided
attention to Sulaco affairs. At the same time the
material interests of all sorts, backed up by the in,
fluence of the San Tomé mine, were quietly gathering
substance in that part of the Republic. If, for instance,
the Sulaco Collectorship was generally understood, in
the political world of the capital, to open the way to the
Ministry of Finance, and so on for every official post,
then, on the other hand, the despondent business circles
of the Republic had come to consider the Occidental
Province as the promised land of safety, especially if a
man managed to get on good terms with the administration of the mine. "Charles Gould; excellent fellow!
Absolutely necessary to make sure of him before taking
a single step. Get an introduction to him from Moraga
if you can—the agent of the King of Sulaco, don't you
know."

No wonder, then, that Sir John, coming from Europe
to smooth the path for his railway, had been meeting the
name (and even the nickname) of Charles Gould at

every turn in Costaguana.   The agent of the San Tomé
Administration in Sta. Marta (a polished, well-informed
gentleman, Sir John thought him) had certainly helped
so greatly in bringing about the presidential tour that he
began to think that there was something in the faint
whispers hinting at the immense occult influence of
the Gould Concession.   What was currently whispered
was this—that the San Tomé Administration had, in
part, at least, financed the last revolution, which had
brought into a five-year dictatorship Don Vincente
Ribiera, a man of culture and of unblemished character,
invested with a mandate of reform by the best elements
of the State.   Serious, well-informed men seemed to
believe the fact, to hope for better things, for the
establishment of legality, of good faith and order in
public life.   So much the better, then, thought Sir John.
He worked always on a great scale; there was a loan to
the State, and a project for systematic colonization of
the Occidental Province, involved in one vast scheme
with the construction of the National Central Railway.
Good faith, order, honesty, peace, were badly wanted
for this great development of material interests.   Anybody on the side of these things, and especially if able
to help, had an importance in Sir John's eyes.   He had
not been disappointed in the "King of Sulaco."   The
local difficulties had fallen away, as the engineer-in-chief
had foretold they would, before Charles Gould's medi-
ation.   Sir John had been extremely fêted in Sulaco,
next to the President-Dictator, a fact which might have
accounted for the evident ill-humour General Montero
displayed at lunch given on board the *Juno* just before
she was to sail, taking away from Sulaco the President-
Dictator and the distinguished foreign guests in his
train.

The Excellentissimo ("the hope of honest men," as

Don José had addressed him in a public speech delivered
in the name of the Provincial Assembly of Sulaco) sat at
the head of the long table; Captain Mitchell, positively
stony-eyed and purple in the face with the solemnity of
this "historical event," occupied the foot as the representative of the O.S.N. Company in Sulaco, the hosts of
that informal function, with the captain of the ship and
some minor officials from the shore around him. Those
cheery, swarthy little gentlemen cast jovial side-glances
at the bottles of champagne beginning to pop behind
the guests' backs in the hands of the ship's stewards.
The amber wine creamed up to the rims of the glasses.

Charles Gould had his place next to a foreign envoy,
who, in a listless undertone, had been talking to him
fitfully of hunting and shooting. The well-nourished,
pale face, with an eyeglass and drooping yellow moustache, made the Señor Administrador appear by contrast twice as sunbaked, more flaming red, a hundred
times more intensely and silently alive. Don José
Avellanos touched elbows with the other foreign diplo-
mat, a dark man with a quiet, watchful, self-confident
demeanour, and a touch of reserve. All etiquette being
laid aside on the occasion, General Montero was the
only one there in full uniform, so stiff with embroideries
in front that his broad chest seemed protected by a
cuirass of gold. Sir John at the beginning had got
away from high places for the sake of sitting near Mrs.
Gould.

The great financier was trying to express to her his
grateful sense of her hospitality and of his obligation to
her husband's "enormous influence in this part of the
country," when she interrupted him by a low "Hush!"
The President was going to make an informal pronouncement.

The Excellentissimo was on his legs. He said only a

few words, evidently deeply felt, and meant perhaps mostly for Avellanos—his old friend—as to the necessity of unremitting effort to secure the lasting welfare of the country emerging after this last struggle, he hoped, into a period of peace and material prosperity.

Mrs. Gould, listening to the mellow, slightly mournful voice, looking at this rotund, dark, spectacled face, at the short body, obese to the point of infirmity, thought that this man of delicate and melancholy mind, physically almost a cripple, coming out of his retirement into a dangerous strife at the call of his fellows, had the right to speak with the authority of his self-sacrifice. And yet she was made uneasy. He was more pathetic than promising; this first civilian Chief of the State Costaguana had ever known, pronouncing, glass in hand, his simple watchwords of honesty, peace, respect for law, political good faith abroad and at home—the safeguards of national honour.

He sat down. During the respectful, appreciative buzz of voices that followed the speech, General Montero raised a pair of heavy, drooping eyelids and rolled his eyes with a sort of uneasy dullness from face to face. The military backwoods hero of the party, though secretly impressed by the sudden novelties and splendours of his position (he had never been on board a ship before, and had hardly ever seen the sea except from a distance), understood by a sort of instinct the advantage his surly, unpolished attitude of a savage fighter gave him amongst all these refined Blanco aristocrats. But why was it that nobody was looking at him? he wondered to himself angrily. He was able to spell out the print of newspapers, and knew that he had performed the "greatest military exploit of modern times."

"My husband wanted the railway," Mrs. Gould said

to Sir John in the general murmur of resumed conversations. "All this brings nearer the sort of future we desire for the country, which has waited for it in sorrow long enough, God knows. But I will confess that the other day, during my afternoon drive when I suddenly saw an Indian boy ride out of a wood with the red flag of a surveying party in his hand, I felt something of a shock. The future means change—an utter change. And yet even here there are simple and picturesque things that one would like to preserve."

Sir John listened, smiling. But it was his turn now to hush Mrs. Gould.

"General Montero is going to speak," he whispered, and almost immediately added, in comic alarm, "Heavens! he's going to propose my own health, I believe."

General Montero had risen with a jingle of steel scabbard and a ripple of glitter on his gold-embroidered breast; a heavy sword-hilt appeared at his side above the edge of the table. In this gorgeous uniform, with his bull neck, his hooked nose flattened on the tip upon a blue-black, dyed moustache, he looked like a disguised and sinister vaquero. The drone of his voice had a strangely rasping, soulless ring. He floundered, lowering, through a few vague sentences; then suddenly raising his big head and his voice together, burst out harshly—

"The honour of the country is in the hands of the army. I assure you I shall be faithful to it." He hesitated till his roaming eyes met Sir John's face upon which he fixed a lurid, sleepy glance; and the figure of the lately negotiated loan came into his mind. He lifted his glass. "I drink to the health of the man who brings us a million and a half of pounds."*

He tossed off his champagne, and sat down heavily with a half-surprised, half-bullying look all round the faces in the profound, as if appalled, silence which succeeded the felicitous toast. Sir John did not move.

"I don't think I am called upon to rise," he murmured to Mrs. Gould. "That sort of thing speaks for itself." But Don José Avellanos came to the rescue with a short oration, in which he alluded pointedly to England's goodwill towards Costaguana—"a goodwill," he continued, significantly, "of which I, having been in my time accredited to the Court of St. James, am able to speak with some knowledge."

Only then Sir John thought fit to respond, which he did gracefully in bad French, punctuated by bursts of applause and the "Hear! Hears!" of Captain Mitchell, who was able to understand a word now and then. Directly he had done, the financier of railways turned to Mrs. Gould—

"You were good enough to say that you intended to ask me for something," he reminded her, gallantly. "What is it? Be assured that any request from you would be considered in the light of a favour to myself."

She thanked him by a gracious smile. Everybody was rising from the table.

"Let us go on deck," she proposed, "where I'll be able to point out to you the very object of my request."

An enormous national flag of Costaguana, diagonal red and yellow, with two green palm trees in the middle, floated lazily at the mainmast head of the *Juno*. A multitude of fireworks being let off in their thousands at the water's edge in honour of the President kept up a mysterious crepitating noise half round the harbour. Now and then a lot of rockets, swishing upwards invisibly, detonated overhead with only a puff of smoke in the bright sky. Crowds of people could be seen between the town gate and the harbour, under the bunches of multicoloured flags fluttering on tall poles.

Faint bursts of military music would be heard suddenly, and the remote sound of shouting. A knot of ragged negroes at the end of the wharf kept on loading and firing a small iron cannon time after time. A greyish haze of dust hung thin and motionless against the sun.

Don Vincente Ribiera made a few steps under the deck-awning, leaning on the arm of Señor Avellanos; a wide circle was formed round him, where the mirthless smile of his dark lips and the sightless glitter of his spectacles could be seen turning amiably from side to side. The informal function arranged on purpose on board the *Juno* to give the President-Dictator an opportunity to meet intimately some of his most notable adherents in Sulaco was drawing to an end. On one side, General Montero, his bald head covered now by a plumed cocked hat, remained motionless on a skylight seat, a pair of big gauntleted hands folded on the hilt of the sabre standing upright between his legs. The white plume, the coppery tint of his broad face, the blue-black of the moustaches under the curved beak, the mass of gold on sleeves and breast, the high shining boots with enormous spurs, the working nostrils, the imbecile and domineering stare of the glorious victor of Rio Seco had in them something ominous and incredible; the exaggeration of a cruel caricature, the fatuity of solemn masquerading, the atrocious grotesqueness of some military idol of Aztec conception and European bedecking, awaiting the homage of worshippers. Don José approached diplomatically this weird and inscrutable portent, and Mrs. Gould turned her fascinated eyes away at last.

Charles, coming up to take leave of Sir John, heard him say, as he bent over his wife's hand, "Certainly. Of course, my dear Mrs. Gould, for a *protégé* of yours! Not the slightest difficulty. Consider it done."

Going ashore in the same boat with the Goulds, Don José Avellanos was very silent. Even in the Gould carriage he did not open his lips for a long time. The mules trotted slowly away from the wharf between the extended hands of the beggars, who for that day seemed to have abandoned in a body the portals of churches. Charles Gould sat on the back seat and looked away upon the plain. A multitude of booths made of green boughs, of rushes, of odd pieces of plank eked out with bits of canvas had been erected all over it for the sale of cana,* of dulces, of fruit, of cigars. Over little heaps of glowing charcoal Indian women, squatting on mats, cooked food in black earthen pots, and boiled the water for the maté gourds, which they offered in soft, caressing voices to the country people. A racecourse had been staked out for the vaqueros; and away to the left, from where the crowd was massed thickly about a huge temporary erection, like a circus tent of wood with a conical grass roof, came the resonant twanging of harp strings, the sharp ping of guitars, with the grave drumming throb of an Indian gombo* pulsating steadily through the shrill choruses of the dancers.

Charles Gould said presently—

"All this piece of land belongs now to the Railway Company. There will be no more popular feasts held here."

Mrs. Gould was rather sorry to think so. She took this opportunity to mention how she had just obtained from Sir John the promise that the house occupied by Giorgio Viola should not be interfered with. She declared she could never understand why the survey engineers ever talked of demolishing that old building. It was not in the way of the projected harbour branch of the line in the least.

She stopped the carriage before the door to reassure at

once the old Genoese, who came out bare-headed and
stood by the carriage step. She talked to him in
Italian, of course, and he thanked her with calm dignity.
An old Garibaldino was grateful to her from the bottom
of his heart for keeping the roof over the heads of his
wife and children. He was too old to wander any more.

"And is it for ever, signora?" he asked.

"For as long as you like."

"Bene. Then the place must be named. It was not
worth while before."

He smiled ruggedly, with a running together of
wrinkles at the corners of his eyes. "I shall set about
the painting of the name to-morrow."

"And what is it going to be, Giorgio?"

"Albergo d'Italia Una,"* said the old Garibaldino,
looking away for a moment. "More in memory of
those who have died," he added, "than for the country
stolen from us soldiers of liberty by the craft of that
accursed Piedmontese race of kings and ministers."

Mrs. Gould smiled slightly, and, bending over a
little, began to inquire about his wife and children. He
had sent them into town on that day. The padrona
was better in health; many thanks to the signora for
inquiring.

People were passing in twos and threes, in whole
parties of men and women attended by trotting children. A horseman mounted on a silver-grey mare drew
rein quietly in the shade of the house after taking off his
hat to the party in the carriage, who returned smiles
and familiar nods. Old Viola, evidently very pleased
with the news he had just heard, interrupted himself for
a moment to tell him rapidly that the house was secured,
by the kindness of the English signora, for as long as he
liked to keep it. The other listened attentively, but
made no response.

When the carriage moved on he took off his hat again, a grey sombrero with a silver cord and tassels. The bright colours of a Mexican serape twisted on the cantle, the enormous silver buttons on the embroidered leather jacket, the row of tiny silver buttons down the seam of the trousers, the snowy linen, a silk sash with embroidered ends, the silver plates on headstall and saddle, proclaimed the unapproachable style of the famous Capataz de Cargadores—a Mediterranean sailor—got up with more finished splendour than any well-to-do young ranchero of the Campo had ever displayed on a high holiday.

"It is a great thing for me," murmured old Giorgio, still thinking of the house, for now he had grown weary of change. "The signora just said a word to the Englishman."

"The old Englishman who has enough money to pay for a railway? He is going off in an hour," remarked Nostromo, carelessly. "Buon viaggio, then. I've guarded his bones all the way from the Entrada pass down to the plain and into Sulaco, as though he had been my own father."

Old Giorgio only moved his head sideways absently. Nostromo pointed after the Goulds' carriage, nearing the grass-grown gate in the old town wall that was like a wall of matted jungle.

"And I have sat alone at night with my revolver in the Company's warehouse time and again by the side of that other Englishman's heap of silver, guarding it as though it had been my own."

Viola seemed lost in thought. "It is a great thing for me," he repeated again, as if to himself.

"It is," agreed the magnificent Capataz de Cargadores, calmly. "Listen, Vecchio—go in and bring me out a cigar, but don't look for it in my room. There's nothing there."

Viola stepped into the *café* and came out directly, still absorbed in his idea, and tendered him a cigar, mumbling thoughtfully in his moustache, "Children growing up—and girls, too! Girls!" He sighed and fell silent.

"What, only one?" remarked Nostromo, looking down with a sort of comic inquisitiveness at the unconscious old man. "No matter," he added, with lofty negligence; "one is enough till another is wanted."

He lit it and let the match drop from his passive fingers. Giorgio Viola looked up, and said abruptly—

"My son would have been just such a fine young man as you, Gian' Battista, if he had lived."

"What? Your son? But you are right, padrone. If he had been like me he would have been a man."

He turned his horse slowly, and paced on between the booths, checking the mare*almost to a standstill now and then for children, for the groups of people from the distant Campo, who stared after him with admiration. The Company's lightermen saluted him from afar; and the greatly envied Capataz de Cargadores advanced, amongst murmurs of recognition and obsequious greetings, towards the huge circus-like erection. The throng thickened; the guitars tinkled louder; other horsemen sat motionless, smoking calmly above the heads of the crowd; it eddied and pushed before the doors of the high-roofed building, whence issued a shuffle and thumping of feet in time to the dance music vibrating and shrieking with a racking rhythm, overhung by the tremendous, sustained, hollow roar of the gombo. The barbarous and imposing noise of the big drum, that can madden a crowd, and that even Europeans cannot hear without a strange emotion, seemed to draw Nostromo on to its source, while a man, wrapped up in a faded, torn poncho, walked by his stirrup, and, buffeted right and left, begged "his worship" insistently for employment on the wharf. He whined, offering the Señor Capataz half his daily pay for the privilege of being admitted to the swaggering fraternity of Cargadores; the other half would be enough for him, he protested. But Captain Mitchell's right-hand man—"invaluable for our work—a perfectly incorruptible fellow"—after looking down critically at the ragged mozo, shook his head without a word in the uproar going on around.

The man fell back; and a little further on Nostromo had to pull up. From the doors of the dance hall men and women emerged tottering, streaming with sweat, trembling in every limb, to lean, panting, with staring eyes and parted lips, against the wall of the structure, where the harps and guitars played on with mad speed in an incessant roll of thunder. Hundreds of hands clapped in there; voices shrieked, and then all at once would sink low, chanting in unison the refrain of a love song, with a dying fall. A red flower, flung with a good aim from somewhere in the crowd, struck the resplendent Capataz on the cheek.

He caught it as it fell, neatly, but for some time did not turn his head. When at last he condescended to look round, the throng near him had parted to make way for a pretty Morenita, her hair held up by a small golden comb, who was walking towards him in the open space.

Her arms and neck emerged plump and bare from a snowy chemisette; the blue woollen skirt, with all the fullness gathered in front, scanty on the hips and tight across the back, disclosed the provoking action of her walk. She came straight on and laid her hand on the mare's neck with a timid, coquettish look upwards out of the corner of her eyes.

"Querido," she murmured, caressingly, "why do you pretend not to see me when I pass?"

"Because I don't love thee any more," said Nostromo, deliberately, after a moment of reflective silence.

The hand on the mare's neck trembled suddenly. She dropped her head before all the eyes in the wide circle formed round the generous, the terrible, the inconstant Capataz de Cargadores, and his Morenita.

Nostromo, looking down, saw tears beginning to fall down her face.

"Has it come, then, ever beloved of my heart?" she whispered. "Is it true?"

"No," said Nostromo, looking away carelessly. "It was a lie. I love thee as much as ever."

"Is that true?" she cooed, joyously, her cheeks still wet with tears.

"It is true."

"True on the life?"

"As true as that; but thou must not ask me to swear it on the Madonna that stands in thy room." And the Capataz laughed a little in response to the grins of the crowd.

She pouted—very pretty—a little uneasy.

"No, I will not ask for that. I can see love in your eyes." She laid her hand on his knee. "Why are you trembling like this? From love?" she continued, while the cavernous thundering of the gombo went on without a pause. "But if you love her as much as that, you must give your Paquita a gold-mounted rosary of beads for the neck of her Madonna."

"No," said Nostromo, looking into her uplifted, begging eyes, which suddenly turned stony with surprise.

"No? Then what else will your worship give me on the day of the fiesta?" she asked, angrily; "so as not to shame me before all these people."

"There is no shame for thee in getting nothing from thy lover for once."

"True! The shame is your worship's—my poor lover's," she flared up, sarcastically.

Laughs were heard at her anger, at her retort. What an audacious spitfire she was! The people aware of this scene were calling out urgently to others in the crowd. The circle round the silver-grey mare narrowed slowly.

The girl went off a pace or two, confronting the mocking curiosity of the eyes, then flung back to the stirrup, tiptoeing, her enraged face turned up to Nostromo with a pair of blazing eyes. He bent low to her in the saddle.

"Juan," she hissed, "I could stab thee to the heart!"

The dreaded Capataz de Cargadores, magnificent and carelessly public in his amours, flung his arm round her neck and kissed her spluttering lips. A murmur went round.

"A knife!" he demanded at large, holding her firmly by the shoulder.

Twenty blades flashed out together in the circle. A young man in holiday attire, bounding in, thrust one in Nostromo's hand and bounded back into the ranks, very proud of himself. Nostromo had not even looked at him.

"Stand on my foot," he commanded the girl, who, suddenly subdued, rose lightly, and when he had her up, encircling her waist, her face near to his, he pressed the knife into her little hand.

"No, Morenita! You shall not put me to shame," he said. "You shall have your present; and so that everyone should know who is your lover to-day, you may cut all the silver buttons off my coat."

There were shouts of laughter and applause at this

witty freak, while the girl passed the keen blade, and the impassive rider jingled in his palm the increasing hoard of silver buttons. He eased her to the ground with both her hands full. After whispering for a while with a very strenuous face, she walked away, staring haughtily, and vanished into the crowd.

The circle had broken up, and the lordly Capataz de Cargadores, the indispensable man, the tried and trusty Nostromo, the Mediterranean sailor come ashore casually to try his luck in Costaguana, rode slowly towards the harbour. The *Juno* was just then swinging round; and even as Nostromo reined up again to look on, a flag ran up on the improvised flagstaff erected in an ancient and dismantled little fort at the harbour entrance. Half a battery of field guns had been hurried over there from the Sulaco barracks for the purpose of firing the regulation salutes for the President-Dictator and the War Minister. As the mail-boat headed through the pass, the badly timed reports announced the end of Don Vincente Ribiera's first official visit to Sulaco, and for Captain Mitchell the end of another "historic occasion." Next time when the "Hope of honest men" was to come that way, a year and a half later, it was unofficially, over the mountain tracks, fleeing after a defeat on a lame mule, to be only just saved by Nostromo from an ignominious death at the hands of a mob. It was a very different event, of which Captain Mitchell used to say—

"It was history—history, sir! And that fellow of mine, Nostromo, you know, was right in it. Absolutely making history, sir."

But this event, creditable to Nostromo, was to lead immediately to another, which could not be classed either as "history" or as "a mistake" in Captain Mitchell's phraseology. He had another word for it.

"Sir," he used to say afterwards, "that was no mistake. It was a fatality. A misfortune, pure and simple, sir. And that poor fellow of mine was right in it—right in the middle of it! A fatality, if ever there was one—and to my mind he has never been the same man since."

PART SECOND

THE ISABELS

CHAPTER ONE

THROUGH good and evil report in the varying fortune of that struggle which Don José had characterized in the phrase, "the fate of national honesty trembles in the balance," the Gould Concession, "Imperium in Imperio," had gone on working; the square mountain had gone on pouring its treasure down the wooden shoots to the unresting batteries of stamps; the lights of San Tomé had twinkled night after night upon the great, limitless shadow of the Campo; every three months the silver escort had gone down to the sea as if neither the war nor its consequences could ever affect the ancient Occidental State secluded beyond its high barrier of the Cordillera. All the fighting took place on the other side of that mighty wall of serrated peaks lorded over by the white dome of Higuerota and as yet unbreached by the railway, of which only the first part, the easy Campo part from Sulaco to the Ivie Valley at the foot of the pass, had been laid. Neither did the telegraph line cross the mountains yet; its poles, like slender beacons on the plain, penetrated into the forest fringe of the foot-hills cut by the deep avenue of the track; and its wire ended abruptly in the construction camp at a white deal table supporting a Morse apparatus, in a long hut of planks with a corrugated iron roof overshadowed by gigantic cedar trees—the quarters of the engineer in charge of the advance section.

The harbour was busy, too, with the traffic in railway material, and with the movements of troops along the coast. The O.S.N. Company found much occupa-

tion for its fleet.   Costaguana had no navy, and, apart
from a few coastguard cutters, there were no national
ships except a couple of old merchant steamers used as
transports.

Captain Mitchell, feeling more and more in the thick
of history, found time for an hour or so during an
afternoon in the drawing-room of the Casa Gould,
where, with a strange ignorance of the real forces at
work around him, he professed himself delighted to get
away from the strain of affairs.   He did not know what
he would have done without his invaluable Nostromo,
he declared.   Those confounded Costaguana politics
gave him more work—he confided to Mrs. Gould—
than he had bargained for.

Don José Avellanos had displayed in the service of the
endangered Ribiera Government an organizing activity
and an eloquence of which the echoes reached even
Europe.   For, after the new loan to the Ribiera Government, Europe had become interested in Costaguana.
The Sala of the Provincial Assembly (in the Municipal
Buildings of Sulaco), with its portraits of the Liberators
on the walls and an old flag of Cortez preserved in a
glass case above the President's chair, had heard all
these speeches—the early one containing the impassioned declaration "Militarism is the enemy," the
famous one of the "trembling balance" delivered on
the occasion of the vote for the raising of a second
Sulaco regiment in the defence of the reforming Government; and when the provinces again displayed their
old flags (proscribed in Guzman Bento's time) there
was another of those great orations, when Don José
greeted these old emblems of the war of Independence,
brought out again in the name of new Ideals.   The
old idea of Federalism had disappeared.   For his part
he did not wish to revive old political doctrines.   They

were perishable. They died. But the doctrine of
political rectitude was immortal. The second Sulaco
regiment, to whom he was presenting this flag, was going
to show its valour in a contest for order, peace, progress;
for the establishment of national self-respect without
which—he declared with energy—"we are a reproach
and a byword amongst the powers of the world."

Don José Avellanos loved his country. He had
served it lavishly with his fortune during his diplomatic
career, and the later story of his captivity and barbarous ill-usage under Guzman Bento was well known
to his listeners. It was a wonder that he had not been
a victim of the ferocious and summary executions which
marked the course of that tyranny; for Guzman had
ruled the country with the sombre imbecility of political
fanaticism. The power of Supreme Government had
become in his dull mind an object of strange worship, as
if it were some sort of cruel deity. It was incarnated in
himself, and his adversaries, the Federalists, were the
supreme sinners, objects of hate, abhorrence, and fear,
as heretics would be to a convinced Inquisitor. For
years he had carried about at the tail of the Army of
Pacification, all over the country, a captive band of
such atrocious criminals, who considered themselves
most unfortunate at not having been summarily executed. It was a diminishing company of nearly naked
skeletons, loaded with irons, covered with dirt, with
vermin, with raw wounds, all men of position, of education, of wealth, who had learned to fight amongst themselves for scraps of rotten beef thrown to them by
soldiers, or to beg a negro cook for a drink of muddy
water in pitiful accents. Don José Avellanos, clanking
his chains amongst the others, seemed only to exist in
order to prove how much hunger, pain, degradation,
and cruel torture a human body can stand without

parting with the last spark of life. Sometimes interrogatories, backed by some primitive method of torture, were administered to them by a commission of officers hastily assembled in a hut of sticks and branches, and made pitiless by the fear for their own lives. A lucky one or two of that spectral company of prisoners would perhaps be led tottering behind a bush to be shot by a file of soldiers. Always an army chaplain—some unshaven, dirty man, girt with a sword and with a tiny cross embroidered in white cotton on the left breast of a lieutenant's uniform—would follow, cigarette in the corner of the mouth, wooden stool in hand, to hear the confession and give absolution; for the Citizen Saviour of the Country (Guzman Bento was called thus officially in petitions) was not averse from the exercise of rational clemency. The irregular report of the firing squad would be heard, followed sometimes by a single finishing shot; a little bluish cloud of smoke would float up above the green bushes, and the Army of Pacification would move on over the savannas, through the forests, crossing rivers, invading rural pueblos, devastating the haciendas of the horrid aristocrats, occupying the inland towns in the fulfilment of its patriotic mission, and leaving behind a united land wherein the evil taint of Federalism could no longer be detected in the smoke of burning houses and the smell of spilt blood.

Don José Avellanos had survived that time.

Perhaps, when contemptuously signifying to him his release, the Citizen Saviour of the Country might have thought this benighted aristocrat too broken in health and spirit and fortune to be any longer dangerous. Or, perhaps, it may have been a simple caprice. Guzman Bento, usually full of fanciful fears and brooding suspicions, had sudden accesses of unreasonable self-confidence when he perceived himself elevated on a pinnacle of power and safety beyond the reach of mere mortal plotters. At such times he would impulsively command the celebration of a solemn Mass of thanksgiving, which would be sung in great pomp in the cathedral of Sta. Marta by the trembling, subservient Archbishop of his creation. He heard it sitting in a gilt armchair placed before the high altar, surrounded by the civil and military heads of his Government. The unofficial world of Sta. Marta would crowd into the cathedral, for it was not quite safe for anybody of mark to stay away from these manifestations of presidential piety. Having thus acknowledged the only power he was at all disposed to recognize as above himself, he would scatter acts of political grace in a sardonic wantonness of clemency. There was no other way left now to enjoy his power but by seeing his crushed adversaries crawl impotently into the light of day out of the dark, noisome cells of the Collegio.* Their harmlessness fed his insatiable vanity, and they could always be got hold of again. It was the rule for all the women of their families to present thanks afterwards in a special audience. The incarnation of that strange god: El Gobierno Supremo, received them standing, cocked hat on head, and exhorted them in a menacing mutter to show their gratitude by bringing up their children in fidelity to the democratic form of government, "which I have established for the happiness of our country." His front teeth having been knocked out in some accident of his former herdsman's life, his utterance was spluttering and indistinct. He had been working for Costaguana alone in the midst of treachery and opposition. Let it cease now lest he should become weary of forgiving!

Don José Avellanos had known this forgiveness.

He was broken in health and fortune deplorably

enough to present a truly gratifying spectacle to the
supreme chief of democratic institutions. He retired
to Sulaco. His wife had an estate in that province, and
she nursed him back to life out of the house of death and
captivity. When she died, their daughter, an only
child, was old enough to devote herself to "poor papa."

Miss Avellanos, born in Europe and educated partly
in England, was a tall, grave girl, with a self-possessed
manner, a wide, white forehead, a wealth of rich brown
hair, and blue eyes.

The other young ladies of Sulaco stood in awe of her
character and accomplishments. She was reputed to
be terribly learned and serious. As to pride, it was
well known that all the Corbelàns were proud, and her
mother was a Corbelàn. Don José Avellanos depended
very much upon the devotion of his beloved Antonia.
He accepted it in the benighted way of men, who,
though made in God's image, are like stone idols without
sense before the smoke of certain burnt offerings. He
was ruined in every way, but a man possessed of passion is not a bankrupt in life. Don José Avellanos
desired passionately for his country: peace, prosperity,
and (as the end of the preface to "Fifty Years of Misrule" has it) "an honourable place in the comity of
civilized nations." In this last phrase the Minister
Plenipotentiary, cruelly humiliated by the bad faith
of his Government towards the foreign bondholders,
stands disclosed in the patriot.

The fatuous turmoil of greedy factions succeeding the
tyranny of Guzman Bento seemed to bring his desire to
the very door of opportunity. He was too old to
descend personally into the centre of the arena at Sta.
Marta. But the men who acted there sought his advice at every step. He himself thought that he could
be most useful at a distance, in Sulaco. His name, his

connections, his former position, his experience commanded the respect of his class. The discovery that this man, living in dignified poverty in the Corbelàn town residence (opposite the Casa Gould), could dispose of material means towards the support of the cause increased his influence. It was his open letter of appeal that decided the candidature of Don Vincente Ribiera for the Presidency. Another of these informal State papers drawn up by Don José (this time in the shape of an address from the Province) induced that scrupulous constitutionalist to accept the extraordinary powers conferred upon him for five years by an overwhelming vote of congress in Sta. Marta. It was a specific mandate to establish the prosperity of the people on the basis of firm peace at home, and to redeem the national credit by the satisfaction of all just claims abroad.

In the afternoon the news of that vote had reached Sulaco by the usual roundabout postal way through Cayta, and up the coast by steamer. Don José, who had been waiting for the mail in the Goulds' drawing-room, got out of the rocking-chair, letting his hat fall off his knees. He rubbed his silvery, short hair with both hands, speechless with the excess of joy.

"Emilia, my soul," he had burst out, "let me embrace you! Let me——"

Captain Mitchell, had he been there, would no doubt have made an apt remark about the dawn of a new era; but if Don José thought something of the kind, his eloquence failed him on this occasion. The inspirer of that revival of the Blanco party tottered where he stood. Mrs. Gould moved forward quickly and, as she offered her cheek with a smile to her old friend, managed very cleverly to give him the support of her arm he really needed.

Don José had recovered himself at once, but for a time he could do no more than murmur, "Oh, you two patriots! Oh, you two patriots!"—looking from one to the other. Vague plans of another historical work, wherein all the devotions to the regeneration of the country he loved would be enshrined for the reverent worship of posterity, flitted through his mind. The historian who had enough elevation of soul to write of Guzman Bento: "Yet this monster, imbrued in the blood of his countrymen, must not be held unreservedly to the execration of future years. It appears to be true that he, too, loved his country. He had given it twelve years of peace; and, absolute master of lives and fortunes as he was, he died poor. His worst fault, perhaps, was not his ferocity, but his ignorance;" the man who could write thus of a cruel persecutor (the passage occurs in his "History of Misrule") felt at the foreshadowing of success an almost boundless affection for his two helpers, for these two young people from over the sea.*

Just as years ago, calmly, from the conviction of practical necessity, stronger than any abstract political doctrine, Henry Gould had drawn the sword, so now, the times being changed, Charles Gould had flung the silver of the San Tomé into the fray. The Inglez of Sulaco, the "Costaguana Englishman" of the third generation, was as far from being a political intriguer as his uncle from a revolutionary swashbuckler. Springing from the instinctive uprightness of their natures their action was reasoned. They saw an opportunity and used the weapon to hand.

Charles Gould's position—a commanding position in the background of that attempt to retrieve the peace and the credit of the Republic—was very clear. At the beginning he had had to accommodate himself to existing circumstances of corruption so naïvely brazen as to disarm the hatred of a man courageous enough not to be afraid of its irresponsible potency to ruin everything it touched. It seemed to him too contemptible for hot anger even. He made use of it with a cold, fearless scorn, manifested rather than concealed by the forms of stony courtesy which did away with much of the ignominy of the situation. At bottom, perhaps, he suffered from it, for he was not a man of cowardly illusions, but he refused to discuss the ethical view with his wife. He trusted that, though a little disenchanted, she would be intelligent enough to understand that his character safeguarded the enterprise of their lives as much or more than his policy. The extraordinary development of the mine had put a great power into his hands. To feel that prosperity always at the mercy of unintelligent greed had grown irksome to him. To Mrs. Gould it was humiliating. At any rate, it was dangerous. In the confidential communications passing between Charles Gould, the King of Sulaco, and the head of the silver and steel interests far away in California, the conviction was growing that any attempt made by men of education and integrity ought to be discreetly supported. "You may tell your friend Avellanos that I think so," Mr. Holroyd had written at the proper moment from his inviolable sanctuary within the eleven-storey high factory of great affairs. And shortly afterwards, with a credit opened by the Third Southern Bank (located next door but one to the Holroyd Building), the Ribierist party in Costaguana took a practical shape under the eye of the administrator of the San Tomé mine. And Don José, the hereditary friend of the Gould family, could say: "Perhaps, my dear Carlos, I shall not have believed in vain."

CHAPTER TWO

AFTER another armed struggle, decided by Montero's victory of Rio Seco, had been added to the tale of civil wars, the "honest men," as Don José called them, could breathe freely for the first time in half a century. The Five-Year-Mandate law became the basis of that regeneration, the passionate desire and hope for which had been like the elixir of everlasting youth for Don José Avellanos.

And when it was suddenly—and not quite unexpectedly—endangered by that "brute Montero," it was a passionate indignation that gave him a new lease of life, as it were. Already, at the time of the President-Dictator's visit to Sulaco, Moraga had sounded a note of warning from Sta. Marta about the War Minister. Montero and his brother made the subject of an earnest talk between the Dictator-President and the Nestor-inspirer of the party. But Don Vincente, a doctor of philosophy from the Cordova University,* seemed to have an exaggerated respect for military ability, whose mysteriousness—since it appeared to be altogether independent of intellect—imposed upon his imagination. The victor of Rio Seco was a popular hero. His services were so recent that the President-Dictator quailed before the obvious charge of political ingratitude. Great regenerating transactions were being initiated—the fresh loan, a new railway line, a vast colonization scheme. Anything that could unsettle the public opinion in the capital was to be avoided. Don José bowed to these arguments and tried to dismiss

from his mind the gold-laced portent in boots, and with
a sabre, made meaningless now at last, he hoped, in the
new order of things.

Less than six months*after the President-Dictator's
visit, Sulaco learned with stupefaction of the military
revolt in the name of national honour. The Minister
of War, in a barrack-square allocution to the officers of
the artillery regiment he had been inspecting, had
declared the national honour sold to foreigners. The
Dictator, by his weak compliance with the demands of
the European powers—for the settlement of long out-
standing money claims—had showed himself unfit to
rule. A letter from Moraga explained afterwards that
the initiative, and even the very text, of the incendiary
allocution came, in reality, from the other Montero, the
ex-guerillero, the Commandante de Plaza. The energetic treatment of Dr. Monygham, sent for in haste "to
the mountain," who came galloping three leagues in the
dark, saved Don José from a dangerous attack of
jaundice.

After getting over the shock, Don José refused to let
himself be prostrated. Indeed, better news succeeded
at first. The revolt in the capital had been suppressed
after a night of fighting in the streets. Unfortunately,
both the Monteros had been able to make their escape
south, to their native province of Entre-Montes. The
hero of the forest march, the victor of Rio Seco, had
been received with frenzied acclamations in Nicoya, the
provincial capital. The troops in garrison there had
gone to him in a body. The brothers were organizing
an army, gathering malcontents, sending emissaries
primed with patriotic lies to the people, and with
promises of plunder to the wild llaneros. Even a
Monterist press had come into existence, speaking
oracularly of the secret promises of support given by

"our great sister Republic of the North" against the sinister land-grabbing designs of European powers, cursing in every issue the "miserable Ribiera," who had plotted to deliver his country, bound hand and foot, for a prey to foreign speculators.

Sulaco, pastoral and sleepy, with its opulent Campo and the rich silver mine, heard the din of arms fitfully in its fortunate isolation. It was nevertheless in the very forefront of the defence with men and money; but the very rumours reached it circuitously—from abroad even, so much was it cut off from the rest of the Republic, not only by natural obstacles, but also by the vicissitudes of the war. The Monteristos were besieging Cayta, an important postal link. The overland couriers ceased to come across the mountains, and no muleteer would consent to risk the journey at last; even Bonifacio on one occasion failed to return from Sta. Marta, either not daring to start, or perhaps captured by the parties of the enemy raiding the country between the Cordillera and the capital. Monterist publications, however, found their way into the province, mysteriously enough; and also Monterist emissaries preaching death to aristocrats in the villages and towns of the Campo. Very early, at the beginning of the trouble, Hernandez, the bandit, had proposed (through the agency of an old priest of a village in the wilds) to deliver two of them to the Ribierist authorities in Tonoro. They had come to offer him a free pardon and the rank of colonel from General Montero in consideration of joining the rebel army with his mounted band. No notice was taken at the time of the proposal. It was joined, as an evidence of good faith, to a petition praying the Sulaco Assembly for permission to enlist, with all his followers, in the forces being then raised in Sulaco for the defence of the Five-

Year Mandate of regeneration. The petition, like everything else, had found its way into Don José's hands. He had showed to Mrs. Gould these pages of dirty-greyish rough paper (perhaps looted in some village store), covered with the crabbed, illiterate handwriting of the old padre, carried off from his hut by the side of a mud-walled church to be the secretary of the dreaded Salteador. They had both bent in the lamplight of the Gould drawing-room over the document containing the fierce and yet humble appeal of the man against the blind and stupid barbarity turning an honest ranchero into a bandit. A postscript of the priest stated that, but for being deprived of his liberty for ten days, he had been treated with humanity and the respect due to his sacred calling. He had been, it appears, confessing and absolving the chief and most of the band, and he guaranteed the sincerity of their good disposition. He had distributed heavy penances, no doubt in the way of litanies and fasts; but he argued shrewdly that it would be difficult for them to make their peace with God durably till they had made peace with men.

Never before, perhaps, had Hernandez's head been in less jeopardy than when he petitioned humbly for permission to buy a pardon for himself and his gang of deserters by armed service. He could range afar from the waste lands protecting his fastness, unchecked, because there were no troops left in the whole province. The usual garrison of Sulaco had gone south to the war, with its brass band playing the Bolivar march on the bridge of one of the O.S.N. Company's steamers. The great family coaches drawn up along the shore of the harbour were made to rock on the high leathern springs by the enthusiasm of the señoras and the señoritas standing up to wave their lace handkerchiefs, as lighter after lighter packed full of troops left the end of the jetty.

Nostromo directed the embarkation, under the super-intendendence of Captain Mitchell, red-faced in the sun, conspicuous in a white waistcoat, representing the allied and anxious goodwill of all the material interests of civilization. General Barrios, who commanded the troops, assured Don José on parting that in three weeks he would have Montero in a wooden cage drawn by three pair of oxen ready for a tour through all the towns of the Republic.

"And then, señora," he continued, baring his curly iron-grey head to Mrs. Gould in her landau—"and then, señora, we shall convert our swords into plough-shares and grow rich. Even I, myself, as soon as this little business is settled, shall open a fundacion on some land I have on the llanos and try to make a little money in peace and quietness. Señora, you know, all Costa-guana knows—what do I say?—this whole South American continent knows, that Pablo Barrios has had his fill of military glory."

Charles Gould was not present at the anxious and patriotic send-off. It was not his part to see the soldiers embark. It was neither his part, nor his inclination, nor his policy. His part, his inclination, and his policy were united in one endeavour to keep unchecked the flow of treasure he had started single-handed from the re-opened scar in the flank of the mountain. As the mine developed he had trained for himself some native help. There were foremen, artificers and clerks, with Don Pépé for the gobernador of the mining population. For the rest his shoulders alone sustained the whole weight of the "Imperium in Imperio," the great Gould Concession whose mere shadow had been enough to crush the life out of his father.

Mrs. Gould had no silver mine to look after. In the general life of the Gould Concession she was represented by her two lieutenants, the doctor and the priest, but she fed her woman's love for excitement on events whose significance was purified to her by the fire of her imaginative purpose. On that day she had brought the Avellanos, father and daughter, down to the harbour with her.

Amongst his other activities of that stirring time, Don José had become the chairman of a Patriotic Committee which had armed a great proportion of troops in the Sulaco command with an improved model of a military rifle. It had been just discarded for something still more deadly by one of the great European powers. How much of the market-price for second-hand weapons was covered by the voluntary contributions of the principal families, and how much came from those funds Don José was understood to command abroad, remained a secret which he alone could have disclosed; but the Ricos, as the populace called them, had contributed under the pressure of their Nestor's eloquence. Some of the more enthusiastic ladies had been moved to bring offerings of jewels into the hands of the man who was the life and soul of the party.

There were moments when both his life and his soul seemed overtaxed by so many years of undiscouraged belief in regeneration. He appeared almost inanimate, sitting rigidly by the side of Mrs. Gould in the landau, with his fine, old, clean-shaven face of a uniform tint as if modelled in yellow wax, shaded by a soft felt hat, the dark eyes looking out fixedly. Antonia, the beautiful Antonia, as Miss Avellanos was called in Sulaco, leaned back, facing them; and her full figure, the grave oval of her face with full red lips, made her look more mature than Mrs. Gould, with her mobile expression and small, erect person under a slightly swaying sunshade.

Whenever possible Antonia attended her father; her recognized devotion weakened the shocking effect of her scorn for the rigid conventions regulating the life of Spanish-American girlhood. And, in truth, she was no longer girlish. It was said that she often wrote State papers from her father's dictation, and was allowed to read all the books in his library. At the receptions—where the situation was saved by the presence of a very decrepit old lady (a relation of the Corbelàns), quite deaf and motionless in an armchair—Antonia could hold her own in a discussion with two or three men at a time. Obviously she was not the girl to be content with peeping through a barred window at a cloaked figure of a lover ensconced in a doorway opposite—which is the correct form of Costaguana courtship. It was generally believed that with her foreign upbringing and foreign ideas the learned and proud Antonia would never marry—unless, indeed, she married a foreigner from Europe or North America, now that Sulaco seemed on the point of being invaded by all the world.

CHAPTER THREE

WHEN General Barrios stopped to address Mrs.
Gould, Antonia raised negligently her hand holding an
open fan, as if to shade from the sun her head, wrapped
in a light lace shawl. The clear gleam of her blue eyes
gliding behind the black fringe of eyelashes paused for a
moment upon her father, then travelled further to the
figure of a young man of thirty at most, of medium
height, rather thick-set, wearing a light overcoat.
Bearing down with the open palm of his hand upon the
knob of a flexible cane, he had been looking on from a
distance; but directly he saw himself noticed, he approached quietly and put his elbow over the door of the
landau.

The shirt collar, cut low in the neck, the big bow of
his cravat, the style of his clothing, from the round hat
to the varnished shoes, suggested an idea of French
elegance; but otherwise he was the very type of a fair
Spanish creole. The fluffy moustache and the short,
curly, golden beard did not conceal his lips, rosy, fresh,
almost pouting in expression. His full, round face was
of that warm, healthy creole white which is never
tanned by its native sunshine. Martin Decoud was
seldom exposed to the Costaguana sun under which he
was born. His people had been long settled in Paris,
where he had studied law, had dabbled in literature, had
hoped now and then in moments of exaltation to become a poet like that other foreigner of Spanish blood,
José Maria Herédia.* In other moments he had, to pass
the time, condescended to write articles on European

affairs for the *Semenario*,* the principal newspaper in
Sta. Marta, which printed them under the heading
"From our special correspondent," though the author-
ship was an open secret. Everybody in Costaguana,
where the tale of compatriots in Europe is jealously
kept, knew that it was "the son Decoud," a talented
young man, supposed to be moving in the higher
spheres of Society. As a matter of fact, he was an idle
boulevardier, in touch with some smart journalists,
made free of a few newspaper offices, and welcomed in
the pleasure haunts of pressmen. This life, whose
dreary superficiality is covered by the glitter of universal blague, like the stupid clowning of a harlequin by
the spangles of a motley costume, induced in him a
Frenchified—but most un-French—cosmopolitanism, in
reality a mere barren indifferentism* posing as intellectual superiority. Of his own country he used to say to
his French associates:—Imagine an atmosphere of
opera-bouffe in which all the comic business of stage
statesmen, brigands, etc., etc., all their farcical stealing,
intriguing, and stabbing is done in dead earnest. It is
screamingly funny, the blood flows all the time, and
the actors believe themselves to be influencing the fate
of the universe. Of course, government in general, any
government anywhere, is a thing of exquisite comicality
to a discerning mind; but really we Spanish-Americans
do overstep the bounds. No man of ordinary intelligence can take part in the intrigues of *une farce macabre*.
However, these Ribierists, of whom we hear so much
just now, are really trying in their own comical way to
make the country habitable, and even to pay some of
its debts. My friends, you had better write up Señor
Ribiera all you can in kindness to your own bondholders.
Really, if what I am told in my letters is true, there is
some chance for them at last."

And he would explain with railing verve what Don Vincente Ribiera stood for—a mournful little man oppressed by his own good intentions, the significance of battles won, who Montero was (*un grotesque vaniteux et féroce*),*and the manner of the new loan connected with railway development, and the colonization of vast tracts of land in one great financial scheme.

And his French friends would remark that evidently this little fellow Decoud *connaissait la question à fond.* An important Parisian review asked him for an article on the situation. It was composed in a serious tone and in a spirit of levity. Afterwards he asked one of his intimates——

"Have you read my thing about the regeneration of Costaguana—*une bonne blague, hein?*"*

He imagined himself Parisian to the tips of his fingers. But far from being that he was in danger of remaining a sort of nondescript dilettante all his life. He had pushed the habit of universal raillery to a point where it blinded him to the genuine impulses of his own nature. To be suddenly selected for the executive member of the patriotic small-arms committee of Sulaco seemed to him the height of the unexpected, one of those fantastic moves of which only his "dear countrymen" were capable.

"It's like a tile falling on my head. I—I—executive member! It's the first I hear of it! What do I know of military rifles? *C'est funambulesque !*"*he had exclaimed to his favourite sister; for the Decoud family—except the old father and mother—used the French language amongst themselves. "And you should see the explanatory and confidential letter! Eight pages of it—no less!"

This letter, in Antonia's handwriting, was signed by Don José, who appealed to the "young and gifted

Costaguanero" on public grounds, and privately opened
his heart to his talented god-son, a man of wealth and
leisure, with wide relations, and by his parentage and
bringing-up worthy of all confidence.

"Which means," Martin commented, cynically, to
his sister, "that I am not likely to misappropriate
the funds, or go blabbing to our Chargé d'Affaires
here."

The whole thing was being carried out behind the
back of the War Minister, Montero, a mistrusted
member of the Ribiera Government, but difficult to
get rid of at once. He was not to know anything of it
till the troops under Barrios's command had the new
rifle in their hands. The President-Dictator, whose
position was very difficult, was alone in the secret.

"How funny!" commented Martin's sister and con-
fidant; to which the brother, with an air of best Parisian
blague, had retorted—

"It's immense! The idea of that Chief of the State
engaged, with the help of private citizens, in digging a
mine under his own indispensable War Minister. No!
We are unapproachable!" And he laughed immoder-
ately.

Afterwards his sister was surprised at the earnestness
and ability he displayed in carrying out his mission,
which circumstances made delicate, and his want of
special knowledge rendered difficult. She had never
seen Martin take so much trouble about anything in his
whole life.

"It amuses me," he had explained, briefly. "I am
beset by a lot of swindlers trying to sell all sorts of gas-
pipe weapons. They are charming; they invite me to
expensive luncheons; I keep up their hopes; it's extremely entertaining. Meanwhile, the real affair is
being carried through in quite another quarter."

When the business was concluded he declared suddenly his intention of seeing the precious consignment delivered safely in Sulaco. The whole burlesque business, he thought, was worth following up to the end. He mumbled his excuses, tugging at his golden beard, before the acute young lady who (after the first wide stare of astonishment) looked at him with narrowed eyes, and pronounced slowly—

"I believe you want to see Antonia."

"What Antonia?" asked the Costaguana boulevardier, in a vexed and disdainful tone. He shrugged his shoulders, and spun round on his heel. His sister called out after him joyously—

"The Antonia you used to know when she wore her hair in two plaits down her back."

He had known her some eight years since, shortly before the Avellanos had left Europe for good, as a tall girl of sixteen, youthfully austere, and of a character already so formed that she ventured to treat slightingly his pose of disabused wisdom. On one occasion, as though she had lost all patience, she flew out at him about the aimlessness of his life and the levity of his opinions. He was twenty then, an only son, spoiled by his adoring family. This attack disconcerted him so greatly that he had faltered in his affection of amused superiority before that insignificant chit of a school-girl. But the impression left was so strong that ever since all the girl friends of his sisters recalled to him Antonia Avellanos by some faint resemblance, or by the great force of contrast. It was, he told himself, like a ridiculous fatality. And, of course, in the news the Decouds received regularly from Costaguana, the name of their friends, the Avellanos, cropped up frequently—the arrest and the abominable treatment of the ex-Minister, the dangers and hardships endured by the family, its withdrawal in poverty to Sulaco, the death of the mother.

The Monterist pronunciamento had taken place before Martin Decoud reached Costaguana. He came out in a roundabout way, through Magellan's Straits by the main line and the West Coast Service of the O.S.N. Company. His precious consignment arrived just in time to convert the first feelings of consternation into a mood of hope and resolution. Publicly he was made much of by the *familias principales*. Privately Don José, still shaken and weak, embraced him with tears in his eyes.

"You have come out yourself! No less could be expected from a Decoud. Alas! our worst fears have been realized," he moaned, affectionately. And again he hugged his god-son. This was indeed the time for men of intellect and conscience to rally round the endangered cause.

It was then that Martin Decoud, the adopted child of Western Europe, felt the absolute change of atmosphere. He submitted to being embraced and talked to without a word. He was moved in spite of himself by that note of passion and sorrow unknown on the more refined stage of European politics. But when the tall Antonia, advancing with her light step in the dimness of the big bare Sala of the Avellanos house, offered him her hand (in her emancipated way), and murmured, "I am glad to see you here, Don Martin," he felt how impossible it would be to tell these two people that he had intended to go away by the next month's packet. Don José, meantime, continued his praises. Every accession added to public confidence, and, besides, what an example to the young men at home from the brilliant defender of the country's regeneration, the worthy expounder of the party's political faith before the world!

Everybody had read the magnificent article in the famous Parisian Review. The world was now informed: and the author's appearance at this moment was like a public act of faith. Young Decoud felt overcome by a feeling of impatient confusion. His plan had been to return by way of the United States through California, visit Yellowstone Park, see Chicago, Niagara, have a look at Canada, perhaps make a short stay in New York, a longer one in Newport, use his letters of introduction. The pressure of Antonia's hand was so frank, the tone of her voice was so unexpectedly unchanged in its approving warmth, that all he found to say after his low bow was—

"I am inexpressibly grateful for your welcome; but why need a man be thanked for returning to his native country? I am sure Doña Antonia does not think so."

"Certainly not, señor," she said, with that perfectly calm openness of manner which characterized all her utterances. "But when he returns, as you return, one may be glad—for the sake of both."

Martin Decoud said nothing of his plans. He not only never breathed a word of them to any one, but only a fortnight later asked the mistress of the Casa Gould (where he had of course obtained admission at once), leaning forward in his chair with an air of well-bred familiarity, whether she could not detect in him that day a marked change—an air, he explained, of more excellent gravity. At this Mrs. Gould turned her face full towards him with the silent inquiry of slightly widened eyes and the merest ghost of a smile, an habitual movement with her, which was very fascinating to men by something subtly devoted, finely selfforgetful in its lively readiness of attention. Because, Decoud continued imperturbably, he felt no longer an idle cumberer of the earth. She was, he assured her, actually beholding at that moment the Journalist of Sulaco. At once Mrs. Gould glanced towards Antonia, posed upright in the corner of a high, straight-backed Spanish sofa, a large black fan waving slowly against the curves of her fine figure, the tips of crossed feet peeping from under the hem of the black skirt. Decoud's eyes also remained fixed there, while in an undertone he added that Miss Avellanos was quite aware of his new and unexpected vocation, which in Costaguana was generally the speciality of half-educated negroes and wholly penniless lawyers. Then, confronting with a sort of urbane effrontery Mrs. Gould's gaze, now turned sympathetically upon himself, he breathed out the words, "Pro Patria!"*

What had happened was that he had all at once yielded to Don José's pressing entreaties to take the direction of a newspaper that would "voice the aspirations of the province." It had been Don José's old and cherished idea. The necessary plant (on a modest scale) and a large consignment of paper had been received from America some time before; the right man alone was wanted. Even Señor Moraga in Sta. Marta had not been able to find one, and the matter was now becoming pressing; some organ was absolutely needed to counteract the effect of the lies disseminated by the Monterist press: the atrocious calumnies, the appeals to the people calling upon them to rise with their knives in their hands and put an end once for all to the Blancos, to these Gothic remnants, to these sinister mummies, these impotent paraliticos, who plotted with foreigners for the surrender of the lands and the slavery of the people.

The clamour of this *Negro Liberalism* frightened Señor Avellanos. A newspaper was the only remedy. And now that the right man had been found in Decoud, great black letters appeared painted between the windows above the arcaded ground floor of a house on the Plaza. It was next to Anzani's great emporium of boots, silks, ironware, muslins, wooden toys, tiny silver arms, legs, heads, hearts (for ex-voto offerings), rosaries, champagne, women's hats, patent medicines, even a few dusty books in paper covers and mostly in the French language. The big black letters formed the words, "Offices of the *Porvenir*."* From these offices a single folded sheet of Martin's journalism issued three times a week; and the sleek yellow Anzani prowling in a suit of ample black and carpet slippers, before the many doors of his establishment, greeted by a deep, side-long inclination of his body the Journalist of Sulaco going to and fro on the business of his august calling.

CHAPTER FOUR

PERHAPS it was in the exercise of his calling that he had come to see the troops depart. The *Porvenir* of the day after next would no doubt relate the event, but its editor, leaning his side against the landau, seemed to look at nothing. The front rank of the company of infantry drawn up three deep across the shore end of the jetty when pressed too close would bring their bayonets to the charge ferociously, with an awful rattle; and then the crowd of spectators swayed back bodily, even under the noses of the big white mules. Notwithstanding the great multitude there was only a low, muttering noise; the dust hung in a brown haze, in which the horsemen, wedged in the throng here and there, towered from the hips upwards, gazing all one way over the heads. Almost every one of them had mounted a friend, who steadied himself with both hands grasping his shoulders from behind; and the rims of their hats touching, made like one disc sustaining the cones of two pointed crowns with a double face underneath. A hoarse mozo would bawl out something to an acquaintance in the ranks, or a woman would shriek suddenly the word *Adios!* followed by the Christian name of a man.

General Barrios, in a shabby blue tunic and white peg-top trousers falling upon strange red boots, kept his head uncovered and stooped slightly, propping himself up with a thick stick. No! He had earned enough military glory to satiate any man, he insisted to Mrs. Gould, trying at the same time to put an air of gallantry into his attitude. A few jetty hairs hung sparsely from

160

his upper lip, he had a salient nose, a thin, long jaw, and
a black silk patch over one eye. His other eye, small
and deep-set, twinkled erratically in all directions,
aimlessly affable. The few European spectators, all
men, who had naturally drifted into the neighbourhood
of the Gould carriage, betrayed by the solemnity of their
faces their impression that the general must have had too
much punch (Swedish punch, imported in bottles by
Anzani) at the Amarilla*Club before he had started with
his Staff on a furious ride to the harbour. But Mrs.
Gould bent forward, self-possessed, and declared her
conviction that still more glory awaited the general in
the near future.

"Señora!" he remonstrated, with great feeling, "in
the name of God, reflect! How can there be any glory
for a man like me in overcoming that bald-headed
embustero with the dyed moustaches?"

Pablo Ignacio Barrios, son of a village alcade, general
of division, commanding in chief the Occidental Military district, did not frequent the higher society of the
town. He preferred the unceremonious gatherings of
men where he could tell jaguar-hunt stories, boast of
his powers with the lasso, with which he could perform
extremely difficult feats of the sort "no married man
should attempt," as the saying goes amongst the
llaneros; relate tales of extraordinary night rides, encounters with wild bulls, struggles with crocodile,
adventures in the great forests, crossings of swollen
rivers. And it was not mere boastfulness that prompted
the general's reminiscences, but a genuine love of that
wild life which he had led in his young days before he
turned his back for ever on the thatched roof of the
parental tolderia in the woods. Wandering away as
far as Mexico he had fought against the French by the
side (as he said) of Juarez,* and was the only military

man of Costaguana who had ever encountered European troops in the field. That fact shed a great lustre upon his name till it became eclipsed by the rising star of Montero. All his life he had been an inveterate gambler. He alluded himself quite openly to the current story how once, during some campaign (when in command of a brigade), he had gambled away his horses, pistols, and accoutrements, to the very epaulettes, playing *monte**with his colonels the night before the battle. Finally, he had sent under escort his sword (a presentation sword, with a gold hilt) to the town in the rear of his position to be immediately pledged for five hundred pesetas with a sleepy and frightened shop-keeper. By daybreak he had lost the last of that money, too, when his only remark, as he rose calmly, was, "Now let us go and fight to the death." From that time he had become aware that a general could lead his troops into battle very well with a simple stick in his hand. "It has been my custom ever since," he would say.

He was always overwhelmed with debts; even during the periods of splendour in his varied fortunes of a Costaguana general, when he held high military commands, his gold-laced uniforms were almost always in pawn with some tradesman. And at last, to avoid the incessant difficulties of costume caused by the anxious lenders, he had assumed a disdain of military trappings, an eccentric fashion of shabby old tunics, which had become like a second nature. But the faction Barrios joined needed to fear no political betrayal. He was too much of a real soldier for the ignoble traffic of buying and selling victories. A member of the foreign diplomatic body in Sta. Marta had once passed a judgment upon him: "Barrios is a man of perfect honesty and even of some talent for war, *mais il manque*

de tenue.* After the triumph of the Ribierists he had
obtained the reputedly lucrative Occidental command,
mainly through the exertions of his creditors (the Sta.
Marta shopkeepers, all great politicians), who moved
heaven and earth in his interest publicly, and privately
besieged Señor Moraga, the influential agent of the
San Tomé mine, with the exaggerated lamentations
that if the general were passed over, "We shall all be
ruined." An incidental but favourable mention of his
name in Mr. Gould senior's long correspondence with
his son had something to do with his appointment, too;
but most of all undoubtedly his established political
honesty. No one questioned the personal bravery of
the Tiger-killer, as the populace called him. He was,
however, said to be unlucky in the field—but this was
to be the beginning of an era of peace. The soldiers
liked him for his humane temper, which was like a
strange and precious flower unexpectedly blooming on
the hotbed of corrupt revolutions; and when he rode
slowly through the streets during some military display,
the contemptuous good humour of his solitary eye roaming over the crowds extorted the acclamations of the
populace. The women of that class especially seemed
positively fascinated by the long dropping nose, the
peaked chin, the heavy lower lip, the black silk eye-
patch and band slanting rakishly over the forehead.
His high rank always procured an audience of Caballeros for his sporting stories, which he detailed very
well with a simple, grave enjoyment. As to the society
of ladies, it was irksome by the restraints it imposed
without any equivalent, as far as he could see. He had
not, perhaps, spoken three times on the whole to Mrs.
Gould since he had taken up his high command; but he
had observed her frequently riding with the Señor
Administrador, and had pronounced that there was

more sense in her little bridle-hand than in all the female heads in Sulaco. His impulse had been to be very civil on parting to a woman who did not wobble in the saddle, and happened to be the wife of a personality very important to a man always short of money. He even pushed his attentions so far as to desire the aide-decamp at his side (a thick-set, short captain with a Tartar physiognomy) to bring along a corporal with a file of men in front of the carriage, lest the crowd in its backward surges should "incommode the mules of the señora." Then, turning to the small knot of silent Europeans looking on within earshot, he raised his voice protectingly—

"Señores, have no apprehension. Go on quietly making your Ferro Carril—your railways, your telegraphs. Your—— There's enough wealth in Costaguana to pay for everything—or else you would not be here. Ha! ha! Don't mind this little picardía of my friend Montero. In a little while you shall behold his dyed moustaches through the bars of a strong wooden cage. Si, señores! Fear nothing, develop the country, work, work!"

The little group of engineers received this exhortation without a word, and after waving his hand at them loftily, he addressed himself again to Mrs. Gould—

"That is what Don José says we must do. Be enterprising! Work! Grow rich! To put Montero in a cage is my work; and when that insignificant piece of business is done, then, as Don José wishes us, we shall grow rich, one and all, like so many Englishmen, because it is money that saves a country, and——"

But a young officer in a very new uniform, hurrying up from the direction of the jetty, interrupted his interpretation of Señor Avellanos's ideals. The general made a movement of impatience; the other went on

talking to him insistently, with an air of respect. The
horses of the Staff had been embarked, the steamer's
gig was awaiting the general at the boat steps; and
Barrios, after a fierce stare of his one eye, began to take
leave. Don José roused himself for an appropriate
phrase pronounced mechanically. The terrible strain
of hope and fear was telling on him, and he seemed to
husband the last sparks of his fire for those oratorical
efforts of which even the distant Europe was to hear.
Antonia, her red lips firmly closed, averted her head
behind the raised fan; and young Decoud, though he
felt the girl's eyes upon him, gazed away persistently,
hooked on his elbow, with a scornful and complete detachment. Mrs. Gould heroically concealed her dismay at the appearance of men and events so remote
from her racial conventions, dismay too deep to be
uttered in words even to her husband. She understood
his voiceless reserve better now. Their confidential
intercourse fell, not in moments of privacy, but precisely in public, when the quick meeting of their glances
would comment upon some fresh turn of events. She
had gone to his school of uncompromising silence, the
only one possible, since so much that seemed shocking,
weird, and grotesque in the working out of their purposes had to be accepted as normal in this country.
Decidedly, the stately Antonia looked more mature and
infinitely calm; but she would never have known how
to reconcile the sudden sinkings of her heart with an
amiable mobility of expression.

Mrs. Gould smiled a good-bye at Barrios, nodded
round to the Europeans (who raised their hats simultaneously) with an engaging invitation, "I hope to
see you all presently, at home"; then said nervously to
Decoud, "Get in, Don Martin," and heard him mutter
to himself in French, as he opened the carriage door,

"*Le sort en est jeté.*"* She heard him with a sort of
exasperation. Nobody ought to have known better
than himself that the first cast of dice had been already
thrown long ago in a most desperate game. Distant
acclamations, words of command yelled out, and a roll
of drums on the jetty greeted the departing general.
Something like a slight faintness came over her, and she
looked blankly at Antonia's still face, wondering what
would happen to Charley if that absurd man failed.
"*A la casa, Ignacio,*" she cried at the motionless broad
back of the coachman, who gathered the reins without
haste, mumbling to himself under his breadth, "*Sí,
la casa. Sí, sí niña.*"*

The carriage rolled noiselessly on the soft track, the
shadows fell long on the dusty little plain interspersed
with dark bushes, mounds of turned-up earth, low
wooden buildings with iron roofs of the Railway
Company; the sparse row of telegraph poles strode
obliquely clear of the town, bearing a single, almost invisible wire far into the great campo—like a slender,
vibrating feeler of that progress waiting outside for a
moment of peace to enter and twine itself about the
weary heart of the land.

The *café* window of the Albergo d'Italia Una was full
of sunburnt, whiskered faces of railway men. But at
the other end of the house, the end of the Signori
Inglesi, old Giorgio, at the door with one of his girls on
each side, bared his bushy head, as white as the snows of
Higuerota. Mrs. Gould stopped the carriage. She
seldom failed to speak to her *protégé;* moreover, the
excitement, the heat, and the dust had made her
thirsty. She asked for a glass of water. Giorgio sent
the children indoors for it, and approached with pleasure
expressed in his whole rugged countenance. It was not
often that he had occasion to see his benefactress,

who was also an Englishwoman—another title to his regard. He offered some excuses for his wife. It was a bad day with her; her oppressions—he tapped his own broad chest. She could not move from her chair that day.

Decoud, ensconced in the corner of his seat, observed gloomily Mrs. Gould's old revolutionist, then, offhand—
"Well, and what do you think of it all, Garibaldino?"

Old Giorgio, looking at him with some curiosity, said civilly that the troops had marched very well. One-eyed Barrios and his officers had done wonders with the recruits in a short time. Those Indios, only caught the other day, had gone swinging past in double quick time, like bersaglieri; they looked well fed, too, and had whole uniforms. "Uniforms!" he repeated with a half-smile of pity. A look of grim retrospect stole over his piercing, steady eyes. It had been otherwise in his time when men fought against tyranny, in the forests of Brazil, or on the plains of Uruguay, starving on half-raw beef without salt, half naked, with often only a knife tied to a stick for a weapon. "And yet we used to prevail against the oppressor," he concluded, proudly.

His animation fell; the slight gesture of his hand expressed discouragement; but he added that he had asked one of the sergeants to show him the new rifle. There was no such weapon in his fighting days; and if Barrios could not—

"Yes, yes," broke in Don José, almost trembling with eagerness. "We are safe. The good Señor Viola is a man of experience. Extremely deadly—is it not so? You have accomplished your mission admirably, my dear Martin."

Decoud, lolling back moodily, contemplated old Viola.

"Ah! Yes. A man of experience. But who are you for, really, in your heart?"

Mrs. Gould leaned over to the children. Linda had brought out a glass of water on a tray, with extreme care; Giselle presented her with a bunch of flowers gathered hastily.

"For the people," declared old Viola, sternly.

"We are all for the people—in the end."

"Yes," muttered old Viola, savagely. "And meantime they fight for you. Blind. Esclavos!"

At that moment young Scarfe of the railway staff emerged from the door of the part reserved for the Signori Inglesi. He had come down to headquarters from somewhere up the line on a light engine, and had had just time to get a bath and change his clothes. He was a nice boy, and Mrs. Gould welcomed him.

"It's a delightful surprise to see you, Mrs. Gould. I've just come down. Usual luck. Missed everything, of course. This show is just over, and I hear there has been a great dance at Don Juste Lopez's last night. Is it true?"

"The young patricians," Decoud began suddenly in his precise English, "have indeed been dancing before they started off to the war with the Great Pompey."*

Young Scarfe stared, astounded. "You haven't met before," Mrs. Gould intervened. "Mr. Decoud— Mr. Scarfe."

"Ah! But we are not going to Pharsalia," protested Don José, with nervous haste, also in English. "You should not jest like this, Martin."

Antonia's breast rose and fell with a deeper breath. The young engineer was utterly in the dark. "Great what?" he muttered, vaguely.

"Luckily, Montero is not a Cæsar," Decoud continued. "Not the two Monteros put together would make a decent parody of a Cæsar." He crossed his arms on his breast, looking at Señor Avellanos, who had returned to his immobility. "It is only you, Don José, who are a genuine old Roman—vir Romanus— eloquent and inflexible."

Since he had heard the name of Montero pronounced, young Scarfe had been eager to express his simple feelings. In a loud and youthful tone he hoped that this Montero was going to be licked once for all and done with. There was no saying what would happen to the railway if the revolution got the upper hand. Perhaps it would have to be abandoned. It would not be the first railway gone to pot in Costaguana. "You know, it's one of their so-called national things," he ran on, wrinkling up his nose as if the world had a suspicious flavour to his profound experience of South American affairs. And, of course, he chatted with animation, it had been such an immense piece of luck for him at his age to get appointed on the staff "of a big thing like that—don't you know." It would give him the pull over a lot of chaps all through life, he asserted. "There- fore—down with Montero! Mrs. Gould." His artless grin disappeared slowly before the unanimous gravity of the faces turned upon him from the carriage; only that "old chap," Don José, presenting a motionless, waxy profile, stared straight on as if deaf. Scarfe did not know the Avellanos very well. They did not give balls, and Antonia never appeared at a ground-floor window, as some other young ladies used to do at- tended by elder women, to chat with the caballeros on horseback in the Calle. The stares of these creoles did not matter much; but what on earth had come to Mrs. Gould? She said, "Go on, Ignacio," and gave him a slow inclination of the head. He heard a short laugh from that round-faced, Frenchified fellow. He coloured up to the eyes, and stared at Giorgio Viola, who had fallen back with the children, hat in hand.

"I shall want a horse presently," he said with some asperity to the old man.

"Si, señor. There are plenty of horses," murmured the Garibaldino, smoothing absently, with his brown hands, the two heads, one dark with bronze glints, the other fair with a coppery ripple, of the two girls by his side. The returning stream of sightseers raised a great dust on the road. Horsemen noticed the group. "Go to your mother," he said. "They are growing up as I am growing older, and there is nobody——"

He looked at the young engineer and stopped, as if awakened from a dream; then, folding his arms on his breast, took up his usual position, leaning back in the doorway with an upward glance fastened on the white shoulder of Higuerota far away.

In the carriage Martin Decoud, shifting his position as though he could not make himself comfortable, muttered as he swayed towards Antonia, "I suppose you hate me." Then in a loud voice he began to congratulate Don José upon all the engineers being convinced Ribierists. The interests of all those foreigners was gratifying. "You have heard this one. He is an enlightened well-wisher. It is pleasant to think that the prosperity of Costaguana is of some use to the world."

"He is very young," Mrs. Gould remarked, quietly.

"And so very wise for his age," retorted Decoud. "But here we have the naked truth from the mouth of that child. You are right, Don José. The natural treasures of Costaguana are of importance to the progressive Europe represented by this youth, just as three hundred years ago the wealth of our Spanish fathers was a serious object to the rest of Europe—as represented by the bold buccaneers. There is a curse of futility upon our character: Don Quixote and Sancho Panza, chivalry and materialism, high-sounding sentiments and a supine morality, violent efforts for an idea and a sullen acquiescence in every form of corruption. We convulsed a continent for our independence only to become the passive prey of a democratic parody, the helpless victims of scoundrels and cut-throats, our institutions a mockery, our laws a farce—a Guzman Bento our master! And we have sunk so low that when a man like you has awakened our conscience, a stupid barbarian of a Montero—Great Heavens! a Montero!—becomes a deadly danger, and an ignorant, boastful Indio, like Barrios, is our defender."

But Don José, disregarding the general indictment as though he had not heard a word of it, took up the defence of Barrios. The man was competent enough for his special task in the plan of campaign. It consisted in an offensive movement, with Cayta as base, upon the flank of the Revolutionist forces advancing from the south against Sta. Marta, which was covered by another army with the President-Dictator in its midst. Don José became quite animated with a great flow of speech, bending forward anxiously under the steady eyes of his daughter. Decoud, as if silenced by so much ardour, did not make a sound. The bells of the city were striking the hour of Oracion when the carriage rolled under the old gateway facing the harbour like a shapeless monument of leaves and stones. The rumble of wheels under the sonorous arch was traversed by a strange, piercing shriek, and Decoud, from his back seat, had a view of the people behind the carriage trudging along the road outside, all turning their heads, in sombreros and rebozos, to look at a locomotive which rolled quickly out of sight behind Giorgio Viola's house, under a white trail of steam that seemed to vanish in the breathless, hysterically prolonged scream of warlike triumph. And it was all like a fleeting vision, the shrieking ghost of a railway engine fleeing across the frame of the archway, behind the startled movement of the people streaming back from a military spectacle with silent footsteps on the dust of the road. It was a material train returning from the Campo to the palisaded yards. The empty cars rolled lightly on the single track; there was no rumble of wheels, no tremor on the ground. The engine-driver, running past the Casa Viola with the salute of an uplifted arm, checked his speed smartly before entering the yard; and when the ear-splitting screech of the steam-whistle for the brakes had stopped, a series of hard, battering shocks, mingled with the clanking of chain-couplings, made a tumult of blows and shaken fetters under the vault of the gate.

CHAPTER FIVE*

THE Gould carriage was the first to return from the harbour to the empty town. On the ancient pavement, laid out in patterns, sunk into ruts and holes, the portly Ignacio, mindful of the springs of the Parisian-built landau, had pulled up to a walk, and Decoud in his corner contemplated moodily the inner aspect of the gate. The squat turreted sides held up between them a mass of masonry with bunches of grass growing at the top, and a grey, heavily scrolled, armorial shield of stone above the apex of the arch with the arms of Spain nearly smoothed out as if in readiness for some new device typical of the impending progress.

The explosive noise of the railway trucks seemed to augment Decoud's irritation. He muttered something to himself, then began to talk aloud in curt, angry phrases thrown at the silence of the two women. They did not look at him at all; while Don José, with his semi-translucent, waxy complexion, overshadowed by the soft grey hat, swayed a little to the jolts of the carriage by the side of Mrs. Gould.

"This sound puts a new edge on a very old truth."

Decoud spoke in French, perhaps because of Ignacio on the box above him; the old coachman, with his broad back filling a short, silver-braided jacket, had a big pair of ears, whose thick rims stood well away from his cropped head.

"Yes, the noise outside the city wall is new, but the principle is old."

He ruminated his discontent for a while, then began afresh with a sidelong glance at Antonia—

"No, but just imagine our forefathers in morions and corselets*drawn up outside this gate, and a band of adventurers just landed from their ships in the harbour there. Thieves, of course. Speculators, too. Their expeditions, each one, were the speculations of grave and reverend persons in England. That is history, as that absurd sailor Mitchell is always saying."

"Mitchell's arrangements for the embarkation of the troops were excellent!" exclaimed Don José.

"That!—that! oh, that's really the work of that Genoese seaman! But to return to my noises; there used to be in the old days the sound of trumpets outside that gate. War trumpets! I'm sure they were trumpets. I have read somewhere that Drake, who was the greatest of these men, used to dine alone in his cabin on board ship to the sound of trumpets. In those days this town was full of wealth. Those men came to take it. Now the whole land is like a treasure-house, and all these people are breaking into it, whilst we are cutting each other's throats. The only thing that keeps them out is mutual jealousy. But they'll come to an agreement some day—and by the time we've settled our quarrels and become decent and honourable, there'll be nothing left for us. It has always been the same. We are a wonderful people, but it has always been our fate to be"—he did not say "robbed," but added, after a pause—"exploited!"

Mrs. Gould said, "Oh, this is unjust!" And Antonia interjected, "Don't answer him, Emilia. He is attacking me."

"You surely do not think I was attacking Don Carlos!" Decoud answered.

And then the carriage stopped before the door of the

Casa Gould. The young man offered his hand to the ladies. They went in first together; Don José walked by the side of Decoud, and the gouty old porter tottered after them with some light wraps on his arm.

Don José slipped his hand under the arm of the journalist of Sulaco.

"The *Porvenir* must have a long and confident article upon Barrios and the irresistibleness of his army of Cayta! The moral effect should be kept up in the country. We must cable encouraging extracts to Europe and the United States to maintain a favourable impression abroad."

Decoud muttered, "Oh, yes, we must comfort our friends, the speculators."

The long open gallery was in shadow, with its screen of plants in vases along the balustrade, holding out motionless blossoms, and all the glass doors of the reception-rooms thrown open. A jingle of spurs died out at the further end.

Basilio, standing aside against the wall, said in a soft tone to the passing ladies, "The Señor Administrador is just back from the mountain."

In the great sala, with its groups of ancient Spanish and modern European furniture making as if different centres under the high white spread of the ceiling, the silver and porcelain of the tea-service gleamed among a cluster of dwarf chairs, like a bit of a lady's boudoir, putting in a note of feminine and intimate delicacy.

Don José in his rocking-chair placed his hat on his lap, and Decoud walked up and down the whole length of the room, passing between tables loaded with knick-knacks and almost disappearing behind the high backs of leathern sofas. He was thinking of the angry face of Antonia; he was confident that he would make his peace with her. He had not stayed in Sulaco to quarrel with Antonia.

Martin Decoud was angry with himself. All he saw and heard going on around him exasperated the preconceived views of his European civilization. To contemplate revolutions from the distance of the Parisian Boulevards was quite another matter. Here on the spot it was not possible to dismiss their tragic comedy with the expression, "*Quelle farce !*"*

The reality of the political action, such as it was, seemed closer, and acquired poignancy by Antonia's belief in the cause. Its crudeness hurt his feelings. He was surprised at his own sensitiveness.

"I suppose I am more of a Costaguanero than I would have believed possible," he thought to himself.

His disdain grew like a reaction of his scepticism against the action into which he was forced by his infatuation for Antonia. He soothed himself by saying he was not a patriot, but a lover.

The ladies came in bareheaded, and Mrs. Gould sank low before the little tea-table. Antonia took up her usual place at the reception hour—the corner of a leathern couch, with a rigid grace in her pose and a fan in her hand. Decoud, swerving from the straight line of his march, came to lean over the high back of her seat.

For a long time he talked into her ear from behind, softly, with a half smile and an air of apologetic familiarity. Her fan lay half grasped on her knees. She never looked at him. His rapid utterance grew more and more insistent and caressing. At last he ventured a slight laugh.

"No, really. You must forgive me. One must be serious sometimes." He paused. She turned her head a little; her blue eyes glided slowly towards him, slightly upwards, mollified and questioning.

"You can't think I am serious when I call Montero a *gran' bestia** every second day in the *Porvenir*? That is not a serious occupation. No occupation is serious, not even when a bullet through the heart is the penalty of failure!"

Her hand closed firmly on her fan.

"Some reason, you understand, I mean some sense, may creep into thinking; some glimpse of truth. I mean some effective truth, for which there is no room in politics or journalism. I happen to have said what I thought. And you are angry! If you do me the kindness to think a little you will see that I spoke like a patriot."

She opened her red lips for the first time, not unkindly.

"Yes, but you never see the aim. Men must be used as they are. I suppose nobody is really disinterested, unless, perhaps, you, Don Martin."

"God forbid! It's the last thing I should like you to believe of me." He spoke lightly, and paused.

She began to fan herself with a slow movement without raising her hand. After a time he whispered passionately—

"Antonia!"

She smiled, and extended her hand after the English manner towards Charles Gould, who was bowing before her; while Decoud, with his elbows spread on the back of the sofa, dropped his eyes and murmured, "*Bonjour*."

The Señor Administrador of the San Tomé mine bent over his wife for a moment. They exchanged a few words, of which only the phrase, "The greatest enthusiasm," pronounced by Mrs. Gould, could be heard.

"Yes," Decoud began in a murmur. "Even he!"

"This is sheer calumny," said Antonia, not very severely.

"You just ask him to throw his mine into the melting-
pot for the great cause," Decoud whispered.

Don José had raised his voice. He rubbed his hands
cheerily. The excellent aspect of the troops and the
great quantity of new deadly rifles on the shoulders of
those brave men seemed to fill him with an ecstatic
confidence.

Charles Gould, very tall and thin before his chair,
listened, but nothing could be discovered in his face
except a kind and deferential attention.

Meantime, Antonia had risen, and, crossing the
room, stood looking out of one of the three long windows
giving on the street. Decoud followed her. The
window was thrown open, and he leaned against the
thickness of the wall. The long folds of the damask
curtain, falling straight from the broad brass cornice,
hid him partly from the room. He folded his arms on
his breast, and looked steadily at Antonia's profile.

The people returning from the harbour filled the
pavements; the shuffle of sandals and a low murmur of
voices ascended to the window. Now and then a coach
rolled slowly along the disjointed roadway of the Calle
de la Constitucion. There were not many private
carriages in Sulaco; at the most crowded hour on the
Alameda they could be counted with one glance of the
eye. The great family arks swayed on high leathern
springs, full of pretty powdered faces in which the eyes
looked intensely alive and black. And first Don Juste
Lopez, the President of the Provincial Assembly,
passed with his three lovely daughters, solemn in a
black frock-coat and stiff white tie, as when directing a
debate from a high tribune. Though they all raised
their eyes, Antonia did not make the usual greeting
gesture of a fluttered hand, and they affected not to see
the two young people, Costaguaneros with European

manners, whose eccentricities were discussed behind the barred windows of the first families in Sulaco. And then the widowed Señora Gavilaso de Valdes rolled by, handsome and dignified, in a great machine in which she used to travel to and from her country house, surrounded by an armed retinue in leather suits and big sombreros, with carbines at the bows of their saddles. She was a woman of most distinguished family, proud, rich, and kind-hearted. Her second son, Jaime, had just gone off on the Staff of Barrios. The eldest, a worthless fellow of a moody disposition, filled Sulaco with the noise of his dissipations, and gambled heavily at the club. The two youngest boys, with yellow Ribierist cockades in their caps, sat on the front seat. She, too, affected not to see the Señor Decoud talking publicly with Antonia in defiance of every convention. And he not even her *novio* as far as the world knew! Though, even in that case, it would have been scandal enough. But the dignified old lady, respected and admired by the first families, would have been still more shocked if she could have heard the words they were exchanging.

"Did you say I lost sight of the aim? I have only one aim in the world."

She made an almost imperceptible negative movement of her head, still staring across the street at the Avellanos's house, grey, marked with decay, and with iron bars like a prison.

"And it would be so easy of attainment," he continued, "this aim which, whether knowingly or not, I have always had in my heart—ever since the day when you snubbed me so horribly once in Paris, you remember."

A slight smile seemed to move the corner of the lip that was on his side.

"You know you were a very terrible person, a sort of Charlotte Corday* in a schoolgirl's dress; a ferocious patriot. I suppose you would have stuck a knife into Guzman Bento?"

She interrupted him. "You do me too much honour."

"At any rate," he said, changing suddenly to a tone of bitter levity, "you would have sent me to stab him without compunction."

"Ah, *par exemple!*" she murmured in a shocked tone

"Well," he argued, mockingly, "you do keep me here writing deadly nonsense. Deadly to me! It has already killed my self-respect. And you may imagine," he continued, his tone passing into light banter, "that Montero, should he be successful, would get even with me in the only way such a brute can get even with a man of intelligence who condescends to call him a *gran' bestia* three times a week. It's a sort of intellectual death; but there is the other one in the background for a journalist of my ability."

"If he is successful!" said Antonia, thoughtfully.

"You seem satisfied to see my life hang on a thread," Decoud replied, with a broad smile. "And the other Montero, the 'my trusted brother' of the proclamations, the guerrillero—haven't I written that he was taking the guests' overcoats and changing plates in Paris at our Legation in the intervals of spying on our refugees there, in the time of Rojas? He will wash out that sacred truth in blood. In my blood! Why do you look annoyed? This is simply a bit of the biography of one of our great men. What do you think he will do to me? There is a certain convent wall round the corner of the Plaza, opposite the door of the Bull Ring. You know? Opposite the door with the inscription, 'Intrada de la Sombra.'* Appropriate, perhaps! That's where the uncle of our host gave up his Anglo-South-American soul. And, note, he might have run away. A man who has fought with weapons may run away. You might have let me go with Barrios if you had cared for me. I would have carried one of those rifles, in which Don José believes, with the greatest satisfaction, in the ranks of poor peons and Indios, that know nothing either of reason or politics. The most forlorn hope in the most forlorn army on earth would have been safer than that for which you made me stay here. When you make war you may retreat, but not when you spend your time in inciting poor ignorant fools to kill and to die."

His tone remained light, and as if unaware of his presence she stood motionless, her hands clasped lightly, the fan hanging down from her interlaced fingers. He waited for a while, and then—

"I shall go to the wall," he said, with a sort of jocular desperation.

Even that declaration did not make her look at him. Her head remained still, her eyes fixed upon the house of the Avellanos, whose chipped pilasters, broken cornices, the whole degradation of dignity was hidden now by the gathering dusk of the street. In her whole figure her lips alone moved, forming the words—

"Martin, you will make me cry."

He remained silent for a minute, startled, as if overwhelmed by a sort of awed happiness, with the lines of the mocking smile still stiffened about his mouth, and incredulous surprise in his eyes. The value of a sentence is in the personality which utters it, for nothing new can be said by man or woman; and those were the last words, it seemed to him, that could ever have been spoken by Antonia. He had never made it up with her so completely in all their intercourse of small encounters; but even before she had time to turn towards him, which she did slowly with a rigid grace, he had begun to plead—

"My sister is only waiting to embrace you. My father is transported with joy. I won't say anything of my mother! Our mothers were like sisters. There is the mail-boat for the south next week—let us go. That Moraga is a fool! A man like Montero is bribed. It's the practice of the country. It's tradition—it's politics. Read 'Fifty Years of Misrule.'"

"Leave poor papa alone, Don Martin. He believes——"

"I have the greatest tenderness for your father," he began, hurriedly. "But I love you, Antonia! And Moraga has miserably mismanaged this business. Perhaps your father did, too; I don't know. Montero was bribeable. Why, I suppose he only wanted his share of this famous loan for national development. Why didn't the stupid Sta. Marta people give him a mission to Europe, or something? He would have taken five years' salary in advance, and gone on loafing in Paris, this stupid, ferocious Indio!"

"The man," she said, thoughtfully, and very calm before this outburst, "was intoxicated with vanity. We had all the information, not from Moraga only; from others, too. There was his brother intriguing, too."

"Oh, yes!" he said. "Of course you know. You know everything. You read all the correspondence, you write all the papers—all those State papers that are inspired here, in this room, in blind deference to a theory of political purity. Hadn't you Charles Gould before your eyes? Rey de Sulaco! He and his mine are the practical demonstration of what could have been done. Do you think he succeeded by his fidelity to a theory of virtue? And all those railway people, with their honest work! Of course, their work is honest! But what if you cannot work honestly till the thieves are satisfied? Could he not, a gentleman, have told this Sir John what's-his-name that Montero had to be bought off—he and all his Negro Liberals hanging on to his gold-laced sleeve? He ought to have been bought off with his own stupid weight of gold—his weight of gold, I tell you, boots, sabre, spurs, cocked hat, and all."

She shook her head slightly. "It was impossible," she murmured.

"He wanted the whole lot? What?"

She was facing him now in the deep recess of the window, very close and motionless. Her lips moved rapidly. Decoud, leaning his back against the wall, listened with crossed arms and lowered eyelids. He drank the tones of her even voice, and watched the agitated life of her throat, as if waves of emotion had run from her heart to pass out into the air in her reasonable words. He also had his aspirations, he aspired to carry her away out of these deadly futilities of pronunciamientos and reforms. All this was wrong —utterly wrong; but she fascinated him, and sometimes the sheer sagacity of a phrase would break the charm, replace the fascination by a sudden unwilling thrill of interest. Some women hovered, as it were, on the threshold of genius, he reflected. They did not want to know, or think, or understand. Passion stood for all that, and he was ready to believe that some startlingly profound remark, some appreciation of character, or a judgment upon an event, bordered on the miraculous. In the mature Antonia he could see with an extraordinary vividness the austere schoolgirl of the earlier days. She seduced his attention; sometimes he could not restrain a murmur of assent; now and then he advanced an objection quite seriously. Gradually they began to argue; the curtain half hid them from the people in the sala.

Outside it had grown dark. From the deep trench of shadow between the houses, lit up vaguely by the glimmer of street lamps, ascended the evening silence of Sulaco; the silence of a town with few carriages, of unshod horses, and a softly sandalled population. The windows of the Casa Gould flung their shining parallelograms upon the house of the Avellanos. Now and then a shuffle of feet passed below with the pulsating red glow of a cigarette at the foot of the walls; and the night air, as if cooled by the snows of Higuerota, refreshed their faces.

"We Occidentals," said Martin Decoud, using the usual term the provincials of Sulaco applied to themselves, "have been always distinct and separated. As long as we hold Cayta nothing can reach us. In all our troubles no army has marched over those mountains. A revolution in the central provinces isolates us at once. Look how complete it is now! The news of Barrios' movement will be cabled to the United States, and only in that way will it reach Sta. Marta by the cable from the other seaboard. We have the greatest riches, the greatest fertility, the purest blood in our great families, the most laborious population. The Occidental Province should stand alone. The early Federalism was not bad for us. Then came this union which Don Henrique Gould resisted. It opened the road to tyranny; and, ever since, the rest of Costaguana hangs like a millstone round our necks. The Occidental territory is large enough to make any man's country. Look at the mountains! Nature itself seems to cry to us 'Separate!'"

She made an energetic gesture of negation. A silence fell.

"Oh, yes, I know it's contrary to the doctrine laid down in the 'History of Fifty Years' Misrule.' I am only trying to be sensible. But my sense seems always to give you cause for offence. Have I startled you very much with this perfectly reasonable aspiration?"

She shook her head. No, she was not startled, but the idea shocked her early convictions. Her patriotism was larger. She had never considered that possibility.

"It may yet be the means of saving some of your convictions," he said, prophetically.

She did not answer. She seemed tired. They leaned side by side on the rail of the little balcony, very friendly, having exhausted politics, giving themselves up to the silent feeling of their nearness, in one of those profound pauses that fall upon the rhythm of passion. Towards the plaza end of the street the glowing coals in the brazeros of the market women cooking their evening meal gleamed red along the edge of the pavement. A man appeared without a sound in the light of a street lamp, showing the coloured inverted triangle of his bordered poncho, square on his shoulders, hanging to a point below his knees. From the harbour end of the Calle a horseman walked his soft-stepping mount, gleaming silver-grey abreast each lamp under the dark shape of the rider.

"Behold the illustrious Capataz de Cargadores," said Decoud, gently, "coming in all his splendour after his work is done. The next great man of Sulaco after Don Carlos Gould. But he is good-natured, and let me make friends with him."

"Ah, indeed!" said Antonia. "How did you make friends?"

"A journalist ought to have his finger on the popular

pulse, and this man is one of the leaders of the populace. A journalist ought to know remarkable men—and this man is remarkable in his way."

"Ah, yes!" said Antonia, thoughtfully. "It is known that this Italian has a great influence."

The horseman had passed below them, with a gleam of dim light on the shining broad quarters of the grey mare, on a bright heavy stirrup, on a long silver spur; but the short flick of yellowish flame in the dusk was powerless against the muffled-up mysteriousness of the dark figure with an invisible face concealed by a great sombrero.

Decoud and Antonia remained leaning over the balcony, side by side, touching elbows, with their heads overhanging the darkness of the street, and the brilliantly lighted sala at their backs. This was a *tête-à-tête* of extreme impropriety; something of which in the whole extent of the Republic only the extraordinary Antonia could be capable—the poor, motherless girl, never accompanied, with a careless father, who had thought only of making her learned. Even Decoud himself seemed to feel that this was as much as he could expect of having her to himself till—till the revolution was over and he could carry her off to Europe, away from the endlessness of civil strife, whose folly seemed even harder to bear than its ignominy. After one Montero there would be another, the lawlessness of a populace of all colours and races, barbarism, irremediable tyranny. As the great Liberator Bolivar had said in the bitterness of his spirit, "America is ungovernable. Those who worked for her independence have ploughed the sea." He did not care, he declared boldly; he seized every opportunity to tell her that though she had managed to make a Blanco journalist of him, he was no patriot. First of all, the word had no sense for cultured minds, to whom the narrowness of every belief is odious; and secondly, in connection with the everlasting troubles of this unhappy country it was hopelessly besmirched; it had been the cry of dark barbarism, the cloak of lawlessness, of crimes, of rapacity, of simple thieving.

He was surprised at the warmth of his own utterance. He had no need to drop his voice; it had been low all the time, a mere murmur in the silence of dark houses with their shutters closed early against the night air, as is the custom of Sulaco. Only the sala of the Casa Gould flung out defiantly the blaze of its four windows, the bright appeal of light in the whole dumb obscurity of the street. And the murmur on the little balcony went on after a short pause.

"But we are labouring to change all that," Antonia protested. "It is exactly what we desire. It is our object. It is the great cause. And the word you despise has stood also for sacrifice, for courage, for constancy, for suffering. Papa, who——"

"Ploughing the sea," interrupted Decoud, looking down.

There was below the sound of hasty and ponderous footsteps.

"Your uncle, the grand-vicar of the cathedral, has just turned under the gate," observed Decoud. "He said Mass for the troops in the Plaza this morning. They had built for him an altar of drums, you know. And they brought outside all the painted blocks to take the air. All the wooden saints stood militarily in a row at the top of the great flight of steps. They looked like a gorgeous escort attending the Vicar-General. I saw the great function from the windows of the *Porvenir*. He is amazing, your uncle, the last of the Corbelàns. He glittered exceedingly in his vestments

with a great crimson velvet cross down his back. And
all the time our saviour Barrios sat in the Amarilla
Club drinking punch at an open window. *Esprit fort*[*]—
our Barrios. I expected every moment your uncle to
launch an excommunication there and then at the black
eye-patch in the window across the Plaza. But not
at all. Ultimately the troops marched off. Later
Barrios came down with some of the officers, and stood
with his uniform all unbuttoned, discoursing at the
edge of the pavement. Suddenly your uncle appeared,
no longer glittering, but all black, at the cathedral door
with that threatening aspect he has—you know, like a
sort of avenging spirit. He gives one look, strides over
straight at the group of uniforms, and leads away the
general by the elbow. He walked him for a quarter of
an hour in the shade of a wall. Never let go his elbow
for a moment, talking all the time with exaltation, and
gesticulating with a long black arm. It was a curious
scene. The officers seemed struck with astonishment.
Remarkable man, your missionary uncle. He hates an
infidel much less than a heretic, and prefers a heathen
many times to an infidel. He condescends graciously
to call me a heathen, sometimes, you know."

Antonia listened with her hands over the balustrade,
opening and shutting the fan gently; and Decoud talked
a little nervously, as if afraid that she would leave him
at the first pause. Their comparative isolation, the
precious sense of intimacy, the slight contact of their
arms, affected him softly; for now and then a tender
inflection crept into the flow of his ironic murmurs.

"Any slight sign of favour from a relative of yours is
welcome, Antonia. And perhaps he understands me,
after all! But I know him, too, our Padre Corbelàn.
The idea of political honour, justice, and honesty for
him consists in the restitution of the confiscated Church

property. Nothing else could have drawn that fierce
converter of savage Indians out of the wilds to work for
the Ribierist cause! Nothing else but that wild hope!
He would make a pronunciamiento himself for such an
object against any Government if he could only get
followers! What does Don Carlos Gould think of
that? But, of course, with his English impenetrability,
nobody can tell what he thinks. Probably he thinks of
nothing apart from his mine; of his 'Imperium in
Imperio.' As to Mrs. Gould, she thinks of her schools, of
her hospitals, of the mothers with the young babies, of
every sick old man in the three villages. If you were to
turn your head now you would see her extracting a report from that sinister doctor in a check shirt—what's
his name? Monygham—or else catechising Don Pépé
or perhaps listening to Padre Romàn. They are all
down here to-day—all her ministers of state. Well,
she is a sensible woman, and perhaps Don Carlos is a
sensible man. It's a part of solid English sense not to
think too much; to see only what may be of practical
use at the moment. These people are not like ourselves.
We have no political reason; we have political passions
—sometimes. What is a conviction? A particular view
of our personal advantage either practical or emotional.
No one is a patriot for nothing. The word serves us
well. But I am clear-sighted, and I shall not use that
word to you, Antonia! I have no patriotic illusions. I
have only the supreme illusion of a lover."

He paused, then muttered almost inaudibly, "That
can lead one very far, though."

Behind their backs the political tide that once in
every twenty-four hours set with a strong flood through
the Gould drawing-room could be heard, rising higher
in a hum of voices. Men had been dropping in singly,
or in twos and threes: the higher officials of the province,

engineers of the railway, sunburnt and in tweeds, with the frosted head of their chief smiling with slow, humorous indulgence amongst the young eager faces. Scarfe, the lover of fandangos, had already slipped out in search of some dance, no matter where, on the outskirts of the town. Don Juste Lopez, after taking his daughters home, had entered solemnly, in a black creased coat buttoned up under his spreading brown beard. The few members of the Provincial Assembly present clustered at once around their President to discuss the news of the war and the last proclamation of the rebel Montero, the miserable Montero, calling in the name of "a justly incensed democracy" upon all the Provincial Assemblies of the Republic to suspend their sittings till his sword had made peace and the will of the people could be consulted. It was practically an invitation to dissolve: an unheard-of audacity of that evil madman.

The indignation ran high in the knot of deputies behind José Avellanos. Don José, lifting up his voice, cried out to them over the high back of his chair, "Sulaco has answered by sending to-day an army upon his flank. If all the other provinces show only half as much patriotism as we, Occidentals——"

A great outburst of acclamations covered the vibrating treble of the life and soul of the party. Yes! Yes! This was true! A great truth! Sulaco was in the forefront, as ever! It was a boastful tumult, the hopefulness inspired by the event of the day breaking out amongst those caballeros of the Campo thinking of their herds, of their lands, of the safety of their families. Everything was at stake. . . . No! It was impossible that Montero should succeed! This criminal, this shameless Indio! The clamour continued for some time, everybody else in the room looking towards the group where Don Juste had put on his air of impartial

solemnity as if presiding at a sitting of the Provincial
Assembly. Decoud had turned round at the noise,
and, leaning his back on the balustrade, shouted into
the room with all the strength of his lungs, "*Gran'
bestia !*"

This unexpected cry had the effect of stilling the
noise. All the eyes were directed to the window with
an approving expectation; but Decoud had already
turned his back upon the room, and was again leaning
out over the quiet street.

"This is the quintessence of my journalism; that is
the supreme argument," he said to Antonia. "I have
invented this definition, this last word on a great
question. But I am no patriot. I am no more of a
patriot than the Capataz of the Sulaco Cargadores, this
Genoese who has done such great things for this harbour
—this active usher-in of the material implements for our
progress. You have heard Captain Mitchell confess
over and over again that till he got this man he could
never tell how long it would take to unload a ship.
That is bad for progress. You have seen him pass by
after his labours on his famous horse to dazzle the girls
in some ballroom with an earthen floor. He is a
fortunate fellow! His work is an exercise of personal
powers; his leisure is spent in receiving the marks of
extraordinary adulation. And he likes it, too. Can
anybody be more fortunate? To be feared and admired is——"

'And are these your highest aspirations, Don
Martin?" interrupted Antonia.

"I was speaking of a man of that sort," said Decoud,
curtly. "The heroes of the world have been feared and
admired. What more could he want?"

Decoud had often felt his familiar habit of ironic
thought fall shattered against Antonia's gravity. She

irritated him as if she, too, had suffered from that inexplicable feminine obtuseness which stands so often
between a man and a woman of the more ordinary sort.
But he overcame his vexation at once. He was very
far from thinking Antonia ordinary, whatever verdict
his scepticism might have pronounced upon himself.
With a touch of penetrating tenderness in his voice he
assured her that his only aspiration was to a felicity so
high that it seemed almost unrealizable on this earth.

She coloured invisibly, with a warmth against which
the breeze from the sierra seemed to have lost its cooling
power in the sudden melting of the snows. His whisper
could not have carried so far, though there was enough
ardour in his tone to melt a heart of ice. Antonia
turned away abruptly, as if to carry his whispered
assurance into the room behind, full of light, noisy with
voices.

The tide of political speculation was beating high
within the four walls of the great sala, as if driven
beyond the marks by a great gust of hope. Don Juste's
fan-shaped beard was still the centre of loud and
animated discussions. There was a self-confident ring
in all the voices. Even the few Europeans around
Charles Gould—a Dane, a couple of Frenchmen, a discreet fat German, smiling, with down-cast eyes, the
representatives of those material interests that had got
a footing in Sulaco under the protecting might of the
San Tomé mine—had infused a lot of good humour into
their deference. Charles Gould, to whom they were
paying their court, was the visible sign of the stability
that could be achieved on the shifting ground of revolutions. They felt hopeful about their various undertakings. One of the two Frenchmen, small, black, with
glittering eyes lost in an immense growth of bushy
beard, waved his tiny brown hands and delicate wrists.

He had been travelling in the interior of the province
for a syndicate of European capitalists. His forcible
"*Monsieur l' Administrateur*"*returning every minute
shrilled above the steady hum of conversations. He
was relating his discoveries. He was ecstatic. Charles
Gould glanced down at him courteously.

At a given moment of these necessary receptions it
was Mrs. Gould's habit to withdraw quietly into a
little drawing-room, especially her own, next to the
great sala. She had risen, and, waiting for Antonia,
listened with a slightly worried graciousness to the
engineer-in-chief of the railway, who stooped over her,
relating slowly, without the slightest gesture, something apparently amusing, for his eyes had a humorous
twinkle. Antonia, before she advanced into the room
to join Mrs. Gould, turned her head over her shoulder
towards Decoud, only for a moment.

"Why should any one of us think his aspirations
unrealizable?" she said, rapidly.

"I am going to cling to mine to the end, Antonia,"
he answered, through clenched teeth, then bowed very
low, a little distantly.

The engineer-in-chief had not finished telling his
amusing story. The humours of railway building in
South America appealed to his keen appreciation of the
absurd, and he told his instances of ignorant prejudice
and as ignorant cunning very well. Now, Mrs. Gould
gave him all her attention as he walked by her side
escorting the ladies out of the room. Finally all three
passed unnoticed through the glass doors in the gallery.
Only a tall priest stalking silently in the noise of the sala
checked himself to look after them. Father Corbelàn,
whom Decoud had seen from the balcony turning into
the gateway of the Casa Gould, had addressed no one
since coming in. The long, skimpy soutane accentu-

ated the tallness of his stature; he carried his powerful torso thrown forward; and the straight, black bar of
his joined eyebrows, the pugnacious outline of the bony
face, the white spot of a scar on the bluish shaven
cheeks (a testimonial to his apostolic zeal from a party
of unconverted Indians), suggested something unlawful
behind his priesthood, the idea of a chaplain of bandits.

He separated his bony, knotted hands clasped behind
his back, to shake his finger at Martin.

Decoud had stepped into the room after Antonia.
But he did not go far. He had remained just within,
against the curtain, with an expression of not quite
genuine gravity, like a grown-up person taking part in a
game of children. He gazed quietly at the threatening
finger.

"I have watched your reverence converting General
Barrios by a special sermon on the Plaza," he said, without making the slightest movement.

"What miserable nonsense!" Father Corbelàn's
deep voice resounded all over the room, making all the
heads turn on the shoulders. "The man is a drunkard.
Señores, the God of your General is a bottle!"

His contemptuous, arbitrary voice caused an uneasy
suspension of every sound, as if the self-confidence of
the gathering had been staggered by a blow. But
nobody took up Father Corbelàn's declaration.

It was known that Father Corbelàn had come out of
the wilds to advocate the sacred rights of the Church
with the same fanatical fearlessness with which he had
gone preaching to bloodthirsty savages, devoid of human compassion or worship of any kind. Rumours of
legendary proportions told of his successes as a missionary beyond the eye of Christian men. He had baptized
whole nations of Indians, living with them like a savage
himself. It was related that the padre used to ride with

his Indians for days, half naked, carrying a bullock-hide
shield, and, no doubt, a long lance, too—who knows?
That he had wandered clothed in skins, seeking for
proselytes somewhere near the snow line of the Cordillera. Of these exploits Padre Corbelàn himself was
never known to talk. But he made no secret of his
opinion that the politicians of Sta. Marta had harder
hearts and more corrupt minds than the heathen to
whom he had carried the word of God. His injudicious
zeal for the temporal welfare of the Church was damag-
ing the Ribierist cause. It was common knowledge
that he had refused to be made titular bishop of the
Occidental diocese till justice was done to a despoiled
Church. The political Géfé of Sulaco (the same
dignitary whom Captain Mitchell saved from the
mob afterwards) hinted with naïve cynicism that
doubtless their Excellencies the Ministers sent the padre
over the mountains to Sulaco in the worst season of the
year in the hope that he would be frozen to death by
the icy blasts of the high paramos. Every year a few
hardy muleteers—men inured to exposure—were known
to perish in that way. But what would you have?
Their Excellencies possibly had not realized what a
tough priest he was. Meantime, the ignorant were
beginning to murmur that the Ribierist reforms meant
simply the taking away of the land from the people.
Some of it was to be given to foreigners who made the
railway; the greater part was to go to the padres.

These were the results of the Grand Vicar's zeal.
Even from the short allocution to the troops on the
Plaza (which only the first ranks could have heard) he
had not been able to keep out his fixed idea of an
outraged Church waiting for reparation from a penitent
country. The political Géfé had been exasperated.
But he could not very well throw the brother-in-law

of Don José into the prison of the Cabildo. The chief magistrate, an easy-going and popular official, visited the Casa Gould, walking over after sunset from the Intendencia, unattended, acknowledging with dignified courtesy the salutations of high and low alike. That evening he had walked up straight to Charles Gould and had hissed out to him that he would have liked to deport the Grand Vicar out of Sulaco, anywhere, to some desert island, to the Isabels, for instance. "The one without water preferably—eh, Don Carlos?" he had added in a tone between jest and earnest. This uncontrollable priest, who had rejected his offer of the episcopal palace for a residence and preferred to hang his shabby hammock amongst the rubble and spiders of the sequestrated Dominican Convent, had taken into his head to advocate an unconditional pardon for Hernandez the Robber! And this was not enough; he seemed to have entered into communication with the most audacious criminal the country had known for years. The Sulaco police knew, of course, what was going on. Padre Corbelàn had got hold of that reckless Italian, the Capataz de Cargadores, the only man fit for such an errand, and had sent a message through him. Father Corbelàn had studied in Rome, and could speak Italian. The Capataz was known to visit the old Dominican Convent at night. An old woman who served the Grand Vicar had heard the name of Hernandez pronounced; and only last Saturday afternoon the Capataz had been observed galloping out of town. He did not return for two days. The police would have laid the Italian by the heels if it had not been for fear of the Cargadores, a turbulent body of men, quite apt to raise a tumult. Nowadays it was not so easy to govern Sulaco. Bad characters flocked into it, attracted by the money in the pockets of the railway workmen. The

populace was made restless by Father Corbelàn's dis-
courses. And the first magistrate explained to Charles
Gould that now the province was stripped of troops any
outbreak of lawlessness would find the authorities with
their boots off, as it were.

Then he went away moodily to sit in an armchair,
smoking a long, thin cigar, not very far from Don
José, with whom, bending over sideways, he exchanged
a few words from time to time. He ignored the entrance of the priest, and whenever Father Corbelàn's
voice was raised behind him, he shrugged his shoulders
impatiently.

Father Corbelàn had remained quite motionless for a
time with that something vengeful in his immobility
which seemed to characterize all his attitudes. A lurid
glow of strong convictions gave its peculiar aspect to the
black figure. But its fierceness became softened as the
padre, fixing his eyes upon Decoud, raised his long,
black arm slowly, impressively—

"And you—you are a perfect heathen," he said, in a
subdued, deep voice.

He made a step nearer, pointing a forefinger at the
young man's breast. Decoud, very calm, felt the wall
behind the curtain with the back of his head. Then,
with his chin tilted well up, he smiled.

"Very well," he agreed with the slightly weary nonchalance of a man well used to these passages. "But
is it perhaps that you have not discovered yet what is
the God of my worship? It was an easier task with our
Barrios."

The priest suppressed a gesture of discouragement.
"You believe neither in stick nor stone," he said.

"Nor bottle," added Decoud without stirring.
"Neither does the other of your reverence's confidants.
I mean the Capataz of the Cargadores. He does not

drink. Your reading of my character does honour to you perspicacity. But why call me a heathen?"

"True," retorted the priest. "You are ten times worse. A miracle could not convert you."

"I certainly do not believe in miracles," said Decoud, quietly. Father Corbelàn shrugged his high, broad shoulders doubtfully.

"A sort of Frenchman—godless—a materialist," he pronounced slowly, as if weighing the terms of a careful analysis. "Neither the son of his own country nor of any other," he continued, thoughtfully.

"Scarcely human, in fact," Decoud commented under his breath, his head at rest against the wall, his eyes gazing up at the ceiling.

"The victim of this faithless age," Father Corbelàn resumed in a deep but subdued voice.

"But of some use as a journalist." Decoud changed his pose and spoke in a more animated tone. "Has your worship neglected to read the last number of the *Porvenir*? I assure you it is just like the others. On the general policy it continues to call Montero a *gran' bestia*, and stigmatize his brother, the guerrillero, for a combination of lacquey and spy. What could be more effective? In local affairs it urges the Provincial Government to enlist bodily into the national army the band of Hernandez the Robber—who is apparently the *protégé* of the Church—or at least of the Great Vicar. Nothing could be more sound."

The priest nodded and turned on the heels of his square-toed shoes with big steel buckles. Again, with his hands clasped behind his back, he paced to and fro, planting his feet firmly. When he swung about, the skirt of his soutane was inflated slightly by the brusqueness of his movements.

The great sala had been emptying itself slowly.

When the Géfé Politico rose to go, most of those still remaining stood up suddenly in sign of respect, and Don José Avellanos stopped the rocking of his chair. But the good-natured First Official made a deprecatory gesture, waved his hand to Charles Gould, and went out discreetly.

In the comparative peace of the room the screaming "*Monsieur l'Administrateur*" of the frail, hairy Frenchman seemed to acquire a preternatural shrillness. The explorer of the Capitalist syndicate was still enthusiastic. "Ten million dollars' worth of copper practically in sight, *Monsieur l'Administrateur*. Ten millions in sight! And a railway coming—a railway! They will never believe my report. *C'est trop beau.*"* He fell a prey to a screaming ecstasy, in the midst of sagely nodding heads, before Charles Gould's imperturbable calm.

And only the priest continued his pacing, flinging round the skirt of his soutane at each end of his beat. Decoud murmured to him ironically: "Those gentlemen talk about their gods."

Father Corbelàn stopped short, looked at the journalist of Sulaco fixedly for a moment, shrugged his shoulders slightly, and resumed his plodding walk of an obstinate traveller.

And now the Europeans were dropping off from the group around Charles Gould till the Administrador of the Great Silver Mine could be seen in his whole lank length, from head to foot, left stranded by the ebbing tide of his guests on the great square of carpet, as it were a multi-coloured shoal of flowers and arabesques under his brown boots. Father Corbelàn approached the rocking-chair of Don José Avellanos.

"Come, brother," he said, with kindly brusqueness and a touch of relieved impatience a man may feel at the end of a perfectly useless ceremony. "*A la Casa ! A la Casa!* This has been all talk. Let us now go and think and pray for guidance from Heaven."

He rolled his black eyes upwards. By the side of the frail diplomatist—the life and soul of the party—he seemed gigantic, with a gleam of fanaticism in the glance. But the voice of the party, or, rather, its mouthpiece, the "son Decoud" from Paris, turned journalist for the sake of Antonia's eyes, knew very well that it was not so, that he was only a strenuous priest with one idea, feared by the women and execrated by the men of the people. Martin Decoud, the dilettante in life, imagined himself to derive an artistic pleasure from watching the picturesque extreme of wrong-headedness into which an honest, almost sacred, conviction may drive a man. "It is like madness. It must be—because it's self-destructive," Decoud had said to himself often. It seemed to him that every conviction, as soon as it became effective, turned into that form of dementia the gods send upon those they wish to destroy. But he enjoyed the bitter flavour of that example with the zest of a connoisseur in the art of his choice. Those two men got on well together, as if each had felt respectively that a masterful conviction, as well as utter scepticism, may lead a man very far on the by-paths of political action.

Don José obeyed the touch of the big hairy hand. Decoud followed out the brothers-in-law. And there remained only one visitor in the vast empty sala, bluishly hazy with tobacco smoke, a heavy-eyed, round-cheeked man, with a drooping moustache, a hide merchant from Esmeralda, who had come overland to Sulaco, riding with a few peons across the coast range. He was very full of his journey, undertaken mostly for the purpose of seeing the Señor Administrador of San Tomé in relation to some assistance he required in his hide-exporting business. He hoped to enlarge it greatly now that the country was going to be settled. It was going to be settled, he repeated several times, degrading by a strange, anxious whine the sonority of the Spanish language, which he pattered rapidly, like some sort of cringing jargon. A plain man could carry on his little business now in the country, and even think of enlarging it—with safety. Was it not so? He seemed to beg Charles Gould for a confirmatory word, a grunt of assent, a simple nod even.

He could get nothing. His alarm increased, and in the pauses he would dart his eyes here and there; then, loth to give up, he would branch off into feeling allusion to the dangers of his journey. The audacious Hernandez, leaving his usual haunts, had crossed the Campo of Sulaco, and was known to be lurking in the ravines of the coast range. Yesterday, when distant only a few hours from Sulaco, the hide merchant and his servants had seen three men on the road arrested suspiciously, with their horses' heads together. Two of these rode off at once and disappeared in a shallow quebrada to the left. "We stopped," continued the man from Esmeralda, "and I tried to hide behind a small bush. But none of my mozos would go forward to find out what it meant, and the third horseman seemed to be waiting for us to come up. It was no use. We had been seen. So we rode slowly on, trembling. He let us pass—a man on a grey horse with his hat down on his eyes—without a word of greeting; but by-and-by we heard him galloping after us. We faced about, but that did not seem to intimidate him. He rode up at speed, and touching my foot with the toe of his boot, asked me for a cigar, with a blood-curdling laugh. He did not seem armed, but when he put his hand back to reach for the matches I saw an enormous revolver

strapped to his waist. I shuddered. He had very
fierce whiskers, Don Carlos, and as he did not offer to go
on we dared not move. At last, blowing the smoke
of my cigar into the air through his nostrils, he said,
'Señor, it would be perhaps better for you if I rode behind your party. You are not very far from Sulaco
now. Go you with God.' What would you? We
went on. There was no resisting him. He might have
been Hernandez himself; though my servant, who has
been many times to Sulaco by sea, assured me that he
had recognized him very well for the Capataz of the
Steamship Company's Cargadores. Later, that same
evening, I saw that very man at the corner of the Plaza
talking to a girl, a Morenita, who stood by the stirrup
with her hand on the grey horse's mane."

"I assure you, Señor Hirsch," murmured Charles
Gould, "that you ran no risk on this occasion."

"That may be, señor, though I tremble yet. A most
fierce man—to look at. And what does it mean? A
person employed by the Steamship Company talking
with salteadores—no less, señor; the other horsemen
were salteadores—in a lonely place, and behaving like
a robber himself! A cigar is nothing, but what was
there to prevent him asking me for my purse?"

"No, no, Señor Hirsch," Charles Gould murmured,
letting his glance stray away a little vacantly from the
round face, with its hooked beak upturned towards him
in an almost childlike appeal. "If it was the Capataz
de Cargadores you met—and there is no doubt, is there?
—you were perfectly safe."

"Thank you. You are very good. A very fierce-
looking man, Don Carlos. He asked me for a cigar in a
most familiar manner. What would have happened if
I had not had a cigar? I shudder yet. What business
had he to be talking with robbers in a lonely place?"

But Charles Gould, openly preoccupied now, gave not a sign, made no sound. The impenetrability of the embodied Gould Concession had its surface shades. To be dumb is merely a fatal affliction; but the King of Sulaco had words enough to give him all the mysterious weight of a taciturn force. His silences, backed by the power of speech, had as many shades of significance as uttered words in the way of assent, of doubt, of negation—even of simple comment. Some seemed to say plainly, "Think it over"; others meant clearly "Go ahead," a simple, low "I see," with an affirmative nod, at the end of a patient listening half-hour was the equivalent of a verbal contract, which men had learned to trust implicitly, since behind it all there was the great San Tomé mine, the head and front of the material interests, so strong that it depended on no man's good-will in the whole length and breadth of the Occidental Province—that is, on no goodwill which it could not buy ten times over. But to the little hook-nosed man from Esmeralda, anxious about the export of hides, the silence of Charles Gould portended a failure. Evidently this was no time for extending a modest man's business. He enveloped in a swift mental malediction the whole country, with all its inhabitants, partisans of Ribiera and Montero alike; and there were incipient tears in his mute anger at the thought of the in-numerable ox-hides going to waste upon the dreamy expanse of the Campo, with its single palms rising like ships at sea within the perfect circle of the horizon, its clumps of heavy timber motionless like solid islands of leaves above the running waves of grass. There were hides there, rotting, with no profit to anybody—rotting where they had been dropped by men called away to attend the urgent necessities of political revolutions. The practical, mercantile soul of Señor Hirsch rebelled against all that foolishness, while he was taking a respectful but disconcerted leave of the might and majesty of the San Tomé mine in the person of Charles Gould. He could not restrain a heart-broken murmur, wrung out of his very aching heart, as it were.

"It is a great, great foolishness, Don Carlos, all this. The price of hides in Hamburg is gone up—up. Of course the Ribierist Government will do away with all that*—when it gets established firmly. Meantime——"

He sighed.

"Yes, meantime," repeated Charles Gould, inscrutably.

The other shrugged his shoulders. But he was not ready to go yet. There was a little matter he would like to mention very much if permitted. It appeared he had some good friends in Hamburg (he murmured the name of the firm) who were very anxious to do business, in dynamite, he explained. A contract for dynamite with the San Tomé mine, and then, perhaps, later on, other mines, which were sure to—— The little man from Esmeralda was ready to enlarge, but Charles interrupted him. It seemed as though the patience of the Señor Administrador was giving way at last.

"Señor Hirsch," he said, "I have enough dynamite stored up at the mountain to send it down crashing into the valley"—his voice rose a little—"to send half Sulaco into the air if I liked."

Charles Gould smiled at the round, startled eyes of the dealer in hides, who was murmuring hastily, "Just so. Just so." And now he was going. It was impossible to do business in explosives with an Administrador so well provided and so discouraging. He had suffered agonies in the saddle and had exposed himself to the atrocities of the bandit Hernandez for nothing at all. Neither hides nor dynamite—and the very shoulders of the enterprising Israelite expressed dejection. At the door he bowed low to the engineer-in-chief. But at the bottom of the stairs in the patio he stopped short, with his podgy hand over his lips in an attitude of meditative astonishment.

"What does he want to keep so much dynamite for?" he muttered. "And why does he talk like this to me?"

The engineer-in-chief, looking in at the door of the empty sala, whence the political tide had ebbed out to the last insignificant drop, nodded familiarly to the master of the house, standing motionless like a tall beacon amongst the deserted shoals of furniture.

"Good-night, I am going. Got my bike downstairs. The railway will know where to go for dynamite should we get short at any time. We have done cutting and chopping for a while now. We shall begin soon to blast our way through."

"Don't come to me," said Charles Gould, with perfect serenity. "I shan't have an ounce to spare for anybody. Not an ounce. Not for my own brother, if I had a brother, and he were the engineer-in-chief of the most promising railway in the world."

"What's that?" asked the engineer-in-chief, with equanimity. "Unkindness?"

"No," said Charles Gould, stolidly. "Policy."

"Radical, I should think," the engineer-in-chief observed from the doorway.

"Is that the right name?" Charles Gould said, from the middle of the room.

"I mean, going to the roots, you know," the engineer explained, with an air of enjoyment.

"Why, yes," Charles pronounced, slowly. "The Gould Concession has struck such deep roots in this country, in this province, in that gorge of the mountains, that nothing but dynamite shall be allowed to dislodge it from there. It's my choice. It's my last card to play."

The engineer-in-chief whistled low. "A pretty game," he said, with a shade of discretion. "And have you told Holroyd of that extraordinary trump card you hold in your hand?"

"Card only when it's played; when it falls at the end of the game. Till then you may call it a—a——"

"Weapon," suggested the railway man.

"No. You may call it rather an argument," corrected Charles Gould, gently. "And that's how I've presented it to Mr. Holroyd."

"And what did he say to it?" asked the engineer, with undisguised interest.

"He"—Charles Gould spoke after a slight pause— "he said something about holding on like grim death and putting our trust in God. I should imagine he must have been rather startled. But then"—pursued the Administrador of the San Tomé mine—"but then, he is very far away, you know, and, as they say in this country, God is very high above."

The engineer's appreciative laugh died away down the stairs, where the Madonna with the Child on her arm seemed to look after his shaking broad back from her shallow niche.

CHAPTER SIX

A PROFOUND stillness reigned in the Casa Gould. The master of the house, walking along the corridor, opened the door of his room, and saw his wife sitting in a big armchair—his own smoking armchair—thoughtful, contemplating her little shoes. And she did not raise her eyes when he walked in.

"Tired?" asked Charles Gould.

"A little," said Mrs. Gould. Still without looking up, she added with feeling, "There is an awful sense of unreality about all this."

Charles Gould, before the long table strewn with papers, on which lay a hunting crop and a pair of spurs, stood looking at his wife: "The heat and dust must have been awful this afternoon by the waterside," he murmured, sympathetically. "The glare on the water must have been simply terrible."

"One could close one's eyes to the glare," said Mrs. Gould. "But, my dear Charley, it is impossible for me to close my eyes to our position; to this awful . . ."

She raised her eyes and looked at her husband's face, from which all sign of sympathy or any other feeling had disappeared. "Why don't you tell me something?" she almost wailed.

"I thought you had understood me perfectly from the first," Charles Gould said, slowly. "I thought we had said all there was to say a long time ago. There is nothing to say now. There were things to be done. We have done them; we have gone on doing them. There is no going back now. I don't suppose that, even

207

from the first, there was really any possible way back. And, what's more, we can't even afford to stand still."

"Ah, if one only knew how far you mean to go," said his wife, inwardly trembling, but in an almost playful tone.

"Any distance, any length, of course," was the answer, in a matter-of-fact tone, which caused Mrs. Gould to make another effort to repress a shudder.

She stood up, smiling graciously, and her little figure seemed to be diminished still more by the heavy mass of her hair and the long train of her gown.

"But always to success," she said, persuasively.

Charles Gould, enveloping her in the steely blue glance of his attentive eyes, answered without hesitation—

"Oh, there is no alternative."

He put an immense assurance into his tone. As to the words, this was all that his conscience would allow him to say.

Mrs. Gould's smile remained a shade too long upon her lips. She murmured—

"I will leave you; I've a slight headache. The heat, the dust, were indeed—— I suppose you are going back to the mine before the morning?"

"At midnight," said Charles Gould. "We are bringing down the silver to-morrow. Then I shall take three whole days off in town with you."

"Ah, you are going to meet the escort. I shall be on the balcony at five o'clock to see you pass. Till then, good-bye."

Charles Gould walked rapidly round the table, and, seizing her hands, bent down, pressing them both to his lips. Before he straightened himself up again to his full height she had disengaged one to smooth his cheek with a light touch, as if he were a little boy.

"Try to get some rest for a couple of hours," she murmured, with a glance at a hammock stretched in a distant part of the room. Her long train swished softly after her on the red tiles. At the door she looked back.

Two big lamps with unpolished glass globes bathed in a soft and abundant light the four white walls of the room, with a glass case of arms, the brass hilt of Henry Gould's cavalry sabre on its square of velvet, and the water-colour sketch of the San Tomé gorge. And Mrs. Gould, gazing at the last in its black wooden frame, sighed out—

"Ah, if we had left it alone, Charley!"

"No," Charles Gould said, moodily; "it was impossible to leave it alone."

"Perhaps it was impossible," Mrs. Gould admitted, slowly. Her lips quivered a little, but she smiled with an air of dainty bravado. "We have disturbed a good many snakes in that Paradise, Charley, haven't we?"

"Yes, I remember," said Charles Gould, "it was Don Pépé who called the gorge the Paradise of snakes. No doubt we have disturbed a great many. But remember, my dear, that it is not now as it was when you made that sketch." He waved his hand towards the small water-colour hanging alone upon the great bare wall. "It is no longer a Paradise of snakes. We have brought mankind into it, and we cannot turn our backs upon them to go and begin a new life elsewhere."

He confronted his wife with a firm, concentrated gaze, which Mrs. Gould returned with a brave assumption of fearlessness before she went out, closing the door gently after her.

In contrast with the white glaring room the dimly lit corridor had a restful mysteriousness of a forest glade, suggested by the stems and the leaves of the plants ranged along the balustrade of the open side. In the streaks of light falling through the open doors of the reception-rooms, the blossoms, white and red and pale lilac, came out vivid with the brilliance of flowers in a stream of sunshine; and Mrs. Gould, passing on, had the vividness of a figure seen in the clear patches of sun that chequer the gloom of open glades in the woods. The stones in the rings upon her hand pressed to her fore-head glittered in the lamplight abreast of the door of the sala.

"Who's there?" she asked, in a startled voice. "Is that you, Basilio?" She looked in, and saw Martin Decoud walking about, with an air of having lost something, amongst the chairs and tables.

"Antonia has forgotten her fan in here," said De-coud, with a strange air of distraction; "so I entered to see."

But, even as he said this, he had obviously given up his search, and walked straight towards Mrs. Gould, who looked at him with doubtful surprise.

"Señora," he began, in a low voice.

"What is it, Don Martin?" asked Mrs. Gould. And then she added, with a slight laugh, "I am so nervous to-day," as if to explain the eagerness of the question.

"Nothing immediately dangerous," said Decoud, who now could not conceal his agitation. "Pray don't distress yourself. No, really, you must not distress yourself."

Mrs. Gould, with her candid eyes very wide open, her lips composed into a smile, was steadying herself in the doorway with a little bejewelled hand.

"Perhaps you don't know how alarming you are, appearing like this unexpectedly——"

"I! Alarming!" he protested, sincerely vexed and surprised. "I assure you that I am not in the least alarmed myself. A fan is lost; well, it will be found again. But I don't think it is here. It is a fan I am looking for. I cannot understand how Antonia could—— Well! Have you found it, amigo?"

"No, señor," said behind Mrs. Gould the soft voice of Basilio, the head servant of the Casa. "I don't think the señorita could have left it in this house at all."

"Go and look for it in the patio again. Go now, my friend; look for it on the steps, under the gate; examine every flagstone; search for it till I come down again. . . . That fellow"—he addressed himself in English to Mrs. Gould—"is always stealing up behind one's back on his bare feet. I set him to look for that fan directly I came in to justify my reappearance, my sudden return."

He paused and Mrs. Gould said, amiably, "You are always welcome." She paused for a second, too. "But I am waiting to learn the cause of your return."

Decoud affected suddenly the utmost nonchalance.

"I can't bear to be spied upon. Oh, the cause? Yes, there is a cause; there is something else that is lost besides Antonia's favourite fan. As I was walking home after seeing Don José and Antonia to their house, the Capataz de Cargadores, riding down the street, spoke to me."

"Has anything happened to the Violas?" inquired Mrs. Gould.

"The Violas? You mean the old Garibaldino who keeps the hotel where the engineers live? Nothing happened there. The Capataz said nothing of them; he only told me that the telegraphist of the Cable Company was walking on the Plaza, bareheaded, looking out for me. There is news from the interior, Mrs. Gould. I should rather say rumours of news."

"Good news?" said Mrs. Gould in a low voice.

"Worthless, I should think. But if I must define them, I would say bad. They are to the effect that a two days' battle had been fought near Sta. Marta, and that the Ribierists are defeated. It must have happened a few days ago—perhaps a week. The rumour has just reached Cayta, and the man in charge of the cable station there has telegraphed the news to his colleague here. We might just as well have kept Barrios in Sulaco."

"What's to be done now?" murmured Mrs. Gould.

"Nothing. He's at sea with the troops. He will get to Cayta in a couple of days' time and learn the news there. What he will do then, who can say? Hold Cayta? Offer his submission to Montero? Disband his army—this last most likely, and go himself in one of the O.S.N. Company's steamers, north or south—to Valparaiso or to San Francisco, no matter where. Our Barrios has a great practice in exiles and repatriations, which mark the points in the political game."

Decoud, exchanging a steady stare with Mrs. Gould, added, tentatively, as it were, "And yet, if we had Barrios with his 2,000 improved rifles here, something could have been done."

"Montero victorious, completely victorious!" Mrs. Gould breathed out in a tone of unbelief.

"A canard, probably. That sort of bird is hatched in great numbers in such times as these. And even if it were true? Well, let us put things at their worst, let us say it is true."

"Then everything is lost," said Mrs. Gould, with the calmness of despair.

Suddenly she seemed to divine, she seemed to see Decoud's tremendous excitement under its cloak of studied carelessness. It was, indeed, becoming visible in his audacious and watchful stare, in the curve, half-reckless, half-contemptuous, of his lips. And a French phrase came upon them as if, for this Costaguanero of the Boulevard, that had been the only forcible language—

"*Non, Madame. Rien n'est perdu.*"*

It electrified Mrs. Gould out of her benumbed attitude, and she said, vivaciously—

"What would you think of doing?"

But already there was something of mockery in Decoud's suppressed excitement.

"What would you expect a true Costaguanero to do? Another revolution, of course. On my word of honour, Mrs. Gould, I believe I am a true *hijo del pays*, a true son of the country, whatever Father Corbelàn may say. And I'm not so much of an unbeliever as not to have faith in my own ideas, in my own remedies, in my own desires."

"Yes," said Mrs. Gould, doubtfully.

"You don't seem convinced," Decoud went on again in French. "Say, then, in my passions."

Mrs. Gould received this addition unflinchingly. To understand it thoroughly she did not require to hear his muttered assurance—

"There is nothing I would not do for the sake of Antonia. There is nothing I am not prepared to undertake. There is no risk I am not ready to run."

Decoud seemed to find a fresh audacity in this voicing of his thoughts. "You would not believe me if I were to say that it is the love of the country which——"

She made a sort of discouraged protest with her arm, as if to express that she had given up expecting that motive from any one.

"A Sulaco revolution," Decoud pursued in a forcible undertone. "The Great Cause may be served here,

on the very spot of its inception, in the place of its
birth, Mrs. Gould."

Frowning, and biting her lower lip thoughtfully, she
made a step away from the door.

"You are not going to speak to your husband?" Decoud arrested her anxiously.

"But you will need his help?"

"No doubt," Decoud admitted without hesitation.
"Everything turns upon the San Tomé mine, but I
would rather he didn't know anything as yet of my—
my hopes."

A puzzled look came upon Mrs. Gould's face, and
Decoud, approaching, explained confidentially—

"Don't you see, he's such an idealist."

Mrs. Gould flushed pink, and her eyes grew darker
at the same time.

"Charley an idealist!" she said, as if to herself,
wonderingly. "What on earth do you mean?"

"Yes," conceded Decoud, "it's a wonderful thing to
say with the sight of the San Tomé mine, the greatest
fact in the whole of South America, perhaps, before our
very eyes. But look even at that, he has idealized this
fact to a point——" He paused. "Mrs. Gould, are
you aware to what point he has idealized the existence,
the worth, the meaning of the San Tomé mine? Are
you aware of it?"

He must have known what he was talking about.

The effect he expected was produced. Mrs. Gould,
ready to take fire, gave it up suddenly with a low little
sound that resembled a moan.

"What do you know?" she asked in a feeble voice.

"Nothing," answered Decoud, firmly. "But, then,
don't you see, he's an Englishman?"

"Well, what of that?" asked Mrs. Gould.

"Simply that he cannot act or exist without idealizing

every simple feeling, desire, or achievement. He could not believe his own motives if he did not make them first a part of some fairy tale. The earth is not quite good enough for him, I fear. Do you excuse my frankness? Besides, whether you excuse it or not, it is part of the truth of things which hurts the—what do you call them?—the Anglo-Saxon's susceptibilities, and at the present moment I don't feel as if I could treat seriously either his conception of things or—if you allow me to say so—or yet yours."

Mrs. Gould gave no sign of being offended. "I suppose Antonia understands you thoroughly?"

"Understands? Well, yes. But I am not sure that she approves. That, however, makes no difference. I am honest enough to tell you that, Mrs. Gould."

"Your idea, of course, is separation," she said.

"Separation, of course," declared Martin. "Yes; separation of the whole Occidental Province from the rest of the unquiet body. But my true idea, the only one I care for, is not to be separated from Antonia."

"And that is all?" asked Mrs. Gould, without severity.

"Absolutely. I am not deceiving myself about my motives. She won't leave Sulaco for my sake, therefore Sulaco must leave the rest of the Republic to its fate. Nothing could be clearer than that. I like a clearly defined situation. I cannot part with Antonia, therefore the one and indivisible Republic of Costaguana must be made to part with its western province. Fortunately it happens to be also a sound policy. The richest, the most fertile part of this land may be saved from anarchy. Personally, I care little, very little; but it's a fact that the establishment of Montero in power would mean death to me. In all the proclamations of general pardon which I have seen,

my name, with a few others, is specially excepted. The
brothers hate me, as you know very well, Mrs. Gould;
and behold, here is the rumour of them having won a
battle. You say that supposing it is true, I have plenty
of time to run away."

The slight, protesting murmur on the part of Mrs.
Gould made him pause for a moment, while he looked
at her with a sombre and resolute glance.

"Ah, but I would, Mrs. Gould. I would run away
if it served that which at present is my only desire. I
am courageous enough to say that, and to do it, too.
But women, even our women, are idealists. It is
Antonia that won't run away. A novel sort of vanity."

"You call it vanity," said Mrs. Gould, in a shocked
voice.

"Say pride, then, which, Father Corbelàn would tell
you, is a mortal sin. But I am not proud. I am simply
too much in love to run away. At the same time I
want to live. There is no love for a dead man. Therefore it is necessary that Sulaco should not recognize the
victorious Montero."

"And you think my husband will give you his support?"

"I think he can be drawn into it, like all idealists,
when he once sees a sentimental basis for his action.
But I wouldn't talk to him. Mere clear facts won't
appeal to his sentiment. It is much better for him to
convince himself in his own way. And, frankly, I could
not, perhaps, just now pay sufficient respect to either
his motives or even, perhaps, to yours, Mrs. Gould."

It was evident that Mrs. Gould was very determined
not to be offended. She smiled vaguely, while she
seemed to think the matter over. As far as she could
judge from the girl's half-confidences, Antonia understood that young man. Obviously there was promise of

safety in his plan, or rather in his idea. Moreover, right or wrong, the idea could do no harm. And it was quite possible, also, that the rumour was false.

"You have some sort of a plan," she said.

"Simplicity itself. Barrios has started, let him go on then; he will hold Cayta, which is the door of the sea route to Sulaco. They cannot send a sufficient force over the mountains. No; not even to cope with the band of Hernandez. Meantime we shall organize our resistance here. And for that, this very Hernandez will be useful. He has defeated troops as a bandit; he will no doubt accomplish the same thing if he is made a colonel or even a general. You know the country well enough not to be shocked by what I say, Mrs. Gould. I have heard you assert that this poor bandit was the living, breathing example of cruelty, injustice, stupidity, and oppression, that ruin men's souls as well as their fortunes in this country. Well, there would be some poetical retribution in that man arising to crush the evils which had driven an honest ranchero into a life of crime. A fine idea of retribution in that, isn't there?"

Decoud had dropped easily into English, which he spoke with precision, very correctly, but with too many z sounds.

"Think also of your hospitals, of your schools, of your ailing mothers and feeble old men, of all that population which you and your husband have brought into the rocky gorge of San Tomé. Are you not responsible to your conscience for all these people? Is it not worth while to make another effort, which is not at all so desperate as it looks, rather than——"

Decoud finished his thought with an upward toss of the arm, suggesting annihilation; and Mrs. Gould turned away her head with a look of horror.

"Why don't you say all this to my husband?" she

asked, without looking at Decoud, who stood watching the effect of his words.

"Ah! But Don Carlos is so English," he began. Mrs. Gould interrupted—

"Leave that alone, Don Martin. He's as much a Costaguanero——No! He's more of a Costaguanero than yourself."

"Sentimentalist, sentimentalist," Decoud almost cooed, in a tone of gentle and soothing deference. "Sentimentalist, after the amazing manner of your people. I have been watching El Rey de Sulaco since I came here on a fool's errand, and perhaps impelled by some treason of fate lurking behind the unaccountable turns of a man's life. But I don't matter, I am not a sentimentalist, I cannot endow my personal desires with a shining robe of silk and jewels. Life is not for me a moral romance derived from the tradition of a pretty fairy tale. No, Mrs. Gould; I am practical. I am not afraid of my motives. But, pardon me, I have been rather carried away. What I wish to say is that I have been observing. I won't tell you what I have discovered——"

"No. That is unnecessary," whispered Mrs. Gould, once more averting her head.

"It is. Except one little fact, that your husband does not like me. It's a small matter, which, in the circumstances, seems to acquire a perfectly ridiculous importance. Ridiculous and immense; for, clearly, money is required for my plan," he reflected; then added, meaningly, "and we have two sentimentalists to deal with."

"I don't know that I understand you, Don Martin," said Mrs. Gould, coldly, preserving the low key of their conversation. "But, speaking as if I did, who is the other?"

"The great Holroyd in San Francisco, of course," Decoud whispered, lightly. "I think you understand me very well. Women are idealists; but then they are so perspicacious."

But whatever was the reason of that remark, disparaging and complimentary at the same time, Mrs. Gould seemed not to pay attention to it. The name of Holroyd had given a new tone to her anxiety.

"The silver escort is coming down to the harbour tomorrow; a whole six months' working, Don Martin!" she cried in dismay.

"Let it come down, then," breathed out Decoud, earnestly, almost into her ear.

"But if the rumour should get about, and especially if it turned out true, troubles might break out in the town," objected Mrs. Gould.

Decoud admitted that it was possible. He knew well the town children of the Sulaco Campo: sullen, thievish, vindictive, and bloodthirsty, whatever great qualities their brothers of the plain might have had. But then there was that other sentimentalist, who attached a strangely idealistic meaning to concrete facts. This stream of silver must be kept flowing north to return in the form of financial backing from the great house of Holroyd. Up at the mountain in the strong room of the mine the silver bars were worth less for his purpose than so much lead, from which at least bullets may be run. Let it come down to the harbour, ready for shipment.

The next north-going steamer would carry it off for the very salvation of the San Tomé mine, which has produced so much treasure. And, moreover, the rumour was probably false, he remarked, with much conviction in his hurried tone.

"Besides, señora," concluded Decoud, "we may

suppress it for many days. I have been talking with
the telegraphist in the middle of the Plaza Mayor; thus
I am certain that we could not have been overheard.
There was not even a bird in the air near us. And also
let me tell you something more. I have been making
friends with this man called Nostromo, the Capataz.
We had a conversation this very evening, I walking by
the side of his horse as he rode slowly out of the town
just now. He promised me that if a riot took place for
any reason—even for the most political of reasons, you
understand—his Cargadores, an important part of the
populace, you will admit, should be found on the side of
the Europeans."

"He has promised you that?" Mrs. Gould inquired,
with interest. "What made him make that promise to
you?"

"Upon my word, I don't know," declared Decoud, in
a slightly surprised tone. "He certainly promised me
that, but now you ask me why I certainly could not tell
you his reasons. He talked with his usual carelessness,
which, if he had been anything else but a common
sailor, I would call a pose or an affectation."

Decoud, interrupting himself, looked at Mrs. Gould
curiously.

"Upon the whole," he continued, "I suppose he
expects something to his advantage from it. You
mustn't forget that he does not exercise his extraordinary power over the lower classes without a certain
amount of personal risk and without a great profusion
in spending his money. One must pay in some way or
other for such a solid thing as individual prestige. He
told me after we made friends at a dance, in a Posada
kept by a Mexican just outside the walls, that he had
come here to make his fortune. I suppose he looks
upon his prestige as a sort of investment."

"Perhaps he prizes it for its own sake," Mrs. Gould said in a tone as if she were repelling an undeserved aspersion. "Viola, the Garibaldino, with whom he has lived for some years, calls him the Incorruptible."

"Ah! he belongs to the group of your *protégés* out there towards the harbour, Mrs. Gould. *Muy bien.* And Captain Mitchell calls him wonderful. I have heard no end of tales of his strength, his audacity, his fidelity. No end of fine things. H'm! incorruptible! It is indeed a name of honour for the Capataz of the Cargadores of Sulaco. Incorruptible! Fine, but vague. However, I suppose he's sensible, too. And I talked to him upon that sane and practical assumption."

"I prefer to think him disinterested, and therefore trustworthy," Mrs. Gould said, with the nearest approach to curtness it was in her nature to assume.

"Well, if so, then the silver will be still more safe. Let it come down, señora. Let it come down, so that it may go north and return to us in the shape of credit."

Mrs. Gould glanced along the corridor towards the door of her husband's room. Decoud, watching her as if she had his fate in her hands, detected an almost imperceptible nod of assent. He bowed with a smile, and, putting his hand into the breast pocket of his coat, pulled out a fan of light feathers set upon painted leaves of sandal-wood. "I had it in my pocket," he murmured, triumphantly, "for a plausible pretext." He bowed again. "Good-night, señora."

Mrs. Gould continued along the corridor away from her husband's room. The fate of the San Tomé mine was lying heavy upon her heart. It was a long time now since she had begun to fear it. It had been an idea. She had watched it with misgivings turning into a fetish, and now the fetish had grown into a monstrous and crushing weight. It was as if the inspiration of their early years had left her heart to turn into a wall of silver-bricks, erected by the silent work of evil spirits, between her and her husband. He seemed to dwell alone within a circumvallation*of precious metal, leaving her outside with her school, her hospital, the sick mothers and the feeble old men, mere insignificant vestiges of the initial inspiration. "Those poor people!" she murmured to herself.

Below she heard the voice of Martin Decoud in the patio speaking loudly:

"I have found Doña Antonia's fan, Basilio. Look, here it is!"

CHAPTER SEVEN

IT WAS part of what Decoud would have called his sane materialism that he did not believe in the possibility of friendship between man and woman.

The one exception he allowed confirmed, he maintained, that absolute rule. Friendship was possible between brother and sister, meaning by friendship the frank unreserve, as before another human being, of thoughts and sensations; all the objectless and necessary sincerity of one's innermost life trying to re-act upon the profound sympathies of another existence.

His favourite sister, the handsome, slightly arbitrary and resolute angel, ruling the father and mother Decoud in the first-floor apartments of a very fine Parisian house, was the recipient of Martin Decoud's confidences as to his thoughts, actions, purposes, doubts, and even failures. . . .

"Prepare our little circle in Paris for the birth of another South American Republic. One more or less, what does it matter? They may come into the world like evil flowers on a hotbed of rotten institutions; but the seed of this one has germinated in your brother's brain, and that will be enough for your devoted assent. I am writing this to you by the light of a single candle, in a sort of inn, near the harbour, kept by an Italian called Viola, a *protégé* of Mrs. Gould. The whole building, which, for all I know, may have been contrived by a Conquistador farmer of the pearl fishery three hundred years ago, is perfectly silent. So is the plain between the town and the harbour; silent, but not so dark as the house, because the pickets of Italian workmen guarding the railway have lighted little fires all along the line. It was not so quiet around here yesterday. We had an awful riot—a sudden outbreak of the populace, which was not suppressed till late to-day. Its object, no doubt, was loot, and that was defeated, as you must have learned already from the cablegram sent via San Francisco and New York last night, when the cables were still open. You have read already there that the energetic action of the Europeans of the railway has saved the town from destruction, and you may believe that. I wrote out the cable myself. We have no Reuter's agency man here. I have also fired at the mob from the windows of the club, in company with some other young men of position. Our object was to keep the Calle de la Constitucion clear for the exodus of the ladies and children, who have taken refuge on board a couple of cargo ships now in the harbour here. That was yesterday. You should also have learned from the cable that the missing President, Ribiera, who had disappeared after the battle of Sta. Marta, has turned up here in Sulaco by one of those strange coincidences that are almost incredible, riding on a lame mule into the very midst of the street fighting. It appears that he had fled, in company of a muleteer called Bonifacio, across the mountains from the threats of Montero into the arms of an enraged mob.

"The Capataz of Cargadores, that Italian sailor of whom I have written to you before, has saved him from an ignoble death. That man seems to have a particular talent for being on the spot whenever there is something picturesque to be done.

"He was with me at four o'clock in the morning at the offices of the *Porvenir*, where he had turned up so early in order to warn me of the coming trouble, and also to assure me that he would keep his Cargadores on the side of order. When the full daylight came we were looking together at the crowd on foot and on horseback, demonstrating on the Plaza and shying stones at the windows of the Intendencia. Nostromo (that is the name they call him by here) was pointing out to me his Cargadores interspersed in the mob.

"The sun shines late upon Sulaco, for it has first to climb above the mountains. In that clear morning light, brighter than twilight, Nostromo saw right across the vast Plaza, at the end of the street beyond the cathedral, a mounted man apparently in difficulties with a yelling knot of leperos. At once he said to me, 'That's a stranger. What is it they are doing to him?' Then he took out the silver whistle he is in the habit of using on the wharf (this man seems to disdain the use of any metal less precious than silver) and blew into it twice, evidently a preconcerted signal for his Cargadores. He ran out immediately, and they rallied round him. I ran out, too, but was too late to follow them and help in the rescue of the stranger, whose animal had fallen. I was set upon at once as a hated aristocrat, and was only too glad to get into the club, where Don Jaime Berges (you may remember him visiting at our house in Paris some three years ago) thrust a sporting gun into my hands. They were already firing from the windows. There were little heaps of cartridges lying about on the open card-tables. I remember a couple of overturned chairs, some bottles rolling on the floor amongst the packs of cards scattered suddenly as the caballeros rose from their game to open fire upon the mob. Most of the young men had spent the night at the club in the expectation of some such disturbance. In two of the candelabra, on the consoles, the candles were burning down in their sockets. A large iron nut, probably stolen from the railway workshops, flew in from the street as I entered, and broke one of the large mirrors set in the wall. I noticed also one of the club servants tied up hand and foot with the cords of the curtain and flung in a corner. I have a vague recollection of Don Jaime assuring me hastily that the fellow had been detected putting poison into the dishes at supper. But I remember distinctly he was shrieking for mercy, without stopping at all, continuously, and so absolutely disregarded that nobody even took the trouble to gag him. The noise he made was so disagreeable that I had half a mind to do it myself. But there was no time to waste on such trifles. I took my place at one of the windows and began firing.

"I didn't learn till later in the afternoon whom it was that Nostromo, with his Cargadores and some Italian workmen as well, had managed to save from those drunken rascals. That man has a peculiar talent when anything striking to the imagination has to be done. I made that remark to him afterwards when we met after some sort of order had been restored in the town, and the answer he made rather surprised me. He said quite moodily, 'And how much do I get for that, señor?' Then it dawned upon me that perhaps this man's vanity has been satiated by the adulation of the common people and the confidence of his superiors!"

Decoud paused to light a cigarette, then, with his head still over his writing, he blew a cloud of smoke, which seemed to rebound from the paper. He took up the pencil again.

"That was yesterday evening on the Plaza, while he sat on the steps of the cathedral, his hands between his knees, holding the bridle of his famous silver-grey mare. He had led his body of Cargadores splendidly all day long. He looked fatigued. I don't know how I looked. Very dirty, I suppose. But I suppose I also looked pleased. From the time the fugitive President had been got off to the S. S. *Minerva*, the tide of success had turned against the mob. They had been driven off the harbour, and out of the better streets of the town, into their own maze of ruins and tolderias. You must understand that this riot, whose primary object was undoubtedly the getting hold of the San Tomé silver stored in the lower rooms of the Custom House (besides the general looting of the Ricos), had acquired a political colouring from the fact of two Deputies to the Provincial Assembly, Señores Gamacho and Fuentes, both from Bolson, putting themselves at the head of it—late in the afternoon, it is true, when the mob, disappointed in their hopes of loot, made a stand in the narrow streets to the cries of 'Viva la Libertad! Down with Feudalism!' (I wonder what they imagine feudalism to be?) 'Down with the Goths and Paralytics.' I suppose the Señores Gamacho and Fuentes knew what they were doing. They are prudent gentlemen. In the Assembly they called themselves Moderates, and opposed every energetic measure with philanthropic pensiveness. At the first rumours of Montero's victory, they began to show a subtle change of the pensive temper, and began to defy poor Don Juste Lopez in his Presidential tribune with an effrontery to which the poor man could only respond by a dazed smoothing of his beard and the ringing of the Presidential bell. Then, when the downfall of the Ribierist cause became confirmed beyond the shadow of a doubt, they have blossomed into convinced Liberals, acting together as if they were Siamese twins, and ultimately taking charge, as it were, of the riot in the name of Monterist principles.

"Their last move of eight o'clock last night was to
organize themselves into a Monterist Committee which
sits, as far as I know, in a posada kept by a retired
Mexican bull-fighter, a great politician, too, whose
name I have forgotten. Thence they have issued a
communication to us, the Goths and Paralytics of the
Amarilla Club (who have our own committee), inviting
us to come to some provisional understanding for a
truce, in order, they have the impudence to say, that
the noble cause of Liberty 'should not be stained by the
criminal excesses of Conservative selfishness!' As I
came out to sit with Nostromo on the cathedral steps
the club was busy considering a proper reply in the
principal room, littered with exploded cartridges, with
a lot of broken glass, blood smears, candlesticks, and all
sorts of wreckage on the floor. But all this is nonsense. Nobody in the town has any real power except
the railway engineers, whose men occupy the dismantled
houses acquired by the Company for their town station
on one side of the Plaza, and Nostromo, whose Cargadores were sleeping under the arcades along the front of
Anzani's shops. A fire of broken furniture out of the
Intendencia saloons, mostly gilt, was burning on the
Plaza, in a high flame swaying right upon the statue of
Charles IV. The dead body of a man was lying on the
steps of the pedestal, his arms thrown wide open, and
his sombrero covering his face—the attention of some
friend, perhaps. The light of the flame touched the
foliage of the first trees on the Alameda, and played on
the end of a side street near by, blocked up by a jumble
of ox-carts and dead bullocks. Sitting on one of the
carcases, a lepero, muffled up, smoked a cigarette. It
was a truce, you understand. The only other living
being on the Plaza besides ourselves was a Cargador
walking to and fro, with a long, bare knife in his hand,

like a sentry before the Arcades, where his friends were sleeping. And the only other spot of light in the dark town were the lighted windows of the club, at the corner of the Calle."

After having written so far, Don Martin Decoud, the exotic dandy of the Parisian boulevard, got up and walked across the sanded floor of the café at one end of the Albergo of United Italy, kept by Giorgio Viola, the old companion of Garibaldi. The highly coloured lithograph of the Faithful Hero seemed to look dimly, in the light of one candle, at the man with no faith in anything except the truth of his own sensations. Looking out of the window, Decoud was met by a darkness so impenetrable that he could see neither the mountains nor the town, nor yet the buildings near the harbour; and there was not a sound, as if the tremendous obscurity of the Placid Gulf, spreading from the waters over the land, had made it dumb as well as blind. Presently Decoud felt a light tremor of the floor and a distant clank of iron. A bright white light appeared, deep in the darkness, growing bigger with a thundering noise. The rolling stock usually kept on the sidings in Rincon was being run back to the yards for safe keeping. Like a mysterious stirring of the darkness behind the headlight of the engine, the train passed in a gust of hollow uproar, by the end of the house, which seemed to vibrate all over in response. And nothing was clearly visible but, on the end of the last flat car, a negro, in white trousers and naked to the waist, swinging a blazing torch basket incessantly with a circular movement of his bare arm. Decoud did not stir.

Behind him, on the back of the chair from which he had risen, hung his elegant Parisian overcoat, with a pearl-grey silk lining. But when he turned back to come to the table the candlelight fell upon a face that was grimy and scratched. His rosy lips were blackened with heat, the smoke of gun-powder. Dirt and rust tarnished the lustre of his short beard. His shirt collar and cuffs were crumpled; the blue silken tie hung down his breast like a rag; a greasy smudge crossed his white brow. He had not taken off his clothing nor used water, except to snatch a hasty drink greedily, for some forty hours. An awful restlessness had made him its own, had marked him with all the signs of desperate strife, and put a dry, sleepless stare into his eyes. He murmured to himself in a hoarse voice, "I wonder if there's any bread here," looked vaguely about him, then dropped into the chair and took the pencil up again. He became aware he had not eaten anything for many hours.

It occurred to him that no one could understand him so well as his sister. In the most sceptical heart there lurks at such moments, when the chances of existence are involved, a desire to leave a correct impression of the feelings, like a light by which the action may be seen when personality is gone, gone where no light of investigation can ever reach the truth which every death takes out of the world. Therefore, instead of looking for something to eat, or trying to snatch an hour or so of sleep, Decoud was filling the pages of a large pocket-book with a letter to his sister.

In the intimacy of that intercourse he could not keep out his weariness, his great fatigue, the close touch of his bodily sensations. He began again as if he were talking to her. With almost an illusion of her presence, he wrote the phrase, "I am very hungry."

"I have the feeling of a great solitude around me," he continued. "Is it, perhaps, because I am the only man with a definite idea in his head, in the complete collapse of every resolve, intention, and hope about me?

But the solitude is also very real. All the engineers are
cut, and have been for two days, looking after the
property of the National Central Railway, of that
great Costaguana undertaking which is to put money
into the pockets of Englishmen, Frenchmen, Americans,
Germans, and God knows who else. The silence about
me is ominous. There is above the middle part of this
house a sort of first floor, with narrow openings like
loopholes for windows, probably used in old times for
the better defence against the savages, when the persistent barbarism of our native continent did not wear the
black coats of politicians, but went about yelling, half-
naked, with bows and arrows in its hands. The woman
of the house is dying up there, I believe, all alone with
her old husband. There is a narrow staircase, the sort
of staircase one man could easily defend against a mob,
leading up there, and I have just heard, through the
thickness of the wall, the old fellow going down into
their kitchen for something or other. It was a sort of
noise a mouse might make behind the plaster of a wall.
All the servants they had ran away yesterday and have
not returned yet, if ever they do. For the rest, there
are only two children here, two girls. The father has
sent them downstairs, and they have crept into this
café, perhaps because I am here. They huddle together
in a corner, in each other's arms; I just noticed them a
few minutes ago, and I feel more lonely than ever."

Decoud turned half round in his chair, and asked,
"Is there any bread here?"

Linda's dark head was shaken negatively in response,
above the fair head of her sister nestling on her breast.

"You couldn't get me some bread?" insisted Decoud.
The child did not move; he saw her large eyes stare at
him very dark from the corner. "You're not afraid
of me?" he said.

"No," said Linda, "we are not afraid of you. You came here with Gian' Battista."

"You mean Nostromo?" said Decoud.

"The English call him so, but that is no name either for man or beast," said the girl, passing her hand gently over her sister's hair.

"But he lets people call him so," remarked Decoud.

"Not in this house," retorted the child.

"Ah! well, I shall call him the Capataz then."

Decoud gave up the point, and after writing steadily for a while turned round again.

"When do you expect him back?" he asked.

"After he brought you here he rode off to fetch the Señor Doctor from the town for mother. He will be back soon."

"He stands a good chance of getting shot somewhere on the road," Decoud murmured to himself audibly; and Linda declared in her high-pitched voice—

"Nobody would dare to fire a shot at Gian' Battista."

"You believe that," asked Decoud, "do you?"

"I know it," said the child, with conviction. "There is no one in this place brave enough to attack Gian' Battista."

"It doesn't require much bravery to pull a trigger behind a bush," muttered Decoud to himself. "Fortunately, the night is dark, or there would be but little chance of saving the silver of the mine."

He turned again to his pocket-book, glanced back through the pages, and again started his pencil.

"That was the position yesterday, after the *Minerva* with the fugitive President had gone out of harbour, and the rioters had been driven back into the side lanes of the town. I sat on the steps of the cathedral with Nostromo, after sending out the cable message for the information of a more or less attentive world.

Strangely enough, though the offices of the Cable
Company are in the same building as the *Porvenir*, the
mob, which has thrown my presses out of the window
and scattered the type all over the Plaza, has been kept
from interfering with the instruments on the other side
of the courtyard. As I sat talking with Nostromo,
Bernhardt, the telegraphist, came out from under the
Arcades with a piece of paper in his hand. The little
man had tied himself up to an enormous sword and
was hung all over with revolvers. He is ridiculous, but
the bravest German of his size that ever tapped the
key of a Morse transmitter. He had received the
message from Cayta reporting the transports with
Barrios's army just entering the port, and ending with
the words, 'The greatest enthusiasm prevails.' I
walked off to drink some water at the fountain, and I
was shot at from the Alameda by somebody hiding
behind a tree. But I drank, and didn't care; with
Barrios in Cayta and the great Cordillera between us
and Montero's victorious army I seemed, notwithstanding Messrs. Gamacho and Fuentes, to hold my
new State in the hollow of my hand. I was ready to
sleep, but when I got as far as the Casa Gould I found
the patio full of wounded laid out on straw. Lights
were burning, and in that enclosed courtyard on that
hot night a faint odour of chloroform and blood hung
about. At one end Doctor Monygham, the doctor of
the mine, was dressing the wounds; at the other, near
the stairs, Father Corbelàn, kneeling, listened to the
confession of a dying Cargador. Mrs. Gould was
walking about through these shambles with a large
bottle in one hand and a lot of cotton wool in the
other. She just looked at me and never even winked.
Her camerista was following her, also holding a bottle,
and sobbing gently to herself.

"I busied myself for some time in fetching water from the cistern for the wounded. Afterwards I wandered upstairs, meeting some of the first ladies of Sulaco, paler than I had ever seen them before, with bandages over their arms. Not all of them had fled to the ships. A good many had taken refuge for the day in the Casa Gould. On the landing a girl, with her hair half down, was kneeling against the wall under the niche where stands a Madonna in blue robes and a gilt crown on her head. I think it was the eldest Miss Lopez; I couldn't see her face, but I remember looking at the high French heel of her little shoe. She did not make a sound, she did not stir, she was not sobbing; she remained there, perfectly still, all black against the white wall, a silent figure of passionate piety. I am sure she was no more frightened than the other white-faced ladies I met carrying bandages. One was sitting on the top step tearing a piece of linen hastily into strips —the young wife of an elderly man of fortune here. She interrupted herself to wave her hand to my bow, as though she were in her carriage on the Alameda. The women of our country are worth looking at during a revolution. The rouge and pearl powder fall off, together with that passive attitude towards the outer world which education, tradition, custom impose upon them from the earliest infancy. I thought of your face, which from your infancy had the stamp of intelligence instead of that patient and resigned cast which appears when some political commotion tears down the veil of cosmetics and usage.

"In the great sala upstairs a sort of Junta of Notables was sitting, the remnant of the vanished Provincial Assembly. Don Juste Lopez had had half his beard singed off at the muzzle of a trabuco loaded with slugs, of which every one missed him, providentially. And as

he turned his head from side to side it was exactly
as if there had been two men inside his frock-coat, one
nobly whiskered and solemn, the other untidy and
scared.

"They raised a cry of 'Decoud! Don Martin!' at
my entrance. I asked them, 'What are you deliberating
upon, gentlemen?' There did not seem to be any
president, though Don José Avellanos sat at the head of
the table. They all answered together, 'On the preservation of life and property.' 'Till the new officials
arrive,' Don Juste explained to me, with the solemn
side of his face offered to my view. It was as if a
stream of water had been poured upon my glowing idea
of a new State. There was a hissing sound in my ears,
and the room grew dim, as if suddenly filled with vapour.

"I walked up to the table blindly, as though I had
been drunk. 'You are deliberating upon surrender,'
I said. They all sat still, with their noses over the
sheet of paper each had before him, God only knows
why. Only Don José hid his face in his hands, muttering, 'Never, never!' But as I looked at him, it
seemed to me that I could have blown him away with
my breath, he looked so frail, so weak, so worn out.
Whatever happens, he will not survive. The deception
is too great for a man of his age; and hasn't he seen the
sheets of 'Fifty Years of Misrule,' which we have begun
printing on the presses of the *Porvenir*, littering the
Plaza, floating in the gutters, fired out as wads for
trabucos loaded with handfuls of type, blown in the
wind, trampled in the mud? I have seen pages floating upon the very waters of the harbour. It would be
unreasonable to expect him to survive. It would be
cruel.

"'Do you know,' I cried, 'what surrender means

to you, to your women, to your children, to your property?'

"I declaimed for five minutes without drawing breath, it seems to me, harping on our best chances, on the ferocity of Montero, whom I made out to be as great a beast as I have no doubt he would like to be if he had intelligence enough to conceive a systematic reign of terror. And then for another five minutes or more I poured out an impassioned appeal to their courage and manliness, with all the passion of my love for Antonia. For if ever man spoke well, it would be from a personal feeling, denouncing an enemy, defending himself, or pleading for what really may be dearer than life. My dear girl, I absolutely thundered at them. It seemed as if my voice would burst the walls asunder, and when I stopped I saw all their scared eyes looking at me dubiously. And that was all the effect I had produced! Only Don José's head had sunk lower and lower on his breast. I bent my ear to his withered lips, and made out his whisper, something like, 'In God's name, then, Martin, my son!' I don't know exactly. There was the name of God in it, I am certain. It seems to me I have caught his last breath—the breath of his departing soul on his lips.

"He lives yet, it is true. I have seen him since; but it was only a senile body, lying on its back, covered to the chin, with open eyes, and so still that you might have said it was breathing no longer. I left him thus, with Antonia kneeling by the side of the bed, just before I came to this Italian's posada, where the ubiquitous death is also waiting. But I know that Don José has really died there, in the Casa Gould, with that whisper urging me to attempt what no doubt his soul, wrapped up in the sanctity of diplomatic treaties and solemn declarations, must have abhorred. I had exclaimed very loud, 'There is never any God in a country where men will not help themselves.'

"Meanwhile, Don Juste had begun a pondered oration whose solemn effect was spoiled by the ridiculous disaster to his beard. I did not wait to make it out. He seemed to argue that Montero's (he called him The General) intentions were probably not evil, though, he went on, 'that distinguished man' (only a week ago we used to call him a *gran' bestia*) 'was perhaps mistaken as to the true means.' As you may imagine, I didn't stay to hear the rest. I know the intentions of Montero's brother, Pedrito, the guerrillero, whom I exposed in Paris, some years ago, in a café frequented by South American students, where he tried to pass himself off for a Secretary of Legation. He used to come in and talk for hours, twisting his felt hat in his hairy paws, and his ambition seemed to become a sort of Duc de Morny to a sort of Napoleon. Already, then, he used to talk of his brother in inflated terms. He seemed fairly safe from being found out, because the students, all of the Blanco families, did not, as you may imagine, frequent the Legation. It was only Decoud, a man without faith and principles, as they used to say, that went in there sometimes for the sake of the fun, as it were to an assembly of trained monkeys. I know his intentions. I have seen him change the plates at table. Whoever is allowed to live on in terror, I must die the death.

"No, I didn't stay to the end to hear Don Juste Lopez trying to persuade himself in a grave oration of the clemency and justice, and honesty, and purity of the brothers Montero. I went out abruptly to seek Antonia. I saw her in the gallery. As I opened the door, she extended to me her clasped hands.

"'What are they doing in there?' she asked.

"'Talking,' I said, with my eyes looking into hers.

"'Yes, yes, but——'

"'Empty speeches,' I interrupted her. 'Hiding their fears behind imbecile hopes. They are all great Parliamentarians there—on the English model, as you know.' I was so furious that I could hardly speak. She made a gesture of despair.

"Through the door I held a little ajar behind me, we heard Don Juste's measured mouthing monotone go on from phrase to phrase, like a sort of awful and solemn madness.

"'After all, the Democratic aspirations have, perhaps, their legitimacy. The ways of human progress are inscrutable, and if the fate of the country is in the hand of Montero, we ought——'

"I crashed the door to on that; it was enough; it was too much. There was never a beautiful face expressing more horror and despair than the face of Antonia. I couldn't bear it; I seized her wrists.

"'Have they killed my father in there?' she asked.

"Her eyes blazed with indignation, but as I looked on, fascinated, the light in them went out.

"'It is a surrender,' I said. And I remember I was shaking her wrists I held apart in my hands. 'But it's more than talk. Your father told me to go on in God's name.'

"My dear girl, there is that in Antonia which would make me believe in the feasibility of anything. One look at her face is enough to set my brain on fire. And yet I love her as any other man would—with the heart, and with that alone. She is more to me than his Church to Father Corbelàn (the Grand Vicar disappeared last night from the town; perhaps gone to join the band or Hernandez). She is more to me than his precious mine to that sentimental Englishman. I won't speak of his wife. She may have been sentimental once. The San Tomé mine stands now between those two people. 'Your father himself, Antonia,' I repeated; 'your father, do you understand? has told me to go on.'

"She averted her face, and in a pained voice—

"'He has?' she cried. 'Then, indeed, I fear he will never speak again.'

"She freed her wrists from my clutch and began to cry in her handkerchief. I disregarded her sorrow; I would rather see her miserable than not see her at all, never any more; for whether I escaped or stayed to die, there was for us no coming together, no future. And that being so, I had no pity to waste upon the passing moments of her sorrow. I sent her off in tears to fetch Doña Emilia and Don Carlos, too. Their sentiment was necessary to the very life of my plan; the sentimentalism of the people that will never do anything for the sake of their passionate desire, unless it comes to them clothed in the fair robes of an idea.

"Late at night we formed a small junta of four—the two women, Don Carlos, and myself—in Mrs. Gould's blue-and-white boudoir.

"El Rey de Sulaco thinks himself, no doubt, a very honest man. And so he is, if one could look behind his taciturnity. Perhaps he thinks that this alone makes his honesty unstained. Those Englishmen live on illusions which somehow or other help them to get a firm hold of the substance. When he speaks it is by a rare 'yes' or 'no' that seems as impersonal as the words of an oracle. But he could not impose on me by his dumb reserve. I knew what he had in his head; he has his mine in his head; and his wife had nothing in her head but his precious person, which he has bound up with the Gould Concession and tied up to that little woman's neck. No matter. The thing was to make

him present the affair to Holroyd (the Steel and Silver
King) in such a manner as to secure his financial support. At that time last night, just twenty-four hours
ago, we thought the silver of the mine safe in the
Custom House vaults till the north-bound steamer
came to take it away. And as long as the treasure
flowed north, without a break, that utter sentimentalist,
Holroyd, would not drop his idea of introducing, not
only justice, industry, peace, to the benighted continents, but also that pet dream of his of a purer form of
Christianity. Later on, the principal European really
in Sulaco, the engineer-in-chief of the railway, came
riding up the Calle, from the harbour, and was admitted
to our conclave. Meantime, the Junta of the Notables
in the great sala was still deliberating; only, one of them
had run out in the corridor to ask the servant whether
something to eat couldn't be sent in. The first words
the engineer-in-chief said as he came into the boudoir
were, 'What is your house, dear Mrs. Gould? A war
hospital below, and apparently a restaurant above. I
saw them carrying trays full of good things into the
sala.'

"'And here, in this boudoir,' I said, 'you behold the
inner cabinet of the Occidental Republic that is to be.'

"He was so preoccupied that he didn't smile at that,
he didn't even look surprised.

"He told us that he was attending to the general
dispositions for the defence of the railway property at
the railway yards when he was sent for to go into the
railway telegraph office. The engineer of the railhead,
at the foot of the mountains, wanted to talk to him from
his end of the wire. There was nobody in the office
but himself and the operator of the railway telegraph,
who read off the clicks aloud as the tape coiled its
length upon the floor. And the purport of that talk,

clicked nervously from a wooden shed in the depths of the forests, had informed the chief that President Ribiera had been, or was being, pursued. This was news, indeed, to all of us in Sulaco. Ribiera himself, when rescued, revived, and soothed by us, had been inclined to think that he had not been pursued.

"Ribiera had yielded to the urgent solicitations of his friends, and had left the headquarters of his discomfited army alone, under the guidance of Bonifacio, the muleteer, who had been willing to take the responsibility with the risk. He had departed at daybreak of the third day. His remaining forces had melted away during the night. Bonifacio and he rode hard on horses towards the Cordillera; then they obtained mules, entered the passes, and crossed the Paramo of Ivie just before a freezing blast swept over that stony plateau, burying in a drift of snow the little shelter-hut of stones in which they had spent the night. Afterwards poor Ribiera had many adventures, got separated from his guide, lost his mount, struggled down to the Campo on foot, and if he had not thrown himself on the mercy of a ranchero would have perished a long way from Sulaco. That man, who, as a matter of fact, recognized him at once, let him have a fresh mule, which the fugitive, heavy and unskilful, had ridden to death. And it was true he had been pursued by a party commanded by no less a person than Pedro Montero, the brother of the general. The cold wind of the Paramo luckily caught the pursuers on the top of the pass. Some few men; and all the animals, perished in the icy blast. The stragglers died, but the main body kept on. They found poor Bonifacio lying half-dead at the foot of a snow slope, and bayoneted him promptly in the true Civil War style. They would have had Ribiera, too, if they had not, for some reason or other, turned off the track of the old Camino Real, only to lose their way in the forests at the foot of the lower slopes. And there they were at last, having stumbled in unexpectedly upon the construction camp. The engineer at the railhead told his chief by wire that he had Pedro Montero absolutely there, in the very office, listening to the clicks. He was going to take possession of Sulaco in the name of the Democracy. He was very overbearing. His men slaughtered some of the Railway Company's cattle without asking leave, and went to work broiling the meat on the embers. Pedrito made many pointed inquiries as to the silver mine, and what had become of the product of the last six months' working. He had said peremptorily, "Ask your chief up there by wire, he ought to know; tell him that Don Pedro Montero, Chief of the Campo and Minister of the Interior of the new Government, desires to be correctly informed.'

"He had his feet wrapped up in blood-stained rags, a lean, haggard face, ragged beard and hair, and had walked in limping, with a crooked branch of a tree for a staff. His followers were perhaps in a worse plight, but apparently they had not thrown away their arms, and, at any rate, not all their ammunition. Their lean faces filled the door and the windows of the telegraph hut. As it was at the same time the bedroom of the engineer-in-charge there, Montero had thrown himself on his clean blankets and lay there shivering and dictating requisitions to be transmitted by wire to Sulaco. He demanded a train of cars to be sent down at once to transport his men up.

"'To this I answered from my end,' the engineer-in-chief related to us, 'that I dared not risk the rolling-stock in the interior, as there had been attempts to wreck trains all along the line several times. I did that for your sake, Gould,' said the chief engineer. 'The answer to this was, in the words of my subordinate, "The filthy brute on my bed said, 'Suppose I were to have you shot?'" To which my subordinate, who, it appears, was himself operating, remarked that it would not bring the cars up. Upon that, the other, yawning, said, "Never mind, there is no lack of horses on the Campo." And, turning over, went to sleep on Harris's bed.'

"This is why, my dear girl, I am a fugitive to-night. The last wire from railhead says that Pedro Montero and his men left at daybreak, after feeding on asado beef all night. They took all the horses; they will find more on the road; they'll be here in less than thirty hours, and thus Sulaco is no place either for me or the great store of silver belonging to the Gould Concession.

"But that is not the worst. The garrison of Esmeralda has gone over to the victorious party. We have heard this by means of the telegraphist of the Cable Company, who came to the Casa Gould in the early morning with the news. In fact, it was so early that the day had not yet quite broken over Sulaco. His colleague in Esmeralda had called him up to say that the garrison, after shooting some of their officers, had taken possession of a Government steamer laid up in the harbour. It is really a heavy blow for me. I thought I could depend on every man in this province. It was a mistake. It was a Monterist Revolution in Esmeralda, just such as was attempted in Sulaco, only that *that* one came off. The telegraphist was signalling to Bernhardt all the time, and his last transmitted words were, 'They are bursting in the door, and taking possession of the cable office. You are cut off. Can do no more.'

"But, as a matter of fact, he managed somehow to

escape the vigilance of his captors, who had tried to stop the communication with the outer world. He did manage it. How it was done I don't know, but a few hours afterwards he called up Sulaco again, and what he said was, 'The insurgent army has taken possession of the Government transport in the bay and are filling her with troops, with the intention of going round the coast to Sulaco. Therefore look out for yourselves. They will be ready to start in a few hours, and may be upon you before daybreak.'

"This is all he could say. They drove him away from his instrument this time for good, because Bernhardt has been calling up Esmeralda ever since without getting an answer."

After setting these words down in the pocket-book which he was filling up for the benefit of his sister, Decoud lifted his head to listen. But there were no sounds, neither in the room nor in the house, except the drip of the water from the filter into the vast earthenware jar under the wooden stand. And outside the house there was a great silence. Decoud lowered his head again over the pocket-book.

"I am not running away, you understand," he wrote on. "I am simply going away with that great treasure of silver which must be saved at all costs. Pedro Montero from the Campo and the revolted garrison of Esmeralda from the sea are converging upon it. That it is there lying ready for them is only an accident. The real objective is the San Tomé mine itself, as you may well imagine; otherwise the Occidental Province would have been, no doubt, left alone for many weeks, to be gathered at leisure into the arms of the victorious party. Don Carlos Gould will have enough to do to save his mine, with its organization and its people; this 'Imperium in Imperio,' this wealth-producing thing, to which his sentimentalism attaches a strange idea of justice. He holds to it as some men hold to the idea of love or revenge. Unless I am much mistaken in the man, it must remain inviolate or perish by an act of his will alone. A passion has crept into his cold and idealistic life. A passion which I can only comprehend intellectually. A passion that is not like the passions we know, we men of another blood. But it is as dangerous as any of ours.

"His wife has understood it, too. That is why she is such a good ally of mine. She seizes upon all my suggestions with a sure instinct that in the end they make for the safety of the Gould Concession. And he defers to her because he trusts her perhaps, but I fancy more rather as if he wished to make up for some subtle wrong, for that sentimental unfaithfulness which surrenders her happiness, her life, to the seduction of an idea. The little woman has discovered that he lives for the mine rather than for her. But let them be. To each his fate, shaped by passion or sentiment. The principal thing is that she has backed up my advice to get the silver out of the town, out of the country, at once, at any cost, at any risk. Don Carlos' mission is to preserve unstained the fair fame of his mine; Mrs. Gould's mission is to save him from the effects of that cold and overmastering passion, which she dreads more than if it were an infatuation for another woman. Nostromo's mission is to save the silver. The plan is to load it into the largest of the Company's lighters, and send it across the gulf to a small port out of Costaguana territory just on the other side the Azuera, where the first north-bound steamer will get orders to pick it up. The waters here are calm. We shall slip away into the darkness of the gulf before the Esmeralda rebels arrive ιd by the time the day breaks over the ocean we shall be

out of sight, invisible, hidden by Azuera, which itself
looks from the Sulaco shore like a faint blue cloud on the
horizon.

"The incorruptible Capataz de Cargadores is the man
for that work; and I, the man with a passion, but without a mission, I go with him to return—to play my part
in the farce to the end, and, if successful, to receive my
reward, which no one but Antonia can give me.

"I shall not see her again now before I depart. I
left her, as I have said, by Don José's bedside. The
street was dark, the houses shut up, and I walked out
of the town in the night. Not a single street-lamp had
been lit for two days, and the archway of the gate was
only a mass of darkness in the vague form of a tower, in
which I heard low, dismal groans, that seemed to answer
the murmurs of a man's voice.

"I recognized something impassive and careless in its
tone, characteristic of that Genoese sailor who, like me,
has come casually here to be drawn into the events for
which his scepticism as well as mine seems to entertain
a sort of passive contempt. The only thing he seems to
care for, as far as I have been able to discover, is to be
well spoken of. An ambition fit for noble souls, but
also a profitable one for an exceptionally intelligent
scoundrel. Yes. His very words, 'To be well spoken
of. Si, señor.' He does not seem to make any difference between speaking and thinking. Is it sheer
naïveness or the practical point of view, I wonder?
Exceptional individualities always interest me, because
they are true to the general formula expressing the
moral state of humanity.

"He joined me on the harbour road after I had
passed them under the dark archway without stopping.
It was a woman in trouble he had been talking to.
Through discretion I kept silent while he walked by my

side. After a time he began to talk himself. It was
not what I expected. It was only an old woman, an
old lace-maker, in search of her son, one of the street-
sweepers employed by the municipality. Friends had
come the day before at daybreak to the door of their
hovel calling him out. He had gone with them, and
she had not seen him since; so she had left the food she
had been preparing half-cooked on the extinct embers
and had crawled out as far as the harbour, where she
had heard that some town mozos had been killed on the
morning of the riot. One of the Cargadores guarding
the Custom House had brought out a lantern, and had
helped her to look at the few dead left lying about there.
Now she was creeping back, having failed in her search.
So she sat down on the stone seat under the arch, moaning, because she was very tired. The Capataz had
questioned her, and after hearing her broken and groaning tale had advised her to go and look amongst the
wounded in the patio of the Casa Gould. He had also
given her a quarter dollar, he mentioned carelessly.

"'Why did you do that?' I asked. 'Do you know
her?'

"'No, señor. I don't suppose I have ever seen her
before. How should I? She has not probably been
out in the streets for years. She is one of those old
women that you find in this country at the back of huts,
crouching over fireplaces, with a stick on the ground by
their side, and almost too feeble to drive away the
stray dogs from their cooking-pots. Caramba! I
could tell by her voice that death had forgotten her.
But, old or young, they like money, and will speak well
of the man who gives it to them.' He laughed a little.
'Señor, you should have felt the clutch of her paw as I
put the piece in her palm.' He paused. 'My last, too,'
he added.

"I made no comment. He's known for his liberality and his bad luck at the game of monte, which keeps him as poor as when he first came here.

"'I suppose, Don Martin,' he began, in a thoughtful, speculative tone, 'that the Señor Administrador of San Tomé will reward me some day if I save his silver?'

"I said that it could not be otherwise, surely. He walked on, muttering to himself. 'Si, si, without doubt, without doubt; and, look you, Señor Martin, what it is to be well spoken of! There is not another man that could have been even thought of for such a thing. I shall get something great for it some day. And let it come soon,' he mumbled. 'Time passes in this country as quick as anywhere else.'

"This, *sœur chérie*,* is my companion in the great escape for the sake of the great cause. He is more naïve than shrewd, more masterful than crafty, more generous with his personality than the people who make use of him are with their money. At least, that is what he thinks himself with more pride than sentiment. I am glad I have made friends with him. As a companion he acquires more importance than he ever had as a sort of minor genius in his way—as an original Italian sailor whom I allowed to come in in the small hours and talk familiarly to the editor of the *Porvenir* while the paper was going through the press. And it is curious to have met a man for whom the value of life seems to consist in personal prestige.

"I am waiting for him here now. On arriving at the posada kept by Viola we found the children alone down below, and the old Genoese shouted to his countryman to go and fetch the doctor. Otherwise we would have gone on to the wharf, where it appears Captain Mitchell with some volunteer Europeans and a few picked Cargadores are loading the lighter with the silver that must be saved from Montero's clutches in order to be used for Montero's defeat. Nostromo galloped furiously back towards the town. He has been long gone already. This delay gives me time to talk to you. By the time this pocket-book reaches your hands much will have happened. But now it is a pause under the hovering wing of death in that silent house buried in the black night, with this dying woman, the two children crouching without a sound, and that old man whom I can hear through the thickness of the wall passing up and down with a light rubbing noise no louder than a mouse. And I, the only other with them, don't really know whether to count myself with the living or with the dead. 'Quien sabe?' as the people here are prone to say in answer to every question. But no! feeling for you is certainly not dead, and the whole thing, the house, the dark night, the silent children in this dim room, my very presence here—all this is life, must be life, since it is so much like a dream."

With the writing of the last line there came upon Decoud a moment of sudden and complete oblivion. He swayed over the table as if struck by a bullet. The next moment he sat up, confused, with the idea that he had heard his pencil roll on the floor. The low door of the café, wide open, was filled with the glare of a torch in which was visible half of a horse, switching its tail against the leg of a rider with a long iron spur strapped to the naked heel. The two girls were gone, and Nostromo, standing in the middle of the room, looked at him from under the round brim of the sombrero low down over his brow.

"I have brought that sour-faced English doctor in Señora Gould's carriage," said Nostromo. "I doubt if, with all his wisdom, he can save the Padrona this time. They have sent for the children. A bad sign that."

He sat down on the end of a bench. "She wants to give them her blessing, I suppose."

Dazedly Decoud observed that he must have fallen sound asleep, and Nostromo said, with a vague smile, that he had looked in at the window and had seen him lying still across the table with his head on his arms. The English señora had also come in the carriage, and went upstairs at once with the doctor. She had told him not to wake up Don Martin yet; but when they sent for the children he had come into the café.

The half of the horse with its half of the rider swung round outside the door; the torch of tow and resin in the iron basket which was carried on a stick at the saddle-bow flared right into the room for a moment, and Mrs. Gould entered hastily with a very white, tired face. The hood of her dark, blue cloak had fallen back. Both men rose.

"Teresa wants to see you, Nostromo," she said.

The Capataz did not move. Decoud, with his back to the table, began to button up his coat.

"The silver, Mrs. Gould, the silver," he murmured in English. "Don't forget that the Esmeralda garrison have got a steamer. They may appear at any moment at the harbour entrance."

"The doctor says there is no hope," Mrs. Gould spoke rapidly, also in English. "I shall take you down to the wharf in my carriage and then come back to fetch away the girls." She changed swiftly into Spanish to address Nostromo. "Why are you wasting time? Old Giorgio's wife wishes to see you."

"I am going to her, señora," muttered the Capataz.

Dr. Monygham now showed himself, bringing back the children. To Mrs. Gould's inquiring glance he only shook his head and went outside at once, followed by Nostromo.

The horse of the torch-bearer, motionless, hung his head low, and the rider had dropped the reins to light a cigarette. The glare of the torch played on the front of the house crossed by the big black letters of its inscription in which only the word ITALIA was lighted fully. The patch of wavering glare reached as far as Mrs. Gould's carriage waiting on the road, with the yellow-faced, portly Ignacio apparently dozing on the box. By his side Basilio, dark and skinny, held a Winchester carbine in front of him, with both hands, and peered fearfully into the darkness. Nostromo touched lightly the doctor's shoulder.

"Is she really dying, señor doctor?"

"Yes," said the doctor, with a strange twitch of his scarred cheek. "And why she wants to see you I cannot imagine."

"She has been like that before," suggested Nostromo, looking away.

"Well, Capataz, I can assure you she will never be like that again," snarled Dr. Monygham. "You may go to her or stay away. There is very little to be got from talking to the dying. But she told Doña Emilia in my hearing that she has been like a mother to you ever since you first set foot ashore here."

"Si! And she never had a good word to say for me to anybody. It is more as if she could not forgive me for being alive, and such a man, too, as she would have liked her son to be."

"Maybe!" exclaimed a mournful deep voice near them. "Women have their own ways of tormenting themselves." Giorgio Viola had come out of the house. He threw a heavy black shadow in the torchlight, and the glare fell on his big face, on the great bushy head of white hair. He motioned the Capataz indoors with his extended arm.

Dr. Monygham, after busying himself with a little medicament box of polished wood on the seat of the landau, turned to old Giorgio and thrust into his big, trembling hand one of the glass-stoppered bottles out of the case.

"Give her a spoonful of this now and then, in water," he said. "It will make her easier."

"And there is nothing more for her?" asked the old man, patiently.

"No. Not on earth," said the doctor, with his back to him, clicking the lock of the medicine case.

Nostromo slowly crossed the large kitchen, all dark but for the glow of a heap of charcoal under the heavy mantel of the cooking-range, where water was boiling in an iron pot with a loud bubbling sound. Between the two walls of a narrow staircase a bright light streamed from the sick-room above; and the magnificent Capataz de Cargadores stepping noiselessly in soft leather sandals, bushy whiskered, his muscular neck and bronzed chest bare in the open check shirt, resembled a Mediterranean sailor just come ashore from some wine or fruit-laden felucca. At the top he paused, broad shouldered, narrow hipped and supple, looking at the large bed, like a white couch of state, with a profusion of snowy linen, amongst which the Padrona sat unpropped and bowed, her handsome, black-browed face bent over her chest. A mass of raven hair with only a few white threads in it covered her shoulders; one thick strand fallen forward half veiled her cheek. Perfectly motionless in that pose, expressing physical anxiety and unrest, she turned her eyes alone towards Nostromo.

The Capataz had a red sash wound many times round his waist, and a heavy silver ring on the forefinger of the hand he raised to give a twist to his moustache.

"Their revolutions, their revolutions," gasped Señora Teresa. "Look, Gian' Battista, it has killed me at last!"

Nostromo said nothing, and the sick woman with an upward glance insisted. "Look, this one has killed me, while you were away fighting for what did not concern you, foolish man."

"Why talk like this?" mumbled the Capataz between his teeth. "Will you never believe in my good sense? It concerns me to keep on being what I am: every day alike."

"You never change, indeed," she said, bitterly. "Always thinking of yourself and taking your pay out in fine words from those who care nothing for you."

There was between them an intimacy of antagonism as close in its way as the intimacy of accord and affection. He had not walked along the way of Teresa's expectations. It was she who had encouraged him to leave his ship, in the hope of securing a friend and defender for the girls. The wife of old Giorgio was aware of her precarious health, and was haunted by the fear of her aged husband's loneliness and the unprotected state of the children. She had wanted to annex that apparently quiet and steady young man, affectionate and pliable, an orphan from his tenderest age, as he had told her, with no ties in Italy except an uncle, owner and master of a felucca, from whose ill-usage he had run away before he was fourteen. He had seemed to her courageous, a hard worker, determined to make his way in the world. From gratitude and the ties of habit he would become like a son to herself and Giorgio; and then, who knows, when Linda had grown up. . . . Ten years' difference between husband and wife was not so much. Her own great man was nearly twenty years older than herself. Gian' Battista was an attractive young fellow, besides; attractive to men, women, and children, just by that profound quietness of personality which, like a serene twilight, rendered more seductive the promise of his vigorous form and the resolution of his conduct.

Old Giorgio, in profound ignorance of his wife's views and hopes, had a great regard for his young countryman. "A man ought not to be tame," he used to tell her, quoting the Spanish proverb in defence of the splendid Capataz. She was growing jealous of his success. He was escaping from her, she feared. She was practical, and he seemed to her to be an absurd spendthrift of these qualities which made him so valuable. He got too little for them. He scattered them with both hands amongst too many people, she thought. He laid no money by. She railed at his poverty, his exploits, his adventures, his loves and his reputation; but in her heart she had never given him up, as though, indeed, he had been her son.

Even now, ill as she was, ill enough to feel the chill, black breath of the approaching end, she had wished to see him. It was like putting out her benumbed hand to regain her hold. But she had presumed too much on her strength. She could not command her thoughts; they had become dim, like her vision. The words faltered on her lips, and only the paramount anxiety and desire of her life seemed to be too strong for death.

The Capataz said, "I have heard these things many times. You are unjust, but it does not hurt me. Only now you do not seem to have much strength to talk, and I have but little time to listen. I am engaged in a work of very great moment."

She made an effort to ask him whether it was true that he had found time to go and fetch a doctor for her. Nostromo nodded affirmatively.

She was pleased: it relieved her sufferings to know that the man had condescended to do so much for those who really wanted his help. It was a proof of his friendship. Her voice became stronger.

"I want a priest more than a doctor," she said, pathetically. She did not move her head; only her eyes ran into the corners to watch the Capataz standing by the side of her bed. "Would you go to fetch a priest for me now? Think! A dying woman asks you!"

Nostromo shook his head resolutely. He did not believe in priests in their sacerdotal character. A doctor was an efficacious person; but a priest, as priest, was nothing, incapable of doing either good or harm. Nostromo did not even dislike the sight of them as old Giorgio did. The utter uselessness of the errand was what struck him most.

"Padrona," he said, "you have been like this before, and got better after a few days. I have given you already the very last moments I can spare. Ask Señora Gould to send you one."

He was feeling uneasy at the impiety of this refusal. The Padrona believed in priests, and confessed herself to them. But all women did that. It could not be of much consequence. And yet his heart felt oppressed for a moment—at the thought what absolution would mean to her if she believed in it only ever so little. No matter. It was quite true that he had given her already the very last moment he could spare.

"You refuse to go?" she gasped. "Ah! you are always yourself, indeed."

"Listen to reason, Padrona," he said. "I am needed to save the silver of the mine. Do you hear? A greater treasure than the one which they say is guarded by ghosts and devils in Azuera. It is true. I am re-

solved to make this the most desperate affair I was
ever engaged on in my whole life."

She felt a despairing indignation. The supreme test
had failed. Standing above her, Nostromo did not
see the distorted features of her face, distorted by a
paroxysm of pain and anger. Only she began to
tremble all over. Her bowed head shook. The broad
shoulders quivered.

"Then God, perhaps, will have mercy upon me!
But do you look to it, man, that you get something for
yourself out of it, besides the remorse that shall over-
take you some day."

She laughed feebly. "Get riches at least for once,
you indispensable, admired Gian' Battista, to whom
the peace of a dying woman is less than the praise of
people who have given you a silly name—and nothing
besides—in exchange for your soul and body."

The Capataz de Cargadores swore to himself under
his breath.

"Leave my soul alone, Padrona, and I shall know
how to take care of my body. Where is the harm of
people having need of me? What are you envying me
that I have robbed you and the children of? Those
very people you are throwing in my teeth have done
more for old Giorgio than they ever thought of doing
for me."

He struck his breast with his open palm; his
voice had remained low though he had spoken in a
forcible tone. He twisted his moustaches one after
another, and his eyes wandered a little about the
room.

"Is it my fault that I am the only man for their purposes? What angry nonsense are you talking, mother?
Would you rather have me timid and foolish, selling
water-melons on the market-place or rowing a boat for

passengers along the harbour, like a soft Neapolitan without courage or reputation? Would you have a young man live like a monk? I do not believe it. Would you want a monk for your eldest girl? Let her grow. What are you afraid of? You have been angry with me for everything I did for years; ever since you first spoke to me, in secret from old Giorgio, about your Linda. Husband to one and brother to the other, did you say? Well, why not! I like the little ones, and a man must marry some time. But ever since that time you have been making little of me to everyone. Why? Did you think you could put a collar and chain on me as if I were one of the watch-dogs they keep over there in the railway yards? Look here, Padrona, I am the same man who came ashore one evening and sat down in the thatched ranche you lived in at that time on the other side of the town and told you all about himself. You were not unjust to me then. What has happened since? I am no longer an insignificant youth. A good name, Giorgio says, is a treasure, Padrona."

"They have turned your head with their praises," gasped the sick woman. "They have been paying you with words. Your folly shall betray you into poverty, misery, starvation. The very leperos shall laugh at you—the great Capataz."

Nostromo stood for a time as if struck dumb. She never looked at him. A self-confident, mirthless smile passed quickly from his lips, and then he backed away. His disregarded figure sank down beyond the doorway. He descended the stairs backwards, with the usual sense of having been somehow baffled by this woman's disparagement of this reputation he had obtained and desired to keep.

Downstairs in the big kitchen a candle was burning, surrounded by the shadows of the walls, of the ceiling,

but no ruddy glare filled the open square of the outer
door. The carriage with Mrs. Gould and Don Martin,
preceded by the horseman bearing the torch, had gone
on to the jetty. Dr. Monygham, who had remained,
sat on the corner of a hard wood table near the candlestick, his seamed, shaven face inclined sideways, his
arms crossed on his breast, his lips pursed up, and his
prominent eyes glaring stonily upon the floor of black
earth. Near the overhanging mantel of the fireplace,
where the pot of water was still boiling violently, old
Giorgio held his chin in his hand, one foot advanced, as
if arrested by a sudden thought.

"*Adios, viejo,*" said Nostromo, feeling the handle of
his revolver in the belt and loosening his knife in its
sheath. He picked up a blue poncho lined with red
from the table, and put it over his head. "Adios, look
after the things in my sleeping-room, and if you hear
from me no more, give up the box to Paquita. There
is not much of value there, except my new serape from
Mexico, and a few silver buttons on my best jacket.
No matter! The things will look well enough on the
next lover she gets, and the man need not be afraid I
shall linger on earth after I am dead, like those Gringos
that haunt the Azuera."

Dr. Monygham twisted his lips into a bitter smile.
After old Giorgio, with an almost imperceptible nod and
without a word, had gone up the narrow stairs, he
said—

"Why, Capataz! I thought you could never fail in
anything."

Nostromo, glancing contemptuously at the doctor,
lingered in the doorway rolling a cigarette, then struck a
match, and, after lighting it, held the burning piece of
wood above his head till the flame nearly touched his
fingers.

"No wind!" he muttered to himself. "Look here, señor—do you know the nature of my undertaking?"

Dr. Monygham nodded sourly.

"It is as if I were taking up a curse upon me, señor doctor. A man with a treasure on this coast will have every knife raised against him in every place upon the shore. You see that, señor doctor? I shall float along with a spell upon my life till I meet somewhere the north-bound steamer of the Company, and then indeed they will talk about the Capataz of the Sulaco Cargadores from one end of America to another."

Dr. Monygham laughed his short, throaty laugh. Nostromo turned round in the doorway.

"But if your worship can find any other man ready and fit for such business I will stand back. I am not exactly tired of my life, though I am so poor that I can carry all I have with myself on my horse's back."

"You gamble too much, and never say 'no' to a pretty face, Capataz," said Dr. Monygham, with sly simplicity. "That's not the way to make a fortune. But nobody that I know ever suspected you of being poor. I hope you have made a good bargain in case you come back safe from this adventure."

"What bargain would your worship have made?" asked Nostromo, blowing the smoke out of his lips through the doorway.

Dr. Monygham listened up the staircase for a moment before he answered, with another of his short, abrupt laughs—

"Illustrious Capataz, for taking the curse of death upon my back, as you call it, nothing else but the whole treasure would do."

Nostromo vanished out of the doorway with a grunt of discontent at this jeering answer. Dr. Monygham heard him gallop away. Nostromo rode furiously in

the dark. There were lights in the buildings of the
O.S.N. Company near the wharf, but before he got
there he met the Gould carriage. The horseman preceded it with the torch, whose light showed the white
mules trotting, the portly Ignacio driving, and Basilio
with the carbine on the box. From the dark body of
the landau Mrs. Gould's voice cried, "They are waiting
for you, Capataz!" She was returning, chilly and excited, with Decoud's pocket-book still held in her hand.
He had confided it to her to send to his sister. "Perhaps my last words to her," he had said, pressing Mrs.
Gould's hand.

The Capataz never checked his speed. At the head
of the wharf vague figures with rifles leapt to the head of
his horse; others closed upon him—cargadores of the
company posted by Captain Mitchell on the watch. At
a word from him they fell back with subservient murmurs, recognizing his voice. At the other end of the
jetty, near a cargo crane, in a dark group with glowing
cigars, his name was pronounced in a tone of relief.
Most of the Europeans in Sulaco were there, rallied
round Charles Gould, as if the silver of the mine had
been the emblem of a common cause, the symbol of the
supreme importance of material interests. They had
loaded it into the lighter with their own hands. Nostromo recognized Don Carlos Gould, a thin, tall shape,
standing a little apart and silent, to whom another tall
shape, the engineer-in-chief, said aloud, "If it must be
lost, it is a million times better that it should go to the
bottom of the sea."

Martin Decoud called out from the lighter, "Au
revoir, messieurs, till we clasp hands again over the
new-born Occidental Republic." Only a subdued murmur responded to his clear, ringing tones; and then it
seemed to him that the wharf was floating away into the

night; but it was Nostromo, who was already pushing against a pile with one of the heavy sweeps. Decoud did not move; the effect was that of being launched into space. After a splash or two there was not a sound but the thud of Nostromo's feet leaping about the boat. He hoisted the big sail; a breath of wind fanned Decoud's cheek. Everything had vanished but the light of the lantern Captain Mitchell had hoisted upon the post at the end of the jetty to guide Nostromo out of the harbour.

The two men, unable to see each other, kept silent till the lighter, slipping before the fitful breeze, passed out between almost invisible headlands into the still deeper darkness of the gulf. For a time the lantern on the jetty shone after them. The wind failed, then fanned up again, but so faintly that the big, half-decked boat slipped along with no more noise than if she had been suspended in the air.

"We are out in the gulf now," said the calm voice of Nostromo. A moment after he added, "Señor Mitchell has lowered the light."

"Yes," said Decoud; "nobody can find us now."

A great recrudescence* of obscurity embraced the boat. The sea in the gulf was as black as the clouds above. Nostromo, after striking a couple of matches to get a glimpse of the boat-compass he had with him in the lighter, steered by the feel of the wind on his cheek.

It was a new experience for Decoud, this mysteriousness of the great waters spread out strangely smooth, as if their restlessness had been crushed by the weight of that dense night. The Placido was sleeping profoundly under its black poncho.

The main thing now for success was to get away from the coast and gain the middle of the gulf before day broke. The Isabels were somewhere at hand. "On your left as you look forward, señor," said Nostromo, suddenly. When his voice ceased, the enormous stillness, without light or sound, seemed to affect Decoud's senses like a powerful drug. He didn't even know at times whether he were asleep or awake. Like a man lost in slumber, he heard nothing, he saw nothing. Even his hand held before his face did not exist for his eyes. The change from the agitation, the passions and the dangers, from the sights and sounds of the shore, was so complete that it would have resembled death had it not been for the survival of his thoughts. In this foretaste of eternal peace they floated vivid and light, like unearthly clear dreams of earthly things that may haunt the souls freed by death from the misty atmosphere of regrets and hopes. Decoud shook himself, shuddered a bit, though the air that drifted past him was warm. He had the strangest sensation of his soul having just returned into his body from the circumambient darkness in which land, sea, sky, the mountains, and the rocks were as if they had not been.

Nostromo's voice was speaking, though he, at the tiller, was also as if he were not. "Have you been asleep, Don Martin? *Caramba*! If it were possible I would think that I, too, have dozed off. I have a strange notion somehow of having dreamt that there was a sound of blubbering, a sound a sorrowing man could make, somewhere near this boat. Something between a sigh and a sob."

"Strange!" muttered Decoud, stretched upon the pile of treasure boxes covered by many tarpaulins. "Could it be that there is another boat near us in the gulf? We could not see it, you know."

Nostromo laughed a little at the absurdity of the idea. They dismissed it from their minds. The solitude could almost be felt. And when the breeze ceased, the blackness seemed to weigh upon Decoud like a stone.

"This is overpowering," he muttered. "Do we move at all, Capataz?"

"Not so fast as a crawling beetle tangled in the grass," answered Nostromo, and his voice seemed deadened by the thick veil of obscurity that felt warm and hopeless all about them. There were long periods when he made no sound, invisible and inaudible as if he had mysteriously stepped out of the lighter.

In the featureless night Nostromo was not even certain which way the lighter headed after the wind had completely died out. He peered for the islands. There was not a hint of them to be seen, as if they had sunk to the bottom of the gulf. He threw himself down by the side of Decoud at last, and whispered into his ear that if daylight caught them near the Sulaco shore through want of wind, it would be possible to sweep the lighter behind the cliff at the high end of the Great Isabel, where she would lie concealed. Decoud was surprised at the grimness of his anxiety. To him the removal of the treasure was a political move. It was necessary for several reasons that it should not fall into the hands of Montero, but here was a man who took another view of this enterprise. The Caballeros over there did not seem to have the slightest idea of what they had given him to do. Nostromo, as if affected by the gloom around, seemed nervously resentful. Decoud was surprised. The Capataz, indifferent to those dangers that seemed obvious to his companion, allowed himself to become scornfully exasperated by the deadly nature of the trust put, as a matter of course, into his hands. It was more dangerous, Nostromo said, with a laugh and a curse, than sending a man to get the treasure that people said was guarded by devils and ghosts in the deep ravines of Azuera. "Señor," he said, "we must catch the steamer at sea. We must keep out in the open looking for her till we have eaten and drunk all that has been put on board here. And if we miss her by some mischance, we must keep away from the land till we grow weak, and perhaps mad, and die, and drift dead, until one or another of the steamers of the Compania comes upon the boat with the two dead men who have saved the treasure. That, señor, is the only way to save it; for, don't you see? for us to come to the land anywhere in a hundred miles along this coast with this silver in our possession is to run the naked breast against the point of a knife. This thing has been given to me like a deadly disease. If men discover it I am dead, and you, too, señor, since you would come with me. There is enough silver to make a whole province rich, let alone a seaboard pueblo inhabited by thieves and vagabonds. Señor, they would think that heaven itself sent these riches into their hands, and would cut our throats without hesitation. I would trust no fair words from the best man around the shores of this wild gulf. Reflect that, even by giving up the treasure at the first demand, we would not be able to save our lives. Do you understand this, or must I explain?"

"No, you needn't explain," said Decoud, a little listlessly. "I can see it well enough myself, that the possession of this treasure is very much like a deadly disease for men situated as we are. But it had to be removed from Sulaco, and you were the man for the task."

"I was; but I cannot believe," said Nostromo, "that its loss would have impoverished Don Carlos Gould very much. There is more wealth in the mountain. I have heard it rolling down the shoots on quiet nights when I used to ride to Rincon to see a certain girl, after my work at the harbour was done. For years the rich rocks have been pouring down with a noise like thunder, and the miners say that there is enough at the heart of the mountain to thunder on for years and years to come. And yet, the day before yesterday, we have been fighting to save it from the mob, and to-night I am sent out with it into this darkness, where there is no wind to get away with; as if it were the last lot of silver on earth to get bread for the hungry with. Ha! ha! Well, I am going to make it the most famous and desperate affair of my life—wind or no wind. It shall be talked about when the little children are grown up and the grown men are old. Aha! the Monterists must not get hold of it, I am told, whatever happens to Nostromo the Capataz; and they shall not have it, I tell you, since it has been tied for safety round Nostromo's neck."

"I see it," murmured Decoud. He saw, indeed, that his companion had his own peculiar view of this enterprise.

Nostromo interrupted his reflections upon the way men's qualities are made use of, without any fundamental knowledge of their nature, by the proposal they should slip the long oars out and sweep the lighter in the direction of the Isabels. It wouldn't do for daylight to reveal the treasure floating within a mile or so of the harbour entrance. The denser the darkness generally, the smarter were the puffs of wind on which he had reckoned to make his way; but to-night the gulf, under its poncho of clouds, remained breathless, as if dead rather than asleep.

Don Martin's soft hands suffered cruelly, tugging at the thick handle of the enormous oar. He stuck to it manfully, setting his teeth. He, too, was in the toils of an imaginative existence, and that strange work of pulling a lighter seemed to belong naturally to the

inception of a new state, acquired an ideal meaning
from his love for Antonia. For all their efforts, the
heavily laden lighter hardly moved. Nostromo could
be heard swearing to himself between the regular
splashes of the sweeps. "We are making a crooked
path," he muttered to himself. "I wish I could see the
islands."

In his unskilfulness Don Martin over-exerted himself.
Now and then a sort of muscular faintness would run
from the tips of his aching fingers through every fibre
of his body, and pass off in a flush of heat. He had
fought, talked, suffered mentally and physically,
exerting his mind and body for the last forty-eight hours
without intermission. He had had no rest, very little
food, no pause in the stress of his thoughts and his
feelings. Even his love for Antonia, whence he drew
his strength and his inspiration, had reached the point
of tragic tension during their hurried interview by Don
José's bedside. And now, suddenly, he was thrown
out of all this into a dark gulf, whose very gloom, silence, and breathless peace added a torment to the
necessity for physical exertion. He imagined the
lighter sinking to the bottom with an extraordinary
shudder of delight. "I am on the verge of delirium,"
he thought. He mastered the trembling of all his
limbs, of his breast, the inward trembling of all his
body exhausted of its nervous force.

"Shall we rest, Capataz?" he proposed in a careless
tone. "There are many hours of night yet before us."

"True. It is but a mile or so, I suppose. Rest your
arms, señor, if that is what you mean. You will find
no other sort of rest, I can promise you, since you let
yourself be bound to this treasure whose loss would
make no poor man poorer. No, señor; there is no rest
till we find a north-bound steamer, or else some ship

finds us drifting about stretched out dead upon the
Englishman's silver. Or rather—no; *por Dios!* I shall
cut down the gunwale with the axe right to the water's
edge before thirst and hunger rob me of my strength.
By all the saints and devils I shall let the sea have the
treasure rather than give it up to any stranger. Since
it was the good pleasure of the Caballeros to send me off
on such an errand, they shall learn I am just the man
they take me for."

Decoud lay on the silver boxes panting. All his
active sensations and feelings from as far back as he
could remember seemed to him the maddest of dreams.
Even his passionate devotion to Antonia into which he
had worked himself up out of the depths of his scepticism had lost all appearance of reality. For a moment
he was the prey of an extremely languid but not unpleasant indifference.

"I am sure they didn't mean you to take such a
desperate view of this affair," he said.

"What was it, then? A joke?" snarled the man, who
on the pay-sheets of the O.S.N. Company's establishment in Sulaco was described as "Foreman of the
wharf" against the figure of his wages. "Was it for a
joke they woke me up from my sleep after two days of
street fighting to make me stake my life upon a bad
card? Everybody knows, too, that I am not a lucky
gambler."

"Yes, everybody knows of your good luck with
women, Capataz," Decoud propitiated his companion
in a weary drawl.

"Look here, señor," Nostromo went on. "I never
even remonstrated about this affair. Directly I heard
what was wanted I saw what a desperate affair it must
be, and I made up my mind to see it out. Every
minute was of importance. I had to wait for you first.

Then, when we arrived at the Italia Una, old Giorgio shouted to me to go for the English doctor. Later on, that poor dying woman wanted to see me, as you know. Señor, I was reluctant to go. I felt already this cursed silver growing heavy upon my back, and I was afraid that, knowing herself to be dying, she would ask me to ride off again for a priest. Father Corbelàn, who is fearless, would have come at a word; but Father Corbelàn is far away, safe with the band of Hernandez, and the populace, that would have liked to tear him to pieces, are much incensed against the priests. Not a single fat padre would have consented to put his head out of his hiding-place to-night to save a Christian soul, except, perhaps, under my protection. That was in her mind. I pretended I did not believe she was going to die. Señor, I refused to fetch a priest for a dying woman . . ."

Decoud was heard to stir.

"You did, Capataz!" he exclaimed. His tone changed. "Well, you know—it was rather fine."

"You do not believe in priests, Don Martin? Neither do I. What was the use of wasting time? But she—she believes in them. The thing sticks in my throat. She may be dead already, and here we are floating helpless with no wind at all. Curse on all superstition. She died thinking I deprived her of Paradise, I suppose. It shall be the most desperate affair of my life."

Decoud remained lost in reflection. He tried to analyze the sensations awaked by what he had been told. The voice of the Capataz was heard again:

"Now, Don Martin, let us take up the sweeps and try to find the Isabels. It is either that or sinking the lighter if the day overtakes us. We must not forget that the steamer from Esmeralda with the soldiers may be coming along. We will pull straight on now. I have discovered a bit of a candle here, and we must take the risk of a small light to make a course by the boat compass. There is not enough wind to blow it out—may the curse of Heaven fall upon this blind gulf!"

A small flame appeared burning quite straight. It showed fragmentarily the stout ribs and planking in the hollow, empty part of the lighter. Decoud could see Nostromo standing up to pull. He saw him as high as the red sash on his waist, with a gleam of a white-handled revolver and the wooden haft of a long knife protruding on his left side. Decoud nerved himself for the effort of rowing. Certainly there was not enough wind to blow the candle out, but its flame swayed a little to the slow movement of the heavy boat. It was so big that with their utmost efforts they could not move it quicker than about a mile an hour. This was sufficient, however, to sweep them amongst the Isabels long before daylight came. There was a good six hours of darkness before them, and the distance from the harbour to the Great Isabel did not exceed two miles. Decoud put this heavy toil to the account of the Capataz's impatience. Sometimes they paused, and then strained their ears to hear the boat from Esmeralda. In this perfect quietness a steamer moving would have been heard from far off. As to seeing anything it was out of the question. They could not see each other. Even the lighter's sail, which remained set, was invisible. Very often they rested.

"Caramba!" said Nostromo, suddenly, during one of those intervals when they lolled idly against the heavy handles of the sweeps. "What is it? Are you distressed, Don Martin?"

Decoud assured him that he was not distressed in the least. Nostromo for a time kept perfectly still, and then in a whisper invited Martin to come aft.

With lips touching Decoud's ear he declared his belief that there was somebody else besides themselves upon the lighter. Twice now he had heard the sound of stifled sobbing.

"Señor," he whispered with awed wonder, "I am certain that there is somebody weeping in this lighter."

Decoud had heard nothing. He expressed his incredulity. However, it was easy to ascertain the truth of the matter.

"It is most amazing," muttered Nostromo. "Could anybody have concealed himself on board while the lighter was lying alongside the wharf?"

"And you say it was like sobbing?" asked Decoud, lowering his voice, too. "If he is weeping, whoever he is he cannot be very dangerous."

Clambering over the precious pile in the middle, they crouched low on the foreside of the mast and groped under the half-deck. Right forward, in the narrowest part, their hands came upon the limbs of a man, who remained as silent as death. Too startled themselves to make a sound, they dragged him aft by one arm and the collar of his coat. He was limp—lifeless.

The light of the bit of candle fell upon a round, hook-nosed face with black moustaches and little side-whiskers. He was extremely dirty. A greasy growth of beard was sprouting on the shaven parts of the cheeks. The thick lips were slightly parted, but the eyes remained closed. Decoud, to his immense astonishment, recognized Señor Hirsch, the hide merchant from Esmeralda. Nostromo, too, had recognized him. And they gazed at each other across the body, lying with its naked feet higher than its head, in an absurd pretence of sleep, faintness, or death.

CHAPTER EIGHT

For a moment, before this extraordinary find, they forgot their own concerns and sensations. Señor Hirsch's sensations as he lay there must have been those of extreme terror. For a long time he refused to give a sign of life, till at last Decoud's objurgations, and, perhaps more, Nostromo's impatient suggestion that he should be thrown overboard, as he seemed to be dead, induced him to raise one eyelid first, and then the other.

It appeared that he had never found a safe opportunity to leave Sulaco. He lodged with Anzani, the universal storekeeper, on the Plaza Mayor. But when the riot broke out he had made his escape from his host's house before daylight, and in such a hurry that he had forgotten to put on his shoes. He had run out impulsively in his socks, and with his hat in his hand, into the garden of Anzani's house. Fear gave him the necessary agility to climb over several low walls, and afterwards he blundered into the overgrown cloisters of the ruined Franciscan convent in one of the by-streets. He forced himself into the midst of matted bushes with the recklessness of desperation, and this accounted for his scratched body and his torn clothing. He lay hidden there all day, his tongue cleaving to the roof of his mouth with all the intensity of thirst engendered by heat and fear. Three times different bands of men invaded the place with shouts and imprecations, looking for Father Corbelàn; but towards the evening, still lying on his face in the bushes, he thought he would die from the fear of silence. He was not very clear as to what had induced him to leave the place, but evidently he had got out and slunk successfully out of town along the deserted back lanes. He wandered in the darkness near the railway, so maddened by apprehension that he dared not even approach the fires of the pickets of Italian workmen guarding the line. He had a vague idea evidently of finding refuge in the railway yards, but the dogs rushed upon him, barking; men began to shout; a shot was fired at random. He fled away from the gates. By the merest accident, as it happened, he took the direction of the O.S.N. Company's offices. Twice he stumbled upon the bodies of men killed during the day. But everything living frightened him much more. He crouched, crept, crawled, made dashes, guided by a sort of animal instinct, keeping away from every light and from every sound of voices. His idea was to throw himself at the feet of Captain Mitchell and beg for shelter in the Company's offices. It was all dark there as he approached on his hands and knees, but suddenly someone on guard challenged loudly, "*Quien vive?*" There were more dead men lying about, and he flattened himself down at once by the side of a cold corpse. He heard a voice saying, "Here is one of those wounded rascals crawling about. Shall I go and finish him?" And another voice objected that it was not safe to go out without a lantern upon such an errand; perhaps it was only some negro Liberal looking for a chance to stick a knife into the stomach of an honest man. Hirsch didn't stay to hear any more, but crawling away to the end of the wharf, hid himself amongst a lot of empty casks. After a while some people came along, talking, and with glowing cigarettes. He did not stop to ask himself whether they would be likely to do him any harm, but bolted incontinently along the jetty, saw a lighter lying moored at the end, and threw himself into it. In his desire to find cover he crept right forward under the half-deck, and he had remained there more dead than alive, suffering agonies of hunger and thirst, and almost fainting with terror, when he heard numerous footsteps and the voices of the Europeans who came in a body escorting the wagon-load of treasure, pushed along the rails by a squad of Cargadores. He understood perfectly what was being done from the talk, but did not disclose his presence from the fear that he would not be allowed to remain. His only idea at the time, overpowering and masterful, was to get away from this terrible Sulaco. And now he regretted it very much. He had heard Nostromo talk to Decoud, and wished himself back on shore. He did not desire to be involved in any desperate affair —in a situation where one could not run away. The involuntary groans of his anguished spirit had betrayed him to the sharp ears of the Capataz.

They had propped him up in a sitting posture against the side of the lighter, and he went on with the moaning account of his adventures till his voice broke, his head fell forward. "Water," he whispered, with difficulty. Decoud held one of the cans to his lips. He revived after an extraordinarily short time, and scrambled up to his feet wildly. Nostromo, in an angry and threatening voice, ordered him forward. Hirsch was one of those men whom fear lashes like a whip, and he must have had an appalling idea of the Capataz's ferocity. He displayed an extraordinary agility in disappearing forward into the darkness. They heard him getting over the tarpaulin; then there was the sound of a heavy fall, followed by a weary sigh. Afterwards all was still in the fore-part of the lighter, as though he had killed himself in his headlong tumble. Nostromo shouted in a menacing voice—

"Lie still there! Do not move a limb. If I hear as much as a loud breath from you I shall come over there and put a bullet through your head."

The mere presence of a coward, however passive, brings an element of treachery into a dangerous situation. Nostromo's nervous impatience passed into gloomy thoughtfulness. Decoud, in an undertone, as if speaking to himself, remarked that, after all, this bizarre event made no great difference. He could not conceive what harm the man could do. At most he would be in the way, like an inanimate and useless object—like a block of wood, for instance.

"I would think twice before getting rid of a piece of wood," said Nostromo, calmly. "Something may happen unexpectedly where you could make use of it. But in an affair like ours a man like this ought to be thrown overboard. Even if he were as brave as a lion we would not want him here. We are not running away for our lives. Señor, there is no harm in a brave man trying to save himself with ingenuity and courage; but you have heard his tale, Don Martin. His being here is a miracle of fear——" Nostromo paused. "There is no room for fear in this lighter," he added through his teeth.

Decoud had no answer to make. It was not a position for argument, for a display of scruples or feelings. There were a thousand ways in which a panic-stricken man could make himself dangerous. It was evident that Hirsch could not be spoken to, reasoned with, or persuaded into a rational line of conduct. The story of his own escape demonstrated that clearly enough. Decoud thought that it was a thousand pities the wretch had not died of fright. Nature, who had made him what he was, seemed to have calculated cruelly how much he could bear in the way of atrocious anguish without actually expiring. Some compassion was due to so much terror. Decoud, though imaginative enough for sympathy, resolved not to interfere with any action that Nostromo would take. But Nostromo did nothing. And the fate of Señor Hirsch remained suspended in the darkness of the gulf at the mercy of events which could not be foreseen.

The Capataz, extending his hand, put out the candle suddenly. It was to Decoud as if his companion had destroyed, by a single touch, the world of affairs, of loves, of revolution, where his complacent superiority analyzed fearlessly all motives and all passions, including his own.

He gasped a little. Decoud was affected by the novelty of his position. Intellectually self-confident, he suffered from being deprived of the only weapon he could use with effect. No intelligence could penetrate the darkness of the Placid Gulf. There remained only one thing he was certain of, and that was the over-weening vanity of his companion. It was direct, uncomplicated, naïve, and effectual. Decoud, who had been making use of him, had tried to understand his man thoroughly. He had discovered a complete singleness of motive behind the varied manifestations of a consistent character. This was why the man remained so astonishingly simple in the jealous greatness of his conceit. And now there was a complication. It was evident that he resented having been given a task in which there were so many chances of failure. "I wonder," thought Decoud, "how he would behave if I were not here."

He heard Nostromo mutter again, "No! there is no room for fear on this lighter. Courage itself does not seem good enough. I have a good eye and a steady hand; no man can say he ever saw me tired or uncer-

tain what to do; but *por Dios*, Don Martin, I have been
sent out into this black calm on a business where neither
a good eye, nor a steady hand, nor judgment are any
use. . . ." He swore a string of oaths in Spanish
and Italian under his breath. "Nothing but sheer
desperation will do for this affair."

These words were in strange contrast to the prevailing peace—to this almost solid stillness of the gulf.
A shower fell with an abrupt whispering sound all
round the boat, and Decoud took off his hat, and, letting
his head get wet, felt greatly refreshed. Presently a
steady little draught of air caressed his cheek. The
lighter began to move, but the shower distanced it. The
drops ceased to fall upon his head and hands, the whispering died out in the distance. Nostromo emitted a
grunt of satisfaction, and grasping the tiller, chirruped
softly, as sailors do, to encourage the wind. Never for
the last three days had Decoud felt less the need for
what the Capataz would call desperation.

"I fancy I hear another shower on the water," he observed in a tone of quiet content. "I hope it will catch
us up."

Nostromo ceased chirruping at once. "You hear
another shower?" he said, doubtfully. A sort of thin-
ning of the darkness seemed to have taken place, and
Decoud could see now the outline of his companion's
figure, and even the sail came out of the night like a
square block of dense snow.

The sound which Decoud had detected came along
the water harshly. Nostromo recognized that noise
partaking of a hiss and a rustle which spreads out on all
sides of a steamer making her way through a smooth
water on a quiet night. It could be nothing else but
the captured transport with troops from Esmeralda.
She carried no lights. The noise of her steaming, grow-

ing louder every minute, would stop at times altogether, and then begin again abruptly, and sound startlingly nearer, as if that invisible vessel, whose position could not be precisely guessed, were making straight for the lighter. Meantime, that last kept on sailing slowly and noiselessly before a breeze so faint that it was only by leaning over the side and feeling the water slip through his fingers that Decoud convinced himself they were moving at all. His drowsy feeling had departed. He was glad to know that the lighter was moving. After so much stillness the noise of the steamer seemed uproarious and distracting. There was a weirdness in not being able to see her. Suddenly all was still. She had stopped, but so close to them that the steam, blowing off, sent its rumbling vibration right over their heads.

"They are trying to make out where they are," said Decoud in a whisper. Again he leaned over and put his fingers into the water. "We are moving quite smartly," he informed Nostromo.

"We seem to be crossing her bows," said the Capataz in a cautious tone. "But this is a blind game with death. Moving on is of no use. We mustn't be seen or heard."

His whisper was hoarse with excitement. Of all his face there was nothing visible but a gleam of white eyeballs. His fingers gripped Decoud's shoulder. "That is the only way to save this treasure from this steamer full of soldiers. Any other would have carried lights. But you observe there is not a gleam to show us where she is."

Decoud stood as if paralyzed; only his thoughts were wildly active. In the space of a second he remembered the desolate glance of Antonia as he left her at the bedside of her father in the gloomy house of Avellanos, with shuttered windows, but all the doors standing open, and

deserted by all the servants except an old negro at the
gate. He remembered the Casa Gould on his last visit.
the arguments, the tones of his voice, the impenetrable
attitude of Charles, Mrs. Gould's face so blanched with
anxiety and fatigue that her eyes seemed to have
changed colour, appearing nearly black by contrast.
Even whole sentences of the proclamation which he
meant to make Barrios issue from his headquarters at
Cayta as soon as he got there passed through his mind;
the very germ of the new State, the Separationist proclamation which he had tried before he left to read hurriedly to Don José, stretched out on his bed under the
fixed gaze of his daughter. God knows whether the old
statesman had understood it; he was unable to speak,
but he had certainly lifted his arm off the coverlet; his
hand had moved as if to make the sign of the cross in the·
air, a gesture of blessing, of consent. Decoud had that
very draft in his pocket, written in pencil on several
loose sheets of paper, with the heavily-printed heading,
"Administration of the San Tomé Silver Mine. Sulaco.
Republic of Costaguana." He had written it furiously,
snatching page after page on Charles Gould's table.
Mrs. Gould had looked several times over his shoulder
as he wrote; but the Señor Administrador, standing
straddle-legged, would not even glance at it when it was
finished. He had waved it away firmly. It must have
been scorn, and not caution, since he never made a
remark about the use of the Administration's paper
for such a compromising document. And that showed
his disdain, the true English disdain of common prudence, as if everything outside the range of their own
thoughts and feelings were unworthy of serious recognition. Decoud had the time in a second or two to become furiously angry with Charles Gould, and even resentful against Mrs. Gould, in whose care, tacitly it

is true, he had left the safety of Antonia. Better
perish a thousand times than owe your preservation to
such people, he exclaimed mentally. The grip of
Nostromo's fingers never removed from his shoulder,
tightening fiercely, recalled him to himself.

"The darkness is our friend," the Capataz murmured
into his ear. "I am going to lower the sail, and trust
our escape to this black gulf. No eyes could make us
out lying silent with a naked mast. I will do it now, before this steamer closes still more upon us. The faint
creak of a block would betray us and the San Tomé
treasure into the hands of those thieves."

He moved about as warily as a cat. Decoud heard
no sound; and it was only by the disappearance of the
square blotch of darkness that he knew the yard had
come down, lowered as carefully as if it had been made
of glass. Next moment he heard Nostromo's quiet
breathing by his side.

"You had better not move at all from where you are,
Don Martin," advised the Capataz, earnestly. "You
might stumble or displace something which would make
a noise. The sweeps and the punting poles are lying
about. Move not for your life. *Por Dios*, Don Martin,"
he went on in a keen but friendly whisper, "I am so
desperate that if I didn't know your worship to be a
man of courage, capable of standing stock still whatever
happens, I would drive my knife into your heart."

A deathlike stillness surrounded the lighter. It was
difficult to believe that there was near a steamer full of
men with many pairs of eyes peering from her bridge for
some hint of land in the night. Her steam had ceased
blowing off, and she remained stopped too far off apparently for any other sound to reach the lighter.

"Perhaps you would, Capataz," Decoud began in a
whisper. "However, you need not trouble. There

are other things than the fear of your knife to keep my heart steady. It shall not betray you. Only, have you forgotten——"

"I spoke to you openly as to a man as desperate as myself," explained the Capataz. "The silver must be saved from the Monterists. I told Captain Mitchell three times that I preferred to go alone. I told Don Carlos Gould, too. It was in the Casa Gould. They had sent for me. The ladies were there; and when I tried to explain why I did not wish to have you with me, they promised me, both of them, great rewards for your safety. A strange way to talk to a man you are sending out to an almost certain death. Those gentlefolk do not seem to have sense enough to understand what they are giving one to do. I told them I could do nothing for you. You would have been safer with the bandit Hernandez. It would have been possible to ride out of the town with no greater risk than a chance shot sent after you in the dark. But it was as if they had been deaf. I had to promise I would wait for you under the harbour gate. I did wait. And now because you are a brave man you are as safe as the silver. Neither more nor less."

At that moment, as if by way of comment upon Nostromo's words, the invisible steamer went ahead at half speed only, as could be judged by the leisurely beat of her propeller. The sound shifted its place markedly, but without coming nearer. It even grew a little more distant right abeam of the lighter, and then ceased again.

"They are trying for a sight of the Isabels," muttered Nostromo, "in order to make for the harbour in a straight line and seize the Custom House with the treasure in it. Have you ever seen the Commandant of Esmeralda, Sotillo? A handsome fellow, with a soft

voice. When I first came here I used to see him in the
Calle talking to the señoritas at the windows of the
houses, and showing his white teeth all the time. But
one of my Cargadores, who had been a soldier, told me
that he had once ordered a man to be flayed alive in the
remote Campo, where he was sent recruiting amongst
the people of the Estancias. It has never entered his
head that the Compania had a man capable of baffling
his game."

The murmuring loquacity of the Capataz disturbed
Decoud like a hint of weakness. And yet, talkative
resolution may be as genuine as grim silence.

"Sotillo is not baffled so far," he said. "Have you
forgotten that crazy man forward?"

Nostromo had not forgotten Señor Hirsch. He re-
proached himself bitterly for not having visited the
lighter carefully before leaving the wharf. He re-
proached himself for not having stabbed and flung
Hirsch overboard at the very moment of discovery without even looking at his face. That would have been
consistent with the desperate character of the affair.
Whatever happened, Sotillo *was* already baffled. Even
if that wretch, now as silent as death, did anything to
betray the nearness of the lighter, Sotillo—if Sotillo
it was in command of the troops on board—would be
still baffled of his plunder.

"I have an axe in my hand," Nostromo whispered,
wrathfully, "that in three strokes would cut through
the side down to the water's edge. Moreover, each
lighter has a plug in the stern, and I know exactly where
it is. I feel it under the sole of my foot."

Decoud recognized the ring of genuine determination
in the nervous murmurs, the vindictive excitement of
the famous Capataz. Before the steamer, guided by a
shriek or two (for there could be no more than that,

Nostromo said, gnashing his teeth audibly), could find the lighter there would be plenty of time to sink this treasure tied up round his neck.

The last words he hissed into Decoud's ear. Decoud said nothing. He was perfectly convinced. The usual characteristic quietness of the man was gone. It was not equal to the situation as he conceived it. Something deeper, something unsuspected by everyone, had come to the surface. Decoud, with careful movements, slipped off his overcoat and divested himself of his boots; he did not consider himself bound in honour to sink with the treasure. His object was to get down to Barrios, in Cayta, as the Capataz knew very well; and he, too, meant, in his own way, to put into that attempt all the desperation of which he was capable. Nostromo muttered, "True, true! You are a politician, señor. Rejoin the army, and start another revolution." He pointed out, however, that there was a little boat belonging to every lighter fit to carry two men, if not more. Theirs was towing behind.

Of that Decoud had not been aware. Of course, it was too dark to see, and it was only when Nostromo put his hand upon its painter fastened to a cleat in the stern that he experienced a full measure of relief. The prospect of finding himself in the water and swimming, overwhelmed by ignorance and darkness, probably in a circle, till he sank from exhaustion, was revolting. The barren and cruel futility of such an end intimidated his affectation of careless pessimism. In comparison to it, the chance of being left floating in a boat, exposed to thirst, hunger, discovery, imprisonment, execution, presented itself with an aspect of amenity worth securing even at the cost of some self-contempt. He did not accept Nostromo's proposal that he should get into the boat at once. "Something sudden may overwhelm us.

señor," the Capataz remarked promising faithfully, at the same time, to let go the painter at the moment when the necessity became manifest.

But Decoud assured him lightly that he did not mean to take to the boat till the very last moment, and that then he meant the Capataz to come along, too. The darkness of the gulf was no longer for him the end of all things. It was part of a living world since, pervading it, failure and death could be felt at your elbow. And at the same time it was a shelter. He exulted in its impenetrable obscurity. "Like a wall, like a wall," he muttered to himself.

The only thing which checked his confidence was the thought of Señor Hirsch. Not to have bound and gagged him seemed to Decoud now the height of improvident folly. As long as the miserable creature had the power to raise a yell he was a constant danger. His abject terror was mute now, but there was no saying from what cause it might suddenly find vent in shrieks.

This very madness of fear which both Decoud and Nostromo had seen in the wild and irrational glances, and in the continuous twitchings of his mouth, protected Señor Hirsch from the cruel necessities of this desperate affair. The moment of silencing him for ever had passed. As Nostromo remarked, in answer to Decoud's regrets, it was too late! It could not be done without noise, especially in the ignorance of the man's exact position. Wherever he had elected to crouch and tremble, it was too hazardous to go near him. He would begin probably to yell for mercy. It was much better to leave him quite alone since he was keeping so still. But to trust to his silence became every moment a greater strain upon Decoud's composure.

"I wish, Capataz, you had not let the right moment pass," he murmured.

"What! To silence him for ever! I thought it good to hear first how he came to be here. It was too strange. Who could imagine that it was all an accident? Afterwards, señor, when I saw you giving him water to drink, I could not do it. Not after I had seen you holding up the can to his lips as though he were your brother. Señor, that sort of necessity must not be thought of too long. And yet it would have been no cruelty to take away from him his wretched life. It is nothing but fear. Your compassion saved him then, Don Martin, and now it is too late. It couldn't be done without noise."

In the steamer they were keeping a perfect silence, and the stillness was so profound that Decoud felt as if the slightest sound conceivable must travel unchecked and audible to the end of the world. What if Hirsch coughed or sneezed? To feel himself at the mercy of such an idiotic contingency was too exasperating to be looked upon with irony. Nostromo, too, seemed to be getting restless. Was it possible, he asked himself, that the steamer, finding the night too dark altogether, intended to remain stopped where she was till daylight? He began to think that this, after all, was the real danger. He was afraid that the darkness, which was his protection, would, in the end, cause his undoing.

Sotillo, as Nostromo had surmised, was in command on board the transport. The events of the last forty-eight hours in Sulaco were not known to him; neither was he aware that the telegraphist in Esmeralda had managed to warn his colleague in Sulaco. Like a good many officers of the troops garrisoning the province, Sotillo had been influenced in his adoption of the Ribierist cause by the belief that it had the enormous wealth of the Gould Concession on its side. He had been one of the frequenters of the Casa Gould, where he

had aired his Blanco convictions and his ardour for reform before Don José Avellanos, casting frank, honest
glances towards Mrs. Gould and Antonia the while. He
was known to belong to a good family persecuted and
impoverished during the tyranny of Guzman Bento.
The opinions he expressed appeared eminently natural
and proper in a man of his parentage and antecedents.
And he was not a deceiver; it was perfectly natural for
him to express elevated sentiments while his whole
faculties were taken up with what seemed then a solid
and practical notion—the notion that the husband of
Antonia Avellanos would be, naturally, the intimate
friend of the Gould Concession. He even pointed this
out to Anzani once, when negotiating the sixth or
seventh small loan in the gloomy, damp apartment
with enormous iron bars, behind the principal shop in
the whole row under the Arcades. He hinted to the
universal shopkeeper at the excellent terms he was on
with the emancipated señorita, who was like a sister
to the Englishwoman. He would advance one leg and
put his arms akimbo, posing for Anzani's inspection, and
fixing him with a haughty stare.

"Look, miserable shopkeeper! How can a man like
me fail with any woman, let alone an emancipated girl
living in scandalous freedom?" he seemed to say.

His manner in the Casa Gould was, of course, very
different—devoid of all truculence, and even slightly
mournful. Like most of his countrymen, he was carried
away by the sound of fine words, especially if uttered
by himself. He had no convictions of any sort upon
anything except as to the irresistible power of his
personal advantages. But that was so firm that even
Decoud's appearance in Sulaco, and his intimacy with
the Goulds and the Avellanos, did not disquiet him.
On the contrary, he tried to make friends with that

rich Costaguanero from Europe in the hope of borrow-
ing a large sum by-and-by. The only guiding motive
of his life was to get money for the satisfaction of his
expensive tastes, which he indulged recklessly, having
no self-control. He imagined himself a master of
intrigue, but his corruption was as simple as an animal
instinct. At times, in solitude, he had his moments of
ferocity, and also on such occasions as, for instance,
when alone in a room with Anzani trying to get a loan.

He had talked himself into the command of the
Esmeralda garrison. That small seaport had its importance as the station of the main submarine cable connecting the Occidental Provinces with the outer world,
and the junction with it of the Sulaco branch. Don
José Avellanos proposed him, and Barrios, with a rude
and jeering guffaw, had said, "Oh, let Sotillo go. He is
a very good man to keep guard over the cable, and the
ladies of Esmeralda ought to have their turn." Barrios,
an indubitably brave man, had no great opinion of Sotillo.

It was through the Esmeralda cable alone that the
San Tomé mine could be kept in constant touch with
the great financier, whose tacit approval made the
strength of the Ribierist movement. This movement
had its adversaries even there. Sotillo governed
Esmeralda with repressive severity till the adverse
course of events upon the distant theatre of civil war
forced upon him the reflection that, after all, the great
silver mine was fated to become the spoil of the victors.
But caution was necessary. He began by assuming
a dark and mysterious attitude towards the faithful
Ribierist municipality of Esmeralda. Later on, the
information that the commandant was holding assemblies of officers in the dead of night (which had
leaked out somehow) caused those gentlemen to neglect

their civil duties altogether, and remain shut up in their houses. Suddenly one day all the letters from Sulaco by the overland courier were carried off by a file of soldiers from the post-office to the Commandancia, without disguise, concealment, or apology. Sotillo had heard through Cayta of the final defeat of Ribiera.

This was the first open sign of the change in his convictions. Presently notorious democrats, who had been living till then in constant fear of arrest, leg irons, and even floggings, could be observed going in and out at the great door of the Commandancia, where the horses of the orderlies doze under their heavy saddles, while the men, in ragged uniforms and pointed straw hats, lounge on a bench, with their naked feet stuck out beyond the strip of shade; and a sentry, in a red baize coat with holes at the elbows, stands at the top of the steps glaring haughtily at the common people, who uncover their heads to him as they pass.

Sotillo's ideas did not soar above the care for his personal safety and the chance of plundering the town in his charge, but he feared that such a late adhesion would earn but scant gratitude from the victors. He had believed just a little too long in the power of the San Tomé mine. The seized correspondence had confirmed his previous information of a large amount of silver ingots lying in the Sulaco Custom House. To gain possession of it would be a clear Monterist move; a sort of service that would have to be rewarded. With the silver in his hands he could make terms for himself and his soldiers. He was aware neither of the riots, nor of the President's escape to Sulaco and the close pursuit led by Montero's brother, the guerrillero. The game seemed in his own hands. The initial moves were the seizure of the cable telegraph office and the securing of the Government steamer lying in the narrow creek

which is the harbour of Esmeralda. The last was ef-
fected without difficulty by a company of soldiers
swarming with a rush over the gangways as she lay
alongside the quay; but the lieutenant charged with the
duty of arresting the telegraphist halted on the way before the only café in Esmeralda, where he distributed
some brandy to his men, and refreshed himself at the
expense of the owner, a known Ribierist. The whole
party became intoxicated, and proceeded on their
mission up the street yelling and firing random shots at
the windows. This little festivity, which might have
turned out dangerous to the telegraphist's life, enabled
him in the end to send his warning to Sulaco. The
lieutenant, staggering upstairs with a drawn sabre, was
before long kissing him on both cheeks in one of those
swift changes of mood peculiar to a state of drunken-
ness. He clasped the telegraphist close round the neck,
assuring him that all the officers of the Esmeralda
garrison were going to be made colonels, while tears of
happiness streamed down his sodden face. Thus it
came about that the town major, coming along later,
found the whole party sleeping on the stairs and in
passages, and the telegraphist (who scorned this chance
of escape) very busy clicking the key of the transmitter.
The major led him away bareheaded, with his hands tied
behind his back, but concealed the truth from Sotillo,
who remained in ignorance of the warning despatched
to Sulaco.

The colonel was not the man to let any sort of darkness stand in the way of the planned surprise. It appeared to him a dead certainty; his heart was set upon
his object with an ungovernable, childlike impatience.
Ever since the steamer had rounded Punta Mala, to
enter the deeper shadow of the gulf, he had remained on
the bridge in a group of officers as excited as himself.

Distracted between the coaxings and menaces of Sotillo
and his Staff, the miserable commander of the steamer
kept her moving with as much prudence as they would
let him exercise. Some of them had been drinking
heavily, no doubt; but the prospect of laying hands
on so much wealth made them absurdly foolhardy, and,
at the same time, extremely anxious. The old major
of the battalion, a stupid, suspicious man, who had
never been afloat in his life, distinguished himself by
putting out suddenly the binnacle light, the only one
allowed on board for the necessities of navigation. He
could not understand of what use it could be for finding
the way. To the vehement protestations of the ship's
captain, he stamped his foot and tapped the handle of
his sword. "Aha! I have unmasked you," he cried,
triumphantly. "You are tearing your hair from
despair at my acuteness. Am I a child to believe that
a light in that brass box can show you where the harbour is? I am an old soldier, I am. I can smell a
traitor a league off. You wanted that gleam to betray
our approach to your friend the Englishman. A thing
like that show you the way! What a miserable lie!
Que picardia! You Sulaco people are all in the pay of
those foreigners. You deserve to be run through the
body with my sword." Other officers, crowding round,
tried to calm his indignation, repeating persuasively,
"No, no! This is an appliance of the mariners, major.
This is no treachery." The captain of the transport
flung himself face downwards on the bridge, and refused to rise. "Put an end to me at once," he repeated
in a stifled voice. Sotillo had to interfere.

The uproar and confusion on the bridge became so
great that the helmsman fled from the wheel. He took
refuge in the engine-room, and alarmed the engineers,
who, disregarding the threats of the soldiers set on

guard over them, stopped the engines, protesting that they would rather be shot than run the risk of being drowned down below.

This was the first time Nostromo and Decoud heard the steamer stop. After order had been restored, and the binnacle lamp relighted, she went ahead again, passing wide of the lighter in her search for the Isabels. The group could not be made out, and, at the pitiful entreaties of the captain, Sotillo allowed the engines to be stopped again to wait for one of those periodical lightenings of darkness caused by the shifting of the cloud canopy spread above the waters of the gulf.

Sotillo, on the bridge, muttered from time to time angrily to the captain. The other, in an apologetic and cringing tone, begged *su merced* the colonel to take into consideration the limitations put upon human faculties by the darkness of the night. Sotillo swelled with rage and impatience. It was the chance of a lifetime.

"If your eyes are of no more use to you than this, I shall have them put out," he burst out.

The captain of the steamer made no answer, for just then the mass of the Great Isabel loomed up darkly after a passing shower, then vanished, as if swept away by a wave of greater obscurity preceding another downpour. This was enough for him. In the voice of a man come back to life again, he informed Sotillo that in an hour he would be alongside the Sulaco wharf. The ship was put then full speed on the course, and a great bustle of preparation for landing arose among the soldiers on her deck.

It was heard distinctly by Decoud and Nostromo. The Capataz understood its meaning. They had made out the Isabels, and were going on now in a straight line for Sulaco. He judged that they would pass close; but believed that lying still like this, with the sail lowered, the lighter could not be seen. "No, not even if they rubbed sides with us," he muttered.

The rain began to fall again; first like a wet mist, then with a heavier touch, thickening into a smart, perpendicular downpour; and the hiss and thump of the approaching steamer was coming extremely near. Decoud, with his eyes full of water, and lowered head, asked himself how long it would be before she drew past, when unexpectedly he felt a lurch. An inrush of foam broke swishing over the stern, simultaneously with a crack of timbers and a staggering shock. He had the impression of an angry hand laying hold of the lighter and dragging it along to destruction. The shock, of course, had knocked him down, and he found himself rolling in a lot of water at the bottom of the lighter. A violent churning went on alongside; a strange and amazed voice cried out something above him in the night. He heard a piercing shriek for help from Señor Hirsch. He kept his teeth hard set all the time. It was a collision!

The steamer had struck the lighter obliquely, heeling her over till she was half swamped, starting some of her timbers, and swinging her head parallel to her own course with the force of the blow. The shock of it on board of her was hardly perceptible. All the violence of that collision was, as usual, felt only on board the smaller craft. Even Nostromo himself thought that this was perhaps the end of his desperate adventure. He, too, had been flung away from the long tiller, which took charge in the lurch. Next moment the steamer would have passed on, leaving the lighter to sink or swim after having shouldered her thus out of her way, and without even getting a glimpse of her form, had it not been that, being deeply laden with stores and the great number of people on board, her anchor was low enough to hook itself into one of the wire shrouds of the lighter's mast. For the space of two or three gasping breaths that new rope held against the sudden strain. It was this that gave Decoud the sensation of the snatching pull, dragging the lighter away to destruction. The cause of it, of course, was inexplicable to him. The whole thing was so sudden that he had no time to think. But all his sensations were perfectly clear; he had kept complete possession of himself; in fact, he was even pleasantly aware of that calmness at the very moment of being pitched head first over the transom, to struggle on his back in a lot of water. Señor Hirsch's shriek he had heard and recognized while he was regaining his feet, always with that mysterious sensation of being dragged headlong through the darkness. Not a word, not a cry escaped him; he had no time to see anything; and following upon the despairing screams for help, the dragging motion ceased so suddenly that he staggered forward with open arms and fell against the pile of the treasure boxes. He clung to them instinctively, in the vague apprehension of being flung about again; and immediately he heard another lot of shrieks for help, prolonged and despairing, not near him at all, but unaccountably in the distance, away from the lighter altogether, as if some spirit in the night were mocking at Señor Hirsch's terror and despair.

Then all was still—as still as when you wake up in your bed in a dark room from a bizarre and agitated dream. The lighter rocked slightly; the rain was still falling. Two groping hands took hold of his bruised sides from behind, and the Capataz's voice whispered, in his ear, "Silence, for your life! Silence! The steamer has stopped."

Decoud listened. The gulf was dumb. He felt the

water nearly up to his knees. "Are we sinking?" he asked in a faint breath.

"I don't know," Nostromo breathed back to him. "Señor, make not the slightest sound."

Hirsch, when ordered forward by Nostromo, had not returned into his first hiding-place. He had fallen near the mast, and had no strength to rise; moreover, he feared to move. He had given himself up for dead, but not on any rational grounds. It was simply a cruel and terrifying feeling. Whenever he tried to think what would become of him his teeth would start chattering violently. He was too absorbed in the utter misery of his fear to take notice of anything.

Though he was stifling under the lighter's sail which Nostromo had unwittingly lowered on top of him, he did not even dare to put out his head till the very moment of the steamer striking. Then, indeed, he leaped right out, spurred on to new miracles of bodily vigour by this new shape of danger. The inrush of water when the lighter heeled over unsealed his lips. His shriek, "Save me!" was the first distinct warning of the collision for the people on board the steamer. Next moment the wire shroud parted, and the released anchor swept over the lighter's forecastle. It came against the breast of Señor Hirsch, who simply seized hold of it, without in the least knowing what it was, but curling his arms and legs upon the part above the fluke with an invincible, unreasonable tenacity. The lighter yawed off wide, and the steamer, moving on, carried him away, clinging hard, and shouting for help. It was some time, however, after the steamer had stopped that his position was discovered. His sustained yelping for help seemed to come from somebody swimming in the water. At last a couple of men went over the bows and hauled him on board. He was carried straight off to

Sotillo on the bridge. His examination confirmed the
impression that some craft had been run over and sunk,
but it was impracticable on such a dark night to look for
the positive proof of floating wreckage. Sotillo was
more anxious than ever now to enter the harbour without loss of time; the idea that he had destroyed the
principal object of his expedition was too intolerable to
be accepted. This feeling made the story he had heard
appear the more incredible. Señor Hirsch, after being
beaten a little for telling lies, was thrust into the chart-
room. But he was beaten only a little. His tale had
taken the heart out of Sotillo's Staff, though they all
repeated round their chief, "Impossible! impossible!"
with the exception of the old major, who triumphed
gloomily.

"I told you; I told you," he mumbled. "I could
smell some treachery, some *diableria* a league off."

Meantime, the steamer had kept on her way towards
Sulaco, where only the truth of that matter could be
ascertained. Decoud and Nostromo heard the loud
churning of her propeller diminish and die out; and
then, with no useless words, busied themselves in making for the Isabels. The last shower had brought with
it a gentle but steady breeze. The danger was not
over yet, and there was no time for talk. The lighter
was leaking like a sieve. They splashed in the water
at every step. The Capataz put into Decoud's hands
the handle of the pump which was fitted at the side aft,
and at once, without question or remark, Decoud began to pump in utter forgetfulness of every desire but
that of keeping the treasure afloat. Nostromo hoisted
the sail, flew back to the tiller, pulled at the sheet like
mad. The short flare of a match (they had been kept
dry in a tight tin box, though the man himself was
completely wet), the vivid flare of a match, disclosed to

the toiling Decoud the eagerness of his face, bent low over the box of the compass, and the attentive stare of his eyes. He knew now where he was, and he hoped to run the sinking lighter ashore in the shallow cove where the high, cliff-like end of the Great Isabel is divided in two equal parts by a deep and overgrown ravine.

Decoud pumped without intermission. Nostromo steered without relaxing for a second the intense, peering effort of his stare. Each of them was as if utterly alone with his task. It did not occur to them to speak. There was nothing in common between them but the knowledge that the damaged lighter must be slowly but surely sinking. In that knowledge, which was like the crucial test of their desires, they seemed to have become completely estranged, as if they had discovered in the very shock of the collision that the loss of the lighter would not mean the same thing to them both. This common danger brought their differences in aim, in view, in character, and in position, into absolute prominence in the private vision of each. There was no bond of conviction, of common idea; they were merely two adventurers pursuing each his own adventure, involved in the same imminence of deadly peril. Therefore they had nothing to say to each other. But this peril, this only incontrovertible truth in which they shared, seemed to act as an inspiration to their mental and bodily powers.

There was certainly something almost miraculous in the way the Capataz made the cove with nothing but the shadowy hint of the island's shape and the vague gleam of a small sandy strip for a guide. Where the ravine opens between the cliffs, and a slender, shallow rivulet meanders out of the bushes to lose itself in the sea, the lighter was run ashore; and the two men, with

a taciturn, undaunted energy, began to discharge her
precious freight, carrying each ox-hide box up the bed
of the rivulet beyond the bushes to a hollow place which
the caving in of the soil had made below the roots of a
large tree. Its big smooth trunk leaned like a falling
column far over the trickle of water running amongst
the loose stones.

A couple of years before Nostromo had spent a whole
Sunday, all alone, exploring the island. He explained
this to Decoud after their task was done, and they sat,
weary in every limb, with their legs hanging down the
low bank, and their backs against the tree, like a pair
of blind men aware of each other and their surroundings
by some indefinable sixth sense.

"Yes," Nostromo repeated, "I never forget a place
I have carefully looked at once." He spoke slowly, almost lazily, as if there had been a whole leisurely life
before him, instead of the scanty two hours before daylight. The existence of the treasure, barely concealed
in this improbable spot, laid a burden of secrecy upon
every contemplated step, upon every intention and plan
of future conduct. He felt the partial failure of this
desperate affair entrusted to the great reputation he had
known how to make for himself. However, it was also
a partial success. His vanity was half appeased. His
nervous irritation had subsided.

"You never know what may be of use," he pursued
with his usual quietness of tone and manner. "I spent
a whole miserable Sunday in exploring this crumb of
land."

"A misanthropic sort of occupation," muttered Decoud, viciously. "You had no money, I suppose, to
gamble with, and to fling about amongst the girls in
your usual haunts, Capataz."

"*E vero!*" exclaimed the Capataz, surprised into the

use of his native tongue by so much perspicacity. "I had not! Therefore I did not want to go amongst those beggarly people accustomed to my generosity. It is looked for from the Capataz of the Cargadores, who are the rich men, and, as it were, the Caballeros amongst the common people. I don't care for cards but as a pastime; and as to those girls that boast of having opened their doors to my knock, you know I wouldn't look at any one of them twice except for what the people would say. They are queer, the good people of Sulaco, and I have got much useful information simply by listening patiently to the talk of the women that everybody believed I was in love with. Poor Teresa could never understand that. On that particular Sunday, señor, she scolded so that I went out of the house swearing that I would never darken their door again unless to fetch away my hammock and my chest of clothes. Señor, there is nothing more exasperating than to hear a woman you respect rail against your good reputation when you have not a single brass coin in your pocket. I untied one of the small boats and pulled myself out of the harbour with nothing but three cigars in my pocket to help me spend the day on this island. But the water of this rivulet you hear under your feet is cool and sweet and good, señor, both before and after a smoke." He was silent for a while, then added reflectively, "That was the first Sunday after I brought down the white-whiskered English *rico* all the way down the mountains from the Paramo on the top of the Entrada Pass—and in the coach, too! No coach had gone up or down that mountain road within the memory of man, señor, till I brought this one down in charge of fifty peons working like one man with ropes, pickaxes, and poles under my direction. That was the rich Englishman who, as people say, pays for the making of

this railway. He was very pleased with me. But my
wages were not due till the end of the month."

He slid down the bank suddenly. Decoud heard the
splash of his feet in the brook and followed his footsteps
down the ravine. His form was lost among the bushes
till he had reached the strip of sand under the cliff.
As often happens in the gulf when the showers
during the first part of the night had been frequent and
heavy, the darkness had thinned considerably towards
the morning though there were no signs of daylight
as yet.

The cargo-lighter, relieved of its precious burden,
rocked feebly, half-afloat, with her fore-foot on the sand.
A long rope stretched away like a black cotton thread
across the strip of white beach to the grapnel Nostromo
had carried ashore and hooked to the stem of a tree-like
shrub in the very opening of the ravine.

There was nothing for Decoud but to remain on the
island. He received from Nostromo's hands whatever
food the foresight of Captain Mitchell had put on
board the lighter and deposited it temporarily in the
little dinghy which on their arrival they had hauled up
out of sight amongst the bushes. It was to be left with
him. The island was to be a hiding-place, not a prison;
he could pull out to a passing ship. The O.S.N. Company's mail boats passed close to the islands when going
into Sulaco from the north. But the *Minerva*, carrying
off the ex-president, had taken the news up north of the
disturbances in Sulaco. It was possible that the next
steamer down would get instructions to miss the port
altogether since the town, as far as the *Minerva's*
officers knew, was for the time being in the hands of the
rabble. This would mean that there would be no
steamer for a month, as far as the mail service went; but
Decoud had to take his chance of that. The island was

his only shelter from the proscription hanging over his head. The Capataz was, of course, going back. The unloaded lighter leaked much less, and he thought that she would keep afloat as far as the harbour.

He passed to Decoud, standing knee-deep alongside, one of the two spades which belonged to the equipment of each lighter for use when ballasting ships. By working with it carefully as soon as there was daylight enough to see, Decoud could loosen a mass of earth and stones overhanging the cavity in which they had deposited the treasure, so that it would look as if it had fallen naturally. It would cover up not only the cavity, but even all traces of their work, the footsteps, the displaced stones, and even the broken bushes.

"Besides, who would think of looking either for you or the treasure here?" Nostromo continued, as if he could not tear himself away from the spot. "Nobody is ever likely to come here. What could any man want with this piece of earth as long as there is room for his feet on the mainland! The people in this country are not curious. There are even no fishermen here to intrude upon your worship. All the fishing that is done in the gulf goes on near Zapiga, over there. Señor, if you are forced to leave this island before anything can be arranged for you, do not try to make for Zapiga. It is a settlement of thieves and matreros, where they would cut your throat promptly for the sake of your gold watch and chain. And, señor, think twice before confiding in any one whatever; even in the officers of the Company's steamers, if you ever get on board one. Honesty alone is not enough for security. You must look to discretion and prudence in a man. And always remember, señor, before you open your lips for a confidence, that this treasure may be left safely here for hundreds of years. Time is on its side, señor. And silver is an incorruptible metal that can be trusted to keep its value for ever. . . . An incorruptible metal," he repeated, as if the idea had given him a profound pleasure.

"As some men are said to be," Decoud pronounced, inscrutably, while the Capataz, who busied himself in baling out the lighter with a wooden bucket, went on throwing the water over the side with a regular splash. Decoud, incorrigible in his scepticism, reflected, not cynically, but with general satisfaction, that this man was made incorruptible by his enormous vanity, that finest form of egoism which can take on the aspect of every virtue.

Nostromo ceased baling, and, as if struck with a sudden thought, dropped the bucket with a clatter into the lighter.

"Have you any message?" he asked in a lowered voice. "Remember, I shall be asked questions."

"You must find the hopeful words that ought to be spoken to the people in town. I trust for that your intelligence and your experience, Capataz. You understand?"

"Si, señor. . . . For the ladies."

"Yes, yes," said Decoud, hastily. "Your wonderful reputation will make them attach great value to your words; therefore be careful what you say. I am looking forward," he continued, feeling the fatal touch of contempt for himself to which his complex nature was subject, "I am looking forward to a glorious and successful ending to my mission. Do you hear, Capataz? Use the words glorious and successful when you speak to the señorita. Your own mission is accomplished gloriously and successfully. You have indubitably saved the silver of the mine. Not only this silver, but probably all the silver that shall ever come out of it."

Nostromo detected the ironic tone. "I dare say, Señor Don Martin," he said, moodily. "There are very few things that I am not equal to. Ask the foreign signori. I, a man of the people, who cannot always understand what you mean. But as to this lot which I must leave here, let me tell you that I would believe it in greater safety if you had not been with me at all."

An exclamation escaped Decoud, and a short pause followed. "Shall I go back with you to Sulaco?" he asked in an angry tone.

"Shall I strike you dead with my knife where you stand?" retorted Nostromo, contemptuously. "It would be the same thing as taking you to Sulaco. Come, señor. Your reputation is in your politics, and mine is bound up with the fate of this silver. Do you wonder I wish there had been no other man to share my knowledge? I wanted no one with me, señor."

"You could not have kept the lighter afloat without me," Decoud almost shouted. "You would have gone to the bottom with her."

"Yes," uttered Nostromo, slowly; "alone."

Here was a man, Decoud reflected, that seemed as though he would have preferred to die rather than deface the perfect form of his egoism. Such a man was safe. In silence he helped the Capataz to get the grapnel on board. Nostromo cleared the shelving shore with one push of the heavy oar, and Decoud found himself solitary on the beach like a man in a dream. A sudden desire to hear a human voice once more seized upon his heart. The lighter was hardly distinguishable from the black water upon which she floated.

"What do you think has become of Hirsch?" he shouted.

"Knocked overboard and drowned," cried Nos-

tromo's voice confidently out of the black wastes of sky
and sea around the islet. "Keep close in the ravine,
señor. I shall try to come out to you in a night or
two."

A slight swishing rustle showed that Nostromo was
setting the sail. It filled all at once with a sound as of
a single loud drum-tap. Decoud went back to the
ravine. Nostromo, at the tiller, looked back from
time to time at the vanishing mass of the Great Isabel,
which, little by little, merged into the uniform texture
of the night. At last, when he turned his head
again, he saw nothing but a smooth darkness, like a
solid wall.

Then he, too, experienced that feeling of solitude
which had weighed heavily on Decoud after the lighter
had slipped off the shore. But while the man on the
island was oppressed by a bizarre sense of unreality
affecting the very ground upon which he walked, the
mind of the Capataz of the Cargadores turned alertly
to the problem of future conduct. Nostromo's faculties,
working on parallel lines, enabled him to steer straight,
to keep a look-out for Hermosa, near which he had to
pass, and to try to imagine what would happen to-
morrow in Sulaco. To-morrow, or, as a matter of fact,
to-day, since the dawn was not very far, Sotillo would
find out in what way the treasure had gone. A gang of
Cargadores had been employed in loading it into a railway truck from the Custom House store-rooms, and
running the truck on to the wharf. There would be
arrests made, and certainly before noon Sotillo would
know in what manner the silver had left Sulaco, and
who it was that took it out.

Nostromo's intention had been to sail right into the
harbour; but at this thought by a sudden touch of the
tiller he threw the lighter into the wind and checked

her rapid way. His re-appearance with the very boat would raise suspicions, would cause surmises, would absolutely put Sotillo on the track. He himself would be arrested; and once in the Calabozo there was no saying what they would do to him to make him speak. He trusted himself, but he stood up to look round. Near by, Hermosa showed low its white surface as flat as a table, with the slight run of the sea raised by the breeze washing over its edges noisily. The lighter must be sunk at once.

He allowed her to drift with her sail aback. There was already a good deal of water in her. He allowed her to drift towards the harbour entrance, and, letting the tiller swing about, squatted down and busied himself in loosening the plug. With that out she would fill very quickly, and every lighter carried a little iron ballast—enough to make her go down when full of water. When he stood up again the noisy wash about the Hermosa sounded far away, almost inaudible; and already he could make out the shape of land about the harbour entrance. This was a desperate affair, and he was a good swimmer. A mile was nothing to him, and he knew of an easy place for landing just below the earthworks of the old abandoned fort. It occurred to him with a peculiar fascination that this fort was a good place in which to sleep the day through after so many sleepless nights.

With one blow of the tiller he unshipped for the purpose, he knocked the plug out, but did not take the trouble to lower the sail. He felt the water welling up heavily about his legs before he leaped on to the taffrail. There, upright and motionless, in his shirt and trousers only, he stood waiting. When he had felt her settle he sprang far away with a mighty splash.

At once he turned his head. The gloomy, clouded

dawn from behind the mountains showed him on the smooth waters the upper corner of the sail, a dark wet triangle of canvas waving slightly to and fro. He saw it vanish, as if jerked under, and then struck out for the shore.

PART THIRD

THE LIGHTHOUSE

CHAPTER ONE

DIRECTLY the cargo boat had slipped away from the wharf and got lost in the darkness of the harbour the Europeans of Sulaco separated, to prepare for the coming of the Monterist *régime*, which was approaching Sulaco from the mountains, as well as from the sea.

This bit of manual work in loading the silver was their last concerted action. It ended the three days of danger, during which, according to the newspaper press of Europe, their energy had preserved the town from the calamities of popular disorder. At the shore end of the jetty, Captain Mitchell said good-night and turned back. His intention was to walk the planks of the wharf till the steamer from Esmeralda turned up. The engineers of the railway staff, collecting their Basque and Italian workmen, marched them away to the railway yards, leaving the Custom House, so well defended on the first day of the riot, standing open to the four winds of heaven. Their men had conducted themselves bravely and faithfully during the famous "three days" of Sulaco. In a great part this faithfulness and that courage had been exercised in self-defence rather than in the cause of those material interests to which Charles Gould had pinned his faith. Amongst the cries of the mob not the least loud had been the cry of death to foreigners. It was, indeed, a lucky circumstance for Sulaco that the relations of those imported workmen with the people of the country had been uniformly bad from the first.

Doctor Monygham, going to the door of Viola's

kitchen, observed this retreat marking the end of the foreign interference, this withdrawal of the army of material progress from the field of Costaguana revolutions.

Algarrobe torches carried on the outskirts of the moving body sent their penetrating aroma into his nostrils. Their light, sweeping along the front of the house, made the letters of the inscription, "Albergo d'Italia Una," leap out black from end to end of the long wall. His eyes blinked in the clear blaze. Several young men, mostly fair and tall, shepherding this mob of dark bronzed heads, surmounted by the glint of slanting rifle barrels, nodded to him familiarly as they went by. The doctor was a well-known character. Some of them wondered what he was doing there. Then, on the flank of their workmen they tramped on, following the line of rails.

"Withdrawing your people from the harbour?" said the doctor, addressing himself to the chief engineer of the railway, who had accompanied Charles Gould so far in his way to the town, walking by the side of the horse, with his hand on the saddle-bow. They had stopped just outside the open door to let the workmen cross the road.

"As quick as I can. We are not a political faction," answered the engineer, meaningly. "And we are not going to give our new rulers a handle against the railway. You approve me, Gould?"

"Absolutely," said Charles Gould's impassive voice, high up and outside the dim parallelogram of light falling on the road through the open door.

With Sotillo expected from one side, and Pedro Montero from the other, the engineer-in-chief's only anxiety now was to avoid a collision with either. Sulaco, for him, was a railway station, a terminus, workshops, a great accumulation of stores. As against the mob the railway defended its property, but politically the railway was neutral. He was a brave man; and in that spirit of neutrality he had carried proposals of truce to the self-appointed chiefs of the popular party, the deputies Fuentes and Gamacho. Bullets were still flying about when he had crossed the Plaza on that mission, waving above his head a white napkin belonging to the table linen of the Amarilla Club.

He was rather proud of this exploit; and reflecting that the doctor, busy all day with the wounded in the patio of the Casa Gould, had not had time to hear the news, he began a succinct narrative. He had communicated to them the intelligence from the Construction Camp as to Pedro Montero. The brother of the victorious general, he had assured them, could be expected at Sulaco at any time now. This news (as he anticipated), when shouted out of the window by Señor Gamacho, induced a rush of the mob along the Campo Road towards Rincon. The two deputies also, after shaking hands with him effusively, mounted and galloped off to meet the great man. "I have misled them a little as to the time," the chief engineer confessed. "However hard he rides, he can scarcely get here before the morning. But my object is attained. I've secured several hours' peace for the losing party. But I did not tell them anything about Sotillo, for fear they would take it into their heads to try to get hold of the harbour again, either to oppose him or welcome him—there's no saying which. There was Gould's silver, on which rests the remnant of our hopes. Decoud's retreat had to be thought of, too. I think the railway has done pretty well by its friends without compromising itself hopelessly. Now the parties must be left to themselves."

"Costaguana for the Costaguaneros," interjected the doctor, sardonically. "It is a fine country, and they have raised a fine crop of hates, vengeance, murder, and rapine—those sons of the country."

"Well, I am one of them," Charles Gould's voice sounded, calmly, "and I must be going on to see to my own crop of trouble. My wife has driven straight on, doctor?"

"Yes. All was quiet on this side. Mrs. Gould has taken the two girls with her."

Charles Gould rode on, and the engineer-in-chief followed the doctor indoors.

"That man is calmness personified," he said, appreciatively, dropping on a bench, and stretching his well-shaped legs in cycling stockings nearly across the doorway. "He must be extremely sure of himself."

"If that's all he is sure of, then he is sure of nothing," said the doctor. He had perched himself again on the end of the table. He nursed his cheek in the palm of one hand, while the other sustained the elbow. "It is the last thing a man ought to be sure of." The candle, half-consumed and burning dimly with a long wick, lighted up from below his inclined face, whose expression affected by the drawn-in cicatrices in the cheeks, had something vaguely unnatural, an exaggerated remorseful bitterness. As he sat there he had the air of meditating upon sinister things. The engineer-in-chief gazed at him for a time before he protested.

"I really don't see that. For me there seems to be nothing else. However——"

He was a wise man, but he could not quite conceal his contempt for that sort of paradox; in fact, Dr. Monygham was not liked by the Europeans of Sulaco. His outward aspect of an outcast, which he preserved even in Mrs. Gould's drawing-room, provoked unfavourable criticism. There could be no doubt of his intelligence; and as he had lived for over twenty years in the country, the pessimism of his outlook could not be altogether ignored. But instinctively, in self-defence of their activities and hopes, his hearers put it to the account of some hidden imperfection in the man's character. It was known that many years before, when quite young, he had been made by Guzman Bento chief medical officer of the army. Not one of the Europeans then in the service of Costaguana had been so much liked and trusted by the fierce old Dictator.

Afterwards his story was not so clear. It lost itself amongst the innumerable tales of conspiracies and plots against the tyrant as a stream is lost in an arid belt of sandy country before it emerges, diminished and troubled, perhaps, on the other side. The doctor made no secret of it that he had lived for years in the wildest parts of the Republic, wandering with almost unknown Indian tribes in the great forests of the far interior where the great rivers have their sources. But it was mere aimless wandering; he had written nothing, collected nothing, brought nothing for science out of the twilight of the forests, which seemed to cling to his battered personality limping about Sulaco, where it had drifted in casually, only to get stranded on the shores of the sea.

It was also known that he had lived in a state of destitution till the arrival of the Goulds from Europe. Don Carlos and Doña Emilia had taken up the mad English doctor, when it became apparent that for all his savage independence he could be tamed by kindness. Perhaps it was only hunger that had tamed him. In years gone by he had certainly been acquainted with Charles Gould's father in Sta. Marta; and now, no matter what were the dark passages of his history, as the medical officer of the San Tomé mine he became a recognized personality. He was recognized, but not unreservedly accepted. So much defiant eccentricity and such an outspoken scorn for mankind seemed to point to mere recklessness of judgment, the bravado of guilt. Besides, since he had become again of some account, vague whispers had been heard that years ago, when fallen into disgrace and thrown into prison by Guzman Bento at the time of the so-called Great Conspiracy, he had betrayed some of his best friends amongst the conspirators. Nobody pretended to believe that whisper; the whole story of the Great Conspiracy was hopelessly involved and obscure; it is admitted in Costaguana that there never had been a conspiracy except in the diseased imagination of the Tyrant; and, therefore, nothing and no one to betray; though the most distinguished Costaguaneros had been imprisoned and executed upon that accusation. The procedure had dragged on for years, decimating the better class like a pestilence. The mere expression of sorrow for the fate of executed kinsmen had been punished with death. Don José Avellanos was perhaps the only one living who knew the whole story of those unspeakable cruelties. He had suffered from them himself, and he, with a shrug of the shoulders and a nervous, jerky gesture of the arm, was wont to put away from him, as it were, every allusion to it. But whatever the reason, Dr. Monygham, a personage in the administration of the Gould Concession, treated with reverent awe by the miners, and indulged in his peculiarities by Mrs. Gould, remained somehow outside the pale.

It was not from any liking for the doctor that the engineer-in-chief had lingered in the inn upon the plain. He liked old Viola much better. He had come to look upon the Albergo d'Italia Una as a dependence of the railway. Many of his subordinates had their quarters there. Mrs. Gould's interest in the family conferred upon it a sort of distinction. The engineer-in-chief, with an army of workers under his orders, appreciated the moral influence of the old Garibaldino upon his countrymen. His austere, old-world Republicanism had a severe, soldier-like standard of faithfulness and duty, as if the world were a battlefield where men had to fight for the sake of universal love and brotherhood, instead of a more or less large share of booty.

"Poor old chap!" he said, after he had heard the doctor's account of Teresa. "He'll never be able to keep the place going by himself. I shall be sorry."

"He's quite alone up there," grunted Doctor Monygham, with a toss of his heavy head towards the narrow staircase. "Every living soul has cleared out, and Mrs. Gould took the girls away just now. It might not be over-safe for them out here before very long. Of course, as a doctor I can do nothing more here; but she has asked me to stay with old Viola, and as I have no horse to get back to the mine, where I ought to be, I made no difficulty to stay. They can do without me in the town."

"I have a good mind to remain with you, doctor, till we see whether anything happens to-night at the harbour," declared the engineer-in-chief. "He must not be molested by Sotillo's soldiery, who may push on as far as this at once. Sotillo used to be very cordial to me at the Goulds' and at the club. How that man'll ever dare to look any of his friends here in the face I can't imagine."

"He'll no doubt begin by shooting some of them to get over the first awkwardness," said the doctor. "Nothing in this country serves better your military man who has changed sides than a few summary executions." He spoke with a gloomy positiveness

that left no room for protest. The engineer-in-chief
did not attempt any. He simply nodded several
times regretfully, then said—

"I think we shall be able to mount you in the morning, doctor. Our peons have recovered some of our
stampeded horses. By riding hard and taking a wide
circuit by Los Hatos and along the edge of the forest,
clear of Rincon altogether, you may hope to reach the
San Tomé bridge without being interfered with. The
mine is just now, to my mind, the safest place for anybody at all compromised. I only wish the railway was
as difficult to touch."

"Am I compromised?" Doctor Monygham brought
out slowly after a short silence.

"The whole Gould Concession is compromised. It
could not have remained for ever outside the political
life of the country—if those convulsions may be called
life. The thing is—can it be touched? The moment
was bound to come when neutrality would become impossible, and Charles Gould understood this well. I
believe he is prepared for every extremity. A man of
his sort has never contemplated remaining indefinitely
at the mercy of ignorance and corruption. It was like
being a prisoner in a cavern of banditti with the price of
your ransom in your pocket, and buying your life from
day to day. Your mere safety, not your liberty, mind,
doctor. I know what I am talking about. The image
at which you shrug your shoulders is perfectly correct,
especially if you conceive such a prisoner endowed with
the power of replenishing his pocket by means as remote
from the faculties of his captors as if they were magic.
You must have understood that as well as I do, doctor.
He was in the position of the goose with the golden
eggs. I broached this matter to him as far back as Sir
John's visit here. The prisoner of stupid and greedy

banditti is always at the mercy of the first imbecile
ruffian, who may blow out his brains in a fit of temper or
for some prospect of an immediate big haul. The tale of
killing the goose with the golden eggs has not been
evolved for nothing out of the wisdom of mankind. It
is a story that will never grow old. That is why
Charles Gould in his deep, dumb way has countenanced
the Ribierist Mandate, the first public act that promised
him safety on other than venal grounds. Ribierism has
failed, as everything merely rational fails in this
country. But Gould remains logical in wishing to save
this big lot of silver. Decoud's plan of a counter-
revolution may be practicable or not, it may have a
chance, or it may not have a chance. With all my
experience of this revolutionary continent, I can hardly
yet look at their methods seriously. Decoud has been
reading to us his draft of a proclamation, and talking
very well for two hours about his plan of action. He
had arguments which should have appeared solid
enough if we, members of old, stable political and
national organizations, were not startled by the mere
idea of a new State evolved like this out of the head of a
scoffing young man fleeing for his life, with a proclamation in his pocket, to a rough, jeering, half-bred swashbuckler, who in this part of the world is called a general.
It sounds like a comic fairy tale—and behold, it may
come off; because it is true to the very spirit of the
country."

"Is the silver gone off, then?" asked the doctor,
moodily.

The chief engineer pulled out his watch. "By
Captain Mitchell's reckoning—and he ought to know—
it has been gone long enough now to be some three or
four miles outside the harbour; and, as Mitchell say,
Nostromo is the sort of seaman to make the best of his

opportunities." Here the doctor grunted so heavily that
the other changed his tone.

"You have a poor opinion of that move, doctor? But
why? Charles Gould has got to play his game out,
though he is not the man to formulate his conduct even
to himself, perhaps, let alone to others. It may be that
the game has been partly suggested to him by Holroyd;
but it accords with his character, too; and that is why it
has been so successful. Haven't they come to calling
him 'El Rey de Sulaco' in Sta. Marta? A nickname
may be the best record of a success. That's what I call
putting the face of a joke upon the body of a truth. My
dear sir, when I first arrived in Sta. Marta I was struck
by the way all those journalists, demagogues, members
of Congress, and all those generals and judges cringed
before a sleepy-eyed advocate without practice simply
because he was the plenipotentiary of the Gould Concession. Sir John when he came out was impressed, too."

"A new State, with that plump dandy, Decoud, for
the first President," mused Dr. Monygham, nursing his
cheek and swinging his legs all the time.

"Upon my word, and why not?" the chief engineer
retorted in an unexpectedly earnest and confidential
voice. It was as if something subtle in the air of
Costaguana had inoculated him with the local faith in
"pronunciamientos." All at once he began to talk, like
an expert revolutionist, of the instrument ready to hand
in the intact army at Cayta, which could be brought
back in a few days to Sulaco if only Decoud managed to
make his way at once down the coast. For the military
chief there was Barrios, who had nothing but a bullet to
expect from Montero, his former professional rival and
bitter enemy. Barrios's concurrence was assured. As
to his army, it had nothing to expect from Montero
either; not even a month's pay. From that point of

view the existence of the treasure was of enormous importance. The mere knowledge that it had been saved from the Monterists would be a strong inducement for the Cayta troops to embrace the cause of the new State.

The doctor turned round and contemplated his companion for some time.

"This Decoud, I see, is a persuasive young beggar," he remarked at last. "And pray is it for this, then, that Charles Gould has let the whole lot of ingots go out to sea in charge of that Nostromo?"

"Charles Gould," said the engineer-in-chief, "has said no more about his motive than usual. You know, he doesn't talk. But we all here know his motive, and he has only one—the safety of the San Tomé mine with the preservation of the Gould Concession in the spirit of his compact with Holroyd. Holroyd is another uncommon man. They understand each other's imaginative side. One is thirty, the other nearly sixty, and they have been made for each other. To be a millionaire, and such a millionaire as Holroyd, is like being eternally young. The audacity of youth reckons upon what it fancies an unlimited time at its disposal; but a millionaire has unlimited means in his hand—which is better. One's time on earth is an uncertain quantity, but about the long reach of millions there is no doubt. The introduction of a pure form of Christianity into this continent is a dream for a youthful enthusiast, and I have been trying to explain to you why Holroyd at fifty-eight is like a man on the threshold of life, and better, too. He's not a missionary, but the San Tomé mine holds just that for him. I assure you, in sober truth, that he could not manage to keep this out of a strictly business conference upon the finances of Costaguana he had with Sir John a couple of years ago.

Sir John mentioned it with amazement in a letter he wrote to me here, from San Francisco, when on his way home. Upon my word, doctor, things seem to be worth nothing by what they are in themselves. I begin to believe that the only solid thing about them is the spiritual value which everyone discovers in his own form of activity——"

"Bah!" interrupted the doctor, without stopping for an instant the idle swinging movement of his legs. "Self-flattery. Food for that vanity which makes the world go round. Meantime, what do you think is going to happen to the treasure floating about the gulf with the great Capataz and the great politician?"

"Why are you uneasy about it, doctor?"

"I uneasy! And what the devil is it to me? I put no spiritual value into my desires, or my opinions, or my actions. They have not enough vastness to give me room for self-flattery. Look, for instance, I should certainly have liked to ease the last moments of that poor woman. And I can't. It's impossible. Have you met the impossible face to face—or have you, the Napoleon of railways, no such word in your dictionary?"

"Is she bound to have a very bad time of it?" asked the chief engineer, with humane concern.

Slow, heavy footsteps moved across the planks above the heavy hard wood beams of the kitchen. Then down the narrow opening of the staircase made in the thickness of the wall, and narrow enough to be defended by one man against twenty enemies, came the murmur of two voices, one faint and broken, the other deep and gentle answering it, and in its graver tone covering the weaker sound.

The two men remained still and silent till the murmurs ceased, then the doctor shrugged his shoulders and muttered—

"Yes, she's bound to. And I could do nothing if I went up now."

A long period of silence above and below ensued.

"I fancy," began the engineer, in a subdued voice, "that you mistrust Captain Mitchell's Capataz."

"Mistrust him!" muttered the doctor through his teeth. "I believe him capable of anything—even of the most absurd fidelity. I am the last person he spoke to before he left the wharf, you know. The poor woman up there wanted to see him, and I let him go up to her. The dying must not be contradicted, you know. She seemed then fairly calm and resigned, but the scoundrel in those ten minutes or so has done or said something which seems to have driven her into despair. You know," went on the doctor, hesitatingly, "women are so very unaccountable in every position, and at all times of life, that I thought sometimes she was in a way, don't you see? in love with him—the Capataz. The rascal has his own charm indubitably, or he would not have made the conquest of all the populace of the town. No, no, I am not absurd. I may have given a wrong name to some strong sentiment for him on her part, to an unreasonable and simple attitude a woman is apt to take up emotionally towards a man. She used to abuse him to me frequently, which, of course, is not inconsistent with my idea. Not at all. It looked to me as if she were always thinking of him. He was something important in her life. You know, I have seen a lot of those people. Whenever I came down from the mine Mrs. Gould used to ask me to keep my eye on them. She likes Italians; she has lived a long time in Italy, I believe, and she took a special fancy to that old Garibaldino. A remarkable chap enough. A rugged and dreamy character, living in the republicanism of his young days as if in a cloud.

He has encouraged much of the Capataz's confounded nonsense—the high-strung, exalted old beggar!"

"What sort of nonsense?" wondered the chief engineer. "I found the Capataz always a very shrewd and sensible fellow, absolutely fearless, and remarkably useful. A perfect handy man. Sir John was greatly impressed by his resourcefulness and attention when he made that overland journey from Sta. Marta. Later on, as you might have heard, he rendered us a service by disclosing to the then chief of police the presence in the town of some professional thieves, who came from a distance to wreck and rob our monthly pay train. He has certainly organized the lighterage service of the harbour for the O.S.N. Company with great ability. He knows how to make himself obeyed, foreigner though he is. It is true that the Cargadores are strangers here, too, for the most part—immigrants, Isleños."

"His prestige is his fortune," muttered the doctor, sourly.

"The man has proved his trustworthiness up to the hilt on innumerable occasions and in all sorts of ways," argued the engineer. "When this question of the silver arose, Captain Mitchell naturally was very warmly of the opinion that his Capataz was the only man fit for the trust. As a sailor, of course, I suppose so. But as a man, don't you know, Gould, Decoud, and myself judged that it didn't matter in the least who went. Any boatman would have done just as well. Pray, what could a thief do with such a lot of ingots? If he ran off with them he would have in the end to land somewhere, and how could he conceal his cargo from the knowledge of the people ashore? We dismissed that consideration from our minds. Moreover, Decoud was going. There have been occasions when the Capataz has been more implicitly trusted."

"He took a slightly different view," the doctor said. "I heard him declare in this very room that it would be the most desperate affair of his life. He made a sort of verbal will here in my hearing, appointing old Viola his executor; and, by Jove! do you know, he—he's not grown rich by his fidelity to you good people of the railway and the harbour. I suppose he obtains some—how do you say that?—some spiritual value for his labours, or else I don't know why the devil he should be faithful to you, Gould, Mitchell, or anybody else. He knows this country well. He knows, for instance, that Gamacho, the Deputy from Javira, has been nothing else but a 'tramposo' of the commonest sort, a petty pedlar of the Campo, till he managed to get enough goods on credit from Anzani to open a little store in the wilds, and got himself elected by the drunken mozos that hang about the Estancias and the poorest sort of rancheros who were in his debt. And Gamacho, who to-morrow will be probably one of our high officials, is a stranger, too—an Isleño. He might have been a Cargador on the O. S. N. wharf had he not (the posadero of Rincon is ready to swear it) murdered a pedlar in the woods and stolen his pack to begin life on. And do you think that Gamacho, then, would have ever become a hero with the democracy of this place, like our Capataz? Of course not. He isn't half the man. No; decidedly, I think that Nostromo is a fool."

The doctor's talk was distasteful to the builder of railways. "It is impossible to argue that point," he said, philosophically. "Each man has his gifts. You should have heard Gamacho haranguing his friends in the street. He has a howling voice, and he shouted like mad, lifting his clenched fist right above his head, and throwing his body half out of the window. At every pause the rabble below yelled, 'Down with the Oligarchs! *Viva* la Libertad!'* Fuentes inside looked extremely miserable. You know, he is the brother of Jorge Fuentes, who has been Minister of the Interior for six months or so, some few years back. Of course, he has no conscience; but he is a man of birth and education—at one time the director of the Customs of Cayta. That idiot-brute Gamacho fastened himself upon him with his following of the lowest rabble. His sickly fear of that ruffian was the most rejoicing sight imaginable."

He got up and went to the door to look out towards the harbour. "All quiet," he said; "I wonder if Sotillo really means to turn up here?"

CHAPTER TWO

CAPTAIN MITCHELL, pacing the wharf, was asking himself the same question. There was always the doubt whether the warning of the Esmeralda telegraphist— a fragmentary and interrupted message—had been properly understood. However, the good man had made up his mind not to go to bed till daylight, if even then. He imagined himself to have rendered an enormous service to Charles Gould. When he thought of the saved silver he rubbed his hands together with satisfaction. In his simple way he was proud at being a party to this extremely clever expedient. It was he, who had given it a practical shape by suggesting the possibility of intercepting at sea the north-bound steamer. And it was advantageous to his Company, too, which would have lost a valuable freight if the treasure had been left ashore to be confiscated. The pleasure of disappointing the Monterists was also very great. Authoritative by temperament and the long habit of command, Captain Mitchell was no democrat. He even went so far as to profess a contempt for parliamentarism itself. "His Excellency Don Vincente Ribiera," he used to say, "whom I and that fellow of mine, Nostromo, had the honour, sir, and the pleasure of saving from a cruel death, deferred too much to his Congress. It was a mistake—a distinct mistake, sir."

The guileless old seaman superintending the O.S.N. service imagined that the last three days had exhausted every startling surprise the political life of Costaguana could offer. He used to confess afterwards that the events which followed surpassed his imagination. To begin with, Sulaco (because of the seizure of the cables and the disorganization of the steam service) remained for a whole fortnight cut off from the rest of the world like a besieged city.

"One would not have believed it possible; but so it was, sir. A full fortnight."

The account of the extraordinary things that happened during that time, and the powerful emotions he experienced, acquired a comic*impressiveness from the pompous manner of his personal narrative. He opened it always by assuring his hearer that he was "in the thick of things from first to last." Then he would begin by describing the getting away of the silver, and his natural anxiety lest "his fellow" in charge of the lighter should make some mistake. Apart from the loss of so much precious metal, the life of Señor Martin Decoud, an agreeable, wealthy, and well-informed young gentleman, would have been jeopardized through his falling into the hands of his political enemies. Captain Mitchell also admitted that in his solitary vigil on the wharf he had felt a certain measure of concern for the future of the whole country.

"A feeling, sir," he explained, "perfectly comprehensible in a man properly grateful for the many kindnesses received from the best families of merchants and other native gentlemen of independent means, who, barely saved by us from the excesses of the mob, seemed, to my mind's eye, destined to become the prey in person and fortune of the native soldiery, which, as is well known, behave with regrettable barbarity to the inhabitants during their civil commotions. And then, sir, there were the Goulds, for both of whom, man and wife, I could not but entertain the warmest feelings deserved by their hospitality and kindness. I felt, too,

the dangers of the gentlemen of the Amarilla Club, who
had made me honorary member, and had treated me
with uniform regard and civility, both in my capacity
of Consular Agent and as Superintendent of an important Steam Service. Miss Antonia Avellanos,
the most beautiful and accomplished young lady whom
it had ever been my privilege to speak to, was not a
little in my mind, I confess. How the interests of my
Company would be affected by the impending change
of officials claimed a large share of my attention, too.
In short, sir, I was extremely anxious and very tired, as
you may suppose, by the exciting and memorable events
in which I had taken my little part. The Company's
building containing my residence was within five
minutes' walk, with the attraction of some supper and of
my hammock (I always take my nightly rest in a hammock, as the most suitable to the climate); but somehow, sir, though evidently I could do nothing for any
one by remaining about, I could not tear myself away
from that wharf, where the fatigue made me stumble
painfully at times. The night was excessively dark—
the darkest I remember in my life; so that I began to
think that the arrival of the transport from Esmeralda
could not possibly take place before daylight, owing
to the difficulty of navigating the gulf. The mosquitoes
bit like fury. We have been infested here with mosquitoes before the late improvements; a peculiar harbour brand, sir, renowned for its ferocity. They were
like a cloud about my head, and I shouldn't wonder
that but for their attacks I would have dozed off as I
walked up and down, and got a heavy fall. I kept on
smoking cigar after cigar, more to protect myself from
being eaten up alive than from any real relish for the
weed. Then, sir, when perhaps for the twentieth time
I was approaching my watch to the lighted end in order

to see the time, and observing with surprise that it
wanted yet ten minutes to midnight, I heard the splash
of a ship's propeller—an unmistakable sound to a
sailor's ear on such a calm night. It was faint indeed,
because they were advancing with precaution and dead
slow, both on account of the darkness and from their
desire of not revealing too soon their presence: a very
unnecessary care, because, I verily believe, in all the
enormous extent of this harbour I was the only living
soul about. Even the usual staff of watchmen and
others had been absent from their posts for several
nights owing to the disturbances. I stood stock still,
after dropping and stamping out my cigar—a circumstance highly agreeable, I should think, to the mosquitoes, if I may judge from the state of my face next morning. But that was a trifling inconvenience in comparison with the brutal proceedings I became victim of
on the part of Sotillo. Something utterly inconceiv-
able, sir; more like the proceedings of a maniac than the
action of a sane man, however lost to all sense of honour
and decency. But Sotillo was furious at the failure of
his thievish scheme."

In this Captain Mitchell was right. Sotillo was indeed infuriated. Captain Mitchell, however, had not
been arrested at once; a vivid curiosity induced him to
remain on the wharf (which is nearly four hundred feet
long) to see, or rather hear, the whole process of dis-
embarkation. Concealed by the railway truck used
for the silver, which had been run back afterwards to
the shore end of the jetty, Captain Mitchell saw the
small detachment thrown forward, pass by, taking
different directions upon the plain. Meantime, the
troops were being landed and formed into a column,
whose head crept up gradually so close to him that he
made it out, barring nearly the whole width of the

wharf, only a very few yards from him. Then the low, shuffling, murmuring, clinking sounds ceased, and the whole mass remained for about an hour motionless and silent, awaiting the return of the scouts. On land nothing was to be heard except the deep baying of the mastiffs at the railway yards, answered by the faint barking of the curs infesting the outer limits of the town. A detached knot of dark shapes stood in front of the head of the column.

Presently the picket at the end of the wharf began to challenge in undertones single figures approaching from the plain. Those messengers sent back from the scouting parties flung to their comrades brief sentences and passed on rapidly, becoming lost in the great motionless mass, to make their report to the Staff. It occurred to Captain Mitchell that his position could become disagreeable and perhaps dangerous, when suddenly, at the head of the jetty, there was a shout of command, a bugle call, followed by a stir and a rattling of arms, and a murmuring noise that ran right up the column. Near by a loud voice directed hurriedly, "Push that railway car out of the way!" At the rush of bare feet to execute the order Captain Mitchell skipped back a pace or two; the car, suddenly impelled by many hands, flew away from him along the rails, and before he knew what had happened he found himself surrounded and seized by his arms and the collar of his coat.

"We have caught a man hiding here, *mi teniente!*" cried one of his captors.

"Hold him on one side till the rearguard comes along," answered the voice. The whole column streamed past Captain Mitchell at a run, the thundering noise of their feet dying away suddenly on the shore. His captors held him tightly, disregarding his declaration that he was an Englishman and his loud demands to

be taken at once before their commanding officer.
Finally he lapsed into dignified silence. With a hollow
rumble of wheels on the planks a couple of field guns,
dragged by hand, rolled by. Then, after a small body
of men had marched past escorting four or five figures
which walked in advance, with a jingle of steel scabbards, he felt a tug at his arms, and was ordered to come
along. During the passage from the wharf to the
Custom House it is to be feared that Captain Mitchell
was subjected to certain indignities at the hands of the
soldiers—such as jerks, thumps on the neck, forcible
application of the butt of a rifle to the small of his back.
Their ideas of speed were not in accord with his notion
of his dignity. He became flustered, flushed, and helpless. It was as if the world were coming to an end.

The long building was surrounded by troops, which
were already piling arms by companies and preparing
to pass the night lying on the ground in their ponchos
with their sacks under their heads. Corporals moved
with swinging lanterns posting sentries all round the
walls wherever there was a door or an opening. Sotillo
was taking his measures to protect his conquest as if
it had indeed contained the treasure. His desire to
make his fortune at one audacious stroke of genius had
overmastered his reasoning faculties. He would not
believe in the possibility of failure; the mere hint of
such a thing made his brain reel with rage. Every
circumstance pointing to it appeared incredible. The
statement of Hirsch, which was so absolutely fatal to his
hopes, could by no means be admitted. It is true, too,
that Hirsch's story had been told so incoherently, with
such excessive signs of distraction, that it really looked
improbable. It was extremely difficult, as the saying
is, to make head or tail of it. On the bridge of the
steamer, directly after his rescue, Sotillo and his officers,

in their impatience and excitement, would not give
the wretched man time to collect such few wits as remained to him. He ought to have been quieted,
soothed, and reassured, whereas he had been roughly
handled, cuffed, shaken, and addressed in menacing
tones. His struggles, his wriggles, his attempts to get
down on his knees, followed by the most violent efforts
to break away, as if he meant incontinently to jump
overboard, his shrieks and shrinkings and cowering
wild glances had filled them first with amazement, then
with a doubt of his genuineness, as men are wont to suspect the sincerity of every great passion. His Spanish,
too, became so mixed up with German that the better
half of his statements remained incomprehensible. He
tried to propitiate them by calling them *hochwohlgeboren herren,*[*] which in itself sounded suspicious. When
admonished sternly not to trifle he repeated his entreaties and protestations of loyalty and innocence again
in German, obstinately, because he was not aware in
what language he was speaking. His identity, of
course, was perfectly known as an inhabitant of Esmeralda, but this made the matter no clearer. As he
kept on forgetting Decoud's name, mixing him up with
several other people he had seen in the Casa Gould, it
looked as if they all had been in the lighter together;
and for a moment Sotillo thought that he had drowned
every prominent Ribierist of Sulaco. The improb-
ability of such a thing threw a doubt upon the whole
statement. Hirsch was either mad or playing a part—
pretending fear and distraction on the spur of the moment to cover the truth. Sotillo's rapacity, excited to
the highest pitch by the prospect of an immense booty,
could believe in nothing adverse. This Jew might have
been very much frightened by the accident, but he
knew where the silver was concealed, and had invented

this story, with his Jewish cunning, to put him entirely
off the track as to what had been done.

Sotillo had taken up his quarters on the upper floor
in a vast apartment with heavy black beams. But
there was no ceiling, and the eye lost itself in the darkness under the high pitch of the roof. The thick shutters stood open. On a long table could be seen a large
inkstand, some stumpy, inky quill pens, and two
square wooden boxes, each holding half a hundred-
weight of sand. Sheets of grey coarse official paper
bestrewed the floor. It must have been a room occupied by some higher official of the Customs, because
a large leathern armchair stood behind the table,
with other high-backed chairs scattered about. A net
hammock was swung under one of the beams—for the
official's afternoon siesta, no doubt. A couple of
candles stuck into tall iron candlesticks gave a dim
reddish light. The colonel's hat, sword, and revolver
lay between them, and a couple of his more trusty
officers lounged gloomily against the table. The
colonel threw himself into the armchair, and a big
negro with a sergeant's stripes on his ragged sleeve,
kneeling down, pulled off his boots. Sotillo's ebony
moustache contrasted violently with the livid colouring
of his cheeks. His eyes were sombre and as if sunk very
far into his head. He seemed exhausted by his per-
plexities, languid with disappointment; but when the
sentry on the landing thrust his head in to announce the
arrival of a prisoner, he revived at once.

"Let him be brought in," he shouted, fiercely.

The door flew open, and Captain Mitchell, bareheaded, his waistcoat open, the bow of his tie under his
ear, was hustled into the room.

Sotillo recognized him at once. He could not have
hoped for a more precious capture; here was a man who

Since his arrival in Sulaco the colonel's ideas had undergone some modification.

He no longer wished for a political career in Montero's administration. He had always doubted the safety of that course. Since he had learned from the chief engineer that at daylight most likely he would be confronted by Pedro Montero his misgivings on that point had considerably increased. The guerrillero brother of the general—the Pedrito of popular speech—had a reputation of his own. He wasn't safe to deal with. Sotillo had vaguely planned seizing not only the treasure but the town itself, and then negotiating at leisure. But in the face of facts learned from the chief engineer (who had frankly disclosed to him the whole situation) his audacity, never of a very dashing kind, had been replaced by a most cautious hesitation.

"An army—an army crossed the mountains under Pedrito already," he had repeated, unable to hide his consternation. "If it had not been that I am given the news by a man of your position I would never have believed it. Astonishing!"

"An armed force," corrected the engineer, suavely.

His aim was attained. It was to keep Sulaco clear of any armed occupation for a few hours longer, to let those whom fear impelled leave the town. In the general dismay there were families hopeful enough to fly upon the road towards Los Hatos, which was left open by the withdrawal of the armed rabble under Señores Fuentes and Gamacho, to Rincon, with their enthusiastic welcome for Pedro Montero. It was a hasty and risky exodus, and it was said that Hernandez, occupying with his band the woods about Los Hatos, was receiving the fugitives. That a good many people he knew were contemplating such a flight had been well known to the chief engineer.

Father Corbelàn's efforts in the cause of that most
pious robber had not been altogether fruitless. The
political chief of Sulaco had yielded at the last moment
to the urgent entreaties of the priest, had signed a
provisional nomination appointing Hernandez a general,
and calling upon him officially in this new capacity to
preserve order in the town. The fact is that the
political chief, seeing the situation desperate, did not
care what he signed. It was the last official document
he signed before he left the palace of the Intendencia
for the refuge of the O.S.N. Company's office. But
even had he meant his act to be effective it was already
too late. The riot which he feared and expected broke
out in less than an hour after Father Corbelàn had left
him. Indeed, Father Corbelàn, who had appointed a
meeting with Nostromo in the Dominican Convent,
where he had his residence in one of the cells, never
managed to reach the place. From the Intendencia he
had gone straight on to the Avellanos's house to tell
his brother-in-law, and though he stayed there no
more than half an hour he had found himself cut off
from his ascetic abode. Nostromo, after waiting there
for some time, watching uneasily the increasing uproar
in the street, had made his way to the offices of the
Porvenir, and stayed there till daylight, as Decoud had
mentioned in the letter to his sister. Thus the Capataz, instead of riding towards the Los Hatos woods as
bearer of Hernandez's nomination, had remained in
town to save the life of the President Dictator, to assist
in repressing the outbreak of the mob, and at last to sail
out with the silver of the mine.

But Father Corbelàn, escaping to Hernandez, had the
document in his pocket, a piece of official writing turning a bandit into a general in a memorable last official
act of the Ribierist party, whose watchwords were

honesty, peace, and progress. Probably neither the priest nor the bandit saw the irony of it. Father Corbelàn must have found messengers to send into the town, for early on the second day of the disturbances there were rumours of Hernandez being on the road to Los Hatos ready to receive those who would put themselves under his protection. A strange-looking horseman, elderly and audacious, had appeared in the town, riding slowly while his eyes examined the fronts of the houses, as though he had never seen such high buildings before. Before the cathedral he had dismounted, and, kneeling in the middle of the Plaza, his bridle over his arm and his hat lying in front of him on the ground, had bowed his head, crossing himself and beating his breast for some little time. Remounting his horse, with a fearless but not unfriendly look round the little gathering formed about his public devotions, he had asked for the Casa Avellanos. A score of hands were extended in answer, with fingers pointing up the Calle de la Constitucion.

The horseman had gone on with only a glance of casual curiosity upwards to the windows of the Amarilla Club at the corner. His stentorian voice shouted periodically in the empty street, "Which is the Casa Avellanos?" till an answer came from the scared porter, and he disappeared under the gate. The letter he was bringing, written by Father Corbelàn with a pencil by the camp-fire of Hernandez, was addressed to Don José, of whose critical state the priest was not aware. Antonia read it, and, after consulting Charles Gould, sent it on for the information of the gentlemen garrisoning the Amarilla Club. For herself, her mind was made up; she would rejoin her uncle; she would entrust the last day—the last hours perhaps—of her father's life to the keeping of the bandit, whose existence was a protest against the irresponsible tyranny of all parties alike, against the moral darkness of the land. The gloom of Los Hatos woods was preferable; a life of hardships in the train of a robber band less debasing. Antonia embraced with all her soul her uncle's obstinate defiance of misfortune. It was grounded in the belief in the man whom she loved.

In his message the Vicar-General answered upon his head for Hernandez's fidelity. As to his power, he pointed out that he had remained unsubdued for so many years. In that letter Decoud's idea of the new Occidental State (whose flourishing and stable condition is a matter of common knowledge now) was for the first time made public and used as an argument. Hernandez, ex-bandit and the last general of Ribierist creation, was confident of being able to hold the tract of country between the woods of Los Hatos and the coast range till that devoted patriot, Don Martin Decoud, could bring General Barrios back to Sulaco for the reconquest of the town.

"Heaven itself wills it. Providence is on our side," wrote Father Corbelàn; there was no time to reflect upon or to controvert his statement; and if the discussion started upon the reading of that letter in the Amarilla Club was violent, it was also shortlived. In the general bewilderment of the collapse some jumped at the idea with joyful astonishment as upon the amazing discovery of a new hope. Others became fascinated by the prospect of immediate personal safety for their women and children. The majority caught at it as a drowning man catches at a straw. Father Corbelàn was unexpectedly offering them a refuge from Pedrito Montero with his llaneros allied to Señores Fuentes and Gamacho with their armed rabble.

All the latter part of the afternoon an animated

discussion went on in the big rooms of the Amarilla
Club. Even those members posted at the windows
with rifles and carbines to guard the end of the street
in case of an offensive return of the populace shouted
their opinions and arguments over their shoulders. As
dusk fell Don Juste Lopez, inviting those caballeros who
were of his way of thinking to follow him, withdrew
into the corridor, where at a little table in the light of
two candles he busied himself in composing an address,
or rather a solemn declaration to be presented to Pedrito Montero by a deputation of such members of
Assembly as had elected to remain in town. His idea
was to propitiate him in order to save the form at least
of parliamentary institutions. Seated before a blank
sheet of paper, a goose-quill pen in his hand and surged
upon from all sides, he turned to the right and to the
left, repeating with solemn insistence—

"Caballeros, a moment of silence! A moment of
silence! We ought to make it clear that we bow in all
good faith to the accomplished facts."

The utterance of that phrase seemed to give him a
melancholy satisfaction. The hubbub of voices round
him was growing strained and hoarse. In the sudden
pauses the excited grimacing of the faces would sink all
at once into the stillness of profound dejection.

Meantime, the exodus had begun. Carretas full of
ladies and children rolled swaying across the Plaza, with
men walking or riding by their side; mounted parties
followed on mules and horses; the poorest were setting
out on foot, men and women carrying bundles, clasping
babies in their arms, leading old people, dragging along
the bigger children. When Charles Gould, after leaving
the doctor and the engineer at the Casa Viola, entered
the town by the harbour gate, all those that had meant
to go were gone, and the others had barricaded them-

selves in their houses. In the whole dark street there
was only one spot of flickering lights and moving figures,
where the Señor Administrador recognized his wife's
carriage waiting at the door of the Avellanos's house.
He rode up, almost unnoticed, and looked on without a
word while some of his own servants came out of the
gate carrying Don José Avellanos, who, with closed eyes
and motionless features, appeared perfectly lifeless.
His wife and Antonia walked on each side of the improvised stretcher, which was put at once into the
carriage. The two women embraced; while from the
other side of the landau Father Corbelàn's emissary,
with his ragged beard all streaked with grey, and high,
bronzed cheek-bones, stared, sitting upright in the
saddle. Then Antonia, dry-eyed, got in by the side of
the stretcher, and, after making the sign of the cross
rapidly, lowered a thick veil upon her face. The
servants and the three or four neighbours who had come
to assist, stood back, uncovering their heads. On the
box, Ignacio, resigned now to driving all night (and to
having perhaps his throat cut before daylight) looked
back surlily over his shoulder.

"Drive carefully," cried Mrs. Gould in a tremulous
voice.

"*Si*, carefully, *si nina*," he mumbled, chewing his
lips, his round leathery cheeks quivering. And the
landau rolled slowly out of the light.

"I will see them as far as the ford," said Charles
Gould to his wife. She stood on the edge of the sidewalk with her hands clasped lightly, and nodded to him
as he followed after the carriage. And now the windows of the Amarilla Club were dark. The last spark
of resistance had died out. Turning his head at the
corner, Charles Gould saw his wife crossing over to their
own gate in the lighted patch of the street. One of their

neighbours, a well-known merchant and landowner of the province, followed at her elbow, talking with great gestures. As she passed in all the lights went out in the street, which remained dark and empty from end to end.

The houses of the vast Plaza were lost in the night. High up, like a star, there was a small gleam in one of the towers of the cathedral; and the equestrian statue gleamed pale against the black trees of the Alameda, like a ghost of royalty haunting the scenes of revolution. The rare prowlers they met ranged themselves against the wall. Beyond the last houses the carriage rolled noiselessly on the soft cushion of dust, and with a greater obscurity a feeling of freshness seemed to fall from the foliage of the trees bordering the country road. The emissary from Hernandez's camp pushed his horse close to Charles Gould.

"Caballero," he said in an interested voice, "you are he whom they call the King of Sulaco, the master of the mine? Is it not so?"

"Yes, I am the master of the mine," answered Charles Gould.

The man cantered for a time in silence, then said, "I have a brother, a sereño in your service in the San Tomé valley. You have proved yourself a just man. There had been no wrong done to any one since you called upon the people to work in the mountains. My brother says that no official of the Government, no oppressor of the Campo, had been seen on your side of the stream. Your own officials do not oppress the people in the gorge. Doubtless they are afraid of your severity. You are a just man and a powerful one," he added.

He spoke in an abrupt, independent tone, but evidently he was communicative with a purpose. He told Charles Gould that he had been a ranchero in one of the

lower valleys, far south, a neighbour of Hernandez in
the old days, and godfather to his eldest boy; one of
those who joined him in his resistance to the recruiting
raid which was the beginning of all their misfortunes.
It was he that, when his compadre had been carried off,
had buried his wife and children, murdered by the
soldiers.

"Si, señor," he muttered, hoarsely, "I and two or three
others, the lucky ones left at liberty, buried them all in
one grave near the ashes of their ranch, under the tree
that had shaded its roof."

It was to him, too, that Hernandez came after he had
deserted, three years afterwards. He had still his
uniform on with the sergeant's stripes on the sleeve, and
the blood of his colonel upon his hands and breast.
Three troopers followed him, of those who had started
in pursuit but had ridden on for liberty. And he told
Charles Gould how he and a few friends, seeing those
soldiers, lay in ambush behind some rocks ready to pull
the trigger on them, when he recognized his compadre
and jumped up from cover, shouting his name, because
he knew that Hernandez could not have been coming
back on an errand of injustice and oppression. Those
three soldiers, together with the party who lay behind
the rocks, had formed the nucleus of the famous band;
and he, the narrator, had been the favourite lieutenant
of Hernandez for many, many years. He mentioned
proudly that the officials had put a price upon his head,
too; but it did not prevent it getting sprinkled with grey
upon his shoulders. And now he had lived long enough
to see his compadre made a general.

He had a burst of muffled laughter. "And now from
robbers we have become soldiers. But look, Caballero,
at those who made us soldiers and him a general! Look
at these people!"

Ignacio shouted. The light of the carriage lamps, running along the nopal hedges that crowned the bank on each side, flashed upon the scared faces of people standing aside in the road, sunk deep, like an English country lane, into the soft soil of the Campo. They cowered; their eyes glistened very big for a second; and then the light, running on, fell upon the half-denuded roots of a big tree, on another stretch of nopal hedge, caught up another bunch of faces glaring back apprehensively. Three women—of whom one was carrying a child—and a couple of men in civilian dress—one armed with a sabre and another with a gun—were grouped about a donkey carrying two bundles tied up in blankets. Further on Ignacio shouted again to pass a carreta, a long wooden box on two high wheels, with the door at the back swinging open. Some ladies in it must have recognized the white mules, because they screamed out, "Is it you, Doña Emilia?"

At the turn of the road the glare of a big fire filled the short stretch vaulted over by the branches meeting overhead. Near the ford of a shallow stream a roadside rancho of woven rushes and a roof of grass had been set on fire by accident, and the flames, roaring viciously, lit up an open space blocked with horses, mules, and a distracted, shouting crowd of people. When Ignacio pulled up, several ladies on foot assailed the carriage, begging Antonia for a seat. To their clamour she answered by pointing silently to her father.

"I must leave you here," said Charles Gould, in the uproar. The flames leaped up sky-high, and in the recoil from the scorching heat across the road the stream of fugitives pressed against the carriage. A middle-aged lady dressed in black silk, but with a coarse manta over her head and a rough branch for a stick in her hand, staggered against the front wheel. Two young girls, frightened and silent, were clinging to her arms. Charles Gould knew her very well.

"*Misericordia!* We are getting terribly bruised in this crowd!" she exclaimed, smiling up courageously to him. "We have started on foot. All our servants ran away yesterday to join the democrats. We are going to put ourselves under the protection of Father Corbelàn, of your sainted uncle, Antonia. He has wrought a miracle in the heart of a most merciless robber. A miracle!"

She raised her voice gradually up to a scream as she was borne along by the pressure of people getting out of the way of some carts coming up out of the ford at a gallop, with loud yells and cracking of whips. Great masses of sparks mingled with black smoke flew over the road; the bamboos of the walls detonated in the fire with the sound of an irregular fusillade. And then the bright blaze sank suddenly, leaving only a red dusk crowded with aimless dark shadows drifting in contrary directions; the noise of voices seemed to die away with the flame; and the tumult of heads, arms, quarrelling, and imprecations passed on fleeing into the darkness.

"I must leave you now," repeated Charles Gould to Antonia. She turned her head slowly and uncovered her face. The emissary and compadre of Hernandez spurred his horse close up.

"Has not the master of the mine any message to send to Hernandez, the master of the Campo?"

The truth of the comparison struck Charles Gould heavily. In his determined purpose he held the mine, and the indomitable bandit held the Campo by the same precarious tenure. They were equals before the lawlessness of the land. It was impossible to disentangle one's activity from its debasing contacts. A close-meshed net of crime and corruption lay upon the whole country. An immense and weary discouragement sealed his lips for a time.

"You are a just man," urged the emissary of Hernandez. "Look at those people who made my compadre a general and have turned us all into soldiers. Look at those oligarchs fleeing for life, with only the clothes on their backs. My compadre does not think of that, but our followers may be wondering greatly, and I would speak for them to you. Listen, señor! For many months now the Campo has been our own. We need ask no man for anything; but soldiers must have their pay to live honestly when the wars are over. It is believed that your soul is so just that a prayer from you would cure the sickness of every beast, like the orison*of the upright judge. Let me have some words from your lips that would act like a charm upon the doubts of our *partida,*where all are men."

"Do you hear what he says?" Charles Gould said in English to Antonia.

"Forgive us our misery!" she exclaimed, hurriedly. "It is your character that is the inexhaustible treasure which may save us all yet; your character, Carlos, not your wealth. I entreat you to give this man your word that you will accept any arrangement my uncle may make with their chief. One word. He will want no more."

On the site of the roadside hut there remained nothing but an enormous heap of embers, throwing afar a darkening red glow, in which Antonia's face appeared deeply flushed with excitement. Charles Gould, with only a short hesitation, pronounced the required pledge. He was like a man who had ventured on a precipitous path with no room to turn, where the only chance of safety is to press forward. At that moment he understood it thoroughly as he looked down at Don José stretched out, hardly breathing, by the side of the erect Antonia, vanquished in a lifelong struggle with the powers of moral darkness, whose stagnant depths breed monstrous crimes and monstrous illusions. In a few words the emissary from Hernandez expressed his complete satisfaction. Stoically Antonia lowered her veil, resisting the longing to inquire about Decoud's escape. But Ignacio leered morosely over his shoulder.

"Take a good look at the mules, *mi amo*," he grumbled. "You shall never see them again!"

CHAPTER FOUR

CHARLES GOULD turned towards the town. Before him jagged peaks of the Sierra came out all black in the clear dawn. Here and there a muffled lepero whisked round the corner of a grass-grown street before the ringing hoofs of his horse. Dogs barked behind the walls of the gardens; and with the colourless light the chill of the snows seemed to fall from the mountains upon the disjointed pavements and the shuttered houses with broken cornices and the plaster peeling in patches between the flat pilasters of the fronts. The daybreak struggled with the gloom under the arcades on the Plaza, with no signs of country people disposing their goods for the day's market, piles of fruit, bundles of vegetables ornamented with flowers, on low benches under enormous mat umbrellas; with no cheery early morning bustle of villagers, women, children, and loaded donkeys. Only a few scattered knots of revolutionists stood in the vast space, looking all one way from under their slouched hats for some sign of news from Rincon. The largest of those groups turned about like one man as Charles Gould passed, and shouted, "*Viva la libertad!*" after him in a menacing tone.

Charles Gould rode on, and turned into the archway of his house. In the patio littered with straw, a practicante, one of Dr. Monygham's native assistants, sat on the ground with his back against the rim of the fountain, fingering a guitar discreetly, while two girls of the lower class, standing up before him, shuffled their feet a little and waved their arms, humming a popular dance tune.

Most of the wounded during the two days of rioting had
been taken away already by their friends and relations,
but several figures could be seen sitting up balancing
their bandaged heads in time to the music.   Charles
Gould dismounted.   A sleepy mozo coming out of the
bakery door took hold of the horse's bridle; the practicante endeavoured to conceal his guitar hastily; the
girls, unabashed, stepped back smiling; and Charles
Gould, on his way to the staircase, glanced into a dark
corner of the patio at another group, a mortally
wounded Cargador with a woman kneeling by his side;
she mumbled prayers rapidly, trying at the same time
to force a piece of orange between the stiffening lips
of the dying man.

The cruel futility of things stood unveiled in the levity
and sufferings of that incorrigible people; the cruel
futility of lives and of deaths thrown away in the vain
endeavour to attain an enduring solution of the problem. Unlike Decoud, Charles Gould could not play
lightly a part in a tragic farce.   It was tragic enough for
him in all conscience, but he could see no farcical element. He suffered too much under a conviction of
irremediable folly. He was too severely practical and
too idealistic to look upon its terrible humours with
amusement, as Martin Decoud, the imaginative materialist, was able to do in the dry light of his scepticism.
To him, as to all of us, the compromises with his conscience appeared uglier than ever in the light of failure.
His taciturnity, assumed with a purpose, had prevented
him from tampering openly with his thoughts; but the
Gould Concession had insidiously corrupted his judgment. He might have known, he said to himself, leaning over the balustrade of the corridor, that Ribierism
could never come to anything. The mine had corrupted his judgment by making him sick of bribing and

intriguing merely to have his work left alone from day
to day. Like his father, he did not like to be robbed.
It exasperated him. He had persuaded himself that,
apart from higher considerations, the backing up of Don
José's hopes of reform was good business. He had gone
forth into the senseless fray as his poor uncle, whose
sword hung on the wall of his study, had gone forth—in
the defence of the commonest decencies of organized
society. Only his weapon was the wealth of the mine,
more far-reaching and subtle than an honest blade of
steel fitted into a simple brass guard.

More dangerous to the wielder, too, this weapon of
wealth, double-edged with the cupidity and misery of
mankind, steeped in all the vices of self-indulgence as
in a concoction of poisonous roots, tainting the very
cause for which it is drawn, always ready to turn awk-
wardly in the hand. There was nothing for it now but
to go on using it. But he promised himself to see it
shattered into small bits before he let it be wrenched
from his grasp.

After all, with his English parentage and English
upbringing, he perceived that he was an adventurer in
Costaguana, the descendant of adventurers enlisted in a
foreign legion, of men who had sought fortune in a
revolutionary war, who had planned revolutions, who
had believed in revolutions. For all the uprightness of
his character, he had something of an adventurer's easy
morality which takes count of personal risk in the
ethical appraising of his action. He was prepared, if
need be, to blow up the whole San Tomé mountain sky
high out of the territory of the Republic. This resolution expressed the tenacity of his character, the remorse of that subtle conjugal infidelity through which
his wife was no longer the sole mistress of his thoughts,
something of his father's imaginative weakness, and

something, too, of the spirit of a buccaneer throwing a
lighted match into the magazine rather than surrender
his ship.

Down below in the patio the wounded Cargador had
breathed his last. The woman cried out once, and her
cry, unexpected and shrill, made all the wounded sit
up. The practicante scrambled up to his feet, and,
guitar in hand, gazed steadily in her direction with
elevated eyebrows. The two girls—sitting now one on
each side of their wounded relative, with their knees
drawn up and long cigars between their lips—nodded
at each other significantly.

Charles Gould, looking down over the balustrade, saw
three men dressed ceremoniously in black frock-coats
with white shirts, and wearing European round hats,
enter the patio from the street. One of them, head and
shoulders taller than the two others, advanced with
marked gravity, leading the way. This was Don Juste
Lopez, accompanied by two of his friends, members of
Assembly, coming to call upon the Administrador of the
San Tomé mine at this early hour. They saw him, too,
waved their hands to him urgently, walking up the
stairs as if in procession.

Don Juste, astonishingly changed by having shaved
off altogether his damaged beard, had lost with it nine-
tenths of his outward dignity. Even at that time of
serious pre-occupation Charles Gould could not help
noting the revealed ineptitude in the aspect of the man.
His companions looked crestfallen and sleepy. One
kept on passing the tip of his tongue over his parched
lips; the other's eyes strayed dully over the tiled floor of
the corridor, while Don Juste, standing a little in advance, harangued the Señor Administrador of the San
Tomé mine. It was his firm opinion that forms had to
be observed. A new governor is always visited by

deputations from the Cabildo, which is the Municipal Council, from the Consulado, the commercial Board, and it was proper that the Provincial Assembly should send a deputation, too, if only to assert the existence of parliamentary institutions. Don Juste proposed that Don Carlos Gould, as the most prominent citizen of the province, should join the Assembly's deputation. His position was exceptional, his personality known through the length and breadth of the whole Republic. Official courtesies must not be neglected, if they are gone through with a bleeding heart. The acceptance of accomplished facts may save yet the precious vestiges of parliamentary institutions. Don Juste's eyes glowed dully; he believed in parliamentary institutions—and the convinced drone of his voice lost itself in the stillness of the house like the deep buzzing of some ponderous insect.

Charles Gould had turned round to listen patiently, leaning his elbow on the balustrade. He shook his head a little, refusing, almost touched by the anxious gaze of the President of the Provincial Assembly. It was not Charles Gould's policy to make the San Tomé mine a party to any formal proceedings.

"My advice, señores, is that you should wait for your fate in your houses. There is no necessity for you to give yourselves up formally into Montero's hands. Submission to the inevitable, as Don Juste calls it, is all very well, but when the inevitable is called Pedrito Montero there is no need to exhibit pointedly the whole extent of your surrender. The fault of this country is the want of measure in political life. Flat acquiescence in illegality, followed by sanguinary reaction—that, señores, is not the way to a stable and prosperous future."

Charles Gould stopped before the sad bewilderment of the faces, the wondering, anxious glances of the eyes. The feeling of pity for those men, putting all their trust into words of some sort, while murder and rapine stalked over the land, had betrayed him into what seemed empty loquacity. Don Juste murmured—

"You are abandoning us, Don Carlos. . . . And yet, parliamentary institutions——"

He could not finish from grief. For a moment he put his hand over his eyes. Charles Gould, in his fear of empty loquacity, made no answer to the charge. He returned in silence their ceremonious bows. His taciturnity was his refuge. He understood that what they sought was to get the influence of the San Tomé mine on their side. They wanted to go on a conciliating errand to the victor under the wing of the Gould Concession. Other public bodies—the Cabildo, the Consulado—would be coming, too, presently, seeking the support of the most stable, the most effective force they had ever known to exist in their province.

The doctor, arriving with his sharp, jerky walk, found that the master had retired into his own room with orders not to be disturbed on any account. But Dr. Monygham was not anxious to see Charles Gould at once. He spent some time in a rapid examination of his wounded. He gazed down upon each in turn, rubbing his chin between his thumb and forefinger; his steady stare met without expression their silently inquisitive look. All these cases were doing well; but when he came to the dead Cargador he stopped a little longer, surveying not the man who had ceased to suffer, but the woman kneeling in silent contemplation of the rigid face, with its pinched nostrils and a white gleam in the imperfectly closed eyes. She lifted her head slowly, and said in a dull voice—

"It is not long since he had become a Cargador—only a few weeks. His worship the Capataz had accepted him after many entreaties."

"I am not responsible for the great Capataz," muttered the doctor, moving off.

Directing his course upstairs towards the door of Charles Gould's room, the doctor at the last moment hesitated; then, turning away from the handle with a shrug of his uneven shoulders, slunk off hastily along the corridor in search of Mrs. Gould's camerista.

Leonarda told him that the señora had not risen yet. The señora had given into her charge the girls belonging to that Italian posadero. She, Leonarda, had put them to bed in her own room. The fair girl had cried herself to sleep, but the dark one—the bigger—had not closed her eyes yet. She sat up in bed clutching the sheets right up under her chin and staring before her like a little witch. Leonarda did not approve of the Viola children being admitted to the house. She made this feeling clear by the indifferent tone in which she inquired whether their mother was dead yet. As to the señora, she must be asleep. Ever since she had gone into her room after seeing the departure of Doña Antonia with her dying father, there had been no sound behind her door.

The doctor, rousing himself out of profound reflection, told her abruptly to call her mistress at once. He hobbled off to wait for Mrs. Gould in the sala. He was very tired, but too excited to sit down. In this great drawing-room, now empty, in which his withered soul had been refreshed after many arid years and his outcast spirit had accepted silently the toleration of many side-glances, he wandered haphazard amongst the chairs and tables till Mrs. Gould, enveloped in a morning wrapper, came in rapidly.

"You know that I never approved of the silver being sent away," the doctor began at once, as a preliminary to the narrative of his night's adventures in association

with Captain Mitchell, the engineer-in-chief, and old
Viola, at Sotillo's headquarters. To the doctor, with
his special conception of this political crisis, the removal
of the silver had seemed an irrational and ill-omened
measure. It was as if a general were sending the best
part of his troops away on the eve of battle upon some
recondite pretext. The whole lot of ingots might have
been concealed somewhere where they could have been
got at for the purpose of staving off the dangers which
were menacing the security of the Gould Concession.
The Administrador had acted as if the immense and
powerful prosperity of the mine had been founded on
methods of probity, on the sense of usefulness. And it
was nothing of the kind. The method followed had
been the only one possible. The Gould Concession had
ransomed its way through all those years. It was a
nauseous process. He quite understood that Charles
Gould had got sick of it and had left the old path to
back up that hopeless attempt at reform. The doctor
did not believe in the reform of Costaguana. And now
the mine was back again in its old path, with the disadvantage that henceforth it had to deal not only with
the greed provoked by its wealth, but with the resentment awakened by the attempt to free itself from its
bondage to moral corruption. That was the penalty of
failure. What made him uneasy was that Charles
Gould seemed to him to have weakened at the decisive
moment when a frank return to the old methods was the
only chance. Listening to Decoud's wild scheme had
been a weakness.

The doctor flung up his arms, exclaiming, "Decoud!
Decoud!" He hobbled about the room with slight,
angry laughs. Many years ago both his ankles had
been seriously damaged in the course of a certain
investigation conducted in the castle of Sta. Marta by a

commission composed of military men. Their nomination had been signified to them unexpectedly at the dead of night, with scowling brow, flashing eyes, and in a tempestuous voice, by Guzman Bento. The old tyrant, maddened by one of his sudden accesses of suspicion, mingled spluttering appeals to their fidelity with imprecations and horrible menaces. The cells and casements of the castle on the hill had been already filled with prisoners. The commission was charged now with the task of discovering the iniquitous conspiracy against the Citizen-Saviour of his country.

The dread of the raving tyrant translated itself into a hasty ferocity of procedure. The Citizen-Saviour was not accustomed to wait. A conspiracy had to be discovered. The courtyards of the castle resounded with the clanking of leg-irons, sounds of blows, yells of pain; and the commission of high officers laboured feverishly, concealing their distress and apprehensions from each other, and especially from their secretary, Father Beron, an army chaplain, at that time very much in the confidence of the Citizen-Saviour. That priest was a big round-shouldered man, with an unclean-looking, overgrown tonsure on the top of his flat head, of a dingy, yellow complexion, softly fat, with greasy stains all down the front of his lieutenant's uniform, and a small cross embroidered in white cotton on his left breast. He had a heavy nose and a pendant lip. Dr. Monygham remembered him still. He remembered him against all the force of his will striving its utmost to forget. Father Beron had been adjoined to the commission by Guzman Bento expressly for the purpose that his enlightened zeal should assist them in their labours. Dr. Monygham could by no manner of means forget the zeal of Father Beron, or his face, or the pitiless, monotonous voice in which he pronounced the words, "Will you confess now?"

The memory did not make him shudder, but it had made of him what he was in the eyes of respectable people, a man careless of common decencies, something between a clever vagabond and a disreputable doctor. But not all respectable people would have had the necessary delicacy of sentiment to understand with what trouble of mind and accuracy of vision Dr. Monygham, medical officer of the San Tomé mine, remembered Father Beron, army chaplain, and once a secretary of a military commission. After all these years Dr. Monygham, in his rooms at the end of the hospital building in the San Tomé gorge, remembered Father Beron as distinctly as ever. He remembered that priest at night, sometimes, in his sleep. On such nights the doctor waited for daylight with a candle lighted, and walking the whole length of his rooms to and fro, staring down at his bare feet, his arms hugging his sides tightly. He would dream of Father Beron sitting at the end of a long black table, behind which, in a row, appeared the heads, shoulders, and epaulettes of the military members, nibbling the feather of a quill pen, and listening with weary and impatient scorn to the protestations of some prisoner calling heaven to witness of his innocence, till he burst out, "What's the use of wasting time over that miserable nonsense! Let me take him outside for a while." And Father Beron would go outside after the clanking prisoner, led away between two soldiers. Such interludes happened on many days, many times, with many prisoners. When the prisoner returned he was ready to make a full confession, Father Beron would declare, leaning forward with that dull, surfeited look which can be seen in the eyes of gluttonous persons after a heavy meal.

The priest's inquisitorial instincts suffered but little from the want of classical apparatus of the Inquisition.

At no time of the world's history have men been at a loss how to inflict mental and bodily anguish upon their fellow-creatures. This aptitude came to them in the growing complexity of their passions and the early refinement of their ingenuity. But it may safely be said that primeval man did not go to the trouble of inventing tortures. He was indolent and pure of heart. He brained his neighbour ferociously with a stone axe from necessity and without malice. The stupidest mind may invent a rankling phrase or brand the innocent with a cruel aspersion. A piece of string and a ramrod; a few muskets in combination with a length of hide rope; or even a simple mallet of heavy, hard wood applied with a swing to human fingers or to the joints of a human body is enough for the infliction of the most exquisite torture. The doctor had been a very stubborn prisoner, and, as a natural consequence of that "bad disposition" (so Father Beron called it), his subjugation had been very crushing and very complete. That is why the limp in his walk, the twist of his shoulders, the scars on his cheeks were so pronounced. His confessions, when they came at last, were very complete, too. Sometimes on the nights when he walked the floor, he wondered, grinding his teeth with shame and rage, at the fertility of his imagination when stimulated by a sort of pain which makes truth, honour, self-respect, and life itself matters of little moment.

And he could not forget Father Beron with his monotonous phrase, "Will you confess now?" reaching him in an awful iteration and lucidity of meaning through the delirious incoherence of unbearable pain. He could not forget. But that was not the worst. Had he met Father Beron in the street after all these years Dr. Monygham was sure he would have quailed before him. This contingency was not to be feared now. Father

Beron was dead; but the sickening certitude prevented Dr. Monygham from looking anybody in the face.

Dr. Monygham had become, in a manner, the slave of a ghost. It was obviously impossible to take his knowledge of Father Beron home to Europe. When making his extorted confessions to the Military Board, Dr. Monygham was not seeking to avoid death. He longed for it. Sitting half-naked for hours on the wet earth of his prison, and so motionless that the spiders, his companions, attached their webs to his matted hair, he consoled the misery of his soul with acute reasonings that he had confessed to crimes enough for a sentence of death—that they had gone too far with him to let him live to tell the tale.

But, as if by a refinement of cruelty, Dr. Monygham was left for months to decay slowly in the darkness of his grave-like prison. It was no doubt hoped that it would finish him off without the trouble of an execution; but Dr. Monygham had an iron constitution. It was Guzman Bento who died, not by the knife thrust of a conspirator, but from a stroke of apoplexy, and Dr. Monygham was liberated hastily. His fetters were struck off by the light of a candle, which, after months of gloom, hurt his eyes so much that he had to cover his face with his hands. He was raised up. His heart was beating violently with the fear of this liberty. When he tried to walk the extraordinary lightness of his feet made him giddy, and he fell down. Two sticks were thrust into his hands, and he was pushed out of the passage. It was dusk; candles glimmered already in the windows of the officers' quarters round the courtyard; but the twilight sky dazed him by its enormous and overwhelming brilliance. A thin poncho hung over his naked, bony shoulders; the rags of his trousers came down no lower than his knees; an eighteen months' growth of hair fell in dirty grey locks on each side of his sharp cheek-bones. As he dragged himself past the guard-room door, one of the soldiers, lolling outside, moved by some obscure impulse, leaped forward with a strange laugh and rammed a broken old straw hat on his head. And Dr. Monygham, after having tottered, continued on his way. He advanced one stick, then one maimed foot, then the other stick; the other foot followed only a very short distance along the ground, toilfully, as though it were almost too heavy to be moved at all; and yet his legs under the hanging angles of the poncho appeared no thicker than the two sticks in his hands. A ceaseless trembling agitated his bent body, all his wasted limbs, his bony head, the conical, ragged crown of the sombrero, whose ample flat rim rested on his shoulders.

In such conditions of manner and attire did Dr. Monygham go forth to take possession of his liberty. And these conditions seemed to bind him indissolubly to the land of Costaguana like an awful procedure of naturalization, involving him deep in the national life, far deeper than any amount of success and honour could have done. They did away with his Europeanism; for Dr. Monygham had made himself an ideal conception of his disgrace. It was a conception eminently fit and proper for an officer and a gentleman. Dr. Monygham, before he went out to Costaguana, had been surgeon in one of Her Majesty's regiments of foot. It was a conception which took no account of physiological facts or reasonable arguments; but it was not stupid for all that. It was simple. A rule of conduct resting mainly on severe rejections is necessarily simple. Dr. Monygham's view of what it behoved him to do was severe; it was an ideal view, in so much that it was the imaginative exaggeration of a correct feeling. It was also, in its

force, influence, and persistency, the view of an eminently loyal nature.

There was a great fund of loyalty in Dr. Monygham's
nature. He had settled it all on Mrs. Gould's head. He
believed her worthy of every devotion. At the bottom
of his heart he felt an angry uneasiness before the prosperity of the San Tomé mine, because its growth was
robbing her of all peace of mind. Costaguana was no
place for a woman of that kind. What could Charles
Gould have been thinking of when he brought her out
there! It was outrageous! And the doctor had
watched the course of events with a grim and distant
reserve which, he imagined, his lamentable history imposed upon him.

Loyalty to Mrs. Gould could not, however, leave out
of account the safety of her husband. The doctor had
contrived to be in town at the critical time because he
mistrusted Charles Gould. He considered him hopelessly infected with the madness of revolutions. That
is why he hobbled in distress in the drawing-room of the
Casa Gould on that morning, exclaiming, "Decoud,
Decoud!" in a tone of mournful irritation.

Mrs. Gould, her colour heightened, and with glistening eyes, looked straight before her at the sudden
enormity of that disaster. The finger-tips on one hand
rested lightly on a low little table by her side, and the
arm trembled right up to the shoulder. The sun,
which looks late upon Sulaco, issuing in all the fulness of
its power high up on the sky from behind the dazzling
snow-edge of Higuerota, had precipitated the delicate,
smooth, pearly greyness of light, in which the town lies
steeped during the early hours, into sharp-cut masses of
black shade and spaces of hot, blinding glare. Three
long rectangles of sunshine fell through the windows of
the sala; while just across the street the front of the

Avellanos's house appeared very sombre in its own shadow seen through the flood of light.

A voice said at the door, "What of Decoud?"

It was Charles Gould. They had not heard him coming along the corridor. His glance just glided over his wife and struck full at the doctor.

"You have brought some news, doctor?"

Dr. Monygham blurted it all at once, in the rough. For some time after he had done, the Administrador of the San Tomé mine remained looking at him without a word. Mrs. Gould sank into a low chair with her hands lying on her lap. A silence reigned between those three motionless persons. Then Charles Gould spoke—

"You must want some breakfast."

He stood aside to let his wife pass first. She caught up her husband's hand and pressed it as she went out, raising the handkerchief to her eyes. The sight of her husband had brought Antonia's position to her mind, and she could not contain her tears at the thought of the poor girl. When she rejoined the two men in the dining-room after having bathed her face, Charles Gould was saying to the doctor across the table—

"No, there does not seem any room for doubt."

And the doctor assented.

"No, I don't see myself how we could question that wretched Hirsch's tale. It's only too true, I fear."

She sat down desolately at the head of the table and looked from one to the other. The two men, without absolutely turning their heads away, tried to avoid her glance. The doctor even made a show of being hungry; he seized his knife and fork, and began to eat with emphasis, as if on the stage. Charles Gould made no pretence of the sort; with his elbows raised squarely, he twisted both ends of his flaming moustaches—they were so long that his hands were quite away from his face.

"I am not surprised," he muttered, abandoning his moustaches and throwing one arm over the back of his chair. His face was calm with that immobility of expression which betrays the intensity of a mental struggle. He felt that this accident had brought to a point all the consequences involved in his line of conduct, with its conscious and subconscious intentions. There must be an end now of this silent reserve, of that air of impenetrability behind which he had been safeguarding his dignity. It was the least ignoble form of dissembling forced upon him by that parody of civilized institutions which offended his intelligence, his uprightness, and his sense of right. He was like his father. He had no ironic eye. He was not amused at the absurdities that prevail in this world. They hurt him in his innate gravity. He felt that the miserable death of that poor Decoud took from him his inaccessible position of a force in the background. It committed him openly unless he wished to throw up the game—and that was impossible. The material interests required from him the sacrifice of his aloofness—perhaps his own safety too. And he reflected that Decoud's separationist plan had not gone to the bottom with the lost silver.

The only thing that was not changed was his position towards Mr. Holroyd. The head of silver and steel interests had entered into Costaguana affairs with a sort of passion. Costaguana had become necessary to his existence; in the San Tomé mine he had found the imaginative satisfaction which other minds would get from drama, from art, or from a risky and fascinating sport. It was a special form of the great man's extravagance, sanctioned by a moral intention, big enough to flatter his vanity. Even in this aberration of his genius he served the progress of the world. Charles Gould felt sure of being understood with precision and judged with the indulgence of their common passion. Nothing now could surprise or startle this great man. And Charles Gould imagined himself writing a letter to San Francisco in some such words: ". . . . The men at the head of the movement are dead or have fled; the civil organization of the province is at an end for the present; the Blanco party in Sulaco has collapsed inexcusably, but in the characteristic manner of this country. But Barrios, untouched in Cayta, remains still available. I am forced to take up openly the plan of a provincial revolution as the only way of placing the enormous material interests involved in the prosperity and peace of Sulaco in a position of permanent safety. . . ." That was clear. He saw these words as if written in letters of fire upon the wall at which he was gazing abstractedly.

Mrs Gould watched his abstraction with dread. It was a domestic and frightful phenomenon that darkened and chilled the house for her like a thundercloud passing over the sun. Charles Gould's fits of abstraction depicted the energetic concentration of a will haunted by a fixed idea. A man haunted by a fixed idea is insane. He is dangerous even if that idea is an idea of justice; for may he not bring the heaven down pitilessly upon a loved head? The eyes of Mrs. Gould, watching her husband's profile, filled with tears again. And again she seemed to see the despair of the unfortunate Antonia.

"What would I have done if Charley had been drowned while we were engaged?" she exclaimed, mentally, with horror. Her heart turned to ice, while her cheeks flamed up as if scorched by the blaze of a funeral pyre consuming all her earthly affections. The tears burst out of her eyes.

"Antonia will kill herself!" she cried out.

This cry fell into the silence of the room with strangely little effect. Only the doctor, crumbling up a piece of bread, with his head inclined on one side, raised his face, and the few long hairs sticking out of his shaggy eyebrows stirred in a slight frown. Dr. Monygham thought quite sincerely that Decoud was a singularly unworthy object for any woman's affection. Then he lowered his head again, with a curl of his lip, and his heart full of tender admiration for Mrs. Gould.

"She thinks of that girl," he said to himself; "she thinks of the Viola children; she thinks of me; of the wounded; of the miners; she always thinks of everybody who is poor and miserable! But what will she do if Charles gets the worst of it in this infernal scrimmage those confounded Avellanos have drawn him into? No one seems to be thinking of her."

Charles Gould, staring at the wall, pursued his reflections subtly.

"I shall write to Holroyd that the San Tomé mine is big enough to take in hand the making of a new State. It'll please him. It'll reconcile him to the risk."

But was Barrios really available? Perhaps. But he was inaccessible. To send off a boat to Cayta was no longer possible, since Sotillo was master of the harbour, and had a steamer at his disposal. And now, with all the democrats in the province up, and every Campo township in a state of disturbance, where could he find a man who would make his way successfully overland to Cayta with a message, a ten days' ride at least; a man of courage and resolution, who would avoid arrest or murder, and if arrested would faithfully eat the paper? The Capataz de Cargadores would have been just such a man. But the Capataz of the Cargadores was no more.

And Charles Gould, withdrawing his eyes from the

wall, said gently, "That Hirsch! What an extraordinary thing! Saved himself by clinging to the anchor, did he? I had no idea that he was still in Sulaco. I thought he had gone back overland to Esmeralda more than a week ago. He came here once to talk to me about his hide business and some other things. I made it clear to him that nothing could be done."

"He was afraid to start back on account of Hernandez being about," remarked the doctor.

"And but for him we might not have known anything of what has happened," marvelled Charles Gould.

Mrs. Gould cried out—

"Antonia must not know! She must not be told. Not now."

"Nobody's likely to carry the news," remarked the doctor. "It's no one's interest. Moreover, the people here are afraid of Hernandez as if he were the devil." He turned to Charles Gould. "It's even awkward, because if you wanted to communicate with the refugees you could find no messenger. When Hernandez was ranging hundreds of miles away from here the Sulaco populace used to shudder at the tales of him roasting his prisoners alive."

"Yes," murmured Charles Gould; "Captain Mitchell's Capataz was the only man in the town who had seen Hernandez eye to eye. Father Corbelàn employed him. He opened the communications first. It is a pity that——"

His voice was covered by the booming of the great bell of the cathedral. Three single strokes, one after another, burst out explosively, dying away in deep and mellow vibrations. And then all the bells in the tower of every church, convent, or chapel in town, even those that had remained shut up for years, pealed out together with a crash. In this furious flood of metallic

uproar there was a power of suggesting images of strife
and violence which blanched Mrs. Gould's cheek.
Basilio, who had been waiting at table, shrinking within
himself, clung to the sideboard with chattering teeth.
It was impossible to hear yourself speak.

"Shut these windows!" Charles Gould yelled at him,
angrily. All the other servants, terrified at what they
took for the signal of a general massacre, had rushed upstairs, tumbling over each other, men and women, the
obscure and generally invisible population of the ground
floor on the four sides of the patio. The women, screaming "Misericordia!" ran right into the room, and, falling on their knees against the walls, began to cross themselves convulsively. The staring heads of men blocked
the doorway in an instant—mozos from the stable,
gardeners, nondescript helpers living on the crumbs of
the munificent house—and Charles Gould beheld all
the extent of his domestic establishment, even to the
gatekeeper. This was a half-paralyzed old man, whose
long white locks fell down to his shoulders: an heirloom
taken up by Charles Gould's familial piety. He could
remember Henry Gould, an Englishman and a Costaguanero of the second generation, chief of the Sulaco
province; he had been his personal mozo years and
years ago in peace and war; had been allowed to attend
his master in prison; had, on the fatal morning, followed the firing squad; and, peeping from behind one
of the cypresses growing along the wall of the Franciscan
Convent, had seen, with his eyes starting out of his
head, Don Enrique throw up his hands and fall with
his face in the dust. Charles Gould noted particularly
the big patriarchal head of that witness in the rear of the
other servants. But he was surprised to see a shrivelled
old hag or two, of whose existence within the walls of his
house he had not been aware. They must have been the

mothers, or even the grandmothers of some of his people. There were a few children, too, more or less naked, crying and clinging to the legs of their elders. He had never before noticed any sign of a child in his patio. Even Leonarda, the camerista, came in a fright, pushing through, with her spoiled, pouting face of a favourite maid, leading the Viola girls by the hand. The crockery rattled on table and sideboard, and the whole house seemed to sway in the deafening wave of sound.

CHAPTER FIVE

DURING the night the expectant populace had taken
possession of all the belfries in the town in order to welcome Pedrito Montero, who was making his entry after
having slept the night in Rincon. And first came strag-
gling in through the land gate the armed mob of all
colours, complexions, types, and states of raggedness,
calling themselves the Sulaco National Guard, and
commanded by Señor Gamacho. Through the middle
of the street streamed, like a torrent of rubbish, a mass
of straw hats, ponchos, gun-barrels, with an enormous
green and yellow flag flapping in their midst, in a
cloud of dust, to the furious beating of drums. The
spectators recoiled against the walls of the houses
shouting their *Vivas!* Behind the rabble could be seen
the lances of the cavalry, the "army" of Pedro Montero.
He advanced between Señores Fuentes and Gamacho
at the head of his llaneros, who had accomplished the
feat of crossing the Paramos of the Higuerota in a
snow-storm. They rode four abreast, mounted on
confiscated Campo horses, clad in the heterogeneous
stock of roadside stores they had looted hurriedly in
their rapid ride through the northern part of the province; for Pedro Montero had been in a great hurry
to occupy Sulaco. The handkerchiefs knotted loosely
around their bare throats were glaringly new, and all
the right sleeves of their cotton shirts had been cut
off close to the shoulder for greater freedom in throwing
the lazo. Emaciated greybeards rode by the side of
lean dark youths, marked by all the hardships of cam-

paigning, with strips of raw beef twined round the crowns of their hats,* and huge iron spurs fastened to their naked heels. Those that in the passes of the mountain had lost their lances had provided themselves with the goads used by the Campo cattlemen: slender shafts of palm fully ten feet long, with a lot of loose rings jingling under the ironshod point. They were armed with knives and revolvers. A haggard fearlessness characterized the expression of all these sun-blacked countenances; they glared down haughtily with their scorched eyes at the crowd, or, blinking upwards insolently, pointed out to each other some particular head amongst the women at the windows. When they had ridden into the Plaza and caught sight of the equestrian statue of the King dazzlingly white in the sunshine, towering enormous and motionless above the surges of the crowd, with its eternal gesture of saluting, a murmur of surprise ran through their ranks. "What is that saint in the big hat?" they asked each other.

They were a good sample of the cavalry of the plains with which Pedro Montero had helped so much the victorious career of his brother the general. The influence which that man, brought up in coast towns, acquired in a short time over the plainsmen of the Republic can be ascribed only to a genius for treachery of so effective a kind that it must have appeared to those violent men but little removed from a state of utter savagery, as the perfection of sagacity and virtue. The popular lore* of all nations testifies that duplicity and cunning, together with bodily strength, were looked upon, even more than courage, as heroic virtues by primitive mankind. To overcome your adversary was the great affair of life. Courage was taken for granted. But the use of intelligence awakened wonder and respect. Stratagems, providing they did not fail, were honourable;

the easy massacre of an unsuspecting enemy evoked
no feelings but those of gladness, pride, and admiration.
Not perhaps that primitive men were more faithless
than their descendants of to-day, but that they went
straighter to their aim, and were more artless in their
recognition of success as the only standard of morality.
We have changed since. The use of intelligence
awakens little wonder and less respect. But the ignorant
and barbarous plainsmen engaging in civil strife followed
willingly a leader who often managed to deliver their
enemies bound, as it were, into their hands. Pedro Montero had a talent for lulling his adversaries into a sense
of security. And as men learn wisdom with extreme
slowness, and are always ready to believe promises that
flatter their secret hopes, Pedro Montero was successful
time after time. Whether only a servant or some inferior
official in the Costaguana Legation in Paris, he had
rushed back to his country directly he heard that his
brother had emerged from the obscurity of his frontier
commandancia. He had managed to deceive by his
gift of plausibility the chiefs of the Ribierist movement
in the capital, ·and even the acute agent of the San
Tomé mine had failed to understand him thoroughly.
At once he had obtained an enormous influence over
his brother. They were very much alike in appearance,
both bald, with bunches of crisp hair above their ears,
arguing the presence of some negro blood. Only Pedro
was smaller than the general, more delicate altogether,
with an ape-like faculty for imitating all the outward
signs of refinement and distinction, and with a parrot-
like talent for languages. Both brothers had received
some elementary instruction by the munificence of a
great European traveller, to whom their father had been
a body-servant during his journeys in the interior of
the country. In General Montero's case it enabled

him to rise from the ranks. Pedrito, the younger, in-corrigibly lazy and slovenly, had drifted aimlessly from one coast town to another, hanging about counting-houses, attaching himself to strangers as a sort of *valet-de-place*, picking up an easy and disreputable living. His ability to read did nothing for him but fill his head with absurd visions. His actions were usually deter-mined by motives so improbable in themselves as to escape the penetration of a rational person.

Thus at first sight the agent of the Gould Concession in Sta. Marta had credited him with the possession of sane views, and even with a restraining power over the general's everlastingly discontented vanity. It could never have entered his head that Pedrito Montero, lackey or inferior scribe, lodged in the garrets of the various Parisian hotels where the Costaguana Legation used to shelter its diplomatic dignity, had been devour-ing the lighter sort of historical works in the French language, such, for instance as the books of Imbert de Saint Amand*upon the Second Empire. But Pedrito had been struck by the splendour of a brilliant court, and had conceived the idea of an existence for himself where, like the Duc de Morny, he would associate the command of every pleasure with the conduct of political affairs and enjoy power supremely in every way. No-body could have guessed that. And yet this was one of the immediate causes of the Monterist Revolution. This will appear less incredible by the reflection that the fundamental causes were the same as ever, rooted in the political immaturity of the people, in the indo-lence of the upper classes and the mental darkness of the lower.

Pedrito Montero saw in the elevation of his brother the road wide open to his wildest imaginings. This was what made the Monterist pronunciamiento so unpre-

ventable. The general himself probably could have been
bought off, pacified with flatteries, despatched on a
diplomatic mission to Europe. It was his brother who
had egged him on from first to last. He wanted to become the most brilliant statesman of South America.
He did not desire supreme power. He would have been
afraid of its labour and risk, in fact. Before all, Pedrito
Montero, taught by his European experience, meant
to acquire a serious fortune for himself. With this
object in view he obtained from his brother, on the
very morrow of the successful battle, the permission
to push on over the mountains and take possession
of Sulaco. Sulaco was the land of future prosperity,
the chosen land of material progress, the only province
in the Republic of interest to European capitalists.
Pedrito Montero, following the example of the Duc de
Morny, meant to have his share of this prosperity.
This is what he meant literally. Now his brother was
master of the country, whether as president, dictator,
or even as Emperor—why not as an Emperor?—he
meant to demand a share in every enterprise—in railways, in mines, in sugar estates, in cotton mills, in land
companies, in each and every undertaking—as the price
of his protection. The desire to be on the spot early
was the real cause of the celebrated ride over the mountains with some two hundred llaneros, an enterprise of
which the dangers had not appeared at first clearly to
his impatience. Coming from a series of victories, it
seemed to him that a Montero had only to appear
to be master of the situation. This illusion had betrayed him into a rashness of which he was becoming
aware. As he rode at the head of his llaneros he regretted that there were so few of them. The enthusiasm
of the populace reassured him. They yelled "*Viva*
Montero! *Viva* Pedrito!" In order to make them still

more enthusiastic, and from the natural pleasure he had in dissembling, he dropped the reins on his horse's neck, and with a tremendous effect of familiarity and confidence slipped his hands under the arms of Señores Fuentes and Gamacho. In that posture, with a ragged town mozo holding his horse by the bridle, he rode triumphantly across the Plaza to the door of the Intendencia. Its old gloomy walls seemed to shake in the acclamations that rent the air and covered the crashing peals of the cathedral bells.

Pedro Montero, the brother of the general, dismounted into a shouting and perspiring throng of enthusiasts whom the ragged Nationals were pushing back fiercely. Ascending a few steps he surveyed the large crowd gaping at him and the bullet-speckled walls of the houses opposite lightly veiled by a sunny haze of dust. The word "PORVENIR" in immense black capitals, alternating with broken windows, stared at him across the vast space; and he thought with delight of the hour of vengeance, because he was very sure of laying his hands upon Decoud. On his left hand, Gamacho, big and hot, wiping his hairy wet face, uncovered a set of yellow fangs in a grin of stupid hilarity. On his right, Señor Fuentes, small and lean, looked on with compressed lips. The crowd stared literally open-mouthed, lost in eager stillness, as though they had expected the great guerrillero, the famous Pedrito, to begin scattering at once some sort of visible largesse. What he began was a speech. He began it with the shouted word "Citizens!" which reached even those in the middle of the Plaza. Afterwards the greater part of the citizens remained fascinated by the orator's action alone, his tip-toeing, the arms flung above his head with the fists clenched, a hand laid flat upon the heart, the silver gleam of rolling

eyes, the sweeping, pointing, embracing gestures, a
hand laid familiarly on Gamacho's shoulder; a hand
waved formally towards the little black-coated person
of Señor Fuentes, advocate and politician and a true
friend of the people. The *vivas* of those nearest to the
orator bursting out suddenly propagated themselves ir-
regularly to the confines of the crowd, like flames running over dry grass, and expired in the opening of the
streets. In the intervals,* over the swarming Plaza
brooded a heavy silence, in which the mouth of the
orator went on opening and shutting, and detached
phrases—"The happiness of the people," "Sons of
the country," "The entire world, *el mundo entiero*"—
reached even the packed steps of the cathedral with
a feeble clear ring, thin as the buzzing of a mosquito.
But the orator struck his breast; he seemed to prance
between his two supporters. It was the supreme effort
of his peroration. Then the two smaller figures disappeared from the public gaze and the enormous Gamacho, left alone, advanced, raising his hat high above
his head. Then he covered himself proudly and yelled
out, "Ciudadanos!" A dull roar greeted Señor Gamacho, ex-pedlar of the Campo, Commandante of the
National Guards.

Upstairs Pedrito Montero walked about rapidly from
one wrecked room of the Intendencia to another, snarling incessantly—

"What stupidity! What destruction!"

Señor Fuentes, following, would relax his taciturn
disposition to murmur—

"It is all the work of Gamacho and his Nationals;"
and then, inclining his head on his left shoulder,
would press together his lips so firmly that a little
hollow would appear at each corner. He had his
nomination for Political Chief of the town in his

pocket, and was all impatience to enter upon his functions.

In the long audience room, with its tall mirrors all starred by stones, the hangings torn down and the canopy over the platform at the upper end pulled to pieces, the vast, deep muttering of the crowd and the howling voice of Gamacho speaking just below reached them through the shutters as they stood idly in dimness and desolation.

"The brute!" observed his Excellency Don Pedro Montero through clenched teeth. "We must contrive as quickly as possible to send him and his Nationals out there to fight Hernandez."

The new Géfé Político only jerked his head sideways, and took a puff at his cigarette in sign of his agreement with his method for ridding the town of Gamacho and his inconvenient rabble.

Pedrito Montero looked with disgust at the absolutely bare floor, and at the belt of heavy gilt picture-frames running round the room, out of which the remnants of torn and slashed canvases fluttered like dingy rags.

"We are not barbarians," he said.

This was what said his Excellency, the popular Pedrito, the guerrillero skilled in the art of laying ambushes, charged by his brother at his own demand with the organization of Sulaco on democractic principles. The night before, during the consultation with his partisans, who had come out to meet him in Rincon, he had opened his intentions to Señor Fuentes—

"We shall organize a popular vote, by yes or no, confiding the destinies of our beloved country to the wisdom and valiance of my heroic brother, the invincible general. A plebiscite. Do you understand?"

And Señor Fuentes, puffing out his leathery cheeks, had inclined his head slightly to the left, letting a thin, bluish jet of smoke escape through his pursed lips. He had understood.

His Excellency was exasperated at the devastation. Not a single chair, table, sofa, *étagère* or console had been left in the state rooms of the Intendencia. His Excellency, though twitching all over with rage, was restrained from bursting into violence by a sense of his remoteness and isolation. His heroic brother was very far away. Meantime, how was he going to take his siesta? He had expected to find comfort and luxury in the Intendencia after a year of hard camp life, ending with the hardships and privations of the daring dash upon Sulaco—upon the province which was worth more in wealth and influence than all the rest of the Republic's territory. He would get even with Gamacho by-and-by. And Señor Gamacho's oration, delectable to popular ears, went on in the heat and glare of the Plaza like the uncouth howlings of an inferior sort of devil cast into a white-hot furnace. Every moment he had to wipe his streaming face with his bare fore-arm; he had flung off his coat, and had turned up the sleeves of his shirt high above the elbows; but he kept on his head the large cocked hat with white plumes. His ingenuousness cherished this sign of his rank as Commandante of the National Guards. Approving and grave murmurs greeted his periods. His opinion was that war should be declared at once against France, England, Germany, and the United States, who, by introducing railways, mining enterprises, colonization, and under such other shallow pretences, aimed at robbing poor people of their lands, and with the help of these Goths and paralytics, the aristocrats would convert them into toiling and miserable slaves. And the leperos, flinging about the corners of their dirty white mantas, yelled their approbation. General

Montero, Gamacho howled with conviction, was the only man equal to the patriotic task. They assented to that, too.

The morning was wearing on; there were already signs of disruption, currents and eddies in the crowd. Some were seeking the shade of the walls and under the trees of the Alameda. Horsemen spurred through, shouting; groups of sombreros set level on heads against the vertical sun were drifting away into the streets, where the open doors of pulperias revealed an enticing gloom resounding with the gentle tinkling of guitars. The National Guards were thinking of siesta, and the eloquence of Gamacho, their chief, was exhausted. Later on, when, in the cooler hours of the afternoon, they tried to assemble again for further consideration of public affairs, detachments of Montero's cavalry camped on the Alameda charged them without parley, at speed, with long lances levelled at their flying backs as far as the ends of the streets. The National Guards of Sulaco were surprised by this proceeding. But they were not indignant. No Costaguanero had ever learned to question the eccentricities of a military force. They were part of the natural order of things. This must be, they concluded, some kind of administrative measure, no doubt. But the motive of it escaped their unaided intelligence, and their chief and orator, Gamacho, Commandante of the National Guard, was lying drunk and asleep in the bosom of his family. His bare feet were upturned in the shadows repulsively, in the manner of a corpse. His eloquent mouth had dropped open. His youngest daughter, scratching her head with one hand, with the other waved a green bough over his scorched and peeling face.

CHAPTER SIX

THE declining sun had shifted the shadows from west
to east amongst the houses of the town. It had shifted
them upon the whole extent of the immense Campo,
with the white walls of its haciendas on the knolls
dominating the green distances; with its grass-thatched
ranchos crouching in the folds of ground by the banks
of streams; with the dark islands of clustered trees on a
clear sea of grass, and the precipitous range of the
Cordillera, immense and motionless, emerging from the
billows of the lower forests like the barren coast of a
land of giants. The sunset rays striking the snow-slope
of Higuerota from afar gave it an air of rosy youth,
while the serrated mass of distant peaks remained black,
as if calcined in the fiery radiance. The undulating
surface of the forests seemed powdered with pale gold
dust; and away there, beyond Rincon, hidden from
the town by two wooded spurs, the rocks of the San
Tomé gorge, with the flat wall of the mountain itself
crowned by gigantic ferns, took on warm tones of brown
and yellow, with red rusty streaks, and the dark green
clumps of bushes rooted in crevices. From the plain
the stamp sheds and the houses of the mine appeared
dark and small, high up, like the nests of birds clustered
on the ledges of a cliff. The zigzag paths resembled
faint tracings scratched on the wall of a cyclopean
blockhouse. To the two sereños of the mine on
patrol duty, strolling, carbine in hand, and watchful
eyes, in the shade of the trees lining the stream near
the bridge, Don Pépé, descending the path from

the upper plateau, appeared no bigger than a large beetle.

With his air of aimless, insect-like going to and fro upon the face of the rock, Don Pépé's figure kept on descending steadily, and, when near the bottom, sank at last behind the roofs of store-houses, forges, and workshops. For a time the pair of sereños strolled back and forth before the bridge, on which they had stopped a horseman holding a large white envelope in his hand. Then Don Pépé, emerging in the village street from amongst the houses, not a stone's throw from the frontier bridge, approached, striding in wide dark trousers tucked into boots, a white linen jacket, sabre at his side, and revolver at his belt. In this disturbed time nothing could find the Señor Gobernador with his boots off, as the saying is.

At a slight nod from one of the sereños, the man, a messenger from the town, dismounted, and crossed the bridge, leading his horse by the bridle.

Don Pépé received the letter from his other hand, slapped his left side and his hips in succession, feeling for his spectacle case. After settling the heavy silver-mounted affair astride his nose, and adjusting it carefully behind his ears, he opened the envelope, holding it up at about a foot in front of his eyes. The paper he pulled out contained some three lines of writing. He looked at them for a long time. His grey moustache moved slightly up and down, and the wrinkles, radiating at the corners of his eyes, ran together. He nodded serenely. "*Bueno*," he said. "There is no answer."

Then, in his quiet, kindly way, he engaged in a cautious conversation with the man, who was willing to talk cheerily, as if something lucky had happened to him recently. He had seen from a distance Sotillo's infantry camped along the shore of the harbour on each

side of the Custom House. They had done no damage
to the buildings. The foreigners of the railway remained shut up within the yards. They were no longer
anxious to shoot poor people. He cursed the foreigners;
then he reported Montero's entry and the rumours of
the town. The poor were going to be made rich now.
That was very good. More he did not know, and,
breaking into propitiatory smiles, he intimated that he
was hungry and thirsty. The old major directed him to
go to the alcalde of the first village. The man rode off,
and Don Pépé, striding slowly in the direction of a little
wooden belfry, looked over a hedge into a little garden,
and saw Father Romàn sitting in a white hammock slung
between two orange trees in front of the presbytery.

An enormous tamarind shaded with its dark foliage
the whole white framehouse. A young Indian girl with
long hair, big eyes, and small hands and feet, carried out
a wooden chair, while a thin old woman, crabbed and
vigilant, watched her all the time from the verandah.

Don Pépé sat down in the chair and lighted a cigar;
the priest drew in an immense quantity of snuff out
of the hollow of his palm. On his reddish-brown
face, worn, hollowed as if crumbled, the eyes, fresh
and candid, sparkled like two black diamonds.

Don Pépé, in a mild and humorous voice, informed
Father Romàn that Pedrito Montero, by the hand of
Señor Fuentes, had asked him on what terms he would
surrender the mine in proper working order to a legally
constituted commission of patriotic citizens, escorted
by a small military force. The priest cast his eyes up
to heaven. However, Don Pépé continued, the mozo
who brought the letter said that Don Carlos Gould
was alive, and so far unmolested.

Father Romàn expressed in a few words his thankfulness at hearing of the Señor Administrador's safety.

The hour of oration had gone by in the silvery ringing of a bell in the little belfry. The belt of forest
closing the entrance of the valley stood like a screen
between the low sun and the street of the village. At
the other end of the rocky gorge, between the walls of
basalt and granite, a forest-clad mountain, hiding all
the range from the San Tomé dwellers, rose steeply,
lighted up and leafy to the very top. Three small rosy
clouds hung motionless overhead in the great depth
of blue. Knots of people sat in the street between the
wattled huts. Before the casa of the alcalde, the foremen of the night-shift, already assembled to lead their
men, squatted on the ground in a circle of leather skull-
caps, and, bowing their bronze backs, were passing
round the gourd of maté. The mozo from the town,
having fastened his horse to a wooden post before
the door, was telling them the news of Sulaco as the
blackened gourd of the decoction passed from hand to
hand. The grave alcalde himself, in a white waistcloth
and a flowered chintz gown with sleeves, open wide upon
his naked stout person with an effect of a gaudy bathing
robe, stood by, wearing a rough beaver hat at the back
of his head, and grasping a tall staff with a silver knob
in his hand. These insignia of his dignity had been
conferred upon him by the Administration of the mine,
the fountain of honour, of prosperity, and peace. He
had been one of the first immigrants into this valley;
his sons and sons-in-law worked within the mountain
which seemed with its treasures to pour down the
thundering ore shoots of the upper mesa, the gifts of
well-being, security, and justice upon the toilers. He
listened to the news from the town with curiosity
and indifference, as if concerning another world than
his own. And it was true that they appeared to
him so. In a very few years the sense of belong-

ing to a powerful organization had been developed in these harassed, half-wild Indians. They were proud of, and attached to, the mine. It had secured their confidence and belief. They invested it with a protecting and invincible virtue as though it were a fetish made by their own hands, for they were ignorant, and in other respects did not differ appreciably from the rest of mankind which puts infinite trust in its own creations. It never entered the alcalde's head that the mine could fail in its protection and force. Politics were good enough for the people of the town and the Campo. His yellow, round face, with wide nostrils, and motionless in expression, resembled a fierce full moon. He listened to the excited vapourings of the mozo without misgivings, without surprise, without any active sentiment whatever.

Padre Román sat dejectedly balancing himself, his feet just touching the ground, his hands gripping the edge of the hammock. With less confidence, but as ignorant as his flock, he asked the major what did he think was going to happen now.

Don Pépé, bolt upright in the chair, folded his hands peacefully on the hilt of his sword, standing perpendicular between his thighs, and answered that he did not know. The mine could be defended against any force likely to be sent to take possession. On the other hand, from the arid character of the valley, when the regular supplies from the Campo had been cut off, the population of the three villages could be starved into submission. Don Pépé exposed these contingencies with serenity to Father Román, who, as an old campaigner, was able to understand the reasoning of a military man. They talked with simplicity and directness. Father Román was saddened at the idea of his flock being scattered or else enslaved. He had no illusions as to their fate, not from penetration, but from long experience of political atrocities, which seemed to him fatal and unavoidable in the life of a State. The working of the usual public institutions presented itself to him most distinctly as a series of calamities overtaking private individuals and flowing logically from each other through hate, revenge, folly, and rapacity, as though they had been part of a divine dispensation. Father Romàn's clear-sightedness was served by an uninformed intelligence; but his heart, preserving its tenderness amongst scenes of carnage, spoliation, and violence, abhorred these calamities the more as his association with the victims was closer. He entertained towards the Indians of the valley feelings of paternal scorn. He had been marrying, baptizing, confessing, absolving, and burying the workers of the San Tomé mine with dignity and unction for five years or more; and he believed in the sacredness of these ministrations, which made them his own in a spiritual sense. They were dear to his sacerdotal supremacy. Mrs. Gould's earnest interest in the concerns of these people enhanced their importance in the priest's eyes, because it really augmented his own. When talking over with her the innumerable Marias and Brigidas of the villages, he felt his own humanity expand. Padre Romàn was incapable of fanaticism to an almost reprehensible degree. The English señora was evidently a heretic; but at the same time she seemed to him wonderful and angelic. Whenever that confused state of his feelings occurred to him, while strolling, for instance, his breviary under his arm, in the wide shade of the tamarind, he would stop short to inhale with a strong snuffling noise a large quantity of snuff, and shake his head profoundly. At the thought of what might befall the illustrious señora presently, he became gradually overcome with dismay.

He voiced it in an agitated murmur. Even Don Pépé lost his serenity for a moment. He leaned forward stiffly.

"Listen, Padre. The very fact that those thieving macaques in Sulaco are trying to find out the price of my honour proves that Señor Don Carlos and all in the Casa Gould are safe. As to my honour, that also is safe, as every man, woman, and child knows. But the negro Liberals who have snatched the town by surprise do not know that. Bueno. Let them sit and wait. While they wait they can do no harm."

And he regained his composure. He regained it easily, because whatever happened his honour of an old officer of Paez was safe. He had promised Charles Gould that at the approach of an armed force he would defend the gorge just long enough to give himself time to destroy scientifically the whole plant, buildings, and workshops of the mine with heavy charges of dynamite; block with ruins the main tunnel, break down the pathways, blow up the dam of the water-power, shatter the famous Gould Concession into fragments, flying sky high out of a horrified world. The mine had got hold of Charles Gould with a grip as deadly as ever it had laid upon his father. But this extreme resolution had seemed to Don Pépé the most natural thing in the world. His measures had been taken with judgment. Everything was prepared with a careful completeness. And Don Pépé folded his hands pacifically on his sword hilt. and nodded at the priest. In his excitement, Father Romàn had flung snuff in handfuls at his face, and, all besmeared with tobacco, round-eyed, and beside himself, had got out of the hammock to walk about, uttering exclamations.

Don Pépé stroked his grey and pendant moustache, whose fine ends hung far below the clean-cut line of his jaw, and spoke with a conscious pride in his reputation.

"So, Padre, I don't know what will happen. But I know that as long as I am here Don Carlos can speak to that macaque, Pedrito Montero, and threaten the destruction of the mine with perfect assurance that will be taken seriously. For people know me."

He began to turn the cigar in his lips a little nervously, and went on—

"But that is talk—good for the politicos. I am a military man. I do not know what may happen. But I know what ought to be done—the mine should march upon the town with guns, axes, knives tied up to sticks —*por Dios*. That is what should be done. Only——"

His folded hands twitched on the hilt. The cigar turned faster in the corner of his lips.

"And who should lead but I? Unfortunately—observe—I have given my word of honour to Don Carlos not to let the mine fall into the hands of these thieves. In war—you know this, Padre—the fate of battles is uncertain, and whom could I leave here to act for me in case of defeat? The explosives are ready. But it would require a man of high honour, of intelligence, of judgment, of courage, to carry out the prepared destruction. Somebody I can trust with my honour as I can trust myself. Another old officer of Paez, for instance. Or—or—perhaps one of Paez's old chaplains would do."

He got up, long, lank, upright, hard, with his martial moustache and the bony structure of his face, from which the glance of the sunken eyes seemed to transfix the priest, who stood still, an empty wooden snuff-box held upside down in his hand, and glared back, speechless, at the governor of the mine.

CHAPTER SEVEN

AT ABOUT that time, in the Intendencia of Sulaco, Charles Gould was assuring Pedrito Montero, who had sent a request for his presence there, that he would never let the mine pass out of his hands for the profit of a Government who had robbed him of it. The Gould Concession could not be resumed. His father had not desired it. The son would never surrender it. He would never surrender it alive. And once dead, where was the power capable of resuscitating such an enterprise in all its vigour and wealth out of the ashes and ruin of destruction? There was no such power in the country. And where was the skill and capital abroad that would condescend to touch such an ill-omened corpse? Charles Gould talked in the impassive tone which had for many years served to conceal his anger and contempt. He suffered. He was disgusted with what he had to say. It was too much like heroics. In him the strictly practical instinct was in profound discord with the almost mystic view he took of his right. The Gould Concession was symbolic of abstract justice. Let the heavens fall. But since the San Tomé mine had developed into world-wide fame his threat had enough force and effectiveness to reach the rudimentary intelligence of Pedro Montero, wrapped up as it was in the futilities of historical anecdotes. The Gould Concession was a serious asset in the country's finance, and, what was more, in the private budgets of many officials as well. It was traditional. It was known. It was said. It was credible. Every Minister of

Interior drew a salary from the San Tomé mine. It was natural. And Pedrito intended to be Minister of the Interior and President of the Council in his brother's Government. The Duc de Morny had occupied those high posts during the Second French Empire with conspicuous advantage to himself.

A table, a chair, a wooden bedstead had been procured for His Excellency, who, after a short siesta, rendered absolutely necessary by the labours and the pomps of his entry into Sulaco, had been getting hold of the administrative machine by making appointments, giving orders, and signing proclamations. Alone with Charles Gould in the audience room, His Excellency managed with his well-known skill to conceal his annoyance and consternation. He had begun at first to talk loftily of confiscation, but the want of all proper feeling and mobility in the Señor Administrador's features ended by affecting adversely his power of masterful expression. Charles Gould had repeated: "The Government can certainly bring about the destruction of the San Tomé mine if it likes; but without me it can do nothing else." It was an alarming pronouncement, and well calculated to hurt the sensibilities of a politician whose mind is bent upon the spoils of victory. And Charles Gould said also that the destruction of the San Tomé mine would cause the ruin of other undertakings, the withdrawal of European capital, the withholding, most probably, of the last instalment of the foreign loan. That stony fiend of a man said all these things (which were accessible to His Excellency's intelligence) in a cold-blooded manner which made one shudder.

A long course of reading historical works, light and gossipy in tone, carried out in garrets of Parisian hotels, sprawling on an untidy bed, to the neglect of his duties, menial or otherwise, had affected the manners of Pedro

Montero. Had he seen around him the splendour of
the old Intendencia, the magnificent hangings, the gilt
furniture ranged along the walls; had he stood upon a
daïs on a noble square of red carpet, he would have probably been very dangerous from a sense of success and
elevation. But in this sacked and devastated residence,
with the three pieces of common furniture huddled up
in the middle of the vast apartment, Pedrito's imagination was subdued by a feeling of insecurity and
impermanence. That feeling and the firm attitude
of Charles Gould who had not once, so far, pronounced
the word "Excellency," diminished him in his own eyes.
He assumed the tone of an enlightened man of the world,
and begged Charles Gould to dismiss from his mind
every cause for alarm. He was now conversing, he
reminded him, with the brother of the master of the
country, charged with a reorganizing mission. The
trusted brother of the master of the country, he repeated. Nothing was further from the thoughts of
that wise and patriotic hero than ideas of destruction.
"I entreat you, Don Carlos, not to give way to your
anti-democratic prejudices," he cried, in a burst of
condescending effusion.

Pedrito Montero surprised one at first sight by the
vast development of his bald forehead, a shiny yellow
expanse between the crinkly coal-black tufts of hair
without any lustre, the engaging form of his mouth,
and an unexpectedly cultivated voice. But his eyes,
very glistening as if freshly painted on each side of his
hooked nose, had a round, hopeless, birdlike stare when
opened fully. Now, however, he narrowed them agreeably, throwing his square chin up and speaking with
closed teeth slightly through the nose, with what he
imagined to be the manner of a grand seigneur.

In that attitude, he declared suddenly that the highest

expression of democracy was Cæsarism: the imperial rule based upon the direct popular vote. Cæsarism was conservative. It was strong. It recognized the legitimate needs of democracy which requires orders, titles, and distinctions. They would be showered upon deserving men. Cæsarism was peace. It was progressive. It secured the prosperity of a country. Pedrito Montero was carried away. Look at what the Second Empire had done for France. It was a régime which delighted to honour men of Don Carlos's stamp. The Second Empire fell, but that was because its chief was devoid of that military genius which had raised General Montero to the pinnacle of fame and glory. Pedrito elevated his hand jerkily to help the idea of pinnacle, of fame. "We shall have many talks yet. We shall understand each other thoroughly, Don Carlos!" he cried in a tone of fellowship. Republicanism had done its work. Imperial democracy was the power of the future. Pedrito, the guerrillero, showing his hand, lowered his voice forcibly. A man singled out by his fellow-citizens for the honourable nickname of El Rey de Sulaco could not but receive a full recognition from an imperial democracy as a great captain of industry and a person of weighty counsel, whose popular designation would be soon replaced by a more solid title. "Eh, Don Carlos? No! What do you say? Conde de Sulaco—Eh?—or marquis . . ."

He ceased. The air was cool on the Plaza, where a patrol of cavalry rode round and round without penetrating into the streets, which resounded with shouts and the strumming of guitars issuing from the open doors of pulperias. The orders were not to interfere with the enjoyments of the people. And above the roofs, next to the perpendicular lines of the cathedral towers the snowy curve of Higuerota blocked a large space of

darkening blue sky before the windows of the Intendencia. After a time Pedrito Montero, thrusting his
hand in the bosom of his coat, bowed his head with
slow dignity. The audience was over.

Charles Gould on going out passed his hand over his
forehead as if to disperse the mists of an oppressive
dream, whose grotesque extravagance leaves behind a
subtle sense of bodily danger and intellectual decay.
In the passages and on the staircases of the old palace
Montero's troopers lounged about insolently, smoking
and making way for no one; the clanking of sabres
and spurs resounded all over the building. Three silent
groups of civilians in severe black waited in the main
gallery, formal and helpless, a little huddled up, each
keeping apart from the others, as if in the exercise of a
public duty they had been overcome by a desire to shun
the notice of every eye. These were the deputations
waiting for their audience. The one from the Provincial Assembly, more restless and uneasy in its corporate
expression, was overtopped by the big face of Don Juste
Lopez, soft and white, with prominent eyelids and
wreathed in impenetrable solemnity as if in a dense
cloud. The President of the Provincial Assembly,
coming bravely to save the last shred of parliamentary
institutions (on the English model), averted his eyes
from the Administrador of the San Tomé mine as a
dignified rebuke of his little faith in that only saving
principle.

The mournful severity of that reproof did not affect
Charles Gould, but he was sensible to the glances of the
others directed upon him without reproach, as if only to
read their own fate upon his face. All of them had
talked, shouted, and declaimed in the great sala of the
Casa Gould. The feeling of compassion for those men,
struck with a strange impotence in the toils of moral

degradation, did not induce him to make a sign. He suffered from his fellowship in evil with them too much. He crossed the Plaza unmolested. The Amarilla Club was full of festive ragamuffins. Their frowsy heads protruded from every window, and from within came drunken shouts, the thumping of feet, and the twanging of harps. Broken bottles strewed the pavement below. Charles Gould found the doctor still in his house.

Dr. Monygham came away from the crack in the shutter through which he had been watching the street.

"Ah! You are back at last!" he said in a tone of relief. "I have been telling Mrs. Gould that you were perfectly safe, but I was not by any means certain that the fellow would have let you go."

"Neither was I," confessed Charles Gould, laying his hat on the table.

"You will have to take action."

The silence of Charles Gould seemed to admit that this was the only course. This was as far as Charles Gould was accustomed to go towards expressing his intentions.

"I hope you did not warn Montero of what you mean to do," the doctor said, anxiously.

"I tried to make him see that the existence of the mine was bound up with my personal safety," continued Charles Gould, looking away from the doctor, and fixing his eyes upon the water-colour sketch upon the wall.

"He believed you?" the doctor asked, eagerly.

"God knows'" said Charles Gould. "I owed it to my wife to say that much. He is well enough informed. He knows that I have Don Pépé there. Fuentes must have told him. They know that the old major is perfectly capable of blowing up the San Tomé mine without hesitation or compunction. Had it not been for that I don't think I'd have left the Intendencia a free

man. He would blow everything up from loyalty
and from hate—from hate of these Liberals, as they
call themselves. Liberals! The words one knows so
well have a nightmarish meaning in this country.
Liberty, democracy, patriotism, government—all of
them have a flavour of folly and murder. Haven't
they, doctor? . . . I alone can restrain Don Pépé.
If they were to—to do away with me, nothing could
prevent him."

"They will try to tamper with him," the doctor
suggested, thoughtfully.

"It is very possible," Charles Gould said very low,
as if speaking to himself, and still gazing at the sketch
of the San Tomé gorge upon the wall. "Yes, I expect
they will try that." Charles Gould looked for the first
time at the doctor. "It would give me time," he added.

"Exactly," said Dr. Monygham, suppressing his excitement. "Especially if Don Pépé behaves diplomatically. Why shouldn't he give them some hope of success?
Eh? Otherwise you wouldn't gain so much time.
Couldn't he be instructed to——"

Charles Gould, looking at the doctor steadily, shook
his head, but the doctor continued with a certain
amount of fire—

"Yes, to enter into negotiations for the surrender of
the mine. It is a good notion. You would mature
your plan. Of course, I don't ask what it is. I don't
want to know. I would refuse to listen to you if you
tried to tell me. I am not fit for confidences."

"What nonsense!" muttered Charles Gould, with
displeasure.

He disapproved of the doctor's sensitiveness about
that far-off episode of his life. So much memory
shocked Charles Gould. It was like morbidness. And
again he shook his head. He refused to tamper with

the open rectitude of Don Pépé's conduct, both from taste and from policy. Instructions would have to be either verbal or in writing. In either case they ran the risk of being intercepted. It was by no means certain that a messenger could reach the mine; and, besides, there was no one to send. It was on the tip of Charles's tongue to say that only the late Capataz de Cargadores could have been employed with some chance of success and the certitude of discretion. But he did not say that. He pointed out to the doctor that it would have been bad policy. Directly Don Pépé let it be supposed that he could be bought over, the Administrador's personal safety and the safety of his friends would become endangered. For there would be then no reason for moderation. The incorruptibility of Don Pépé was the essential and restraining fact. The doctor hung his head and admitted that in a way it was so.

He couldn't deny to himself that the reasoning was sound enough. Don Pépé's usefulness consisted in his unstained character. As to his own usefulness, he reflected bitterly it was also his own character. He declared to Charles Gould that he had the means of keeping Sotillo from joining his forces with Montero, at least for the present.

"If you had had all this silver here," the doctor said, "or even if it had been known to be at the mine, you could have bribed Sotillo to throw off his recent Monterism. You could have induced him either to go away in his steamer or even to join you."

"Certainly not that last," Charles Gould declared, firmly. "What could one do with a man like that, afterwards—tell me, doctor? The silver is gone, and I am glad of it. It would have been an immediate and strong temptation. The scramble for that visible plunder would have precipitated a disastrous ending.

I would have had to defend it, too. I am glad we've removed it—even if it is lost. It would have been a danger and a curse."

"Perhaps he is right," the doctor, an hour later, said hurriedly to Mrs. Gould, whom he met in the corridor. "The thing is done, and the shadow of the treasure may do just as well as the substance. Let me try to serve you to the whole extent of my evil reputation. I am off now to play my game of betrayal with Sotillo, and keep him off the town."

She put out both her hands impulsively. "Dr. Monygham, you are running a terrible risk," she whispered, averting from his face her eyes, full of tears, for a short glance at the door of her husband's room. She pressed both his hands, and the doctor stood as if rooted to the spot, looking down at her, and trying to twist his lips into a smile.

"Oh, I know you will defend my memory," he uttered at last, and ran tottering down the stairs across the patio, and out of the house. In the street he kept up a great pace with his smart hobbling walk, a case of instruments under his arm. He was known for being *loco*. Nobody interfered with him. From under the seaward gate, across the dusty, arid plain, interspersed with low bushes, he saw, more than a mile away, the ugly enormity of the Custom House, and the two or three other buildings which at that time constituted the seaport of Sulaco. Far away to the south groves of palm trees edged the curve of the harbour shore. The distant peaks of the Cordillera had lost their identity of clear-cut shapes in the steadily deepening blue of the eastern sky. The doctor walked briskly. A darkling shadow seemed to fall upon him from the zenith. The sun had set. For a time the snows of Higuerota continued to glow with the reflected glory of the west. The doctor, holding a straight course for the Custom House, appeared lonely, hopping amongst the dark bushes like a tall bird with a broken wing.

Tints of purple, gold, and crimson were mirrored in the clear water of the harbour. A long tongue of land, straight as a wall, with the grass-grown ruins of the fort making a sort of rounded green mound, plainly visible from the inner shore, closed its circuit; while beyond the Placid Gulf repeated those splendours of colouring on a greater scale and with a more sombre magnificence. The great mass of cloud filling the head of the gulf had long red smears amongst its convoluted folds of grey and black, as of a floating mantle stained with blood. The three Isabels, overshadowed and clear cut in a great smoothness confounding the sea and sky, appeared suspended, purple-black, in the air. The little wavelets seemed to be tossing tiny red sparks upon the sandy beaches. The glassy bands of water along the horizon gave out a fiery red glow, as if fire and water had been mingled together in the vast bed of the ocean.

At last the conflagration of sea and sky, lying embraced and still in a flaming contact upon the edge of the world, went out. The red sparks in the water vanished together with the stains of blood in the black mantle draping the sombre head of the Placid Gulf; a sudden breeze sprang up and died out after rustling heavily the growth of bushes on the ruined earthwork of the fort. Nostromo woke up from a fourteen hours' sleep, and arose full length from his lair in the long grass. He stood knee deep amongst the whispering undulations of the green blades with the lost air of a man just born into the world. Handsome, robust, and supple, he threw back his head, flung his arms open, and stretched himself with a slow twist of the waist and a leisurely

growling yawn of white teeth, as natural and free from
evil in the moment of waking as a magnificent and
unconscious wild beast. Then, in the suddenly steadied
glance fixed upon nothing from under a thoughtful
frown, appeared the man.

CHAPTER EIGHT

After landing from his swim Nostromo had scrambled up, all dripping, into the main quadrangle of the old fort; and there, amongst ruined bits of walls and rotting remnants of roofs and sheds, he had slept the day through. He had slept in the shadow of the mountains, in the white blaze of noon, in the stillness and solitude of that overgrown piece of land between the oval of the harbour and the spacious semi-circle of the gulf. He lay as if dead. A rey-zamuro, appearing like a tiny black speck in the blue, stooped, circling prudently with a stealthiness of flight startling in a bird of that great size. The shadow of his pearly-white body, of his black-tipped wings, fell on the grass no more silently than he alighted himself on a hillock of rubbish within three yards of that man, lying as still as a corpse. The bird stretched his bare neck, craned his bald head, loathsome in the brilliance of varied colouring, with an air of voracious anxiety towards the promising stillness of that prostrate body. Then, sinking his head deeply into his soft plumage, he settled himself to wait. The first thing upon which Nostromo's eyes fell on waking was this patient watcher for the signs of death and corruption. When the man got up the vulture hopped away in great, side-long, fluttering jumps. He lingered for a while, morose and reluctant, before he rose, circling noiselessly with a sinister droop of beak and claws.

Long after he had vanished, Nostromo, lifting his eyes up to the sky, muttered, "I am not dead yet."*

The Capataz of the Sulaco Cargadores had lived in
splendour and publicity up to the very moment, as it
were, when he took charge of the lighter containing the
treasure of silver ingots.

The last act he had performed in Sulaco was in complete harmony with his vanity, and as such perfectly
genuine. He had given his last dollar to an old woman
moaning with the grief and fatigue of a dismal search
under the arch of the ancient gate. Performed in
obscurity and without witnesses, it had still the characteristics of splendour and publicity, and was in strict
keeping with his reputation. But this awakening in
solitude, except for the watchful vulture, amongst
the ruins of the fort, had no such characteristics. His
first confused feeling was exactly this—that it was not
in keeping. It was more like the end of things. The
necessity of living concealed somehow, for God knows
how long, which assailed him on his return to consciousness, made everything that had gone before for years
appear vain and foolish, like a flattering dream come
suddenly to an end.

He climbed the crumbling slope of the rampart, and,
putting aside the bushes, looked upon the harbour. He
saw a couple of ships at anchor upon the sheet of water
reflecting the last gleams of light, and Sotillo's steamer
moored to the jetty. And behind the pale long front of
the Custom House, there appeared the extent of the
town like a grove of thick timber on the plain with a
gateway in front, and the cupolas, towers, and miradors
rising above the trees, all dark, as if surrendered already
to the night. The thought that it was no longer open
to him to ride through the streets, recognized by everyone, great and little, as he used to do every evening
on his way to play *monte* in the posada of the Mexican
Domingo; or to sit in the place of honour, listening to

songs and looking at dances, made it appear to him as a town that had no existence.

For a long time he gazed on, then let the parted bushes spring back, and, crossing over to the other side of the fort, surveyed the vaster emptiness of the great gulf. The Isabels stood out heavily upon the narrowing long band of red in the west, which gleamed low between their black shapes, and the Capataz thought of Decoud alone there with the treasure. That man was the only one who cared whether he fell into the hands of the Monterists or not, the Capataz reflected bitterly. And that merely would be an anxiety for his own sake. As to the rest, they neither knew nor cared. What he had heard Giorgio Viola say once was very true. Kings, ministers, aristocrats, the rich in general, kept the people in poverty and subjection; they kept them as they kept dogs, to fight and hunt for their service.

The darkness of the sky had descended to the line of the horizon, enveloping the whole gulf, the islets, and the lover of Antonia alone with the treasure on the Great Isabel. The Capataz, turning his back on these things invisible and existing, sat down and took his face between his fists. He felt the pinch of poverty for the first time in his life. To find himself without money after a run of bad luck at *monte* in the low, smoky room of Domingo's posada, where the fraternity of Cargadores gambled, sang, and danced of an evening; to remain with empty pockets after a burst of public generosity to some *peyne d'oro* girl or other (for whom he did not care), had none of the humiliation of destitution. He remained rich in glory and reputation. But since it was no longer possible for him to parade the streets of the town, and be hailed with respect in the usual haunts of his leisure, this sailor felt himself destitute indeed.

His mouth was dry. It was dry with heavy sleep and extremely anxious thinking, as it had never been dry before. It may be said that Nostromo tasted the dust and ashes of the fruit of life into which he had bitten deeply in his hunger for praise. Without removing his head from between his fists, he tried to spit before him—"Tfui"—and muttered a curse upon the selfishness of all the rich people.*

Since everything seemed lost in Sulaco (and that was the feeling of his waking), the idea of leaving the country altogether had presented itself to Nostromo. At that thought he had seen, like the beginning of another dream, a vision of steep and tideless shores, with dark pines on the heights and white houses low down near a very blue sea. He saw the quays of a big port, where the coasting feluccas, with their lateen sails* outspread like motionless wings, enter gliding silently between the end of long moles of squared blocks that project angularly towards each other, hugging a cluster of shipping to the superb bosom of a hill covered with palaces. He remembered these sights not without some filial emotion, though he had been habitually and severely beaten as a boy on one of these feluccas by a short-necked, shaven Genoese, with a deliberate and distrustful manner, who (he firmly believed) had cheated him out of his orphan's inheritance. But it is mercifully decreed that the evils of the past should appear but faintly in retrospect. Under the sense of loneliness, abandonment, and failure, the idea of return to these things appeared tolerable. But, what? Return? With bare feet and head, with one check shirt and a pair of cotton calzoneros for all worldly possessions?

The renowned Capataz, his elbows on his knees and a fist dug into each cheek, laughed with self-derision, as he had spat with disgust, straight out before him into

the night. The confused and intimate impressions of
universal dissolution which beset a subjective nature at
any strong check to its ruling passion had a bitterness
approaching that of death itself.* He was simple. He
was as ready to become the prey of any belief, superstition, or desire as a child.

The facts of his situation he could appreciate like a
man with a distinct experience of the country. He saw
them clearly. He was as if sobered after a long bout
of intoxication. His fidelity had been taken advantage
of. He had persuaded the body of Cargadores to side
with the Blancos against the rest of the people; he had
had interviews with Don José; he had been made use
of by Father Corbelàn for negotiating with Hernandez; it was known that Don Martin Decoud had admitted him to a sort of intimacy, so that he had been
free of the offices of the *Porvenir*. All these things had
flattered him in the usual way. What did he care about
their politics? Nothing at all. And at the end of it all
—Nostromo here and Nostromo there—where is Nostromo? Nostromo can do this and that—work all day
and ride all night—behold! he found himself a marked
Ribierist for any sort of vengeance Gamacho, for instance, would choose to take, now the Montero party,
had, after all, mastered the town. The Europeans
had given up; the Caballeros had given up. Don
Martin had indeed explained it was only temporary—
that he was going to bring Barrios to the rescue. Where
was that now—with Don Martin (whose ironic manner
of talk had always made the Capataz feel vaguely uneasy) stranded on the Great Isabel? Everybody had
given up. Even Don Carlos had given up. The
hurried removal of the treasure out to sea meant nothing
else than that. The Capataz de Cargadores, on a re-
vulsion of subjectiveness, exasperated almost to insanity,

beheld all his world without faith and courage. He had
been betrayed!

With the boundless shadows of the sea behind him,
out of his silence and immobility, facing the lofty shapes
of the lower peaks crowded around the white, misty
sheen of Higuerota, Nostromo laughed aloud again,
sprang abruptly to his feet, and stood still. He must
go. But where?

"There is no mistake. They keep us and encourage
us as if we were dogs born to fight and hunt for them.
The vecchio is right," he said, slowly and scathingly.
He remembered old Giorgio taking his pipe out of his
mouth to throw these words over his shoulder at the
café, full of engine-drivers and fitters from the railway
workshops. This image fixed his wavering purpose.
He would try to find old Giorgio if he could. God
knows what might have happened to him! He made
a few steps, then stopped again and shook his head.
To the left and right, in front and behind him, the
scrubby bush rustled mysteriously in the darkness.

"Teresa was right, too," he added in a low tone
touched with awe. He wondered whether she was
dead in her anger with him or still alive. As if in answer
to this thought, half of remorse and half of hope, with a
soft flutter and oblique flight, a big owl, whose appalling
cry: "Ya-acabo! Ya-acabo!—it is finished; it is finished"—announces calamity and death in the popular
belief, drifted vaguely like a large dark ball across his
path. In the downfall of all the realities that made his
force, he was affected by the superstition, and shuddered
slightly. Signora Teresa must have died, then. It
could mean nothing else. The cry* of the ill-omened
bird, the first sound he was to hear on his return, was a
fitting welcome for his betrayed individuality. The
unseen powers which he had offended by refusing

to bring a priest to a dying woman were lifting up
their voice against him. She was dead. With admirable and human consistency he referred everything to
himself. She had been a woman of good counsel always. And the bereaved old Giorgio remained stunned
by his loss just as he was likely to require the advice
of his sagacity. The blow would render the dreamy
old man quite stupid for a time.

As to Captain Mitchell, Nostromo, after the manner
of trusted subordinates, considered him as a person
fitted by education perhaps to sign papers in an office
and to give orders, but otherwise of no use whatever,
and something of a fool. The necessity of winding
round his little finger, almost daily, the pompous and
testy self-importance of the old seaman had grown
irksome with use to Nostromo. At first it had given
him an inward satisfaction. But the necessity of
overcoming small obstacles becomes wearisome to a
self-confident personality as much by the certitude
of success as by the monotony of effort. He mistrusted
his superior's proneness to fussy action. That old
Englishman had no judgment, he said to himself. It
was useless to suppose that, acquainted with the true
state of the case, he would keep it to himself. He
would talk of doing impracticable things. Nostromo
feared him as one would fear saddling one's self
with some persistent worry. He had no discretion.
He would betray the treasure. And Nostromo had
made up his mind that the treasure should not be
betrayed.

The word had fixed itself tenaciously in his intelligence. His imagination had seized upon the clear and
simple notion of betrayal to account for the dazed feeling of enlightenment as to being done for, of having
inadvertently gone out of his existence on an issue in

which his personality had not been taken into account.
A man betrayed is a man destroyed. Signora Teresa
(may God have her soul!) had been right. He had
never been taken into account. Destroyed! Her
white form sitting up bowed in bed, the falling black
hair, the wide-browed suffering face raised to him, the
anger of her denunciations appeared to him now majestic with the awfulness of inspiration and of death.
For it was not for nothing that the evil bird had uttered
its lamentable shriek over his head. She was dead—
may God have her soul!

Sharing in the anti-priestly freethought of the masses,
his mind used the pious formula from the superficial
force of habit, but with a deep-seated sincerity. The
popular mind is incapable of scepticism; and that incapacity delivers their helpless strength to the wiles of
swindlers and to the pitiless enthusiasms of leaders
inspired by visions of a high destiny. She was dead.
But would God consent to receive her soul? She had
died without confession or absolution, because he had
not been willing to spare her another moment of his
time. His scorn of priests as priests remained; but
after all, it was impossible to know whether what they
affirmed was not true. Power, punishment, pardon,
are simple and credible notions. The magnificent
Capataz de Cargadores, deprived of certain simple
realities, such as the admiration of women, the adulation of men, the admired publicity of his life, was ready
to feel the burden of sacrilegious guilt descend upon his
shoulders.

Bareheaded, in a thin shirt and drawers, he felt the
lingering warmth of the fine sand under the soles of his
feet. The narrow strand gleamed far ahead in a long
curve, defining the outline of this wild side of the
harbour. He flitted along the shore like a pursued

shadow between the sombre palm-groves and the sheet of water lying as still as death on his right hand. He strode with headlong haste in the silence and solitude as though he had forgotten all prudence and caution. But he knew that on this side of the water he ran no risk of discovery. The only inhabitant was a lonely, silent, apathetic Indian in charge of the palmarias,* who brought sometimes a load of cocoanuts to the town for sale. He lived without a woman in an open shed, with a perpetual fire of dry sticks smouldering near an old canoe lying bottom up on the beach. He could be easily avoided.

The barking of the dogs about that man's ranche was the first thing that checked his speed. He had forgotten the dogs. He swerved sharply, and plunged into the palm-grove, as into a wilderness of columns in an immense hall, whose dense obscurity seemed to whisper and rustle faintly high above his head. He traversed it, entered a ravine, climbed to the top of a steep ridge free of trees and bushes.

From there, open and vague in the starlight, he saw the plain between the town and the harbour. In the woods above some night-bird made a strange drumming noise. Below beyond the palmaria on the beach, the Indian's dogs continued to bark uproariously. He wondered what had upset them so much, and, peering down from his elevation, was surprised to detect unaccountable movements of the ground below, as if several oblong pieces of the plain had been in motion. Those dark, shifting patches, alternately catching and eluding the eye, altered their place always away from the harbour, with a suggestion of consecutive order and purpose. A light dawned upon him. It was a column of infantry on a night march towards the higher broken country at the foot of the hills. But he was too much in the dark about everything for wonder and speculation.

The plain had resumed its shadowy immobility. He descended the ridge and found himself in the open solitude, between the harbour and the town. Its spaciousness, extended indefinitely by an effect of obscurity, rendered more sensible his profound isolation. His pace became slower. No one waited for him; no one thought of him; no one expected or wished his return. "Betrayed! Betrayed!" he muttered to himself. No one cared. He might have been drowned by this time. No one would have cared—unless, perhaps, the children, he thought to himself. But they were with the English signora, and not thinking of him at all.

He wavered in his purpose of making straight for the Casa Viola. To what end? What could he expect there? His life seemed to fail him in all its details, even to the scornful reproaches of Teresa. He was aware painfully of his reluctance. Was it that remorse which she had prophesied with, what he saw now, was her last breath?

Meantime, he had deviated from the straight course, inclining by a sort of instinct to the right, towards the jetty and the harbour, the scene of his daily labours. The great length of the Custom House loomed up all at once like the wall of a factory. Not a soul challenged his approach, and his curiosity became excited as he passed cautiously towards the front by the unexpected sight of two lighted windows.

They had the fascination of a lonely vigil kept by some mysterious watcher up there, those two windows shining dimly upon the harbour in the whole vast extent of the abandoned building. The solitude could almost be felt. A strong smell of wood smoke hung about in a thin haze, which was faintly perceptible to his raised eyes against the glitter of the stars. As he advanced in the profound silence, the shrilling of innumerable cicalas in the dry grass seemed positively deafening to his strained ears. Slowly, step by step, he found himself in the great hall, sombre and full of acrid smoke.

A fire built against the staircase had burnt down impotently to a low heap of embers. The hard wood had failed to catch; only a few steps at the bottom smouldered, with a creeping glow of sparks defining their charred edges. At the top he saw a streak of light from an open door. It fell upon the vast landing, all foggy with a slow drift of smoke. That was the room. He climbed the stairs, then checked himself, because he had seen within the shadow of a man cast upon one of the walls. It was a shapeless, high-shouldered shadow of somebody standing still, with lowered head, out of his line of sight. The Capataz, remembering that he was totally unarmed, stepped aside, and, effacing himself upright in a dark corner, waited with his eyes fixed on the door.

The whole enormous ruined barrack of a place, unfinished, without ceilings under its lofty roof, was pervaded by the smoke swaying to and fro in the faint cross draughts playing in the obscurity of many lofty rooms and barnlike passages. Once one of the swinging shutters came against the wall with a single sharp crack, as if pushed by an impatient hand. A piece of paper scurried out from somewhere, rustling along the landing. The man, whoever he was, did not darken the lighted doorway. Twice the Capataz, advancing a couple of steps out of his corner, craned his neck in the hope of catching sight of what he could be at, so quietly, in there. But every time he saw only the distorted shadow of broad shoulders and bowed head.

He was doing apparently nothing, and stirred not from the spot, as though he were meditating—or, perhaps, reading a paper. And not a sound issued from the room.

Once more the Capataz stepped back. He wondered who it was—some Monterist? But he dreaded to show himself. To discover his presence on shore, unless after many days, would, he believed, endanger the treasure. With his own knowledge possessing his whole soul, it seemed impossible that anybody in Sulaco should fail to jump at the right surmise. After a couple of weeks or so it would be different. Who could tell he had not returned overland from some port beyond the limits of the Republic? The existence of the treasure confused his thoughts with a peculiar sort of anxiety, as though his life had become bound up with it. It rendered him timorous for a moment before that enigmatic, lighted door. Devil take the fellow! He did not want to see him. There would be nothing to learn from his face, known or unknown. He was a fool to waste his time there in waiting.

Less than five minutes after entering the place the Capataz began his retreat. He got away down the stairs with perfect success, gave one upward look over his shoulder at the light on the landing, and ran stealthily across the hall. But at the very moment he was turning out of the great door, with his mind fixed upon escaping the notice of the man upstairs, somebody he had not heard coming briskly along the front ran full into him. Both muttered a stifled exclamation of surprise, and leaped back and stood still, each indistinct to the other. Nostromo was silent. The other man spoke first, in an amazed and deadened tone.

"Who are you?"

Already Nostromo had seemed to recognize Dr.

Monygham. He had no doubt now. He hesitated the space of a second. The idea of bolting without a word presented itself to his mind. No use! An inexplicable repugnance to pronounce the name by which he was known kept him silent a little longer. At last he said in a low voice—

"A Cargador."

He walked up to the other. Dr. Monygham had received a shock. He flung his arms up and cried out his wonder aloud, forgetting himself before the marvel of this meeting. Nostromo angrily warned him to moderate his voice. The Custom House was not so deserted as it looked. There was somebody in the lighted room above.

There is no more evanescent quality in an accomplished fact than its wonderfulness. Solicited incessantly by the considerations affecting its fears and desires, the human mind turns naturally away from the marvellous side of events. And it was in the most natural way possible that the doctor asked this man whom only two minutes before he believed to have been drowned in the gulf—

"You have seen somebody up there? Have you?"

"No, I have not seen him."

"Then how do you know?"

"I was running away from his shadow when we met."

"His shadow?"

"Yes. His shadow in the lighted room," said Nostromo, in a contemptuous tone. Leaning back with folded arms at the foot of the immense building, he dropped his head, biting his lips slightly, and not looking at the doctor. "Now," he thought to himself, "he will begin asking me about the treasure."

But the doctor's thoughts were concerned with an

event not as marvellous as Nostromo's appearance, but in itself much less clear. Why had Sotillo taken himself off with his whole command with this suddenness and secrecy? What did this move portend? However, it dawned upon the doctor that the man upstairs was one of the officers left behind by the disappointed colonel to communicate with him.

"I believe he is waiting for me," he said.

"It is possible."

"I must see. Do not go away yet, Capataz."

"Go away where?" muttered Nostromo.

Already the doctor had left him. He remained leaning against the wall, staring at the dark water of the harbour; the shrilling of cicalas filled his ears. An invincible vagueness coming over his thoughts took from them all power to determine his will.

"Capataz! Capataz!" the doctor's voice called urgently from above.

The sense of betrayal and ruin floated upon his sombre indifference as upon a sluggish sea of pitch. But he stepped out from under the wall, and, looking up, saw Dr. Monygham leaning out of a lighted window.

"Come up and see what Sotillo has done. You need not fear the man up here."

He answered by a slight, bitter laugh. Fear a man! The Capataz of the Sulaco Cargadores fear a man! It angered him that anybody should suggest such a thing. It angered him to be disarmed and skulking and in danger because of the accursed treasure, which was of so little account to the people who had tied it round his neck. He could not shake off the worry of it. To Nostromo the doctor represented all these people. . . . And he had never even asked after it. Not a word of inquiry about the most desperate undertaking of his life.

Thinking these thoughts, Nostromo passed again through the cavernous hall, where the smoke was considerably thinned, and went up the stairs, not so warm to his feet now, towards the streak of light at the top. The doctor appeared in it for a moment, agitated and impatient.

"Come up! Come up!"

At the moment of crossing the doorway the Capataz experienced a shock of surprise. The man had not moved. He saw his shadow in the same place. He started, then stepped in with a feeling of being about to solve a mystery.

It was very simple. For an infinitesimal fraction of a second, against the light of two flaring and guttering candles, through a blue, pungent, thin haze which made his eyes smart, he saw the man standing, as he had imagined him, with his back to the door, casting an enormous and distorted shadow upon the wall. Swifter than a flash of lightning followed the impression of his constrained, toppling attitude—the shoulders projecting forward, the head sunk low upon the breast. Then he distinguished the arms behind his back, and wrenched so terribly that the two clenched fists, lashed together, had been forced up higher than the shoulder-blades. From there his eyes traced in one instantaneous glance the hide rope going upwards from the tied wrists over a heavy beam and down to a staple in the wall. He did not want to look at the rigid legs, at the feet hanging down nervelessly, with their bare toes some six inches above the floor, to know that the man had been given the estrapade till he had swooned. His first impulse was to dash forward and sever the rope at one blow. He felt for his knife. He had no knife—not even a knife. He stood quivering, and the doctor, perched on the edge of the table, facing thoughtfully the cruel and lamentable sight, his chin in his hand, uttered, without stirring—

"Tortured—and shot dead through the breast—getting cold."

This information calmed the Capataz. One of the candles flickering in the socket went out. "Who did this?" he asked.

"Sotillo, I tell you. Who else? Tortured—of course. But why shot?" The doctor looked fixedly at Nostromo, who shrugged his shoulders slightly. "And mark, shot suddenly, on impulse. It is evident. I wish I had his secret."

Nostromo had advanced, and stooped slightly to look. "I seem to have seen that face somewhere," he muttered. "Who is he?"

The doctor turned his eyes upon him again. "I may yet come to envying his fate. What do you think of that, Capataz, eh?"

But Nostromo did not even hear these words. Seizing the remaining light, he thrust it under the drooping head. The doctor sat oblivious, with a lost gaze. Then the heavy iron candlestick, as if struck out of Nostromo's hand, clattered on the floor.

"Hullo!" exclaimed the doctor, looking up with a start. He could hear the Capataz stagger against the table and gasp. In the sudden extinction of the light within, the dead blackness sealing the window-frames became alive with stars to his sight.

"Of course, of course," the doctor muttered to himself in English. "Enough to make him jump out of his skin."

Nostromo's heart seemed to force itself into his throat. His head swam. Hirsch! The man was Hirsch! He held on tight to the edge of the table.

"But he was hiding in the lighter," he almost shouted His voice fell. "In the lighter, and—and——"

"And Sotillo brought him in," said the doctor. "He is no more startling to you than you were to me. What I want to know is how he induced some compassionate soul to shoot him."

"So Sotillo knows——" began Nostromo, in a more equable voice.

"Everything!" interrupted the doctor.

The Capataz was heard striking the table with his fist. "Everything? What are you saying, there? Everything? Know everything? It is impossible! Everything?"

"Of course. What do you mean by impossible? I tell you I have heard this Hirsch questioned last night, here, in this very room. He knew your name, Decoud's name, and all about the loading of the silver. . . . The lighter was cut in two. He was grovelling in abject terror before Sotillo, but he remembered that much. What do you want more? He knew least about himself. They found him clinging to their anchor. He must have caught at it just as the lighter went to the bottom."

"Went to the bottom?" repeated Nostromo, slowly. "Sotillo believes that? *Bueno!*"

The doctor, a little impatiently, was unable to imagine what else could anybody believe. Yes, Sotillo believed that the lighter was sunk, and the Capataz de Cargadores, together with Martin Decoud and perhaps one or two other political fugitives, had been drowned.

"I told you well, señor doctor," remarked Nostromo at that point, "that Sotillo did not know everything."

"Eh? What do you mean?"

"He did not know I was not dead."

"Neither did we."

"And you did not care—none of you caballeros on

the wharf—once you got off a man of flesh and blood like yourselves on a fool's business that could not end well."

"You forget, Capataz, I was not on the wharf. And I did not think well of the business. So you need not taunt me. I tell you what, man, we had but little leisure to think of the dead. Death stands near behind us all. You were gone."

"I went, indeed!" broke in Nostromo. "And for the sake of what—tell me?"

"Ah! that is your own affair," the doctor said, roughly. "Do not ask me."

Their flowing murmurs paused in the dark. Perched on the edge of the table with slightly averted faces, they felt their shoulders touch, and their eyes remained directed towards an upright shape nearly lost in the obscurity of the inner part of the room, that with projecting head and shoulders, in ghastly immobility, seemed intent on catching every word.

"*Muy bien!*" Nostromo muttered at last. "So be it. Teresa was right. It is my own affair."

"Teresa is dead," remarked the doctor, absently, while his mind followed a new line of thought suggested by what might have been called Nostromo's return to life. "She died, the poor woman."

"Without a priest?" the Capataz asked, anxiously.

"What a question! Who could have got a priest for her last night?"

"May God keep her soul!" ejaculated Nostromo, with a gloomy and hopeless fervour which had no time to surprise Dr. Monygham, before, reverting to their previous conversation, he continued in a sinister tone, "Si, señor doctor. As you were saying, it is my own affair. A very desperate affair."

"There are no two men in this part of the world that

could have saved themselves by swimming as you have done," the doctor said, admiringly.

And again there was silence between those two men. They were both reflecting, and the diversity of their natures made their thoughts born from their meeting swing afar from each other. The doctor, impelled to risky action by his loyalty to the Goulds, wondered with thankfulness at the chain of accident which had brought that man back where he would be of the greatest use in the work of saving the San Tomé mine. The doctor was loyal to the mine. It presented itself to his fifty-years' old eyes in the shape of a little woman in a soft dress with a long train, with a head attractively overweighted by a great mass of fair hair and the delicate preciousness of her inner worth, partaking of a gem and a flower, revealed in every attitude of her person. As the dangers thickened round the San Tomè mine this illusion acquired force, permanency, and authority. It claimed him at last! This claim, exalted by a spiritual detachment from the usual sanctions of hope and reward, made Dr. Monygham's thinking, acting, individuality extremely dangerous to himself and to others, all his scruples vanishing in the proud feeling that his devotion was the only thing that stood between an admirable woman and a frightful disaster.

It was a sort of intoxication which made him utterly indifferent to Decoud's fate, but left his wits perfectly clear for the appreciation of Decoud's political idea. It was a good idea—and Barrios was the only instrument of its realization. The doctor's soul, withered and shrunk by the shame of a moral disgrace, became implacable in the expansion of its tenderness. Nostromo's return was providential. He did not think of him humanely, as of a fellow-creature just escaped from the jaws of death. The Capataz for him was the only possible messenger to Cayta. The very man. The doctor's misanthropic mistrust of mankind (the bitterer because based on personal failure) did not lift him sufficiently above common weaknesses. He was under the spell of an established reputation. Trumpeted by Captain Mitchell, grown in repetition, and fixed in general assent, Nostromo's faithfulness had never been questioned by Dr. Monygham as a fact. It was not likely to be questioned now he stood in desperate need of it himself. Dr. Monygham was human; he accepted the popular conception of the Capataz's incorruptibility simply because no word or fact had ever contradicted a mere affirmation. It seemed to be a part of the man, like his whiskers or his teeth. It was impossible to conceive him otherwise. The question was whether he would consent to go on such a dangerous and desperate errand. The doctor was observant enough to have become aware from the first of something peculiar in the man's temper. He was no doubt sore about the loss of the silver.

"It will be necessary to take him into my fullest confidence," he said to himself, with a certain acuteness of insight into the nature he had to deal with.

On Nostromo's side the silence had been full of black irresolution, anger, and mistrust. He was the first to break it, however.

"The swimming was no great matter," he said. "It is what went before—and what comes after that——"

He did not quite finish what he meant to say, breaking off short, as though his thought had butted against a solid obstacle. The doctor's mind pursued its own schemes with Machiavellian* subtlety. He said as sympathetically as he was able—

"It is unfortunate, Capataz. But no one would think of blaming you. Very unfortunate. To begin

with, the treasure ought never to have left the mountain.
But it was Decoud who—— however, he is dead. There
is no need to talk of him."

"No," assented Nostromo, as the doctor paused,
"there is no need to talk of dead men. But I am not
dead yet."

"You are all right. Only a man of your intrepidity
could have saved himself."

In this Dr. Monygham was sincere. He esteemed
highly the intrepidity of that man, whom he valued
but little, being disillusioned as to mankind in general,
because of the particular instance in which his own manhood had failed. Having had to encounter single-
handed during his period of eclipse many physical
dangers, he was well aware of the most dangerous
element common to them all: of the crushing, paralyzing
sense of human littleness, which is what really defeats
a man struggling with natural forces, alone, far from
the eyes of his fellows. He was eminently fit to appreciate the mental image he made for himself of the
Capataz, after hours of tension and anxiety, precipitated suddenly into an abyss of waters and darkness,
without earth or sky, and confronting it not only with
an undismayed mind, but with sensible success. Of
course, the man was an incomparable swimmer, that
was known, but the doctor judged that this instance
testified to a still greater intrepidity of spirit. It was
pleasing to him; he augured well from it for the success
of the arduous mission with which he meant to entrust
the Capataz so marvellously restored to usefulness.
And in a tone vaguely gratified, he observed—

"It must have been terribly dark!"

"It was the worst darkness of the Golfo," the Capataz
assented, briefly. He was mollified by what seemed a
sign of some faint interest in such things as had befallen

him, and dropped a few descriptive phrases with an
affected and curt nonchalance. At that moment he
felt communicative. He expected the continuance
of that interest which, whether accepted. or rejected,
would have restored to him his personality—the only
thing lost in that desperate affair. But the doctor,
engrossed by a desperate adventure of his own, was
terrible in the pursuit of his idea. He let an exclamation of regret escape him.

"I could almost wish you had shouted and shown a
light."

This unexpected utterance astounded the Capataz
by its character of cold-blooded atrocity. It was as
much as to say, "I wish you had shown yourself a
coward; I wish you had had your throat cut for your
pains." Naturally he referred it to himself, whereas it
related only to the silver, being uttered simply and with
many mental reservations. Surprise and rage rendered
him speechless, and the doctor pursued, practically
unheard by Nostromo, whose stirred blood was beating
violently in his ears.

"For I am convinced Sotillo in possession of the
silver would have turned short round and made for some
small port abroad. Economically it would have been
wasteful, but still less wasteful than having it sunk.
It was the next best thing to having it at hand in some
safe place, and using part of it to buy up Sotillo. But
I doubt whether Don Carlos would have ever made up
his mind to it. He is not fit for Costaguana, and that
is a fact, Capataz."

The Capataz had mastered the fury that was like a
tempest in his ears in time to hear the name of Don
Carlos. He seemed to have come out of it a changed
man—a man who spoke thoughtfully in a soft and even
voice.

"And would Don Carlos have been content if I had surrendered this treasure?"

"I should not wonder if they were all of that way of thinking now," the doctor said, grimly. "I was never consulted. Decoud had it his own way. Their eyes are opened by this time, I should think. I for one know that if that silver turned up this moment miraculously ashore I would give it to Sotillo. And, as things stand, I would be approved."

"Turned up miraculously," repeated the Capataz very low; then raised his voice. "That, señor, would be a greater miracle than any saint could perform."

"I believe you, Capataz," said the doctor, drily.

He went on to develop his view of Sotillo's dangerous influence upon the situation. And the Capataz, listening as if in a dream, felt himself of as little account as the indistinct, motionless shape of the dead man whom he saw upright under the beam, with his air of listening also, disregarded, forgotten, like a terrible example of neglect.

"Is it for an unconsidered and foolish whim that they came to me, then?" he interrupted, suddenly. "Had I not done enough for them to be of some account, *por Dios?* Is it that the *hombres finos*—the gentlemen—need not think as long as there is a man of the people ready to risk his body and soul? Or, perhaps, we have no souls—like dogs?"

"There was Decoud, too, with his plan," the doctor reminded him again.

"Si! And the rich man in San Francisco who had something to do with that treasure, too—what do I know? No! I have heard too many things. It seems to me that everything is permitted to the rich."

"I understand, Capataz," the doctor began.

"What Capataz?" broke in Nostromo, in a forcible

but even voice. "The Capataz is undone, destroyed. There is no Capataz. Oh, no! You will find the Capataz no more."

"Come, this is childish!" remonstrated the doctor; and the other calmed down suddenly.

"I have been indeed like a little child," he muttered.

And as his eyes met again the shape of the murdered man suspended in his awful immobility, which seemed the uncomplaining immobility of attention, he asked, wondering gently—

"Why did Sotillo give the estrapade to this pitiful wretch? Do you know? No torture could have been worse than his fear. Killing I can understand. His anguish was intolerable to behold. But why should he torment him like this? He could tell no more."

"No; he could tell nothing more. Any sane man would have seen that. He had told him everything. But I tell you what it is, Capataz. Sotillo would not believe what he was told. Not everything."

"What is it he would not believe? I cannot understand."

"I can, because I have seen the man. He refuses to believe that the treasure is lost."

"What?" the Capataz cried out in a discomposed tone.

"That startles you—eh?"

"Am I to understand, señor," Nostromo went on in a deliberate and, as it were, watchful tone, "that Sotillo thinks the treasure has been saved by some means?"

"No! no! That would be impossible," said the doctor, with conviction; and Nostromo emitted a grunt in the dark. "That would be impossible. He thinks that the silver was no longer in the lighter when she was sunk. He has convinced himself that the whole show of getting it away to sea is a mere sham got up to deceive

Gamacho and his Nationals, Pedrito Montero, Señor Fuentes, our new.Géfé Político, and himself, too. Only, he says, he is no such fool."

"But he is devoid of sense. He is the greatest imbecile that ever called himself a colonel in this country of evil," growled Nostromo.

"He is no more unreasonable than many sensible men," said the doctor. "He has convinced himself that the treasure can be found because he desires passionately to possess himself of it. And he is also afraid of his officers turning upon him and going over to Pedrito, whom he has not the courage either to fight or trust. Do you see that, Capataz? He need fear no desertion as long as some hope remains of that enormous plunder turning up. I have made it my business to keep this very hope up."

"You have!" the Capataz de Cargadores repeated cautiously. "Well, that is wonderful. And how long do you think you are going to keep it up?"

"As long as I can."

"What does that mean?"

"I can tell you exactly. As long as I live," the doctor retorted in a stubborn voice. Then, in a few words, he described the story of his arrest and the circumstances of his release. "I was going back to that silly scoundrel when we met," he concluded.

Nostromo had listened with profound attention. "You have made up your mind, then, to a speedy death," he muttered through his clenched teeth.

"Perhaps, my illustrious Capataz," the doctor said, testily. "You are not the only one here who can look an ugly death in the face."

"No doubt," mumbled Nostromo, loud enough to be overheard. "There may be even more than two fools in this place. Who knows?"

"And that is my affair," said the doctor, curtly.

"As taking out the accursed silver to sea was my affair," retorted Nostromo. "I see, *Bueno*. Each of us has his reasons. But you were the last man I conversed with before I started, and you talked to me as if I were a fool."

Nostromo had a great distaste for the doctor's sardonic treatment of his great reputation. Decoud's faintly ironic recognition used to make him uneasy; but the familiarity of a man like Don Martin was flattering, whereas the doctor was a nobody. He could remember him a penniless outcast, slinking about the streets of Sulaco, without a single friend or acquaintance, till Don Carlos Gould took him into the service of the mine.

"You may be very wise," he went on, thoughtfully, staring into the obscurity of the room, pervaded by the gruesome enigma of the tortured and murdered Hirsch. "But I am not such a fool as when I started. I have learned one thing since, and that is that you are a dangerous man."

Dr. Monygham was too startled to do more than exclaim—

"What is it you say?"

"If he could speak he would say the same thing," pursued Nostromo, with a nod of his shadowy head silhouetted against the starlit window.

"I do not understand you," said Dr. Monygham, faintly.

"No? Perhaps, if you had not confirmed Sotillo in his madness, he would have been in no haste to give the estrapade to that miserable Hirsch."

The doctor started at the suggestion. But his devotion, absorbing all his sensibilities, had left his heart steeled against remorse and pity. Still, for complete relief, he felt the necessity of repelling it loudly and contemptuously.

"Bah! You dare to tell me that, with a man like Sotillo. I confess I did not give a thought to Hirsch. If I had it would have been useless. Anybody can see that the luckless wretch was doomed from the moment he caught hold of the anchor. He was doomed, I tell you! Just as I myself am doomed—most probably."

This is what Dr. Monygham said in answer to Nostromo's remark, which was plausible enough to prick his conscience. He was not a callous man. But the necessity, the magnitude, the importance of the task he had taken upon himself dwarfed all merely humane considerations. He had undertaken it in a fanatical spirit. He did not like it. To lie, to deceive, to circumvent even the basest of mankind was odious to him. It was odious to him by training, instinct, and tradition. To do these things in the character of a traitor was abhorrent to his nature and terrible to his feelings. He had made that sacrifice in a spirit of abasement. He had said to himself bitterly, "I am the only one fit for that dirty work." And he believed this. He was not subtle. His simplicity was such that, though he had no sort of heroic idea of seeking death, the risk, deadly enough, to which he exposed himself, had a sustaining and comforting effect. To that spiritual state the fate of Hirsch presented itself as part of the general atrocity of things. He considered that episode practically. What did it mean? Was it a sign of some dangerous change in Sotillo's delusion? That the man should have been killed like this was what the doctor could not understand.

"Yes. But why shot?" he murmured to himself.

Nostromo kept very still.

CHAPTER NINE

DISTRACTED between doubts and hopes, dismayed by the sound of bells pealing out the arrival of Pedrito Montero, Sotillo had spent the morning in battling with his thoughts; a contest to which he was unequal, from the vacuity of his mind and the violence of his passions. Disappointment, greed, anger, and fear made a tumult, in the colonel's breast louder than the din of bells in the town. Nothing he had planned had come to pass. Neither Sulaco nor the silver of the mine had fallen into his hands. He had performed no military exploit to secure his position, and had obtained no enormous booty to make off with. Pedrito Montero, either as friend or foe, filled him with dread. The sound of bells maddened him.

Imagining at first that he might be attacked at once, he had made his battalion stand to arms on the shore. He walked to and fro all the length of the room, stopping sometimes to gnaw the finger-tips of his right hand with a lurid sideways glare fixed on the floor; then, with a sullen, repelling glance all round, he would resume his tramping in savage aloofness. His hat, horsewhip, sword, and revolver were lying on the table. His officers, crowding the window giving the view of the town gate, disputed amongst themselves the use of his field-glass bought last year on long credit from Anzani. It passed from hand to hand, and the possessor for the time being was besieged by anxious inquiries.

"There is nothing; there is nothing to see!" he would repeat, impatiently.

There was nothing. And when the picket in the bushes near the Casa Viola had been ordered to fall back upon the main body, no stir of life appeared on the stretch of dusty and arid land between the town and the waters of the port. But late in the afternoon a horseman issuing from the gate was made out riding up fearlessly. It was an emissary from Señor Fuentes. Being all alone he was allowed to come on. Dismounting at the great door he greeted the silent bystanders with cheery impudence, and begged to be taken up at once to the "muy valliente" colonel.*

Señor Fuentes, on entering upon his functions of Géfé Politico, had turned his diplomatic abilities to getting hold of the harbour as well as of the mine. The man he pitched upon to negotiate with Sotillo was a Notary Public, whom the revolution had found languishing in the common jail on a charge of forging documents. Liberated by the mob along with the other "victims of Blanco tyranny," he had hastened to offer his services to the new Government.

He set out determined to display much zeal and eloquence in trying to induce Sotillo to come into town alone for a conference with Pedrito Montero. Nothing was further from the colonel's intentions. The mere fleeting idea of trusting himself into the famous Pedrito's hands had made him feel unwell several times. It was out of the question—it was madness. And to put himself in open hostility was madness, too. It would render impossible a systematic search for that treasure, for that wealth of silver which he seemed to feel somewhere about, to scent somewhere near.

But where? Where? Heavens! Where? Oh! why had he allowed that doctor to go! Imbecile that he was. But no! It was the only right course, he reflected distractedly, while the messenger waited downstairs chat-

ting agreeably to the officers. It was in that scoundrelly
doctor's true interest to return with positive information.
But what if anything stopped him? A general prohibition to leave the town, for instance! There would
be patrols!

The colonel, seizing his head in his hands, turned in
his tracks as if struck with vertigo. A flash of craven
inspiration suggested to him an expedient not unknown
to European statesmen when they wish to delay a difficult negotiation. Booted and spurred, he scrambled
into the hammock with undignified haste. His handsome face had turned yellow with the strain of weighty
cares. The ridge of his shapely nose had grown sharp;
the audacious nostrils appeared mean and pinched.
The velvety, caressing glance of his fine eyes seemed
dead, and even decomposed; for these almond-shaped,
languishing orbs had become inappropriately bloodshot
with much sinister sleeplessness. He addressed the
surprised envoy of Señor Fuentes in a deadened, exhausted voice. It came pathetically feeble from under
a pile of ponchos, which buried his elegant person right
up to the black moustaches, uncurled, pendant, in sign
of bodily prostration and mental incapacity. Fever,
fever—a heavy fever had overtaken the "muy valliente"
colonel. A wavering wildness of expression, caused by
the passing spasms of a slight colic which had declared
itself suddenly, and the rattling teeth of repressed panic,
had a genuineness which impressed the envoy. It was a
cold fit. The colonel explained that he was unable
to think, to listen, to speak. With an appearance of
superhuman effort the colonel gasped out that he was
not in a state to return a suitable reply or to execute
any of his Excellency's orders. But to-morrow!
To-morrow! Ah! to-morrow! Let his Excellency Don
Pedro be without uneasiness. The brave Esmeralda

Regiment held the harbour, held—— And closing his eyes, he rolled his aching head like a half-delirious invalid under the inquisitive stare of the envoy, who was obliged to bend down over the hammock in order to catch the painful and broken accents. Meantime, Colonel Sotillo trusted that his Excellency's humanity would permit the doctor, the English doctor, to come out of town with his case of foreign remedies to attend upon him. He begged anxiously his worship the caballero now present for the grace of looking in as he passed the Casa Gould, and informing the English doctor, who was probably there, that his services were immediately required by Colonel Sotillo, lying ill of fever in the Custom House. Immediately. Most urgently required. Awaited with extreme impatience. A thousand thanks. He closed his eyes wearily and would not open them again, lying perfectly still, deaf, dumb, insensible, overcome, vanquished, crushed, annihilated by the fell disease.

But as soon as the other had shut after him the door of the landing, the colonel leaped out with a fling of both feet in an avalanche of woollen coverings. His spurs having become entangled in a perfect welter of ponchos he nearly pitched on his head, and did not recover his balance till the middle of the room. Concealed behind the half-closed jalousies he listened to what went on below.

The envoy had already mounted, and turning to the morose officers occupying the great doorway, took off his hat formally.

"Caballeros," he said, in a very loud tone, "allow me to recommend you to take great care of your colonel. It has done me much honour and gratification to have seen you all, a fine body of men exercising the soldierly virtue of patience in this exposed situation, where there is much sun, and no water to speak of, while a town full of wine and feminine charms is ready to embrace you for the brave men you are. Caballeros, I have the honour to salute you. There will be much dancing to-night in Sulaco. Good-bye!"

But he reined in his horse and inclined his head sideways on seeing the old major step out, very tall and meagre, in a straight narrow coat coming down to his ankles as it were the casing of the regimental colours rolled round their staff.

The intelligent old warrior, after enunciating in a dogmatic tone the general proposition that the "world was full of traitors," went on pronouncing deliberately a panegyric upon Sotillo. He ascribed to him with leisurely emphasis every virtue under heaven, summing it all up in an absurd colloquialism current amongst the lower class of Occidentals (especially about Esmeralda). "And," he concluded, with a sudden rise in the voice, "a man of many teeth—'*hombre de muchos dientes*.' *Si, señor*. As to us," he pursued, portentous and impressive, "your worship is beholding the finest body of officers in the Republic, men unequalled for valour and sagacity, '*y hombres de muchos dientes*.'"*

"What? All of them?" inquired the disreputable envoy of Señor Fuentes, with a faint, derisive smile.

"*Todos. Si, señor*," the major affirmed, gravely, with conviction. "Men of many teeth."

The other wheeled his horse to face the portal resembling the high gate of a dismal barn. He raised himself in his stirrups, extended one arm. He was a facetious scoundrel, entertaining for these stupid Occidentals a feeling of great scorn natural in a native from the central provinces. The folly of Esmeraldians especially aroused his amused contempt. He began an oration upon Pedro Montero, keeping a solemn countenance. He flourished his hand as if introducing him to their notice. And when he saw every face set, all the eyes fixed upon his lips, he began to shout a sort of catalogue of perfections: "Generous, valorous, affable, profound"—(he snatched off his hat enthusiastically)—"a statesman, an invincible chief of partisans—" He dropped his voice startlingly to a deep, hollow note—"and a dentist."

He was off instantly at a smart walk; the rigid straddle of his legs, the turned-out feet, the stiff back, the rakish slant of the sombrero above the square, motionless set of the shoulders expressing an infinite, awe-inspiring impudence.

Upstairs, behind the jalousies, Sotillo did not move for a long time. The audacity of the fellow appalled him. What were his officers saying below? They were saying nothing. Complete silence. He quaked. It was not thus that he had imagined himself at that stage of the expedition. He had seen himself triumphant, unquestioned, appeased, the idol of the soldiers, weighing in secret complacency the agreeable alternatives of power and wealth open to his choice. Alas! How different! Distracted, restless, supine, burning with fury, or frozen with terror, he felt a dread as fathomless as the sea creep upon him from every side. That rogue of a doctor had to come out with his information. That was clear. It would be of no use to him—alone. He could do nothing with it. Malediction! The doctor would never come out. He was probably under arrest already, shut up together with Don Carlos. He laughed aloud insanely. Ha! ha! ha! ha! It was Pedrito Montero who would get the information. Ha! ha! ha! ha!—and the silver. Ha!

All at once, in the midst of the laugh, he became motionless and silent as if turned into stone. He, too, had a prisoner. A prisoner who must, must know the real truth. He would have to be made to speak. And Sotillo, who all that time had not quite forgotten Hirsch, felt an inexplicable reluctance at the notion of proceeding to extremities.

He felt a reluctance—part of that unfathomable dread that crept on all sides upon him. He remembered reluctantly, too, the dilated eyes of the hide merchant, his contortions, his loud sobs and protestations. It was not compassion or even mere nervous sensibility. The fact was that though Sotillo did never for a moment believe his story—he could not believe it; nobody could believe such nonsense—yet those accents of despairing truth impressed him disagreeably. They made him feel sick. And he suspected also that the man might have gone mad with fear. A lunatic is a hopeless subject. Bah! A pretence. Nothing but a pretence. He would know how to deal with that.

He was working himself up to the right pitch of ferocity. His fine eyes squinted slightly; he clapped his hands; a bare-footed orderly appeared noiselessly; a corporal, with his bayonet hanging on his thigh and a stick in his hand.

The colonel gave his orders, and presently the miserable Hirsch, pushed in by several soldiers, found him frowning awfully in a broad armchair, hat on head, knees wide apart, arms akimbo, masterful, imposing, irresistible, haughty, sublime, terrible.

Hirsch, with his arms tied behind his back, had been bundled violently into one of the smaller rooms. For many hours he remained apparently forgotten, stretched lifelessly on the floor. From that solitude, full of despair and terror, he was torn out brutally, with kicks and blows, passive, sunk in hebetude. He listened to threats and admonitions, and afterwards made his usual answers to questions, with his chin sunk on his breast, his hands tied behind his back, swaying a little in front of Sotillo, and never looking up. When he was forced to hold up his head, by means of a bayonet-point prodding him under the chin, his eyes had a vacant, trance-like stare, and drops of perspiration as big as peas were seen hailing down the dirt, bruises, and scratches of his white face. Then they stopped suddenly.

Sotillo looked at him in silence. "Will you depart from your obstinacy, you rogue?" he asked. Already a rope, whose one end was fastened to Señor Hirsch's wrists, had been thrown over a beam, and three soldiers held the other end, waiting. He made no answer. His heavy lower lip hung stupidly. Sotillo made a sign. Hirsch was jerked up off his feet, and a yell of despair and agony burst out in the room, filled the passage of the great buildings, rent the air outside, caused every soldier of the camp along the shore to look up at the windows, started some of the officers in the hall babbling excitedly, with shining eyes; others, setting their lips, looked gloomily at the floor.

Sotillo, followed by the soldiers, had left the room. The sentry on the landing presented arms. Hirsch went on screaming all alone behind the half-closed jalousies while the sunshine, reflected from the water of the harbour, made an ever-running ripple of light high up on the wall. He screamed with uplifted eyebrows and a wide-open mouth—incredibly wide, black, enormous, full of teeth—comical.

In the still burning air of the windless afternoon he made the waves of his agony travel as far as the O. S. N. Company's offices. Captain Mitchell on the balcony, trying to make out what went on generally, had heard him faintly but distinctly, and the feeble and appalling sound lingered in his ears after he had retreated indoors with blanched cheeks. He had been driven off the balcony several times during that afternoon.

Sotillo, irritable, moody, walked restlessly about, held consultations with his officers, gave contradictory orders in this shrill clamour pervading the whole empty edifice. Sometimes there would be long and awful silences. Several times he had entered the torture-chamber where his sword, horsewhip, revolver, and field-glass were lying on the table, to ask with forced calmness, "Will you speak the truth now? No? I can wait." But he could not afford to wait much longer. That was just it. Every time he went in and came out with a slam of the door, the sentry on the landing presented arms, and got in return a black, venomous, unsteady glance, which, in reality, saw nothing at all, being merely the reflection of the soul within—a soul of gloomy hatred, irresolution, avarice, and fury.

The sun had set when he went in once more. A soldier carried in two lighted candles and slunk out, shutting the door without noise.

"Speak, thou Jewish child of the devil! The silver! The silver, I say! Where it it? Where have you foreign rogues hidden it? Confess or——"

A slight quiver passed up the taut rope from the racked limbs, but the body of Señor Hirsch, enterprising business man from Esmeralda, hung under the heavy beam perpendicular and silent, facing the colonel awfully. The inflow of the night air, cooled by the snows of the Sierra, spread gradually a delicious freshness through the close heat of the room.

"Speak—thief—scoundrel—picaro—or——"

Sotillo had seized the riding-whip, and stood with his arm lifted up. For a word, for one little word, he felt he would have knelt, cringed, grovelled on the floor before the drowsy, conscious stare of those fixed eye-

balls starting out of the grimy, dishevelled head that
drooped very still with its mouth closed askew. The
colonel ground his teeth with rage and struck. The
rope vibrated leisurely to the blow, like the long string
of a pendulum starting from a rest. But no swinging
motion was imparted to the body of Señor Hirsch,
the well-known hide merchant on the coast. With
a convulsive effort of the twisted arms it leaped up a few
inches, curling upon itself like a fish on the end of a line.
Señor Hirsch's head was flung back on his straining
throat; his chin trembled. For a moment the rattle
of his chattering teeth pervaded the vast, shadowy
room, where the candles made a patch of light round
the two flames burning side by side. And as Sotillo,
staying his raised hand, waited for him to speak, with
the sudden flash of a grin and a straining forward of the
wrenched shoulders, he spat violently into his face.*

The uplifted whip fell, and the colonel sprang back
with a low cry of dismay, as if aspersed by a jet of
deadly venom. Quick as thought he snatched up his
revolver, and fired twice. The report and the concus-
sion of the shots seemed to throw him at once from
ungovernable rage into idiotic stupor. He stood with
drooping jaw and stony eyes. What had he done,
Sangre de Dios! What had he done? He was basely
appalled at his impulsive act, sealing for ever these lips
from which so much was to be extorted. What could
he say? How could he explain? Ideas of headlong
flight somewhere, anywhere, passed through his mind;
even the craven and absurd notion of hiding under
the table occurred to his cowardice. It was too late;
his officers had rushed in tumultuously, in a great clatter
of scabbards, clamouring, with astonishment and
wonder. But since they did not immediately proceed
to plunge their swords into his breast, the brazen side

of his character asserted itself. Passing the sleeve of his uniform over his face he pulled himself together, His truculent glance turned slowly here and there, checked the noise where it fell; and the stiff body of the late Señor Hirsch, merchant, after swaying imperceptibly, made a half turn, and came to a rest in the midst of awed murmurs and uneasy shuffling.

A voice remarked loudly, "Behold a man who will never speak again." And another, from the back row of faces, timid and pressing, cried out—

"Why did you kill him, *mi colonel?*"

"Because he has confessed everything," answered Sotillo, with the hardihood of desperation. He felt himself cornered. He brazened it out on the strength of his reputation with very fair success. His hearers thought him very capable of such an act. They were disposed to believe his flattering tale. There is no credulity so eager and blind as the credulity of covetousness, which, in its universal extent, measures the moral misery and the intellectual destitution of mankind. Ah! he had confessed everything, this fractious Jew, this *bribon*. Good! Then he was no longer wanted. A sudden dense guffaw was heard from the senior captain—a big-headed man, with little round eyes and monstrously fat cheeks which never moved. The old major, tall and fantastically ragged like a scarecrow, walked round the body of the late Señor Hirsch, muttering to himself with ineffable complacency that like this there was no need to guard against any future treacheries of that scoundrel. The others stared, shifting from foot to foot, and whispering short remarks to each other.

Sotillo buckled on his sword and gave curt, peremptory orders to hasten the retirement decided upon in the afternoon. Sinister, impressive, his sombrero pulled right down upon his eyebrows, he marched first through the door in such disorder of mind that he forgot utterly to provide for Dr. Monygham's possible return. As the officers trooped out after him, one or two looked back hastily at the late Señor Hirsch, merchant from Esmeralda, left swinging rigidly at rest, alone with the two burning candles. In the emptiness of the room the burly shadow of head and shoulders on the wall had an air of life.

Below, the troops fell in silently and moved off by companies without drum or trumpet. The old scarecrow major commanded the rearguard; but the party he left behind with orders to fire the Custom House (and "burn the carcass of the treacherous Jew where it hung") failed somehow in their haste to set the staircase properly alight. The body of the late Señor Hirsch dwelt alone for a time in the dismal solitude of the unfinished building, resounding weirdly with sudden slams and clicks of doors and latches, with rustling scurries of torn papers, and the tremulous sighs that at each gust of wind passed under the high roof. The light of the two candles burning before the perpendicular and breathless immobility of the late Señor Hirsch threw a gleam afar over land and water, like a signal in the night. He remained to startle Nostromo by his presence, and to puzzle Dr. Monygham by the mystery of his atrocious end.

"But why shot?" the doctor again asked himself, audibly. This time he was answered by a dry laugh from Nostromo.

"You seem much concerned at a very natural thing, señor doctor. I wonder why? It is very likely that before long we shall all get shot one after another, if not by Sotillo, then by Pedrito, or Fuentes, or Gamacho. And we may even get the estrapade, too, or worse—*quien sabe?*—with your pretty tale of the silver you put into Sotillo's head."

"It was in his head already," the doctor protested. "I only——"

"Yes. And you only nailed it there so that the devil himself—"

"That is precisely what I meant to do," caught up the doctor.

"That is what you meant to do. *Bueno.* It is as I say. You are a dangerous man."

Their voices, which without rising had been growing quarrelsome, ceased suddenly. The late Señor Hirsch, erect and shadowy against the stars, seemed to be waiting attentive, in impartial silence.

But Dr. Monygham had no mind to quarrel with Nostromo. At this supremely critical point of Sulaco's fortunes it was borne upon him at last that this man was really indispensable, more indispensable than ever the infatuation of Captain Mitchell, his proud discoverer, could conceive; far beyond what Decoud's best dry raillery about "my illustrious friend, the unique Capataz de Cargadores," had ever intended. The fellow was unique. He was not "one in a thousand." He was absolutely the only one. The doctor surrendered. There was something in the genius of that Genoese seaman which dominated in the destinies of great enterprises and of many people, the fortunes of Charles Gould, the fate of an admirable woman. At this last thought the doctor had to clear his throat before he could speak.

In a completely changed tone he pointed out to the Capataz that, to begin with, he personally ran no great risk. As far as everybody knew he was dead. It was an enormous advantage. He had only to keep out of sight in the Casa Viola. where the old Garibaldino was known to be alone—with his dead wife. The servants had all run away. No one would think of searching for him there, or anywhere else on earth, for that matter.

"That would be very true," Nostromo spoke up, bitterly, "if I had not met you."

For a time the doctor kept silent. "Do you mean to say that you think I may give you away?" he asked in an unsteady voice. "Why? Why should I do that?"

"What do I know? Why not? To gain a day perhaps. It would take Sotillo a day to give me the estrapade, and try some other things perhaps, before he puts a bullet through my heart—as he did to that poor wretch here. Why not?"

The doctor swallowed with difficulty. His throat had gone dry in a moment. It was not from indignation. The doctor, pathetically enough, believed that he had forfeited the right to be indignant with any one—for anything. It was simple dread. Had the fellow heard his story by some chance? If so, there was an end of his usefulness in that direction. The indispensable man escaped his influence, because of that indelible blot which made him fit for dirty work. A feeling as of sickness came upon the doctor. He would have given anything to know, but he dared not clear up the point. The fanaticism of his devotion, fed on the sense of his abasement, hardened his heart in sadness and scorn.

"Why not, indeed?" he reëchoed, sardonically. "Then the safe thing for you is to kill me on the spot. I would defend myself. But you may just as well know I am going about unarmed."

"*Por Dios!*" said the Capataz, passionately. "You fine people are all alike. All dangerous. All betrayers of the poor who are your dogs."

"You do not understand," began the doctor, slowly.

"I understand you all!" cried the other with a violent movement, as shadowy to the doctor's eyes as the persistent immobility of the late Señor Hirsch. "A poor man amongst you has got to look after himself. I say that you do not care for those that serve you. Look at me! After all these years, suddenly, here I find myself like one of these curs that bark outside the walls —without a kennel or a dry bone for my teeth. *Caramba!*" But he relented with a contemptuous fairness. "Of course," he went on, quietly, "I do not suppose that you would hasten to give me up to Sotillo, for example. It is not that. It is that I am nothing! Suddenly——" He swung his arm downwards. "Nothing to any one," he repeated.

The doctor breathed freely. "Listen, Capataz," he said, stretching out his arm almost affectionately towards Nostromo's shoulder. "I am going to tell you a very simple thing. You are safe because you are needed. I would not give you away for any conceivable reason, because I want you."

In the dark Nostromo bit his lip. He had heard enough of that. He knew what that meant. No more of that for him. But he had to look after himself now, he thought. And he thought, too, that it would not be prudent to part in anger from his companion. The doctor, admitted to be a great healer, had, amongst the populace of Sulaco, the reputation of being an evil sort of man. It was based solidly on his personal appearance, which was strange, and on his rough ironic manner—proofs visible, sensible, and incontrovertible of the doctor's malevolent disposition. And Nostromo was of the people. So he only grunted incredulously.

"You, to speak plainly, are the only man," the doctor pursued. "It is in your power to save this town and

. . . everybody from the destructive rapacity of men who——"

"No, señor," said Nostromo, sullenly. "It is not in my power to get the treasure back for you to give up to Sotillo, or Pedrito, or Gamacho. What do I know?"

"Nobody expects the impossible," was the answer.

"You have said it yourself—nobody," muttered Nostromo, in a gloomy, threatening tone.

But Dr. Monygham, full of hope, disregarded the enigmatic words and the threatening tone. To their eyes, accustomed to obscurity, the late Señor Hirsch, growing more distinct, seemed to have come nearer. And the doctor lowered his voice in exposing his scheme as though afraid of being overheard.

He was taking the indispensable man into his fullest confidence. Its implied flattery and suggestion of great risks came with a familiar sound to the Capataz. His mind, floating in irresolution and discontent, recognized it with bitterness. He understood well that the doctor was anxious to save the San Tomé mine from annihilation. He would be nothing without it. It was his interest. Just as it had been the interest of Señor Decoud, of the Blancos, and of the Europeans to get his Cargadores on their side. His thought became arrested upon Decoud. What would happen to him?

Nostromo's prolonged silence made the doctor uneasy. He pointed out, quite unnecessarily, that though for the present he was safe, he could not live concealed for ever. The choice was between accepting the mission to Barrios, with all its dangers and difficulties, and leaving Sulaco by stealth, ingloriously, in poverty.

"None of your friends could reward you and protect you just now, Capataz. Not even Don Carlos himself."

"I would have none of your protection and none of

your rewards. I only wish I could trust your courage and your sense. When I return in triumph, as you say, with Barrios, I may find you all destroyed. You have the knife at your throat now."

It was the doctor's turn to remain silent in the contemplation of horrible contingencies.

"Well, we would trust your courage and your sense. And you, too, have a knife at your throat"

"Ah! And whom am I to thank for that? What are your politics and your mines to me—your silver and your constitutions—your Don Carlos this, and Don José that——"

"I don't know," burst out the exasperated doctor. "There are innocent people in danger whose little finger is worth more than you or I and all the Ribierists together. I don't know. You should have asked yourself before you allowed Decoud to lead you into all this. It was your place to think like a man; but if you did not think then, try to act like a man now. Did you imagine Decoud cared very much for what would happen to you?"

"No more than you care for what will happen to me," muttered the other.

"No; I care for what will happen to you as little as I care for what will happen to myself."

"And all this because you are such a devoted Ribierist?" Nostromo said in an incredulous tone.

"All this because I am such a devoted Ribierist," repeated Dr. Monygham, grimly.

Again Nostromo, gazing abstractedly at the body of the late Señor Hirsch, remained silent, thinking that the doctor was a dangerous person in more than one sense. It was impossible to trust him.

"Do you speak in the name of Don Carlos?" he asked at last.

"Yes. I do," the doctor said, loudly, without hesitation. "He must come forward now. He must," he added in a mutter, which Nostromo did not catch.

"What did you say, señor?"

The doctor started. "I say that you must be true to yourself, Capataz. It would be worse than folly to fail now."

"True to myself," repeated Nostromo. "How do you know that I would not be true to myself if I told you to go to the devil with your propositions?"

"I do not know. Maybe you would," the doctor said, with a roughness of tone intended to hide the sinking of his heart and the faltering of his voice. "All I know is, that you had better get away from here. Some of Sotillo's men may turn up here looking for me."

He slipped off the table, listened intently. The Capataz, too, stood up.

"Suppose I went to Cayta, what would you do meantime?" he asked.

"I would go to Sotillo directly you had left—in the way I am thinking of."

"A very good way—if only that engineer-in-chief consents. Remind him, señor, that I looked after the old rich Englishman who pays for the railway, and that I saved the lives of some of his people that time when a gang of thieves came from the south to wreck one of his pay-trains. It was I who discovered it all at the risk of my life, by pretending to enter into their plans. Just as you are doing with Sotillo."

"Yes. Yes, of course. But I can offer him better arguments," the doctor said, hastily. "Leave it to me."

"Ah, yes! True. I am nothing."

"Not at all. You are everything."

They moved a few paces towards the door. Behind

them the late Señor Hirsch preserved the immobility
of a disregarded man.

"That will be all right. I know what to say to the
engineer," pursued the doctor, in a low tone. "My
difficulty will be with Sotillo."

And Dr. Monygham stopped short in the doorway as
if intimidated by the difficulty. He had made the sacrifice of his life. He considered this a fitting opportunity.
But he did not want to throw his life away too soon.
In his quality of betrayer of Don Carlos' confidence,
he would have ultimately to indicate the hiding-place
of the treasure. That would be the end of his deception,
and the end of himself as well, at the hands of the infuriated colonel. He wanted to delay him to the very last
moment; and he had been racking his brains to invent
some place of concealment at once plausible and difficult of access.

He imparted his trouble to Nostromo, and concluded—

"Do you know what, Capataz? I think that when
the time comes and some information must be given,
I shall indicate the Great Isabel. That is the best
place I can think of. What is the matter?"

A low exclamation had escaped Nostromo. The
doctor waited, surprised, and after a moment of profound silence, heard a thick voice stammer out "Utter
folly," and stop with a gasp.

"Why folly?"

"Ah! You do not see it," began Nostromo, scathingly, gathering scorn as he went on. "Three men in
half an hour would see that no ground had been disturbed anywhere on that island. Do you think that
such a treasure can be buried without leaving traces
of the work—eh! señor doctor? Why! you would not
gain half a day more before having your throat cut by

Sotillo. The Isabel! What stupidity! What miserable invention! Ah! you are all alike, you fine men of intelligence. All you are fit for is to betray men of the people into undertaking deadly risks for objects that you are not even sure about. If it comes off you get the benefit. If not, then it does not matter. He is only a dog. Ah! *Madre de Dios*, I would——"
He shook his fists above his head.

The doctor was overwhelmed at first by this fierce, hissing vehemence.

"Well! It seems to me on your own showing that the men of the people are no mean fools, too," he said, sullenly. "No, but come. You are so clever. Have you a better place?"

Nostromo had calmed down as quickly as he had flared up.

"I am clever enough for that," he said, quietly, almost with indifference. "You want to tell him of a hiding-place big enough to take days in ransacking—a place where a treasure of silver ingots can be buried without leaving a sign on the surface."

"And close at hand," the doctor put in.

"Just so, señor. Tell him it is sunk."

"This has the merit of being the truth," the doctor said, contemptuously. "He will not believe it."

"You tell him that it is sunk where he may hope to lay his hands on it, and he will believe you quick enough. Tell him it has been sunk in the harbour in order to be recovered afterwards by divers. Tell him you found out that I had orders from Don Carlos Gould to lower the cases quietly overboard somewhere in a line between the end of the jetty and the entrance. The depth is not too great there. He has no divers, but he has a ship, boats, ropes, chains, sailors—of a sort. Let him fish for the silver. Let him set his fools to drag backwards and forwards and crossways while he sits and watches till his eyes drop out of his head."

"Really, this is an admirable idea," muttered the doctor.

"Si. You tell him that, and see whether he will not believe you! He will spend days in rage and torment—and still he will believe. He will have no thought for anything else. He will not give up till he is driven off—why, he may even forget to kill you. He will neither eat nor sleep. He——"

"The very thing! The very thing!" the doctor repeated in an excited whisper. "Capataz, I begin to believe that you are a great genius in your way."

Nostromo had paused; then began again in a changed tone, sombre, speaking to himself as though he had forgotten the doctor's existence.

"There is something in a treasure that fastens upon a man's mind. He will pray and blaspheme and still persevere, and will curse the day he ever heard of it, and will let his last hour come upon him unawares, still believing that he missed it only by a foot. He will see it every time he closes his eyes. He will never forget it till he is dead—and even then—— Doctor, did you ever hear of the miserable gringos on Azuera, that cannot die? Ha! ha! Sailors like myself. There is no getting away from a treasure that once fastens upon your mind."

"You are a devil of a man, Capataz. It is the most plausible thing."

Nostromo pressed his arm.

"It will be worse for him than thirst at sea or hunger in a town full of people. Do you know what that is? He shall suffer greater torments than he inflicted upon that terrified wretch who had no invention. None!

none! Not like me. I could have told Sotillo a deadly tale for very little pain."

He laughed wildly and turned in the doorway towards the body of the late Señor Hirsch, an opaque long blotch in the semi-transparent obscurity of the room between the two tall parallelograms of the windows full of stars.

"You man of fear!" he cried. "You shall be avenged by me—Nostromo. Out of my way, doctor! Stand aside—or, by the suffering soul of a woman dead without confession, I will strangle you with my two hands."

He bounded downwards into the black, smoky hall. With a grunt of astonishment, Dr. Monygham threw himself recklessly into the pursuit. At the bottom of the charred stairs he had a fall, pitching forward on his face with a force that would have stunned a spirit less intent upon a task of love and devotion. He was up in a moment, jarred, shaken, with a queer impression of the terrestrial globe having been flung at his head in the dark. But it wanted more than that to stop Dr. Monygham's body, possessed by the exaltation of self-sacrifice; a reasonable exaltation, determined not to lose whatever advantage chance put into its way. He ran with headlong, tottering swiftness, his arms going like a windmill in his effort, to keep his balance on his crippled feet. He lost his hat; the tails of his open gaberdine flew behind him. He had no mind to lose sight of the indispensable man. But it was a long time, and a long way from the Custom House, before he managed to seize his arm from behind, roughly, out of breath.

"Stop! Are you mad?"

Already Nostromo was walking slowly, his head dropping, as if checked in his pace by the weariness of irresolution.

"What is that to you? Ah! I forgot you want me for something. Always. Siempre Nostromo."

"What do you mean by talking of strangling me?" panted the doctor.

"What do I mean? I mean that the king of the devils himself has sent you out of this town of cowards and talkers to meet me to-night of all the nights of my life."

Under the starry sky the Albergo d'Italia Una emerged, black and low, breaking the dark level of the plain. Nostromo stopped altogether.

"The priests say he is a tempter, do they not?" he added, through his clenched teeth.

"My good man, you drivel. The devil has nothing to do with this. Neither has the town, which you may call by what name you please. But Don Carlos Gould is neither a coward nor an empty talker. You will admit that?" He waited. "Well?"

"Could I see Don Carlos?"

"Great heavens! No! Why? What for?" exclaimed the doctor in agitation. "I tell you it is madness. I will not let you go into the town for anything."

"I must."

"You must not!" hissed the doctor, fiercely, almost beside himself with the fear of the man doing away with his usefulness for an imbecile whim of some sort. "I tell you you shall not. I would rather——"

He stopped at loss for words, feeling fagged out, powerless, holding on to Nostromo's sleeve, absolutely for support after his run.

"I am betrayed!" muttered the Capataz to himself; and the doctor, who overheard the last word, made an effort to speak calmly.

"That is exactly what would happen to you. You would be betrayed."

He thought with a sickening dread that the man was so well known that he could not escape recognition.

The house of the Señor Administrador was beset by spies, no doubt. And even the very servants of the casa were not to be trusted. "Reflect, Capataz," he said, impressively. . . . "What are you laughing at?"

"I am laughing to think that if somebody that did not approve of my presence in town, for instance—you understand, señor doctor—if somebody were to give me up to Pedrito, it would not be beyond my power to make friends even with him. It is true. What do you think of that?"

"You are a man of infinite resource, Capataz," said Dr. Monygham, dismally. "I recognize that. But the town is full of talk about you; and those few Cargadores that are not in hiding with the railway people have been shouting 'Viva Montero' on the Plaza all day."

"My poor Cargadores!" muttered Nostromo. "Betrayed! Betrayed!"

"I understand that on the wharf you were pretty free in laying about you with a stick amongst your poor Cargadores," the doctor said in a grim tone, which showed that he was recovering from his exertions. "Make no mistake. Pedrito is furious at Señor Ribiera's rescue, and at having lost the pleasure of shooting Decoud. Already there are rumours in the town of the treasure having been spirited away. To have missed that does not please Pedrito either; but let me tell you that if you had all that silver in your hand for your ransom it would not save you."

Turning swiftly, and catching the doctor by the shoulders, Nostromo thrust his face close to his.

"Maladetta! You follow me speaking of the treasure. You have sworn my ruin. You were the last man who looked upon me before I went out with it. And Sidoni the engine-driver says you have an evil eye."

"He ought to know. I saved his broken leg for him last year," the doctor said, stoically. He felt on his shoulders the weight of these hands famed amongst the populace for snapping thick ropes and bending horse-shoes. "And to you I offer the best means of saving yourself—let me go—and of retrieving your great reputation. You boasted of making the Capataz de Cargadores famous from one end of America to the other about this wretched silver. But I bring you a better opportunity—let me go, hombre!"

Nostromo released him abruptly, and the doctor feared that the indispensable man would run off again. But he did not. He walked on slowly. The doctor hobbled by his side till, within a stone's throw from the Casa Viola, Nostromo stopped again.

Silent in inhospitable darkness, the Casa Viola seemed to have changed its nature; his home appeared to repel him with an air of hopeless and inimical mystery. The doctor said—

"You will be safe there. Go in, Capataz."

"How can I go in?" Nostromo seemed to ask himself in a low, inward tone. "She cannot unsay what she said, and I cannot undo what I have done."

"I tell you it is all right. Viola is all alone in there. I looked in as I came out of the town. You will be perfectly safe in that house till you leave it to make your name famous on the Campo. I am going now to arrange for your departure with the engineer-in-chief, and I shall bring you news here long before daybreak."

Dr. Monygham, disregarding, or perhaps fearing to penetrate the meaning of Nostromo's silence, clapped him lightly on the shoulder, and starting off with his smart, lame walk, vanished utterly at the third or fourth hop in the direction of the railway track. Arrested between the two wooden posts for people to fasten their horses to,

Nostromo did not move, as if he, too, had been planted solidly in the ground. At the end of half an hour he lifted his head to the deep baying of the dogs at the railway yards, which had burst out suddenly, tumultuous and deadened as if coming from under the plain. That lame doctor with the evil eye had got there pretty fast.

Step by step Nostromo approached the Albergo d'Italia Una, which he had never known so lightless, so silent, before. The door, all black in the pale wall, stood open as he had left it twenty-four hours before, when he had nothing to hide from the world. He remained before it, irresolute, like a fugitive, like a man betrayed. Poverty, misery, starvation! Where had he heard these words? The anger of a dying woman had prophesied that fate for his folly. It looked as if it would come true very quickly. And the leperos would laugh—she had said. Yes, they would laugh if they knew that the Capataz de Cargadores was at the mercy of the mad doctor whom they could remember, only a few years ago, buying cooked food from a stall on the Plaza for a copper coin—like one of themselves.

At that moment the notion of seeking Captain Mitchell passed through his mind. He glanced in the direction of the jetty and saw a small gleam of light in the O.S.N. Company's building. The thought of lighted windows was not attractive. Two lighted windows had decoyed him into the empty Custom House, only to fall into the clutches of that doctor. No! He would not go near lighted windows again on that night. Captain Mitchell was there. And what could he be told? That doctor would worm it all out of him as if he were a child.

On the threshold he called out "Giorgio!" in an undertone. Nobody answered. He stepped in. *"Olà!*

viejo! Are you there? . . ." In the impenetrable darkness his head swam with the illusion that the obscurity of the kitchen was as vast as the Placid Gulf, and that the floor dipped forward like a sinking lighter. *"Ola! viejo!"* he repeated, falteringly, swaying where he stood. His hand, extended to steady himself, fell upon the table. Moving a step forward, he shifted it, and felt a box of matches under his fingers. He fancied he had heard a quiet sigh. He listened for a moment, holding his breath; then, with trembling hands, tried to strike a light.

The tiny piece of wood flamed up quite blindingly at the end of his fingers, raised above his blinking eyes. A concentrated glare fell upon the leonine white head of old Giorgio against the black fire-place—showed him leaning forward in a chair in staring immobility, surrounded, overhung, by great masses of shadow, his legs crossed, his cheek in his hand, an empty pipe in the corner of his mouth. It seemed hours before he attempted to turn his face; at the very moment the match went out, and he disappeared, overwhelmed by the shadows, as if the walls and roof of the desolate house had collapsed upon his white head in ghostly silence.

Nostromo heard him stir and utter dispassionately the words—

"It may have been a vision."

"No," he said, softly. "It is no vision, old man."

A strong chest voice asked in the dark—

"Is that you I hear, Giovann' Battista?"

"Si, viejo. Steady. Not so loud."

After his release by Sotillo, Giorgio Viola, attended to the very door by the good-natured engineer-in-chief, had reëntered his house, which he had been made to leave almost at the very moment of his wife's death. All was still. The lamp above was burning. He nearly called out to her by name; and the thought that no call from him would ever again evoke the answer of her voice, made him drop heavily into the chair with a loud groan, wrung out by the pain as of a keen blade piercing his breast.

The rest of the night he made no sound. The darkness turned to grey, and on the colourless, clear, glassy dawn the jagged sierra stood out flat and opaque, as if cut out of paper.

The enthusiastic and severe soul of Giorgio Viola, sailor, champion of oppressed humanity, enemy of kings, and, by the grace of Mrs. Gould, hotel-keeper of the Sulaco harbour, had descended into the open abyss of desolation amongst the shattered vestiges of his past. He remembered his wooing between two campaigns a single short week in the season of gathering olives. Nothing approached the grave passion of that time but the deep, passionate sense of his bereavement. He discovered all the extent of his dependence upon the silenced voice of that woman. It was her voice that he missed. Abstracted, busy, lost in inward contemplation, he seldom looked at his wife in those later years. The thought of his girls was a matter of concern, not of consolation. It was her voice that he would miss. And he remembered the other child—the little boy who died at sea. Ah! a man would have been something to lean upon. And, alas! even Gian' Battista—he of whom, and of Linda, his wife had spoken to him so anxiously before she dropped off into her last sleep on earth, he on whom she had called aloud to save the children, just before she died—even he was dead!

And the old man, bent forward, his head in his hand, sat through the day in immobility and solitude. He never heard the brazen roar of the bells in town. When it ceased the earthenware filter in the corner of the kitchen kept on its swift musical drip, drip into the great porous jar below.

Towards sunset he got up, and with slow movements disappeared up the narrow staircase. His bulk filled it; and the rubbing of his shoulders made a small noise as of a mouse running behind the plaster of a wall. While he remained up there the house was as dumb as a grave. Then, with the same faint rubbing noise, he descended. He had to catch at the chairs and tables to regain his seat. He seized his pipe off the high mantel of the fire-place—but made no attempt to reach the tobacco—thrust it empty into the corner of his mouth, and sat down again in the same staring pose. The sun of Pedrito's entry into Sulaco, the last sun of Señor Hirsch's life, the first of Decoud's solitude on the Great Isabel, passed over the Albergo d'Italia Una on its way to the west. The tinkling drip, drip of the filter had ceased, the lamp upstairs had burnt itself out, and the night beset Giorgio Viola and his dead wife with its obscurity and silence that seemed invincible till the Capataz de Cargadores, returning from the dead, put them to flight with the splutter and flare of a match.

"Si, viejo. It is me. Wait."

Nostromo, after barricading the door and closing the shutters carefully, groped upon a shelf for a candle, and lit it.

Old Viola had risen. He followed with his eyes in the dark the sounds made by Nostromo. The light disclosed him standing without support, as if the mere presence of that man who was loyal, brave, incorruptible, who was all his son would have been, were enough for the support of his decaying strength.

He extended his hand grasping the briar-wood pipe, whose bowl was charred on the edge, and knitted his bushy eyebrows heavily at the light.

"You have returned," he said, with shaky dignity. "Ah! Very well! I——"

He broke off. Nostromo, leaning back against the table, his arms folded on his breast, nodded at him slightly.

"You thought I was drowned! No! The best dog of the rich, of the aristocrats, of these fine men who can only talk and betray the people, is not dead yet."

The Garibaldino, motionless, seemed to drink in the sound of the well-known voice. His head moved slightly once as if in sign of approval; but Nostromo saw clearly that the old man understood nothing of the words. There was no one to understand; no one he could take into the confidence of Decoud's fate, of his own, into the secret of the silver. That doctor was an enemy of the people—a tempter. . . .

Old Giorgio's heavy frame shook from head to foot with the effort to overcome his emotion at the sight of that man, who had shared the intimacies of his domestic life as though he had been a grown-up son.

"She believed you would return," he said, solemnly.

Nostromo raised his head.

"She was a wise woman. How could I fail to come back——?"

He finished the thought mentally: "Since she has prophesied for me an end of poverty, misery, and starvation." These words of Teresa's anger, from the circumstances in which they had been uttered, like the cry of a soul prevented from making its peace with God, stirred the obscure superstition of personal fortune from which even the greatest genius amongst men of adventure and action is seldom free. They reigned over Nostromo's mind with the force of a potent malediction. And what a curse it was that which her words had laid upon him! He had been orphaned so

young that he could remember no other woman whom
he called mother. Henceforth there would be no enterprise in which he would not fail. The spell was working
already. Death itself would elude him now. . . .
He said violently—

"Come, viejo! Get me something to eat. I am
hungry! *Sangre de Dios!* The emptiness of my belly
makes me lightheaded."

With his chin dropped again upon his bare breast
above his folded arms, barefooted, watching from under
a gloomy brow the movements of old Viola foraging
amongst the cupboards, he seemed as if indeed fallen
under a curse—a ruined and sinister Capataz.

Old Viola walked out of a dark corner, and, without a
word, emptied upon the table out of his hollowed palms
a few dry crusts of bread and half a raw onion.

While the Capataz began to devour his beggar's
fare, taking up with stony-eyed voracity piece after
piece lying by his side, the Garibaldino went off, and
squatting down in another corner filled an earthenware
mug with red wine out of a wicker-covered demijohn.
With a familiar gesture, as when serving customers in
the café, he had thrust his pipe between his teeth to
have his hands free.

The Capataz drank greedily. A slight flush deepened
the bronze of his cheek. Before him, Viola, with a
turn of his white and massive head towards the staircase, took his empty pipe out of his mouth, and pronounced slowly—

"After the shot was fired down here, which killed her
as surely as if the bullet had struck her oppressed heart,
she called upon you to save the children. Upon you,
Gian' Battista."

The Capataz looked up.

"Did she do that, Padrone? To save the children!"

They are with the English señora, their rich benefactress. Hey! old man of the people. Thy benefactress. . . ."

"I am old," muttered Giorgio Viola. "An Englishwoman was allowed to give a bed to Garibaldi lying wounded in prison. The greatest man that ever lived. A man of the people, too—a sailor. I may let another keep a roof over my head. *Si* . . . I am old. I may let her. Life lasts too long sometimes."

"And she herself may not have a roof over her head before many days are out, unless I . . . What do you say? Am I to keep a roof over her head? Am I to try—and save all the Blancos together with her?"

"You shall do it," said old Viola in a strong voice. "You shall do it as my son would have. . . ."

"Thy son, viejo! . . . . There never has been a man like thy son. Ha, I must try. . . . But what if it were only a part of the curse to lure me on? . . . And so she called upon me to save—and then——?"

"She spoke no more." The heroic follower of Garibaldi, at the thought of the eternal stillness and silence fallen upon the shrouded form stretched out on the bed upstairs, averted his face and raised his hand to his furrowed brow. "She was dead before I could seize her hands," he stammered out, pitifully.

Before the wide eyes of the Capataz, staring at the doorway of the dark staircase, floated the shape of the Great Isabel, like a strange ship in distress, freighted with enormous wealth and the solitary life of a man. It was impossible for him to do anything. He could only hold his tongue, since there was no one to trust. The treasure would be lost, probably—unless Decoud. . . . And his thought came abruptly to an end. He perceived that he could not imagine in the least what Decoud was likely to do.

Old Viola had not stirred. And the motionless Capataz dropped his long, soft eyelashes, which gave to the upper part of his fierce, black-whiskered face a touch of feminine ingenuousness. The silence had lasted for a long time.

"God rest her soul!" he murmured, gloomily.

CHAPTER TEN

THE next day was quiet in the morning, except for the faint sound of firing to the northward, in the direction of Los Hatos. Captain Mitchell had listened to it from his balcony anxiously. The phrase, "In my delicate position as the only consular agent then in the port, everything, sir, everything was a just cause for anxiety," had its place in the more or less stereotyped relation of the "historical events" which for the next few years was at the service of distinguished strangers visiting Sulaco. The mention of the dignity and neutrality of the flag, so difficult to preserve in his position, "right in the thick of these events between the lawlessness of that piratical villain Sotillo and the more regularly established but scarcely less atrocious tyranny of his Excellency Don Pedro Montero," came next in order. Captain Mitchell was not the man to enlarge upon mere dangers much. But he insisted that it was a memorable day. On that day, towards dusk, he had seen "that poor fellow of mine—Nostromo. The sailor whom I discovered, and, I may say, made, sir. The man of the famous ride to Cayta, sir. An historical event, sir!"

Regarded by the O. S. N. Company as an old and faithful servant, Captain Mitchell was allowed to attain the term of his usefulness in ease and dignity at the head of the enormously extended service. The augmentation of the establishment, with its crowds of clerks, an office in town, the old office in the harbour, the division into departments—passenger, cargo, lighterage, and so on—secured a greater leisure for his last years in the regenerated Sulaco, the capital of the Occidental Republic. Liked by the natives for his good nature and the formality of his manner, self-important and simple, known for years as a "friend of our country," he felt himself a personality of mark in the town. Getting up early for a turn in the market-place while the gigantic shadow of Higuerota was still lying upon the fruit and flower stalls piled up with masses of gorgeous colouring, attending easily to current affairs, welcomed in houses, greeted by ladies on the Alameda, with his entry into all the clubs and a footing in the Casa Gould, he led his privileged old bachelor, man-about-town existence with great comfort and solemnity. But on mail-boat days he was down at the Harbour Office at an early hour, with his own gig, manned by a smart crew in white and blue, ready to dash off and board the ship directly she showed her bows between the harbour heads.

It would be into the Harbour Office that he would lead some privileged passenger he had brought off in his own boat, and invite him to take a seat for a moment while he signed a few papers. And Captain Mitchell, seating himself at his desk, would keep on talking hospitably—

"There isn't much time if you are to see everything in a day. We shall be off in a moment. We'll have lunch at the Amarilla Club—though I belong also to the Anglo-American—mining engineers and business men, don't you know—and to the Mirliflores as well, a new club—English, French, Italians, all sorts—lively young fellows mostly, who wanted to pay a compliment to an old resident, sir. But we'll lunch at the Amarilla. Interest you, I fancy. Real thing of the country. Men of the first families. The President of the Occidental Republic himself belongs to it, sir. Fine old bishop with a broken nose in the patio. Remarkable piece of statuary, I believe. Cavaliere Parrochetti—you know Parrochetti, the famous Italian sculptor—was working here for two years—thought very highly of our old bishop. . . . There! I am very much at your service now."

Proud of his experience, penetrated by the sense of historical importance of men, events, and buildings, he talked pompously in jerky periods, with slight sweeps of his short, thick arm, letting nothing "escape the attention" of his privileged captive.

"Lot of building going on, as you observe. Before the Separation it was a plain of burnt grass smothered in clouds of dust, with an ox-cart track to our Jetty. Nothing more. This is the Harbour Gate. Picturesque, is it not? Formerly the town stopped short there. We enter now the Calle de la Constitution. Observe the old Spanish houses. Great dignity. Eh? I suppose it's just as it was in the time of the Viceroys, except for the pavement. Wood blocks now. Sulaco National Bank there, with the sentry boxes each side of the gate. Casa Avellanos this side, with all the ground-floor windows shuttered. A wonderful woman lives there—Miss Avellanos—the beautiful Antonia. A character, sir! A historical woman! Opposite —Casa Gould. Noble gateway. Yes, *the* Goulds of the original Gould Concession, that all the world knows of now. I hold seventeen of the thousand-dollar shares in the Consolidated San Tomé mines. All the poor savings of my lifetime, sir, and it will be enough to keep me in comfort to the end of my days at home when I retire. I got in on the ground-floor, you see. Don Carlos, great friend of mine. Seventeen shares— quite a little fortune to leave behind one, too. I have a niece—married a parson—most worthy man, incumbent of a small parish in Sussex; no end of children. I was never married myself. A sailor should exercise self-denial. Standing under that very gateway, sir, with some young engineer-fellows, ready to defend that house where we had received so much kindness and hospitality, I saw the first and last charge of Pedrito's horsemen upon Barrios's troops, who had just taken the Harbour Gate. They could not stand the new rifles brought out by that poor Decoud. It was a murderous fire. In a moment the street became blocked with a mass of dead men and horses. They never came on again."

And all day Captain Mitchell would talk like this to his more or less willing victim—

"The Plaza. I call it magnificent. Twice the area of Trafalgar Square."

From the very centre, in the blazing sunshine, he pointed out the buildings—

"The Intendencia, now President's Palace—Cabildo, where the Lower Chamber of Parliament sits. You notice the new houses on that side of the Plaza? Compañia Anzani, a great general store, like those coöperative things at home. Old Anzani was murdered by the National Guards in front of his safe. It was even for that specific crime that the deputy Gamacho, commanding the Nationals, a bloodthirsty and savage brute, was executed publicly by garrotte upon the sentence of a court-martial ordered by Barrios. Anzani's nephews converted the business into a company. All that side of the Plaza had been burnt; used to be colonnaded before. A terrible fire, by the light of which I saw the last of the fighting, the llaneros flying, the Nationals throwing their arms down, and the miners of San Tomé, all Indians from the Sierra, rolling by like a torrent to the sound of pipes and cymbals, green flags flying, a wild mass of men in white ponchos and green hats, on foot, on mules, on donkeys. Such a sight, sir, will never be seen again. The miners, sir, had marched upon the town, Don Pépé leading on his black horse, and their very wives in the rear on burros, screaming encouragement, sir, and beating tambourines. I remember one of these women had a green parrot seated on her shoulder, as calm as a bird of stone. They had just saved their Señor Administrador; for Barrios, though he ordered the assault at once, at night, too, would have been too late. Pedrito Montero had Don Carlos led out to be shot—like his uncle many years ago —and then, as Barrios said afterwards, 'Sulaco would not have been worth fighting for.' Sulaco without the Concession was nothing; and there were tons and tons of dynamite distributed all over the mountain with detonators arranged, and an old priest, Father Romàn, standing by to annihilate the San Tomé mine at the first news of failure. Don Carlos had made up his mind not to leave it behind, and he had the right men to see to it, too."

Thus Captain Mitchell would talk in the middle of the Plaza, holding over his head a white umbrella with a green lining; but inside the cathedral, in the dim light, with a faint scent of incense floating in the cool atmosphere, and here and there a kneeling female figure, black or all white, with a veiled head, his lowered voice became solemn and impressive.

"Here," he would say, pointing to a niche in the wall of the dusky aisle, "you see the bust of Don José Avellanos, 'Patriot and Statesman,' as the inscription says, 'Minister to Courts of England and Spain, etc., etc., died in the woods of Los Hatos worn out with his lifelong struggle for Right and Justice at the dawn of the New Era.' A fair likeness. Parrochetti's work from

some old photographs and a pencil sketch by Mrs.
Gould. I was well acquainted with that distinguished
Spanish-American of the old school, a true Hidalgo,
beloved by everybody who knew him. The marble
medallion in the wall, in the antique style, representing
a veiled woman seated with her hands clasped loosely
over her knees, commemorates that unfortunate young
gentleman who sailed out with Nostromo on that fatal
night, sir. See, 'To the memory of Martin Decoud,
his betrothed Antonia Avellanos.' Frank, simple,
noble. There you have that lady, sir, as she is. An
exceptional woman. Those who thought she would
give way to despair were mistaken, sir. She has been
blamed in many quarters for not having taken the veil.
It was expected of her. But Doña Antonia is not the
stuff they make nuns of. Bishop Corbelàn, her uncle,
lives with her in the Corbelàn town house. He is a
fierce sort of priest, everlastingly worrying the Government about the old Church lands and convents. I believe they think a lot of him in Rome. Now let us go
to the Amarilla Club, just across the Plaza, to get some
lunch."

Directly outside the cathedral on the very top of the
noble flight of steps, his voice rose pompously, his arm
found again its sweeping gesture.

"*Porvenir*, over there on that first floor, above those
French plate-glass shop-fronts; our biggest daily. Conservative, or, rather, I should say, Parliamentary. We
have the Parliamentary party here of which the actual
Chief of the State, Don Juste Lopez, is the head; a very
sagacious man, I think. A first-rate intellect, sir. The
Democratic party in opposition rests mostly, I am sorry
to say, on these socialistic Italians, sir, with their secret
societies, camorras, and such-like. There are lots of
Italians settled here on the railway lands, dismissed

navvies, mechanics, and so on, all along the trunk line. There are whole villages of Italians on the Campo. And the natives, too, are being drawn into these ways . . . American bar? Yes. And over there you can see another. New Yorkers mostly frequent that one—— Here we are at the Amarilla. Observe the bishop at the foot of the stairs to the right as we go in."

And the lunch would begin and terminate its lavish and leisurely course at a little table in the gallery, Captain Mitchell nodding, bowing, getting up to speak for a moment to different officials in black clothes, merchants in jackets, officers in uniform, middle-aged caballeros from the Campo—sallow, little, nervous men, and fat, placid, swarthy men, and Europeans or North Americans of superior standing, whose faces looked very white amongst the majority of dark complexions and black, glistening eyes.

Captain Mitchell would lie back in the chair, casting around looks of satisfaction, and tender over the table a case full of thick cigars.

"Try a weed with your coffee. Local tobacco. The black coffee you get at the Amarilla, sir, you don't meet anywhere in the world. We get the bean from a famous *caféteria* in the foot-hills, whose owner sends three sacks every year as a present to his fellow members in remembrance of the fight against Gamacho's Nationals, carried on from these very windows by the caballeros. He was in town at the time, and took part, sir, to the bitter end. It arrives on three mules—not in the common way, by rail; no fear!—right into the patio, escorted by mounted peons, in charge of the Mayoral of his estate, who walks upstairs, booted and spurred, and delivers it to our committee formally with the words, 'For the sake of those fallen the third of May.' We call it *Très de Mayo* coffee.* Taste it."

Captain Mitchell, with an expression as though making ready to hear a sermon in a church, would lift the tiny cup to his lips. And the nectar would be sipped to the bottom during a restful silence in a cloud of cigar smoke.

"Look at this man in black just going out," he would begin, leaning forward hastily. "This is the famous Hernandez, Minister of War. *The Times'* special correspondent, who wrote that striking series of letters calling the Occidental Republic the 'Treasure House of the World,' gave a whole article to him and the force he has organized—the renowned Carabineers of the Campo."

Captain Mitchell's guest, staring curiously, would see a figure in a long-tailed black coat walking gravely, with downcast eyelids in a long, composed face, a brow furrowed horizontally, a pointed head, whose grey hair, thin at the top, combed down carefully on all sides and rolled at the ends, fell low on the neck and shoulders. This, then, was the famous bandit of whom Europe had heard with interest. He put on a high-crowned sombrero with a wide flat brim; a rosary of wooden beads was twisted about his right wrist. And Captain Mitchell would proceed—

"The protector of the Sulaco refugees from the rage of Pedrito. As general of cavalry with Barrios he distinguished himself at the storming of Tonoro, where Señor Fuentes was killed with the last remnant of the Monterists. He is the friend and humble servant of Bishop Corbelàn. Hears three Masses every day. I bet you he will step into the cathedral to say a prayer or two on his way home to his siesta."

He took several puffs at his cigar in silence; then, in his best important manner, pronounced—

"The Spanish race, sir, is prolific of remarkable characters in every rank of life. . . . I propose we go now into the billiard-room, which is cool, for a quiet chat. There's never anybody there till after five. I could tell you episodes of the Separationist revolution that would astonish you. When the great heat's over, we'll take a turn on the Alameda."

The programme went on relentless, like a law of Nature. The turn on the Alameda was taken with slow steps and stately remarks.

"All the great world of Sulaco here, sir." Captain Mitchell bowed right and left with no end of formality; then with animation, "Doña Emilia, Mrs. Gould's carriage. Look. Always white mules. The kindest, most gracious woman the sun ever shone upon. A great position, sir. A great position. First lady in Sulaco—far before the President's wife. And worthy of it." He took off his hat; then, with a studied change of tone, added, negligently, that the man in black by her side, with a high white collar and a scarred, snarly face, was Dr. Monygham, Inspector of State Hospitals, chief med·cal officer of the Consolidated San Tomé mines. "A familiar of the house. Everlastingly there. No wonder. The Goulds made him. Very clever man and all that, but I never liked him. Nobody does. I can recollect him limping about the streets in a check shirt and native sandals with a watermelon under his arm—all he would get to eat for the day. A big-wig now, sir, and as nasty as ever. However . . . There's no doubt he played his part fairly well at the time. He saved us all from the deadly incubus of Sotillo, where a more particular man might have failed——"

His arm went up.

"The equestrian statue that used to stand on the pedestal over there has been removed. It was an anachronism," Captain Mitchell commented, obscurely. "There is some talk of replacing it by a marble shaft commemorative of Separation, with angels of peace at the four corners, and bronze Justice holding an even balance, all gilt, on the top. Cavaliere Parrochetti was asked to make a design, which you can see framed under glass in the Municipal Sala. Names are to be engraved all round the base. Well! They could do no better than begin with the name of Nostromo. He has done for Separation as much as anybody else, and," added Captain Mitchell, "has got less than many others by it—when it comes to that." He dropped on to a stone seat under a tree, and tapped invitingly at the place by his side. "He carried to Barrios the letters from Sulaco which decided the General to abandon Cayta for a time, and come back to our help here by sea. The transports were still in harbour fortunately. Sir, I did not even know that my Capataz de Cargadores was alive. I had no idea. It was Dr. Monygham who came upon him, by chance, in the Custom House, evacuated an hour or two before by the wretched Sotillo. I was never told; never given a hint, nothing—as if I were unworthy of confidence. Monygham arranged it all. He went to the railway yards, and got admission to the engineer-in-chief, who, for the sake of the Goulds as much as for anything else, consented to let an engine make a dash down the line, one hundred and eighty miles, with Nostromo aboard. It was the only way to get him off. In the Construction Camp at the rail-head, he obtained a horse, arms, some clothing, and started alone on that marvellous ride—four hundred miles in six days, through a disturbed country, ending by the feat of passing through the Monterist lines outside Cayta. The history of that ride, sir, would make a most exciting book. He carried all our lives in his pocket. Devotion, courage, fidelity, intelligence were not enough. Of course, he was perfectly fearless and incorruptible. But a man was wanted that would know how to succeed. He was that man, sir. On the fifth of May, being practically a prisoner in the Harbour Office of my Company, I suddenly heard the whistle of an engine in the railway yards, a quarter of a mile away. I could not believe my ears. I made one jump on to the balcony, and beheld a locomotive under a great head of steam run out of the yard gates, screeching like mad, enveloped in a white cloud, and then, just abreast of old Viola's inn, check almost to a standstill. I made out, sir, a man—I couldn't tell who—dash out of the Albergo d'Italia Una, climb into the cab, and then, sir, that engine seemed positively to leap clear of the house, and was gone in the twinkling of an eye. As you blow a candle out, sir! There was a first-rate driver on the foot-plate, sir, I can tell you. They were fired heavily upon by the National Guards in Rincon and one other place. Fortunately the line had not been torn up. In four hours they reached the Construction Camp. Nostromo had his start. . . . The rest you know. You've got only to look round you. There are people on this Alameda that ride in their carriages, or even are alive at all to-day, because years ago I engaged a runaway Italian sailor for a foreman of our wharf simply on the strength of his looks. And that's a fact. You can't get over it, sir. On the seventeenth of May, just twelve days after I saw the man from the Casa Viola get on the engine, and wondered what it meant, Barrios's transports were entering this harbour, and the 'Treasure House of the World,' as *The Times* man calls Sulaco in his book, was saved intact for civilization—for a great future, sir. Pedrito, with Hernandez on the west, and the San Tomé miners pressing on the land gate, was not able to oppose the landing. He had been sending messages to Sotillo for a week to join him. Had Sotillo done so there would have been massacres and proscription that would have left no man or woman of position alive. But that's where Dr. Monygham comes in. Sotillo, blind and deaf to everything, stuck on board his steamer watching the dragging for silver, which he believed to be sunk at the bottom of the harbour. They say that for the last three days he was out of his mind raving and foaming with disappointment at getting nothing, flying about the deck, and yelling curses at the boats with the drags, ordering them in, and then suddenly stamping his foot and crying out, 'And yet it is there! I see it! I feel it!'

"He was preparing to hang Dr. Monygham (whom he had on board) at the end of the after-derrick, when the first of Barrios's transports, one of our own ships at that, steamed right in, and ranging close alongside opened a small-arm fire without as much preliminaries as a hail. It was the completest surprise in the world, sir. They were too astounded at first to bolt below. Men were falling right and left like ninepins. It's a miracle that Monygham, standing on the after-hatch with the rope already round his neck, escaped being riddled through and through like a sieve. He told me since that he had given himself up for lost, and kept on yelling with all the strength of his lungs: 'Hoist a white flag! Hoist a white flag!' Suddenly an old major of the Esmeralda regiment, standing by, unsheathed his sword with a shriek: 'Die, perjured traitor!' and ran Sotillo clean through the body, just before he fell himself shot through the head."

Captain Mitchell stopped for a while.

"Begad, sir! I could spin you a yarn for hours.

But it's time we started off to Rincon. It would not do
for you to pass through Sulaco and not see the lights of
the San Tomé mine, a whole mountain ablaze like a
lighted palace above the dark Campo. It's a fashionable drive. . . . But let me tell you one little
anecdote, sir; just to show you. A fortnight or more
later, when Barrios, declared Generalissimo, was gone
in pursuit of Pedrito away south, when the Provisional
Junta, with Don Juste Lopez at its head, had promul-
gated the new Constitution, and our Don Carlos
Gould was packing up his trunks bound on a mission to
San Francisco and Washington (the United States, sir,
were the first great power to recognize the Occidental
Republic)—a fortnight later, I say, when we were
beginning to feel that our heads were safe on our
shoulders, if I may express myself so, a prominent man,
a large shipper by our line, came to see me on business,
and, says he, the first thing: 'I say, Captain Mitchell,
is that fellow' (meaning Nostromo) 'still the Capataz of
your Cargadores or not?' 'What's the matter?' says I.
'Because, if he is, then I don't mind; I send and receive
a good lot of cargo by your ships; but I have observed
him several days loafing about the wharf, and just now
he stopped me as cool as you please, with a request for
a cigar. Now, you know, my cigars are rather special,
and I can't get them so easily as all that.' 'I hope
you stretched a point,' I said, very gently. 'Why, yes.
But it's a confounded nuisance. The fellow's everlastingly cadging for smokes.' Sir, I turned my eyes
away, and then asked, 'Weren't you one of the prisoners
in the Cabildo?' 'You know very well I was, and in
chains, too,' says he. 'And under a fine of fifteen
thousand dollars?' He coloured, sir, because it got
about that he fainted from fright when they came to
arrest him, and then behaved before Fuentes in a man-

ner to make the very *policianos*, who had dragged him there by the hair of his head, smile at his cringing. 'Yes,' he says, in a sort of shy way. 'Why?' 'Oh, nothing. You stood to lose a tidy bit,' says I, 'even if you saved your life. . . . But what can I do for you?' He never even saw the point. Not he. And that's how the world wags, sir."

He rose a little stiffly, and the drive to Rincon would be taken with only one philosophical remark, uttered by the merciless cicerone, with his eyes fixed upon the lights of San Tomé, that seemed suspended in the·dark night between earth and heaven.

"A great power, this, for good and evil, sir. A great power."

And the dinner of the Mirliflores would be eaten, excellent as to cooking, and leaving upon the traveller's mind an impression that there were in Sulaco many pleasant, able young men with salaries apparently too large for their discretion, and amongst them a few, mostly Anglo-Saxon, skilled in the art of, as the saying is, "taking a rise" out of his kind host.

With a rapid, jingling drive to the harbour in a two-wheeled machine (which Captain Mitchell called a curricle) behind a fleet and scraggy mule beaten all the time by an obviously Neapolitan driver, the cycle would be nearly closed before the lighted-up offices of the O. S. N. Company, remaining open so late because of the steamer. Nearly—but not quite.

"Ten o'clock. Your ship won't be ready to leave till half-past twelve, if by then. Come in for a brandy-and-soda and one more cigar."

And in the superintendent's private room the privileged passenger by the *Ceres*, or *Juno*, or *Pallas*,·stunned and as it were annihilated mentally by a sudden surfeit of sights, sounds, names, facts, and complicated information imperfectly apprehended, would listen like a tired child to a fairy tale; would hear a voice, familiar and surprising in its pompousness, tell him, as if from another world, how there was "in this very harbour" an international naval demonstration, which put an end to the Costaguana-Sulaco War. How the United States cruiser, *Powhattan*,* was the first to salute the Occidental flag—white, with a wreath of green laurel in the middle encircling a yellow amarilla flower. Would hear how General Montero, in less than a month after proclaiming himself Emperor of Costaguana, was shot dead (during a solemn and public distribution of orders and crosses) by a young artillery officer, the brother of his then mistress.

"The abominable Pedrito, sir, fled the country," the voice would say. And it would continue: "A captain of one of our ships told me lately that he recognized Pedrito the Guerrillero, arrayed in purple slippers and a velvet smoking-cap with a gold tassel, keeping a disorderly house in one of the southern ports."

"Abominable Pedrito! Who the devil was he?" would wonder the distinguished bird of passage hovering on the confines of waking and sleep with resolutely open eyes and a faint but amiable curl upon his lips, from between which stuck out the eighteenth or twentieth cigar of that memorable day.

"He appeared to me in this very room like a haunting ghost, sir"—Captain Mitchell was talking of his Nostromo with true warmth of feeling and a touch of wistful pride. "You may imagine, sir, what an effect it produced on me. He had come round by sea with Barrios, of course. And the first thing he told me after I became fit to hear him was that he had picked up the lighter's boat floating in the gulf! He seemed quite overcome by the circumstance. And a remarkable enough circumstance it was, when you remember that it was then sixteen days since the sinking of the silver.* At once I could see he was another man. He stared at the wall, sir, as if there had been a spider or something running about there. The loss of the silver preyed on his mind. The first thing he asked me about was whether Doña Antonia had heard yet of Decoud's death. His voice trembled. I had to tell him that Doña Antonia, as a matter of fact, was not then back in town yet. Poor girl! And just as I was making ready to ask him a thousand questions, with a sudden, 'Pardon me, señor,' he cleared out of the office altogether. I did not see him again for three days. I was terribly busy, you know. It seems that he wandered about in and out of the town, and on two nights turned up to sleep in the baracoons of the railway people. He seemed absolutely indifferent to what went on. I asked him on the wharf, 'When are you going to take hold again, Nostromo? There will be plenty of work for the Cargadores presently.'

" 'Señor,' says he, looking at me in a slow, inquisitive manner, 'would it surprise you to hear that I am too tired to work just yet? And what work could I do now? How can I look my Cargadores in the face after losing a lighter?'

"I begged him not to think any more about the silver, and he smiled. A smile that went to my heart, sir. 'It was no mistake,' I told him. 'It was a fatality. A thing that could not be helped.' '*Si, si!*' he said, and turned away. I thought it best to leave him alone for a bit to get over it. Sir, it took him years really, to get over it. I was present at his interview with Don Carlos. I must say that Gould is rather a cold man. He had to keep a tight hand on his feelings, dealing with thieves and rascals, in constant danger of ruin for him-

self and wife for so many years, that it had become a
second nature. They looked at each other for a long
time. Don Carlos asked what he could do for him, in
his quiet, reserved way.

"'My name is known from one end of Sulaco to the
other,' he said, as quiet as the other. 'What more can
you do for me?' That was all that passed on that occasion. Later, however, there was a very fine coasting
schooner for sale, and Mrs. Gould and I put our heads
together to get her bought and presented to him.
It was done, but he paid all the price back within the
next three years. Business was booming all along this
seaboard, sir. Moreover, that man always succeeded
in everything except in saving the silver. Poor Doña
Antonia, fresh from her terrible experiences in the
woods of Los Hatos, had an interview with him, too.
Wanted to hear about Decoud: what they said, what
they did, what they thought up to the last on that fatal
night. Mrs. Gould told me his manner was perfect
for quietness and sympathy. Miss Avellanos burst
into tears only when he told her how Decoud had happened to say that his plan would be a glorious success.
. . . And there's no doubt, sir, that it is. It is a
success."

The cycle was about to close at last. And while
the privileged passenger, shivering with the pleasant
anticipations of his berth, forgot to ask himself,
"What on earth Decoud's plan could be?" Captain
Mitchell was saying, "Sorry we must part so soon.
Your intelligent interest made this a pleasant day to
me. I shall see you now on board. You had a
glimpse of the 'Treasure House of the World.' A
very good name that." And the coxswain's voice at
the door, announcing that the gig was ready, closed the
cycle.

Nostromo had, indeed, found the lighter's boat, which he had left on the Great Isabel with Decoud, floating empty far out in the gulf. He was then on the bridge of the first of Barrios's transports, and within an hour's steaming from Sulaco. Barrios, always delighted with a feat of daring and a good judge of courage, had taken a great liking to the Capataz. During the passage round the coast the General kept Nostromo near his person, addressing him frequently in that abrupt and boisterous manner which was the sign of his high favour.

Nostromo's eyes were the first to catch, broad on the bow, the tiny, elusive dark speck, which, alone with the forms of the Three Isabels right ahead, appeared on the flat, shimmering emptiness of the gulf. There are times when no fact should be neglected as insignificant; a small boat so far from the land might have had some meaning worth finding out. At a nod of consent from Barrios the transport swept out of her course, passing near enough to ascertain that no one manned the little cockle-shell. It was merely a common small boat gone adrift with her oars in her. But Nostromo, to whose mind Decoud had been insistently present for days, had long before recognized with excitement the dinghy of the lighter.

There could be no question of stopping to pick up that thing. Every minute of time was momentous with the lives and futures of a whole town. The head of the leading ship, with the General on board, fell off to her course. Behind her, the fleet of transports, scattered haphazard over a mile or so in the offing, like the finish of an ocean race, pressed on, all black and smoking on the western sky.

"Mi General," Nostromo's voice rang out loud, but quiet, from behind a group of officers, "I should like to save that little boat. *Por Dios*, I know her. She belongs to my Company."

"And, *por Dios*," guffawed Barrios, in a noisy, good-humoured voice, "you belong to me. I am going to make you a captain of cavalry directly we get within sight of a horse again."

"I can swim far better than I can ride, mi General," cried Nostromo, pushing through to the rail with a set stare in his eyes. "Let me——"

"Let you? What a conceited fellow that is," bantered the General, jovially, without even looking at him. "Let him go! Ha! ha! ha! He wants me to admit that we cannot take Sulaco without him! Ha! ha! ha! Would you like to swim off to her, my son?"

A tremendous shout from one end of the ship to the other stopped his guffaw. Nostromo had leaped overboard; and his black head bobbed up far away already from the ship. The General muttered an appalled "*Cielo!* Sinner that I am!" in a thunderstruck tone. One anxious glance was enough to show him that Nostromo was swimming with perfect ease; and then he thundered terribly, "No! no! We shall not stop to pick up this impertinent fellow. Let him drown—that mad Capataz."

Nothing short of main force would have kept Nostromo from leaping overboard. That empty boat, coming out to meet him mysteriously, as if rowed by an invisible spectre, exercised the fascination of some sign, of some warning, seemed to answer in a startling and enigmatic way the persistent thought of a treasure and of a man's fate. He would have leaped if there had been death in that half-mile of water. It was as smooth as a pond, and for some reason sharks are unknown in the Placid Gulf, though on the other side of the Punta Mala the coastline swarms with them.

The Capataz seized hold of the stern and blew with force. A queer, faint feeling had come over him while he swam. He had got rid of his boots and coat in the water. He hung on for a time, regaining his breath. In the distance the transports, more in a bunch now, held on straight for Sulaco, with their air of friendly contest, of nautical sport, of a regatta; and the united smoke of their funnels drove like a thin, sulphurous fogbank right over his head. It was his daring, his courage, his act that had set these ships in motion upon the sea, hurrying on to save the lives and fortunes of the Blancos, the taskmasters of the people; to save the San Tomé mine; to save the children.

With a vigorous and skilful effort he clambered over the stern. The very boat! No doubt of it; no doubt whatever. It was the dinghy of the lighter No. 3—the dinghy left with Martin Decoud on the Great Isabel so that he should have some means to help himself if nothing could be done for him from the shore. And here she had come out to meet him empty and inexplicable. What had become of Decoud? The Capataz made a minute examination. He looked for some scratch, for some mark, for some sign. All he discovered was a brown stain on the gunwale*abreast of the thwart.* He bent his face over it and rubbed hard with his finger. Then he sat down in the stern sheets, passive, with his knees close together and legs aslant.

Streaming from head to foot, with his hair and whiskers hanging lank and dripping and a lustreless stare fixed upon the bottom boards, the Capataz of the Sulaco Cargadores resembled a drowned corpse come up from the bottom to idle away the sunset hour in a small boat. The excitement of his adventurous ride, the excitement of the return in time, of achievement, of success, all these excitements centred round the associated ideas of the great treasure and of the only other man who knew of its existence, had departed from him. To the very last moment he had been cudgelling his brains as to how he could manage to visit the Great Isabel without loss of time and undetected. For the idea of secrecy had come to be connected with the treasure so closely that even to Barrios himself he had refrained from mentioning the existence of Decoud and of the silver on the island. The letters he carried to the General, however, made brief mention of the loss of the lighter, as having its bearing upon the situation in Sulaco. In the circumstances, the one-eyed tiger-slayer, scenting battle from afar, had not wasted his time in making inquiries from the messenger. In fact, Barrios, talking with Nostromo, assumed that both Don Martin Decoud and the ingots of San Tomé were lost together, and Nostromo, not questioned directly, had kept silent, under the influence of some indefinable form of resentment and distrust.. Let Don Martin speak of everything with his own lips—was what he told himself mentally.

And now, with the means of gaining the Great Isabel thrown thus in his way at the earliest possible moment, his excitement had departed, as when the soul takes flight leaving the body inert upon an earth it knows no more. Nostromo did not seem to know the gulf. For a long time even his eyelids did not flutter once upon the glazed emptiness of his stare. Then slowly, without a limb having stirred, without a twitch of muscle or quiver of an eyelash, an expression, a living expression came upon the still features, deep thought crept into the empty stare—as if an outcast soul, a quiet, brooding soul, finding that untenanted body in its way, had come in stealthily to take possession.

The Capataz frowned: and in the immense stillness

of sea, islands, and coast, of cloud forms on the sky and
trails of light upon the water, the knitting of that brow
had the emphasis of a powerful gesture. Nothing
else budged for a long time; then the Capataz shook
his head and again surrendered himself to the universal
repose of all visible things. Suddenly he seized the
oars, and with one movement made the dinghy spin
round, head-on to the Great Isabel. But before he
began to pull he bent once more over the brown stain
on the gunwale.

"I know that thing," he muttered to himself, with a
sagacious jerk of the head. "That's blood."

His stroke was long, vigorous, and steady. Now and
then he looked over his shoulder at the Great Isabel,
presenting its low cliff to his anxious gaze like an impenetrable face. At last the stem touched the strand.
He flung rather than dragged the boat up the little
beach. At once, turning his back upon the sunset, he
plunged with long strides into the ravine, making the
water of the stream spurt and fly upwards at every
step, as if spurning its shallow, clear, murmuring spirit
with his feet. He wanted to save every moment of daylight.

A mass of earth, grass, and smashed bushes had fallen
down very naturally from above upon the cavity under
the leaning tree. Decoud had attended to the concealment of the silver as instructed, using the spade with
some intelligence. But Nostromo's half-smile of approval changed into a scornful curl of the lip by the
sight of the spade itself flung there in full view, as if in
utter carelessness or sudden panic, giving away the
whole thing. Ah! They were all alike in their folly,
these *hombres finos* that invented laws and governments
and barren tasks for the people.

The Capataz picked up the spade, and with the feel of

the handle in his palm the desire to have a look at the horse-hide boxes of treasure came upon him suddenly. In a very few strokes he uncovered the edges and corners of several; then, clearing away more earth, became aware that one of them had been slashed with a knife.

He exclaimed at that discovery in a stifled voice, and dropped on his knees with a look of irrational apprehension over one shoulder, then over the other. The stiff hide had closed, and he hesitated before he pushed his hand through the long slit and felt the ingots inside. There they were. One, two, three. Yes, four gone. Taken away. Four ingots. But who? Decoud? Nobody else. And why? For what purpose? For what cursed fancy? Let him explain. Four ingots carried off in a boat, and—blood!

In the face of the open gulf, the sun, clear, unclouded, unaltered, plunged into the waters in a grave and untroubled mystery of self-immolation consummated far from all mortal eyes, with an infinite majesty of silence and peace. Four ingots short!—and blood!

The Capataz got up slowly.

"He might simply have cut his hand," he muttered. "But, then——"

He sat down on the soft earth, unresisting, as if he had been chained to the treasure, his drawn-up legs clasped in his hands with an air of hopeless submission, like a slave set on guard. Once only he lifted his head smartly: the rattle of hot musketry fire had reached his ears, like pouring from on high a stream of dry peas upon a drum. After listening for a while, he said, half aloud—

"He will never come back to explain."

And he lowered his head again.

"Impossible!" he muttered, gloomily.

The sounds of firing died out. The loom of a great

conflagration in Sulaco flashed up red above the coast, played on the clouds at the head of the gulf, seemed to touch with a ruddy and sinister reflection the forms of the Three Isabels. He never saw it, though he raised his head.

"But, then, I cannot know," he pronounced, distinctly, and remained silent and staring for hours.

He could not know. Nobody was to know. As might have been supposed, the end of Don Martin Decoud never became a subject of speculation for any one except Nostromo. Had the truth of the facts been known, there would always have remained the question, Why? Whereas the version of his death at the sinking of the lighter had no uncertainty of motive. The young apostle of Separation had died striving for his idea by an ever-lamented accident. But the truth was that he died from solitude, the enemy known but to few on this earth, and whom only the simplest of us are fit to withstand. The brilliant Costaguanero of the boulevards had died from solitude and want of faith in himself and others.

For some good and valid reasons beyond mere human comprehension, the sea-birds of the gulf shun the Isabels. The rocky head of Azuera is their haunt, whose stony levels and chasms resound with their wild and tumultuous clamour as if they were for ever quarrelling over the legendary treasure.

At the end of his first day on the Great Isabel, Decoud, turning in his lair of coarse grass, under the shade of a tree, said to himself—

"I have not seen as much as one single bird all day."

And he had not heard a sound, either, all day but that one now of his own muttering voice. It had been a day of absolute silence—the first he had known in his life. And he had not slept a wink. Not for all these wakeful nights and the days of fighting, planning, talking; not for all that last night of danger and hard physical toil upon the gulf, had he been able to close his eyes for a moment. And yet from sunrise to sunset he had been lying prone on the ground, either on his back or on his face.

He stretched himself, and with slow steps descended into the gully to spend the night by the side of the silver. If Nostromo returned—as he might have done at any moment—it was there that he would look first; and night would, of course, be the proper time for an attempt to communicate. He remembered with profound indifference that he had not eaten anything yet since he had been left alone on the island.

He spent the night open-eyed, and when the day broke he ate something with the same indifference. The brilliant "Son Decoud," the spoiled darling of the family, the lover of Antonia and journalist of Sulaco, was not fit to grapple with himself single-handed. Solitude from mere outward condition of existence becomes very swiftly a state of soul in which the affectations of irony and scepticism have no place. It takes possession of the mind, and drives forth the thought into the exile of utter unbelief. After three days of waiting for the sight of some human face, Decoud caught himself entertaining a doubt of his own individuality. It had merged into the world of cloud and water, of natural forces and forms of nature. In our activity* alone do we find the sustaining illusion of an independent existence as against the whole scheme of things of which we form a helpless part. Decoud lost all belief in the reality of his action past and to come. On the fifth day an immense melancholy descended upon him palpably. He resolved not to give himself up to these people in Sulaco, who had beset him, unreal and terrible, like jibbering and obscene spectres. He saw himself struggling feebly in their midst, and Antonia, gigantic and lovely like an allegorical statue, looking on with scornful eyes at his weakness.

Not a living being, not a speck of distant sail, appeared within the range of his vision; and, as if to escape from this solitude, he absorbed himself in his melancholy. The vague consciousness of a misdirected life given up to impulses whose memory left a bitter taste in his mouth was the first moral sentiment of his manhood. But at the same time he felt no remorse. What should he regret? He had recognized no other virtue than intelligence, and had erected passions into duties. Both his intelligence and his passion were swallowed up easily in this great unbroken solitude of waiting without faith. Sleeplessness had robbed his will of all energy, for he had not slept seven hours in the seven days. His sadness was the sadness of a sceptical mind. He beheld the universe as a succession of incomprehensible images. Nostromo was dead. Everything had failed ignominiously. He no longer dared to think of Antonia. She had not survived. But if she survived he could not face her. And all exertion seemed senseless.

On the tenth day, after a night spent without even dozing off once (it had occurred to him that Antonia could not possibly have ever loved a being so impalpable as himself), the solitude appeared like a great void, and the silence of the gulf like a tense, thin cord to which he hung suspended by both hands, without fear, without surprise, without any sort of emotion whatever. Only towards the evening, in the comparative relief of coolness, he began to wish that this cord would snap.* He imagined it snapping with a report as of a pistol—a sharp, full crack. And that would be the end of him. He contemplated that eventuality with pleasure, because he dreaded the sleepless nights in which the silence, remaining unbroken in the shape of a cord to which he hung with both hands, vibrated with senseless phrases, always the same but utterly incomprehensible, about Nostromo, Antonia, Barrios, and proclamations mingled into an ironical and senseless buzzing. In the daytime he could look at the silence like a still cord stretched to breaking-point, with his life, his vain life, suspended to it like a weight.

"I wonder whether I would hear it snap before I fell," he asked himself.

The sun was two hours above the horizon when he got up, gaunt, dirty, white-faced, and looked at it with his red-rimmed eyes. His limbs obeyed him slowly, as if full of lead, yet without tremor; and the effect of that physical condition gave to his movements an unhesitating, deliberate dignity. He acted as if accomplishing some sort of rite. He descended into the gully; for the fascination of all that silver, with its potential power, survived alone outside of himself. He picked up the belt with the revolver, that was lying there, and buckled it round his waist. The cord of silence could never snap on the island. It must let him fall and sink into the sea, he thought. And sink! He was looking at the loose earth covering the treasure. In the sea! His aspect was that of a somnambulist. He lowered himself down on his knees slowly and went on grubbing with his fingers with industrious patience till he uncovered one of the boxes. Without a pause, as if doing some work done many times before, he slit it open and took four ingots, which he put in his pockets. He covered up the exposed box again and step by step came out of the gully. The bushes closed after him with a swish.

It was on the third day of his solitude that he had dragged the dinghy near the water with an idea of rowing away somewhere, but had desisted partly at the whisper of lingering hope that Nostromo would return, partly from conviction of utter uselessness of all effort. Now she wanted only a slight shove to be set afloat. He had eaten a little every day after the first, and had some muscular strength left yet. Taking up the oars slowly, he pulled away from the cliff of the Great Isabel, that stood behind him warm with sunshine, as if with the heat of life, bathed in a rich light from head to foot as if in a radiance of hope and joy. He pulled straight towards the setting sun. When the gulf had grown dark, he ceased rowing and flung the sculls in. The hollow clatter they made in falling was the loudest noise he had ever heard in his life. It was a revelation. It seemed to recall him from far away. Actually the thought, "Perhaps I may sleep to-night," passed through his mind. But he did not believe it. He believed in nothing; and he remained sitting on the thwart.

The dawn from behind the mountains put a gleam into his unwinking eyes. After a clear daybreak the sun appeared splendidly above the peaks of the range. The great gulf burst into a glitter all around the boat; and in this glory of merciless solitude the silence appeared again before him, stretched taut like a dark, thin string.

His eyes looked at it while, without haste, he shifted his seat from the thwart to the gunwale. They looked at it fixedly, while his hand, feeling about his waist, unbuttoned the flap of the leather case, drew the revolver, cocked it, brought it forward pointing at his breast, pulled the trigger, and, with convulsive force, sent the still-smoking weapon hurtling through the air. His eyes looked at it while he fell forward and hung with his breast on the gunwale and the fingers of his right hand hooked under the thwart. They looked——

"It is done," he stammered out, in a sudden flow of blood. His last thought was: "I wonder how that Capataz died." The stiffness of the fingers relaxed, and the lover of Antonia Avellanos rolled overboard without having heard the cord of silence snap in the solitude of the Placid Gulf, whose glittering surface remained untroubled by the fall of his body.

A victim of the disillusioned weariness which is the retribution meted out to intellectual audacity, the brilliant Don Martin Decoud, weighted by the bars of San Tomé silver, disappeared without a trace, swallowed up in the immense indifference of things. His sleepless, crouching figure was gone from the side of the San Tomé silver; and for a time the spirits of good and evil that hover near every concealed treasure of the earth might have thought that this one had been forgotten by all mankind. Then, after a few days, another form appeared striding away from the setting sun to sit motionless and awake in the narrow black gully all through the night, in nearly the same pose, in the same place in which had sat that other sleepless man who had gone away for ever so quietly in a small boat, about the time of sunset. And the spirits of good and evil that hover about a forbidden treasure understood well that the silver of San Tomé was provided now with a faithful and lifelong slave.

The magnificent Capataz de Cargadores, victim of the disenchanted vanity which is the reward of audacious action, sat in the weary pose of a hunted outcast through a night of sleeplessness as tormenting as any

known to Decoud, his companion in the most desperate
affair of his life. And he wondered how Decoud had
died. But he knew the part he had played himself.
First a woman, then a man, abandoned each in their
last extremity, for the sake of this accursed treasure.
It was paid for by a soul lost and by a vanished life.
The blank stillness of awe was succeeded by a gust of
immense pride. There was no one in the world but
Gian' Battista Fidanza, Capataz de Cargadores, the
incorruptible and faithful Nostromo, to pay such a
price.

He had made up his mind that nothing should be
allowed now to rob him of his bargain. Nothing. Decoud had died. But how? That he was dead he had
not a shadow of a doubt. But four ingots? . . .
What for? Did he mean to come for more—some
other time?

The treasure was putting forth its latent power.
It troubled the clear mind of the man who had paid
the price. He was sure that Decoud was dead. The
island seemed full of that whisper. Dead? Gone!
And he caught himself listening for the swish of bushes
and the splash of the footfalls in the bed of the brook.
Dead! The talker, the novio of Doña Antonia!

"Ha!" he murmured, with his head on his knees,
under the livid clouded dawn breaking over the liberated Sulaco and upon the gulf as gray as ashes. "It
is to her that he will fly. To her that he will fly!"

And four ingots! Did he take them in revenge, to
cast a spell, like the angry woman who had prophesied
remorse and failure, and yet had laid upon him the
task of saving the children? Well, he had saved the
children. He had defeated*the spell of poverty and
starvation. He had done it all alone—or perhaps
helped by the devil. Who cared? He had done it.

betrayed as he was, and saving by the same stroke the San Tomé mine, which appeared to him hateful and immense, lording it by its vast wealth over the valour, the toil, the fidelity of the poor, over war and peace, over the labours of the town, the sea, and the Campo.

The sun lit up the sky behind the peaks of the Cordillera. The Capataz looked down for a time upon the fall of loose earth, stones, and smashed bushes, concealing the hiding-place of the silver.

"I must grow rich very slowly," he meditated, aloud.

CHAPTER ELEVEN

SULACO outstripped Nostromo's prudence, growing rich swiftly on the hidden treasures of the earth, hovered over by the anxious spirits of good and evil, torn out by the labouring hands of the people. It was like a second youth, like a new life, full of promise, of unrest, of toil, scattering lavishly its wealth to the four corners of an excited world. Material changes swept along in the train of material interests. And other changes more subtle, outwardly unmarked, affected the minds and hearts of the workers. Captain Mitchell had gone home to live on his savings invested in the San Tomé mine; and Dr. Monygham had grown older, with his head steel-grey and the unchanged expression of his face, living on the inexhaustible treasure of his devotion drawn upon in the secret of his heart like a store of unlawful wealth.

The Inspector-General of State Hospitals (whose maintenance is a charge upon the Gould Concession), Official Adviser on Sanitation to the Municipality, Chief Medical Officer of the San Tomé Consolidated Mines (whose territory, containing gold, silver, copper, lead, cobalt, extends for miles along the foot-hills of the Cordillera), had felt poverty-stricken, miserable, and starved during the prolonged, second visit the Goulds paid to Europe and the United States of America. Intimate of the casa, proved friend, a bachelor without ties and without establishment (except of the professional sort), he had been asked to take up his quarters in the Gould house. In the eleven months* of their absence the familiar rooms, recalling at every glance the woman to whom he had given all his loyalty, had grown intolerable. As the day approached for the arrival of the mail boat *Hermes**(the latest addition to the O. S. N. Co.'s splendid fleet), the doctor hobbled about more vivaciously, snapped more sardonically at simple and gentle out of sheer nervousness.

He packed up his modest trunk with speed, with fury, with enthusiasm, and saw it carried out past the old porter at the gate of the Casa Gould with delight, with intoxication; then, as the hour approached, sitting alone in the great landau behind the white mules, a little sideways, his drawn-in face positively venomous with the effort of self-control, and holding a pair of new gloves in his left hand, he drove to the harbour.

His heart dilated within him so, when he saw the Goulds on the deck of the *Hermes*, that his greetings were reduced to a casual mutter. Driving back to town, all three were silent. And in the patio the doctor, in a more natural manner, said—

"I'll leave you now to yourselves. I'll call to-morrow if I may?"

"Come to lunch, dear Dr. Monygham, and come early," said Mrs. Gould, in her travelling dress and her veil down, turning to look at him at the foot of the stairs; while at the top of the flight the Madonna, in blue robes and the Child on her arm, seemed to welcome her with an aspect of pitying tenderness.

"Don't expect to find me at home," Charles Gould warned him. "I'll be off early to the mine."

After lunch, Doña Emilia and the señor doctor came slowly through the inner gateway of the patio. The large gardens of the Casa Gould, surrounded by high walls, and the red-tile slopes of neighbouring roofs, lay open before them, with masses of shade under the trees

and level surfaces of sunlight upon the lawns. A triple
row of old orange trees surrounded the whole. Barefooted, brown gardeners, in snowy white shirts and wide
calzoneras, dotted the grounds, squatting over flower-
beds, passing between the trees, dragging slender indiarubber tubes across the gravel of the paths; and the
fine jets of water crossed each other in graceful curves,
sparkling in the sunshine with a slight pattering noise
upon the bushes, and an effect of showered diamonds
upon the grass.

Doña Emilia, holding up the train of a clear dress,
walked by the side of Dr. Monygham, in a longish
black coat and severe black bow on an immaculate shirt-
front. Under a shady clump of trees, where stood scattered little tables and wicker easy-chairs, Mrs. Gould
sat down in a low and ample seat.

"Don't go yet," she said to Dr. Monygham, who was
unable to tear himself away from the spot. His chin
nestling within the points of his collar, he devoured her
stealthily with his eyes, which, luckily, were round and
hard like clouded marbles, and incapable of disclosing
his sentiments. His pitying emotion at the marks of
time upon the face of that woman, the air of frailty
and weary fatigue that had settled upon the eyes and
temples of the "Never-tired Señora" (as Don Pépê
years ago used to call her with admiration), touched
him almost to tears. "Don't go yet. To-day is all
my own," Mrs. Gould urged, gently. "We are not back
yet officially. No one will come. It's only to-morrow
that the windows of the Casa Gould are to be lit up for
a reception."

The doctor dropped into a chair.

"Giving a tertulia?" he said, with a detached air.

"A simple greeting for all the kind friends who care to
come."

"And only to-morrow?"

"Yes. Charles would be tired out after a day at the mine, and so I—— It would be good to have him to myself for one evening on our return to this house I love. It has seen all my life."

"Ah, yes!" snarled the doctor, suddenly. "Women count time from the marriage feast. Didn't you live a little before?"

"Yes; but what is there to remember? There were no cares."

Mrs. Gould sighed. And as two friends, after a long separation, will revert to the most agitated period of their lives, they began to talk of the Sulaco Revolution. It seemed strange to Mrs. Gould that people who had taken part in it seemed to forget its memory and its lesson.

"And yet," struck in the doctor, "we who played our part in it had our reward. Don Pépé, though super-annuated, still can sit a horse. Barrios is drinking himself to death in jovial company away somewhere on his *fundacion* beyond the Bolson de Tonoro. And the heroic Father Romàn—I imagine the old padre blowing up systematically the San Tomé mine, uttering a pious exclamation at every bang, and taking handfuls of snuff between the explosions—the heroic Padre Romàn says that he is not afraid of the harm Holroyd's missionaries can do to his flock, as long as *he* is alive."

Mrs. Gould shuddered a little at the allusion to the destruction that had come so near to the San Tomé mine.

"Ah, but you, dear friend?"

"I did the work I was fit for."

"You faced the most cruel dangers of all. Something more than death."

"No, Mrs. Gould! Only death—by hanging. And I am rewarded beyond my deserts."

Noticing Mrs. Gould's gaze fixed upon him, he dropped his eyes.

"I've made my career—as you see," said the Inspector-General of State Hospitals, taking up lightly the lapels of his superfine black coat. The doctor's self-respect marked inwardly by the almost complete disappearance from his dreams of Father Beron, appeared visibly in what, by contrast with former carelessness, seemed an immoderate cult of personal appearance. Carried out within severe limits of form and colour, and in perpetual freshness, this change of apparel gave to Dr. Monygham an air at the same time professional and festive; while his gait and the unchanged crabbed character of his face acquired from it a startling force of incongruity.

"Yes," he went on. "We all had our rewards—the engineer-in-chief, Captain Mitchell——"

"We saw him," interrupted Mrs. Gould, in her charming voice. "The poor dear man came up from the country on purpose to call on us in our hotel in London. He comported himself with great dignity, but I fancy he regrets Sulaco. He rambled feebly about 'historical events' till I felt I could have a cry."

"H'm," grunted the doctor; "getting old, I suppose. Even Nostromo is getting older—though he is not changed. And, speaking of that fellow, I wanted to tell you something——"

For some time the house had been full of murmurs, of agitation. Suddenly the two gardeners, busy with rose trees at the side of the garden arch, fell upon their knees with bowed heads on the passage of Antonia Avellanos, who appeared walking beside her uncle.

Invested with the red hat after a short visit to Rome, where he had been invited by the Propaganda,* Father Corbelàn, missionary to the wild Indians, conspirator, friend and patron of Hernandez the robber, advanced with big, slow strides, gaunt and leaning forward, with his powerful hands clasped behind his back. The first Cardinal-Archbishop of Sulaco had preserved his fanatical and morose air; the aspect of a chaplain of bandits. It was believed that his unexpected elevation to the purple was a counter-move to the Protestant invasion of Sulaco organized by the Holroyd Missionary Fund. Antonia, the beauty of her face as if a little blurred, her figure slightly fuller, advanced with her light walk and her high serenity, smiling from a distance at Mrs. Gould. She had brought her uncle over to see dear Emilia, without ceremony, just for a moment before the siesta.

When all were seated again, Dr. Monygham, who had come to dislike heartily everybody who approached Mrs. Gould with any intimacy, kept aside, pretending to be lost in profound meditation. A louder phrase of Antonia made him lift his head.

"How can we abandon, groaning under oppression, those who have been our countrymen only a few years ago, who *are* our countrymen now?" Miss Avellanos was saying. "How can we remain blind, and deaf without pity to the cruel wrongs suffered by our brothers? There is a remedy."

"Annex the rest of Costaguana to the order and prosperity of Sulaco," snapped the doctor. "There is no other remedy."

"I am convinced, señor doctor," Antonia said, with the earnest calm of invincible resolution, "that this was from the first poor Martin's intention."

"Yes, but the material interests will not let you jeopardize their development for a mere idea of pity and justice," the doctor muttered, grumpily. "And it is just as well perhaps."

The Cardinal-Archbishop straightened up his gaunt, bony frame.

"We have worked for them; we have made them, these material interests of the foreigners," the last of the Corbeláns uttered in a deep, denunciatory tone.

"And without them you are nothing," cried the doctor from the distance. "They will not let you."

"Let them beware, then, lest the people, prevented from their aspirations, should rise and claim their share of the wealth and their share of the power," the popular Cardinal-Archbishop of Sulaco declared, significantly, menacingly.

A silence ensued, during which his Eminence stared, frowning at the ground, and Antonia, graceful and rigid in her chair, breathed calmly in the strength of her convictions. Then the conversation took a social turn, touching on the visit of the Goulds to Europe. The Cardinal-Archbishop, when in Rome, had suffered from neuralgia in the head all the time. It was the climate —the bad air.

When uncle and niece had gone away, with the servants again falling on their knees, and the old porter, who had known Henry Gould, almost totally blind and impotent now, creeping up to kiss his Eminence's extended hand, Dr. Monygham, looking after them, pronounced the one word—

"Incorrigible!"

Mrs. Gould, with a look upwards, dropped wearily on her lap her white hands flashing with the gold and stones of many rings.

"Conspiring. Yes!" said the doctor. "The last of the Avellanos and the last of the Corbeláns are conspiring with the refugees from Sta. Marta that flock here after every revolution. The Café Lombroso* at the corner of the Plaza is full of them; you can hear their chatter across the street like the noise of a parrot-house. They are conspiring for the invasion of Costa-guana. And do you know where they go for strength, for the necessary force? To the secret societies amongst immigrants and natives, where Nostromo—I should say Captain Fidanza—is the great man. What gives him that position? Who can say? Genius? He has genius. He is greater with the populace than ever he was before. It was as if he had some secret power; some mysterious means to keep up his influence. He holds conferences with the Archbishop, as in those old days which you and I remember. Bàrrios is useless. But for a military head they have the pious Hernandez. And they may raise the country with the new cry of the wealth for the people."

"Will there be never any peace? Will there be no rest?" Mrs. Gould whispered. "I thought that we——"

"No!" interrupted the doctor. "There is no peace and no rest in the development of material interests. They have their law, and their justice. But it is founded on expediency, and is inhuman; it is without rectitude, without the continuity and the force that can be found only in a moral principle. Mrs. Gould, the time approaches when all that the Gould Concession stands for shall weigh as heavily upon the people as the barbarism, cruelty, and misrule of a few years back."

"How can you say that, Dr. Monygham?" she cried out, as if hurt in the most sensitive place of her soul.

"I can say what is true," the doctor insisted, obstinately. "It'll weigh as heavily, and provoke resentment, bloodshed, and vengeance, because the men have grown different. Do you think that now the mine would march upon the town to save their Señor Administrador? Do you think that?"

She pressed the backs of her entwined hands on her eyes and murmured hopelessly—

"Is it this we have worked for, then?"

The doctor lowered his head. He could follow her silent thought. Was it for this that her life had been robbed of all the intimate felicities of daily affection which her tenderness needed as the human body needs air to breathe? And the doctor, indignant with Charles Gould's blindness, hastened to change the conversation.

"It is about Nostromo that I wanted to talk to you. Ah! that fellow has some continuity and force. Nothing will put an end to him. But never mind that. There's something inexplicable going on—or perhaps only too easy to explain. You know, Linda is practically the lighthouse keeper of the Great Isabel light. The Garibaldino is too old now. His part is to clean the lamps and to cook in the house; but he can't get up the stairs any longer. The black-eyed Linda sleeps all day and watches the light all night. Not all day, though. She is up towards five in the afternoon, when our Nostromo, whenever he is in harbour with his schooner, comes out on his courting visit, pulling in a small boat."

"Aren't they married yet?" Mrs. Gould asked.

"The mother wished it, as far as I can understand, while Linda was yet quite a child. When I had the girls with me for a year or so during the War of Separation, that extraordinary Linda used to declare quite simply that she was going to be Gian' Battista's wife."

"They are not married yet," said the doctor, curtly. "I have looked after them a little."

"Thank you, dear Dr. Monygham," said Mrs. Gould; and under the shade of the big trees her little, even teeth gleamed in a youthful smile of gentle malice. "People don't know how really good you are. You will not let them know, as if on purpose to annoy me, who have put my faith in your good heart long ago."

The doctor, with a lifting up of his upper lip, as though he were longing to bite, bowed stiffly in his chair. With the utter absorption of a man to whom love comes late, not as the most splendid of illusions, but like an enlightening and priceless misfortune, the sight of that woman (of whom he had been deprived for nearly a year) suggested ideas of adoration, of kissing the hem of her robe. And this excess of feeling translated itself naturally into an augmented grimness of speech.

"I am afraid of being overwhelmed by too much gratitude. However, these people interest me. I went out several times to the Great Isabel light to look after old Giorgio."

He did not tell Mrs. Gould that it was because he found there, in her absence, the relief of an atmosphere of congenial sentiment in old Giorgio's austere admiration for the "English signora—the benefactress"; in black-eyed Linda's voluble, torrential, passionate affection for "our Doña Emilia—that angel"; in the white-throated, fair Giselle's adoring upward turn of the eyes, which then glided towards him with a sidelong, half-arch, half-candid glance, which made the doctor exclaim to himself mentally, "If I weren't what I am, old and ugly, I would think the minx is making eyes at me. And perhaps she is. I dare say she would make eyes at anybody." Dr. Monygham said nothing of this to Mrs. Gould, the providence of the Viola family, but reverted to what he called "our great Nostromo."

"What I wanted to tell you is this: Our great Nostromo did not take much notice of the old man and the children for some years. It's true, too, that he was away on his coasting voyages certainly ten months out of the twelve. He was making his fortune, as he told Captain Mitchell once. He seems to have done uncommonly well. It was only to be expected. He is a man full of resource, full of confidence in himself, ready to take chances and risks of every sort. I remember being in Mitchell's office one day, when he came in with that calm, grave air he always carries everywhere. He had been away trading in the Gulf of California, he said, looking straight past us at the wall, as his manner is, and was glad to see on his return that a lighthouse was being built on the cliff of the Great Isabel. Very glad, he repeated. Mitchell explained that it was the O. S. N. Co. who was building it, for the convenience of the mail service, on his own advice. Captain Fidanza was good enough to say that it was excellent advice. I remember him twisting up his moustaches and looking all round the cornice of the room before he proposed that old Giorgio should be made the keeper of that light."

"I heard of this. I was consulted at the time," Mrs. Gould said. "I doubted whether it would be good for these girls to be shut up on that island as if in a prison."

"The proposal fell in with the old Garibaldino's humour. As to Linda, any place was lovely and delightful enough for her as long as it was Nostromo's suggestion. She could wait for her Gian' Battista's good pleasure there as well as anywhere else. My opinion is that she was always in love with that incorruptible Capataz. Moreover, both father and sister were anxious to get Giselle away from the attentions of a certain Ramirez."

"Ah!" said Mrs. Gould, interested. "Ramirez? What sort of man is that?"

"Just a mozo of the town. His father was a Cargador. As a lanky boy he ran about the wharf in rags, till Nostromo took him up and made a man of him. When he got a little older, he put him into a lighter and very soon gave him charge of the No. 3 boat—the boat which took the silver away, Mrs. Gould. Nostromo selected that lighter for the work because she was the best sailing and the strongest boat of all the Company's fleet. Young Ramirez was one of the five Cargadores entrusted with the removal of the treasure from the Custom House on that famous night. As the boat he had charge of was sunk, Nostromo, on leaving the Company's service, recommended him to Captain Mitchell for his successor. He had trained him in the routine of work perfectly, and thus Mr. Ramirez, from a starving waif, becomes a man and the Capataz of the Sulaco Cargadores."

"Thanks to Nostromo," said Mrs. Gould, with warm approval.

"Thanks to Nostromo," repeated Dr. Monygham. "Upon my word, the fellow's power frightens me when I think of it. That our poor old Mitchell was only too glad to appoint somebody trained to the work, who saved him trouble, is not surprising. What is wonderful is the fact that the Sulaco Cargadores accepted Ramirez for their chief, simply because such was Nostromo's good pleasure. Of course, he is not a second Nostromo, as he fondly imagined he would be; but still, the position was brilliant enough. It emboldened him to make up to Giselle Viola, who, you know, is the recognized beauty of the town. The old Garibaldino, however, took a violent dislike to him. I don't know why. Perhaps because he was not a model of perfection like his Gian' Battista, the incarnation of the courage, the fidelity, the honour of 'the people.' Signor Viola does not think much of Sulaco natives. Both of

them, the old Spartan and that white-faced Linda,
with her red mouth and coal-black eyes, were looking
rather fiercely after the fair one. Ramirez was warned
off. Father Viola, I am told, threatened him with his
gun once."

"But what of Giselle herself?" asked Mrs. Gould.

"She's a bit of a flirt, I believe," said the doctor. "I
don't think she cared much one way or another. Of
course she likes men's attentions. Ramirez was not
the only one, let me tell you, Mrs. Gould. There was
one engineer, at least, on the railway staff who got
warned off with a gun, too. Old Viola does not allow
any trifling with his honour. He has grown uneasy
and suspicious since his wife died. He was very pleased
to remove his youngest girl away from the town. But
look what happens, Mrs. Gould. Ramirez, the honest,
lovelorn swain, is forbidden the island. Very well.
He respects the prohibition, but naturally turns his
eyes frequently towards the Great Isabel. It seems as
though he had been in the habit of gazing late at night
upon the light. And during these sentimental vigils
he discovers that Nostromo, Captain Fidanza that is,
returns very late from his visits to the Violas. As
late as midnight at times."

The doctor paused and stared meaningly at Mrs.
Gould.

"Yes. But I don't understand," she began, looking
puzzled.

"Now comes the strange part," went on Dr. Monygham. "Viola, who is king on his island, will allow no
visitor on it after dark. Even Captain Fidanza has
got to leave after sunset, when Linda has gone up to
tend the light. And Nostromo goes away obediently.
But what happens afterwards? What does he do in the
gulf between half-past six and midnight? He has been

seen more than once at that late hour pulling quietly
into the harbour. Ramirez is devoured by jealousy.
He dared not approach old Viola; but he plucked up
courage to rail Linda about it on Sunday morning as she
came on the mainland to hear Mass and visit her
mother's grave. There was a scene on the wharf, which,
as a matter of fact, I witnessed. It was early morning.
He must have been waiting for her on purpose. I was
there by the merest chance, having been called to an
urgent consultation by the doctor of the German gunboat in the harbour. She poured wrath, scorn, and
flame upon Ramirez, who seemed out of his mind. It
was a strange sight, Mrs. Gould: the long jetty, with
this raving Cargador in his crimson sash and the girl
all in black, at the end; the early Sunday morning
quiet of the harbour in the shade of the mountains;
nothing but a canoe or two moving between the ships
at anchor, and the German gunboat's gig coming to
take me off. Linda passed me within a foot. I noticed
her wild eyes. I called out to her. She never heard
me. She never saw me. But I looked at her face. It
was awful in its anger and wretchedness."

Mrs. Gould sat up, opening her eyes very wide.

"What do you mean, Dr. Monygham? Do you
mean to say that you suspect the younger sister?"

"*Quien sabe!* Who can tell?" said the doctor,
shrugging his shoulders like a born Costaguanero.
"Ramirez came up to me on the wharf. He reeled—he
looked insane. He took his head into his hands. He
had to talk to someone—simply had to. Of course
for all his mad state he recognized me. People know
me well here. I have lived too long amongst them to
be anything else but the evil-eyed doctor, who can cure
all the ills of the flesh, and bring bad luck by a glance.
He came up to me. He tried to be calm. He tried

to make it out that he wanted merely to warn me
against Nostromo. It seems that Captain Fidanza at
some secret meeting or other had mentioned me as the
worst despiser of all the poor—of the people. It's very
possible. He honours me with his undying dislike.
And a word from the great Fidanza may be quite enough
to send some fool's knife into my back. The Sanitary
Commission I preside over is not in favour with the
populace. 'Beware of him, señor doctor. Destroy
him, señor doctor,' Ramirez hissed right into my face.
And then he broke out. 'That man,' he spluttered,
'has cast a spell upon both these girls.' As to himself,
he had said too much. He must run away now—run
away and hide somewhere. He moaned tenderly about
Giselle and then, called her names that cannot be repeated. If he thought she could be made to love him
by any means, he would carry her off from the island.
Off into the woods. But it was no good. . . . He
strode away, flourishing his arms above his head. Then
I noticed an old negro, who had been sitting behind a
pile of cases, fishing from the wharf. He wound up his
lines and slunk away at once. But he must have heard
something, and must have talked, too, because some of
the old Garibaldino's railway friends, I suppose, warned
him against Ramirez. At any rate, the father had been
warned. But Ramirez has disappeared from the town."

"I feel I have a duty towards these girls," said Mrs.
Gould, uneasily. "Is Nostromo in Sulaco now?"

"He is, since last Sunday."

"He ought to be spoken to—at once."

"Who will dare speak to him? Even the love-mad
Ramirez runs away from the mere shadow of Captain
Fidanza."

"I can. I will," Mrs. Gould declared. "A word
will be enough for a man like Nostromo."

The doctor smiled sourly.

"He must end this situation which lends itself to——
I can't believe it of that child," pursued Mrs. Gould.

"He's very attractive," muttered the doctor, gloomily.

"He'll see it, I am sure. He must put an end to all this by marrying Linda at once," pronounced the first lady of Sulaco with immense decision.*

Through the garden gate emerged Basilio, grown fat and sleek, with an elderly hairless face, wrinkles at the corners of his eyes, and his jet-black, coarse hair plastered down smoothly. Stooping carefully behind an ornamental clump of bushes, he put down with precaution a small child he had been carrying on his shoulder—his own and Leonarda's last born. The pouting, spoiled Camerista and the head mozo of the Casa Gould had been married for some years now.

He remained squatting on his heels for a time, gazing fondly at his offspring, which returned his stare with imperturbable gravity; then, solemn and respectable, walked down the path.

"What is it, Basilio?" asked Mrs. Gould.

"A telephone came through from the office of the mine. The master remains to sleep at the mountain to-night."

Dr. Monygham had got up and stood looking away. A profound silence reigned for a time under the shade of the biggest trees in the lovely gardens of the Casa Gould.

"Very well, Basilio," said Mrs. Gould. She watched him walk away along the path, step aside behind the flowering bush, and reappear with the child seated on his shoulder. He passed through the gateway between the garden and the patio with measured steps, careful of his light burden.

The doctor, with his back to Mrs. Gould, contemplated a flower-bed away in the sunshine. People believed him scornful and soured. The truth of his nature consisted in his capacity for passion and in the sensitiveness of his temperament. What he lacked was the polished callousness of men of the world, the callousness from which springs an easy tolerance for oneself and others; the tolerance wide as poles asunder from true sympathy and human compassion. This want of callousness accounted for his sardonic turn of mind and his biting speeches.

In profound silence, and glaring viciously at the brilliant flower-bed, Dr. Monygham poured mental imprecations on Charles Gould's head. Behind him the immobility of Mrs. Gould added to the grace of her seated figure the charm of art, of an attitude caught and interpreted for ever. Turning abruptly, the doctor took his leave.

Mrs. Gould leaned back in the shade of the big trees planted in a circle. She leaned back with her eyes closed and her white hands lying idle on the arms of her seat. The half-light under the thick mass of leaves brought out the youthful prettiness of her face; made the clear, light fabrics and white lace of her dress appear luminous. Small and dainty, as if radiating a light of her own in the deep shade of the interlaced boughs, she resembled a good fairy, weary with a long career of well-doing, touched by the withering suspicion of the uselessness of her labours, the powerlessness of her magic.

Had anybody asked her of what she was thinking, alone in the garden of the Casa, with her husband at the mine and the house closed to the street like an empty dwelling, her frankness would have had to evade the question. It had come into her mind that for life to

be large and full, it must contain the care of the past
and of the future in every passing moment of the present. Our daily work must be done to the glory of the
dead, and for the good of those who come after. She
thought that, and sighed without opening her eyes—
without moving at all. Mrs. Gould's face became set and
rigid for a second, as if to receive, without flinching, a
great wave of loneliness that swept over her head. And
it came into her mind, too, that no one would ever ask
her with solicitude what she was thinking of. No one.
No one, but perhaps the man who had just gone away.
No; no one who could be answered with careless sincerity in the ideal perfection of confidence.

The word "incorrigible"—a word lately pronounced
by Dr. Monygham—floated into her still and sad immobility. Incorrigible in his devotion to the great
silver mine was the Señor Administrador! Incorrigible
in his hard, determined service of the material interests
to which he had pinned his faith in the triumph of order
and justice. Poor boy! She had a clear vision of the
grey hairs on his temples. He was perfect—perfect.
What more could she have expected? It was a colossal and lasting success; and love was only a short moment of forgetfulness, a short intoxication, whose delight one remembered with a sense of sadness, as if it
had been a deep grief lived through. There was something inherent in the necessities of successful action
which carried with it the moral degradation of the idea.
She saw the San Tomé mountain hanging over the
Campo, over the whole land, feared, hated, wealthy;
more soulless than any tyrant, more pitiless and auto-
cratic than the worst Government; ready to crush
innumerable lives in the expansion of its greatness.
He did not see it. He could not see it. It was not his
fault. He was perfect, perfect; but she would never

have him to herself. Never; not for one short hour
altogether to herself in this old Spanish house she loved
so well! Incorrigible, the last of the Corbeláns, the
last of the Avellanos, the doctor had said; but she saw
clearly the San Tomé mine possessing, consuming,
burning up the life of the last of the Costaguana Goulds;
mastering the energetic spirit of the son as it had mastered the lamentable weakness of the father. A terrible
success for the last of the Goulds. The last! She had
hoped for a long, long time, that perhaps—— But no!
There were to be no more. An immense desolation, the
dread of her own continued life, descended upon the first
lady of Sulaco. With a prophetic vision she saw herself
surviving alone the degradation of her young ideal of
life, of love, of work—all alone in the Treasure House
of the World. The profound, blind, suffering expression
of a painful dream settled on her face with its closed
eyes. In the indistinct voice of an unlucky sleeper,
lying passive in the grip of a merciless nightmare, she
stammered out aimlessly the words—

"Material interests."

CHAPTER TWELVE*

NOSTROMO had been growing rich very slowly. It was an effect of his prudence. He could command himself even when thrown off his balance. And to become the slave of a treasure with full self-knowledge is an occurrence rare and mentally disturbing. But it was also in a great part because of the difficulty of converting it into a form in which it could become available. The mere act of getting it away from the island piecemeal, little by little, was surrounded by difficulties, by the dangers of imminent detection. He had to visit the Great Isabel in secret, between his voyages along the coast, which were the ostensible source of his fortune. The crew of his own schooner were to be feared as if they had been spies upon their dreaded captain. He did not dare stay too long in port. When his coaster was unloaded, he hurried away on another trip, for he feared arousing suspicion even by a day's delay. Sometimes during a week's stay, or more, he could only manage one visit to the treasure. And that was all. A couple of ingots. He suffered through his fears as much as through his prudence. To do things by stealth humiliated him. And he suffered most from the concentration of his thought upon the treasure.

A transgression, a crime, entering a man's existence, eats it up like a malignant growth, consumes it like a fever. Nostromo had lost his peace; the genuineness of all his qualities was destroyed. He felt it himself, and often cursed the silver of San Tomé. His courage, his magnificence, his leisure, his work, everything was as before, only everything was a sham. But the treasure was real. He clung to it with a more tenacious, mental grip. But he hated the feel of the ingots. Sometimes, after putting away a couple of them in his cabin—the fruit of a secret night expedition to the Great Isabel—he would look fixedly at his fingers, as if surprised they had left no stain on his skin.

He had found means of disposing of the silver bars in distant ports. The necessity to go far afield made his coasting voyages long, and caused his visits to the Viola household to be rare and far between. He was fated to have his wife from there. He had said so once to Giorgio himself. But the Garibaldino had put the subject aside with a majestic wave of his hand, clutching a smouldering black briar-root pipe. There was plenty of time; he was not the man to force his girls upon anybody.

As time went on, Nostromo discovered his preference for the younger of the two. They had some profound similarities of nature, which must exist for complete confidence and understanding, no matter what outward differences of temperament there may be to exercise their own fascination of contrast. His wife would have to know his secret or else life would be impossible. He was attracted by Giselle, with her candid gaze and white throat, pliable, silent, fond of excitement under her quiet indolence; whereas Linda, with her intense, passionately pale face, energetic, all fire and words, touched with gloom and scorn, a chip of the old block, true daughter of the austere republican, but with Teresa's voice, inspired him with a deep-seated mistrust. Moreover, the poor girl could not conceal her love for Gian' Battista. He could see it would be violent, exacting, suspicious, uncompromising—like her soul. Giselle, by her fair but warm beauty, by the surface placidity of her nature holding a promise of submissiveness, by the charm of her girlish mysteriousness, excited his passion and allayed his fears as to the future.

His absences from Sulaco were long. On returning from the longest of them, he made out lighters loaded with blocks of stone lying under the cliff of the Great Isabel; cranes and scaffolding above; workmen's figures moving about, and a small lighthouse already rising from its foundations on the edge of the cliff.

At this unexpected, undreamt-of, startling sight, he thought himself lost irretrievably. What could save him from detection now? Nothing! He was struck with amazed dread at this turn of chance, that would kindle a far-reaching light upon the·only secret spot of his life; that life whose very essence, value, reality, consisted in its reflection from the admiring eyes of men. All of it but that thing which was beyond common comprehension; which stood between him and the power that hears and gives effect to the evil intention of curses. It was dark. Not every man had such a darkness. And they were going to put a light there. A light! He saw it shining upon disgrace, poverty, contempt. Somebody was sure to. . . . Perhaps somebody had already. . . .

The incomparable Nostromo, the Capataz, the respected and feared Captain Fidanza, the unquestioned patron of secret societies, a republican like old Giorgio, and a revolutionist at heart (but in another manner), was on the point of jumping overboard from the deck of his own schooner. That man, subjective almost to insanity, looked suicide deliberately in the face. But he never lost his head. He was checked by the thought that this was no escape. He imagined himself dead, and the disgrace, the shame going on. Or, rather, properly speaking, he could not imagine himself dead. He was possessed too strongly by the sense of his own existence, a thing of infinite duration in its changes, to grasp the notion of finality. The earth goes on for ever.

And he was courageous. It was a corrupt courage, but it was as good for his purposes as the other kind. He sailed close to the cliff of the Great Isabel, throwing a penetrating glance from the deck at the mouth of the ravine, tangled in an undisturbed growth of bushes. He sailed close enough to exchange hails with the workmen, shading their eyes on the edge of the sheer drop of the cliff overhung by the jib-head of a powerful crane. He perceived that none of them had any occasion even to approach the ravine where the silver lay hidden; let alone to enter it. In the harbour he learned that no one slept on the island. The labouring gangs returned to port every evening, singing chorus songs in the empty lighters towed by a harbour tug. For the moment he had nothing to fear.

But afterwards? he asked himself. Later, when a keeper came to live in the cottage that was being built some hundred and fifty yards back from the low light-tower, and four hundred or so from the dark, shaded, jungly ravine, containing the secret of his safety, of his influence, of his magnificence, of his power over the future, of his defiance of ill-luck, of every possible betrayal from rich and poor alike—what then? He could never shake off the treasure. His audacity, greater than that of other men, had welded that vein of silver into his life. And the feeling of fearful and ardent subjection, the feeling of his slavery—so irremediable and profound that often, in his thoughts, he compared himself to the legendary Gringos, neither dead nor alive, bound down to their conquest of unlawful wealth on Azuera—weighed heavily on the independent Captain Fidanza, owner and master of a coasting schooner, whose smart appearance (and fabulous good-luck in trading) were so well known along the western seaboard of a vast continent.

Fiercely whiskered and grave, a shade less supple in his walk, the vigour and symmetry of his powerful limbs lost in the vulgarity of a brown tweed suit, made by Jews in the slums of London, and sold by the clothing department of the Compañia Anzani, Captain Fidanza was seen in the streets of Sulaco attending to his business, as usual, that trip. And, as usual, he allowed it to get about that he had made a great profit on his cargo. It was a cargo of salt fish, and Lent was approaching. He was seen in tramcars going to and fro between the town and the harbour; he talked with people in a café or two in his measured, steady voice. Captain Fidanza was *seen*. The generation that would know nothing of the famous ride to Cayta was not born yet.

Nostromo, the miscalled Capataz de Cargadores, had made for himself, under his rightful name, another public existence, but modified by the new conditions, less picturesque, more difficult to keep up in the increased size and varied population of Sulaco, the progressive capital of the Occidental Republic.

Captain Fidanza, unpicturesque, but always a little mysterious, was recognized quite sufficiently under the lofty glass and iron roof of the Sulaco railway station. He took a local train, and got out in Rincon, where he visited the widow of the Cargador who had died of his wounds (at the dawn of the New Era, like Don José Avellanos) in the patio of the Casa Gould. He consented to sit down and drink a glass of cool lemonade in the hut, while the woman, standing up, poured a perfect torrent of words to which he did not listen.

He left some money with her, as usual. The orphaned
children, growing up and well schooled, calling him
uncle, clamoured for his blessing. He gave that, too;
and in the doorway paused for a moment to look at the
flat face of the San Tomé mountain with a faint frown.
This slight contraction of his bronzed brow casting a
marked tinge of severity upon his usual unbending expression, was observed at the Lodge which he attended
—but went away before the banquet. He wore it at
the meeting of some good comrades, Italians and Occidentals, assembled in his honour under the presidency
of an indigent, sickly, somewhat hunchbacked little
photographer, with a white face and a magnanimous
soul dyed crimson by a bloodthirsty hate of all capitalists, oppressors of the two hemispheres. The heroic
Giorgio Viola, old revolutionist, would have understood nothing of his opening speech; and Captain
Fidanza, lavishly generous as usual to some poor comrades, made no speech at all. He had listened, frowning
with his mind far away, and walked off unapproachable,
silent, like a man full of cares.

His frown deepened as, in the early morning, he
watched the stone-masons go off to the Great Isabel,
in lighters loaded with squared blocks of stone, enough
to add another course to the squat light-tower. That
was the rate of the work. One course per day.

And Captain Fidanza meditated. The presence of
strangers on the island would cut him completely off the
treasure. It had been difficult and dangerous enough
before. He was afraid, and he was angry. He thought
with the resolution of a master and the cunning of a
cowed slave. Then he went ashore.

He was a man of resource and ingenuity; and, as
usual, the expedient he found at a critical moment was
effective enough to alter the situation radically. He

had the gift of evolving safety out of the very danger, this incomparable Nostromo, this "fellow in a thousand." With Giorgio established on the Great Isabel, there would be no need for concealment. He would be able to go openly, in daylight, to see his daughters— one of his daughters—and stay late talking to the old Garibaldino. Then in the dark . . . Night after night . . . He would dare to grow rich quicker now. He yearned to clasp, embrace, absorb, subjugate in unquestioned possession this treasure, whose tyranny had weighed upon his mind, his actions, his very sleep.

He went to see his friend Captain Mitchell—and the thing was done as Dr. Monygham had related to Mrs. Gould. When the project was mooted to the Garibaldino, something like the faint reflection, the dim ghost of a very ancient smile, stole under the white and enormous moustaches of the old hater of kings and ministers. His daughters were the object of his anxious care. The younger, especially. Linda, with her mother's voice, had taken more her mother's place. Her deep, vibrating "Eh, Padre?" seemed, but for the change of the word, the very echo of the impassioned, remonstrating "Eh, Giorgio?" of poor Signora Teresa. It was his fixed opinion that the town was no proper place for his girls. The infatuated but guileless Ramirez was the object of his profound aversion, as resuming the sins of the country whose people were blind, vile *esclavos*.

On his return from his next voyage, Captain Fidanza found the Violas settled in the light-keeper's cottage. His knowledge of Giorgio's idiosyncrasies had not played him false. The Garibaldino had refused to entertain the idea of any companion whatever, except his girls. And Captain Mitchell, anxious to please his poor Nostromo, with that felicity of inspiration which only true affection can give, had formally appointed Linda Viola as under-keeper of the Isabel's Light.

"The light is private property," he used to explain. "It belongs to my Company. I've the power to nominate whom I like, and Viola it shall be. It's about the only thing Nostromo—a man worth his weight in gold, mind you—has ever asked me to do for him."

Directly his schooner was anchored opposite the New Custom House, with its sham air of a Greek temple, flat-roofed, with a colonnade, Captain Fidanza went pulling his small boat out of the harbour, bound for the Great Isabel, openly in the light of a declining day, before all men's eyes, with a sense of having mastered the fates. He must establish a regular position. He would ask him for his daughter now. He thought of Giselle as he pulled. Linda loved him, perhaps, but the old man would be glad to keep the elder, who had his wife's voice.

He did not pull for the narrow strand where he had landed with Decoud, and afterwards alone on his first visit to the treasure. He made for the beach at the other end, and walked up the regular and gentle slope of the wedge-shaped island. Giorgio Viola, whom he saw from afar, sitting on a bench under the front wall of the cottage, lifted his arm slightly to his loud hail. He walked up. Neither of the girls appeared.

"It is good here," said the old man, in his austere, far-away manner.

Nostromo nodded; then, after a short silence—

"You saw my schooner pass in not two hours ago? Do you know why I am here before, so to speak, my anchor has fairly bitten into the ground of this port of Sulaco?"

"You are welcome like a son," the old man declared, quietly, staring away upon the sea.

"Ah! thy son. I know. I am what thy son would have been. It is well, viejo. It is a very good welcome. Listen, I have come to ask you for——"

A sudden dread came upon the fearless and incorruptible Nostromo. He dared not utter the name in his mind. The slight pause only imparted a marked weight and solemnity to the changed end of the phrase.

"For my wife!" . . . His heart was beating fast. "It is time you——"

The Garibaldino arrested him with an extended arm. "That was left for you to judge."

He got up slowly. His beard, unclipped since Teresa's death, thick, snow-white, covered his powerful chest. He turned his head to the door, and called out in his strong voice—

"Linda."

Her answer came sharp and faint from within; and the appalled Nostromo stood up, too, but remained mute, gazing at the door. He was afraid. He was not afraid of being refused the girl he loved—no mere refusal could stand between him and a woman he desired— but the shining spectre of the treasure rose before him, claiming his allegiance in a silence that could not be gainsaid. He was afraid, because, neither dead nor alive, like the Gringos on Azuera, he belonged body and soul to the unlawfulness of his audacity. He was afraid of being forbidden the island. He was afraid, and said nothing.

Seeing the two men standing up side by side to await her, Linda stopped in the doorway. Nothing could alter the passionate dead whiteness of her face; but her black eyes seemed to catch and concentrate all the light of the low sun in a flaming spark within the black depths, covered at once by the slow descent of heavy eyelids.

"Behold thy husband, master, and benefactor." Old

Viola's voice resounded with a force that seemed to fill the whole gulf.

She stepped forward with her eyes nearly closed, like a sleep-walker in a beatific dream.

Nostromo made a superhuman effort. "It is time, Linda, we two were betrothed," he said, steadily, in his level, careless, unbending tone.

She put her hand into his offered palm, lowering her head, dark with bronze glints, upon which her father's hand rested for a moment.

"And so the soul of the dead is satisfied."

This came from Giorgio Viola, who went on talking for a while of his dead wife; while the two, sitting side by side, never looked at each other. Then the old man ceased; and Linda, motionless, began to speak.

"Ever since I felt I lived in the world, I have lived for you alone, Gian' Battista. And that you knew! You knew it . . . Battistino."

She pronounced the name exactly with her mother's intonation. A gloom as of the grave covered Nostromo's heart.

"Yes. I knew," he said.

The heroic Garibaldino sat on the same bench bowing his hoary head, his old soul dwelling alone with its memories, tender and violent, terrible and dreary—solitary on the earth full of men.

And Linda, his best-loved daughter, was saying, "I was yours ever since I can remember. I had only to think of you for the earth to become empty to my eyes. When you were there, I could see no one else. I was yours. Nothing is changed. The world belongs to you, and you let me live in it," . . . She dropped her low, vibrating voice to a still lower note, and found other things to say—torturing for the man at her side. Her murmur ran on ardent and voluble. She did not seem to see her sister, who came out with an altar-cloth she was embroidering in her hands, and passed in front of them, silent, fresh, fair, with a quick glance and a faint smile, to sit a little away on the other side of Nostromo.

The evening was still. The sun sank almost to the edge of a purple ocean; and the white lighthouse, livid against the background of clouds filling the head of the gulf, bore the lantern red and glowing, like a live ember kindled by the fire of the sky. Giselle, indolent and demure, raised the altar-cloth from time to time to hide nervous yawns, as of a young panther.

Suddenly Linda rushed at her sister, and seizing her head, covered her face with kisses. Nostromo's brain reeled. When she left her, as if stunned by the violent caresses, with her hands lying in her lap, the slave of the treasure felt as if he could shoot that woman. Old Giorgio lifted his leonine head.

"Where are you going, Linda?"

"To the light, padre mio."

"Si, si—to your duty."

He got up, too, looked after his eldest daughter; then, in a tone whose festive note seemed the echo of a mood lost in the night of ages—

"I am going in to cook something. Aha! Son! The old man knows where to find a bottle of wine, too."

He turned to Giselle, with a change to austere tenderness.

"And you, little one, pray not to the God of priests and slaves, but to the God of orphans, of the oppressed, of the poor, of little children, to give thee a man like this one for a husband."

His hand rested heavily for a moment on Nostromo's shoulder; then he went in. The hopeless slave of the San Tomé silver felt at these words the venomous fangs of jealousy biting deep into his heart. He was appalled by the novelty of the experience, by its force, by its physical intimacy. A husband! A husband for her! And yet it was natural that Giselle should have a husband at some time or other. He had never realized that before. In discovering that her beauty could belong to another he felt as though he could kill this one of old Giorgio's daughters also. He muttered moodily—

"They say you love Ramirez."

She shook her head without looking at him. Coppery glints rippled to and fro on the wealth of her gold hair. Her smooth forehead had the soft, pure sheen of a priceless pearl in the splendour of the sunset, mingling the gloom of starry spaces, the purple of the sea, and the crimson of the sky in a magnificent stillness.

"No," she said, slowly. "I never loved him. I think I never . . . He loves me—perhaps."

The seduction of her slow voice died out of the air, and her raised eyes remained fixed on nothing, as if indifferent and without thought.

"Ramirez told you he loved you?" asked Nostromo, restraining himself.

"Ah! once—one evening . . ."

"The miserable . . . Ha!"

He had jumped up as if stung by a gad-fly, and stood before her mute with anger.

"*Misericordia Divina!* You, too, Gian' Battista! Poor wretch that I am!" she lamented in ingenuous tones. "I told Linda, and she scolded—she scolded. Am I to live blind, dumb, and deaf in this world? And she told father, who took down his gun and cleaned it. Poor Ramirez! Then you came, and she told you."

He looked at her. He fastened his eyes upon the hollow of her white throat, which had the invincible

charm of things young, palpitating, delicate, and alive.
Was this the child he had known? Was it possible?
It dawned upon him that in these last years he had
really seen very little—nothing—of her. Nothing.
She had come into the world like a thing unknown.
She had come upon him unawares. She was a danger.
A frightful danger.* The instinctive mood of fierce
determination that had never failed him before the
perils of this life added its steady force to the violence
of his passion. She, in a voice that recalled to him the
song of running water, the tinkling of a silver bell,
continued—

"And between you three you have brought me here
into this captivity to the sky and water. Nothing else.
Sky and water. Oh, *Sanctissima Madre.* My hair
shall turn grey on this tedious island. I could hate you,
Gian' Battista!"

He laughed loudly. Her voice enveloped him like a
caress. She bemoaned her fate, spreading unconsciously,
like a flower its perfume in the coolness of the evening,
the indefinable seduction of her person. Was it her
fault that nobody ever had admired Linda? Even
when they were little, going out with their mother to
Mass, she remembered that people took no notice of
Linda, who was fearless, and chose instead to frighten
her, who was timid, with their attention. It was her
hair like gold, she supposed.

He broke out—

"Your hair like gold, and your eyes like violets, and
your lips like the rose; your round arms, your white
throat." . . .

Imperturbable in the indolence of her pose, she
blushed deeply all over to the roots of her hair. She
was not conceited. She was no more self-conscious than
a flower. But she was pleased. And perhaps even a

flower loves to hear itself praised. He glanced down, and added, impetuously—

"Your little feet!"

Leaning back against the rough stone wall of the cottage, she seemed to bask languidly in the warmth of the rosy flush. Only her lowered eyes glanced at her little feet.

"And so you are going at last to marry our Linda. She is terrible. Ah! now she will understand better since you have told her you love her. She will not be so fierce."

"*Chica!*" said Nostromo, "I have not told her anything."

"Then make haste. Come to-morrow. Come and tell her, so that I may have some peace from her scolding and—perhaps—who knows . . ."

"Be allowed to listen to your Ramirez, eh? Is that it? You . . ."

"Mercy of God! How violent you are, Giovanni," she said, unmoved. "Who is Ramirez . . . Ramirez . . . Who is he?" she repeated, dreamily, in the dusk and gloom of the clouded gulf, with a low red streak in the west like a hot bar of glowing iron laid across the entrance of a world sombre as a cavern, where the magnificent Capataz de Cargadores had hidden his conquests of love and wealth.

"Listen, Giselle," he said, in measured tones; "I will tell no word of love to your sister. Do you want to know why?"

"Alas! I could not understand perhaps, Giovanni. Father says you are not like other men; that no one had ever understood you properly; that the rich will be surprised yet. . . . Oh! saints in heaven! I am weary."

She raised her embroidery to conceal the lower

part of her face, then let it fall on her lap. The lantern was shaded on the land side, but slanting away from the dark column of the lighthouse they could see the long shaft of light, kindled by Linda, go out to strike the expiring glow in a horizon of purple and red.

Giselle Viola, with her head resting against the wall of the house, her eyes half closed, and her little feet, in white stockings and black slippers, crossed over each other, seemed to surrender herself, tranquil and fatal, to the gathering dusk. The charm of her body, the promising mysteriousness of her indolence, went out into the night of the Placid Gulf like a fresh and intoxicating fragrance spreading out in the shadows, impregnating the air. The incorruptible Nostromo breathed her ambient seduction in the tumultuous heaving of his breast. Before leaving the harbour he had thrown off the store clothing of Captain Fidanza, for greater ease in the long pull out to the islands. He stood before her in the red sash and check shirt as he used to appear on the Company's wharf—a Mediterranean sailor come ashore to try his luck in Costaguana. The dusk of purple and red enveloped him, too—close, soft, profound, as no more than fifty yards from that spot it had gathered evening after evening about the self-destructive passion of Don Martin Decoud's utter scepticism, flaming up to death in solitude.

"You have got to hear," he began at last, with perfect self-control. "I shall say no word of love to your sister, to whom I am betrothed from this evening, because it is you that I love. It is you!" . . .

The dusk let him see yet the tender and voluptuous smile that came instinctively upon her lips shaped for love and kisses, freeze hard in the drawn, haggard lines of terror. He could not restrain himself any longer.

While she shrank from his approach, her arms went out to him, abandoned and regal in the dignity of her languid surrender. He held her head in his two hands, and showered rapid kisses upon the upturned face that gleamed in the purple dusk. Masterful and tender, he was entering slowly upon the fulness of his possession. And he perceived that she was crying. Then the incomparable Capataz, the man of careless loves, became gentle and caressing, like a woman to the grief of a child. He murmured to her fondly. He sat down by her and nursed her fair head on his breast. He called her his star and his little flower.

It had grown dark. From the living-room of the light-keeper's cottage, where Giorgio, one of the Immortal Thousand, was bending his leonine and heroic head over a charcoal fire, there came the sound of sizzling and the aroma of an artistic *frittura*.

In the obscure disarray of that thing, happening like a cataclysm, it was in her feminine head that some gleam of reason survived. He was lost to the world in their embraced stillness. But she said, whispering into his ear—

"God of mercy! What will become of me—here—now—between this sky and this water I hate? Linda, Linda—I see her!" . . . She tried to get out of his arms, suddenly relaxed at the sound of that name. But there was no one approaching their black shapes, enlaced and struggling on the white background of the wall. "Linda! Poor Linda! I tremble! I shall die of fear before my poor sister Linda, betrothed to-day to Giovanni—my lover! Giovanni, you must have been mad! I cannot understand you! You are not like other men! I will not give you up—never—only to God himself! But why have you done this blind, mad, cruel, frightful thing?"

Released, she hung her head, let fall her hands. The altar-cloth, as if tossed by a great wind, lay far away from them, gleaming white on the black ground.

"From fear of losing my hope of you," said Nostromo.

"You knew that you had my soul! You know everything! It was made for you! But what could stand between you and me? What? Tell me!" she repeated, without impatience, in superb assurance.

"Your dead mother," he said, very low.

"Ah! . . . Poor mother! She has always . . . She is a saint in heaven now, and I cannot give you up to her. No, Giovanni. Only to God alone. You were mad—but it is done. Oh! what have you done? Giovanni, my beloved, my life, my master, do not leave me here in this grave of clouds. You cannot leave me now. You must take me away—at once—this instant —in the little boat. Giovanni, carry me off to-night, from my fear of Linda's eyes, before I have to look at her again."

She nestled close to him. The slave of the San Tomé silver felt the weight as of chains upon his limbs, a pressure as of a cold hand upon his lips. He struggled against the spell.

"I cannot," he said. "Not yet. There is something that stands between us two and the freedom of the world."

She pressed her form closer to his side with a subtle and naïve instinct of seduction.

"You rave, Giovanni—my lover!" she whispered, engagingly. "What can there be? Carry me off—in thy very hands—to Doña Emilia—away from here. I am not very heavy."

It seemed as though she expected him to lift her up at once in his two palms. She had lost the notion of all impossibility. Anything could happen on this night of wonder. As he made no movement, she almost cried aloud—

"I tell you I am afraid of Linda!" And still he did not move. She became quiet and wily. "What can there be?" she asked, coaxingly.

He felt her warm, breathing, alive, quivering in the hollow of his arm. In the exulting consciousness of his strength, and the triumphant excitement of his mind, he struck out for his freedom.

"A treasure," he said. All was still. She did not understand. "A treasure. A treasure of silver to buy a gold crown for thy brow."

"A treasure?" she repeated in a faint voice, as if from the depths of a dream. "What is it you say?"

She disengaged herself gently. He got up and looked down at her, aware of her face, of her hair, her lips, the dimples on her cheeks—seeing the fascination of her person in the night of the gulf as if in the blaze of noon-day. Her nonchalant and seductive voice trembled with the excitement of admiring awe and ungovernable curiosity.

"A treasure of silver!" she stammered out. Then pressed on faster: "What? Where? How did you get it, Giovanni?"

He wrestled with the spell of captivity. It was as if striking a heroic blow that he burst out—

"Like a thief!"

The densest blackness of the Placid Gulf seemed to fall upon his head. He could not see her now. She had vanished into a long, obscure abysmal silence, whence her voice came back to him after a time with a faint glimmer, which was her face.

"I love you! I love you!"

These words gave him an unwonted sense of freedom; they cast a spell stronger than the accursed spell of the treasure; they changed his weary subjection to that dead thing into an exulting conviction of his power. He would cherish her, he said, in a splendour as great as Doña Emilia's. The rich lived on wealth stolen from the people, but he had taken from the rich nothing—nothing that was not lost to them already by their folly and their betrayal. For he had been betrayed—he said—deceived, tempted. She believed him. . . . He had kept the treasure for purposes of revenge; but now he cared nothing for it. He cared only for her. He would put her beauty in a palace on a hill crowned with olive trees—a white palace above a blue sea. He would keep her there like a jewel in a casket. He would get land for her—her own land fertile with vines and corn —to set her little feet upon. He kissed them. . . . He had already paid for it all with the soul of a woman and the life of a man. . . . The Capataz de Cargadores tasted the supreme intoxication of his generosity. He flung the mastered treasure superbly at her feet in the impenetrable darkness of the gulf, in the darkness defying—as men said—the knowledge of God and the wit of the devil. But she must let him grow rich first—he warned her.

She listened as if in a trance. Her fingers stirred in his hair. He got up from his knees reeling, weak, empty, as though he had flung his soul away.

"Make haste, then," she said. "Make haste, Giovanni, my lover, my master, for I will give thee up to no one but God. And I am afraid of Linda."

He guessed at her shudder, and swore to do his best. He trusted the courage of her love. She promised to be brave in order to be loved always—far away in a white palace upon a hill above a blue sea. Then with a timid, tentative eagerness she murmured—

"Where is it? Where? Tell me that, Giovanni."

He opened his mouth and remained silent—thunder-struck.

"Not that! Not that!" he gasped out, appalled at the spell of secrecy that had kept him dumb before so many people falling upon his lips again with unimpaired force. Not even to her. Not even to her. It was too dangerous. "I forbid thee to ask," he cried at her, deadening cautiously the anger of his voice.

He had not regained his freedom. The spectre of the unlawful treasure arose, standing by her side like a figure of silver, pitiless and secret, with a finger on its pale lips. His soul died within him at the vision of himself creeping in presently along the ravine, with the smell of earth, of damp foliage in his nostrils—creeping in, determined in a purpose that numbed his breast, and creeping out again loaded with silver, with his ears alert to every sound. It must be done on this very night—that work of a craven slave!

He stooped low, pressed the hem of her skirt to his lips, with a muttered command—

"Tell him I would not stay," and was gone suddenly from her, silent, without as much as a footfall in the dark night.

She sat still, her head resting indolently against the wall, and her little feet in white stockings and black slippers crossed over each other. Old Giorgio, coming out, did not seem to be surprised at the intelligence as much as she had vaguely feared. For she was full of inexplicable fear now—fear of everything and everybody except of her Giovanni and his treasure. But that was incredible.

The heroic Garibaldino accepted Nostromo's abrupt departure with a sagacious indulgence. He remembered his own feelings, and exhibited a masculine penetration of the true state of the case.

"*Va bene*. Let him go. Ha! ha! No matter how fair the woman, it galls a little. Liberty, liberty. There's more than one kind! He has said the great word, and son Gian' Battista is not tame." He seemed to be instructing the motionless and scared Giselle. . . . "A man should not be tame," he added, dogmatically out of the doorway. Her stillness and silence seemed to displease him. "Do not give way to the enviousness of your sister's lot," he admonished her, very grave, in his deep voice.

Presently he had to come to the door again to call in his younger daughter. It was late. He shouted her name three times before she even moved her head. Left alone, she had become the helpless prey of astonishment. She walked into the bedroom she shared with Linda like a person profoundly asleep. That aspect was so marked that even old Giorgio, spectacled, raising his eyes from the Bible, shook his head as she shut the door behind her.

She walked right across the room without looking at anything, and sat down at once by the open window. Linda, stealing down from the tower in the exuberance of her happiness, found her with a lighted candle at her back, facing the black night full of sighing gusts of wind and the sound of distant showers—a true night of the gulf, too dense for the eye of God and the wiles of the devil. She did not turn her head at the opening of the door.

There was something in that immobility which reached Linda in the depths of her paradise. The elder sister guessed angrily: the child is thinking of that wretched Ramirez. Linda longed to talk. She said in her arbitrary voice, "Giselle!" and was not answered by the slightest movement.

The girl that was going to live in a palace and walk on

ground of her own was ready to die with terror. Not for anything in the world would she have turned her head to face her sister. Her heart was beating madly. She said with subdued haste—

"Do not speak to me. I am praying."

Linda, disappointed, went out quietly; and Giselle sat on unbelieving, lost, dazed, patient, as if waiting for the confirmation of the incredible. The hopeless blackness of the clouds seemed part of a dream, too. She waited.

She did not wait in vain. The man whose soul was dead within him, creeping out of the ravine, weighted with silver, had seen the gleam of the lighted window, and could not help retracing his steps from the beach.

On that impenetrable background, obliterating the lofty mountains by the seaboard, she saw the slave of the San Tomé silver, as if by an extraordinary power of a miracle. She accepted his return as if henceforth the world could hold no surprise for all eternity.

She rose, compelled and rigid, and began to speak long before the light from within fell upon the face of the approaching man.

"You have come back to carry me off. It is well! Open thy arms, Giovanni, my lover. I am coming."

His prudent footsteps stopped, and with his eyes glistening wildly, he spoke in a harsh voice:

"Not yet. I must grow rich slowly." . . . A threatening note came into his tone. "Do not forget that you have a thief for your lover."

"Yes! Yes!" she whispered, hastily. "Come nearer! Listen! Do not give me up, Giovanni! Never, never! . . . I will be patient! . . ."

Her form drooped consolingly over the low casement

towards the slave of the unlawful treasure.   The light in the room went out, and weighted with silver, the magnificent Capataz clasped her round her white neck in the darkness of the gulf as a drowning man clutches at a straw.

CHAPTER THIRTEEN*

ON THE day Mrs. Gould was going, in Dr. Monygham's words, to "give a tertulia," Captain Fidanza
went down the side of his schooner lying in Sulaco
harbour, calm, unbending, deliberate in the way he sat
down in his dinghy and took up his sculls. He was later
than usual. The afternoon was well advanced before
he landed on the beach of the Great Isabel, and with a
steady pace climbed the slope of the island.

From a distance he made out Giselle sitting in a chair
tilted back against the end of the house, under the window of the girl's room. She had her embroidery in her
hands, and held it well up to her eyes. The tranquillity
of that girlish figure exasperated the feeling of perpetual
struggle and strife he carried in his breast. He became
angry. It seemed to him that she ought to hear the
clanking of his fetters—his silver fetters, from afar.
And while ashore that day, he had met the doctor with
the evil eye, who had looked at him very hard.

The raising of her eyes mollified him. They smiled in
their flower-like freshness straight upon his heart. Then
she frowned. It was a warning to be cautious. He
stopped some distance away, and in a loud, indifferent
tone, said—

"Good day, Giselle. Is Linda up yet?"

"Yes. She is in the big room with father."

He approached then, and, looking through the window into the bedroom for fear of being detected by
Linda returning there for some reason, he said, moving
only his lips—

"You love me?"

"More than my life." She went on with her embroidery under his contemplating gaze and continued to speak, looking at her work, "Or I could not live. I could not, Giovanni. For this life is like death. Oh, Giovanni, I shall perish if you do not take me away."

He smiled carelessly. "I will come to the window when it's dark," he said.

"No, don't, Giovanni. Not-to-night. Linda and father have been talking together for a long time to-day."

"What about?"

"Ramirez, I fancy I heard. I do not know. I am afraid. I am always afraid. It is like dying a thousand times a day. Your love is to me like your treasure to you. It is there, but I can never get enough of it."

He looked at her very still. She was beautiful. His desire had grown within him. He had two masters now. But she was incapable of sustained emotion. She was sincere in what she said, but she slept placidly at night. When she saw him she flamed up always. Then only an increased taciturnity marked the change in her. She was afraid of betraying herself. She was afraid of pain, of bodily harm, of sharp words, of facing anger, and witnessing violence. For her soul was light and tender with a pagan sincerity in its impulses. She murmured—

"Give up the palazzo, Giovanni, and the vineyard on the hills, for which we are starving our love."

She ceased, seeing Linda standing silent at the corner of the house.

Nostromo turned to his affianced wife with a greeting, and was amazed at her sunken eyes, at her hollow cheeks, at the air of illness and anguish in her face.

"Have you been ill?" he asked, trying to put some concern into this question.

Her black eyes blazed at him. "Am I thinner?" she asked.

"Yes—perhaps—a little."

"And older?"

"Every day counts—for all of us."

"I shall go grey, I fear, before the ring is on my finger," she said, slowly, keeping her gaze fastened upon him.

She waited for what he would say, rolling down her turned-up sleeves.

"No fear of that," he said, absently.

She turned away as if it had been something final, and busied herself with household cares while Nostromo talked with her father. Conversation with the old Garibaldino was not easy. Age had left his faculties unimpaired, only they seemed to have withdrawn somewhere deep within him. His answers were slow in coming, with an effect of august gravity. But that day he was more animated, quicker; there seemed to be more life in the old lion. He was uneasy for the integrity of his honour. He believed Sidoni's warning as to Ramirez's designs upon his younger daughter. And he did not trust her. She was flighty. He said nothing of his cares to "Son Gian' Battista." It was a touch of senile vanity. He wanted to show that he was equal yet to the task of guarding alone the honour of his house.

Nostromo went away early. As soon as he had disappeared, walking towards the beach, Linda stepped over the threshold and, with a haggard smile, sat down by the side of her father.

Ever since that Sunday, when the infatuated and desperate Ramirez had waited for her on the wharf, she had no doubts whatever. The jealous ravings of that man were no revelation. They had only fixed with precision, as with a nail driven into her heart, that sense of unreality and deception which, instead of bliss and security, she had found in her intercourse with her promised husband. She had passed on, pouring indignation and scorn upon Ramirez; but, that Sunday, she nearly died of wretchedness and shame, lying on the carved and lettered stone of Teresa's grave, subscribed for by the engine-drivers and the fitters of the railway workshops, in sign of their respect for the hero of Italian Unity. Old Viola had not been able to carry out his desire of burying his wife in the sea; and Linda wept upon the stone.

The gratuitous outrage appalled her. If he wished to break her heart—well and good. Everything was permitted to Gian' Battista. But why trample upon the pieces; why seek to humiliate her spirit? Aha! He could not break that. She dried her tears. And Giselle! Giselle! The little one that, ever since she could toddle, had always clung to her skirt for protection. What duplicity! But she could not help it probably. When there was a man in the case the poor featherheaded wretch could not help herself.

Linda had a good share of the Viola stoicism. She resolved to say nothing. But woman-like she put passion into her stoicism. Giselle's short answers, prompted by fearful caution, drove her beside herself by their curtness that resembled disdain. One day she flung herself upon the chair in which her indolent sister was lying and impressed the mark of her teeth at the base of the whitest neck in Sulaco. Giselle cried out. But she had her share of the Viola heroism. Ready to faint with terror, she only said, in a lazy voice, "*Madre de Dios!* Are you going to eat me alive, Linda?" And this outburst passed off leaving no trace upon the situation. "She knows nothing. She cannot know anything," reflected Giselle. "Perhaps it is not true. It cannot be true," Linda tried to persuade herself.

But when she saw Captain Fidanza for the first time after her meeting with the distracted Ramirez, the certitude of her misfortune returned. She watched him from the doorway go away to his boat, asking herself stoically, "Will they meet to-night?" She made up her mind not to leave the tower for a second. When he had disappeared she came out and sat down by her father.

The venerable Garibaldino felt, in his own words, "a young man yet." In one way or another a good deal of talk about Ramirez had reached him of late; and his contempt and dislike of that man who obviously was not what his son would have been, had made him restless. He slept very little now; but for several nights past instead of reading—or only sitting, with Mrs. Gould's silver spectacles on his nose, before the open Bible, he had been prowling actively all about the island with his old gun, on watch over his honour.

Linda, laying her thin brown hand on his knee, tried to soothe his excitement. Ramirez was not in Sulaco. Nobody knew where he was. He was gone. His talk of what he would do meant nothing.

"No," the old man interrupted. "But son Gian' Battista told me—quite of himself—that the cowardly *esclavo* was drinking and gambling with the rascals of Zapiga, over there on the north side of the gulf. He may get some of the worst scoundrels of that scoundrelly town of negroes to help him in his attempt upon the little one. . . . But I am not so old. No!"

She argued earnestly against the probability of any attempt being made; and at last the old man fell silent, chewing his white moustache. Women had their obstinate notions which must be humoured—his poor wife was like that, and Linda resembled her mother. It was not seemly for a man to argue. "May be. May be," he mumbled.

She was by no means easy in her mind. She loved Nostromo. She turned her eyes upon Giselle, sitting at a distance, with something of maternal tenderness, and the jealous anguish of a rival outraged in her defeat. Then she rose and walked over to her.

"Listen—you," she said, roughly.

The invincible candour of the gaze, raised up all violet and dew, excited her rage and admiration. She had beautiful eyes—the *Chica*—this vile thing of white flesh and black deception. She did not know whether she wanted to tear them out with shouts of vengeance or cover up their mysterious and shameless innocence with kisses of pity and love. And suddenly they became empty, gazing blankly at her, except for a little fear not quite buried deep enough with all the other emotions in Giselle's heart.

Linda said, "Ramirez is boasting in town that he will carry you off from the island."

"What folly!" answered the other, and in a perversity born of long restraint, she added: "He is not the man," in a jesting tone with a trembling audacity.

"No?" said Linda, through her clenched teeth. "Is he not? Well, then, look to it; because father has been walking about with a loaded gun at night."

"It is not good for him. You must tell him not to, Linda. He will not listen to me."

"I shall say nothing—never any more—to anybody," cried Linda, passionately.

This could not last, thought Giselle. Giovanni must take her away soon—the very next time he came. She would not suffer these terrors for ever so much silver.

To speak with her sister made her ill.   But she was not
uneasy at her father's watchfulness.   She had begged
Nostromo not to come to the window that night.   He
had promised to keep away for this once.   And she
did not know, could not guess or imagine, that he had
another reason for coming on the island.

Linda had gone straight to the tower.   It was time to
light up.   She unlocked the little door, and went heavily
up the spiral staircase, carrying her love for the magnificent Capataz de Cargadores like an ever-increasing load
of shameful fetters.   No; she could not throw it off.
No; let Heaven dispose of these two.   And moving
about the lantern, filled with twilight and the sheen of
the moon, with careful movements she lighted the lamp.
Then her arms fell along her body.

"And with our mother looking on," she murmured.
"My own sister—the *Chica!*"

The whole refracting apparatus, with its brass fittings
and rings of prisms, glittered and sparkled like a dome-
shaped shrine of diamonds, containing not a lamp, but
some sacred flame, dominating the sea.   And Linda, the
keeper, in black, with a pale face, drooped low in a
wooden chair, alone with her jealousy, far above the
shames and passions of the earth.   A strange, dragging
pain as if somebody were pulling her about brutally
by her dark hair with bronze glints, made her put her
hands up to her temples.   They would meet.   They
would meet.   And she knew where, too.   At the window.
The sweat of torture fell in drops on her cheeks, while
the moonlight in the offing closed as if with a colossal
bar of silver the entrance of the Placid Gulf—the sombre
cavern of clouds and stillness in the surf-fretted seaboard.

Linda Viola stood up suddenly with a finger on her lip.
He loved neither her nor her sister.   The whole thing

seemed so objectless as to frighten her, and also give her some hope. Why did he not carry her off? What prevented him? He was incomprehensible. What were they waiting for? For what end were these two lying and deceiving? Not for the ends of their love. There was no such thing. The hope of regaining him for herself made her break her vow of not leaving the tower that night. She must talk at once to her father, who was wise, and would understand. She ran down the spiral stairs. At the moment of opening the door at the bottom she heard the sound of the first shot ever fired on the Great Isabel.

She felt a shock, as though the bullet had struck her breast. She ran on without pausing. The cottage was dark. She cried at the door, "Giselle! Giselle!" then dashed round the corner and screamed her sister's name at the open window, without getting an answer; but as she was rushing, distracted, round the house, Giselle came out of the door, and darted past her, running silently, her hair loose, and her eyes staring straight ahead. She seemed to skim along the grass as if on tiptoe, and vanished.

Linda walked on slowly, with her arms stretched out before her. All was still on the island; she did not know where she was going. The tree under which Martin Decoud spent his last days, beholding life like a succession of senseless images, threw a large blotch of black shade upon the grass. Suddenly she saw her father, standing quietly all alone in the moonlight.

The Garibaldino—big, erect, with his snow-white hair and beard—had a monumental repose in his immobility, leaning upon a rifle. She put her hand upon his arm lightly. He never stirred.

"What have you done?" she asked, in her ordinary voice.

"I have shot Ramirez—*infame!*" he answered, with his eyes directed to where the shade was blackest. "Like a thief he came, and like a thief he fell. The child had to be protected."

He did not offer to move an inch, to advance a single step. He stood there, rugged and unstirring, like a statue of an old man guarding the honour of his house. Linda removed her trembling hand from his arm, firm and steady like an arm of stone, and, without a word, entered the blackness of the shade. She saw a stir of formless shapes on the ground, and stopped short. A murmur of despair and tears grew louder to her strained hearing.

"I entreated you not to come to-night. Oh, my Giovanni! And you promised. Oh! Why—why did you come, Giovanni?"

It was her sister's voice. It broke on a heartrending sob. And the voice of the resourceful Capataz de Cargadores, master and slave of the San Tomé treasure, who had been caught unawares by old Giorgio while stealing across the open towards the ravine to get some more silver, answered careless and cool, but sounding startlingly weak from the ground.

"It seemed as though I could not live through the night without seeing thee once more—my star, my little flower."

*   *   *   *   *

The brilliant tertulia was just over, the last guests had departed, and the Señor Administrador had gone to his room already, when Dr. Monygham, who had been expected in the evening but had not turned up, arrived driving along the wood-block pavement under the electric-lamps of the deserted Calle de la Constitucion, and found the great gateway of the Casa still open.

He limped in, stumped up the stairs, and found the fat and sleek Basilio on the point of turning off the lights in the sala. The prosperous majordomo remained open-mouthed at this late invasion.

"Don't put out the lights," commanded the doctor. "I want to see the señora."

"The señora is in the Señor Adminstrador's cancillaria," said Basilio, in an unctuous voice. "The Señor Administrador starts for the mountain in an hour. There is some trouble with the workmen to be feared, it appears. A shameless people without reason and decency. And idle, señor. Idle."

"You are shamelessly lazy and imbecile yourself," said the doctor, with that faculty for exasperation which made him so generally beloved. "Don't put the lights out."

Basilio retired with dignity. Dr. Monygham, waiting in the brilliantly lighted sala, heard presently a door close at the further end of the house. A jingle of spurs died out. The Señor Administrador was off to the mountain.

With a measured swish of her long train, flashing with jewels and the shimmer of silk, her delicate head bowed as if under the weight of a mass of fair hair, in which the silver threads were lost, the "first lady of Sulaco," as Captain Mitchell used to describe her, moved along the lighted corridor, wealthy beyond great dreams of wealth, considered, loved, respected, honoured, and as solitary as any human being had ever been, perhaps, on this earth.

The doctor's "Mrs. Gould! One minute!" stopped her with a start at the door of the lighted and empty sala. From the similarity of mood and circumstance, the sight of the doctor, standing there all alone amongst the groups of furniture, recalled to her emotional memory her unexpected meeting with Martin Decoud; she seemed to hear in the silence the voice of that man, dead miserably so many years ago, pronounce the words, "Antonia left her fan here." But it was the doctor's voice that spoke, a little altered by his excitement. She remarked his shining eyes.

"Mrs. Gould, you are wanted. Do you know what has happened? You remember what I told you yesterday about Nostromo. Well, it seems that a lancha, a decked boat, coming from Zapiga, with four negroes in her, passing close to the Great Isabel, was hailed from the cliff by a woman's voice—Linda's, as a matter of fact—commanding them (it's a moonlight night) to go round to the beach and take up a wounded man to the town. The *patron* (from whom I've heard all this), of course, did so at once. He told me that when they got round to the low side of the Great Isabel, they found Linda Viola waiting for them. They followed her: she led them under a tree not far from the cottage. There they found Nostromo lying on the ground with his head in the younger girl's lap, and father Viola standing some distance off leaning on his gun. Under Linda's direction they got a table out of the cottage for a stretcher, after breaking off the legs. They are here, Mrs. Gould. I mean Nostromo and—and Giselle. The negroes brought him in to the first-aid hospital near the harbour. He made the attendant send for me. But it is not me he wanted to see—it was you, Mrs. Gould! It was you."

"Me?" whispered Mrs. Gould, shrinking a little.

"Yes, you!" the doctor burst out. "He begged me —his enemy, as he thinks—to bring you to him at once. It seems he has something to say to you alone."

"Impossible!" murmured Mrs. Gould.

"He said to me, 'Remind her that I have done some-

thing to keep a roof over her head.' . . . Mrs.
Gould," the doctor pursued, in the greatest excitement. "Do you remember the silver? The silver in
the lighter—that was lost!"

Mrs. Gould remembered. But she did not say she
hated the mere mention of that silver. Frankness
personified, she remembered with an exaggerated horror
that for the first and last time of her life she had concealed the truth from her husband about that very
silver. She had been corrupted by her fears at that
time, and she had never forgiven herself. Moreover,
that silver, which would never have come down if her
husband had been made acquainted with the news
brought by Decoud, had been in a roundabout way
nearly the cause of Dr. Monygham's death. And these
things appeared to her very dreadful.

"Was it lost, though?" the doctor exclaimed. "I've
always felt that there was a mystery about our Nostromo ever since. I do believe he wants now, at the
point of death——"

"The point of death," repeated Mrs. Gould.

"Yes. Yes . . . . He wants perhaps to tell
you something concerning that silver which——"

"Oh, no! No!" exclaimed Mrs. Gould, in a low
voice. "Isn't it lost and done with? Isn't there
enough treasure without it to make everybody in the
world miserable?"

The doctor remained still, in a submissive, disappointed silence. At last he ventured, very low—

"And there is that Viola girl, Giselle. What are
we to do? It looks as though father and sister had——"

Mrs. Gould admitted that she felt in duty bound to
do her best for these girls.

"I have a volante here," the doctor said. "If you
don't mind getting into that——"

He waited, all impatience, till Mrs. Gould reappeared, having thrown over her dress a grey cloak with a deep hood.

It was thus that, cloaked and monastically hooded over her evening costume, this woman, full of endurance and compassion, stood by the side of the bed on which the splendid Capataz de Cargadores lay stretched out motionless on his back. The whiteness of sheets and pillows gave a sombre and energetic relief to his bronzed face, to the dark, nervous hands, so good on a tiller, upon a bridle and on a trigger, lying open and idle upon a white coverlet.

"She is innocent," the Capataz was saying in a deep and level voice, as though afraid that a louder word would break the slender hold his spirit still kept upon his body. "She is innocent. It is I alone. But no matter. For these things I would answer to no man or woman alive."

He paused. Mrs. Gould's face, very white within the shadow of the hood, bent over him with an invincible and dreary sadness. And the low sobs of Giselle Viola, kneeling at the end of the bed, her gold hair with coppery gleams loose and scattered over the Capataz's feet, hardly troubled the silence of the room.

"Ha! Old Giorgio—the guardian of thine honour! Fancy the Vecchio coming upon me so light of foot, so steady of aim. I myself could have done no better. But the price of a charge of powder might have been saved. The honour was safe. . . . Señora, she would have followed to the end of the world Nostromo the thief. . . . I have said the word. The spell is broken!"

A low moan from the girl made him cast his eyes down.

"I cannot see her. . . . No matter," he went on,

with the shadow of the old magnificent carelessness in his voice. "One kiss is enough, if there is no time for more. An airy soul, señora! Bright and warm, like sunshine—soon clouded, and soon serene. They would crush it there between them. Señora, cast on her the eye of your compassion, as famed from one end of the land to the other as the courage and daring of the man who speaks to you. She will console herself in time. And even Ramirez is not a bad fellow. I am not angry. No! It is not Ramirez who overcame the Capataz of the Sulaco Cargadores." He paused, made an effort, and in louder voice, a little wildly, declared—

"I die betrayed—betrayed by——"

But he did not say by whom or by what he was dying betrayed.

"She would not have betrayed me," he began again, opening his eyes very wide. "She was faithful. We were going very far—very soon. I could have torn myself away from that accursed treasure for her. For that child I would have left boxes and boxes of it—full. And Decoud took four. Four ingots. Why? *Picardia!* To betray me? How could I give back the treasure with four ingots missing? They would have said I had purloined them. The doctor would have said that. Alas! it holds me yet!"

Mrs. Gould bent low, fascinated—cold with apprehension.

"What became of Don Martin on that night, Nostromo?"

"Who knows! I wondered what would become of me. Now I know. Death was to come upon me unawares. He went away! He betrayed me. And you think I have killed him! You are all alike, you fine people. The silver has killed me. It has held me. It holds me yet. Nobody knows where it is. But you are the wife of Don Carlos, who put it into my hands and said, 'Save it on your life.' And when I returned, and you all thought it was lost, what do I hear? It was nothing of importance. Let it go. Up, Nostromo, the faithful, and ride away to save us, for dear life!"

"Nostromo!" Mrs. Gould whispered, bending very low. "I, too, have hated the idea of that silver from the bottom of my heart."

"Marvellous!—that one of you should hate the wealth that you know so well how to take from the hands of the poor. The world rests upon the poor, as old Giorgio says. You have been always good to the poor. But there is something accursed in wealth. Señora, shall I tell you where the treasure is? To you alone. . . . Shining! Incorruptible!"

A pained, involuntary reluctance lingered in his tone, in his eyes, plain to the woman with the genius of sympathetic intuition. She averted her glance from the miserable subjection of the dying man, appalled, wishing to hear no more of the silver.

"No, Capataz," she said. "No one misses it now. Let it be lost for ever."

After hearing these words, Nostromo closed his eyes, uttered no word, made no movement. Outside the door of the sick-room Dr. Monygham, excited to the highest pitch, his eyes shining with eagerness, came up to the two women.

"Now, Mrs. Gould," he said, almost brutally in his impatience, "tell me, was I right? There is a mystery. You have got the word of it, have you not? He told you——"

"He told me nothing," said Mrs. Gould, steadily.

The light of his temperamental enmity to Nostromo went out of Dr. Monygham's eyes. He stepped back submissively. He did not believe Mrs. Gould. But her word was law. He accepted her denial like an inexplicable fatality affirming the victory of Nostromo's genius over his own. Even before that woman, whom he loved with secret devotion, he had been defeated by the magnificent Capataz de Cargadores, the man who had lived his own life on the assumption of unbroken fidelity, rectitude, and courage!

"Pray send at once somebody for my carriage," spoke Mrs. Gould from within her hood. Then, turning to Giselle Viola, "Come nearer me, child; come closer. We will wait here."

Giselle Viola, heartbroken and childlike, her face veiled in her falling hair, crept up to her side. Mrs. Gould slipped her hand through the arm of the unworthy daughter of old Viola, the immaculate republican, the hero without a stain. Slowly, gradually, as a withered flower droops, the head of the girl, who would have followed a thief to the end of the world, rested on the shoulder of Doña Emilia, the first lady of Sulaco, the wife of the Señor Administrador of the San Tomé mine. And Mrs. Gould, feeling her suppressed sobbing, nervous and excited, had the first and only moment of bitterness in her life. It was worthy of Dr. Monygham himself.

"Console yourself, child. Very soon he would have forgotten you for his treasure."

"Señora, he loved me. He loved me," Giselle whispered, despairingly. "He loved me as no one had ever been loved before."

"I have been loved, too," Mrs. Gould said in a severe tone.

Giselle clung to her convulsively. "Oh, señora, but you shall live adored to the end of your life," she sobbed out.

Mrs. Gould kept an unbroken silence till the carriage

arrived. She helped in the half-fainting girl. After the doctor had shut the door of the landau, she leaned over to him.

"You can do nothing?" she whispered.

"No, Mrs. Gould. Moreover, he won't let us touch him. It does not matter. I just had one look. . . . Useless."

But he promised to see old Viola and the other girl that very night. He could get the police-boat to take him off to the island. He remained in the street, looking after the landau rolling away slowly behind the white mules.

The rumour of some accident—an accident to Captain Fidanza—had been spreading along the new quays with their rows of lamps and the dark shapes of towering cranes. A knot of night prowlers—the poorest of the poor—hung about the door of the first-aid hospital, whispering in the moonlight of the empty street.

There was no one with the wounded man but the pale photographer, small, frail, bloodthirsty, the hater of capitalists, perched on a high stool near the head of the bed with his knees up and his chin in his hands. He had been fetched by a comrade who, working late on the wharf, had heard from a negro belonging to a lancha, that Captain Fidanza had been brought ashore mortally wounded.

"Have you any dispositions to make, comrade?" he asked, anxiously. "Do not forget that we want money for our work. The rich must be fought with their own weapons."

Nostromo made no answer. The other did not insist, remaining huddled up on the stool, shock-headed, wildly hairy, like a hunchbacked monkey. Then, after a long silence—

"Comrade Fidanza," he began, solemnly, "you have

refused all aid from that doctor. Is he really a dangerous enemy of the people?"

In the dimly lit room Nostromo rolled his head slowly on the pillow and opened his eyes, directing at the weird figure perched by his bedside a glance of enigmatic and profound inquiry.* Then his head rolled back, his eyelids fell, and the Capataz de Cargadores died without a word or moan after an hour of immobility, broken by short shudders testifying to the most atrocious sufferings.

Dr. Monygham, going out in the police-galley to the islands, beheld the glitter of the moon upon the gulf and the high black shape of the Great Isabel sending a shaft of light afar, from under the canopy of clouds.

"Pull easy," he said, wondering what he would find there. He tried to imagine Linda and her father, and discovered a strange reluctance within himself. "Pull easy," he repeated.

*   *   *   *   *   *

From the moment he fired at the thief of his honour, Giorgio Viola had not stirred from the spot. He stood, his old gun grounded, his hand grasping the barrel near the muzzle. After the lancha carrying off Nostromo for ever from her had left the shore, Linda, coming up, stopped before him. He did not seem to be aware of her presence, but when, losing her forced calmness, she cried out—

"Do you know whom you have killed?" he answered—

"Ramirez the vagabond."

White, and staring insanely at her father, Linda laughed in his face. After a time he joined her faintly in a deep-toned and distant echo of her peals. Then she stopped, and the old man spoke as if startled—

"He cried out in son Gian' Battista's voice."

The gun fell from his opened hand, but the arm remained extended for a moment as if still supported. Linda seized it roughly.

"You are too old to understand. Come into the house."

He let her lead him. On the threshold he stumbled heavily, nearly coming to the ground together with his daughter. His excitement, his activity of the last few days, had been like the flare of a dying lamp. He caught at the back of his chair.

"In son Gian' Battista's voice," he repeated in a severe tone. "I heard him—Ramirez—the miserable——"

Linda helped him into the chair, and, bending low, hissed into his ear—

"You have killed Gian' Battista."

The old man smiled under his thick moustache. Women had strange fancies.

"Where is the child?" he asked, surprised at the penetrating chilliness of the air and the unwonted dimness of the lamp by which he used to sit up half the night with the open Bible before him.

Linda hesitated a moment, then averted her eyes.

"She is asleep," she said. "We shall talk of her to-morrow."

She could not bear to look at him. He filled her with terror and with an almost unbearable feeling of pity. She had observed the change that came over him. He would never understand what he had done; and even to her the whole thing remained incomprehensible. He said with difficulty—

"Give me the book."

Linda laid on the table the closed volume in its worn leather cover, the Bible given him ages ago by an Englishman in Palermo.

"The child had to be protected," he said, in a strange, mournful voice.

Behind his chair Linda wrung her hands, crying without noise. Suddenly she started for the door. He heard her move.

"Where are you going?" he asked.

"To the light," she answered, turning round to look at him balefully.

"The light! Si—duty."

Very upright, white-haired, leonine, heroic in his absorbed quietness, he felt in the pocket of his red shirt for the spectacles given him by Doña Emilia. He put them on. After a long period of immobility he opened the book, and from on high looked through the glasses at the small print in double columns. A rigid, stern expression settled upon his features with a slight frown, as if in response to some gloomy thought or unpleasant sensation. But he never detached his eyes from the book while he swayed forward, gently, gradually, till his snow-white head rested upon the open pages. A wooden clock ticked methodically on the white-washed wall, and growing slowly cold the Garibaldino lay alone, rugged, undecayed, like an old oak uprooted by a treacherous gust of wind.

The light of the Great Isabel burned unfailing above the lost treasure of the San Tomé mine. Into the bluish sheen of a night without stars the lantern sent out a yellow beam towards the far horizon. Like a black speck upon the shining panes, Linda, crouching in the outer gallery, rested her head on the rail. The moon, drooping in the western board, looked at her radiantly.

Below, at the foot of the cliff, the regular splash of oars from a passing boat ceased, and Dr. Monygham stood up in the stern sheets.

"Linda!" he shouted, throwing back his head. "Linda!"

Linda stood up.   She had recognized the voice.

"Is he dead?" she cried, bending over.

"Yes, my poor girl.   I am coming round," the doctor answered from below.   "Pull to the beach," he said to the rowers.

Linda's black figure detached itself upright on the light of the lantern with her arms raised above her head as though she were going to throw herself over.

"It is I who loved you," she whispered, with a face as set and white as marble in the moonlight.   "I! Only I!   She will forget thee, killed miserably for her pretty face.   I cannot understand.   I cannot understand.   But I shall never forget thee.   Never!"

She stood silent and still, collecting her strength to throw all her fidelity, her pain, bewilderment, and despair into one great cry.

"Never!   Gian' Battista!"

Dr. Monygham, pulling round in the police-galley, heard the name pass over his head.   It was another of Nostromo's triumphs, the greatest, the most enviable, the most sinister of all.   In that true cry of undying passion that seemed to ring aloud from Punta Mala to Azuera and away to the bright line of the horizon, overhung by a big white cloud shining like a mass of solid silver, the genius of the magnificent Capataz de Cargadores dominated the dark gulf containing his conquests of treasure and love.

THE END

APPENDIX
The serial ending of *Nostromo*

THE last 4,300 words of the final episode of the serial (*T. P. O'Connor's Weekly*, 7 October 1904, pp. 455–7) are reprinted below so that readers may appreciate Conrad's extensive amplifications and changes. Compare *Nostromo* (pp. 517–66; i.e. roughly 16,000 words).

———

'Just a mozo of the town. He was, as a matter of fact, recommended by Nostromo to Captain Mitchell for Capataz of the Company's stevedores. He strutted round, and tried to play the part of a second Nostromo. But the fraternity of the Cargadores very soon put a stop to that. Old Giorgio could not bear him—called him a blind esclavo, an empty head, without sense, a cowardly youth, a heart without honour; not like his model of perfection, his Gian' Battista, the incarnation of the honesty, the fidelity, the superiority of 'the people'. They both, the old Spartan and that great white-faced Linda, with her red mouth and coal-black eyes, are looking rather fiercely after the fair one. Old Viola, who is king on his island, will not allow anyone to remain after half-past six. Even Captain Fidanza, the incorruptible Nostromo, has to take his leave before dark. Why should he stay longer? Linda goes up to the light then. Now comes the strange part. For some time past, Captain Fidanza, whenever his schooner is in Sulaco, has been observed to enter the harbour, pulling himself in a small boat, long after midnight. Where does he spend his time? I mean after he has left the old lighthouse-keeper, and when Linda is up with the light. He ought to be back at eight at the latest. It is impossible to believe that he floats for six hours or so in the Gulf for the fun of the thing. Last time Nostromo was here, Ramirez, who dares not approach old Viola, plucked heart of grace, and spoke about it to Linda one Sunday when she came ashore to go to church and pay a visit to her mother's grave. Linda was never so unrelenting towards Ramirez as the old man himself. I fancy she would not be sorry to see the other fairly married. The question is, at what does Captain Fidanza employ all these hours between seven and midnight. He goes away at seven right enough.'

Mrs Gould had sat up, opening her eyes very wide.

'What do you mean, Dr Monygham? Do you mean to say that you suspect the younger sister?'

'Who can tell. Quien sabe?' said the doctor, rising to take his leave.

'But Nostromo should be spoken to!' cried Mrs Gould. 'That child — '

'It would be the best thing for him,' the doctor remarked dryly. 'But who is to speak to him? Who would dare? No one in Sulaco. Even the miserable Ramirez goes whimpering to Linda rather than face the incomparable man.'

'I will,' cried Mrs Gould. 'Tell him to come and see me.'

'And do you think he would come?' the doctor asked, ironically. 'Even you can't command Captain Fidanza. But if you wish me, I shall try. Only he looks upon me as an enemy of long-standing. And, do you know, he wouldn't even have the trouble of exerting himself. There is not a man in the working population of Sulaco who wouldn't undertake to make me meet with some ugly accident just to ingratiate himself with Captain Fidanza. Half of our new town police are members of one or other of these camorras honoured by the membership of Captain Fidanza. Shall I speak to him?'

'No, no! I forbid you!' Mrs Gould cried hastily. 'I—I think I'll send for the girls—or for the father himself.'

'It would be much better. Old Viola shall know how to take care of his honour.'

Mrs Gould meditated. She had the fate of these girls very much at heart. But to-morrow—officially the first day of her presence in Sulaco—would be very full, with a two o'clock dinner-party for the intimate friends adhering to the ancient style of living, and a great reception in the evening.

'I shall ask the Garibaldino to come and see me the day after,' she thought to herself. The thing was impossible. There would be some very simple explanation. Perhaps the best thing would be to say nothing at all to anybody.

And after the Doctor had gone away she leaned back in her chair, in the shade of big trees planted in a circle. She leaned back with closed eyes and her hand lying idle in her lap, small and dainty, with a youthful prettiness in the half light, clad in gossamer fabrics and delicate laces, like a good fairy wearied with a long career of well-doing, touched by the withering suspicion of the uselessness of her labours, the powerlessness of her magic.

CHAPTER XV

Nostromo had been growing rich very slowly; it was an effect of his prudence, for that man could command himself even when thrown off his balance. And to become the slave of a treasure with full self-knowledge is an occurrence rare and mentally disturbing. But it was also in a great part because of the difficulty of converting it into a form in which it could become available. The mere act of getting hold of it piecemeal, little by little, was surrounded by difficulties, by the dangers of imminent detection. He had to visit the Isabels in secret, between his voyages along the coast, which were the ostensible source of his fortune. The crew of his own schooner were like so many spies upon their dreaded captain. He did not dare stay too long in port. When his coaster was unloaded he had to go out on another trip, for he feared arousing suspicion even by a day's delay. Sometimes during a week's stay, or more, he could only manage one visit—no more. He suffered through his fears as much as through his prudence. To do things by stealth humiliated him. And he suffered most from the concentration of his thought upon the treasure as thought becomes concentrated upon a vision of horror and pain. Never did his unblemished reputation appear more vividly as a matter of life and death.

A transgression, a crime, entering a man's existence eats it up like a malignant growth, consumes it like a fever. Nostromo cursed often the silver of the San Tomé Mine, and cast black looks at Charles Gould when he happened to pass him on the other side of the street. He hated the feel of the touch of the ingots. After handling them, with the door of his cabin on board the schooner locked, he looked fixedly at his fingers, as [if] surprised they had left no stain on his skin.

He had found means of disposing of them in distant ports. This is what made his coasting voyages long, and caused his visits to the Viola household to be rare and far between. He was fated to have his wife from there. He had said so once to Giorgio himself. But the old man had put the question aside with a majestic wave of his hand, clutching a smouldering black briar-root pipe. There was plenty of time; he was not going to force his girls upon anybody.

As time went on he discovered his preference for the younger of the two. This must have been owing to some profound similarities of nature, which must exist for complete confidence and understanding, no matter what outward resemblances of temperament there may be to exercise their own fascination of contrast. His wife would have to know. He was much attracted by Giselle, with candid gaze and white throat, pliable, silent, a lover of indolence and excitement; whereas Linda, with her intense, passionately pale face, energetic, all fire, and words touched with gloom and scorn, a chip of the old block, true daughter of the austere republican, but with Teresa's voice, inspired him with a deep-seated mistrust. Moreover, the poor girl could not conceal her love for Gian' Battista. He could see it would be violent, exacting, suspicious, uncompromising—like her soul. Giselle, by her fair but warm beauty, by the surface quietness of her nature holding a promise of submissiveness, by the charm of girlish mysteriousness, excited his passion and allayed his fears as to the future.

His absences from Sulaco were long. On returning from the longest of them he made out that lighters of material were lying under the cliff of the Great Isabel, with cranes and scaffoldings above, workmen's figures moving about, and the small lighthouse already rising from its foundations on the edge of the cliff.

He thought himself lost. What could save him? Nothing! Nostromo, the splendid Capataz, the feared Captain Fidanza, a power in the bosom of secret societies, the republican like the austere Giorgio, and revolutionist in his heart too (but in another manner), was on the point of jumping overboard. This man, subjective almost to madness, looked suicide in the face for something like a quarter of a second. But he never lost his head. He sailed close. He observed that the workmen had no occasion to come near the ravine. He learned in port that no one slept on the island. They all returned to the harbour at sunset in an empty material lighter, towed by a tug. He breathed freely.

Ah! but what afterwards! When a lighthouse-keeper would come to live in the cottage that was being built some 150 yards from the brow of the cliff, and about four hundred from the edge of the ravine! What then?

And the idea came into his head to get old Viola appointed for the post. He would live there with the girls. He loved solitude. He would probably allow no other man on the island.

'I shall be able to visit them every evening if I like. Nobody will be surprised,' he muttered to himself.

And the thing was done. The influence of Captain Fidanza, ex-Capataz de Cargadores, a man famous through the whole extent of the Occidental Republic for his desperate ride to Cayta, was very great; the man saluted publicly with a touch of the fingers on the hat brim by the Señor Administrador of the San Tomé Mine; the man clapped on the shoulder by General Barrios; the man of great and occult power amongst the new element of political life created by the new conditions.

On the day of the grand reception at the Casa Gould Nostromo got into the little boat of his schooner and pulled out of the harbour towards the Great Isabel about the time of sunset. And the brilliant tertulia was just over, the last guests had departed, and the Señor Administrador had gone to his room when Dr Monygham, who had been expected in the evening but had not turned up, arrived, driving along the wood-block pavement under the electric lights of the deserted Calle de la Constitution, and found the great gateway of the Casa still open.

He ran in, dashed up the stairs, and found Basilio, grown fat and sleek, on the point of turning off the lights. The man turned round open-mouthed.

'Don't put out the lights,' commanded the doctor. 'I want to see the Señora.'

'The Señora is in the Señor Administrador's cancillaria,' said Basilio in an unctuous voice. 'The Señor Administrador starts for the mountain in an hour.'

'Is he going to live there altogether?' hissed the Doctor, very low, through his teeth. 'It'll consume him; it'll burn him; it will have him as it had that poor fool, his father.' He turned upon Basilio. 'Go out. Go away altogether.'

And Basilio hastened to obey, full of awe and dread of that evil-minded Doctor. Dr Monygham heard a door close at the further end of the house.

With a measured swish, swish of the long gown, flashing with jewels and the shimmer of silk, with her delicate head bowed as if under the weight of a mass of fair hair in which the silver threads were lost, the 'first lady in Sulaco,' as Captain Mitchell used to describe her, moved along the lighted corrédor, wealthy beyond many great dreams of wealth, considered, loved, respected, honoured, adored, and as solitary as any human being had ever been, perhaps, on this earth.

The Doctor's 'Mrs Gould! One minute!' stopped her with a start at the door of the lighted and empty sala. From the similarity of mood and circumstance the sight of the Doctor standing there all alone amongst the groups of furniture recalled to her emotional memory her unexpected meeting with Martin Decoud; she seemed to hear in the silence the voice of that man, dead miserably so many years ago, pronounce the words, 'Antonia lost her fan here.' But it was the doctor's voice that spoke, a little changed with excitement. She remarked his shining eyes.

'Mrs Gould, you are wanted. Do you know what has happened? You remember what I've told you yesterday about Nostromo. Well, it seems that a lancha, a decked boat, coming from Zapiga, with four negroes in her, passing close to the Great Isabel, was hailed from the cliff by a woman's voice—Linda's, as a matter of fact—commanding them (it's a moonlight night) to go round to the beach and take up a wounded man to the town. The patron (from whom I've heard all this), of course, did so at once. He told me that when they got round to the low side of the Great Isabel they found Linda Viola waiting for them. They followed her; she led them to the cottage; there they found outside, under an open window, Nostromo lying on the ground, with father Viola standing at the corner with his old blunderbuss in his hand, and the other daughter leaning with her forehead against the wall. Linda said, "Take this man up," and Nostromo said, with dread in his voice, "Gently, hombres."

'Seeing who it was two of the negroes went into the cottage (which was lighted), took out a table without ceremony, and on that, after breaking off the legs, they carried him to the lancha, leaving the others motionless where they stood. Only just as they were about to push their boat afloat they heard light footsteps running, and Giselle came flying down to the water. She cried out, "Take me, Gian' Battista! They will shut me up there till I die. Take me, and kill me rather." He said to them, "Let her come on board and sit by me."

'This she did, holding his hand; and all the time they did not exchange a word. They brought him, still on the table, into the first-aid hospital near the harbour, where the accidents are attended to. I was sent for; but it is not me he was asking for. It was you, Mrs Gould. It was you!'

'Me?' whispered Mrs Gould, shrinking a little.

'Yes, you!' the Doctor burst out. 'He begged me—his enemy, as he thinks—to bring you. He has something to say.'

'Impossible!' murmured Mrs Gould.

'He said to me, "Tell her that I, too, have done something to keep the roof over her head," Mrs Gould,' the Doctor pursued, in the greatest excitement. 'I do believe we are to hear something of the lost silver. I believe it! I've always had a sort of feeling that there was just a chance. I do believe he wishes to tell you something about the treasure—the silver which — '

'Oh, no! No!' exclaimed Mrs Gould, in a low voice. 'Isn't it lost and done with? Isn't there enough treasure without it to make everybody in the world miserable?'

The Doctor, amazed, remained still, in a sort of submissive, disappointed silence. At last he ventured, very low:

'And there is that Viola girl, Giselle. What are we to do? It looks as though father and sister did not care — '

Mrs Gould glanced along the corrédor to the door of her husband's study.

'I have a volante here,' the Doctor said. 'If you don't mind getting into that — '

He waited, all impatience, till Mrs Gould re-appeared, having thrown over her dress a grey silk cloak with a deep hood.

It was thus that, cloaked and monastically hooded over her brilliant evening costume, this woman, full of endurance and compassion, stood by the side of the bed on which the once splendid Capataz de Cargadores lay stretched out motionless on his back. The whiteness of sheets and pillows gave a sombre and energetic relief to his bronzed face, to the big, dark, nervous hands, so good on the tiller, upon a bridle, and on the trigger of the revolver, lying open and idle upon a white coverlet.

'She is innocent,' the Capataz was saying in a deep and level voice, as though afraid that a louder word would break the slender hold his spirit still kept upon his body. 'She is innocent. It is I alone. But no matter. For these things I would answer to no man or woman alive.'

He paused. Mrs Gould stood like a statue. Her face, very white within the shadow of the hood, had an air of invincible and dreary sadness. And the low sobs of Giselle Viola, kneeling at the end of the bed, with her gold hair with coppery gleams loose and scattered over the Capataz's feet, hardly troubled the silence of the room.

'Ha! Old Giorgio—the guardian of thine honour! Fancy the viejo coming round so light of foot, so steady of aim. Nostromo himself could have done no better. But the price of a charge of powder might have been saved. The honour was safe. . . . Señora she would have followed to the end of the world Nostromo the thief. . . . I have said the word. The spell is broken!'

A low moan from the girl made him cast his eyes down.

'I cannot see her. . . . No matter,' he went on, with the shadow of the old magnificent carelessness in his voice. 'One kiss is enough, if there is no time for more. An airy soul, Señora! Bright and warm, like sunshine, soon clouded, and soon serene. They would crush it there between them. Señora, cast the eye of your compassion, as far-famed as the courage and daring of the man who speaks to you, from one end of the land to the other. She will console herself with Ramirez. He is not a bad fellow. I am not angry. No! It is not Ramirez who overcame the Capataz of the Sulaco

Cargadores.' He paused, made an effort, and in louder voice a little wildly declared:

'I die betrayed—betrayed by—'

But he did not say by whom or by what he was dying betrayed.

'But she did not,' he began again, opening his eyes very wide, 'she was faithful. We were going away—soon. I could have torn myself away from that accursed treasure for her. For that child I would have left boxes and boxes of it—full. And Decoud took four. Why? Ha! Picardia. To betray me. How could I give back the treasure with four ingots missing? You would have said I had purloined them.'

Mrs Gould bent low as if fascinated by the horror that trembled in her voice.

'Tell me, Nostromo, have you killed Don Martin Decoud for that silver?'

An expression of unutterable scorn came upon that rigid face.

'You are all alike, you fine people. The silver has killed me. It has held me. It holds me yet. Nobody knows where it is. But you are the wife of Don Carlos, who put it into my hands and said: "Save it on your life." And when I returned, and you all thought it was lost, what do I hear? It was nothing of importance. Let it go. Up, Nostromo, the faithful, and ride away to save us, for dear life!'

'Nostromo!' Mrs Gould whispered, bending very low. 'I, too, have been guilty of deception about that very silver.'

'Marvellous!' breathed out the Capataz, with an imperceptible irony. 'Señora, nobody knows where it is. It is lost!'

His transgression had eaten up his life, seemed to have decomposed, corrupted his personality. A grimace of effort and pain settled on his face.

'Shall I tell you where it is to be found? Is it your wish? I will try to.'

Mrs Gould averted her head in obscure sympathy, in dread, in pity:

'No, Capataz,' she said. 'Let it be lost for ever.'

After hearing these words Nostromo closed his eyes; answered no word, made no movement. At the door of the room Dr Monygham, excited to the highest pitch, his eyes shining with eagerness, ran up to her:

'Now, Mrs Gould,' he said, almost brutally in his impatience, 'tell me, was I right? There is a mystery. You have got the word, have you not? He told you — '

'He told me nothing,' said Mrs Gould steadily.

'Ah!' The light of his temperamental enmity to Nostromo went out of Dr Monygham's eyes. He stepped back submissively. He did not believe Mrs Gould. Her word was law. He accepted her will like an inexplicable fatality affirming the victory of Nostromo's genius over his own. Even before that woman, whom he loved with secret devotion, he had been defeated by the magnificent Capataz de Cargadores, the man who had lived his own life on the assumption of unbroken fidelity and courage!

'Pray send your volante for my carriage,' spoke Mrs Gould from within her hood. Then turning to Giselle Viola, 'Come near me, child; come closer. We will wait here.'

Giselle Viola, heartbroken and childlike, her face veiled in her falling hair, crept closer and closer. Mrs Gould slipped her hand through the arm of the unworthy daughter of old Viola, the immaculate republican, the hero without a stain. Slowly, gradually, as a withered flower droops, the head of the girl who would have followed a thief to the end of the world, rested on the shoulder of Doña Emilia, the first lady in Sulaco, wife of the Señor Administrador of the San Tomé Mine. And Mrs Gould, feeling the suppressed sobbing, nervous and excited, had the first and only movement of cynical bitterness in her life:

'Console yourself, child. Very soon he would have forgotten you, living by his side, for his treasure.'

On seeing his youngest daughter run and disappear in the night, old Viola dropped the gun from his nerveless fingers. Linda, rigid, silent, helped him into the house, then stepped back and looked at her father, with her coal-black eyes blazing in the light of the lamp, with her long face of passionate whiteness, where her red lips seemed like an open wound.

The old Garabaldino looked around; moved three steps with difficulty, and sat down in a chair.

'Give me the book,' he said with an inflexible calm.

'And is the book of avail to you?' she asked.

'Yes,' said the old man, austerely.

She laid it, closed, before him in its worn leather cover, the Bible given him years, ages ago by an Englishman in Palmero [*sic*].

'Where are you going?' he asked mournfully.

'To the light,' she answered in a dead voice, looking at him balefully.

'Si—duty,' he mumbled.

He felt in the pocket of his red flannel shirt for his spectacles, sitting very upright, white haired, leonine, heroic in his terrible quietness. The spectacles given him by Doña Emilia. How could he ever show his face before the English señora? Dishonoured! Disgraced!

Methodically he put on the silver-rimmed glasses, then opened the Book, and looked at the pages of small print in double columns. He looked at them from on high, then fell slowly forward. He fell, rugged, robust, undecayed, like an old oak uprooted by a tempest. His face rested on the open pages, his hands seemed to steady him, spread out and gripping the edges of the table. A wooden clock, of German make, was ticking on the wall; and growing slowly cold the old Garibaldino lay alone, uprooted by the tempest.

It was a moonlight night, and in the wide and placid gulf the light of the Great Isabel burned peacefully above the lost treasure of San Tomé, like bright beacon upon the shoals of crime and corruption. In the cold, bluish sheen of the starless night the lantern was full of a warm yellow glow, on which a black speck might have been detected from afar. It was Linda, crouching in the outside gallery, on her knees, her forehead resting against the rail. She did not move. And the moon from the west seemed to look at her radiantly.

Linda stood. Her black figure detached itself on the lighted background, erect, tense, narrow, with the arms flung up above her head as though she were going to throw herself headlong into the sea.

'Ah! She shall not have thee, Battistino my own,' she whispered madly. 'She shall not have thee. And she will forget thee miserably killed at her feet. But I, unhappy, shall never forget thee. Never!'

Her voice had been rising to the word never. She seized the rail with a convulsive clutch, and leaning out her body, with her face like marble in the moonlight, she cried out in her pain, with a piercing voice, 'Gian' Battista!'

From the deep head of the gulf, full of black vapour, and walled by immense mountains from Punta Mala round to the west of Aznexa, where the obscure gringos, dead in life and living in death, guard the legendary treasure, out upon the ocean with a bright line marking the illusory edge of the world, where a great white cloud hung brighter than a mass of silver in the moonlight, in that cry of a longing heart sending its never-ceasing vibration into a sky empty of stars, the genius of the magnificent Capataz de Cargadores dominated the place.

EXPLANATORY NOTES

THE following notes treat historical and mythical places, events and figures, references to South American culture, and phrases in foreign languages which are too complicated for the glossary. They record some of Conrad's most interesting sources, and both his main emendations of E¹ and his main additions to the late episodes of the serial.

E¹	*Nostromo* (London and New York, Harper and Bros.), 1904
E²	*Nostromo* (London, Dent), 1918
E³	*Nostromo* (London, Heinemann), 1921
CE	*Nostromo*, Collected Edition (Dent), 1947
Eastwick	*Venezuela: Sketches of Life in a South American Republic* (London), 1868
Masterman	*Seven Eventful Years in Paraguay* (London), 1869
Sherry	*Conrad's Western World* (Cambridge), 1971
Watts	(ed.) *Joseph Conrad's Letters to Cunninghame Graham* (Cambridge), 1969
TPW	*T. P. O'Connor's Weekly*

xl *last story*: 'To-morrow', finished in January 1902.

xli *shabby volume*: identified by Mr John Halverson and Ian Watt as Frederick Benton William's *On Many Seas: The Life and Exploits of a Yankee Sailor* (1897); Cp. 'The Original Nostromo: Conrad's Source', *Review of English Studies* X, no. 37 (1959), 45–52.

xlv *Dominic*: Dominic Cervoni in *The Mirror of the Sea* (1906).

xlvi *my first love*: the original (if she ever existed) is the subject of much biographical speculation. Frederick R. Karl's *The Three Lives* contains a full discussion (101–4).

xlviii *so foul . . . a storm*: *King John*, IV. ii. 108.

3 *Costaguana*: coast of bird-dung, of 'palm' and 'palm leaves'. As Costaguana's flag is 'diagonal red and yellow, with two green palm trees in the middle' (121), and as palms and their uses are often mentioned, the latter meaning may be more important.

5 *gringos*: foreigners. The term originally applied to English-speaking (usually American) foreigners.

Cordillera: the most western of Colombia's mountain ranges is called the Cordillera Occidental.

9 *Juno*: wife of Jupiter. She was worshipped as queen of heaven, considered the patroness of womanhood, and, as one of the great goddesses of the Roman state, she was revered as guardian of finances. Under the title Moneta (*It.*) she had a temple which contained the mint.

Saturn: Roman god of sowing or of seed corn and father of Juno and Jupiter, noted for his misanthropic gloom.

10 *Ganymede*: son of Tros, King of Troy. Because of his exceeding beauty he was carried off by Zeus to serve as his cup-bearer. His childishly pretty figure is a favourite in Hellenistic and later literature and art.

Cerberus: hydra-headed monster which guarded the entrance to Hades.

12 *Minerva*: Roman goddess of wisdom and good counsel, identified with the Greek Pallas Athena.

13 *Capataz de Cargadores*: overseer of the dockers.

17 *Gian' Battista*: John the Baptist. He prophesied the coming of Jesus.

20 *conquest of Sicily*: on 5 May 1860 Garibaldi (1807–82) and his Thousand Red Shirts sailed from Genoa to Sicily. On 20 July the Neapolitans were forced to evacuate all of Sicily, except Messina.

24 *Cavour*: Count Camillo Benso di Cavour (1810–61). Italian states-man dedicated to the liberation and regeneration of Italy. Cavour believed in a constitutional monarchy as opposed both to despotism and Republicanism. He submitted to Garibaldi's invasion of Sicily (1860), but opposed his plans to liberate Naples, and to march upon Rome. Cavour's decision (1859) to cede Nice (Garibaldi's birthplace) to Louis Napoleon, in return for the latter's support for Piedmontese plans to annex central Italy, placed further strains on his relations with Garibaldi.

25 *Maldonado*: town in SE Uruguay.

Spezzia: port in NW Italy.

un uragano terribile: a frightful hurricane.

26 *white hair*: as *Sherry* demonstrates Conrad 'actually based Viola's appearance and character upon Garibaldi as an old man' (157–8).

29 *navy of Montevideo*: Garibaldi led a small flotilla to oppose Rosas's forces. When his ammunition was exhausted he burned his ships and escaped.

Italian legion: formed after the loss of his flotilla. His legion won the battles of Cerro and Sant' Antonio in the spring of 1846 and assured the freedom of Uruguay.

Rosas: Juan Manuel de Rosas (1793–1877), Dictator of Argentina (1829–32, 1835–52). He followed an expansionist policy. In the factional strife in Uruguay he supported the Blancos led by Oribe against the Colorados led by Rivera. From 1843–51 Montevideo was besieged by Oribe. During the period of the blockade French and British troops occupied Uruguayan territories as a check to Rosas.

The siege was finally abandoned and the Colorado government remained in power.

Aspromonte: in March 1862 Garibaldi came out of retirement to organize the Society for the Emancipation of Italy. His aim was to oust the French troops from Rome and thus strengthen the newly founded Kingdom of Italy (1861) which he had done much to promote. Defying his own government, he raised the cry of 'Rome or Death', and in the Battle of Aspromonte, 29 Aug. 1862, he and his troops were defeated by government forces. Garibaldi was wounded and captured, and amnestied soon after (5 Oct.).

30 *Palermo*: on 27 May 1860 Garibaldi and his Thousand Red Shirts took Palermo and set up a provincial government.

Samuel: *Sherry* (156) demonstrates that Conrad borrowed these unlikely details concerning Samuel from Garibaldi's *Autobiography*.

31 *in the defence of the Roman Republic*: in the spring and summer of 1849, Garibaldi fought to expel the French from Rome. Besieged, Garibaldi made terms with the French and marched forth with some 5,000 men on his famous retreat pursued by the armies of Spain, France, Austria and Naples. Almost all were presently killed (including Anita his wife), captured or dispersed. Garibaldi escaped, after dramatic adventures, to Piedmont and then New York.

Volturno: on 26 Oct. 1860 Garibaldi again defeated the Neapolitans.

34 *Sta Marta*: Santa Marta, coastal town in Northern Columbia, fronting the Caribbean.

42 *hidalgos*: originally referred to members of the lesser Spanish nobility or gentry, many of whom sought fame and fortune in Latin America in the period of the conquest and colonization.

43 *Captain Mitchell's mispronunciation*: it is generally presumed that Captain Mitchell mispronounces 'nostro uomo', 'our man'. Roger L. Cox disputes the standard reading and reminds us that 'nostromo' is the Italian for 'boatswain' derived from the Spanish 'nostramo' or 'nuestramo' meaning 'our master'. Both meanings are possible. Cp. Cox, 'Conrad's Nostromo as Boatswain', *Modern Language Notes* 74 (1959), pp. 303–6.

47 *Bolívar*: Simon Bolívar (1783–1830), South American soldier, statesman and revolutionary leader. Born in Caracas of distinguished Creole parents he was instrumental in the independence of Peru and the formation of the republic of Bolívar. Interestingly, Bolívar retired to and died in Santa Marta in 1830.

Carabobo: on 24 June 1821 the united forces of Bolívar and Paez defeated the Spanish royalists and thus assured Venezuelan independence. *Eastwick* recounts a visit to the battlefield (Ch. XI).

48 *cantering*: Conrad said in a letter to Cunninghame Graham (31 Oct. 1904): 'But the mistake is in the word *canter* which I wrote persistently while I really meant *amble*, I believe. I am appalled simply.' *Watts*, p. 158.

Charles IV: King of Spain, 1748–1819. Conrad is referring to Manuel Tolsa's (1757–1816) famous bronze equestrian statue in Mexico City (1803). One authority states: 'Royalty never wore a more silly aspect than in the person of Charles IV.'

50 *corrédor*: the accent is incorrect.

52 *pronunciamentos*: a Latin-American phenomenon of the nineteenth and twentieth centuries—a military *coup d'état* or take-over attempt.

53 *fourth in six years*: the serial reads 'the thirteenth in six years', *TPW*, 12 Feb. 1904, p. 205.

55 *Pas moyen . . . sac*: 'Forget it, old son. Pity all the same. Oh damn! I do not steal from my pals. Me—I'm no minister. You can take your present away.'

Allez . . . la pilule: 'Go on and say this to your bloke—understand? You'll have to swallow the pill.'

57 *lecture*: curiously Conrad appears to use the word in the French sense of 'reading', 'perusal'.

60 *Lucca*: town in NW Italy.

68 *Ceres*: Italian fertility goddess and patron of the corn trade.

69 *flor . . . buena*: literally, Christmas Eve Flower.

76 *Atacama nitrate fields*: stretches 600 miles from Copiapo, Chile to Arica in Peru. Their development led to 'The War of the Pacific' (1879–83) between Chile, Peru and Bolivia, which Chile won.

77 *I guess*: Avrom Fleishman notes: 'in the early history of attempts to build a Panama Canal, there is a . . . similar figure, the "mystical and imaginary New York capitalist" Fred. M. Kelley who declared: "Seven years ago my thoughts were directed to this field of honorable enterprise and investigation by HIM who directs the minds of man to what does good or confers distinction, and I have laboured ever since . . . to accomplish what seemed to be quite in accordance with the arrangement of providence."' *Conrad's Politics*, p. 170.

78 *Persona non grata*: an unacceptable person.

86 *my soul*: Conrad apologized to Cunninghame Graham (31 Oct. 1904) for this curious detail: '*Mi alma* is a more serious mistake. I've heard a little girl so address a pet small dog as they swung in a hammock together. What misled me was this, that in Polish that very term of

endearment: "My Soul" has not the passionate significance you point out. I am crestfallen and sorry.' *Watts*, pp. 157–8.

89 *and thieves*: Conrad's first omission from the serial of any consequence provides a powerful gloss upon 'poor Costaguana':

> Young Mrs. Gould took these impressions avidly. . . . She saw the beggars on the steps of the churches besieging the doors of the house of God and the gates of the dwellings of men; they murmured blessings on her charity in resigned voices. At the halting places Don Pepe used to fling out through the door what remained after the meal of the pile of tortillas, and the skinny, dreadful old hags, ragged men, women with hopeless faces, and thin, naked children, stooped to gather this harvest of food out of the dust of the road.
>
> Those were the very poor, the starving fringe outside the body of the people that worked in towns and upon the estancias; and the great, empty vastness of the landscape made their existence incredible and their state appear hopeless, for this was not a question of room to live in. Was the remedy for that, too, in the development of material interests? Charles seemed to hug that belief in his taciturn and observing reserve. He was looking for workmen, and that was proof enough of his theory.
>
> *TPW*, 26 Feb. 1904, 270

90 *Mozart*: Pedro is wrong of course. The opera is by Donizetti (1798–1848).

94 *peyne d'oro* (It.): literally a golden comb. Conrad borrowed the term from *Masterman* who notes that in Paraguay it referred to 'a woman of lower class' (p. 22).

97 *Paez*: José, soldier and statesman. He was President (1830–46) of the newly founded State of Venezuela. He fought with Bolívar against the royalist forces of Spain 1818–22.

100 *primero . . . tercero*: first, second and third.

102 *Sí! . . . Norte*: 'Yes! Yes! A North American woman.'

103 *muy . . . maravillosa*: very pure and marvellous.

104 *yerba*: in Mexican means marijuana. Conrad probably follows *Masterman* who uses the term to describe 'the native tea' (24).

105 *paradise of snakes*: *Eastwick*, after describing a succession of abandoned and beautiful plantations, wryly remarks: 'were it not for snakes, insects, a vertical sun, fever, and a too rank crop of liberty, this valley would be Paradise' (207).

111 *brief . . . authority*: a Shakespearian echo. 'But man, proud man, Dressed in a little brief authority.' *Measure for Measure*, ii. ii. 117–18.

120 *I drink . . . pounds*: *Eastwick* is the source for this anecdote (95–6).

123 *cana*: distilled treacle. *Masterman* describes it as 'a vile spirit when unrectified, which it generally is, of a disgusting smell'. 'The English mechanics in Asuncion, with the usual recklessness and improvidence of their class, consumed it in enormous quantities and the death of nearly half the number could be traced directly or indirectly to its abuse' (58).

   gombo: called 'the gomba' in *Masterman* who describes it as 'an immense Indian drum . . . beaten in turns by hundreds of willing hands' (49).

124 *Albergo d'Italia Una*: Inn of Italian Unity.

126 *the mare*: Conrad wrote to Cunninghame Graham (31 Oct. 1904) re. Nostromo: 'As to his conduct generally and with women in particular I only wish to say that he is not a Spaniard or S. American. I tried to differentiate him even to the point of mounting him upon a mare which I believe is not or *was not* the proper thing to do in Argentina; though in Chile there was never much of that nonsense.' *Watts*, p. 157.

136 *Cortez*: Hernando (1485–1547). Spanish soldier, the conqueror of Mexico (1519–21). Montezuma received him with great pomp, and his subjects, believing Cortez to be a descendant of the sun, prostrated themselves before him. Charles V (1500–58) appointed him governor and captain-general of Mexico. Cortez's successes reflected his genius, valour, and profound, but unscrupulous, policy.

139 *Collegio*: the meaning is not entirely clear. *Colegio* (Sp.) means college, school, or seminary.

142 *twelve years of peace*: said to be 'a whole fifteen years' on p. 115.

   from over the sea: the following sequence, omitted from the serial, may help to clarify the aims and methods of the Ribierists:

   Meantime Charles Gould in riding breeches and leggings (just down 'from the mountain'), his Norfolk coat unbuttoned, had stooped to pick up the hat and newspaper dropped by Avellanos— the just arrived number of the Sta. Marta 'Diario Official.' It contained, printed in heavy type on the first page, the proclamation of the so-called Mandate law of Don Vincente's Dictatorship. Charles Gould ran his eye curiously over the text. . . .

   The Señor Administrador of the Gould concession was pleased with the wording of the Five-year Mandate, which suspended the fundamental laws of the estate, but at the same time aimed at keeping private ambitions from interfering in the work of economical reconstruction. . . . This was not politics; it was the common-sense watchword of material interests which, once established, would safeguard the honest working of these political institutions which, sound in themselves, had been the shield of plundering demagogues.

TPW, 13 Mar. 1904, p. 370

144 *Cordova University*: in Cordoba, S. Spain.

145 *six months*: on pp. 34 and 130 said to be eighteen months. Perhaps an example of Conrad's carelessness; but the following pages suggest we are meant to assume the Monterist revolt smouldered before it caught fire.

151 *Herédia*: José Maria Herédia y Campuzano (1803–39), Cuban poet and patriot. In 1823 he was arrested on a charge of conspiracy against the Spanish government, and was sentenced to banishment for life. He took refuge first in the United States, and then became a naturalized Mexican. He is regarded as one of the greatest Spanish-American poets of the nineteenth century.

152 *Semenario*: weekly paper. Semanario is correct Spanish.

indifferentism: the theory that all religious systems are equally valuable and valid.

153 *un grotesque . . . féroce*: a vain and ferocious grotesque.

connaissait . . . à fond: he has a thorough understanding of the question.

une . . . hein?: a good joke, eh?

C'est funambulesque: That's bizarre.

155 *eight years since*: perhaps the main inconsistency in the novel. As we know Guzman Bento ruled for at least 'twelve years' (142) and his death was followed by 'the long turmoil of pronunciamentos' (52). The inconsistencies spawned by Decoud's memory of the Avellanos family and the curve of Don José's career must, surely, have been apparent to Conrad. In the serial Decoud is said to have known Antonia 'ten years ago' (*TPW*, 25 Mar. 1904, p. 402). Thus Conrad, even in revision, is less concerned to make his characters' case-histories either consistent with each other or with an overall chronology, than he is to render Decoud's behaviour believable.

156 *Magellan's Straits*: the waterway at the extreme southern tip of South America which separates the mainland from Tierra del Fuego.

158 *Pro Patria!*: For my country.

159 *the Porvenir*: the *Future*.

161 *Amarilla*: *Eastwick* recounts how, at a banquet, he thanked the politicians for the gift of an amarilla—'Viva la Amarilla'—unaware 'that yellow was the colour of the party in power' (76).

Juarez: Benito Pablo (1806–72), Mexican statesman, elected president in 1861. His decree of July 1861, suspending for two years all payments of public debts of every kind, led the French to declare war in 1862, and Maximilian was made Emperor. Juarez maintained an obstinate resistance and was elected president again in 1867.

162 *monte*: a Spanish and Spanish-American game of chance played with forty-five cards.

163 *mais . . . tenue*: but he has no breeding.

166 *"Le sort . . . jeté"*: the die is cast.

Si, . . . niña: Yes, to the house. Yes, yes, girl. Correct Spanish would have an accent—Sí. Si (unaccented) means either 'himself', 'herself', 'itself'.

168 *Great Pompey*: Gnaeus Pompeius (106–48 BC), Conqueror of Spain, Africa, and Asia. Member of the first Roman triumvirate. He refused the senate's order to disband his army (50 BC) and was defeated by Caesar at Pharsalia in 48 BC.

173 *Chapter Five*: in the *Nostromo* MS the first thirteen pages of this chapter, which comprised the eleventh instalment of the serial, are written in Ford Madox Ford's hand, and this fact has led to speculation about Ford's contribution overall. Of this period Ford wrote:

> Whilst I was living in London with Conrad almost next door . . . he was taken with so violent an attack of gout and nervous depression that he was quite unable to continue his installments of *Nostromo*. . . . I therefore simply wrote enough from time to time to keep the presses going—a job that presented no difficulty to me. . . . But to argue from that that I had any large share in Conrad's writing would be absurd.
>
> Quoted in Karl's *The Three Lives*, p. 558.

As ever with Ford, a notorious romancer, it is impossible to sort out the wheat from the chaff. He may dismiss as 'absurd' that he had 'any large share' in the writing of *Nostromo*, but he, slyly, emphasizes Conrad's condition ('he was quite unable') and conceitedly declares his capacity for a task 'which presented no difficulty to me'. That a tiny part of the MS is in Ford's handwriting does not, of course, prove Ford wrote it because Conrad may have dictated it.

The issue of Ford's contribution is, clearly, too complex for a footnote. I am inclined to believe, however, that Ford wrote some of this sequence because Decoud especially rings false on occasion ('But to return to my noises'), and because when Conrad revised the serial for the book publication he cut out over 100 words which remind me of Ford at his most facile. For example of Antonia we read 'she was with a sort of reasonable ardour, justifying her father really'. *TPW*, 8 April 1904, p. 467.

174 *morions and corselets*: respectively, a kind of helmet without beaver

or visor, and a piece of armour to protect the body.

176 *Quelle farce!*: what a farce!

177 *gran' bestia*: great beast. *Masterman* refers to the tyrant, Lopez, as 'el gran' bestia' (301).

180 *Corday*: Marie Anne Charlotte Corday D'Armont (1768–93). French revolutionary heroine who murdered Marat in 1793. Brought before the Revolutionary Tribunal she gloried in her act; and, when asked to reply to the indictment against her, answered: 'Nothing, except that I have succeeded.' She was guillotined on 17 July.

Intrada de la Sombra: Entrance to shade seating at (say) a bullfight. Correct Spanish is *Entrade*.

188 *Esprit fort*: free thinker.

193 *Monsieur l'Administrateur*: Mr Administrator.

199 *C'est trop beau*: It's too beautiful.

204 *that*: extremely obscure because Conrad omitted some 100 words from the magazine version in which Hirsch 'dolefully' castigates 'the preposterous export duties' on hides; and confesses he has 'made a confidential arrangement with the Collector of Customs'. *TPW*, 22 April 1904, p. 530.

210 *was . . . bejewelled hand*: evidently these details bothered Conrad. E^1 and E^2 read 'was steadying herself with a little bejewelled hand against the lintel of the door' (176, 181); E^3 corrects 'lintel' and reads 'against the side of the door' (198). This is the only instance when E^2, E^3, and *CE* all differ.

213 *Non . . . perdu*: No, Madame. Nothing is lost.

222 *circumvallation*: a rampart or entrenchment constructed round any place by way of investment or defence.

237 *Duc de Morny*: Charles Auguste Louis Joseph de Morny (1811–65). Half-brother of Louis Napoleon, he helped to engineer the *coup d'état* of 2 December 1851. He was rewarded with the Ministry of the Interior. The liberal traditions which he had retained enabled him to serve the imperial cause by his influence with the leaders of the opposition. Instrumental in laying the foundations of the 'Liberal Empire'.

sort of Napoleon: Charles Louis Napoleon Bonaparte, Napoleon III (1808–73). Third son of Louis Bonaparte, brother of Napoleon I. His liberal ideals were confused with his dream of restoring the Napoleonic dynasty. On 10 December 1848 he was elected President of the French Republic. After the *coup d'état* of 1851 he became Emperor in 1852, presiding over a brilliant court. His Empire fell on 4 September 1870 during the disastrous Franco-Prussian War.

248 *sœur chérie*: dear sister.

261 *recrudescence*: recurrence, especially of disease or evil.

289 *binnacle*: box containing a compass on a ship's deck by the helm.

290 *su merced*: your mercy.

292 *transom*: beam across sternpost.

293 *fluke*: pointed triangular end on each arm of an anchor.

303 *taffrail*: rail round stern of ship.

322 *Viva la Libertad*: Long live Liberty.

324 *comic*: E¹ reads 'wearisome' (303).

329 *hochwohlgeboren herren*: O most noble lords.

340 *the children*: *Sherry* notes that the dying plea of Garibaldi's wife was 'Giuseppe—the children!' (154).

354 *Others became*: the twenty-seventh episode of the serial which begins here and ends 'the Assembly's deputation' (367) was the first to be considerably expanded—by 600 words, or over a sixth. The *main* additions are: 'Others became . . . rabble' (354); '"you have . . . the stream"' (357); 'They cowered . . . blankets' (359); 'At that moment . . . satisfaction' (361–2); 'It was . . . judgment' (364); 'This resolution . . . his ship' (365–66).

361 *orison*: E¹ and E³ read 'oration'.

   partida: band, party. Correct Spanish would end in 'o'.

367 *His position*: episode 28 of the serial begins here and ends 'own safety too' (378). The main additions are: 'His position . . . insect' (367); 'It was a . . . of failure' (370); 'He would dream . . . a heavy meal' (372); 'This aptitude . . . cruel aspersion' (373); 'It was . . . necessarily simple' (375); 'What could . . . upon him' (376).

385 *their hats*: *Eastwick* is the source for this striking detail and for the incident itself (195).

   popular lore: Conrad's main additions to episode 29 are: 'The popular lore . . . their hands' (385–6); 'This will . . . the lower' (387).

387 *the books of Imbert de Saint Amand*: presumably Pedro is referring to the last six volumes of *Les Femmes des Tuileries* published during 1897–9. This suggests a charting of the novel's events which is totally inconsistent with the chronology suggested by either Giorgio's or Gould's careers.

390 *In the intervals*: the thirtieth episode of the serial begins here and ends 'of the mine' (401). Conrad expanded the serial by nearly a fifth (700 words). The main additions are: 'Every moment . . . that, too' (392–3); 'His bare feet . . . peeling face' (393); 'The sunset rays . . . crevices' (394); 'They invested . . . creations', 'Politics . . . whatever'

(398); 'The working . . . dispensation', 'Whenever . . . profoundly' (399).

405 *Caesarism*: absolutism in government.

413 *dead yet*: Conrad cut a 600-word sequence from E[1] (348–50) which briefly describes Nostromo's earlier career as 'a first-rate boatswain' and dwells over-explicitly on his vanity: 'Each man must have some temperamental sense by which to discover himself. With Nostromo it was vanity of an artless sort. Without it he would have been nothing' (349–50).

414 *last dollar*: said to be 'a quarter dollar', p. 247.

416 *rich people*: Conrad wisely cut 250 words from E[1] (352–3) which suggested Nostromo could flee Costaguana on 'an Italian barque' anchored in the harbour. The passage describes man as 'short-sighted in good and evil'—a phrase Conrad retains in his 'Author's Note' (xlii).

lateen sails: type of triangular sail for small boats.

417 *death itself*: Conrad cut the following sequence from E[1] (353–4):

> And no wonder—with no intellectual existence or moral strain to carry on his individuality, unscathed, over the abyss left by the collapse of his vanity; for even that had been simply sensuous and picturesque, and could not exist apart from outward show. He was like many other men of southern races in whom the complexity of simple conceptions is much more apparent than real.

418 *The cry*: to 'for a time' (418–19) added to the serial.

421 *palmarias*: no such word in Spanish. Conrad seems to have meant *palmeras*, i.e. palm trees.

432 *Machiavellian*: byword for political cunning. After Niccolò Machiavelli (1469–1527), Italian statesman and writer. Author of *The Prince*, completed 1513.

441 *muy valliente*: very brave. Correct Spanish is *valiente*.

444 *y hombres de muchos dientes*: man of many teeth. Conrad wrote to Cunninghame Graham 'you must (generously) forgive me for stealing and making use . . . of your excellent 'y dentista' anecdote'. *Watts*, p. 155.

449 *into his face*: *Sherry* argues (158–61) that Conrad's source for this incident is to be found in Garibaldi's *Autobiography*.

464 *off again*: devotees of 'the secret sharer' theme in Conrad's fiction will be pleased to learn that the serial continues: 'Those two men seemed unable to part. They walked together till . . .' *TPW*, 23 September 1904, p. 389.

470 *To save the children*: to 'over my head' (471) plus 'And she . . . and then?' (471) are additions to the serial.

479 *Très de Mayo coffee*: this date is a precious one in Polish history. The Constitution of the Third of May (1791) embodied democratic reforms which were annihilated by a confederacy of Polish magnates backed and financed by Catherine the Great, which led in 1793 to the second Partition of Poland.

486 *Pallas*: presumably Pallas Athena the Greek goddess of wisdom and good counsel, see note to p. 12. Pallas is also the name of the villainous manumitted slave of Claudius's mother, who persuaded Claudius to marry Agrippina the younger (AD 49) and then abetted her in poisoning his master.

487 *Powhattan*: Algonquin Indian chief in Virginia (1550?–1618). He was the father of Pocahontas, who, according to John Smith, adventurer and self promoter, happily pleaded for the preservation of his handsome personage. Conrad's inclusion of this incident probably relates to his reaction to the revolution (3 Nov. 1903), in the Colombian province of Panama. On 26 December 1903 Conrad wrote to Cunninghame Graham: 'And à propos what do you think of the Yankee Conquistadores in Panama? Pretty isn't it?' *Watts* (p. 149). The revolution was backed by the United States who despatched warships to both the Atlantic and Pacific ports of Panama, and was the first country to recognize the 'independence' of the new country. The next step in 1904 was to persuade the grateful nation to cede the Canal Zone to America on a perpetual lease. In 1911 Theodore Roosevelt spoke like a character out of *Nostromo* when he said of the seizure of the Canal Zone: 'Every action taken was not merely proper but was carried out in accordance with the highest, finest and the nicest standards of public and governmental ethics.'

488 *sixteen days since the sinking of the silver*: a slight error—on p. 483 Mitchell says that it took 'twelve days' in all for Nostromo to ride to Cayta and Barrios to return, by sea, with the troops. As Nostromo's journey began the day after the alleged sinking of the silver the actual time was thirteen days.

492 *gunwale*: upper edge of boat's side.

thwart: seat for oarsman.

497 *In our activity*: to 'weakness' (498) is an addition to the serial.

498 *this cord would snap*: a play on Decoud's name. *Découdre* (Fr.) means to unstitch, unpick, to come unstitched.

502 *He had defeated*: to 'Cordillera' (503) an addition to the serial.

504 *the eleven months*: E[1] reads 'eighteen' (p. 428).

505 *Hermes*: a sly name for 'the latest addition to the O.S.N. Co's

splendid fleet'. In Greek mythology Hermes was at once a fertility god; the messenger or herald of the gods; conductor of the dead to Hades; patron of travellers; deity of good luck and of commerce and gain in general. As the deity of 'material interests' he was renowned for his trickery and cunning.

508 *the Propaganda*: committee of cardinals to organize foreign missions.

510 *Café Lombroso*: named after Dr Caesare Lombroso (1836–1909), an Italian criminologist. He theorized that there was a definite relationship between primitive physical structure and primitive social behaviour. Ossipon in *The Secret Agent* is an advocate of Lombrosian 'science'. Cp. Robert G. Jacob's 'Comrade Ossipon's Favourite Saint: Lombroso and Conrad', *Nineteenth Century Fiction* XXIII (June 1968), 74–84.

519 *immense decision*: except for the paragraph beginning 'Mrs. Gould leaned back . . . ' (520) the remainder of this chapter is an addition to the serial.

523 *Chapter Twelve*: the main additions to the serial in this chapter are: 'All this unexpected . . . had already' (525); 'He was checked . . . the other kind' (525–6); 'containing the secret . . . his very sleep' (526–9); from 'when the project . . . ' to the end of the chapter (529–45).

535 *A frightful danger*: in Gautier's 'Adam' ballet Giselle is associated with the Willis, young women who have died between their betrothal and marriage, and who emerge at night to dance and lure to death any young swain unfortunate enough to fall into their clutches.

546 *Chapter Thirteen*: the main additions to the serial in this chapter are: 'He was later . . . "my little flower"' (546–54); '"Who knows . . . " "I have killed him"' (559); '"Senora, he . . . he repeated"' (561–3); 'He did . . . incomprehensible' (563–4); 'Below at . . . to the rowers' (565–6); 'She stood . . . "Never! Gian' Battista!"'; 'Dr. Monygham . . . of all'; 'the dark gulf . . . treasure and love' (566).

555 *cancillaria*: correct Spanish is *cancilleria*, 'chancellor's office'.

563 *inquiry*: E[1] reads 'of enigmatic and mocking scorn' (477).

GLOSSARY OF FOREIGN TERMS

from the Spanish unless otherwise indicated

I would like to thank Dr D. Clark for her generous help in compiling this glossary.

alameda: promenade, avenue
alcalde: mayor
algarobbe: locust-tree
asado: roast
avanti: forward!

baracoon: shed
bersagliere: sharpshooter
blague (Fr.): practical joke
bolson: lagoon
boulevardier (Fr.) man-about-town
bribon: scoundrel
bueno: good
buon viaggio (It.): good journey

caballeros: gentlemen
Cabildo: Town Hall
calabozo: jail
calle: street
calzoneras: trousers
camerista (It.): maid
camino real: royal highway
camorras: wrangles, disputes
campania: company
campo: countryside
Caramba!: Good Lord!
carreta: crude country cart
casa: house
chemisette (Fr.): short-sleeved shirt
Chica!: For heaven's sake girl!
cholo: half-breed
chulo: common chap
cicala: grasshopper
Cielo!: Heaven help us!
ciudadanos: citizens
compadre: friend
condottiere: mercenary leaders
convite: banquet

cordillera: mountain range
cosas: things

diligencia: stage-coach
Diurio official: official newspaper
dulces: sweets

embustero: trickster, impostor
esclavos: slaves
estancia: ranch
etagère (Fr.): rack, shelf
E vero! (It.): It's true!

felucca (It.): small swift boat
ferro carril: railway
fiscale: prosecuting attorney
frittura (It.): fried fish
fundacion: foundation

El señor Gobanador: The Governor

haciendas: estates
hidalgo: gentleman, nobleman
hijo del pays: son of the country

infame!: the villain!
Intendencia (Argentinian): mayoralty
Islenos: Islanders

jalousies (Fr.): slatted window blinds

ladrones: thief
lanceros: lancers
lanchas: lighters
lazo: lassoo
leperos (Mex.): low class person, villain
llaneros: plain dwellers
llanos: plains

macaques: thieves
Madre de Dios: Mother of God
maladetta (It.): cursed one (female)
manta: shawl, wrap
maté: herbal tea
matreros (South Am.): bandit
mesa: plateau
mi amo: master
mirador: balcony, bay window
misericordia: mercy
misericordia divina!: heavens above!
morenita: little dark girl
moreno: dark man
mozo: young man
muchachos: lads
muy bien: very good

novio: fiancé

opéra-bouffe (Fr.): comic opera
oracion: prayer

paraliticos: paralytics
paramo: moor
pasotrote: trot
picardia: roguery, mischief
picaro: rogue
Plaza Mayor: Main Square
pobrecitos!: poor things!
poncho: cloak, blanket
Por Dios: for heaven's sake
posada: tavern, inn
posadero: innkeeper
potalon: large anchor stone
potreros (South Am.): cattle ranches, pastures
practicante: doctor's assistant

pueblo: village
pulperias: bars

quebrada: ravine
Que picardia!: What treachery!
querido: darling
Quien sabe!: Who knows!
Quien vive?: Who goes there?

rancheros: ranch owner
rebozos: mufflers
ricos: the rich
rio seco: dry river
rubia: blonde
rubianta: little blonde

sala: drawing room
salteador: highwayman
Sanctissima Madre: Most Blessed Mother
Sangre de Dios: Blood of God!
serenos: night watchman
siempre: always
Signori Inglesi (It.): English gentlemen

teniente: lieutenant
tertulia: reunion, gathering
todos: all of them
tolderia: Indian hut
trabuco: blunderbuss
tropilla: herd

va bene (It.): all right
valet de place (Fr.): manservant, usher
vaqueros: cowboys
vecchio: old one
vivas: cheers, hurrahs
volante: carriage

WIDOW FOR HIRE

MARGARET WESTHAVEN

Harlequin Books

TORONTO • NEW YORK • LONDON
AMSTERDAM • PARIS • SYDNEY • HAMBURG
STOCKHOLM • ATHENS • TOKYO • MILAN

Published October 1990

ISBN 0-373-31135-4

Printed in U.S.A.

CHAPTER ONE

"Madam!"

The narrow white face of Higgins, the footman, peeked round the doorway of Amelia's small sitting-room. "I swear I only went to the Swan with Two Necks to collect your ladyship's messages, but—"

"Oh, Higgins, do come all the way in," said Amelia, laughing. "I didn't really expect an answer to my advertisement on the first day. We'll come about, but it's bound to take longer than this for a response."

"But, madam—" Higgins's voice was nearly frantic, and his watery eyes positively bulged as he kept his body hidden behind the door.

"Higgins," said Amelia in a warning tone. Her footman was a loyal creature, one of her best friends, but he was inclined to take disappointment too much to heart, and he was given to outbursts of silliness to alleviate his feelings.

This was evidently one of those times. Higgins appeared to stagger, those prominent eyes nearly popping while his head bobbed up and down. The door creaked, and Amelia frowned in disapproval. She exchanged a glance with Lewes, the abigail, a pretty blonde who sat sewing in the chair by her lady's side.

Before either Amelia or Higgins could say anything more, the door burst open. Amelia stared and nearly jumped out of her seat. Higgins hadn't been acting fool-

ish. He had been holding the door closed against an in-
truder. A tall, almost cadaverous man now strode into the
room, brushing off a last, timid attempt by Higgins to
stay his progress.

"Ah, that's better," said the man. Amelia, overcome
by surprise, was at least reassured that they weren't being
attacked by a common cutpurse, the sort of person she
suspected inhabited this grim lodging-house. The
stranger's clothing, though sadly rumpled, was that of a
gentleman, and his voice was cultivated. Friendly steel-
coloured eyes twinkled from behind a pair of spectacles,
and the man's sparse gingery hair was standing up in a
wild manner.

"Your servant is very protective, ma'am, but when
opportunity strikes, be ready, I always say. And your
advertisement is the opportunity I've waited for. You *are*
Lady J-H?" The gentleman unfurled a copy of the *Gazette* as he spoke, held it far away from his face and read,
"'Widow for hire. A titled dowager with the entrée to
good society would be glad to undertake the chaperonage of a young lady for the coming Season. Enquire Lady
J-H, et cetera.' You placed this, ma'am?"

Higgins had shuffled into the room behind the
stranger, and now he mumbled, before the astonished
Amelia could get a word out, "Sorry, madam. I wanted
to take a message to you from the gentleman, knowing
you'd like to prepare, but the gentleman insisted—
wouldn't even let me come in first to warn you—"

"Don't distress yourself, Higgins," said Amelia. She
laid her white-work down in her lap and held out an unfortunately needle-pricked hand. "I am Lady Jeffries-
Hodge, sir. And now you have the advantage of me."

The strange man approached while Higgins hovered warily in the background and Lewes, startled out of her seat, disappeared into the inner room of the lodgings.

"Sir Ethelred Crane, at your service," said the stranger, bowing over Amelia's hand. "Lady Jeffries-Hodge, a pleasure. I—"

"Pardon me," Amelia interrupted. "Did you say Crane? *The* Sir Ethelred Crane?"

"You've heard of me?" Sir Ethelred's thin chest puffed out ever so slightly.

"I've heard of your work, of course," said Amelia. "And it's a pleasure to meet one of our most noted scientists. But—you must excuse me, sir, it simply seems so odd that *you* should answer my advertisement."

"Why is that?" Sir Ethelred said. With no further ado and without an invitation, he lowered his thin frame into the hard chair lately vacated by Lewes, the only seat in the room besides Amelia's. "You wish to chaperon a young lady, do you not? Well, ma'am, I've a daughter in pressing need of a sponsor this Season. Seems logical to me. Perfectly logical."

Amelia remained silent for a little. She was hard pressed to answer his question. By inserting that audacious advertisement in the paper she had thought to attract the notice of some City papa or mama who would be impressed by the words "title" and "good society" and hire her. Indeed, if no one did hire her she didn't know what she and her two loyal servants were to do next. She could not afford to stay in town much longer, even in these horrid lodgings in this offal-strewn lane in Seven Dials. She had pawned her pearl necklace to get her little ménage to London, and she had no resources left. One could hardly count the needlework she and Lewes had been doing on commission for a nearby seamstress.

Their efforts brought in scarcely enough to keep a bird alive, let alone three hungry adults.

In the year of her widowhood, Amelia had done nothing but think what to do after her small savings ran out, and the best and most lucrative idea she had conceived of was to move to London from her tiny rented cottage in Hampshire, hire herself out as a young lady's sponsor, which would give her and, she hoped, her servants, room and board, and collect the customary fee for such services at the end of the Season. She even understood that a supplemental payment to the chaperon was common if the young lady in question ended the Season suitably betrothed.

"Ma'am?" Sir Ethelred appeared to be vexed by Amelia's extended silence. He was fidgeting in his chair quite like a small boy.

"I—Sir Ethelred, I don't quite know how to say this, but I expected to offer my services to a family of City merchants, perhaps. At any rate to someone without good connections. I know you must move in the highest circles, sir, and I can't believe that someone in your own family wouldn't be more suitable to take charge of your daughter."

"But there's no one, ma'am," exclaimed Sir Ethelred. "Never was a family more short on females. Oh, there's the old party, late wife's cousin, who keeps my house, but she's a homely sort of woman, not fit to act as sponsor to a young girl. I don't have too much to do with Society, mind you, but even I know that appearing under Mrs. Winkle's wing wouldn't give a girl any more distinction than a fly on the wall. And my daughter, ma'am, must do the Season thing if she's to marry. I think, you see, that she's sacrificing herself to me. Means to stay by me and be my hostess, but that won't do. The girl must have her own life, and you, Lady Jeffries-Hodge, must help her."

Amelia was overwhelmed by this flood of words, and she once again took refuge in silence. "I—I have two servants whom I've sworn to provide for," she finally said in a faltering tone. Sir Ethelred's offer seemed too good to be true. She must make all her admissions at once and let him change his mind before she became too set on the plan.

Higgins was standing behind Sir Ethelred, waving his hands and shaking his head as though to warn her not to miss this chance upon his account. She smiled at both him and Sir Ethelred. "Very loyal servants," she elaborated."

Sir Ethelred nodded. "I see nothing out of the way in a lady bringing along her own staff. You would live in my house in Portman Square, ma'am." He looked around the bare, sordid little room. "I'm correct in thinking your circumstances are somewhat straitened? Should be a nice change for you if that's the case."

No, this proposed happy ending was too rosy. Amelia took a deep breath and said, "Sir Ethelred, I must be completely honest with you. Perhaps you didn't catch my name. I am Lady Jeffries-Hodge."

The ominous pause which followed her words was broken by Sir Ethelred's puzzled, "Yes, I heard you. And I've heard the name, ma'am, but can't say in what connection."

"Perhaps you're familiar with a scandal which broke over a year ago, sir. You must have heard of the One-Guinea Widow? It was all over the papers and all over Society when my husband left me the sum of one guinea in his will."

Sir Ethelred looked concerned as he said, "I beg your pardon, ma'am, I don't live much in the world. Perhaps I've heard the tale, but I certainly don't remember. Dashed unkind of your husband to leave you in these circumstances, if you don't mind my saying so." Again he indicated the cheerless room. "There were no relations?"

Amelia shrugged. "My late husband's brother, the present baron, agreed with my husband's opinion of me and tossed me out on my ear the day after the funeral. And as for my family—my father and I haven't spoken since my marriage for, well, personal reasons, but he is Lord Alfred Montresor, seventh son of the old Marquis of Haverstock. You needn't worry about bringing bad blood into your household." She thought a moment, then added, "I still correspond with several friends from my early days in London. During my marriage I spent most of my time in the country; my husband was the one who came to town. But I have no reason to believe I would not be received in the circles I was born to. I must warn you, though, that there could be talk, and as it's your daughter's first Season, such an important time in her life—"

Sir Ethelred held up a long hand to halt her words. "I am prepared to take you on faith, ma'am. I can see you've all the qualities my Calliope requires in a chaperon. You're good-looking and young; bound to bring her out of her shell where some starchy old harridan would only make her lock herself in her room for the Season. Your connections appear to be quite respectable. And the talk? Well, let 'em talk."

Amelia dropped her eyes at these flattering words, hoping Sir Ethelred couldn't guess how young she really was. The widow's cap she affected made her look older, she fondly believed, but she was only four-and-twenty. Though technically a dowager, she couldn't lay claim to a quarter of the typical dowager's dignity.

Sir Ethelred was scrutinizing the young woman who sat before him. What could have made a husband use his wife in such a way? he wondered for an instant before his brain moved on to something else. Sir Ethelred's mind could never keep steadily on anything but his scientific experiments.

He looked at the young woman as though she were an experiment, as she was, in her way. A very neat figure in a shabby black dress. Didn't look to be very tall, and Sir Ethelred admired tall women. In all other respects Lady Jeffries-Hodge was quite the pattern-card of beauty. Her waving black hair escaped to frame her face despite her best efforts to confine it under that dashed cap; and the face itself, a lovely face, if a little pale, was dominated by a pair of large blue eyes.

Sir Ethelred admired Lady Jeffries-Hodge as he might a statue and didn't even consider that having such a lovely woman living in the house might put him in danger. His mind was too much on other things, and so it would remain until the unlikely day he found a female who touched his heart as his late wife had. Somehow he knew that Lady Jeffries-Hodge was not that person.

Lady Jeffries-Hodge was, though, the answer to his prayers. He had to force Calliope out of her study and into the world this Season. The girl was already nineteen and hadn't attended one party since coming out of the schoolroom. Not that Sir Ethelred liked parties. He loathed them, but where else was a girl to meet young men? Lady Jeffries-Hodge could take Calliope about with perfect propriety, leaving Sir Ethelred to the peace of his many projects.

"Well, my lady," he said, giving no further thought to the young woman's confession of what amounted to a scandal in her past, "are we agreed, then? You and your servants will move to Portman Square as soon as possible, and, ah, yes, we must discuss the fee." He searched in the pocket of his coat and came up with a small battered notebook. "I'm a bargain hunter, madam, I don't mind telling you, and before coming here I asked some friends at the club what the going rate is for this kind of service. Where—oh, here it is." He named a sum which made Amelia gasp. "Oh, and of course something by way of our thanks if you fire the girl off successfully. The custom, I'm told."

Amelia, in a shaky voice, was just consenting to the arrangement when Lewes entered the room with a tray of tea things.

"No, no, never take the stuff," said Sir Ethelred, jumping up. Amelia thought his eyes lingered on the cracked crockery and the wooden tray which was only as clean as Lewes could make it. He made his adieux in a rushed manner, leaving his card and saying he would send a carriage for Lady Jeffries-Hodge's party on the morrow.

When the door had closed behind the volatile baronet, Amelia jumped up from her chair and hugged Lewes, then Higgins. "My dears, you needn't look quite so much like surprised fish. It's true! We're saved."

Higgins, who at the best of times did rather resemble a denizen of Neptune's realm, ran a finger under his collar. "I witnessed the whole thing, madam. If the cove—er, the gentleman tries to back out of this, he'll have me to deal with."

Amelia beamed on her two servants. "I've often wished the two of you would go and find employment with someone who could afford to pay you, but now I'm glad we've stayed together. Good times are coming to us, I know it. You will be an abigail again, Nan Lewes, not a maid of all work, and you, Higgins, will lounge about a hallway as a footman should rather than spending all your waking hours trying to bring me in the odd shilling."

"Really, madam," said the quiet Lewes, with a little sniff which called attention to her upturned nose, "as if we ever would have left you. We've been through the worst together, madam, and that don't mean nothing."

"No, it don't—er, does not, and now we'll begin our new lives by having this tea Sir Ethelred couldn't bring himself to touch. Perhaps it's the smell that put him off. What sort of leaves did you put in this time, Lewes?" Amelia sat down to pour, thinking pleasant thoughts of performing the same duty on the morrow in a grand house in Portman Square.

A rare smile crooked the corner of Lewes' mouth. "Don't know, madam, but Higgins brought it back to me from the Park the day we arrived in London."

Higgins shrugged. "Some greenery or other, ma'am, we thought it would dry up and pass for tea. Not much blooming this time of year."

Amelia laughed. "Well, find a third cup, Lewes, and we'll all try it. Didn't you say but a moment ago that we must stand together?"

It was a merry little group that sat down to the unspecified herbal brew. Hope filled each heart as it hadn't since the day Lord Jeffries-Hodge had died.

"Why, ma'am," said Lewes. Good fortune had made the quiet girl quite talkative. "With you out in Society, there's no doubt in my mind that you'll marry again."

Higgins drew in his breath, and Amelia, who had suddenly turned stiff as a poker in her chair, set down her cup with deliberate slowness. "Lewes, you are never to say such things. You know I refuse to marry again, and you, of all people, should know why. I don't care to expose myself in that way again. Ever."

"We quite understand, madam," said Higgins in his best formal voice, casting a disgusted glance at Lewes, who had begun to weep into her apron. "Some of us do, at any rate."

"Of course I understand, m'lady," cried the girl. Her voice was muffled through the apron's folds. "I simply—it's—"

Amelia relaxed somewhat and patted her abigail on the shoulder. "It's London, isn't it? There's such an atmosphere of hope here, of expectation. One can sense it even from this dreadful neighbourhood. I certainly felt it in my first Season, and feel it again now. Yet, even with renewed hope for the future, I cannot allow myself to indulge in wishful thinking. Some doors are closed forever."

"Oh, ma'am," sniffed the abigail, "it's such a shame. You're so young, and your life is—is—"

"Changed," said Amelia. "My life is only changed a little." She looked at Lewes keenly and surmised that the girl was crying not only over her mistress's situation, but her own. The abigail considered that she, as well as her mistress, had no right to marry, and who was Amelia to contradict her?

"I can have a perfectly reasonable, contented life, Lewes. And so can you. We are both so skilled with the needle. Perhaps we'll use my salary to set ourselves up in business in a millinery shop of our own come summer."

Lewes giggled through her tears. "Oh, ma'am," she cried, "that would be ever so pleasant."

The conversation luckily turned to this new plan, which both Amelia and Higgins embroidered upon until all three were laughing so hard their sides ached.

CHAPTER TWO

THE MARCH SUNRISE SEEMED to arrive early at a certain distinguished house in Portman Square, as if in recognition of the fact that Sir Ethelred Crane insisted upon starting the day promptly.

In the wainscotted breakfast room, Sir Ethelred's place had long since been cleared, but two women still sat at table, both ploughing their way in a sensible manner through a breakfast much more substantial than was generally thought acceptable for ladies of fashion.

The elder lady, a stout woman in a fussy purple gown which shouted to the world a lack of care for the newest mode, managed to talk quite actively as she ate. "I can't believe it," she stated for the third time, buttering another muffin while she nodded to an attendant footman to fill her chocolate cup. "Sir Ethelred must be losing his mind at last. All those powders and potions he's always messing about with have finally permeated to his brain, I shouldn't wonder."

Calliope Crane, a slender young lady with flaming red hair and a pretty, pointed face, didn't dignify the older woman's words with an answer. Adjusting her tiny gold-rimmed spectacles on her straight little nose, she went on reading the botanical journal beside her plate and plying her fork.

"Calliope! Are you listening?"

The girl looked up and blinked. "Why, you were questioning Papa's judgement, were you not, Cousin Dorinda?"

Dorinda Winkle sighed and spoke her next words very slowly. "If you, my child, would ever take your nose out of a book long enough to learn what's going on in the world, you would be questioning dear Sir Ethelred's wisdom in this case even as I do. Really! The One-Guinea Widow, to live in this house and take you about for the Season! It's the outside of enough."

Calliope shrugged. "She sounds a rather interesting woman to me. I was afraid he'd find some starched-up dowager with nothing to recommend her but her title."

"You call it interesting for the woman to have so displeased her husband that his will left her a pauper? The rumours that flew about town a year ago, when the contents of the will got out! They say she—" Mrs. Winkle cut off her words abruptly. Calliope might be disturbingly calm and even daunting in those ridiculous spectacles she affected, but she was still a young girl. Not for her ears the story of Lady Jeffries-Hodge, a tantalizing bit of gossip never proven, never spoken of but in whispers.

"Oh, dear," said Calliope with a sigh. "Something shocking, and you can't let it sully my innocent ears. What a dreadful shame. Well, I'm glad Lady Jeffries-Hodge is coming. From what Papa said, she's been reduced to the veriest penury, and it will show charity on our part to welcome her even if we don't like her. I expect I shall, though."

"If she were the most respectable woman in the world—and she's not—the waste of your papa's money! Quite unnecessary, as I should be glad..."

The girl went back to half-listening, making the occasional murmur of interest as she tried to concentrate on her periodical, which described the newest breed of conifer to be introduced to England's shores. There was no use in telling Cousin Dorinda point-blank that she didn't have any claim to fashion, didn't know anyone but her superannuated cronies, and would be of no use to a young girl making her come-out.

Calliope shivered. Her life had come to this! She would be a young lady making her first appearance in Society. The prospect didn't terrify her, but it exasperated her mightily. She knew, though, that for Papa's sake she must give the Season, and the world of young, marriageable men, a fair trial. The article on conifers blurred before her eyes as she contemplated the dismal way in which she would be passing the next months.

The butler entered. "Miss Crane, Madam, Lady Jeffries-Hodge has arrived. I've put her into the morning-room. Shall I have her luggage carried up?"

Calliope stifled a giggle as Mrs. Winkle choked out, "Her luggage! The absolute gall."

"Papa has already said that Lady Jeffries-Hodge is to be made comfortable as soon as she arrives. There are also a couple of servants, I believe, who are to be shown quarters," Calliope said, emphasizing the reference to her father. "You may see to it, Green. We'll go to the morning-room directly."

The butler, a tall individual with eyes that would twinkle when he meant them to be impassive, bowed and left the room. Calliope soon followed him, trailed by a muttering Mrs. Winkle.

In the entry hall Calliope caught a glimpse of two strangers, one likely a maid by her respectable black cloak and straw bonnet worn over a frilled mobcap, one a lanky young man with a receding hairline and bulging eyes whose worn livery proclaimed his profession to be that of a footman. Calliope and Lady Jeffries-Hodge would confer and find occupation for the servants, as Papa had directed. He hadn't mentioned that Mrs. Winkle, his nominal housekeeper, was to be included in the making of that decision, probably because that dame had fussed so at the very notion of having the One-Guinea Widow in the house.

In the morning-room a small, rather forlorn-looking figure in a black pelisse and a substantial widow's bonnet was standing before the fire.

"Lady Jeffries-Hodge?" The woman turned around at the address, and Calliope was shocked to see a face of innocent beauty peeking out from the large black bonnet. "I am Calliope Crane, your charge." For some reason, Calliope wished that her dress were neater and that she were not quite so tall. This lady was so delicate, and her ensemble, though depressingly black in the most dreadful of styles, mysteriously gave the impression that she had been dressed by the first modistes.

Amelia smiled warmly. The girl was pretty; Sir Ethelred hadn't mentioned that. And the family resemblance between Miss Crane and her father struck the eye immediately. They were both so tall, with that bright hair and obviously near-sighted grey eyes. And the fierce-looking old lady who had just stepped to Miss Crane's side, arms folded over a rigid bombazine bodice, must be—

"I am Mrs. Winkle," said the woman in a hard voice. "Miss Crane forgets her manners, but then you are here to attend to that, are you not—my lady?"

Despite a certain degree of familiarity with Society, Amelia hardly knew what to say in response to this. In diplomatic silence, she held out her hand to each lady in turn. So Mrs. Winkle was no cozy housekeeper, but a jealous rival of sorts! Well, the situation would have been too perfect without some such trial.

"I'm so glad you've come," said Calliope. Cousin Dorinda's surliness was bringing out a side of her she hadn't known existed. Calliope never bothered to play hostess or do the pretty, yet here she was motioning Lady Jeffries-Hodge to the best chair in the room, sitting down next to her quite as if she didn't wish to be anywhere else in the world but London at the beginning of the Season.

"Let me leave the two of you to get acquainted," said Mrs. Winkle. Her small dark eyes ran over Lady Jeffries-Hodge, and she shrugged. "I must respect Sir Ethelred's decision," she added, and was gone as quickly as her rather bulky form could manage.

When the door had clicked shut Calliope burst out laughing. "My lady, you must pay no attention to my cousin. She will be a little jealous of you, I'm afraid. She has no title, and no position in Society. She's from Manchester, and since she's come to live with us she has met a few old cats at church and so forth. But she is a bit insulted that even an unworldly sort such as Papa recognises her lack of connections and doesn't consider her fit to take charge of me for the Season."

"I quite understand," said Amelia. She undid her bonnet strings and took off the ponderous widow's headgear, revealing a small, perfectly shaped head of black curls done in a vaguely Grecian topknot.

Calliope all but gasped upon seeing how pretty Lady Jeffries-Hodge really was. A tiny suspicion passed through her mind—but no, Papa had never yet succumbed to feminine charms. As she did with every new acquaintance, Calliope next looked deeply into Lady

Jeffries-Hodge's eyes for some hint of intelligence. Seeming to find what she was seeking in the clear blue depths, she said, "I believe it would be best if we were quite honest with each other, my lady. Chance—or Papa—has thrown us together for a Season, and we won't get far as companions unless we understand one another."

"Why—as you say," said Amelia. She was thoroughly enjoying this odd girl.

Calliope's smile lit her freckled face like sunshine. Much better than that unnerving stare into one's eyes, Amelia thought. "You see, Lady Jeffries-Hodge, Papa has his heart set on my enduring the Season because he has some absurd idea that I wish to marry. Well, I don't, but that's nothing to the purpose. I will go about this Season to please Papa, make no mistake, and you're not to worry that I'll try to hide from Society or play any other tricks a younger girl might get up to. I'm nineteen, you see, and I know my way about as well as I know my own mind. I'm telling you all this so that you won't feel yourself a failure when we end the Season with me unbetrothed."

"Thank you for your honesty, my dear," said Amelia. "Since we are to be such friends, do you think you could call me by my Christian name? It's Amelia. And I shall call you Calliope if I may. Well, Calliope, you put me in a difficult position. Your father has hired me to bring you out and, let's be honest, find you a husband, and you want no part of his scheme. Doesn't that mean I would be accepting a generous salary under false pretenses?"

Calliope's frown was thoughtful as she took off her spectacles and rubbed them on her muslin shirt, then replaced them on her nose. "No, I don't see it that way," she declared after a short silence. "You will be doing as Papa wishes. I am the one who won't, and Papa isn't paying *me*. I would also expect that you should be paid for services rendered whether or not I choose to marry. And," she finished with a serious nod, "I think it will be fun to have you here."

"Thank you," said Amelia, holding back a laugh. "I have to agree that I've landed soft, as the saying goes. After my little hardships it will be delightful to be here with your family."

"Except Cousin Dorinda, I'll wager," said Calliope. "Oh, that reminds me. My cousin will have it that you've some dreadful secret in your past. That's part of the reason for her terrific rudeness a moment ago. Shall you tell me now, or do we wait until I find it out on my own?"

Amelia stared. "Do you know, my dear, you are the first person to ask me a direct question about my—my past. I feel you deserve an answer." She paused, thinking of all the well-meaning as well as ill-natured souls who had pried and poked at her for information in recent years, never quite asking her what they most wanted to. Nor had they even been honest enough to tell her what the rumours were which circulated about her. She could do no more than guess what Society said about her, never having heard anything.

"I married in my first Season, when I was seventeen," she said simply. She couldn't confide every detail of her story to this young girl, but there was no reason not to give Calliope an accurate idea of the woman who would be living in her house. "My marriage was for the wrong reasons; many wrong reasons which I can't discuss, but I can say that I let my father bully me into a step I shouldn't have taken. And my husband and I didn't deal together. It's really as simple as that. When Lord

Jeffries-Hodge died he disinherited me. I suspect that the terms of his will were to further embarrass me. To announce to the world at large that he had been most displeased. No doubt you have heard of the One-Guinea Widow? Well, you're sitting with her now."

"And you had no money of your own, and ever since your husband's death you've been living in dreadful poverty. Papa told me about your rooms, you see. My goodness!" said Calliope. She knew very well that there must be something more to Amelia's story. Hardly a husband and wife in the world "dealt together," Calliope was reasonably certain even with her limited experience, but that was never a reason for leaving a widow destitute. Why, even Cousin Dorinda, who must have led Mr. Winkle a merry dance, had a respectable jointure. Calliope wisely decided not to press Amelia for details. It was no doubt a case of those mysterious things young girls weren't supposed to hear about.

Amelia was saying, "I know your father must have been shocked by my living conditions, but I was really in much better circumstances in the little country cottage I lived in before coming to London. I had no idea of the price of things, you see, and even the meanest lodgings here were ruinously expensive. I brought my household to town because we were running out of money, nothing left to sell, and I knew that only in London could I find a position such as this one. I've been very lucky, my dear."

Calliope dimpled. "I've a feeling that we're the ones in luck. Now, do let's talk over what to do with your maid and footman. Naturally you'll want your maid to care for you, but the footman? Perhaps we could fasten him to Papa; does he like scientific experiments? Oh, I don't suppose you'd know...."

Amelia settled down to the welcome task of organizing her new life. Despite the indignantly rigid purple bodice of Mrs. Winkle, the Crane household was shaping up to be quite as pleasant as one had imagined.

A FEW DAYS AFTER HER arrival, Amelia emerged from her comfortable bedroom and headed for the stairs on her way to the breakfast parlour. She was humming a little tune as she walked along, looking forward to the shopping trip she and Calliope were to set out upon today. Madame Gilberte, Amelia was sure, was still all the fashion and the properest person to dress a young lady of Calliope's originality. The question was, did Amelia dare to anticipate her salary and order a few things for herself on credit?

The only command Sir Ethelred had given her so far had been an order to dispense with her blacks, and Amelia, her year of mourning up, had been quick to comply. She had, however, only brought with her the most sedate and chaperon-like of her pre-widowhood wardrobe, well-made and not much more than a year out of date. She did wish for something new.

This morning she was wearing a blue gown with a flattering white lace ruff. To be in colours once again cheered her and as she walked down the stairs, she enjoyed the feel of thick carpet which she had once taken so for granted, and wondered what Madame Gilberte would do about Calliope's height and red hair.

"Good lord!" said a voice at the foot of the stairs. "It's Miss Montresor. No, I ought to say Lady Jeffries-Hodge. May I say that the years have been kind to your ladyship?"

Amelia stared down into a darkly handsome face. "Jeremy!" she whispered, clutching the banister.

CHAPTER THREE

"PARDON ME," said Amelia, her voice faint. "I ought to have said Lord Doncastle. Do forgive me, sir."

The gentleman's snapping dark eyes seemed to bore into Amelia's very soul. With difficulty she kept from lowering her eyes before the piercing gaze.

She had not seen Jeremy since she was seventeen, and on that last occasion he had gazed on her with love, not with the cool distaste now so blatantly apparent. Why wouldn't he say something else? Amelia knew she had earned his hatred, but it was still a shock to see it, so clearly expressed, on the face she had once thought the dearest on earth.

The years had certainly been kind to the new Lord Doncastle. Amelia had read about Major Jeremy Searle's elevation to a viscountcy two years before, at the time of Waterloo. Not that he hadn't changed in seven years. He seemed taller, more muscular than ever, and he had never been slightly built. Amelia still remembered what a strange sensation it had been to fancy herself the equal in every way of this man, so closely did their minds commune, then to catch a glimpse of their two figures in a mirror and realize that she scarcely came up to his shoulder. His hair was still as crisp and dark as it had ever been, and his features more rugged though no less handsome. But his eyes! Amelia never would have thought that the warm brown eyes of the Jeremy of her youth would be able to communicate such cynicism, such disdain.

"Well, madam," said that well-loved voice. "At last we have our confrontation. You were too cowardly to give me a meeting when you jilted me, but Providence—dare I call it Providence?—has at last brought us together." Doncastle flicked an imaginary speck of dust from the lapel of his well-cut morning coat in an unsettling, dandified motion which Amelia instinctively knew was not his usual style. "I won't even ask what you're doing in my friend's house, and looking quite at home. You're out of weeds, I see. I would have thought your sorrow over losing Lord Jeffries-Hodge would outlast the proper term of mourning. You were anxious enough to snare him."

Amelia could say nothing to defend herself against this battery of angry words. She *had* thrown Jeremy over to elope with Lord Jeffries-Hodge, not even granting the man to whom she had considered herself betrothed a last interview or an explanation. No explanation had been possible, of course, under the dreadful circumstances, but Jeremy had no way of knowing that. In his eyes Amelia was only a heartless jilt, someone who had accepted his love, agreed to a secret engagement until she could placate her father. Then she had run off to Gretna Green with another man.

Jeremy had bought a commission not long after that time. Amelia had never chanced to meet him on her rare visits to London in all the years since, for he had been serving abroad. She had kept informed about his life though, reading every word she could of the military news with an interest her husband would sneer at habitually. Yet she scanned every list of casualties in dread of seeing one certain name.

"I didn't know you were back in England, my lord," she said in her best imitation of a normal, polite tone of voice. Thank heaven she was now mature enough not to stammer and quake and make a fool of herself. "Nor that you knew Sir Ethelred." She did remember that her Jeremy had been enthralled by matters scientific. It was for this reason she had kept abreast of the doings of the scientific community over the years. Sir Ethelred hadn't thought it strange that a lady should have heard of him as Amelia had; but her knowledge was a product of her careful study, not his general fame.

"Ah, how regretfully you style me 'my lord,'" said Doncastle. That cynical twist of his lips was nearly unbearable. "Do I dare to hope that, had I only been created a viscount seven years sooner, you would have been true?"

"Sir!" Amelia's eyes flashed. "Perhaps I deserve this, but no gentleman would continue to taunt me. I cannot allow it." And, carefully gauging the space which remained clear on either side of his solid form at the foot of the stairs, she decided not to slip past him and instead turned on her heel. Lewes would bring her some breakfast in her room, and she would be able to calm herself.

She did not know what she had expected. Perhaps that Jeremy—how hard it was to think of him as Doncastle!—would rush up the stairs after her and kiss her with all the fire she could sense beneath his consciously cool manner.

He did no such thing. Amelia reached her room unkissed and oddly frustrated. She did not wish to see Jeremy again.

IN THE FRONT HALL, LORD Doncastle stepped back from the stairs and snapped his fingers. "You, fellow. Have

you been eavesdropping? I ought to warn your master of
your lurking tendencies.''

From the shadows near the green baize door at the rear
of the hall stepped a footman, a lanky individual in worn
livery which did not match that of the house. His prominent light eyes put Doncastle in mind of a mackerel—a
frightened mackerel—and the viscount decided on the
spot not to be too severe.

''Your pardon, m'lord,'' mumbled the man.

''You may tell Sir Ethelred I've arrived. The footman
who let me in must have gotten lost. And don't make a
habit of listening to your betters. You will rarely learn
anything of value.''

This statement was so patently untrue that Higgins's
long mouth nearly twisted in a grin. He bowed to hide
this unfortunate tendency to levity. ''Your lordship's
name? I will carry it in.''

So the fellow meant to preserve the fiction that he
hadn't just heard Amelia Montresor address him as
Doncastle. The viscount's voice was wry as he gave his
name. He shook his head as he watched the footman
disappear down the hall. Another man, the one who had
let him in, appeared in an instant with apologies for
keeping Doncastle waiting and conducted him by another route to Sir Ethelred's study. Doncastle forgot
about the strange, piscine footman in the tattered livery.

''Delighted to see you here at last, m'lord,'' said Sir
Ethelred, springing up from his desk accompanied by a
shower of papers. He held out his hand, realized belat-
edly that the appendage still held a quill pen, and gri-
maced at the splotches of ink spattering across his cuff
and the manuscript pages of his latest work.

Doncastle laughed along with Sir Ethelred at this mishap and sacrificed his own handkerchief to mop up the

spill when it became apparent that Sir Ethelred could not lay hands on one. The two men eventually found themselves seated before the fire while they enjoyed a glass of warm ale, which Sir Ethelred preferred to any other morning beverage and never failed to inflict upon his guests.

The two men had been corresponding for several years on matters such as Sir Ethelred's latest effort to ally the harnessing of electricity to his chemical practices. The friendship, begun when Doncastle read and commented on one of Sir Ethelred's articles in a scientific journal, had blossomed on paper without Sir Ethelred, at least, knowing or caring what sort of human being was behind the intelligent writing of his military, and later noble, correspondent.

They had met quite recently at one of the clubs on Lord Doncastle's return to England. And Sir Ethelred, to do him credit as a father, immediately noticed that the fine mind he had enjoyed at long distance was encased in the agreeable form of a handsome viscount not much above the age of thirty. Calliope, he was tolerably certain, would find such a man the perfect mate. She must still do the Season—that would give her polish and experience, not to mention other eligible beaus should Doncastle prove intractable—but Sir Ethelred was rather proud to have come up with the first and most likely candidate all on his own, without the assistance of the worthy Lady Jeffries-Hodge.

He was surprised, therefore, when practically the first words out of his guest's mouth had to do, not with the daughter he had just been extolling with his own peculiar form of subtlety, but his daughter's chaperon.

"I chanced to meet your—I suppose she was your house guest, as I was coming in," said Doncastle casually. One booted leg crossed over the other, he was doing his best to enjoy the warm ale which had been pressed upon him. "A Lady Jeffries-Hodge."

"Ahem! Yes, Lady Jeffries-Hodge. She is to be my daughter's chaperon for the Season. Do you know her?"

Doncastle shook his head. He counted it one of life's greatest blessings that his engagement to Amelia Montresor had never been made public, and that he had never become a laughing-stock when the young lady absconded. "We met once or twice, years ago, but nothing more than that. She is to chaperon your daughter? Interesting. She is a family friend or a relation of yours, perhaps?"

"No," said Sir Ethelred, "I hired her. The lady was in search of a post, and my daughter in pressing need of a chaperon. Calliope and her ladyship are friends already. A most fortuitous meeting for all of us."

"Including yourself?" Doncastle let a note of slyness slip into his voice. Amelia was a lovely creature, and no sane man could be blamed for thinking she would make a perfect household ornament.

"Naturally including myself. I was at my wit's end to get my daughter fired off. Calliope is a serious girl, and she wouldn't have consented to be presented, between you and me, if she hadn't heard Lady Jeffries-Hodge's story and determined to help the woman." There was absolutely no hint in Sir Ethelred's voice or manner that he had understood Doncastle's allusion to a special interest in the lady, and the viscount was forced to conclude that the arrangement was innocent.

Amelia hired as a chaperon! She must have run through her husband's fortune in record time, thought Doncastle. He studiously kept a bland expression on his face, all the while wishing he could laugh aloud. He did not consider himself a vindictive man. Yet he could not help being glad that justice had been done in the end. Amelia had at last gotten what she deserved.

Money and rank, he believed, had made her run away from his love seven years ago. It was a fitting punishment for her to be destitute now. As he often did, he marvelled over the treachery, over the carefully created innocent façade of Amelia and women such as herself. Never in their glorious season of dawning love would he have thought Amelia's a mercenary soul. He had reeled from the shock of her elopement with another man, an older, more sophisticated man with the money and title Jeremy Searle had not.

He dismissed the unlucky Amelia from his thoughts and returned his attention to his host. His conversation with Sir Ethelred, which dwelt heavily on the baronet's pretty and intelligent daughter, made Doncastle realize that Miss Calliope Crane was to be flung at his head by this doting father. Never having met Miss Crane, he couldn't say whether this would be a penance or no. He did suppose that being thrown together with Sir Ethelred's daughter would mean being thrown together with her chaperon.

The said chaperon returned forthwith to Doncastle's mind. He took a sort of fiendish pleasure in the prospect of disconcerting Amelia Jeffries-Hodge by his presence.

AMELIA RETURNED SAFELY to her bedroom, sat on her bed awhile and trembled, then rang the bell. To her surprise, both Lewes and Higgins answered her summons.

Higgins, knowing that another footman was on the task, hadn't bothered to announce Lord Doncastle to anyone at all. He had instead waited in the servants' hall, for something told him Amelia would need the assistance of her friends before long. While he waited he took the opportunity to reveal to Lewes the odd conversation her ladyship had had with a handsome stranger in the front hall.

"I only met my lady after she was married," said Lewes thoughtfully. "The way she cried, though, night and day when the master first brought her home. I thought it was only that she woke up to find herself wed to the master, but if she lost the young man she loved— yes, that would explain it."

"This Doncastle cove don't seem to have an inkling of the way things was," said Higgins, "for he was near to biting her head off. Seems she jilted him to run off with the master. Madam must have kept her troubles a secret from him. A mystery how she could do so. *We* knew all about it."

"We have our ways," said Lewes. "*They* often do not."

"Well, whatever he was to Madam, he had no right to speak to her as he did. Her ladyship did well to send him off with a flea in his ear, and that's the truth. This cove probably wasn't good enough for her, and it's a small loss."

Lewes opened her blue eyes wide. "You know better than that. If this gentleman is the veriest devil, she would have done better to stay by him than to marry the master."

Higgins did know. He shrugged. "She might have thought, after what happened, that she was no longer good enough for him."

Tears appeared in the corners of Lewes's eyes.

"Oh, I'm sorry, lass. I forgot," said Higgins, stricken. He wished the girl wouldn't be so sensitive on that particular subject. What was done was done.

Both servants answered Amelia's bell with quick steps and anxious faces.

Amelia managed a weak smile upon their entrance. "Higgins, I'm feeling a little unwell this morning. Only a little. Please tell Miss Crane that I won't be joining the ladies in the breakfast room, though I can still go shopping with her later, and then go to the kitchen and see if the cook will put a few things on a tray. Some bread and coffee is all I require. Lewes, I'll need you here to help me make ready for our outing."

Higgins and Lewes exchanged glances. "Madam," said the footman, "may we serve you in any other way? You seem out of sorts. Has something happened to vex you?"

"Not really," said Amelia. "Why should I be vexed that my past is now rising up to haunt me? I knew such things might happen if I re-entered Society. It was a calculated risk." At the servants' puzzled looks, she added, "It doesn't signify, really. I've just encountered someone, a friend from happier days, and the meeting gave me no pleasure. Dear me, you are such inquisitive creatures. If you weren't such good friends I'd turn you off without a character."

"Yes, madam," said Lewes. "You must know we wouldn't go."

Higgins brought up the breakfast tray in record time, along with a message from Miss Crane that Lady Jeffries-Hodge wasn't to overtax herself. He also offered as a casual tidbit the fact that Sir Ethelred's guest, a dark gentleman, had but a moment ago been seen to leave the house.

Amelia shrugged at this news. It was to be expected that servants would know one's business, especially such intimate servants as hers. She hadn't seen Higgins in the hall earlier that morning and could only wonder at his powers of divination, for he had obviously learned somehow that the person from her past and Sir Ethelred's friend were one and the same. Perhaps Higgins had only guessed.

Thanks to the footman's information, Amelia did go downstairs later, followed by Lewes, with a pleased sense of security. She might see Jeremy in the future, indeed she would have to if they were both in London, but she needed time to collect herself.

Calliope, dressed in a schoolgirlish outdoor garment of tobacco brown and the close bonnet of the girl not yet out, was all concern when she met Amelia at the door. "Amelia, you can't go out if you're not well. Heaven knows a shopping tour isn't at the top of my list of pleasures; I can very well stay home today and do some work I've been wishing I could get to."

"Don't give it another thought, my dear. A momentary touch of the megrims, but I'm perfectly fit now. And I'm longing to see you on the way to a new wardrobe. Don't you like new clothes? Your father has given us free rein."

Calliope shrugged. "Clothes. To keep one warm in winter and decent in summer. I couldn't possibly care for a man who was attracted to my clothes, and I've never understood what all the fuss was about."

"Hmm." Amelia considered this carefully as the two of them, and Lewes, were settled in Sir Ethelred's town chariot. "I begin to see, my dear, that you have much to learn about—biology."

"Biology?" Calliope stared, never having thought to hear such a word from the lips of her decidedly unscientific chaperon.

Amelia held back a smile. "Doesn't even the butterfly dress in bright colours to attract a mate?"

"Well, I don't think that's why, but I'd have to research the point," said Calliope, pushing her spectacles up her nose. "Oh! You're funning me." She had caught the glint of amusement in Amelia's eye. "And you must admit, Amelia, that the butterflies don't have to waste their precious mornings at the modiste."

They were still arguing the point when the carriage pulled up in front of the Bruxton Street establishment of Madame Gilberte, modiste extraordinaire. Amelia hadn't been in the way of buying clothes, aside from the obligatory widow's weeds which she had had made up in the country, since before her husband's death, but Madame Gilberte remembered her. Lady Jeffries-Hodge and her charge were ushered into a lush private sitting-room and plied with tea and cakes while a swarm of assistants rushed in and out with lengths of fabric and piles of fashion plates.

Madame Gilberte, a sharp-featured woman with dark auburn hair, began by offering her condolences on milady's loss. A flicker of awareness in the dressmaker's eyes made Amelia certain that Madame had heard the myriad rumours surrounding Amelia's husband's death and the reading of his will. Madame Gilberte had doubtless heard more about the situation than had Amelia herself. Impossible to question the modiste; impossible not to be curious. Amelia sighed and turned the conversation to Calliope's wardrobe.

"Ah, yes, milady's charge," said Madame Gilberte. "I have two things to observe: tall, red hair."

Calliope bristled, but Amelia knew what was coming next.

"We must emphasize these, your best qualities," said Madame Gilberte with a decided nod of the head. "Mademoiselle, you will be a credit to my genius."

Calliope burst out laughing, which didn't endear her to the modiste. Amelia leaned over to whisper into Madame Gilberte's ear that Miss Crane was a veritable ascetic and would have to be prodded into becoming costumes.

"It's true," said Calliope, who had overheard. "I have no real interest in the Season, and I wouldn't care if I wore a sack."

Madame Gilberte's sharp eyebrows shot up, but she said nothing, merely nodded thoughtfully and drew forth a book of fashion plates.

An exhausting three hours later, Amelia and Calliope were ready to depart. Clothes for every sort of occasion were on order, to be made from the best and most costly materials in shades becoming to redheads. Several costumes would be ready within the week, Madame Gilberte assured her clients. Now if her ladyship would but order something new...

"No," said Amelia. "When I have the means I'll be back, madame, but I simply can't buy from you on credit."

"You cannot? But you were used to, milady, all the time," said Madame Gilberte, eyes widening.

"That was different," said Amelia with a shrug. "I knew I could pay my account at any moment, don't you see?"

"Nonsense," said Calliope. "Papa said I was to buy you a gown or two, as a thank-you for helping me, and it would be absurd not to. After all, you're the one who wants one."

The couturière flashed an irritated glance at the young lady she had spent the morning turning into a prospective and quite respectable debutante for the Season. Were one's taste, one's flawless judgement to be offered such ingratitude? her look seemed to say. She was careful not to offend a wealthy customer out loud, though, and merely urged Lady Jeffries-Hodge to take a new evening gown and a walking costume, "For now."

When Amelia finally did quit the shop she was the proud owner of two new costumes which were to be made up post-haste: a sophisticated evening gown in a style deemed by all to be quite suitable for a stylish widow, as well as a walking dress in the very newest mode, to be fashioned in a lovely twilled silk newly arrived from Paris.

"I was right," said Calliope. "You have a spring in your step! My word, I wish *I* could understand this fuss about clothes."

"I admit it. I take every feminine enjoyment in new clothes," said Amelia. "That must make me a frivolous creature in your eyes."

"Yes," said Calliope, a dimple appearing at the corner of her mouth, "but there's something so—so abandoned about your enjoyment. As if you haven't been frivolous in a very long time. It's a pleasure to watch you."

Lewes, a silent spectator in the morning's excursion, looked at her mistress anxiously, in the hopes her ladyship would not take offence. If the foolish Miss Crane only knew exactly how long it had been since Lady Jeffries-Hodge had had any sort of real amusement in her life!

Her ladyship was laughing; that was a good sign. She had taken the girl's remark in her stride, then. The abigail realized, with a start, that her mistress had a pretty laugh, and that her friends had only heard it on rare occasions. The rich matron, Lady Jeffries-Hodge, who could buy at will on credit from Madame Gilberte and every other establishment in Mayfair, had never laughed.

Lewes herself had shed tears of relief on Master's death, but she realized that there were many individual ways to mourn the demise of such a man.

CHAPTER FOUR

"I REPEAT, YOU CHUCKLEHEAD, I did not ask for any of the ladies. Show me in to Sir Ethelred. Now!"

Green, the Crane butler, had become accustomed to many strange things in his years of employment in Sir Ethelred's household, but being called names was not one of them. Looking down his long nose, he said with a perceptible sniff, "The baronet insists on the proper form. May I take in your card, madam?"

"Blast you for an ignoramus. I said show me in! Oh, never mind." And before Green could straighten from his half-mocking bow, an umbrella of puce silk and ivory walloped him across the small of the back. With that, a little, round woman in late middle age stormed past him, the canary plumes of her high-crowned bonnet wagging above her like flags.

A moment later Sir Ethelred's study door was flung open, and a piercing scream rent the air.

Sir Ethelred Crane unwound himself from his awkward position on the floor. "Good Lord! Lady Manville! Confound it, I tell Green to deny me to all visitors when I'm doing my exercises. Oh, drat." He rushed forward just in time to catch the dumpling-shaped mass of puce and canary-colour as Lady Manville toppled to the ground. "Green!" he bellowed out the door.

The butler arrived, with apologies for letting her ladyship slip past him, and helped Sir Ethelred transport the visitor to the study sofa. "I'll call one of the maids, sir, to loosen clothing and bring whatever restoratives ladies commonly use," said Green, exchanging a glance with his master which bespoke his own desire to have nothing whatever to do with Lady Manville's reviving.

"A glass of cold water in the face is more like, and that I can do! Never heard of such a thing, a thick-skinned woman like her ladyship to be overset to the point of insensibility by the sight of a man peacefully stretching his leg muscles on his own carpet," grumbled Sir Ethelred.

"If you will permit me to say so, sir, I have the distinct impression that her ladyship would have been less overset were it not for your habit of leaving off your nether garments during the morning session...."

"Oh." Sir Ethelred glanced down at himself. Then he snatched a pair of grey kerseymere pantaloons from a nearby chair and began to hop his way into them, muttering, "Better be decent before the old harridan revives. What possessed you, Green? Should have been able to guard the door better than that."

Green mumbled some incoherent apology, repeated his intention of fetching a female servant, and left the room.

Lady Manville began to moan in a theatrical style. Sir Ethelred called after the butler, "Never mind, she's come to!" and approached the sofa. "Lady Manville? You're all right and tight? Your own fault, you know, you shouldn't break in on people unannounced."

The lady opened one baleful eye and glared up at the baronet. "You, sir, are impossible! Ah, I see you've made yourself a bit more formal. Assist me!" She held out an arm, and Sir Ethelred obligingly aided her to sit upright. Lady Manville was such a wide and well-rounded female that he had to resist the temptation to roll her about, purely in the interests of physiology, to see if she would turn equally on all sides.

With every appearance of the proper deference, he next pulled up a chair near the sofa, sat down, and said, "To what do I owe the honour of this visit, my lady?"

Lady Manville was some distant connection of the Cranes and from time to time would blaze into the household intent upon ministering to the motherless Calliope. So alarming was she to one of Sir Ethelred's quiet manner that it had never crossed his mind to commit his daughter to her charge for the Season.

Before speaking, the lady surveyed Sir Ethelred's private sanctum with apparent distaste, her eyes lingering on the mountains of scribbled-on paper, the chemical stains on the Axminster, the classical busts festooned, as often as not, with a hat or cravat. Sir Ethelred did not permit the maids to clean in this room for fear they might displace something only he could locate. "I am here," Lady Manville said in stagy tones, turning her malignant gaze from her surroundings to Sir Ethelred, "out of the love I bore your late lady, and by extension your daughter. You, Sir Ethelred, are a hopeless case. And this latest rig proves it."

Sir Ethelred blinked. "If a man can't stretch out on his own carpet, Lady Manville—"

"Oh, I'm not talking about your obscene behaviour of a moment ago. *That* sort of thing is only to be expected from an eccentric such as yourself. No, I'm here to speak on a serious matter. What does it mean, you unnatural father, that you've let a wicked, scandal-bound woman into your home to care for your innocent daughter?" Lady Manville regarded her companion as though he were vermin.

"Is that it?" Sir Ethelred laughed. "Madam, Lady Jeffries-Hodge is a fine woman, the salt of the earth and all of that. Her husband left her one guinea in his will, I hear. For that I should blame the lady? I don't know much of the late baron, but his action seemed dashed impolite, to say the least."

"Naturally, you clunch, a widow could only be so treated if her behaviour during her husband's lifetime had been reprehensible," snapped Lady Manville in return. "I have done my research before coming to you, and it's only fair to warn you that the woman is said to have been well deserving of her lord's shabby treatment. Infidelities, disgusting carnal appetites—heavens, but the rumour mill is difficult to sort through! I have some sort of edge since my second cousin lives near the place in Hampshire where Lady Jeffries-Hodge spent most of her married life. No one is certain what she did, but one thing is sure: it must have been dreadful. And what amazes me most is that there is every intent in Society to receive her when she appears. Morbid curiosity, no doubt."

"Ah! Thank you for coming to me with that information, Lady Manville," said Sir Ethelred. "It relieves my mind that there will be no attempt to cut the poor lady, and on the eve of Calliope's come-out. Whispering behind her back's bound to be more amusing than not letting her into rooms in the first place, what?"

"Well!" Lady Manville rose in a sweep of vari-coloured garments, leaned forward and poked Sir Ethelred on the shirt front at intervals with a plump, kid-covered finger to punctuate her next words. "You pla-guey man, I came here only for your good, to keep you from making the worst mistake of your life and to offer the sheltering wings of my dignity to repair your daughter's little lapse. For even going round to the shops with that woman is bound to be seen as a dreadful gaffe once the whole scandal comes out.''

''Ah, yes, the scandal no one is certain of, but everyone talks of.'' Sir Ethelred's mind worked busily behind his spectacles, and he realized at last that Lady Manville was insulted that she hadn't been asked to chaperon Calliope. Gad, he couldn't have played such a trick on his own daughter had he and this small woman been the best of friends. ''My lady, it gives me great pleasure to inform you that I don't listen to gossip. Neither does my daughter. And both of us are pleased with Lady Jeffries-Hodge.''

''So that's where the wind lies! You've designs upon her, you libertine!''

''Designs?'' Sir Ethelred's face was a blank for an instant. ''Oh, you mean evil masculine intentions, I see. Sorry to disappoint you, madam, but you'll find no meat for gossip there.''

Lady Manville sniffed. ''What Dorinda Winkle can be thinking to allow this—''

''Oh, she's quite as cut up as you over the arrangement,'' said Sir Ethelred cheerfully. ''Same reason, too. She expected to take charge of Calliope for the Season.''

''That nobody? Ridiculous. And I, sir, have made the offer solely out of friendship to your late wife, not, I assure you, from any wish to expend what little remains of my energy on the rigorous demands of a young lady's Season.'' Lady Manville's little red cheeks puffed up in alarm at the very thought.

''Yes. To be sure. Well, have no fear, my lady, I wouldn't think of trespassing upon your good nature or endangering your health. The very idea is absurd, when I've been able to come up with a young, strong dowager who's eager for the occupation.''

"Eager! I'd wager the trollop is more than eager."

"The . . . the what? I'm certain I can't have heard your ladyship properly." Sir Ethelred suddenly drew himself up to his full height and regarded Lady Manville with his most steely gaze, which, given his long, cadaverous form and thick spectacles, was rather terrifying. Lady Manville, no small contender herself in the basilisk department, stared him down.

"The trollop!" she finally repeated. "That's the rumour going about, you know. That she hastened her husband's death to have more scope for her disgusting pleasures, little knowing that poor Jeffries-Hodge was on to her game and had altered his will."

"Good Lord! Lady Manville, I must ask you to remove yourself from my house," said Sir Ethelred, opening the study door and executing a stiff bow. "Green!" he called down the corridor. "Lady Manville is leaving." Turning back to his guest, he added, "Though I assume you know your own way out, ma'am? You certainly knew your way in."

"Precisely as I thought! Trapped by that woman's wiles." With this parting shot, Lady Manville gathered up her umbrella, seemed to consider connecting it with Sir Ethelred's head, and turned on her heel. She stalked down the hall as majestically as possible for one of her size and overly narrow skirt.

Sir Ethelred shrugged, closed the door again, and immediately undid his pantaloons.

"GOODNESS!" SAID CALLIOPE, bursting into the morning-room where Amelia and Mrs. Winkle sat in uncompanionable silence over their work. "I ran into Lady Manville in the hall just now. She was here to see Papa, of all things. And she looked angry as a bear. I wonder what can have vexed her? When I said good day and invited her in to sit with us, she merely glared at me, then called me a poor, benighted child, and went on her way to her carriage. How very strange. Do you know Lady Manville, Amelia?''

Shrugging, Amelia replied, ''I may have met her once or twice. The name sounds familiar.'' In reality she did remember the lady very well, as one of the topmost dragons of the ton. And she had a good idea of the woman's mission with Sir Ethelred. Amelia had been in residence in Portman Square barely two weeks, but already the gossips would be having a field day, questioning the motives of both herself and Sir Ethelred in much the same way Mrs. Winkle was wont to do at the breakfast table. Glancing at the stiffly starched figure across the room, Amelia thought she noted a flash of pleasure cross the elder woman's face at Calliope's news.

''Well, you'll meet her soon enough. Lady Manville is hard to avoid in Society, I would imagine,'' said Calliope, sitting down and stretching her long legs out on the sofa in a charming, uninhibited way that Amelia supposed she ought to squelch. But Calliope's spontaneity was such an attractive trait that Amelia hadn't the heart to correct her manners, and she supposed Mrs. Winkle had given up the effort long ago.

''Lady Manville is one of the *crème de la crème*,'' contributed Mrs. Winkle, with a sharp look at Amelia. As it happened, Dorinda Winkle and Lady Manville enjoyed a mutual dislike based on their differing ideas of the former lady's consequence, but Mrs. Winkle would be prepared to defend her enemy in this case. Obviously her ladyship had come to warn Sir Ethelred of the viper he harboured in his bosom, and Dorinda Winkle endorsed this behaviour whole-heartedly. Everything she

herself said to Sir Ethelred on the subject went un-
heeded.

Amelia decided to turn the conversation, but didn't
know what to say. If she mentioned Calliope's first appearance in Society, which was fast approaching and the
only thing on her own mind, Mrs. Winkle would be
newly offended because not only wasn't she chaperoning Calliope, she hadn't even been invited to the event in
question. Would she be offended enough to leave the
room, Amelia wondered idly? Well, it wasn't worth the
gamble to find out.

Before she could think of any safe subject, Calliope
broke the silence with a frank, "Come away to my room,
Amelia. I have your advice to ask on my costume for that
dreadful ball. I'd hate to bother Cousin Dorinda with
such frivolous talk."

The two younger women excused themselves and had
left the morning-room before Mrs. Winkle could think of
a suitable retort.

"Well, what is it you really want to say to me?" enquired Amelia as the two made their way up the stairs.
"Never tell me you care what you're wearing, even to
your first appearance."

"Oh, I'm simply feeling stifled," said Calliope. "This
infernal preoccupation with dress and Society is hurting
my concentration. I was going to spend the morning
writing that article I've been telling you of, for the *Lady's
Magazine*, on the dangers of the terrible things ladies use
to paint themselves up with, but it's the oddest thing. I
can't organize my thoughts."

Amelia smiled. She was certain that the *Lady's Magazine* would reject out of hand any such article, and that
the project was best left half-finished. Should she tell
Calliope that her distraction meant she was likely suffer-

ing from a normal attack of nerves on the eve of her introduction to Society?

Calliope saw the smile. "Well, you needn't laugh at me," she said as she opened the door to her bedroom and motioned Amelia inside, "and as it happens, I do have a slight problem I'd like your advice on, something I wouldn't wish to come to Cousin Dorinda's ears. Not that I want anything to, come to think of it."

"I'd be delighted to offer my advice. I'm surprised, though, that you feel you need it," said Amelia, sitting down before the fire. It always shocked her a little to come into Calliope's room, such an ascetic chamber as it was, free of any of the feminine furbelows usually to be seen in a young lady's private quarters. Calliope had done her best to make her sanctum the combination of a book room and a medieval monk's cell, choosing straight, unrounded furnishings in a dark wood, a narrow white bed unadorned by such frivolities as curtains, and plain whitewashed walls rather than silk or paper, the better to display her collection of antiquarian maps and original botanical drawings.

"It's Papa," said Calliope, sitting down across from her chaperon. "He's—well, Amelia, he seems determined that I marry."

"Didn't you know that already, dear? He's fastened me to you for the Season and is forcing you to enter Society, isn't he?"

"Yes, yes, but he's even taken it upon himself to find me a suitable candidate! I can't endure being paraded before this Lord What's-his-name as a possible match. But so Papa will have it. He's coyly suggested to me a number of times that I'm bound to like his friend."

"Who is this friend?" asked Amelia. She already had a very good idea.

"I can't remember the name. You will know him when Papa pushes me into a closed room with the man. Someone with a title and an interest in the sciences, that's all I know. I haven't met many of Papa's friends because of my absurd status as 'not out,' but I shall see this paragon at the ball."

"What if you like him?" Amelia's heart thudded. Something told her that Sir Ethelred had hit on his friend Doncastle as the perfect mate for his daughter. How logical, for Jeremy was good-looking and suitable in every worldly way besides being a personal friend of Sir Ethelred's.

So Jeremy would be at tomorrow's ball! And not only would he meet Calliope, he would be forced to encounter Amelia. She and Calliope had done nothing but shop and go on healthy morning walks in the days since Amelia had first happened upon Lord Doncastle on the stairs, but everywhere she did go she found herself craning her neck and looking over her shoulder, fearing—or hoping—to see again the new, sardonic smile on that once-beloved face. She hadn't glimpsed him, but tomorrow she would.

"Like him? Absurd! As if I could like anyone I did not choose for myself. This marriage business is getting out of hand." Calliope sighed, pushing her unruly red hair back from her temples. "Papa has lost all sense of logic. Can't he see how suitable it would be for me simply to come out and act his hostess? He couldn't find anyone so useful to him if he searched England and the Continent. I understand his work; I'd love to meet his friends on an equal footing—any friends he doesn't want me to marry, that is—and I have no desire in the world to be wed."

"Why not?" asked Amelia.

"Well." Calliope leaned forward as if to emphasize the importance of her next statement. "I haven't failed to observe, Amelia, that married women are not *free*."

This was such an understatement in Amelia's mind, and such an obvious truth, that she remained silent for fear of laughing.

"I suppose you will say that unmarried women are not free, either," Calliope went on, "but that's where my peculiar situation with Papa works to my advantage. Can you even imagine him gathering his forces to act the stern parent, or cutting me out of his will—oh, pardon my wretched tongue!" The girl paused, obviously stricken.

Amelia waved away the remark. "My situation is no secret, and I don't mind its being referred to among friends. I do admit, Calliope, that you have quite an example before you of what marriage—and men's wills—can do to a female's consequence *and* her peace of mind. And I think you're showing all the sense you were born with in thinking your father would never subject you to such shabby treatment as you might experience with a husband—or another sort of father. But, my dear, doesn't this plan of yours reveal a certain lack of courage?"

Calliope opened her grey eyes wide. "Lack of courage? I? I am a scholar, Amelia. I never think of myself as either lacking courage or possessing it."

"But don't scholars, and scientists, make a habit of chancing the unknown?" Amelia wracked her brain for some names. "Sir Isaac Newton, Copernicus, er, Aristotle?"

"Oh, Amelia! As though any of those *men* had to endure a ton party, or be the powerless partner in a marriage, or anything I'm talking about." Calliope paused.

"Though you've given me something to think on, to be sure. Courage, you say?"

Amelia nodded. She would be glad if any idea she hit upon could reconcile Calliope to an honest trial, not a mere walking through, of her coming Season. Despite her difficulties, Amelia was still romantic enough to believe that the right man existed for every girl. He could hardly be found if the girl in question did not go seeking him.

Courage! She knew that quality was something which she, Amelia, would need in abundance for her coming encounter with Lord Doncastle.

CHAPTER FIVE

AMELIA COULD NOT HAVE imagined a more uncomfortable situation had she spent years struggling to do so. Her career as a chaperon could hardly be starting less auspiciously.

True, upon her entrance into Buckley House, the crowds gathered for this gala ball had not as a body turned their backs on her. In the inner recesses of her mind, Amelia had feared some such tragedy would occur, and she was quite glad, for the sake of the Cranes who walked beside her, that she was apparently to be received. Also comforting was the fact that Lady Buckley's greeting had been all that was cordial. Amelia had thought, though, that she noticed a hint of something in her hostess's eyes when they met hers—something resembling a look of sisterhood. Lady Buckley, though received everywhere, was rumoured to be a little fast. Lord Buckley, smiling beside his wife, was known to be very fast indeed, and he most definitely leered.

But once Amelia and her companions passed safely into the ballroom, there to mingle under the glittering chandeliers with all of fashionable London, a definite sense of panic set in. Sir Ethelred soon deserted his womenfolk. Once his protecting presence was removed, Amelia grew more nervous than ever.

She was surreptitiously scanning the crowd, both hoping and fearing to see Lord Doncastle, when a small, ex-

traordinarily dressed female tapped her on the shoulder
rather hard with an ostrich-plume fan.

"Good evening to you, Lady Jeffries-Hodge. Calliope," said Lady Manville. She put up a lorgnette and
examined Amelia's gown. "What? Have you spent so
long out of Society, ma'am, that you call that proper garb
for a widow?"

"I believe you are a widow yourself, Lady Manville."
Amelia spoke in a smooth, outwardly confident voice.
"And my year of mourning is past." Her attack of nerves
was forgotten as she defended herself, and she privately
rejoiced at this new feeling of near-relaxation.

"Humph," said the small rotund woman. Her purple
satin gown, with its unexpected green trimmings, gave her
a startling likeness to a grape, but in no way did it signify bereavement. She was not willing to concede the
point, however. "There is the younger generation for
you. One year, if you please, and back into colours! You
might at least have trimmed *that* in black."

Amelia was silent, trying with difficulty to suppress a
smile at the thought of Madame Gilberte's elegant creation banded in the black grosgrain favoured by the economical bereaved. The sapphire-blue sarcenet tunic,
embroidered in silver and cut away to reveal an under-
dress of filmy, silver-spotted white, was the most flattering gown Amelia had ever owned. She didn't even feel
that the matching, silver-embroidered evening toque, the
modiste's grudging concession to widowhood, spoiled the
effect, though this was the first time she had appeared at
a ball in any sort of headgear save a plume or flower.

Amelia supposed, as Lady Manville's voice droned on,
that she ought to be grateful that the woman was even
speaking to her. For this was what she must do from now
on: mix with other dowagers in public places.

"Amelia, I see some people over the way who wish to speak to us," broke in Calliope, interrupting Lady Manville's tirade in a style which really should not have been tolerated in a young girl just out.

Lady Manville began to tell her so, in a threatening tone, and Amelia and her charge were only able to curtsey and escape when the small lioness of the ton was hailed by a crony.

"So this is Society," said Calliope with a sigh. "Trussed up like a chicken in these woefully unhealthy stays, barked at by Lady Manville...no wonder Papa escaped to the card room as soon as we were announced. He hates cards."

"Try not to think about the unpleasant parts, my love. Isn't this a pretty room? Lady Buckley has redecorated since I was last here—oh, above three years ago." Amelia looked about at the ornate ballroom, remembering. She had been in the company of a friend, for Lord Jeffries-Hodge and she never attended the same parties if they could help it. The hangings had been dark red then. Now they had been changed to a lovely old gold, which worked extremely well with the ornate gold mouldings and the new gold-tapestried chairs which lined the room.

The new décor served quite well to set off Calliope's appearance, thought Amelia with pleasure. The girl was striking in a cream-coloured tamboured muslin, banded in a gold Greek key pattern, her curly red hair just contained in a pretty knot by a bandeau of golden leaves. Her little spectacles, which she refused to leave off, added a jarring, original note and, along with her stately height, ensured that she would not be lost in the crowd.

"You didn't really see someone who wanted to speak to us, did you?" Amelia said as the two ladies edged through the throng. "I suppose we ought to find seats and wait for the young men to form a queue. That, I think, is the proper procedure.''

"Fiddle! I don't expect to dance a step tonight," said Calliope. She looked down at her golden dancing slippers in scorn. "Nor do I want to."

Amelia laughed. "You seem determined to make me lose my job, my dear. You are here to dance, and dance you will or I'll know the reason why."

"Amelia!" shrieked someone quite nearby. "It *is* Amelia. My dear, how perfectly enchanting to see you in town."

Amelia recognized the voice and turned about in pleasure, just in time to clasp the hands of a pretty, elegantly dressed blonde. "Sarah! I'm so glad."

Calliope was soon making her curtsey to Sarah, Lady St. Cloud, Lady Jeffries-Hodge's oldest friend from Miss Towers' Select Seminary.

"How well you look, Amelia!"

"And you, my dear. You are so—"

"Fat? It's not an excess of sweets, I assure you, merely that I couldn't expect to keep secret forever the fact I'm increasing. Soon I must begin declining invitations, but I'm so delighted I accepted this one. The Season promises to be so tedious, you can't think, but with you back in town to amuse me—where are you living?"

The moment had come. Amelia had waited, silently, through Sarah's kind chatter, but now she must make her confession. "I'm chaperoning Miss Crane this Season, Sarah. Her father hired me."

The dread words were out, and Amelia searched her friend's face, expecting to see disdain in the china-blue eyes, a moue of distaste on the pretty rosebud mouth.

Sarah was staring in honest surprise. "You are! He did!" she exclaimed. "Well, come, both of you, there are seats in this corner. You must tell me how this came about. It sounds dreadfully amusing." And she led the way, moving in a slightly ungainly fashion, to a sofa in a secluded area behind a forest of flower vases.

Amelia remembered why she had always liked Sarah so much. She settled herself on the white-and-gold striped satin next to her friend before saying, "I do think, Sarah, that you ought to hear my story some other time. This spot is much too out of the way for Calliope. She's here to dance, you know." It was the more imperative not to let Calliope stick herself in a corner, since Amelia already knew, from the satisfied look on her young friend's face, that such a situation suited Calliope down to the ground.

Lady St. Cloud sighed. "Yes, dancing. I can barely remember what it was like. Next year, as my lord keeps promising me. Well, we'll soon attend to Miss Crane's needs."

"I'm perfectly comfortable, my lady. I urge you not to bother—" Calliope was beginning, with an irritated look at Amelia, when her words were cut off by Sarah's imperious hailing of a nearby young man.

"Penton! Over here, sir," said Sarah in a carrying voice, waving her feather fan as a signal flag.

Amelia wondered why on earth Sarah would request the presence of such a middling young man: round of face, unprepossessing of figure. The very young gentleman hurrying around the flower vases to their sofa looked not at all interesting. Certainly not the type of male to captivate Calliope.

"The Marquis of Penton, fabulously rich, and my husband's relation," murmured Sarah behind her fan into Amelia's ear. "It will not hurt the girl to cut her wisdoms on the Season's greatest catch."

"Sarah, you are a wonder," Amelia said as softly. Soon she was holding out her hand to the young marquis, trying to eye him with the severity required of a young lady's chaperon.

When presented to Miss Crane, the marquis dutifully begged the honour of the first set, which was just forming.

Calliope clamped her mouth shut and scowled.

"I say, ma'am, I know it ain't nothing to taking a fence, but do come along." Penton, Amelia was relieved to note, would not take silence and scowls for an answer. Evidently his rank had made him bold.

"Miss Crane is delighted," Amelia prompted.

Calliope finally gave a gracious nod in assent and stood up to give her hand to her first partner. As the young couple moved away, the ladies were able to observe that Calliope topped her new swain by a good half a head.

"Oh, dear, I didn't think. She is such a maypole. I mean to say, so statuesque," said Sarah with a sigh. "Well, you can't expect me to do perfectly on my first try."

"I'm well satisfied. The child is dancing, and with a marquis. You're making my duties as chaperon begin as they should, and I thank you."

"Chaperon. You were going to explain how you came to be hired for such an office. Is it true, then, what the gossips say about your husband's will?"

Amelia had no hesitation in admitting to her old friend the particulars of Lord Jeffries-Hodge's last testament, though she did not detail the extreme poverty which had led her to take the step of obtaining a post. Let the world suppose she had some private means. She presented her decision instead as somewhat of a lark, a way to ease back into Society.

"Well, I call it great good luck that you came to do it, whatever your reason," said Sarah, squeezing her friend's hand. "To think of seeing you here! Let us take a turn about the room, shall we, after the next set begins. What say you to the Duke of Devonshire for Miss Crane's next partner? Perfectly safe, I fear. Word has it he will never marry. We're distantly connected, he and I, also through my husband, and he owes me a favour. Every young lady in town would be willing to cast herself into a fire if he would but glance her way."

"Sarah, you are a wonder," said Amelia. She paused to ask herself how Calliope would be faring if she had had to rely only upon her chaperon for introductions.

Amelia had no leisure to indulge in such grim thoughts. The magic hand of Lady St. Cloud saw to it that Calliope went from partner to partner without a pause. Amelia began to enjoy herself, especially once she and her *enceinte* friend were stationed in chairs which commanded a better view of the dancers than had their first confidential corner.

"How I do love to dance," said Sarah with regret, nodding her head in time to the music.

Amelia was watching Calliope go down the dance with a raw-boned and blessedly tall young man, a second cousin of a great friend of Lady St. Cloud's. "So did I," she returned.

"Did? What's to stop you from dancing now if you wish? You're out of mourning, and *you* aren't hampered by a midsection the size of St. Paul's."

"As a dignified chaperon," said Amelia with a smile, "I am here merely to watch the dancing."

"Nonsense," said Sarah with a snort. "There is nothing out of the way about a *young* chaperon taking the floor if she might wish."

Amelia could not remember the last time she had felt truly young, and she was considering making some rejoinder to that effect. She remembered that she and Sarah were of an age, though, and hesitated. "But I don't wish to dance," she said, wondering if that really was the truth.

As though to test her resolve, a gentleman approached her chair and bowed over her hand. He was a beefy, red-faced individual of perhaps forty, a member of one of her late husband's clubs, as he did not hesitate to inform Lady Jeffries-Hodge to excuse his boldness in approaching a female to whom he had not been formally introduced. He begged the honour of a dance.

"No, thank you, Mr.—Johnstone," said Amelia, raising large, wondering eyes to the bloodshot ones of her would-be partner. "I do not mean to dance."

"A pity, ma'am," returned the gentleman. "A glass of punch, then? A turn about the rooms?"

"No, thank you. I'm chaperoning a young lady, and I must stay here."

"Pity," repeated Mr. Johnstone. He had not yet let go of her gloved hand, and he gave it a definite squeeze before he bowed once more and excused himself. "Until later, then, fair lady."

Sarah St. Cloud had stayed motionless and silent throughout this encounter. "What could that man mean, to approach you in such a manner?" she whispered as soon as they saw his back.

"I have no idea," said Amelia. "Let's hope he doesn't return. He was probably in his cups. Lord Jeffries-Hodge did have some rather rough friends."

"I should say so," said Sarah. "I wonder how that Johnstone got in here. The Buckleys might be rogues, but they are usually so exclusive—oh, is that your Sir Ethelred? I'd recognize him anywhere from your description.''

Amelia looked in the direction Sarah had indicated, a smile of welcome and affection bedecking her face. For some unknown reason, though his evening clothes fit perfectly, as always, Sir Ethelred gave the impression of being too long for his garments. He was forever rumpled, as if he had but that moment emerged from his study after an immersion of several days. His friendly eyes were beaming from behind his thick spectacles as he elbowed his way through the well-dressed crowd on the edge of the dance floor.

"Well, my dear, you've done splendidly," he said in greeting, giving Amelia an approving nod. "Calliope's danced every dance, some old biddy told me a second ago, and with a clutch of titled young chaps. Can't ask for more. You may be sure I commended your efforts."

"And with no reason at all, sir, for it's thanks to my old friend, Lady St. Cloud, that your daughter is such a success. Are you acquainted?"

They were not, Sarah living as much in the world as Sir Ethelred did not, and Amelia smoothly performed introductions.

"Hope this reel, or what d'you call it, is near an end, for I've someone to present to you, ma'am, and Calliope," said Sir Ethelred. "A good friend. I told him to follow me over here—ah, here he comes now."

Amelia let a shiver of apprehension escape her. Then she had to look up with friendly interest into the cold brown eyes of Jeremy Searle, Lord Doncastle.

She had to admit he was more handsome than any man in the room. His only sartorial fault—if a fault it could be called—was that his broad shoulders looked ready to burst from his precisely fitting coat of corbeau-coloured superfine. He was now affecting a quizzing-glass, she noted with a little start, and was surveying her through it with all the fastidiousness of a Brummell.

"Lord Doncastle and I are already acquainted," she said, looking away.

"To be sure. You were Mr. Searle, were you not, when you danced with both of us at Almack's in the old days? I won't say how long ago, for I expect you to remember me, my lord," put in Sarah with a practiced air of social flirtation only slightly hampered by her physical state.

"Miss Guildford, of course," said Doncastle, smiling an enchanting smile which he had not vouchsafed Amelia.

As Sarah and Jeremy renewed their acquaintance, Amelia willed herself not to think back to those innocent days. Jeremy Searle had indeed made it a practice to distinguish her friends as well as Amelia: at first, because they were a gaggle of pleasant girls, and later to hide the particularity of his attachment to the then Miss Montresor.

"Splendid, we're all friends together," said Sir Ethelred.

If anyone would be oblivious to tense undercurrents, it would be the baronet. Amelia only hoped that Sarah St. Cloud, as well, would not feel the distressing nervous tension which was making Amelia's own eardrums pound. How could anyone breathing not sense the hatred emanating from Jeremy's eyes whenever his glance lit upon her? Not to mention the misguided longing in her own heart, which she could not but feel must be radiating from her in a sort of cloud for all the world to see.

"May I have this dance, madam?" said Doncastle unexpectedly.

He could not be addressing Sarah. Amelia was forced to conclude that he must want to torment her, Amelia, in the privacy of the waltz which she could hear the musicians striking up. She resolutely stifled a wish to rise and join him. How would it feel to be in his arms again? She must not let herself wonder. "I do not mean to dance, sir," she said with what she hoped was a distant nod.

Sarah and Sir Ethelred both urged her to change her mind, but Amelia was adamant.

"My loss, I'm sure," said Doncastle with a slight bow. He quirked a dark brow at Amelia as if to impress upon her a special meaning in his words.

Or was she only imagining that every phrase he uttered must relate to his anger at her, his resentment at their blighted love?

At this point Calliope was delivered back to her chaperon's side. She could have no part in the waltz until she had passed muster with the patronesses of Almack's and would thus be excused from the chore of the next dance. The thrill of this knowledge was sparkling in her fine grey eyes. Her erstwhile partner disappeared a little too quickly, Amelia thought.

"The dolt!" exclaimed Calliope as she took the vacant chair next to her chaperon. "He wished to speak only of some silly cockfight he had placed money on. Not another thought in his head but that barbarous—I can't even call it a sport. Can you even feature such a thing as watching two fowls pull one another apart? You may be sure I told him—oh, hello, Papa." She noticed her sire for the first time and nodded pleasantly.

"My dear, I wish to present you to a gentleman with whom you'll have a great deal more in common than that unlucky sprig," said Sir Ethelred, eyes twinkling with pleasure. "Doncastle? My daughter, Calliope. I have corresponded with Lord Doncastle for years on scientific matters, my dear.''

The baronet was canny enough not to rub his hands in glee as his handsome and eligible friend bowed over the hand of his daughter, but his wishes were evident.

Calliope gave a cool nod and lapsed into the pose of mute young schoolgirl. She averted her eyes.

"You never told me your daughter was such a beauty, Crane," said Doncastle. He favoured the silent young lady with the full power of his most enchanting smile, a smile Lady Jeffries-Hodge, looking on in helpless frustration, had not seen from him in seven years.

Amelia's heart sank. The match was made.

"SHE WILL NOT DANCE," said Count Riccoli, touching a hand to his overly pomaded black locks as he leered across the room at a certain lovely lady, clad in deep blue and sparkling white, who sat tamely in a gilt chair. "A pity. My Lady Buckley orders so many waltzes, for she is not averse to a little play, that one, and the mazy waltz is a service to us all. How better to start a friendship, *vero*? But the Jeffries-Hodge means to cause me more effort."

"Lay you a wager I'll win her favours before you manage to kiss her hand," challenged Captain Dawber. His luxurious military mustachios twitching in excitement, he followed the Italian's gaze.

"No, I shall," put in Mr. Johnstone.

Lord Doncastle glared from his position on the other side of a Doric column just behind the little congress. This gathering of rakes made it clear: the former Amelia Montresor had no honour left. Why did the thought that she was really no better than she should be, no better than he thought her, give him no pleasure?

He looked across the room as the three roués were scheming. Amelia was smiling up at a young partner of Miss Crane's. How innocent she appeared from this distance, how unlikely it seemed that any scandal could touch her. Doncastle had never seen her look lovelier. That gown! When he had been near her earlier, he had had to bite his tongue to keep from telling her how beautiful she looked in the shimmering sapphire silk. She hadn't lost her fashion sense in the seven years since their parting. She had only changed into a woman with more licence to dress alluringly than the young girl he had known. He had to admit that every other fashionable matron in the room wore a similar low neck. Why, on Amelia, did the style seem virtually indecent?

And now, to hear these bounders speculate upon the bestowing of her favours nearly drove him to distraction. He stifled the urge to throttle that irritating expatriot, Count Riccoli, and instead strolled around the column in a casual manner.

"Well, gentlemen," he said, "I overheard you discussing a certain lady. Someone who's known to be fast, I take it? I've been out of the country till recently. Haven't kept up on the latest." He winked.

"Lord Doncastle," said Mr. Johnstone with an overly respectful bow. "We were merely singing the praises of the newest widow to appear upon the scene."

"Ah! A widow." Doncastle deliberately looked knowing, hoping to draw his companions out.

They hardly needed that inducement, he was reflecting in disgust a moment later.

"The One-Guinea Widow, no less," said Count Riccoli without hesitation. "Left penniless by her husband. And do you suppose, milord, it was for her great fidelity? Now that she's unfettered, she'll be—lonely."

"Rumoured to be a regular tigress," said Captain Dawber, who had served in India.

"And where she's getting the funds to do the Season, who can tell? I've a good idea. I'd pay a pretty penny myself. Who knows how many others were called upon to dig into their pockets for that creation on her back?" said Mr. Johnstone, nudging the viscount.

That gentleman ignored the boorish touch of his social inferior, and Johnstone looked suitably chastened.

By this time Doncastle had heard the One-Guinea Widow story and had revised his opinion of Amelia's ability to run through funds. "She is staying with Sir Ethelred Crane's family this Season, to bring out the daughter," he informed the three. "For the usual stipend, I believe, which would explain where she gets the wherewithal to make an appearance." He wondered in passing why he was doing what amounted to defending the woman who had wronged him. He assured himself he would do the same for any human creature he heard slandered.

"Look there!" spoke up Captain Dawber. "There goes Lord Clayville to steal a march on all of us. Shouldn't wonder *he* will succeed. She's said to have a taste for the unusual. And his lordship was a friend of her husband's."

"So was I," put in Johnstone. "Don't see why—"

Doncastle didn't bother to listen to Johnstone's babbling. He followed the captain's ill-bred, pointing finger with his eyes and saw, across the room, a wolfish, leering man with light hair bending over Amelia's hand. Lady St. Cloud, still stationed beside her friend, was looking quite alarmed. And why should she not? Lord Clayville's amorous exploits were rumoured to put Lord Byron's worst transgressions in the shade.

Amelia maintained her mild and serene attitude as she gave a frosty stare to Lord Clayville, shook her head, and went back to her conversation with Sarah St. Cloud.

Doncastle frowned. Amelia's behaviour was as modest as a maiden's. Too modest to be genuine. She must be a clever one indeed, to think she could indulge in romantic exploits with the ton none the wiser.

Perhaps she was hanging out for another rich husband, and that was why she had denied all these rakes the pleasure of her company. Well, she would catch cold at that game! Her reputation among the gentlemen assured that she would never marry again, unless to some Cit too dazzled by her beauty to mind her ill fame.

Doncastle kept looking at her, observing her pure profile, her delightful figure, with a studious attention which he attributed to morbid curiosity. His ears pricked up as he heard the musicians strike up a certain tune.

He felt his heart contract. Now, at the very moment he was looking at Amelia, to hear that particular piece! Without pausing to consider, he strode across the room and bowed stiffly before the lady.

"Lady Jeffries-Hodge, you will dance with me."

Amelia looked up. She was flushed, and her blue eyes were overbright; could she have recognised the tune as well as he had? "I never dance, sir," she said dismissively. "I have already told you so."

Doncastle responded by grasping her arm and lifting her, gently but firmly, out of her chair while Sarah St. Cloud looked on with avid interest. He had propelled Amelia out onto the floor and put his arm about her before she had time to do more than gasp out her protests in a soft voice, mindful of the sharp ears in their vicinity. "We are dancing, madam," he said coldly. "It is either that or cause a scene."

Amelia wished she could close her eyes and forget that
this wasn't her Jeremy who held her. It was only the cold
and cynical Lord Doncastle he had become. Her steps
fitted to his as neatly as they ever had, though they had
not waltzed before. Despite her best efforts, she began to
enjoy the feel of being in his arms, not remembering the
past, simply enjoying the present. The folly of such an
occupation soon struck her. She shivered.

"Cold, my lady?" drawled her partner as he swept her
into a difficult turn.

"Yes, my lord," she returned as calmly as she could.

"It was a country dance that we engaged in in the old
days, wasn't it? The powers that be didn't allow this
public embracing seven years ago," said Doncastle in a
conversational tone. He held her tighter, as though to
demonstrate the loose morals of the present age.

Amelia stared. "You do remember!"

He glanced down at her for one telling instant, then
quickly directed his gaze over her shoulder. "How could
I not remember the tune I fell in love to? Callow youth
that I was."

"I was quite as callow," Amelia said with a sigh.

He looked at her again, sharply. "But you quickly
gleaned enough town-bronze to understand that your best
interest lay in a rich marriage."

Amelia was silent. She could never answer that charge.
To Lord Doncastle, the facts were irrevocably against
her.

They spent the rest of the dance in frosty silence, a
drifting iceberg in the sea of chattering couples who surrounded them.

When the music stopped, Doncastle formally conducted Amelia back to her chair. A bevy of rakes, including the obnoxious and licentious Lord Clayville, was

waiting beside the seat, all evidently oblivious to the un-
welcoming frowns of Lady St. Cloud.

Amelia's heart sank as she saw the men. She had done
so well in not dancing until Jeremy had captured her, and
now that she had broken her vow, what was she to say to
these wolves? She was no more than a helpless creature
about to be thrown into their jaws. Sarah met her eyes
and gave her a defeated little shrug.

Doncastle saw her seated with all the courtesy due any
partner. He bowed. "My thanks, Lady Jeffries-Hodge,
and your pardon for using you to win my wager," he
said. Acknowledging the eager gentlemen with a smile,
he added in a confiding tone, "A friend of mine bet me
I couldn't waltz with this lady, who is determined never
to dance again. I am afraid I bullied her onto the floor. I
know none of you will be as ungentlemanly as I was."

"Don't worry, my lord, none of them will," spoke up
Lady St. Cloud.

Amelia gave Doncastle a grateful glance, wondering
why on earth he should bother to save her from these
men. He ought to be glad she was to be persecuted. Or
was he trying to spoil what he supposed must be her
pleasure? Did he think that she wished to dance with her
motley admirers? That she had only been waiting for the
opportunity to break her own rule? Had he made up that
story about a wager to spite her? Or—dreadful thought—
had there really been a wager?

She said with a cool look around, "His lordship is
correct, gentlemen. He virtually captured me, and I cannot allow that sort of disreputable behaviour again. Next
time I would be forced to scream aloud and cause a
scandal."

Even the boldest of the surrounding rakehells was not
willing to risk such a spectacle. All of them, including the

great Lord Clayville, had only a tenuous entrée to gatherings of any respectability. A public contretemps would ensure that the one of them who provoked the scene would do no more in the future than hang about the fringes of society, where no rich matrons or tempting widows would cross his path.

"I am desolated, *signora*. Desolated," said Count Riccoli in a passionate voice.

"And I," piped up Mr. Johnstone.

"Respect a lady's wishes, though," said Captain Dawber. "Can't do less, can we?" Favouring his companions with a look of shared irritation, his red-veined blue eyes turned to Lord Doncastle.

That gentleman shrugged, smiled, and walked away, quite pleased with himself for putting a spoke in the wheel of Amelia's would-be lovers.

Heaven only knew if she wanted any of them. Perhaps she was only pretending reluctance because of her position in Sir Ethelred's household. If she was respectable, how would she have earned that fast reputation among the rakes?

How right she had felt in his arms, though! He had been hard pressed to believe that so many years had gone by. And she had seemed so sincerely dismayed to see the crowd of rakehells ready to pounce upon her.

Resolutely, Doncastle pushed these thoughts to the back of his mind. Amelia had bewitched him years ago. He must not allow her to work on his feelings again, however practiced her imitation of an innocent woman in difficulties.

CHAPTER SIX

"I THINK IT A CRIME AGAINST nature to take flowers out of their habitat," said Calliope the next morning, frowning over the array of bouquets the footman, Amelia's faithful Higgins, was ranging on the sideboard in the breakfast room.

"If it makes you feel any better, my dear, remember that these blossoms have lived all their lives in hothouses," said Amelia. She exchanged a surreptitious wink with Higgins as that individual left the room.

He was back again in an instant, to Calliope's evident disgust, near staggering under the weight of an especially gaudy floral offering. He placed it in the middle of the collection. "That's all, madam," he then said, executing a smooth bow.

"Thank you, Higgins," said Amelia. The servant left the room, and Calliope, with a sigh, sat down opposite the blooms and scowled.

"This is nonsense," she proclaimed.

"I call it an excellent sign that your Season is a success already," said Amelia. "I didn't receive a quarter so many after my first ball. Did I receive any? I really can't remember." She crossed the room to sniff at a bouquet of pure white roses. The card clipped to one stem caught her eye, and she drew in her breath.

The card was Lord Clayville's. Amelia turned it over and read the message scrawled on the back. She turned bright red and crumpled the bit of pasteboard up in her hand, pricking herself on the pin which had secured the card to the ribbons of the bouquet. She continued down the row of flowers, carefully examining each card.

Calliope had lost interest in the mistreated blossoms and was studying a pamphlet on the Corn Laws, for she prided herself on being a young lady who, despite her love of more scholarly pursuits, did know what was going on in the world about her.

Amelia had to remove two more cards with suggestive notes addressed to her before she came to the last bouquet. She read Calliope's name on this tasteful offering of hothouse lilies. As though she had last seen it yesterday, not seven years before, she recognised the strong hand of Jeremy Searle.

Her enjoyment in Calliope's triumph was destroyed. She supposed she ought not to feel any emotion other than gratitude that so many young men, including the desirable Jeremy, had distinguished her young charge. Why must such a sick feeling wash over her merely because the event she so dreaded was indeed well on the way to happening? Lord Doncastle was evidently commencing his courtship of his friend's daughter. Amelia took a deep breath and vowed not to let a tear fall. She would need plenty of practice by the time of the wedding.

And what was she to do about the other flowers, the ones for her, all from men with dalliance on their minds?

There was no problem with the flowers themselves. Calliope would probably not even read the cards, let alone notice which messages were missing. The bouquets all would pass as being sent for Calliope.

As if to test this theory, Mrs. Winkle bustled into the room, the stiff draperies of her fringed and braid-trimmed morning robe trailing behind her. ''I didn't believe it when that dreadful Jeffries-Hodge footman told me why the bell had been ringing all the morning. So it's true. All these flowers for Calliope! Well, my dear, I congratulate you. Wasn't I right to tell you that looks aren't everything?''

"Thank you," said Calliope, not looking up.

Mrs. Winkle went through the flowers as carefully as had Amelia. "Why, there are several without cards. What could this mean?" she exclaimed.

"The usual," said Amelia. "Many men wish to be anonymous when they distinguish a young lady for the first time."

"Oh. How strange," said Calliope.

"How timid the young men of today must be, indeed. Three anonymous offerings," said Mrs. Winkle.

Amelia thought the older lady looked at her hard, and she even fancied that Mrs. Winkle could tell she held the three missing cards crumpled up in one fist. How this lady would stare could she read the licentious message Lord Clayville had dared to write! Amelia hid her hand in the folds of her skirt.

"Oh, this pretty arrangement is from your father's friend, Lord Doncastle," said Mrs. Winkle, bending her bulky form over the bouquet of lilies. "A flattering attention."

"Flattering," muttered Calliope, still engrossed in her reading.

"I believe I'll go up to my room for a bit," Amelia said. "It must be the scent of the flowers—I have the headache."

"What a shame," said Calliope. "I was going to suggest you take some of these plaguey things to your bedchamber. I know you usually enjoy them."

"I think, dear, it would be better if you were to order them dispersed about the public rooms, if you don't care for them in your own chamber," said Amelia. She left the room just as Mrs. Winkle was beginning to hint to Calliope that her own room would be much improved by the addition of those lovely white roses, the ones with no card.

In Amelia's bedroom, Lewes was still doing the morning cleaning. "I hear some bouquets came for you, my lady," said the maid with a sympathetic look.

Servants! Once again Amelia marvelled at how they knew everything. "I haven't had so many indecent proposals since—well, I've never had that many indecent proposals all at once," said Amelia, sighing.

"Oh! Then they were all of them—"

Amelia shook her head at the girl's disappointed face. "Lewes, you will please discontinue at once your absurd fancies that I will meet a man I like. I will never marry again, and that is final. I'm rather relieved that the gentlemen seem united in their desire to give me a disgust of them. I certainly won't be tempted by an offer of an interlude at a country inn, which was Count Riccoli's suggestion."

"You don't say so, madam!" Lewes' eyes were wide.

"It seems my vile reputation has preceded me into Society," said Amelia with a sigh. "I only wish I knew how vile I was supposed to be, and who is the one who started the rumours. That's the difficulty with being the object of gossip: one seldom hears it oneself."

"Oh, madam," said Lewes in a mournful tone.

Amelia had to laugh at the abigail's tragic air. "It's not so bad—yet. But do you keep it quiet, Lewes, that any of those flowers were for me. I am certain I can count on

Higgins, too. I've removed the cards, and I'm saying the bouquets are anonymous gifts for Miss Crane.''

''Most wise, my lady.''

''I think, Lewes, that my Season here will be more difficult than I had anticipated. Never did I expect to attract that kind of notice. Lord Jeffries-Hodge likely gave a false idea of me to the men he knew, for I can't imagine how else the rumour started that I was free with my favours. Only think! A woman of ill repute chaperoning a young lady! Perhaps I have done the wrong thing by taking this post.''

''Oh, never say that, ma'am,'' said Lewes. ''It is ever so much nicer here than in that little hole across town. And so many of the flowers were for Miss Crane, you must be doing the proper thing as her watch-dog.''

''I hope so, Lewes. I hope so. But I fear that Miss Crane would be better off if she had never met me.''

Lewes shook her head in disagreement, but she dared say nothing further.

LATER THAT DAY, AMELIA got into her best walking ensemble and stopped by Calliope's room to collect the girl for their outing. Upon entering, the first thing Amelia saw was Doncastle's bouquet of lilies, ornamenting a plain table near a window.

Calliope, who was tying her bonnet in a severe bow beneath her chin with the aid of the one looking-glass the room boasted, a small one inside the wardrobe door, saw Amelia's start of surprise. ''I had to bring that bunch up here with me. Cousin Dorinda kept hinting that I should give it her, as well as the white roses, and I finally got disgusted with my Cousin's greed and determined to foil her.''

This explanation was reasonable, but Amelia found it a little too glib. "I thought you might be reconsidering Lord Doncastle's attentions to you," she said, hating herself for her misplaced jealousy. Why should she care if Doncastle sent flowers to all the girls in London? But she did.

"Lord Doncastle's attentions to me," said Calliope succinctly, "are entirely motivated by Papa's nonsensical encouraging. I don't like his lordship at all."

"Don't you?" Amelia opened her eyes wide in astonishment. For all Calliope's prior assertions that she would not like her father's friend, Amelia had been certain that actually meeting the charming man would change the girl's mind, and she had been steeling herself to watch their romance develop under her reluctant chaperonage.

"I find Lord Doncastle to be too sure of himself. Too satirical. Too insincere," said Calliope, shaking her head.

"Plain speaking indeed." Amelia suddenly felt almost giddy with relief. "What do you think of the other young men you met last night?"

"They were all too stupid to be borne," said Calliope. "I knew it would be so, but it was still a shock to find that gentlemen talk, and think, of nothing but their silly sports. Occasionally they seem compelled to offer an inane compliment which has nothing to do with the girl they're speaking to. Do you know one of the clunches told me how much he admired my lovely auburn hair? My hair is red, and I'm not to be flattered."

"I'm sure you're not," said Amelia, smiling. "I do hope you meet someone more to your taste, my dear. Perhaps at Lady St. Cloud's. Unless she's changed beyond reason, and I don't think she has, one can meet the most interesting people at her house."

"She is a nice enough woman, but too interested in how others go on," said Calliope. "I don't wish to speak ill of your old friend, Amelia, but she would do well not to meddle in other people's affairs. The way she kept pushing dancing partners on me last night! I never saw the like."

Amelia hid her amusement, nodded, and led the way down to the carriage.

Their goal this afternoon was a Venetian breakfast at Lady St. Cloud's in Mount Street. Sarah had explained to Amelia the night before when begging her friends to attend, that though her delicate situation was forcing her more and more to stay at home, neither her apothecary nor her accoucheur could find fault with an entertainment which featured eating as its main focus and took place in the lady's own home.

Sarah's house was like Sarah herself: beautiful, light-hearted, and in excellent taste. As Amelia and her charge were shown into the salon where her ladyship was receiving, Amelia marvelled that her old friend had been able to impress her own style upon the place so thoroughly. Sarah had only been married four years and had a large and censorious troupe of in-laws to bemoan every change she made. Yet every light, elegant stick of furniture, each cheerful picture and tasteful ornament, had evidently been selected by the present Lady St. Cloud herself.

The gathering was a crush. Amelia would have expected no less of the friendly and hospitable Sarah, who used to host secret midnight suppers when boxes of cake from home arrived for her at the seminary. Looking about anxiously, Amelia saw that none of the horrid men from the night before were present. Her instinct had been right, then. None of the blades who had sent her flowers were good ton.

Thankfully, though a good many curious stares were directed her way, here as at the Buckley ball nobody pointedly turned a back or otherwise distressed her.

One youngish, rather pretty woman who looked slightly familiar, but whom Amelia could not place, did cast an eager, amused look her way. Amelia could not respond other than to nod slightly, in case the woman was someone she had met and forgotten—a lady with such startling brassy-blond curls, though, and such very elaborate clothing—surely one would remember meeting such a creature. The female acknowledged the nod with only a lowering of long, thickly lashed eyelids and what Amelia thought was a knowing expression.

She had no time to meditate further upon the incident.

"Dearest creatures! I'm so thrilled you could come," Sarah said, breaking from a group of fashionable people to come and kiss first Amelia's cheek, then Calliope's, for which latter operation she had to stand on tiptoe. "You are both elegance itself. That pale russet is divine on you, Miss Crane, and you are looking particularly fine yourself, Amelia. I can't wait for you both to meet my friends. There are several here who are known to you, Amelia. As for Miss Crane, I have a set of remarkably lively young people already in the dining-room setting upon the food, including several of the young men you danced with last night, my dear, and I shall have you conducted to them at once. Sam!"

Lady St. Cloud beckoned in her imperious manner to a young man across the way. She paid no attention to Calliope's mumbled request not to bother. Amelia had seen the involuntary shudder shake Calliope's shoulders at the mention of a lively group of young people, but

Sarah could not know that her debutante guest would not be delighted by the prospect of callow companions.

The man Sarah had summoned came over, and Amelia flushed with pleasure as she recognized him. "Mr. Guildford!" she cried, holding out her hand.

Sarah's twin brother, Samuel Guildford, smiled widely. His narrow long face and lank blond hair had not changed, though Amelia could tell at a glance that he was vastly more confident than the bookish young Cambridge man she remembered from her earlier acquaintance with Sarah's family. His clothes were in the first style of elegance, too, a change from the flyaway costumes of his student years.

"You were used to call me Sam, were you not?" he said, taking Amelia's hand. "I don't think I can get used to styling you Lady Jeffries-Hodge."

"No, it must be Amelia." She beamed with the pure pleasure of meeting an old friend, a friend who had not changed at all in his manner towards her.

"And I must present you to Amelia's charge, Miss Crane, so that you may take her off to join the younger set in the dining parlour," put in Sarah. "Odd, is it not, brother, that you're one of the young people, and by some quirk of fate Amelia and I are sedate old ladies? We're all of an age." She paused for breath. "Miss Crane, my twin brother—Mr. Guildford."

For the first time Sam Guildford's eyes lit on Calliope, who had been doing her insufficient best to hide behind Amelia.

"Miss Crane!" said Sam. He looked into her face for a long and thoughtful moment; then he spoke a phrase in some foreign tongue which Amelia did not understand at all.

Calliope apparently did. Her eyes widened slightly, her face took on a wary expression, and she inclined her head. "Thank you, sir," she said, dropping a small curtsey. When she rose from it Amelia noted that the girl was actually blushing. Amelia took care to note further that Sam was a good few inches taller than Calliope.

"Do you call that plain speaking?" said Sarah with a laugh. "I know you are pleased to call yourself a plain-spoken man."

Her brother took his eyes off Calliope and turned to Sarah. "Oh, beg pardon, sister. I merely told Miss Crane, in Greek, that the flames of her hair burn as brightly as the fires of love."

Amelia stared. "Are we to recognize the quotation, Sam?"

"Not likely. I made it up this instant. So you understand me, Miss Crane? Fancy meeting a female in my sister's circle who reads Greek. Forgive me for the boldness, but your hair struck me. I expect I needed an inspiration as I've spent the morning trying to compose something in that style of the ancients with no success. Yet now I make no doubt that if I had some more to go with that line I might come up with a tolerable poem. What do you think?"

His manner was so matter of fact, his expression so open and friendly, that Amelia couldn't believe he was trying to flirt. She carefully gauged Calliope's reaction.

After the first shock of being addressed in Greek, the girl was smiling back in a friendlier manner than Amelia had yet seen her exhibit in front of a young man. "I might advise you, Mr. Guildford," she said, "if I had some idea of what sort of poem you intend."

"You children may carry that prosy discussion right into the dining-room, if you please," said Sarah with a wave of her hand.

"Pleasure to see you again, Amelia," said Sam with a frank smile. He tucked Calliope's hand into his arm, and the two were off.

"That was well done," said Amelia.

"What, my sending her off with Sam? I thought she would be safe with him, for a less dangerous young man has yet to walk the earth. He isn't an eligible parti, you understand, for he's readying himself to go to Edinburgh in the fall, where he is actually to take up a post at the University. My mama is heartsick."

Amelia smiled, digesting this information. Promising, very promising. She knew Sir Ethelred Crane cared nothing for rank or fortune. Only his daughter's happiness would matter to him. "I meant, actually, that it was well done of Sam to say something to her in Greek. Calliope has been bewailing the sad fact that all the young men in Society are stupid."

"Fancy! She didn't know that already?" And Sarah, with a tinkling laugh, led her friend over towards a group of ladies. "And, now, since we're renewing old acquaintances, here's someone I swear you won't have forgotten."

A stately young woman with smooth brown hair turned from the circle of females just as Sarah had finished her words. A lovely smile broke out on a pale, oval face as the lady's eyes met Amelia's.

Amelia couldn't have been happier to greet Lady Margot Jamieson. She had corresponded intermittently with the young woman, as she had with Sarah, ever since their Season in London, and had seen her but rarely on her few flying visits to town in the company of Lord Jeffries-Hodge. Lady Margot was wealthy and independent save for a doting father, and a couple of years older than Sarah and Amelia. She had grown from an awkward girl suffering through the obligatory Season into a blue-stocking well-known for her frank opinions and her disdain of the men who still tried to distinguish her.

She either affected or really was afflicted by the same carelessness with clothes that she had exhibited in schoolgirl days. Her outfits were fashionable though sober, but she always seemed to forget about them, sometimes to the extent of treading on her own gown or letting a shawl drag in the dirt. Amelia remembered this distinguishing mark of Margot's when she saw that the lace edge of her friend's long sleeve had caught and torn on a ring she wore. No doubt such nonchalance was a trait of the true scholar.

Margot had written Amelia that she was trying her best to grow into a formidable intellectual, the type of woman no man would approach but with a respectful question about a literary problem. Amelia could tell at a glance that the programme was successful.

Fortunately, she could also tell that the formidable manner was a pose pure and simple, to save Margot trouble, and that her old friend was still the same kind soul she had always been. Amelia and Margot found themselves on a sofa, catching up on old times, while Sarah fluttered away—though her fluttering was somewhat comical in her situation—to see to other guests.

"Sarah has told me of your new position, and I call chaperoning a young lady a fine, sensible thing to do," said Lady Margot decidedly. "You must let me be of use in any way I can."

"Oh, Margot, both you and Sarah are too kind," said Amelia. To her astonishment, she actually felt a tear well up in her eye. "I don't deserve such friends."

"But you do. Am I not right, Amelia, that you haven't had many friends in late years?"

"Truthfully," said Amelia, "sometimes, if it hadn't been for two loyal servants of mine, I don't know how I would have gone on."

Margot nodded. "We have never spoken of it, my dear, or written of it, but your marriage to Lord Jeffries-Hodge wasn't the romantic escapade it was made out to be, was it?"

Amelia stared. She supposed, upon consideration, that an elopement would be assumed to be a romantic escapade, but those words were so far from being descriptive of her relations with her late husband that her face was a complete blank.

"Sarah thought, at the time, that you were seized suddenly by a grand passion," said Margot, a dimple appearing at the corner of her straight, serious mouth, "but I always knew that wasn't the case."

"How did you know?" asked Amelia.

"Logic, my dear. After turning the event over carefully in my mind, it became clear to me that you not only weren't in love, you were probably in difficulties of some sort. I won't question you further, but do know that I am your friend, and should you wish to confide in me—"

"No, thank you, Margot," said Amelia, her face stern. "My marriage is something I never discuss."

Margot was often somewhat insensitive to the moods of others, but in this case she could hardly mistake the matter. She laughed to break the sudden tension. "If only some of my friends followed your example! And now tell me more about your situation here. Is the young lady pleasant?''

Amelia was quite glad to give her curious friend all the particulars of her post, including an expurgated, but still wicked, sketch of Mrs. Winkle.

"Seeing you ladies here together has brought back some fond memories for me," said a masculine voice near Amelia's ear. She found herself looking into Lord Doncastle's eyes. To her astonishment, those eyes were gleaming with friendliness, and for a moment her heartbeat quickened. Then she noticed that his gaze was fixed on Lady Margot.

"Lord Doncastle, you are quite welcome to join us, so long as you don't concern yourself solely with the past," stated Margot.

"I can hardly lose myself completely in the long ago, with two such fine examples of the present-day female before me," returned the gentleman. "A dignified dowager, and the kingdom's foremost authority on the works of Chaucer."

Margot quipped something in return which Amelia did not even hear. She was too upset by the definite satirical glint in Doncastle's eye as he had included her in his comment. Dignified dowager, indeed!

She began to wish—a very little—that she and Jeremy had not succeeded so thoroughly in keeping their long-ago attachment a secret. She would give much to be able to confide in one of her kind friends the present trouble the former Mr. Jeremy Searle was causing her heart.

"Wool-gathering, my dear?" The voice of Lady Margot brought Amelia out of her daze. "Sarah has started the procession to the breakfast part of this entertainment."

"Perhaps Lady Jeffries-Hodge is fatigued after the exertions of her night. At the Buckley ball, I mean to say," said Doncastle with a maddening smile.

Amelia had the unsettling feeling that he was baiting her with an obvious double meaning; that he had heard stories of her, likely the same stories that had given her would-be swains the gall to pelt her with insulting messages disguised by flowers. "I am unused to late hours, but reaccustoming myself," she said.

"And getting back into Society ought to be a gradual thing, as I'm sure you both know," said Lady Margot. She hadn't seemed to remark any irony in Doncastle's words.

A lady upon each arm, Doncastle moved into the dining parlour. The meal was to be informal, and small tables were placed here and there quite in the style of a ballroom supper. The viscount had no trouble in securing the best situated of these tables by means of fixing his most haughty stare on a very young gentleman who was evidently attempting to save places for friends. The unlucky boy bowed and hurried away.

"That wasn't kind of you," said Amelia, glancing round the room and seeing, with relief, that Calliope was well settled with Sam Guildford and a circle of pleasant-looking young ladies and gentlemen.

Doncastle smiled. Again it was a genuine smile, and again he directed it to Lady Margot, quite as though that lady had been the one to address him. "I don't, as a rule, use the privilege of rank, but there are these rare occasions when it comes in very handy. That young man served under me in Belgium." He put the ladies in two chairs and went off to join the gentlemen milling about the buffet tables.

"Doncastle is an odd sort," said Lady Margot, directing a piercing stare at Amelia. "Seems quite taken with you. Quite as it was in the old days, when he hovered about all of us, pretending there was no particularity in his attentions."

"Taken with me? How can you say so, Margot? He holds me in disgust, I promise you," said Amelia, speaking lightly. She ignored the comment about their younger days. She and Jeremy had been so careful, so secret in their attachment in those days that it was a shock to know that anyone had suspected the truth.

"He holds you in disgust?" Her friend repeated Amelia's words in astonishment.

"Depend upon it, he's heard about my husband's will and has listened to Lady Manville and her set. I happen to know he considered me a mercenary wretch before I was widowed, and now he is probably thinking, along with so many others, that I well deserved Lord Jeffries-Hodge's Turkish treatment." Amelia shrugged, willing her voice to remain casual, uncaring.

She reckoned without Margot's piercing hazel eyes and sharp ears. "I see," said the lady shortly, frowning at Amelia. "You know, my dear, that of all things I deplore secretiveness."

Amelia shrugged and turned the conversation. She could think of nothing else to do and hoped the discussion of Margot's present activities in town would distract her friend as well as herself.

Lord Doncastle, followed by a footman bearing a tray with three laden plates, soon returned to distract them further.

"Now, ladies," he said with a suave smile, placing himself opposite Lady Jeffries-Hodge with a flourish and looking directly into Amelia's eyes, "tell me what life in town is like these days. I've been away so long I've forgotten everything."

"Everything, my lord?" queried Margot with a severely raised eyebrow.

"Everything," said Doncastle, still looking, with a disconcerting shrewdness, at Amelia.

"Good," said Amelia. "How pleasant it must be for a gentleman like yourself to begin life anew."

"I haven't forgotten quite that much, madam," he returned. Amelia had no recourse but to smile, shrug, and apply herself to her meal. She had to struggle not to notice that all the while they ate, and Margot entertained them with a description of the latest offerings of the Society of Ancient Music, Jeremy was regarding her closely. Likely with the same attention he only otherwise applied to some dreadful insect he wished to dissect for scientific purposes.

CHAPTER SEVEN

DONCASTLE SURVEYED THE PARK from the back of his newest acquisition, a highly bred Arabian stallion. In a riding coat of severe dark grey, cut in the most dashing mode, the viscount was the cynosure of many an appraising and approving female eye.

His companion, an acquaintance chance-met in the bridle-path, had not that same advantage, for he was a small and wiry individual whose lank brown hair rebelled at all attempts to curl it into a fashionable crop. His clothes, though tailored by the best, did not become him, and the manner in which he sat his highly-bred roan gelding was clumsy compared to Lord Doncastle's perfection.

Doncastle and the other were at the moment surveying a barouche-landau occupied by a dark-haired lady and a younger female redhead. The vehicle was surrounded by a half-dozen gentlemen, mounted and on foot, and even from a distance of ten yards the discomfort on the dark-haired lady's face was evident.

"Look at her," said Doncastle's companion with a sneer, "my brother barely cold, and already up to her vile tricks. I tell you, my lord, it was not for no reason that she was left with that famous single guinea."

"I am rather shocked that you, as her brother-in-law, did not provide for her," said Doncastle, quirking a dark brow. The One-Guinea story made perfect sense to him, and he called it a good joke on Amelia. Evidently her husband hadn't liked finding out he had been wed for his money. Doncastle could not fathom, though, why Amelia's husband's family had not given her at least a small stipend. Since she bore their name, her staying in want must be to their disgrace.

"I would have been going against my late brother's wishes," exclaimed the present Lord Jeffries-Hodge in some heat. "He particularly wished her to live in poverty. That's why he took care to settle even her dowry away from her, you know. She is a pretty woman, but not an innocent. I saw her at the time of my brother's death as I see her now: a female who can shift very well for herself. We do not speak, naturally. To do so would defame my brother's memory. Besides, I could hardly ask my lady to receive such a one into her home."

Doncastle wondered why the condemnation of this sharp-nosed, shifty-eyed baron was not sinking Amelia in his own estimation. On the contrary, he felt his opinion of her undergoing a certain change. Anyone but a fool could see that, far from basking in the attention of all those rogues about her carriage, as Jeffries-Hodge pretended, Amelia was wild to be out of the Park and safe at home. If she did not wish herself away upon her own account—and Doncastle must assume, from the talk going about London, that she eagerly courted male gallantries—she did not appear to like exposing Miss Crane to such company.

Doncastle glanced about, beginning to worry in earnest. Only upon Miss Crane's account, naturally. Now would be the time for one of Amelia's friends to save the situation, and he looked in vain for Lady St. Cloud or Lady Margot Jamieson. There were several respectable matrons driving or walking near Amelia's carriage, but none looked ready to lend countenance to the motley collection of beaus that surrounded the dowager Lady Jeffries-Hodge.

"Fascinates you, does she?" said her brother-in-law, seeing the viscount's attention still directed to Amelia's carriage. "I don't wonder. She's a pretty wench. Beware, though, Doncastle. There is some question about the way my brother met his death."

Amelia a murderess? This was a new idea, and hardly a believable one. Doncastle looked his astonishment.

Though the two horsemen were quite alone, Jeffries-Hodge leaned towards the viscount to whisper, "Nothing that can be proven, more's the pity. But my brother died suddenly. I was not with them in Hampshire at the time, but the rumours there, sir, are not pretty. I did nothing to investigate it, of course, being unwilling to besmirch my family name with a scandal of the worst sort."

"Of course." Doncastle observed the other man narrowly. What was he doing now, if not spreading scandal? "Then you are telling me your sister-in-law is likely a criminal."

"Oh, nothing like that. I would never even hint at such a shocking thing," said Lord Jeffries-Hodge with a small smile. "Now I must leave you, Doncastle. See you at the club. There are some people over the way I must say how d'ye do to. Goodbye."

Doncastle nodded his head in leave-taking and watched the baron spring his horse over to the carriage path, where a couple in a small, somehow pinched-looking low phaeton greeted him. The female, a gaudy creature with improbably golden hair, was cool but friendly. The gentleman with her, a grey-haired, high-nosed individual in late middle age, scowled at Jeffries-Hodge's approach but was tolerably polite after that one lapse.

Doncastle wondered in passing who the lady could be. He believed he had seen her from a distance at Lady St. Cloud's breakfast, for that hair and that gaudy style in dress did stand out in a crowd.

As for the aging gentleman, Doncastle remembered very well that stern profile, those small, calculating eyes. Even seeing the man from across the park, he shuddered. Now why the devil should Amelia's brother-in-law be acquainted with Lord Alfred Montresor, Amelia's father?

There was no telling. He guided his horse in the direction of Amelia's carriage. Miss Crane was his object. He had been meaning to spend more time with Sir Ethelred's daughter in any case. One could scarcely marry a chit with whom one had not exchanged two words.

AMELIA WISHED SHE WERE driving. Not even fear of hurting the horses would have kept her from springing the beasts right through this crowd. Anything to escape the leering attentions of all these dreadful men. She knew, however, that Sir Ethelred's sedate coachman would never be so careless of his master's cattle, and her orders to him to drive on had not yet been obeyed. Lord Clayville had purposely positioned his own high-perch vehicle directly in their path and delighted in his captive audience as he shouted down his compliments with a knowing smile.

Count Riccoli, Captain Dawber, a loud and leering Major Webb, and an unfastidious Mr. Halliford joined the notorious Lord Clayville in Lady Jeffries-Hodge's court. Mr. Johnstone had had to take his leave, to Amelia's relief, but his departure had unfortunately not dispersed his friends.

"Perhaps we could turn the carriage about, Miles, in order not to disturb Lord Clayville's cattle," Amelia suggested desperately.

The coachman merely gave her a disgusted look and kept still.

Calliope was looking stormy. "Sir, you must have other appointments," she said to Count Riccoli.

"None at all, *signorina*, I assure you. Nothing is more important than your entertainment this fine spring day."

"We might pray for rain," Calliope said quite loudly to Amelia, with an impish smile.

"For the tenth time, gentlemen, my charge and I must be going," Amelia said. She was beginning to feel ready to scream. These men were outwardly admiring, true, but she knew they were really surrounding her in a threatening manner. Not for her sort the respect due an ordinary titled dowager. That her supposed adorers would not follow her wishes was proof that they were scornful of her, to a man.

She gritted her teeth. Never again would she dare to bring Calliope out for a drive. The girl must not be exposed to this kind of nonsense. No young woman's reputation could bear many encounters like this one. In grim decision, Amelia resolved to offer Sir Ethelred her resignation. What good was a sponsor who attracted this kind of a motley crowd?

"My lady Jeffries-Hodge. And Miss Crane, upon my word. Have you forgotten our appointment?"

Surprised, Amelia looked up into the face of Lord Doncastle. "Oh, sir, we are merely having a little difficulty with the horses."

"Well, resolve it quickly, coachman, for I'm late getting these two ladies to Lady Manville's," Doncastle improvised with a superior grin for the lesser males of Amelia's court. "Miss Crane, may I say you are looking lovely."

Calliope nodded, eyeing him suspiciously.

Amelia's heart sank. She might have known Jeremy had not seen the situation and determined to rescue her, his former love. No, his concern was all for Calliope. And why should it not be? Though he had as yet paid no further attention to the girl than dancing with her at the Buckley ball and sending her flowers the morning after, he was bound to consider her a suitable wife. She was young, pretty, and extremely intelligent.

And Calliope *was* looking lovely. Her costume was perfection, and she had been blushing like a rose ever since their brief encounter with Sam Guildford shortly after they had entered the Park. The colour was quite becoming to her normally pale freckled face.

Lord Doncastle determinedly ignored Calliope's icy reception of his compliment and continued with the intended rescue. "If you will excuse us, gentlemen? You know Lady Manville. She hates to be kept waiting." He said this in the secure knowledge that the haughty portals of Manville House had never opened to any of this ragtag and bobtail.

Count Riccoli's nostrils flared in anger; he looked as if he might pull forth a dueling foil at any moment. Captain Dawber twirled his luxuriant mustachios and looked stormy enough to call the viscount out for this insult. Then reason presumably reasserted itself. The count and the captain left tamely, each sparing only one regretful, raking glance for Lady Jeffries-Hodge. The other gentlemen perforce did likewise.

"You will be hearing from me, my lady," said Lord Clayville, the last to go. He nearly shouted the words from his phaeton, then wheeled it away at last, freeing up the Crane barouche-landau.

"You aren't really taking us to Lady Manville, are you?" demanded Calliope. "That would not be much of a rescue."

"Rest assured I would never play such a trick on two charming ladies," said Doncastle with a special smile for the younger of them. His eyes flickered over Amelia. "A pity you should need saving."

"We do thank you, my lord, and I agree with you completely. A dreadful shame that things should have come to such a pass. Never you fear, though, Miss Crane will soon be safe from any further insult," said Amelia stiffly. Her face was serious, thoughtful, as she added, "Perhaps we ought to go to Lady Manville after all."

"Amelia! In heaven's name, why?" asked Calliope in horror.

Her chaperon hesitated, choosing her words carefully. "Why, to put you under her wing for the rest of the Season. My dear, Lord Doncastle would be the first to agree, as your father's friend, that your present chaperon is hardly in a position to see you placed in the best Society."

"What? Who is Lady St. Cloud, if not the best Society?" said Calliope scornfully.

"If it were only a question of her and her kind, there would be no problem," said Amelia. "I have many friends. However, I do have enemies. I can't dignify those dreadful gentlemen we just escaped from with any other title. They would offer either of us an insult as soon as look at us."

Calliope nodded in agreement. "But we can't give in to them. We can't let them win."

"Miss Crane has a point," said Doncastle. He was amazed at Amelia's correct reading of the situation and rather gratified that despite her cold and mercenary streak she was not quite lost to all proper feeling. His own poor judgement in falling in love with her long ago was somewhat vindicated by the knowledge that she did at least have some correct notions. "You might try a compromise, Lady Jeffries-Hodge. I agree with you that your young charge must never again be exposed to the society of those boors. Rather than avoid the Park, though, simply see to it that a respectable gentleman or two escorts you. I would be glad to offer my services."

"Oh, and I'm certain Mr. Guildford would, too," said Calliope.

Amelia nodded, noticing the way Calliope brought Sam Guildford into the conversation. Gratifying, most gratifying, but Sarah's brother had quite a rival in Doncastle. "The—boors are at least somewhat more controlled at social functions within doors," Amelia said. "And I always deny them when they try to visit the house. It's only out in the open that they become a problem."

"Precisely," said Doncastle. "Don't let your fears overcome your good sense." He smiled at Amelia, and, for just an instant, a look of real understanding passed between them.

Amelia's heart sang, in spite of her remonstrations to the errant organ that one little smile meant nothing to one so estranged from her as Lord Doncastle. Then the moment ended with the gentleman's next words.

"Did you know your brother-in-law was in town, my lady?" he asked with a keen look, a look almost of suspicion.

"No, I did not," said Amelia. "I have nothing to do with my late husband's family."

"I would keep it that way if I were you, madam. It strikes me that the new Lord Jeffries-Hodge is not a proper acquaintance for—for Miss Crane."

"I must agree with you there, sir," said Amelia. Once again she and Jeremy looked at each other, seeming to search one another's eyes for—something. Amelia wondered what her brother-in-law was doing in town, and what sorts of stories he was telling about her.

This line of thought was ended effectively when Doncastle turned from Amelia in rather an abrupt style and asked Calliope for the favour of a dance at the upcoming assembly at Almack's.

Amelia summoned up all her staunchest notions of dignity and listened, as gooseberry, to a gentleman arranging his next meeting with the girl he was courting. It took all her strength.

NEXT DAY, WHEN AMELIA and Lewes were out upon some errands in Bond Street, Amelia had the odd, not entirely unprecedented sensation of being watched. She turned about several times, in fact, so strong was the feeling that sharp eyes were boring into her back, but no one in particular was there.

Finally, on coming out of a milliner's, she ran right into a lady who, she realized, had been several steps behind her once that morning, had been seated in a carriage by the pavement another time, and now stood looking at her with a curious, half-friendly smile.

"The time has come, Amelia, dear," said the woman. "It is Amelia, is it not?"

Amelia nodded, mystified. She recognised the violently golden curls peeking from beneath the lady's red-plumed bonnet. She had seen this woman from a distance at least once before, but try though she might, she could not come up with a name to match the face. A round, pretty face, highly rouged but set in an expression of simple friendliness.

The blonde grasped Amelia's hands with no further ado, pressed them, and then cast herself into the startled arms of Lady Jeffries-Hodge, to the entertainment of several passers-by. Amelia, who was quite a bit smaller than the well-padded stranger, nearly staggered. She exchanged a shocked glance with Lewes, who pinched her mouth in disapproval.

"Amelia, my dear," said the fair-haired lady, "I am your mama."

Amelia pulled back. "You are the new Lady Alfred? My stepmother?"

Lewes let out a little shriek. Lady Alfred Montresor spared a glare for the maid and turned back to Amelia, a sweet smile immediately returning to her countenance.

"Indeed, my dear, I am your father's wife. Do come with me. We have such a lot to talk about. Fancy us never meeting before now! But your papa is so inflexible in his prejudices, my dear, and I did not dare to come up to you at a party. This, though, a chance meeting in the street: what could be more natural? Shall I take you up in my coach? We might drive about the Green Park at this hour without the matter coming to Lord Alfred's ears. I so long to be acquainted with my stepdaughter."

Amelia did not know how to refuse this offer. She wished she could forget the niggling little sensation of

doubt she had. Never would she have expected her father's second wife to speak in such consciously refined
tones. And as for her obviously dyed hair and flamboy-
ant clothes! It was almost as if she might have a past not
befitting her new station. But no, Amelia was certain she
must be mistaken. Lord Alfred Montresor would surely
never marry anyone of doubtful gentility, although the
ripe figure and cheery smiles of the new Lady Alfred did
make it obvious that marriage to her would have its
compensations, whatever its social cost. Amelia knew
men's foibles well, or thought she did. She had never
expected her father to be one to succumb to ordinary
feminine lures.

Telling Lewes to wait for her in the Crane coach, which
was stationed nearby, Amelia followed Lady Alfred to a
smart closed town carriage, gaily painted in blue with
silver trim, and got in beside the lady. They drove off
down Bond Street to the Green Park, the showy pair of
whites moving at a good clip.

Amelia had not communicated with her father since
her own marriage seven years before. This estrangement
was by mutual desire. She wondered if she should explain as much to her new—yes, she would have to say her
new stepmother. She had read of Lord Alfred's marriage to a Miss—somebody, she had not recognized the
name—about a six-month before.

Lady Alfred, once she had got her quarry alone,
showed that her only desire was to end the long-standing
quarrel between father and daughter. "For I know that
he ain't spoken to you since you eloped, my dear. Knowing Lord Alfred as I am coming to do, I don't call it a
wonder he drew the line at a runaway marriage, though
you did well enough for yourself after all. A baron, and
you only seventeen! So prudish as Lord Alfred is,

though, he'd probably have disowned you had you eloped with a royal duke! But he's softened in late years, and I hope you have, and I shall call it a fine day's work if I can reconcile the two of you and make you be friends again."

Amelia looked carefully at the other woman. Could she be sincere? She sounded quite serious, but Amelia didn't know this lady well enough to judge of her character and probable motives. What other motive could she have, though, than the one she stated?

"You are very kind, Lady Alfred, but my father and I have parted ways, and that is that," Amelia said with a smile in which she sought to blend gratitude and a definite refusal. She gazed out of the window, trying to enjoy the sight of the cows grazing on the green turf.

Lady Alfred pouted, frowned, and took out a highly scented handkerchief. "You are quite like him, you know," she said, sniffling delicately into the scrap of embroidered lawn. "Both stubborn as donkeys. No, Amelia, I won't take no for an answer. You must come to dinner—you haven't seen your childhood home in years, have you?—and your father will see reason once he looks upon your lovely face. You are so like your mother, you know. I have seen her portrait in the lumber room."

Amelia struggled to contain her fury that her mother's beautiful portrait, by Mr. Romney, had been consigned to a lumber room. Perhaps, if she did go to dinner, become friends with this woman, she might procure the portrait for herself. No. The momentary temptation passed. She would not be cozened into the society of her father.

She managed a mild smile.

"My father may see reason," she said, though she doubted this, "but I won't. Thank you for the thought, Lady Alfred. And I am so glad to have met you. But my father and I will never be in the same room again if I can help it. I'm terribly grateful he doesn't go out anymore. I've never had to be afraid of meeting him at parties."

Lady Alfred sighed rather theatrically one last time and signalled to her coachman to return the equipage to Bond Street. The ladies rode for the most part in silence, and Lady Alfred let Amelia go with only a parting promise to answer any notes she might write her stepdaughter.

Amelia escaped from the carriage, more pleased than she had hoped to be with her father's wife, but still disturbed. What an encounter! The subject of her father brought back, with a rush, that whole sad business seven years ago, at the time of her marriage. Papa was a cruel and cold parent, and she never wanted to see him again, though she did wish him joy of Lady Alfred. Something told her he had much on his plate with that one.

Lewes took one look at her mistress's face when she entered the Crane carriage and said, "Home with the headache, ma'am?"

"You are on the mark as usual, my dear," said Amelia. "With a very large headache."

"I can't believe that female is married to madam's father," burst out Lewes unexpectedly, when the carriage had gone some distance up Bond Street.

Amelia was startled out of her reverie. "What, do you know the lady?" she asked with interest.

"I might have seen her once or twice, at home in Hampshire," said the maid. "Could be wrong, though. There's a lot can be done with hair dye and such. I might have mistaken her for someone else."

"If you did know her, who would she be?" asked Amelia, wondering if a meeting in Hampshire could be the reason for her own nagging sense that Lady Alfred's face was more familiar than a couple of sightings at recent parties would account for.

"Nobody, my lady," said Lewes. "That's why I can't believe she would be married to my lady's father."

Amelia did not press further, but the thought of fastidious Lord Alfred being saddled for life to a Hampshire "nobody" known to Lewes did have its elements of humour.

CHAPTER EIGHT

"WE ARE COME TO HAVE A council of war, my dear," said Lady Margot Jamieson, smiling in her mild way as she entered Amelia's chamber. The train of her sober riding habit caught on the door, and she had to stop to pull at it.

Lady St. Cloud took over the explanation. "You see, Amelia, there is a lot of talk going about, so here we are, quite informally, to consider what is to be done."

Amelia was still in her bed, for the ladies' call had come at an unprecedentedly early hour and as a complete surprise to her. She rubbed her eyes and automatically straightened her lace nightcap. "Shall I ring for early tea?" she said with a touch of sarcasm. "Do take the long chair, Sarah, you probably shouldn't be on your feet. I am astonished to see you abroad so early in your situation."

"Ah, bliss, to have the world urging one into a horizontal position," said Sarah with a laugh. She was looking lovely, but undeniably large, in a loosely cut walking costume of rose velvet. She crossed the room and stretched out obligingly on the French chaise longue. "Do you know, that footman of yours, the one with the watery eyes, is the most helpful creature. He didn't hesitate to let us in when I explained that we had to see you quietly, and on a matter of the utmost importance. Oh, by the bye, your maid will be up in a moment with the tea and some bread and cheese. I have a most particular fancy for bread and cheese."

Lady Margot freed her train from the door and was finally able to finish her entrance into the room. She poked up the fire before arranging herself in a wing chair near it.

Amelia, seeing that her guests were comfortable and had attended to their own needs, saw no reason to rise from her bed. She tucked a couple of extra pillows behind her back and sat up straighter.

"There is a lot of talk going about?" she said with interest. "Could you tell me, either of you, exactly what that talk is?"

"What?" Lady Margot stared. "Don't you know?"

Amelia sighed. "This talk is presumably about me. Don't you understand that I would be the last person to hear about it? I've been curious as a cat for so many years, for I know people gossiped about me even before I was widowed, and I've never heard a thing." There was more than a touch of resentment in her tone, and not a little apprehension.

Sarah seemed to understand. "Yes, isn't it vexing not to hear the latest on-dits. One scarcely knows how to go on when one is supposed to have done some shocking thing, and hasn't. I always feel that it's much better really to do it. Do you remember that time in our first Season, when everyone was saying I'd swum the Serpentine? The swimmer turned out to be that madcap Eugenia Simond, who ended by marrying the bishop. How I did wish I had been the one to do it, though! But that would not do in your case, dear Amelia. I don't think it would have been wise for you to really kill your husband."

"Kill my husband?" gasped Amelia, falling back on the pillows. She remembered at the last moment to keep her voice down, but no one could have blamed her for giving way to a shriek at this news.

"It is merely a rumour, not an outright accusation," said Lady Margot. "And I am able to date the start of the shocking tale almost to the moment your brother-in-law, the present Lord Jeffries-Hodge, arrived in town."

"I heard he was here," said Amelia. "And I'm not surprised that he should dare to spread such lies about me, for he has always hated me, ever since—for a long time."

"Ever since when, my dear?" asked Margot, with one of her most piercing stares.

Amelia hesitated. Two pairs of sympathetic, friendly eyes were fixed on her. What a comfort it would be to let at least a small portion of her many trials out into the open. She had sworn to herself never to reveal the true circumstances of her marriage. But her husband's brother, Darwin! His wretched attitude had been vexing her for months, and why shouldn't she confide his black designs to her dearest friends?

"Well?" Sarah, evidently realizing by the ominous silence that some important revelation was in the offing, learned forward eagerly.

Amelia was about to speak when Lewes entered with a large tray full of tea things.

The three maintained a scrupulous silence before the maid, who quickly arranged a small table by the side of Lady St. Cloud, placed a generous plateful of bread and cheese upon it, and left the other things near Lady Margot, who indicated that she would pour and hand round the cups.

The door shut behind the efficient Lewes. "We really didn't need to do that, you know," said Amelia. "My maid knows all my secrets."

"You don't say!" cried Sarah. "My Céline would sell me to the gypsies if it would do her any economic good."

"Lewes wouldn't," said Amelia. "Now shall we wait for tea before I satisfy your curiosity?"

"You do, and I'll pour it over the counterpane," declared Sarah. "Out with your secret."

Margot said, "What she means to say, my dear, is that we are at your service and quite willing to keep your confidence. Aren't we, Sarah?"

"To be sure."

Amelia managed a smile. "It means so much to me to have the two of you as friends. The business about my brother-in-law is a very sordid little thing, really. I believe Darwin—that is, Lord Jeffries-Hodge—hates me because of a certain offer he made me after his brother's funeral."

She hesitated, and the ladies silently waited for her to continue, the tension in the room broken only by the sound of Sarah munching on a hard roll.

"He said that if I would be kind to him, as he put it, he would see to it that I was made an allowance," said Amelia. She pushed a loose curl back under her nightcap, remembering that bleak occasion, in the library directly after the reading of her husband's will. She had been forced to slap Darwin's sharp, commonplace face when he had actually grabbed her and initiated a seduction, and he had said that he would be pleased to see her starve if she would withhold from him what she had doubtless given any number of others. She decided to edit the incident properly for her audience. "I refused, of course. And I believe there's no more to his hatred than that."

"Infamous!" said Margot, while Sarah nearly choked on the bread.

"That horrid, ferret-like rake," said Sarah as soon as she was able. "The more I learn of men's characters, the luckier I feel to have found St. Cloud."

She discussed her husband's many virtues for a little. Amelia leaned back on her pillows, relieved that someone else but she at last knew her brother-in-law's true character. Margot poured tea.

"Well," said Margot, when she had supplied her friends with that restorative beverage, "if he was so monstrous as to try to seduce you, he must also be the one spreading the rumours that you are a free and easy widow."

"How do you deduce that? From the hordes of eager rakes all clamouring for my attention?" asked Amelia in a slightly bitter tone.

"In a word, yes," said Margot. "And Lady Manville and her set are saying it, too."

"No doubt aided, in her small way, by Mrs. Winkle, Sir Ethelred's cousin. The female who keeps this house," said Amelia. "Well, my dears, it is kind of you to visit me and tell me both of these tales. I truly do appreciate knowing for a fact what is being said of me. I won't be surprised if I begin to be cut very soon if I am to be not only a wanton, but a murderess. Doesn't anyone stop to think how absurd such charges are?" This was spoken with a weary sigh. "But I don't see how anything can be done about it."

"Come now, Amelia, you certainly don't mean to underestimate our power in the world of wagging tongues," said Sarah with a laugh. "Margot shall take the sensible people, and I the fribbles. We will put our own words in people's ears and see what happens. What we need from you is some sort of story we can use, as the reason these vile rumours have been spread about you. I believe that the true tale, of your dreadful brother-in-law's proposition to you, is too detrimental to you in itself to be of use.''

"Yes, it can easily be made to seem that I am lying about him to be vindictive," said Amelia. "Because he made me no allowance."

"If only the world did not believe that your late husband was such a paragon among men," said Margot. "I feel in my bones he was not."

She and Sarah looked at Amelia, but no more revelations were forthcoming. Lady Jeffries-Hodge had set her small jaw stubbornly.

Sarah sighed. "Well, let him rest in peace, then. We shall think of something. What do you say to this? The new Lord Jeffries-Hodge—rigged a horse race, and you found out and upbraided him for it, and so he detests you enough to start these rumours."

Amelia burst out laughing.

"Never have I heard anything so absurd," said Margot. "Do think before you speak, Sarah."

"But, Margot, sometimes thinking while I speak is the only way I come up with anything at all."

"Come, my dear, we must allow her some latitude for her interesting condition," said Amelia as her rather hysterical hoots wound down to chuckles.

Margot looked severe, but said nothing more. The three ladies sat in silence for some moments, trying to come up with a suggestion more sensible than Sarah's melodramatics.

Finally Margot spoke. "There is nothing for it but the truth, my dears," she said firmly. "We must take the risk that you will be thought vindictive, Amelia. It is better than being murderous and wanton. Once the world knows that you spurned that vile creature's advances, people of sense will not doubt that he made up this horrid murder story, not to mention the story about you being free with your favours, all out of anger at being refused."

"People of sense! We are talking about the ton. And I'm afraid both stories are probably not the sole inventions of my brother-in-law," said Amelia. "The rumours grew out of the circumstances of my husband's death and his will. He deliberately left me a pauper, and people will supply their own reasons for his actions. Nobody will believe it is simply that we did not deal well together."

"And no wonder they won't! An obvious bouncer," said Sarah.

"There is no more to it than that," said Amelia.

"No more that you'll tell us," corrected Margot. "Well, we shall do our best to counteract these tales with the story of your horrid brother-in-law's infamy, Amelia, but I warn you: the damage has already been done."

"I know it has," said Amelia. "I am seriously thinking of leaving Sir Ethelred's employ before I do Calliope more harm than good. Though I do have reason to believe that my charge is about to receive a most suitable offer."

"Oh, is she?" asked Sarah with interest.

"A connection both Sir Ethelred and the gentleman would find most advantageous," Amelia elaborated.

"Sir Ethelred and the gentleman! Doesn't that leave someone out?" Sarah spoke in a teasing tone, but her eyes were suddenly quite thoughtful.

"Calliope will do nothing if it does not please her," Amelia said, though she wondered, uneasily, if the child might not think it wise, upon consideration of the Season's crop of mostly unbearable young men, to marry the

gentleman her father had selected. There was Sam
Guildford, of course, but it was quite possible that nothing would develop there, for Sam had told Amelia he
thought himself ineligible. No matter what his feelings,
he might not offer for a girl he would be casting into a life
of retrenchment.

"Who is offering for her?" asked Margot.

"Doncastle. But it must go no further than this room,
for he hasn't declared himself yet," said Amelia.

"I should think not, with the Season barely begun,"
said Sarah, looking quite worried. "What a coup that
would be for the child, indeed. Doncastle did tell me, the
last time we were together, that he meant to marry this
year. He wishes to settle. All men come to it. That is, all
the ones do who are worth the inordinate time we spend
trying to entrap them."

Amelia felt herself sinking under a sudden weight of
gloom. She had brought up the possibility of Calliope's
engagement to become used to speaking of it, but she had
not expected Sarah to add new information which confirmed so neatly the thing she dreaded most: that the man
she still loved was going to be married, and not to herself. It didn't help matters that Margot was looking
sharply at her. Margot had on more than one occasion
indicated that she knew there was something more than
a mere casual acquaintance between Amelia and the former Mr. Searle.

"Well," said Amelia briskly, "I don't know if you ladies have accomplished your kind mission, but what time
is it?"

Margot glanced at the sensible watch pinned to the
bosom of her habit. "Nearly seven."

Amelia's eyes widened. "I suppose it is quite the
proper time to make a secret visit." She brightened as a

new thought struck her. She had been meaning for some time to organize a certain opportunity, and here it was in her lap. "What do you say to making your visit a bit less secret? I'll hurry into some clothes, and we'll go down to join Sir Ethelred for breakfast. He always eats at this hour, though no one else in the house does."

"Breakfast sounds delightful," said Sarah, who had devoured the last of the bread and cheese. "But why should we intrude upon Sir Ethelred at this hour of the morning? I don't believe Margot has even met him."

"That," said Amelia, with a mysterious smile, "is a fine reason all by itself."

LATER ON THAT SAME DAY, Viscount Doncastle knocked on the door of the Crane establishment, and, on being admitted directly to Sir Ethelred's study, came right to the point of his visit.

"Well, you've done it, old fellow," he said matter of factly, shaking the baronet's hand. "I'm here to ask for your daughter's hand in marriage."

"Are you, by Jove?" Sir Ethelred smiled broadly. He had been sitting idle, for once, twirling a desk ornament around on one finger while he gazed into the distance. Now he turned bright and alert. "So you've fallen in love with her?"

"I am quite wishful to make her my wife," said Doncastle.

Sir Ethelred nodded in a distracted fashion and rang the bell. "I'll have Calliope summoned to the music room, and you may burst in on her with the news. She'll be delighted, I'll wager. And not least of her pleasures will be an end to all these social occasions. The Season is annoying her mightily, I believe. I know the couple of parties I found myself squiring the ladies to drove me into

Bedlam, and I don't wish to prolong my daughter's torture."

"I hope my suit will be acceptable," said Doncastle, though he had no reason to believe it would not. Miss Crane looked a sensible girl. He could tell she was irritated by the social whirl and would probably be distressed by the inanities of a long courtship. Much better, he felt, to secure her now. Then they could both stop worrying about it.

His decision to marry Calliope was not sudden. He had been mulling it over ever since he had met the girl, found her attractive, and put this fact together with the need he saw to provide an heir to his new-found estate. It would be pleasant to be closely connected to Sir Ethelred, too. Doncastle's mind was made up, and his fate was settled.

He felt no great relief at the prospect of marriage, nor any pleasure, but from the way his male acquaintances talked, this was normal.

The desire to show that irritating dowager, Lady Jeffries-Hodge, a thing or two played no part in his decision. He was certain of that much.

When he entered the Crane music room sometime later, Miss Crane, in a simple white gown, was waiting for him before the fire. Her arms were folded, and she looked quite severe.

"The purpose of this interview, sir, if you please?" she said crisply.

Doncastle started. He had no preconceived notion of how a sensible proposal scene ought to go, but he had the definite feeling that this was not the usual thing.

"I came to ask you for your hand in marriage," he stated, wondering why the words felt so wrong, uttered to this young woman who was practically a stranger. It came to him that once, long ago, he had proposed to

Amelia Montresor when he had known her scarcely any longer than he had been acquainted with Calliope. Yet there was a definite difference between that scene and this.

"Well, I thank you for the, er, flattering offer, but I must refuse, as any woman of sense would," said Calliope.

Doncastle found himself groping for a chair. Calliope came to stand over him, looking like a virago. Her grey eyes flashed behind her spectacles, and she actually shook a finger at him. She resembled nothing so much as an angry nursemaid.

"You, sir, are the stupidest of all the men I've met this season, and that, I may tell you, is saying a great deal." Calliope was frowning awfully, and her cheeks were growing very white under her freckles. "I happen to know that you have no feelings for me, Lord Doncastle. I suppose it is your right to tie yourself in a loveless marriage, but to endeavour to make that choice for me as well—it's infamous! I've never heard of anything worse."

Doncastle gazed up at her. He suspected he ought to say something at this point about having very warm feelings for the young lady. He realized he could not.

"And," Calliope continued her tirade, scarcely taking a breath, "I have done nothing to earn your disfavour, my lord. Your intended cruelty to me is unprovoked. That, sir, is inexcusable, and I demand an apology."

There was a silence. Then, "You deserve one," said Doncastle. He rose from the chair and held out his hand to the young lady. "I am deeply sorry for my unprovoked offer, ma'am. Can you shake hands and forgive me?"

"Willingly," said Calliope, favouring him with a firm hand-clasp. "I realize you are only thoughtless, as most men are, and I know you must lead quite an unhappy life, if you are willing to throw the rest of it away. Tell me. Was it only my father's suggestion that made you offer for me?"

"I have to be honest with you," said Doncastle, staring at her in a bemused way, "it was." He shrugged. "It was wrong of me. I can see that clearly now that you've explained. But the time is right for me to marry, and you seemed to fill the bill of Lady Doncastle in every particular. A dashed shame, though, as you've pointed out, for me to embroil you in my schemes for a loveless union. I take it you have a match of quite another kind in your eye?"

Calliope blushed and looked innocent and maidenly for the first time during their interview. "Well, I cannot say there is anything to it as yet, but . . ."

"Say no more, my dear. I am a beast," said Doncastle. He stared into space, aghast at the liberty he had not hesitated to take. This young lady obviously cared for someone else, and he had been quite ready to have her without making enquiries into the state of her heart. Assuming, in effect, that she had no more use for that recalcitrant organ than did he.

His thoughts jumped back once more to that proposal scene of long ago—the incoherent words of passion, the promises and stolen embraces which had marked his asking Amelia Montresor to be his wife. He had been quite ready to deny any experience of that nature to Miss Calliope Crane.

"I ought to be horsewhipped," he said.

"It's not that bad—yet," said Calliope. "But I wish I could have your promise, my lord, that if you are set on marrying you will choose someone who you are certain thinks as you do on these matters. If you should simply single out another debutante and angle for her, ten to one she won't have as understanding a father as I do. An ordinary young lady would be hard put to refuse your offer, sir. I mean to say that she would not be allowed to. Or, worse, she might cherish hopes of your really being attached to her, which we both know would be false."

"A champion of her fellows and a secret romantic," said Doncastle with a smile. "I would never have thought it of one of your scientific bent, Miss Crane."

"We all have our embarrassing quirks," said Calliope gruffly. "May I have that promise I requested?"

"With all my heart," said Doncastle. In an excess of some sentiment which mingled relief and respect, he pressed both the young lady's hands in his and kissed them.

It was at this identical moment that Amelia, holding a sheet of music and humming a snatch of the song she wished to practise, walked into the music room.

CHAPTER NINE

AMELIA TOOK ONE HORRIFIED look at the tender scene in progress, turned on her heel, and fumbled for the door handle. She didn't even notice that the sheet of music had dropped from her hands.

"Don't go, Lady Jeffries-Hodge." Doncastle's voice came from behind her shoulder. "Miss Crane and I are just concluding our interview."

"That's right, Amelia," said Calliope. "He was on the point of leaving."

Without turning around, Amelia said, "Please forget you saw me. I'll leave you alone. It's quite all right." She was astonished, and deeply embarrassed, that her voice was quivering slightly.

"You don't understand, do you?" Doncastle said. His own tones were matter of fact, reasonable. "Miss Crane has just made me the happiest of men."

Drat the man for being so persistent about the matter! So it was done. He had gotten back at her, at last, in the way which hurt her most. A lump in her throat, Amelia turned, the proper expression of joy arranged upon her face, and her hand outstretched. "Then you must allow me to be the first to congratulate you, my lord."

Doncastle was smiling, and his eyes twinkled. Amelia had not seen such an expression of sincere pleasure on his face since before she had jilted him. He seemed to have grown younger by seven years. "I shouldn't have teased you, madam," he said. "What Miss Crane has done is point out to me my folly in endeavouring to stick us both in a marriage of convenience. Naturally, I made my apologies and withdrew my offer. And for that you may congratulate me." He took Amelia's hand before she could withdraw it and shook it heartily. A shock went through her at his touch, and his words took time to sink in.

She was silent. She looked from Calliope to Jeremy and back again, her expression puzzled. "You didn't want to marry him?" she addressed her charge. Though she didn't know it, the disbelief in her voice was most flattering to Lord Doncastle.

"Amelia," said Calliope sternly, "there is nothing I want less, and you know it."

Though this statement was supremely *un*flattering to Lord Doncastle, there seemed to be nothing left to say on the subject, at least from the young lady's point of view. Doncastle, who had been declared to have just been leaving, was obliged to be off.

"It would be folly, would it not," he said in parting, "to marry simply to anger another person?"

Amelia started. He had not been looking at her when he spoke, but she wondered all the same if his words weren't meant to refer to her. So it seemed she had not been wrong to suspect revenge as at least one of his ulterior motives.

Calliope, from her lack of interest in his remark, evidently had no inkling that there could be any special meaning in the conversation, and Amelia breathed easier.

The viscount left the room, still smiling. The ladies could hear him begin to whistle as he went on his way down the corridor.

"I still can't believe it," said Amelia, weakly sitting down in the very chair Doncastle had thrown himself into when Calliope announced that she would not marry him.

"My first proposal," said Calliope. "I think I handled it quite well. I called it infamous."

"Did you?" Amelia looked at the younger girl in amazement. "Have you hurt him? Is he in love with you?"

"By no means. That is why I did not hesitate to be honest with him. I told him precisely what I think of a man who would offer a girl he cares nothing for a marriage of convenience." Calliope's eyes were shining in her triumph, and she sat down opposite Amelia looking rather like an Amazon warrior. "And you can see how relieved Lord Doncastle was to be free of me. What he was whistling just now was the 'Marseilles March', which the French sang as their anthem when they overthrew their king. Now I must find a way to tell Papa that his fond dream of having his friend and his daughter marry is not to be. Not that I haven't told him a dozen times already; but it will be so much more final now I've refused the offer."

Calliope looked so genuinely glad about the situation that Amelia felt weeks of worries drain rapidly away. Whatever indignities were ahead for her this Season, at least she would not have to smile and look gratified at the wedding of her charge and the man she herself loved.

The one disadvantage of Calliope's refusal of Doncastle was that Amelia would definitely have to leave the Cranes' employ as soon as possible. With no suitor already secure, Calliope must be put under the wing of someone of undoubted respectability for, due to her brother-in-law's latest attempt to sink her, Amelia could no longer be sure of even being received. Calliope required a more suitable chaperon if she were to make a suitable match. The Season was fast flying by.

Amelia said nothing of this to Calliope, but as soon as she was able, later that day, she confronted Sir Ethelred in his study. As always, the baronet was busily writing something at his desk. Amelia was used to seeing a welter of unintelligible-looking equations and drawings of complex machines on the paper before Sir Ethelred, for so he organized his thoughts. She was a bit shocked when, on casually glancing at the sheet of foolscap he was scribbling over, she observed a jumble of hearts and singing birds in splotchy ink.

"Lady Jeffries-Hodge!" the baronet greeted her. He had a strange grin on his face, most unlike his usual pensive demeanour. That, and the hearts, made Amelia begin to worry that he was counting upon Calliope's marriage to Lord Doncastle and had as yet no inkling of the truth.

She couldn't do more than speculate, though, for there was no polite way to question him on the subject. Instead she began her rehearsed speech, before she should lose courage.

"Sir Ethelred, I find it is time for me to leave your employ," she stated, looking him in the eye.

He had risen to greet her. Now he sat back down in his chair in surprise, motioning her to take the one opposite his desk. "Madam, I understood that we had a contract for the Season."

Amelia sat down and took a deep breath. "We did indeed, but something has happened which must override any agreement between you and me."

"And that is?" Sir Ethelred looked at her in concern.

"I fear that I shall soon begin to be cut, and that would do Calliope no good at all." The words rushed out.

Amelia was amazed at how easy it was to be completely candid. "It is essential that she have a proper sponsor, so that she may have the best chance of marrying as you would wish. And I—well, sir, not to put too fine a point on it, few people will be sending invitations in the future to a reputed murderess."

Sir Ethelred's gingery eyebrows flew up, and his spectacles slid down his bony nose. "A murderess?"

Amelia explained as best she could that a couple of her friends had warned her of that particular piece of malicious gossip. "And I assure you, sir, that it is not true," she felt bound to add. "Neither am I a loose woman, as the tattlemongers also have it." She blushed deeply at the last comment. Her evident embarrassment would have done much to confirm her claim of innocence had Sir Ethelred been disposed to think ill of her.

He was not, however. "My dear young woman, I am hurt that you would even consider me a person who might believe such calumny," said the baronet.

"I beg your pardon." Amelia couldn't help being gratified by his instant reaction. "But do not you see that I must leave? For Calliope's sake?"

"Calliope needs you, ma'am. You've gotten her entrée to the best houses, and you help bring her out of that scholar's shell she gets from me. I suppose you're already privy to the offer Doncastle made her today?" At Amelia's conscious nod he continued. "I was surprised she refused him, but there you have it. You're more necessary to her than ever, for she must pick someone in earnest now and go after him."

"Calliope will never do that, sir."

"If I may presume to correct you, my lady, she will never mean to do that. She might fall into the situation of courtship, though. Stranger things have happened, and to more unlikely people. And talking of strange things, I mean to give a dinner party. For a mixed group of Society,'' he added, for it was a common thing for Sir Ethelred to give all-male dinners to the scholars and scientists of his circle.

"You do?'' Of all the things that had happened that day, including being bearded in her bed by her two friends, and hearing that Calliope had refused Jeremy, this qualified as the most unusual in Amelia's mind. Never would she have thought to hear Sir Ethelred, of his own free will, engage to give a dinner party.

"You tell Mrs. Winkle, and we'll set it for Thursday week. You have Almack's on Wednesday, isn't that correct? And let us have some new faces.''

"Anyone in particular?'' asked Amelia. She hid a smile. Since Sir Ethelred never entertained in the ordinary way, any face at his board might be said to be new.

"That friend of yours I met this morning at breakfast. Lady Margot, I mean to say. Don't suppose Lady What's-her-name, the other one, cares to go about in the evening what with the blessed event so close at hand.'' Sir Ethelred's voice was casual, but his rather prominent ears turned a telling shade of vermilion.

"I don't suppose Sarah is going out in the evenings anymore. Lady Margot, then,'' said Amelia, with no trace of triumph or special knowledge in her voice. "Is there anyone else whom you most particularly wish to see, or to avoid?''

Sir Ethelred grinned. "Invite Lady Manville at your peril, but you have free rein aside from that. Oh, please do ask Doncastle. I want to show him our friendship for him is unchanged even if Calliope did refuse him. She indicated she wants that also. Seems to be so friendly with the man, I wonder she didn't take him.''

"I think, Sir Ethelred, that you'll have better luck with Calliope's marriage plans if you leave them to her. She is quite a logical and practical young lady, and I'm certain she won't choose unwisely."

"You may be right, my lady. You may be right. The Lord knows trying it my way didn't serve." Sir Ethelred spoke in a light tone which set Amelia's mind at rest. He wasn't too terribly disappointed that Calliope and Doncastle were not to be man and wife.

Amelia's own feelings on that point wavered between blazing joy and the sense of an inevitable hardship delayed for only a little while. Doncastle must marry someday. And when he did, she did not doubt that she would suffer very much.

MRS. WINKLE, UPON HEARING Sir Ethelred meant to entertain, flew into a pet. "What? Sir Ethelred dine in company with females? He's never done so before. You must be mistaken," she informed Amelia, and, without waiting to discuss the situation further, she went to confer directly with Sir Ethelred.

Amelia sighed and continued with her task of composing a plausible list of guests. She was in the drawing-room at an escritoire, and there she remained, waiting for Mrs. Winkle to return with the inevitable news that Sir Ethelred did, indeed, wish to give a dinner to some friends he had not hosted before.

"You're sending Lady Manville a card, of course." Mrs. Winkle moved importantly back into the room as though there had been no question of doubt over Sir Ethelred's plans. She observed over Amelia's shoulder the task at hand. "She is a most particular friend and a close connection of the family."

"Sir Ethelred asked me not to invite her." Amelia, toying with her quill, was concentrating on the question of whether she ought to suggest to Lady Margot that she ask Sarah's brother, that serious and scholarly Sam Guildford, to escort her. Amelia decided this would be a fine idea and bent to write the note.

Mrs. Winkle was still fixed on the question of Lady Manville. "Oh. Well, perhaps he's right. One as high in Society as her ladyship would be insulted if anyone were to presume she was not already busy for Thursday week. Now I must go to confer with cook. Sir Ethelred's dinners with the Scientific Society are never any problem, for those men wouldn't know what they were eating unless it rose up to bite them. But for Society we must have two full courses, and we shall order in a delightful piece of confectionery by way of a centrepiece. There is a new pastry cook's in Oxford Street that does wonderful renditions of the battle of Waterloo in spun sugar, and..." Mrs. Winkle went off talking to herself. Amelia sighed with relief and completed her invitations in peace.

THE DINNER WENT OFF splendidly despite the unfortunate fact that the pastry cook mistakenly delivered a spun-sugar rendition of the battle of Vittoria. Mrs. Winkle bemoaned this tragedy for weeks. There was a joint, and a salmon, and a turkey, and a welter of side-dishes of varying degrees of success. Amelia, who had recommended that Mrs. Winkle act as hostess for the meal and be given the seat of honour, found herself overridden by her employer and his daughter. As a result, she was herself acting as hostess presiding over one end of the table, with Lord Doncastle on one side of her and the noted mathematician, Sir Lumley Martinstone, on the other.

Mrs. Winkle, frightening in mouse-coloured bombazine, glared at Lady Jeffries-Hodge from lower down.

Amelia had never been more oddly situated. To sit beside Doncastle was almost more than she could bear. She
tried to forget him, and, since he was studiously ignor-
ing her, this ruse at least appeared to be successful. A
bright spot in the evening was that Lady Margot Jamieson, seated not quite strictly by protocol at Sir Ethelred's right hand, was having an animated conversation
with the baronet. Amelia had rarely, if ever, had the opportunity to try her luck at matchmaking. Would this
maiden attempt succeed? She had never known two people to be more ideally suited. They would sink in a sea of
science and literary study, of course, but neither would
mind.

Then there was Calliope, looking quite pleased as she
discussed something or other, undoubtedly a serious
question, with her own dinner partner, Sam Guildford.
Amelia, who had made out the seating arrangements,
smiled to herself in an unguarded moment. The smile was
fleeting, though, and the look of discomfort was back on
her face as she dealt with the issue of Sir Lumley Martinstone.

Doncastle saw that brief smile, though, and was attracted despite himself to the honest pleasure which
flashed across his former fiancée's face. And he wondered, as he applied himself to his meal in order to avoid
conversation with his hostess, why he had accepted this
invitation. He had told himself that he wished to show
Calliope and Sir Ethelred that the girl's refusal of him
meant nothing, but both the Cranes were too intelligent
to need that type of assurance.

He certainly hadn't wished to be thrust into the company of Amelia, the one woman on earth he had most reason to avoid.

He gave her many sidelong looks, wondering how her mind worked these days. Her behaviour was so very modest. True, the dinner gown she had on, a wine-red silk of less suitable cut than a dowager ought to wear, did draw a man's attention, but she seemed not to know she had a body, let alone that it was being displayed to its best advantage. As Doncastle watched and listened, Amelia gently discouraged Martinstone's scholarly attempts at flirtation, refusing to drive with him and saying she did not receive callers in Portman Square upon her own account.

Doncastle knew very well why she would avoid the obvious rakehells, the Count Riccolis and Captain Dawbers who were so blatantly anxious to seduce her. Living with the Cranes, she could hardly abandon herself to impropriety. But why would she put on the same quelling manners with Sir Lumley, who, Doncastle had reason to know, was reputed to be rich as well as respectable? For a mercenary widow like Amelia, he would seem the perfect quarry.

Well, perhaps she was after a higher title, although, with the rumours circulating about her, she ought to be grateful if a baronet so much as glanced her way. Doncastle furrowed his brow, perplexed, and had to apologize to the lady on his other side for not having heard her last remark. Amelia's behaviour might be a mystery, but it was a mystery he cared nothing for. He would not try to find reasons for her actions.

After the meal, tables for cards were set up in the drawing-room, and Amelia opened the large, ornamental instrument in the adjoining music room in order to encourage music-making by the young ladies. She was longing for this evening to be over. She was still tense from sitting next to Doncastle for the duration of an entire dinner, something she had not done since . . . had she ever done it?

She forced herself to forget him. He was not even in the room, the gentlemen still being at their port, and she must not let him distress her in absentia.

Firmly putting herself in the role of hostess, she approached Lady Margot Jamieson. "Are you enjoying yourself, my dear?"

Lady Margot smiled, her usual calm self. "Oh, vastly, dear Amelia. I rarely have a chance for true intelligent conversation at a dinner in the Season. Your Sir Ethelred is a highly gifted man. I don't wonder I haven't seen him out in Society. He is much too good for it."

"He is not *my* Sir Ethelred," said Amelia. "I believe he is entirely unfettered at present."

She had the satisfaction of seeing a blush rise to the cheeks of her usually unflappable friend, Margot.

Mrs. Winkle bustled over. "I am sure, dear Lady Jeffries-Hodge, that no one would take it amiss if you were to retire. You look so ill."

"Do I?" Amelia, rather than being insulted by such an obvious ploy, was struck by the delightful prospect of spending the remainder of the party in her room. She knew Mrs. Winkle had made the suggestion only out of a wish to move into the position of hostess for the balance of the evening, and Amelia could think of nothing that would please herself more. "I quite agree with you, Mrs. Winkle. I'm really quite pulled. Do give Sir Ethelred my apologies when he comes in."

"He is bound to understand. You look like death," said Mrs. Winkle cheerfully, prompting Amelia to take a worried glance into the nearest pier glass in the full expectation of seeing a veritable gorgon stare back at her. She seemed to look much as usual, even a bit flushed, and she couldn't help sighing with relief.

"You look fine to me, Amelia," said Margot with a keen look, first appraising Amelia's condition, then suspiciously fixing her lorgnette on Mrs. Winkle.

"But I feel most unwell. I'll slip out now, before the gentlemen join us," said Amelia.

She had not yet finished speaking when a rumble of masculine voices announced the arrival of the very creatures she wished most to avoid. Sir Ethelred led the procession, arm in arm with Sir Lumley Martinstone and closely followed by Doncastle. The three seemed to be discussing some unintelligible matter of mathematics.

Doncastle happened to meet Amelia's eye as the men broke off their various conversations and went to join the ladies. He bowed slightly and crossed the room immediately to join another woman.

Amelia, frozen motionless by his look, was a prime target for Sir Lumley. This gentleman advanced to her side and guided Lady Jeffries-Hodge to a small sofa in one corner of the room.

"Sir, you must forgive me, but I was on the point of retiring with the headache...." Amelia began.

"Nonsense, my dear, what is a headache? A much overrated ailment. There is no need for you to miss the evening. The pressure of my thumbs upon your, er, alabaster brow will soon set matters to rights," said Sir Lumley. He was a small, rodent-like man with the soothing manner of a physician. Without waiting for Amelia's concurrence, he proceeded to act upon his recommendations.

"Sir!" said Amelia weakly, raising her hands to his, which now held her forehead in an iron grip. She hated to refuse what she sensed was an honest offer of help, unmotivated by flirtatious considerations, but this scene was surely most improper.

As though to confirm her thoughts, Doncastle strode quickly across the room to their sofa. Amelia noticed the lady he had left was looking rather miffed. "I beg your pardon, Lady Jeffries-Hodge, Sir Lumley," he said with a lifting of eyebrows, "should you wish to be more private for your interview, I am certain Sir Ethelred would not take it amiss were you to leave the room."

Amelia frowned at him. Sir Lumley's small hands left her forehead like guilty pigeons fleeing a coop.

"Sir, we do not wish for privacy," said Amelia with dignity. "Sir Lumley was merely trying to cure my headache."

"Of course," said Doncastle, his voice ironic.

"Sir!" spoke up the quiet Sir Lumley. His narrow face had flushed into blotchy splendour. "I take leave to object to your tone."

"My tone," said Doncastle coldly, "matched the situation perfectly. You were taking a liberty, which the lady was permitting."

Amelia drew in her breath. To her astonishment, Sir Lumley rose from the sofa, drew off a glove, and swatted Doncastle on the nose with it. "You have defamed this lady's reputation, sir, and you shall pay for this outrage. Name your friends."

Amelia put her hand to her head as a genuine headache suddenly pounded at her temples. What could be worse? Sir Lumley, if he wished to fight for her honour, would deem her the prize for his valour. She had no wish to encourage the man.

Doncastle was looking amused but interested at the prospect of a duel with a small mathematician. As for the rest of the room, all other conversation had halted, and the guests were craning their necks in order to see the little drama more clearly.

Reason reasserted itself. Doncastle's expression changed to one of conciliation, and he bowed. "I do not wish to fight, Sir Lumley. Would you accept my apology now, both of you? And I'll beg both of your pardons in writing tomorrow."

Amelia breathed easier. Forcing a smile, she cast a pleading look at Calliope across the room. That damsel, who was becoming quite adept at the social niceties, commenced a loud conversation with her father and Sam Guildford on the subject of Archimedes. The rest of the room obligingly buzzed, once more, with varied snatches of talk.

Sir Lumley, meanwhile, had not altered his terrier-like stance before the much taller viscount. "Sir, I consider you a coward. Your friends, if you please! Sir Ethelred will, I am sure, act for me."

Doncastle appeared to be fascinated. "But I had thought to ask him to act for me."

"Nonsense! You must have other friends, sir."

"Double nonsense!" put in Amelia, truly alarmed. "Sir Lumley, surely you cannot mean to pursue this. I am quite willing to accept Lord Doncastle's apology."

"You, madam, are a kind and generous lady, but you know little of the ways of the world. This, er, gentleman has pleased to offer you, a delicate lady without protectors, an insult in a public place. He has accused us before this company of dallying. He must be chastised," said the earnest Sir Lumley.

"Don't worry, ma'am. We won't fight," said Doncastle with a piercing look at Amelia.

She couldn't help it. She burst out laughing.

At this Sir Lumley bristled, and even Doncastle looked less than pleased.

"I'm sorry. Forgive me, gentlemen, but I've tried so desperately to avoid the wrong kind of notice, and here I am the object of a prospective duel, to be fought because I had a headache. I—I must be overtired," said Amelia, wiping her wet eyes on a handkerchief.

Sir Lumley looked worried at the unmistakably hysterical note in her voice. "Ma'am, you are overwrought. How thoughtless of us to enact such a scene of masculine violence before you. I'll go this instant to procure you a glass of water. Doncastle, do you stay by her. She may have another attack."

The room watched surreptitiously as Sir Lumley hurried away, and Lord Doncastle sat down by Amelia.

"Well," he said conversationally, "this tête-à-tête should help to allay any rumour that Martinstone and I are to fight a duel for your honour."

"Of course I have little enough, as your satirical tone implies," said Amelia. She was still feeling a bit strange, but she was able to utter the words with the blandest of social smiles and to wonder at herself for being so bold. Had she taken too much wine at dinner? No, she had been as abstemious as usual.

"Madam," said Doncastle, "your activities are of little interest to me, as is your honour. It is a mystery to me how you managed to arouse the protective instinct in that odd little scholar. Your wiles must be more subtle than I, a poor ordinary male, can observe. And you must know best whether you are worth fighting over."

"I am not," said Amelia without hesitation. "And I beg you to do anything, up to and including sending Sir Lumley flowers, to see to it that this charade goes no further than this room. The gossips can't be stopped altogether, but the story will fade to nothing if nothing comes of it. Poor Sir Lumley must not be thinking quite straight this evening."

"I won't fight that odd little man. Don't worry," said Doncastle.

"Good. And there's no need to call him names."

"Do you indeed intend him for your next victim in the matrimonial snares, then? You are so careful of him." Doncastle smiled in an unbearably contemptuous manner.

Amelia was silent for a little. "If it will save you the trouble of speculating on my every action, I will tell you, sir, that I'm sworn never to marry again. Never."

Doncastle's answer was instant. "That, Lady Jeffries-Hodge, would be a fine piece of news for the innocent male community. But do forgive me if I doubt your sincerity. Was it not Dr. Johnson who said that, when widows exclaim loudly against second marriages, the man, if not the wedding day, is absolutely fixed on?"

Amelia was stung by a mixture of outrage and hurt, but she kept her dignity. "I must forgive you, of all people, for doubting my sincerity on any subject. But it is the truth nevertheless. I won't marry again, and not a man in the world is in any danger from my wiles." The allusion to Dr. Johnson nearly broke her heart, for it took her back to earlier times, when she and her Jeremy had been pleased to discuss literature. They had been terribly pedantic in their zeal to outquote each other. And now he was using their favourite game of those younger days as a weapon against her! What was worse, he was probably doing it unconsciously. He would not remember their former intimacy as she did.

She could not resist correcting him, however. "And I believe it was Fielding you quoted, not Johnson," she said, unable to keep a little tinge of triumph out of her voice.

He stared at her, and she wondered if he could possibly be remembering that game they had been used to play.

Sir Lumley bustled up with a tumbler full of water at this point, and Doncastle, rising from his place beside the lady, was again entreated by Sir Lumley to name his friends before he went back to his conversation with Lady Barnstickle.

"Friends? Oh, yes, your wish to duel. I will have to think on the matter and send to you. That is, to your own man, Sir Ethelred. We will be in touch," said Doncastle with every appearance of seriousness. Shaking his head slightly, he took himself off.

"That's more like it. I was afraid the man was a coward," said Sir Lumley to Amelia. "Are you better, my dear? Can't be too careful with these attacks of hysteria."

Amelia finished the water and smiled at her companion. "My dear sir, you have been so good to me. I really must retire to my room now, though, for I fear my headache is growing worse by the minute."

Sir Lumley was profuse in his desire to have her remain, but Amelia finally made good her escape from the party, which she did as though all the demons of mythology were nipping at her heels.

She had no wish to stay longer in the room. Within five minutes of the gentlemen joining the ladies, she had become the object of a duel between the man she had jilted and a man she suspected had never held a weapon of any sort.

She shuddered to think what would happen if she were to remain ten minutes more.

CHAPTER TEN

"THIS WAS DELIVERED BY special messenger, madam," said Lewes with a curtsy, presenting an ominous-looking package. "Higgins happened to open the door, so the other servants have no inkling you've received anything. I do hope it is nothing you will not like."

Amelia was seated at her dressing-table, concluding her toilette for the morning. She took the long flat box from Lewes' hands, dreading to open it. She was grateful that Higgins did tend to hover by the door these days, seeing to it that the possibly gossip-prone Crane servants knew less about Amelia's affairs than they might otherwise have done.

"Probably another bibelot from Lord Clayville," Amelia said in her best joking manner. "That man simply will not be discouraged. I have tried everything, including turning my back on him in a public place."

"Thinks he's irresistible, I'll wager," said Lewes with a sniff. "Well, I hear he ain't too proud to traffic with his own staff, and them not always willing. Does it sound like anyone we used to know?"

"Too much so for comfort." Amelia paused, and she and her maid both looked thoughtful. Amelia was first to speak. "How these domestic secrets do get about," she said briskly. "Who told you?"

"Green, madam." And Lewes lowered her round blue eyes in a sudden attack of confusion.

Amelia had her sources, too, including Higgins and the evidence of her own eyes, and she had heard of Lewes' flirtation with the Crane butler. Could anything come of it? Looking at Lewes' troubled face, Amelia doubted it.

Amelia busied herself with undoing the package, carefully, since she would have to wrap it right up again to send it back. To her surprise, it was not Clayville's familiar card which fell from the wrappings, but a strange one.

"Good heavens," she cried, taking it up. "Sir Lumley Martinstone has sent me a—" quickly she opened the box, revealing a supremely ugly cameo on a thin chain "—a token of his esteem, so the card says. Oh, dear."

"The gentleman who wants to duel over you, with Lord Doncastle?" asked Lewes with eagerness.

Amelia rolled her eyes. "What would you do for entertainment belowstairs if it weren't for the antics of Society? It never does fail to amaze me how quickly you and Higgins come to know all."

"I expect, ma'am," said Lewes in an injured tone, "if there wasn't high Society, with antics to go with it, there'd be no belowstairs, and you wouldn't have to worry about us knowing nothing."

"I don't worry," said Amelia. "At least not about you and Higgins. I beg your pardon for my hasty words. But since you know that sordid little story from last night, all of London must know it as well, for the rest of the staff has no reason for discretion when telling a perfectly fascinating tale. Especially—" she smiled, remembering the little scholar standing right up to the tall, broad Doncastle "—when it was such an amusing spectacle."

"True, madam."

Amelia consoled herself with the fact that she had verbally forbidden the duel and Doncastle had promised that no meeting would take place. These two pieces of information would soon put paid to any tales that might be flitting about Society.

Meanwhile she was faced with a problem new in her experience: how to find the proper language to use when she sent back this well-meant, but still unacceptable gift. It had presented no difficulty to send back the sapphire earrings Lord Clayville had dared to give her. The unwelcome offering had arrived with an infuriating note stating that they matched milady's eyes, and that the giver would love to see her wearing the earrings—and nothing else. She had returned the sapphires without comment. The same treatment had been right for other too-intimate articles which had arrived from the gallants of what Amelia must consider her motley court.

Sir Lumley was a different story. Amelia had to spend the better part of an hour composing a note which expressed her gratitude, yet held out no encouragement whatsoever and refused the gift absolutely. By the time she sealed the note and rewrapped the jeweller's box, she was exhausted.

Amelia was an early riser, and she commonly dressed and spent some quiet time in her room before descending to breakfast with the ladies. Sir Lumley's package and her note she saw safely into the hands of Higgins before she gave herself over to the public portion of her day.

"Well," said Mrs. Winkle, as Amelia entered the breakfast parlour, "I made sure you'd remain abed, Lady Jeffries-Hodge. You were looking so unwell last night, and you still appear quite drawn."

Calliope merely looked up from the journal she was studying and smiled. Mrs. Winkle could always be counted upon for some astringent comment, and, as both

Amelia and Calliope knew, there was really nothing to be done about it save to take her words lightly.

Amelia sat down to her usual boiled egg, bread, and coffee, murmuring her greetings.

"Oh, here is something for you," said Mrs. Winkle, letting fly an engraved card of invitation across the table. "It got into my letters by mistake, and I opened the thing without noticing it was your ladyship's. An invitation to drink tea at your father's, I believe."

Amelia was as appalled at Mrs. Winkle's rudeness as by the fact of such a summons. So the new Lady Alfred had made good her pledge to reconcile father and daughter.

The note was brief and to the point. Amelia was requested to appear at Lord Alfred Montresor's in three days' time in the evening for a "companionable chat."

She sighed. She wouldn't go, of course.

"You'll go, of course," said Mrs. Winkle decisively. "I can't tell you how it mortifies me to hear how you and your dear papa have become estranged over the years. We know he had his reasons, for your runaway marriage would have hardened a less highly principled man than he, and to hear Lady Manville tell it, you and he have not spoken since your elopement. This is quite a Christian gesture on the part of his wife, and . . ."

Amelia let the words flow over her without paying them much heed. She understood the main points of the lady's monologue. If Amelia did not choose to go to her father's house for tea, the story of her unwillingness to make amends would be all over town within the day.

Calliope was listening with an unusual attention to Mrs. Winkle's revelations. "Only fancy!" she said, looking over the tops of her spectacles at Amelia. "I didn't know you made a runaway marriage, Amelia."

"Yes, and my father was very strait-laced. It quite ruined his good opinion of me," said Amelia. She tried to speak as though the matter had meant nothing to her.

How it had, though...and how doubly difficult it was to let this false story stand, when she was longing to unburden herself of the secret she had sworn to carry to her grave.

As for her father, she had no desire in the world to see Lord Alfred Montresor again. Yet, for the sake of what remained of her reputation, she supposed she was engaged to do so. She turned over the card of invitation, puzzled by her new stepmother's rangy and untutored handwriting. There was another odd circumstance which continued to trouble her. How in heaven's name had her hard-to-please papa ever taken a wife who lacked any but the crudest pretensions to gentility?

Shrugging, she opened the next missive in her little stack and read a formal note of apology from Lord Doncastle, begging her pardon for so misconstruing the situation with Sir Lumley Martinstone the evening before. He entreated her forgiveness most humbly and praised the sterling behaviour of Sir Lumley. Evidently, the note was meant to be shown to Martinstone for corroboration should that chivalrous scholar doubt that Doncastle had made amends.

Amelia found herself smiling over this message. When, in the ordinary course of events, would Lord Doncastle have sent her such a conciliatory letter? She knew that, even though his sentiments were facetious, she would preserve this note among her private papers forever.

AMELIA PRESENTED HERSELF on the night Lady Alfred had requested in a small, elegant house in Half-Moon Street which she had not seen—except, to be sure, from the outside—since she was seventeen. She was accompanied only by Lewes, who engaged to wait in the servants' hall while Lady Jeffries-Hodge paid her duty call. Lewes, who had bristled up at the very idea that her lady must enter the house of her cruel father, was somewhat mollified when she learned she might come along and lend her protection. The practical Higgins urged her privately to find out any tidbits she could from Lord Alfred's staff regarding their master and his lady while she was about it.

Lewes duly disappeared belowstairs, carrying the cloak which she had removed with her own hands from her mistress's shoulders, not trusting this duty to the pudding-faced butler. Amelia, feeling very small, was left alone in the entry hall. The place, once her home, had changed in seven years. The paper and ornaments of the entry were different; even the carpet on the stairs had been changed for a newer, brighter one.

Amelia was wearing her best dinner gown, the wine-red silk, and only hoped she would not be overdressed for a private family evening. The butler, a stranger to her, moved to the doors of the drawing-room she remembered well. Here she and Jeremy, accompanied by her chaperon of those days, Miss Finch, had been wont to sit much longer than they ought at cribbage or chess.

The butler flung open the doors. "Lady Jeffries-Hodge," he announced loudly, over the chattering of many voices.

Amelia struggled to contain her surprise. She was facing, not her stepmother and her father alone, but a roomful of people.

Lady Alfred breezed up, brassy curls glittering in the light of a hundred wax tapers. Her gown was cut shockingly low, and she was smiling in friendly welcome.

"Dear Amelia, how happy I am you could come to drink tea. We have been having a little dinner party this evening, and between you and me, we have need of a pretty face. All these dowagers are so many bracket-faced lumps!" This last was uttered in a slightly lowered voice, but not low enough, judging from the shocked reaction of a nearby turbaned lady in rusty olive green.

"Where is my father?" asked Amelia coldly. She had been offered an insult, and she didn't know whether this woman was aware of it or no. Someone who lacked breeding wouldn't necessarily know that an invitation to come in after a dinner party was a slight. Especially when the party was in one's own father's house.

"Lord Alfred is over here in the corner. He likes to sit still these days, you know, since his gout has been paining him so," chattered Lady Alfred. Taking her stepdaughter familiarly by the hand, she tripped across the room, leaving staring guests in her wake. Amelia recognized none of the people. Some looked vulgar to her eye. Probably Lady Alfred's set. Once again, Amelia wondered what her father had been thinking of to marry this woman.

In a comfortable fauteuil, ensconced in a quiet corner, sat a slight, grey man with a stern profile and a firm, unyielding jaw. He was dressed more foppishly than Amelia had ever seen him. Was this Lady Alfred's influence, or had her father's taste simply deteriorated with age? One bandaged foot was resting on a stool. He had lost some hair.

"Papa," said Amelia, offering him the slightest of curtseys, "it is good of you to invite me here."

"It's her doing," said Lord Alfred Montresor, pointing an ebony walking stick at his lady.

Lady Alfred laughed as she untangled the stick from the gauzy folds of her golden gown. "Oh, you've made a sad tear here, Alfie."

Alfie? Amelia hid a smile. Her father had been variously described by those who knew him as stiff-rumped, strait-laced, high-nosed, and above his company—whatever that company might be. Never had he been known as Alfie.

"How good of Lady Alfred," said Amelia with the same icy dignity. She was dimly aware that the party was going on around her. These people, whoever they might be, were luckily not interested in the reunion of a long-estranged father and daughter. This fact gave her courage. Also helpful was the knowledge that she did not care what happened. She had no more wish to reconcile with her father than to fly to the moon; she reminded herself that she was only here because Mrs. Winkle had got wind of the invitation and would gossip to her cost if she had remained at home. Serenity flowed through Amelia, serenity and detachment. Let Lord Alfred Montresor be as rude as he wished.

"You must call me Sukey, Amelia, dear," said Lady Alfred with a most winning smile. "There, now, it isn't so hard to be friends again, is it?" She batted her eyelashes at her husband. "I was right, as you must admit, my dear."

"I admit only that my daughter is now in my house, and that seven years ago I quite clearly told her never to darken my door again," said Lord Alfred.

Amelia's eyes widened at these cruel words, but her father's animosity was strangely comforting to her. No, he hadn't changed. And she had never had trouble standing up to him in the ordinary way of things. There had been that one last time, of course, when no assertive behaviour of her own could have saved her. Best not dwell on that. "I never did listen to you, did I, Papa?" she said in her best conversational tone. "If truth be told, I thought that since you and, er, Sukey are now man and wife, you might give me my mother's portrait if I came to you and did the pretty. I have no more wish to reconcile with you than you with me—and I believe you know why."

"You're an honest girl, I will give you that," said Lord Alfred. A glint of respect dawned in his slate-grey eyes. "I'll think about the portrait."

Amelia considered her parent with calm eyes. He was cold, virtually unforgiving, and just this side of ill-mannered. No, some things never changed. Lady Alfred—Sukey—had gone through the house with her own brand of tastelessness, if the hall and this drawing-room were any judge, but she hadn't made serious inroads into the man who went with the trappings. Lord Alfred would never alter, though Amelia had to acknowledge that he must now possess some strange new quality. Whatever strange flight of fancy had made him take this particular woman as his second wife, she couldn't feature.

Lady Alfred was talking at a good clip of how poor dear Alfie had had this latest attack of the gout come on during their wedding tour, and hadn't been the same since. He was so patient, poor man. They were going to Bath after the Season, or maybe Brighton, or maybe both. Did Amelia think the Bath waters would be better than sea bathing?

"I should think my father would enjoy the inland spring more than the seashore," said Amelia. She knew the stodgy society of Bath would not welcome Lady Alfred, and that this would embarrass her father no end. In

Brighton, the lady would fit right in with the bright, varied crowds.

"You've guessed it," said Lord Alfred. "Off we go to Bath as soon as the Season winds down. But don't think you're coming with us. Lady Alfred speaks of inviting you, but I say draw the line at that. We don't like each other, do we, girl?"

"No, Papa," said Amelia, "we do not. And I would rather travel with a cageful of lions than with you."

Lord Alfred gave a matter-of-fact nod.

Sukey made some clucking sounds, slapped Lord Alfred playfully with her feather fan, and announced her intention to invite her dear stepdaughter where she would, with or without his consent. Lord Alfred snarled, but he made no demur. Amelia, looking on in fascination at this domestic byplay, saw that, if she wished it, she could be welcomed back into the bosom of her father's family by a sort of default. Lord Alfred would complain, but he would not insist. Lady Alfred would go her own way with no interference from a mere provider of luxuries who couldn't even walk some days.

Of course, Amelia would not give Lady Alfred the chance to work her wiles and insinuate her stepdaughter into the family circle. She would never forgive her father for what he had done to her. Their estrangement would be a lasting one, she was determined on that.

Lord Alfred's second marriage did please her, though. She had never really seen her father with a woman, for her mother had died in her early childhood. She would never have thought that her sire would be most comfortable under the cat's paw, but so it appeared. Lady Alfred would run through Lord Alfred's fortune and bully him.

"I am so happy you have made such a good match, Papa," she said with another curtsey. Sukey twittered in pleasure and hit Lord Alfred with the fan again. He glared. Amelia turned from him, meaning to make her way to the door and thence to freedom. She would collect Lewes and be gone, and nobody in Society would be able to say she had not offered her father at least as much politeness as he had deigned to give her.

"Madam, I congratulate you on your father's forgiving nature," someone said. Amelia looked around; the voice was disturbingly familiar.

Facing her was her husband's brother, the present Lord Jeffries-Hodge. She nearly shuddered upon seeing the neat, well-turned-out figure she had thought she had left behind for the last time in her husband's library in the country.

"Brother Darwin, what in the name of heaven are you doing here?" she asked before she could stop herself.

"Brother! Ah, don't give me such a close relationship in your mind. I would prefer something quite as close, yet more intimate than brother," he said, leaning near.

"I would not," said Amelia, and turned to move on.

He caught at her arm. "You asked me why I am here. Well, the truth is I am an old comrade of her ladyship's—she's like a sister to me. I asked her to invite me since you would be here. There is something I have to say to you."

Amelia stared.

"That sentimental Sukey is convinced that I long to see you back in the bosom of my family," he continued. "Now there are elements of truth to that. Why don't we leave the room? I know the way to the study, and we must be private." His eyes held the familiar leer which Amelia

had been seeing so frequently from all the bucks of Society.

"I prefer to stay with the rest of the company," she
said in a dismissive tone.

"Very well." He still held her arm in a tight grip, and
now he propelled her to a slightly more private area, behind the very Broadwood pianoforte Amelia used to
practise on. Nobody had opened the instrument this
evening. The crowd was not a musical one, and the area
around the pianoforte was as private as any place in the
room.

"Please let me go," said Amelia.

"Not before I give you this one message." Darwin's
little eyes, so like her late husband's that Amelia nearly
shook, were glittering at her. "You've been starved out,
haven't you? Forced to take a post, and now to be
drummed out of that because of the scandal of my
brother's death—"

Amelia interrupted him. "You more than anyone
know that I had nothing to do with your brother's death.
And I suspect you, sir, of being the one to spread these
slanderous rumours."

He smiled, and Amelia was sure she had the right of it.
"It matters little how rumours start. What is important
is that you have no means of support now, nowhere to
turn now that your chaperoning venture is as good as at
an end. There is still the allowance I am quite willing to
give you. A country cottage near my estate—a little
company to ease the lonely hours of widowhood now and
again...." His voice trailed off, and he stroked the arm
he still held tightly.

Amelia took the opportunity to pull her arm away. She
was sure it would show bruises come morning. Her hand
raised automatically, but she was able to snatch it back

before she actually slapped him. "You are despicable," she whispered. "And your touch disgusts me. Never dare to come near me again."

His face darkened in anger as Amelia rustled away from him, heading straight for the door. Her cheeks were burning. Had he really started that damning rumour about her, merely so that she would have no other choice but to become his mistress?

She wasn't surprised that the new Lord Jeffries-Hodge and Lady Alfred should be acquainted. Darwin had always mixed with a less than genteel crowd.

From a safe station beside a large vase, Lord Doncastle surreptitiously watched Amelia as he pretended to attend to the gushing conversation of a less than fashionable, but very bold matron.

He had accepted this invitation out of curiosity. Lady Alfred wrote that she had not yet met him, but hoped to strike up a rewarding acquaintance, and such artless familiarity had intrigued him, especially since he was being invited to the very house he had entered so often seven years before.

Doncastle had worried a bit over Lord Alfred's reaction when that crotchety gentleman should see again the man he had warned off his daughter so long ago. He needn't have done so. Lord Alfred, grown a bit dotty with the passage of time, made no connection between the poor Mr. Searle of former days and the Viscount Doncastle whom he had met ever so briefly this evening.

It became clear, during a very long dinner spent at Lady Alfred's right hand, that Doncastle had been selected for the lady's cicisbeo. He was amused but not interested, and he didn't know if he had managed to convey this message. He hoped he would not have to reject Lady Alfred's outright proposition, for she seemed vulgar enough to make it if the more subtle techniques failed. He found himself liking her in an odd way, and he didn't wish to hurt her feelings.

His surprise was great when Amelia was announced after dinner. He had never expected to see her in her father's house. He witnessed from afar the scene of reconciliation between her and Lord Alfred. Doncastle had heard at the time of Amelia's elopement that her rigidly moral father had cast her off for her henwitted and scandalous behaviour. Jeremy Searle had been glad, for at that time he wished nothing but evil to Amelia, the girl who had blasted his hopes.

Now, it seemed, she was halfway back into the fold. The invitation to join the party after dinner was a definite insult to a daughter of the house, however estranged, and Doncastle was amazed Amelia had so little pride that she would countenance it. He kept watching her, simply as a curiosity, of course, and saw her meet with her brother-in-law in the middle of the room.

What happened then was clear enough. Doncastle saw the insolent leer on Jeffries-Hodge's face; Amelia's raised hand which did not quite connect with her brother-in-law's cheek; her angry expression as she jerked herself away. He resisted the temptation to follow her out of the room, though he would have liked an opportunity to tell her that he and Sir Ethelred had subdued the chivalrous pretensions of her newest admirer, Sir Lumley Martinstone, and that there would be no duel.

More abstracted than ever, he returned his attention to his one-sided conversation with the talkative woman.

He was thinking of making his excuses and going on to some other amusement, or even home to bed, when Lord Jeffries-Hodge nodded to him in passing.

"I say, Doncastle, did you notice my brother's widow was here earlier?"

Wondering why on earth Jeffries-Hodge would allude to Amelia, Doncastle gave a tight nod.

The baron's eyes were shifting about as he said, leaning towards the viscount, "You might have noticed she was angry with me. Well, I seized this opportunity of meeting her to let her know I've my suspicions about my brother's death. I told her she needn't think the whole story won't come out even though I, out of delicacy to my brother's memory, would never prosecute her."

"Oh," said Doncastle. "Is that what you told her?" He had the unpleasant feeling that he was being used to spread gossip. Knowing Amelia as he once had, observing her present-day manners, he could not believe this story was anything but outright slander.

"I did indeed," said Jeffries-Hodge. "My brother's memory is sacred to me, my lord. Sacred."

"To be sure," said Doncastle. But he wondered, all the same, why Amelia's short interview with her brother-in-law had resembled so much a lady fending off improper attentions.

Doncastle decided to trust the evidence of his own eyes. He would take any statements her brother-in-law made about Amelia with a grain of salt, as coming from a rejected lover.

CHAPTER ELEVEN

BY THE NEXT MORNING, Amelia had managed to sort through her mixed feelings about her visit to Lord Alfred Montresor's.

Though she had not expected to derive any pleasure from her father's second marriage, she *was* pleased, albeit for not the usual reasons. She somehow knew that Lady Alfred would lead her lord into more frustrations than he thought possible. Whatever momentary impulse had led to his capture, he would pay for that weakness, and Amelia, who believed in retribution when all was said and done, was content.

And Sukey was a good-hearted soul. Amelia would not have liked to see him caught in the clutches of a cold and mercenary shrew. But a merry and vulgar adventuress? He deserved no better, and Amelia looked forward to reading in the Society columns of the Montresor menage's expensive movements from one spa to another, trailing new carriages loaded with expensive clothes and jewels.

As for Amelia's short but telling interview with her brother-in-law, Darwin, a night of sober reflection had convinced her that he had indeed circulated the horrid new rumours about her, solely to remove her from Society and leave her no other choice than to give in to his lecherous designs. She wished she had not forgotten to ask him how she was supposed to have murdered her husband. It would be most interesting to know.

Darwin had no way of knowing how kind, how understanding Sir Ethelred was on the subject of her respectability. He would never ask Amelia to leave his employ. Yet, this time, she had quite made up her mind to deliver her resignation.

Her days in the ton were numbered, and, wishing very much for her young charge to be settled before she took her leave, she rejoiced when Calliope received yet another morning call from Sam Guildford on the very day after Amelia's visit to the Montresors.

The young people, as Amelia persisted in calling them, despite the fact that she was of an age with Sam, put their heads together on one side of the drawing-room while Amelia bent her head to her work on the other. Glancing up now and again she had to smile at Calliope's serious, intense face as she discussed the Greek poets with Mr. Guildford, whose rapt attention betrayed an unscholarly infatuation with the girl by his side.

Amelia knew that Sam's fortune was middling if not non-existent, and that his greatest claim to good connections was his sister Sarah's lucky marriage to Lord St. Cloud. He would not be much of a catch, certainly nothing to the grand matrimonial prize Lord Doncastle had represented. As a chaperon, Amelia was expected to bring about a brilliant match. But as a friend of the family, she would be well-pleased with what seemed to be developing into a love-match.

She knew, too, that any bringing about would be the work of Sam and Calliope. Being duenna to an opinionated young lady who would marry where she chose was an easy task after all.

When Green opened the door and cleared his throat, his habit when announcing visitors, Amelia looked up in some irritation. She had no wish for Calliope's near tête-à-tête with the man of her choice to be interrupted. From time to time one of the callow troupe which still clustered about Miss Crane at balls and parties, thanks to the efforts of Sarah St. Cloud, would buzz into the house despite—or perhaps because of—Calliope's total lack of interest in any of the boneheaded young men.

To Amelia's surprise, it was no untried sprig who walked in at the door, but Doncastle. He was followed closely by Sir Lumley Martinstone. The two did not look out of charity with one another.

Brief all-around greetings ensued; then, with a sly glance of understanding directed at the courting couple, Doncastle steered Sir Lumley away from Calliope and Mr. Guildford, into Amelia's corner.

"Would you like to begin, Sir Lumley?" he said with a knowing smile at Amelia.

The small mathematician bowed. "I would be honoured, sir." He proceeded to take the astonished Amelia's hand and launched into what she recognized as a prepared speech.

"Fair lady, his lordship has made me realize that our coming to blows would only distress you and would serve no useful purpose to your reputation, as it would make you notorious."

"Indeed, yes," added Doncastle as Martinstone came to a pausing place. "And since we are both dedicated to serving you, we must put aside our differences and unite in that delightful project."

Both gentlemen beamed at Amelia. Their respective smiles had very different effects on her heart, but she managed a uniform graciousness as she said, "I thank you, gentlemen, and I trust we can put the whole unfortunate mishap behind us now.''

''By all means,'' said Sir Lumley eagerly, sitting down beside her.

''As my lady wishes,'' said Doncastle with an ironic look. He bowed, then strolled across the room to Calliope and Guildford, leaving Amelia alone with her scholarly admirer.

While she had to appreciate Lord Doncastle's amusement at having deliberately left her in a sticky situation, she doubted whether she was ever to make any progress in her campaign to depress Sir Lumley's pretensions to her favour. He did not refer to the present she had sent back and began to insist upon a drive in the Park. He would borrow a friend's tilbury if Lady Jeffries-Hodge would but grant him the pleasure of her company.

Amelia was halfway tempted to accept his invitation as the easy way out of her predicament. Perhaps he would try to take a liberty, and she might slap him and have the whole unfortunate affair at an end.

Instead she made a last effort at a reasonable denial, using a new excuse. ''Sir, I've let you know before that I don't even normally receive callers in this house upon my own account. How could I drive with you when it is my constant task to act as Miss Crane's chaperon? Besides,'' and she presented her newly-formed reason, ''my time in London is drawing to a close. I will be leaving soon for—for the country, and it would be unwise for us to strike up a closer acquaintance now.''

There, it was out. Sir Ethelred might again press her to stay, but as soon as the Season could possibly be said to be winding down, off she would go. ''The country'' would be her story, and she must get out of the gossip-mill of London, but in reality, she had no idea where she and her servants would be bound. A minor spa, perhaps, where Amelia might hire herself out once more upon the strength of Sir Ethelred's reference. She could only hope that her brother-in-law's vicious campaign against her would not soon reach her new employers' ears.

"The country!" exclaimed Sir Lumley. "I must hope you will change your intention, dear lady. Any thinking person would be stifled to death in the country, for though the frivolity of the Metropolis is tiring, to be sure, the great minds still congregate here. How tedious it would be for you to have to rely solely on correspondence with your friend Lady Margot, to take but one instance, rather than the free exchange of ideas which must now delight you."

Amelia wondered for the first time if her close acquaintance with the noted bluestocking, Lady Margot Jamieson, was some explanation for Sir Lumley's attraction to her. She had found it hard to believe that a man of his temperament could be taken in solely by her beautiful eyes.

She made some noncommittal answer while her glance strayed to the tableau across the room. Doncastle was definitely no rival to Calliope's attentions in the mind of Sam Guildford. The viscount was taking part in the rather esoteric conversation, playing gooseberry with the cheerful concurrence of the two lovers. Amelia knew she could consider Sam and Calliope undeclared lovers by this time. So many dances, chaperoned drives, and morning calls could mean only one thing.

How she and Jeremy had once struggled to hide any such signs of particularity in their own dealings!

She gave a start at these thoughts, which caused Sir Lumley to pause in his dissertation on the joys of the

Metropolis. Amelia apologized, assured Sir Lumley that she had merely felt a chill and did not object on ethical grounds to Davy's experiments with laughing gas. She then forced her expression into one of rapt attention to disguise her roving thoughts, as Sir Lumley, with a bright nod, continued his lecture.

For seven years she had been in the habit of thinking fondly about her one true romance, her too-short time with Jeremy Searle. It was a habit she had not yet tried to break, though it was surely most improper and quite dangerous to her own peace to think nostalgic thoughts of a gentleman who was in her present circle. What a different experience it was to remember what Jeremy had said or done and not have to conjure up his image in her mind. To look across the room and see him, handsomer even than he was in her memory, yet totally oblivious to her!

But was he quite oblivious? Today she sensed a certain tension between them as if neither could deny the other's presence. She felt it quite keenly, but had nearly convinced herself that it was only her imagination playing tricks upon her.

He was coming towards her, she noticed suddenly. He had taken a ceremonious leave of Calliope and shaken Guildford's hand.

"I have another appointment, my lady, and I regret I must leave you now," he said gravely. "Martinstone, are you coming? I will be taking my way through Albemarle Street, where you mentioned you wished to stop by at the Royal Institution."

Sir Lumley took the obvious hint that he had long ago outstayed the proper length of a morning call. He stood up and made his devoirs to Amelia. "And let us not hear any more nonsense of leaving town," he said with a playful wag of his finger.

Amelia was more disturbed by the intimacy of the wiggling digit than by his words. She made some neutral murmur.

"Leaving town?" asked Doncastle. His eyes searched Amelia's.

"You know, my lord, that there are pressing reasons for me to leave this household," said Amelia with a telling glance in the direction of Calliope. Doncastle actually looked concerned. How different from his ordinary cold manner.

"I had understood that Sir Ethelred would not accept your decision to go," said Doncastle.

Amelia was shocked that her affairs had been matter for discussion between her employer and Doncastle. "Did he ask your advice?"

"By no means, ma'am, he merely asked me to be of use in scotching the scurrilous talk going about town."

"He did!" Amelia was struck that unworldly Sir Ethelred should be so kind or, for that matter, so worldly-wise as to enlist the help of one of the foremost bucks of the ton to mend her reputation. Sir Ethelred could know nothing of her former association with Lord Doncastle, of course, nor that the said Lord Doncastle would wish nothing less than to come to the aid of the former Miss Montresor. "How kind of Sir Ethelred," she said.

She had forgotten that Sir Lumley still stood at her elbow. He was glancing from Amelia to Doncastle with an expression of puzzlement. "What's this about scurrilous talk?" he demanded. "Has someone dared to spread word of our duel already?"

"Something of the sort," said Doncastle. With a private wink for Amelia, he went away with Martinstone.

Not wishing to repeat the latest on-dit, Doncastle was able to satisfy Sir Lumley's concern with an innocuous story about the duel. The anxious baronet was all concern for Lady Jeffries-Hodge. By the time Doncastle parted from Sir Lumley in Albemarle Street, the small scholar was sworn to defend Lady Jeffries-Hodge to the best of his ability, and above all things to use discretion in so doing.

Amelia was left to puzzle over Doncastle's manner. He seemed to be on her side for some reason. By now he must have heard the worst of the gossip about her. He believed her to be vile and mercenary and yet, he had just now shown her a kindness. Could it be possible that he was beginning to doubt the reputation given her by the tattlemongers?

"Amelia," said Calliope, "aren't you listening? Mr. Guildford just asked permission to escort us to Drury Lane tonight. Shall we go or not?"

Amelia managed to focus her attention on the world around her and the hoped-for happy ending to at least one romance.

DONCASTLE WAS DOING SOME hard thinking as he strolled along by a somewhat indirect route to his appointment in Half-Moon Street. Amelia was modest and retiring at all times. She seemed the most upright of widows, and she lived in a situation of the utmost respectability. In addition, Amelia refused even the most unexceptionable attentions of every male who approached her. Sir Lumley had bemoaned to Doncastle during their walk the way Lady Jeffries-Hodge denied him the innocent pleasure of a drive with her in the Park.

Doncastle knew for a fact that whatever else Amelia was, she was an impoverished widow. It was surely economic and social folly for a woman in her position to say no to a legitimate suitor. Why, then, did she make a practice of doing so?

He remembered that evening when she had told him she would never wed again. He had flatly refused to believe her. Yet, looking back, had there not been a certain sureness in her voice, a fire in her eyes when she insisted she would not remarry? And a widow without a jointure must marry again if she could.

Amelia was only four-and-twenty. Did she honestly plan to spend the rest of her life alone? If so, why? Had Lord Jeffries-Hodge been so important to her that she could not think of giving him a successor?

This thought was not pleasant, and Doncastle put it to the back of his mind. He had never believed that Amelia had run away with Jeffries-Hodge in a fit of passion, and he was not about to start believing it now. Money and position had been her driving force, that he knew. All the love her cold heart had been capable of had been lavished upon himself. Hadn't it?

So unaccountable was the widow's behaviour that Doncastle actually wondered if she could have in her eye not marriage, but living under the protection of some prince of the realm, perhaps even the Regent himself. She was beautiful enough to catch any notice. Some such worldly ambition would explain her refusal of Sir Lumley's proper attentions. But Doncastle discarded this thought as soon as he'd formed it. The picture simply did not suit.

When he was ushered into the sitting-room of the lady who had summoned him, he was wearing a thoughtful frown.

"My dear Doncastle, why so Friday-faced?" said Lady Alfred Montresor, rising from her chaise longue to drift towards him, hand outstretched so as to show to best advantage a shapely white arm draped in lace.

The rest of Lady Alfred, Doncastle could not help noting, was attired in a garment much too provocative for an ordinary morning visit.

"Forgive me, my lady," he said with just the proper touch of contrition, "I was thinking of—business."

"Business, on such a fine morning?" the lady teased, tossing her guinea-gold curls. She moved to a sofa and sat herself down, patting the place beside her.

Doncastle pretended not to notice this sign and placed himself a safe distance away, on a stiff brocade chair. He knew already, or thought he knew, why he had been called to this interview. He wasn't surprised to see that Lady Alfred entertained no other callers, and that her husband was not present. Not even the boldest lady would wish an audience to observe her blatant attempt to snare a lover.

Events proved Doncastle not a coxcomb. The hint, if hint it could be called, was not long in coming. "My dear Doncastle, it is so kind of you to take pity on a neglected wife," said Lady Alfred, shooting him a glance of unmistakable meaning before she modestly lowered sooty eyelashes to the scarf she was drawing back and forth between her hands.

"Neglected? You? But you are virtually a newlywed, ma'am." Doncastle tried to appear properly shocked without letting his humour slip through.

She heard it nevertheless and laughed. "Newlywed, forsooth! It should make not a bit of difference were I married to Lord Alfred for a hundred years. Never let it be said Susan Moffitt would wed a man of Lord Alfred's stamp and expect not to be neglected. I am trying to catch you, sir, for our mutual pleasure. Are you to be taken?''

Doncastle laughed in pure delight and gently told her he was not. ''I make it a rule never to cuckold anyone,'' he explained. If he were a different sort of man, though, there might be no little pleasure in straying with the wife of Lord Alfred Montresor. Lady Alfred's blatancy was most attractive. He would find her person attractive also, he admitted to himself, were it not that he was already in the snare of—

His thoughts halted abruptly.

''It was worth a try,'' Lady Alfred was saying with a wink. She was evidently not one to bear a grudge. ''My first effort, you must know, at this sort of game. I've never been a wife before, Lord knows, and instinct told me the approach in such a case as this would best contain no roundaboutation. Was I wrong?''

''Oh, no,'' Doncastle made haste to assure her. ''If I had been susceptible to dalliance with a married woman, my lady, rest assured your approach would have worked marvellously well. Your honesty is refreshing.''

Lady Alfred looked at him keenly. ''Are you really such a stickler, my lord? Is it only that I've a husband, or is it that you've already someone else?''

Doncastle hardly knew how to respond to this. He said nothing.

That nothing was enough to make the lady sure she was on the mark. ''Well, what measures can I take against an unknown rival? I won't cut up your peace, you may rest assured. Doncastle, may I be frank with you?''

''You have already been more than frank, ma'am.''

''I mean to be franker still. My lord, I find myself in a sorry situation. You have met Lord Alfred. You can see that if I'm to be amused in any sense of the word, I must take a—a—there is a word that is French or some such . . ."

"Cicisbeo?" suggested Doncastle, with a smile.

"Just so. What a funny word. So much more genteel than lover," said Lady Alfred in satisfaction. "I am new on the town, sir, and I find myself quite at a standstill before I've begun, simply because I can't get into the best Society where the most attractive men are. Can you suggest anyone who would be suitable to my purposes? A pity that dandy whom everyone admired, that Mr. Brummell, has left the country. But I am willing to entertain any idea." She leaned back on the sofa, exposing her figure in a way that left no doubt as to her willingness to entertain ideas by the score.

Doncastle saw the opportunity to find out some information about a problem that had been preying on his mind. In fact, he had accepted the lady's invitation solely for the purpose of gleaning knowledge about certain of her friends. "How about—what was his name?—oh, yes, Lord Jeffries-Hodge, the baron from Hampshire. I met him at your dinner. He's of rank, and married already—which would be most suitable to your needs, would it not?—and his wife would seem to live entirely in the country, which would be convenience itself. Lessen the need for discretion, don't you know." He paused. "You know him well, I assume?"

Lady Alfred let out a rather braying laugh. "Oh, him! But of course you wouldn't know, sir, that Lord Jeffries-Hodge has nothing to recommend him to a female who ain't in need of money. I've known him for years, you see, him and his late brother. I can think of nothing that would tempt me to allow him—of all people—"

"You do know him well," said Doncastle. "I don't, and he interests me. What can you tell me about him?"

She shrugged. "He is from my own neighbourhood in the country. And brother-in-law to my new stepdaughter, the dowager, whom I mean to love dearly. What a tangle that would be! I'm mortal glad he's not one to attach a woman of my spirit."

"Your stepdaughter is a dowager?" enquired Doncastle with a politely raised eyebrow, as though to doubt that anyone of Lady Alfred's youth could have a relation so styled.

"Yes, my husband's daughter, Amelia, who is only in her twenties now. Hardly older than me." Lady Alfred would never see thirty again, but Doncastle made no reaction to her low estimate of her own age, and she went on talking. "The poor child was fairly sold to the present baron's brother—Thomas, the old Lord Jeffries-Hodge—as a chit of seventeen. I do think it heartless of Lord Alfred to have insisted she marry Jeffries-Hodge. For the late baron might have had his good points, as most men do, but they were not of a sort to appeal to an innocent young girl."

"What?" said Doncastle. "Amelia's—her ladyship's father forced her to have Jeffries-Hodge?"

He looked so stricken that Lady Alfred peered at him with definite suspicion.

"That is not the talk which went about town at the time," said Doncastle, recovering himself with difficulty. His view of Amelia had been absolutely settled for so many years. When he and she had formed their secret engagement, she had promised to stand firm in the face of her father's disapproval of Jeremy. She had not done so. But now it seemed her defection was for a very different reason than the one Doncastle had accused her of for so long.

"Oh, yes, I know there was a runaway marriage," said Lady Alfred. "But Lord Alfred arranged that. He told me so himself."

"Is that so?" Doncastle knew that he should turn the subject so that he would not betray his interest in Amelia more than he had done, but he could not resist the opportunity to find out more. "And you said that the late Lord Jeffries-Hodge was not the sort of man a young girl would like. Could you elaborate on that? I know Lady Jeffries-Hodge slightly, and it concerns me that her married life might have been less than ideal."

"Less than ideal!" Lady Alfred leaned closer. "As I'm from their part of Hampshire, I was well-acquainted with the late baron. Never met his wife, which turns out to be convenient, for here I am her stepmother through the merest coincidence. But the stories of their domestic life were clear enough. The poor child cried for the first year, so my old auntie told me, for Auntie was the housekeeper at the Jeffries-Hodge estate. Then poor Amelia found her salvation in dignity and became quite beloved in the neighbourhood, doing charitable works and whatnot, for she really had to do something, what with her married life a shambles. *She* lived in the country, and there aren't a lot of gallants available, especially in that part of Hampshire. One was quite at a loss." This with a wink. "I haven't told her I knew of her in those days, and you must not tell her, either. How well are you acquainted with her?"

"Not well," said Doncastle, struggling to disguise his avid interest. "And you have my promise. I won't repeat a word of this conversation. To anyone. I must tell you, Lady Alfred, that I think it monstrous kind of you to try to reconcile father and daughter as you did the other night. Only think, Society assumes Lord Alfred is estranged from his daughter because he objected to her elopement, and you say he forced the marriage? Extraordinary. Then why has he been angry with her all these years?''

''It never does occur to anyone,'' said Lady Alfred, ''that all the time it might have been Amelia angry with him.''

She was right; this explanation had never occurred to Doncastle. What a different version of his long-ago disappointment was hurtling through his brain at the moment! Amelia had disappeared so suddenly. His last meeting with her had been all that was affectionate. They had talked of somehow reconciling her father to their engagement. She had promised Jeremy that, if Lord Alfred remained intractable, she would wait for the man she loved until she was one-and-twenty and her own mistress.

Then she had disappeared, and word seeped through Society of her elopement with Lord Jeffries-Hodge.

Doncastle, or Mr. Searle, as he had been at the time, had formerly noticed Jeffries-Hodge, a burly man in early middle age. The baron had evidently been attracted to the lovely Amelia, who, having eyes only for one man, had not paid this would-be suitor the least heed.

Had Jeffries-Hodge gone to her father and been accepted? Had Amelia crumbled in the face of her father's insistence? That would be weak, but it would hardly be the heartless conduct Jeremy had believed her guilty of for seven years.

There was only one way to find out. Doncastle said goodbye to Lady Alfred, thanked her for the amusing visit, and directed his steps once more to Portman Square.

CHAPTER TWELVE

AMELIA WAS SITTING ALONE. She had seen Sam Guildford on his way and Calliope off to her room for an afternoon of diligent study.

Love was making Calliope bloom in looks as well as in scholarship. Amelia would swear the girl's freckles were fading, but perhaps this was because they were less visible with her cheeks always so rosy with excitement. As for her eyesight, it must have improved, for Amelia noticed that the spectacles were more often missing from Calliope's small, neat nose, leaving her clear grey eyes to shine forth without any obstacle.

Thank goodness Mrs. Winkle's habit was to take a long nap every afternoon, Amelia was thinking as she opened *Discipline*, a novel she had been longing to read ever since she had enjoyed the author's first effort, *Self-Control*. She might count upon another two hours of peace.

There was a scratch at the door, and Higgins peeked his head into the room in his singular way. "Madam," said the footman with an apologetic smile, "Green is off about some errand, and I happened to answer the front door."

"Yes?" Amelia motioned him to continue, thinking that she really would have to speak to him about this annoying habit of not appearing in the room in his entirety. "Do you have something for me?" she asked as the thought struck her that Higgins might have received delivery of another distressing gift from a rakish admirer of hers.

"There is a visitor, ma'am. I know we are to deny you, but the gentleman says it is most important he see you, and I—I believe him, m'lady." Higgins bowed his head, as though already ashamed to have been so taken in.

"Who is it?" asked Amelia. A note of displeasure was clear in her voice.

"Lord Doncastle, madam," said Higgins quickly. The long head disappeared, the door clicking behind.

Before Amelia could collect herself the door was pushed all the way open by a firm hand, and Doncastle entered the room. Amelia sprang to her feet.

"*You* wished to see me?" she said in a shaky voice. Her eyes surveyed the floor, the ceiling: anything but him.

"Amelia," he said. "Look at me."

He had not called her Amelia in seven years. Her eyes raised to his of their own accord.

"Much better." Doncastle crossed to her side, took her hand in his, and without any sort of introduction, said what was uppermost in his mind. "Amelia, my dear, you must tell me the truth. What was it made you run off with Jeffries-Hodge years ago? I know now that you were pushed into the match. Please tell me why."

Amelia's sensations on having her hand held for such a long time by the man she most cared for were many and varied, but they all came down to one thing. If there had been any doubt in her mind, it was no longer present. She did love this man. She always had, and, heaven help her, she always would.

Gently, she withdrew her hand from his grasp. "I can't tell you," she said softly. "I can never tell."

"Why not?" he demanded. This time he grasped her shoulders, not hard, gently in fact, but the contact was sudden.

Amelia reacted as if he had approached her with a hatchet. She tore herself away and retreated across the room. Doncastle was too startled to follow her.

"I simply can't," she said, sounding almost frantic. "Please go. And why this sudden interest in my past, Lord Doncastle? Is it idle curiosity? Why must I open all my private business to you?"

"I didn't know until today, but here is my reason. I am your friend," he said.

Amelia remained silent, and the words echoed in the room as words will. She wished nobody need say anything ever again. It was a perfect moment. Unfortunately, the past seven years had not been perfect and if she took exception to Jeremy's touch, she could never tell him why. But his words were more welcome than she could ever say. She wanted to reassure him but she couldn't speak; she could only look at him with the sentiments she felt clearly to be read in her eyes.

He made a move towards her.

She stayed him with a raised hand. "Please don't. Don't touch me."

"Why, in God's name, won't you trust me? Tell me why you married that blasted Jeffries-Hodge. If it's some deep, dark secret, why worry now? The man is dead. And I suspect he was served right."

"He was," said Amelia.

Struck by the matter of factness of her tone, Doncastle stared at her lovely, innocent face and was startled by the hatred blazing in the blue eyes. "Good lord, Amelia, did you kill him?" he asked in horror. "Was he so cruel to you that you killed him?"

Amelia's eyes widened until they seemed to fill her face. "You think that of me? Leave me at once!"

Doncastle knew instantly that he had made the biggest mistake of his life to accuse her so. "I didn't mean—please, my darling, listen to me—it was only the tone of your voice just now, and your expression—"

"No excuses," said Amelia coldly. Somewhere in the back of her mind registered the delightful fact that he had called her his darling, but that was unimportant in the face of his insult. "Good day, sir." And she ran out of the room before he could stop her.

Doncastle waited a moment before he left the drawing-room, too, shaking his head at his folly.

He had accused the woman he loved of committing murder. There could be no excuse.

What could he do to make amends?

The trite symbol of flowers must serve as a start, for no respectable woman would accept a more intimate gift. Which blossoms stood for forgiveness? He would find out and send her a quantity before night fell.

In the entrance hall the footman who had let him in waited with his hat and cane. Doncastle accepted both, put on the hat, and headed for the door, thinking confused thoughts of Ophelia's mad scene in *Hamlet*. Pansies? No, they weren't for forgiveness, they were for thoughts....

"My lord," said the footman who was now holding the door, "if I might beg a moment of your time? It has to do with Lady Jeffries-Hodge."

Doncastle paused and looked the footman in his pale eyes. "You wish to gossip about her ladyship?" he said with hauteur.

"No, begging your lordship's pardon, I wish to help her," said Higgins desperately. "I and a friend. Her personal servants, my lord."

"Her personal servants!" There was a moment of hesitation. Then, "By all means, my good man, meet me at the corner tavern in five minutes," said Doncastle. Without another word, only an eloquent look exchanged with the lanky footman, he left the house.

Higgins rushed to the servants' hall and told Lewes, whom he found having a blushing conversation with Green, the butler, of Lord Doncastle's wish to speak to them. Once the two servants were out of the house themselves and on the way to the rendezvous, Higgins explained what he had learned by the simple expediency of listening at the door during Amelia's interview with his lordship.

Lewes was round-eyed. She agreed wholeheartedly. She and Higgins had a duty, if they could, to save Madam from her own misguided pride.

"The truth must out, and Madam will never say naught unless we help her along," said Lewes virtuously. "I—I have told Green the truth about myself, Higgins. He is so kind, so generous!"

"Then I'm to be wishing you happy, lass?"

"Not quite that. Not yet," said Lewes, but her smiles and blushes left no doubt that at least an engagement was in the offing.

In tolerably good cheer, the two entered the local tavern, where the neighbourhood's upper servants were wont to gather for a good gossip—one of the first means of spreading news throughout the complex maze of London Society.

Doncastle had procured them a corner table and had three tankards of ale waiting. When he saw that Higgins was accompanied by a female, by her looks a refined ladies' abigail, he signalled to the barman and had one tankard changed for a glass of lemonade.

The three sat in silence for a little. When Lewes had been served, and they were left alone, Doncastle spoke.

"You two serve Lady Jeffries-Hodge and wish to help her. What do you know about my dealings with the lady?"

Lewes spoke up quickly, as though she were a scholar reciting an important lesson. "We know you were the man our lady loved when she was married to our old master, sir. She wept for you for years, she did, for I came to her right after her wedding. Real sad it was, and we didn't know at the time why she should cry so very much. When Higgins—when we found out later she had jilted you to run off with master, we knew the secret at last, sir."

"You know my secret, then," said Doncastle. He was sensible of some measure of relief that he did not have to explain himself. "May I be allowed to know hers? She cried for me, did she? Why the devil did she marry Lord Jeffries-Hodge, then? Was it only her father's bullying? She had sworn to stand up to him. What made her change? Can you tell me that?"

The servants exchanged looks, and Higgins nodded. He took a deep breath. "My lord, we wish not to be vulgar. My lady—she was forced."

"Yes, I have learned she was forced to marry him," said Doncastle impatiently. "But why?"

"You don't understand, sir," spoke up Lewes. She turned a fiery shade of red. "She was forced. Old master forced her, my lord. She—she felt she had no choice but to marry him after it happened."

Doncastle stared in disbelief. "Are you saying he ruined her? He ravished my Amelia?" Rage simmered in his every vein. He regretted for the first time that Lord Jeffries-Hodge was already beneath the ground. Oh, for the pleasure of putting him there!

Higgins cast his eyes down to the table. "My lady confided in us as we came to know each other well," he said. "After it happened, her wish was to live as a spinster for the rest of her life since she was ruined. But his lordship went to her father, told him what he'd done, and demanded our lady's hand, along with her dowry, to be sure. Her father bullied her into the marriage, sir. She couldn't do nothing else, for he as much as kicked her out of her home, and she was only seventeen. Her father told Jeffries-Hodge to carry her off, for he'd have no soiled goods being wed in a church with his blessing. A patched-up business it was, but it appeared no more than a runaway marriage."

"The old weasel," muttered Doncastle. "I hope that tart he's married to cuckolds him soon and often."

"Please, your lordship?" said Lewes with a mystified look.

"Never mind. Tell me more." Doncastle maintained an admirable calm for one whose world was crumbling about him. For years he had relied upon his idea of Amelia as the mercenary witch, the false lover. His life had made sense that way; his opinion of women had not changed with the passing of time.

Now Amelia, the woman who had started him on his cynical path, stood revealed before him as a victim of circumstances. A victim of a violent attack!

"Why didn't she come to me?" he murmured.

"If you please, sir." It was the maid Lewes again, speaking in her soft, clear country accent. "No woman would ask a man to take a bad bargain."

"How could she be so foolish?"

Lewes turned angry eyes on him; then, presumably aghast at her own daring, she studied her glass.

"Tell me about your late master," were Doncastle's next words, addressed to both servants.

They exchanged looks again. "He was not a good man, sir," said Higgins after a meaningful moment of silence.

"I've gathered that," said Doncastle. "And he was not a good husband, I take it?"

"A husband may do as he likes," said Lewes primly. "But late Master carried that to extreme, if you'll forgive my saying so."

"He made a practice of trafficking with all the ladies in the neighbourhood who would take him," said Higgins with a wise nod.

"And some as weren't ladies," said Lewes. "And some as weren't willing." She had been red; now she turned white. Doncastle noticed that her hands were shaking as she put down her glass of lemonade.

He looked at Higgins, for there was no way he could persuade Lewes to meet his eye. The footman nodded.

The story was near an end. Lord Jeffries-Hodge had used brute force to obtain a wife, and had not cared a snap for any vows of fidelity he might have made in that transaction. He had ravished those of his servants who appealed to him. Pretty Lewes had evidently been one of those.

Doncastle wished anew that Lord Jeffries-Hodge had not been carried off the year before. He could not really kill a man in cold blood. But what a pleasure it would have been indeed to throttle him, challenge him to a duel, at least to have him horsewhipped.

"My foolish Amelia," he said, half to himself. "If only she had come to me."

"I wish she had, too, sir," said Lewes fervently. "You are kind. You wouldn't have cast her off. And you wouldn't have died in a duel, as she told me recently she feared at the time."

"No, young woman, I wouldn't have," said Doncastle. "Tell me one thing more about your master. How did he die? Is there any doubt about the matter?"

The servants hesitated a moment, long enough to make Doncastle fear they were thinking how best to protect their mistress. Higgins spoke. "There's no doubt, my lord, embarrassing though it were for all concerned. Three of our staff including me went looking for him when he failed to keep an appointment with the squire. Found him. In the village inn he was, with a female in hysterics in the room with him. They had been—his heart must have given way, sir, in the act of, er—"

"Say no more," interrupted Doncastle. "Witnesses, and his wife nowhere near him when he died. How do you suppose the new Lord Jeffries-Hodge has managed to spread the rumour that Amelia—that her ladyship had something to do with her husband's death?"

"Nothing easier," said Higgins in surprise. He had heard the rumours, of course, and had been doing his best to scotch them from his end, but with limited success. "Hampshire is the country, sir, and this is London. Who's to pay attention to what really happened? Who's to find out, when a lie is so much more interesting?"

There was really no more to it than that. Doncastle knew in his bones that Amelia had had nothing to do with her husband's death. Indeed, he had known it all along, misled for only a moment by the note of hatred in her voice and the flash of loathing in her eyes when she spoke of the late Lord Jeffries-Hodge. And now those sentiments were amply explained.

"We hope we've done well, sir," said Lewes in a shaking voice. "We wouldn't do anything to hurt madam. We know she must love you, and we want her to be happy."

"She must love me! Has she told you that?" asked Doncastle in eagerness.

"No," Lewes had to admit.

"We're her servants, my lord," said Higgins, puffing out his thin chest. "We know."

"I have a feeling you are much more than her servants," said Doncastle, "and rest assured you will have honoured places in our establishment when she and I marry."

Lewes burst into tears.

"Now what's wrong?" said Higgins in irritation.

"You know she's said she will never remarry," said Lewes into her handkerchief.

"Oh, that's all in the past," said Doncastle. "She wasn't thinking of me, girl. She could have had no idea—"

"Begging your pardon, my lord," said Lewes, "sometimes I have a feeling she meant you more than anyone." She took a deep breath, peeking over her handkerchief, and then the words rushed out. "She don't want to be bound to anyone, sir. How could she risk the same thing as happened to her once happening with the one she loved?"

Doncastle could not quite comprehend this logic. "She has no idea what marriage to me could be like," he said. "Do you say she thinks that I would use her so?"

"A husband has a right," said Lewes stoutly. "To do anything he might wish with any woman he likes. To beat you if he wants to. To—"

"He beat her?" roared out Doncastle. Heads turned, and, considering that those heads were all attached to elegant upper servants of the best houses in Mayfair, the viscount quickly lowered his voice. "He dared to lay hands on her?" he said in a murmur. He remembered, in a sudden flash, Amelia's odd reaction when he had grasped her shoulders unexpectedly, earlier that day. She had torn herself away in desperation. Quite as though she expected only pain to come from a touch....

"No 'dare' about it, sir," said Higgins with a shrug. "It's as Lewes says. The master may do what he wishes in his own house."

"My poor Amelia," said Doncastle, staring at her two loyal retainers. "What can I do to make this up to her?"

"Love her, sir," said Lewes with a twist of her handkerchief.

But Doncastle wondered for the first time in his rather egotistical life if anything he could give would be enough.

CHAPTER THIRTEEN

MY LOVE, MY LOVE, JEREMY was murmuring, *can you ever forgive me?*

Amelia's eyes popped open, and she found herself staring only at the darkness. What had startled her? A noise? Or was it merely that she had been arriving at an intimate place in her dream which she would not know how to deal with in reality?

How very real some dreams were, to be sure. Amelia closed her eyes and burrowed down into her pillows, only to have someone pull the bed curtains aside and shake her gently by the shoulder.

"Madam!" It was Lewes, Amelia found as she focused her bleary eyes a second time. The maid was smiling broadly. "Lady St. Cloud sent word to you first thing it happened. She's been brought to bed, my lady, of a fine boy, and both are safe as houses."

"Great news!" cried Amelia. Instantly awake, she bounded out of bed and hurried to the small table where she kept her work-basket. She took out a small white garment. "And to think I haven't even finished this yet, for Sarah was certain the baby would never be born. What time is it, Lewes?"

"Three in the morning, madam."

Amelia sighed. "Then I suppose I shall have to wait . . . but I can't sleep, either."

"Then perhaps your ladyship would like me to fetch up the bouquet which arrived this evening while you were at the theatre? It was put in the kitchen till you returned and I forgot it by mistake when you came home," said Lewes.

"A bouquet? You know what sorts of bouquets I receive," said Amelia, shaking her head. She sat down by her table and fiddled with the infant dress, wondering if she could possibly finish the embroidery by morning, if she worked very hard. "Bring me candles, Lewes."

The maid was still stuck on the idea of the flowers. "This bouquet is different, madam," she insisted. "Won't you have it? I might carry it up when I bring the candles."

"Very well," said Amelia, but she didn't hold out much hope that yet another offering from Lord Clayville or Captain Dawber would make her feel anything other than persecuted. Neither, though, would it put her into the depths of despair. Nothing could do that on a night when she was so relieved, so happy over Sarah's safe delivery.

When Lewes arrived, staggering under the weight of a voluptuous basket of varicolored flowers, with the candles her mistress had requested positioned unsteadily under one arm, Amelia let a gasp escape her. None of her admirers tended to quite this style of showy generosity. At least not in the realm of flora. Amelia had sent back some remarkably gaudy jewels in this misbegotten Season, some of which must have been paste, and others which she knew to be as genuine as the black designs of the givers.

She rushed to grab the candles from Lewes just as they were about to tumble to the floor. The maid placed the flowers on the nearest flat surface and stood back admiringly. "There! Is it not lovely, ma'am?"

"Striking," was Amelia's less enthusiastic comment. She walked all around the table, warily, as though the bouquet were a wild beast. Her initial impression was that there must have been every flower in the world bunched together. And on closer inspection she discovered that there was indeed a sample of every blossom that had ever bloomed in a conservatory or a cottage garden. Roses of all colours vied with carnations, violets, lilies, jonquils, hyacinths, pansies, columbine, orchids—Amelia grew dazed as she tried to identify all the types. Attached to a sturdy gladiolus was a sealed note.

She broke the wafer and read, in a most distinctive hand which she recognised instantly,

> I have been unable to find which flower signifies forgiveness. Please forgive my lack of knowledge as well as my crass behaviour.
>
>   Jeremy

Amelia's hand shook. For whatever reason, forgetfulness or a wish for further intimacy, he had not styled himself "Doncastle."

Lewes had been setting out and lighting the candles and only now had leisure to turn to her mistress and say, in an excited voice, "From Lord Doncastle, madam. He has not sent flowers before. Are you not pleased?"

"A most surprising attention," said Amelia. She managed to speak in a cool and matter-of-fact voice and did not deign to notice Lewes' disappointment. Amelia sat down near a pair of brightly glowing candles and began to wrestle with the intricacies of the embroidery on the infant dress. For more than one reason now, she knew that sleep was over for her that night.

THE LADIES OF THE CRANE household were settled late at their breakfast table, and Amelia was wondering how many days she must wait before she could properly call on Sarah. For all her zeal of the middle of the night, and her conviction that she would go to Mount Street at first light, the notion had passed with the reason of sunrise. Perhaps it would be prudent to allow Sarah to recover her strength before besetting her with visitors, however eager. When Lady Margot Jamieson walked into the room, closely followed by Sir Ethelred, who had breakfasted hours before, thoughts of Sarah flew out the window.

The three females all looked their shock at this double surprise. Sir Ethelred rarely showed himself during the day and certainly not with a lady. He compounded their amazement by stealing his arm about Lady Margot's waist. He was smiling broadly.

"I came to collect Lady Jeffries-Hodge and take her to Lady St. Cloud's, when I happened to meet Sir Ethelred in the hall," said Lady Margot, clearing her throat self-consciously.

"And?" Amelia could not tear her fascinated eyes away from the bony hand which was now caressing Margot's middle.

"And we decided, while we were about it, to get ourselves betrothed," said Sir Ethelred. At this Lady Margot blushed, which Amelia had rarely seen her do.

"Why, Papa, this is beyond anything grand," said Calliope. She dropped her fork and her scientific journal, both of which had been motionless in mid-air for the last little while, and rose from her place to kiss both Lady Margot and her father.

Mrs. Winkle had begun to frown. She no doubt saw the end of her reign in the Crane household. "Lady Jeffries-Hodge, I thought we had agreed, at your own suggestion, that you would have no callers upon your own account," she said in a low tone, under cover of a happy burst of chatter from Sir Ethelred and his two women.

Amelia was too happy herself to take offence. "Evidently Lady Margot came to see Sir Ethelred. At least so it has turned out." She felt rather smug. The first successful matchmaking of her life! For she could not count Sam Guildford's association with Calliope, that being entirely due to Sarah St. Cloud.

Mrs. Winkle sighed and wiped the awful scowl from her face before she turned to the engaged couple with the most apparently genuine of good wishes.

"How fortuitous," Calliope found a moment to whisper to Amelia. "Now Papa won't be lonely when he finds I'm going to Scotland."

"What?" Amelia thought of her own miserable trip to Scotland years ago in the disgusting company of Lord Jeffries-Hodge. "You aren't eloping?"

"Heavens, no. Sam—Mr. Guildford is to take up a post at the University of Edinburgh, and naturally I shall go with him," responded Calliope.

"As his wife, I would hope?"

"But of course. Anything else would be most improper," said the girl calmly, but her eyes were sparkling, and she hugged Amelia. "I had to override Sam's scruples, for he was set on leaving without me simply because he has not much fortune. I soon convinced him how foolish that would be. We haven't found the proper moment to tell Papa—or you—but any time ought to be safe now."

"I should think so," agreed Amelia. She felt rather dazed by the superfluity of happy courtships as she went up to embrace her friend Margot and offer her congratulations to Sir Ethelred. The two were just breaking free from the obsequious Mrs. Winkle.

Before long Amelia found herself in Margot's carriage and on the way to Sarah's house, for the practical Margot, though slightly distracted by Sir Ethelred's offer, would not be deterred from her original purpose. She would not listen to Amelia's protests that perhaps they might want to delay the actual visit a day or two—or a week—and simply leave their cards in Mount Street.

"Sarah is healthy as a horse," said Lady Margot. "And she'd hate to be the last to hear the news I bring."

"I must agree with you there," said Amelia, eyes twinkling at her grave friend's carefully hidden excitement.

Sarah turned out to be in that peculiar state of high energy which sometimes follows a lying-in. News of Margot's engagement nearly brought her out of bed to dance about the room with her two schoolfellows—or so she said.

"We will leave the dancing for later," said Amelia. "Well, Sarah, your little boy is delightful, but I suppose we ought to let you rest now. Lord St. Cloud asked us to join him in the drawing-room for a few moments before we leave. From the noise, he seems to have collected both your families for the occasion."

"Isn't he silly?" said Sarah blithely. "The two sides cannot bear each other, and it would be quite funny to see them forced to be civil—almost worth going down to see for myself."

"No, you don't," said Amelia.

"I suppose you are right. I must wait for news to be brought me on how they're brangling. I don't expect all the news I get to be as charming as Margot's! This is your doing, Amelia."

"Certainly not," said Margot with dignity. "Sir Ethelred and I have made a mutual decision based on reason and esteem."

"Which you could hardly have made if Amelia had not introduced you," said Sarah. "Reason and esteem, indeed! Fudge. I have never seen you look so happy."

"Nor have I," Amelia felt bound to add.

Margot looked thoughtful at this, and to her friends' amusement she went to the nearest looking-glass to peer with interest at her own reflection.

Amelia thought Sarah's peals of laughter at this sight might be more tiring than Lady St. Cloud knew, so she ended the visit. She and Margot each gave Sarah a parting kiss. Then it was down to the drawing-room for the promised congratulatory toast with Lord St. Cloud.

Sarah's lord was a thinly elegant, slightly dandified young man whose present mood of elation did not match his usual pose of ennui. He welcomed his lady's two friends into a crowded room in which crusty dowagers and stout middle-aged men, as well as a representative or two of the younger generation, all mingled about in an atmosphere charged with tension.

"Family," said St. Cloud with a wink, helping the ladies to wine. "Shall we have a little game? You pick out the Guildfords, Lady Margot, and you, Lady Jeffries-Hodge, shall have the honour of naming my family. Shall we start with those two great-aunts over by the fire, the ones in puce and pea-green who are about to come to blows?"

The two friends laughed at him. The proposed game was brought to a premature end when Sam Guildford strolled up and bowed over both ladies' hands. Lord St. Cloud clapped his brother-in-law on the back, commended the ladies to his care, and strolled away.

Amelia could not resist a little hint at Sam's romance with Calliope; nor could she resist announcing the news which Margot would probably be too reticent to utter. "Sam, you've known us all for years, and you ought to be told that Margot and Sir Ethelred Crane are to make a match of it. I believe you have a near interest in the doings of the Crane family."

Sam pushed back a lank strand of blond hair and grinned as he said, "You have it, Amelia! Calliope and I mean to marry before the fall. She has convinced me that if I give her up, she will simply come after me. I know Calliope well enough to believe her. And you, Margot, have made life a bit easier for us. Calliope has been worrying over leaving her father to a life of loneliness in the grip of that old cousin, Mrs. Winkle. You'll see to that problem first thing, though."

Lady Margot, very much on her dignity, admitted that her intention was to remove Mrs. Winkle, a woman she could not like, from the Crane household as soon as she could see to another comfortable situation for the tiresome female.

"This is too perfect," said Amelia, clasping her hands. "I've never liked her, and I hate to give her the satisfaction of having successfully chased me out of the house. But now I may leave in peace, knowing she's in for a less than pleasant surprise."

"Leave?" Margot looked keenly at her friend. "You mean to leave the Cranes?"

"Naturally I do," said Amelia with the brightest smile she could come up with at that grim thought. "My task is complete. I was hired to chaperon Miss Crane into a life of wedded bliss, and so I have done. Now it's off to the next young woman in need of my expert care."

Sam and Lady Margot looked at each other in concern, over the top of Amelia's head.

The family gathering soon palled on two who were not family members, and Amelia and Margot took their leave of Sam and decided to be on their way. When they had left the St. Cloud residence, and were about to step up into Margot's chariot, the sound of horses stamping to a halt made Amelia turn around.

Doncastle was bringing his curricle to a standstill right beside Margot's vehicle.

He threw the ribbons to his tiger and leapt down onto the street, then hurried to Amelia's side while Margot looked on, an interested and keenly observant third.

"I found you." He clasped Amelia's hands and smiled into her astonished face.

"You did indeed find me," she said in wonder. "Why were you looking for me?"

"Why, to ask you to drive," said Doncastle. "If Lady Margot will forgive us, we can drive to the Park from here."

"But…" Amelia hesitated, still too amazed at the mere fact of his presence to be able to think up excuses or question him further.

Margot assessed the situation in a glance and took up the gentleman's cause. "I was on the point of returning to my father's, Amelia, and you would save me a trip back to Portman Square if you were to go with his lordship. Nothing could be more proper than an afternoon drive with a friend of your employer's family," she said in a tone of voice which made it clear that no objections would be tolerated.

Amelia could hardly refuse in the face of this blatant attempt at matchmaking and she managed to take leave of her friend with only one dark look of disapprobation, which Margot gaily shrugged off. Before she knew it, Amelia was settled in beside Doncastle in his shiny curricle and headed off down Mount Street, in the direction of Hyde Park. She spared one thought to her costume and was relieved that today, of all days, she had chosen to put on her best walking dress of dark green twilled silk, and a new plumed bonnet which was of Parisian elegance, though it had been concocted in her own bedchamber.

"My friend is quite zealous to deliver me into your company." Amelia began the conversation by striving for a normal tone. She glanced behind her and noticed for the first time that Doncastle's tiger had been left standing on the pavement. "But I'm certain you understand, my lord, how shocking it is to me to be singled out like this. I would have sooner expected one of the lamp-posts in Mount Street to rush up and ask me to drive."

"I won't say that your comparison of me to an inanimate object isn't on the mark," said Doncastle, in as cheerful a voice as Amelia's. "I have been little more than a stone in my dealings with you."

Amelia was totally confused. Did he indeed mean what he had said yesterday, when he had said he was her friend and wished to help her? She had to test the waters and said, "Do you remember who I am, sir? I'm the one who jilted you seven years ago, as you've been reminding me all the Season."

"It was wrong of me to throw that in your teeth," said Doncastle, still in that strangely good-humoured tone. "The past is long gone, my dear Amelia, and the future is before us." He gestured to the quickly approaching greenery of the Park and bestowed upon his companion a bright smile.

She could respond only by staring.

"The practicality of our drive must also be considered," said Doncastle, his voice confidential. "As you may know, my dear, I have turned out to be a figure of no little power in the ton. Probably my deuced distinction as a matrimonial prize. If you are seen driving with me, it will do much to end the rumours that have been circulating about you. That silly on-dit about your husband's death is the prime example. Imagine! When any fool might know for the asking that Jeffries-Hodge died in his bed, although that bed was in a hedge-tavern, and his companion a female other than his wife."

Amelia gasped and turned quite red. "You know *that?*"

"I had only to ask," said Doncastle. He did not mention whom he had asked, though Amelia could well suppose someone from Hampshire had given Doncastle the information. He turned his attention to his driving until they had safely navigated the Stanhope Gate.

Amelia took advantage of this pause in the conversation to study him carefully, if surreptitiously, from beneath her bonnet. She could accept without too much trouble that Doncastle had united with Sir Ethelred to make her less of a favourite of the gossip-mongers. She could not but agree that such a ploy as driving with Doncastle would do wonders for her reputation, and, by extension, for Calliope's.

But . . . she thought back to her last interview with Doncastle, the day before. He had demanded to know her secrets, and she had run from the room in imminent tears. Their next contact had been those flowers, asking for forgiveness. What had he found out about her? Surely not the truth!

Her brows nearly came together as she puzzled over this. Finally she decided that Doncastle must simply have dug up the secret of her husband's embarrassing demise. He was therefore aware of how cruel he had been to suspect her, even for a moment, of bringing Thomas's life to an end. This would more than explain Doncastle's abject apologies. But would it explain his newly cordial manner?

She decided it could not, and reached for the truth once more. "Sir, I've just remembered that I forgot to thank you for the flowers."

He smiled. "An inadequate gesture, I know, but as good a place as any to begin."

"Are you pretending to—to like me to help me socially, too?" she asked. "It is most kind of you to do so, but most upsetting to me, and I beg—"

Doncastle took his eyes off the road to look straight into her face. "I never pretend," he said.

Now Amelia was truly at a loss. Her eyes opened wide in horror as a thought struck her. "Surely you don't mean to offer me a *carte blanche*!" she exclaimed.

His hands must have tightened on the ribbons, for the horses made some slight alteration in their path, and he had to work to steady the pair. "No. I might be despicable in my treatment of you, but I don't meant to sink that low."

"Oh." With this Amelia had to be satisfied, for she could hardly demand to be told if his intentions were honourable.

"Do you know, my lady, you might consider going out of town for a bit," said Doncastle.

The change of subject was a little jarring, and Amelia looked at him questioningly.

"I agree with you, sir," she said. "I will be looking for a new post as soon as possible."

"A post? That isn't what I meant. You need a rest after the Season's labours. Some friend must invite you to a country place. If you leave town, the rumours will die a natural death."

Amelia had to agree with this, and the notion of resting in the country was most appealing. "Unfortunately, I have no friends likely to be so kind," she said, shaking her head. Sarah would not be leaving town for some weeks; Margot was a town-bred creature who loathed the quiet of rural life; and Amelia knew no one else well enough to ask such a favour.

"Your parents, perhaps?" Doncastle suggested.

She puzzled over this for a moment before she realized that Doncastle was referring to Lord and Lady Alfred. "No, I don't think so," she said with a half smile.

He nodded, looking vaguely troubled, and Amelia wondered if he had a particular reason for wishing her to rusticate. If he merely wanted to avoid her society, he was more able than she to leave town. Thankfully, he turned the subject.

Amelia sat through a perfectly genteel drive in the Park, her appearance in Lord Doncastle's curricle noticed by a gratifying number of gossipy matrons and sly dandies. Doncastle's plan was working. Several people in the Park, who had failed to see her the last time she had driven there, nodded to Amelia this time.

The only upsetting moment came when Captain Dawber, evidently assuming that Doncastle had succeeded in storming the citadel, rode up to the carriage and offered the viscount his best wishes on the new conquest. Doncastle's reply was by way of a smooth but devastating setdown that sent Captain Dawber away with a stiff back and a grim face.

As for Doncastle's treatment of her, he was polite, kind, and a tiny bit distant, leaving Amelia in a quandary as to what he meant to do or say next. Nothing, perhaps. He had helped her by taking her on this drive, he had sent her flowers to make up for his dreadful aspersions on her character, and now he could in good conscience forget her. He did not refer to a future meeting when he escorted her to the door of Sir Ethelred's house.

"I am in your debt, sir," Amelia said as he lifted her gloved hand to his lips. As always, his touch jarred her badly, and she had to hide a pressing desire to fling herself into his arms.

"Oh, no. If there is to be talk of debts, I am in yours." He appeared to release the hand regretfully. "You have brightened an otherwise dull day with your charming company."

With that he left her. Amelia went into the house to spend the rest of the day in confusion.

Doncastle apparently wished to become her friend again. How lucky indeed that she planned for her next post to take her away from town. Friendship would never be enough for her.

CHAPTER FOURTEEN

"LORD DONCASTLE!" LADY Alfred fluttered into her drawing-room. She wore a much less revealing morning ensemble than the viscount had been treated to on his last visit to her home. She smiled at him, nevertheless, as though she had nothing on at all. "To what do we owe the pleasure?"

"My dear Lady Alfred, how kind of you to grant me a private interview." Doncastle made his most charming bow over her hand, being careful to dodge the many huge rings. In an effort to show her that he was not reconsidering her amatory proposition, he said immediately, "I've come to see you because I need your help." He glanced about the room, thinking of the many visits he had made to this very salon in the past, when he and Amelia had first fallen in love. How the place had changed, its furnishings reflecting the taste of its current mistress; yet the shadows of those youthful lovers Amelia and Jeremy seemed to reach out, to give him courage.

At Lady Alfred's questioning look Doncastle plunged into his planned speech. "I know you wish your stepdaughter well. I am her friend, and I asked you to receive me so I might beg you to convince your husband to leave town for a period of time, taking Amelia along on perhaps a tour to some watering place." He hesitated and added, "Such a visit would not come untimely, considering his lordship's state of health, and Lady Jeffries-Hodge would be much better out of town while the talk about her dies down. As it will, you know. Talk is easily forgotten, but the healing process must hasten if the object of that talk leaves the scene for a time.''

"You are infatuated with Amelia! So that's it," said Lady Alfred in smug satisfaction.

Doncastle could easily conjecture the meaning of her ladyship's words. She was now happier with him, for she had guessed that his rejection of her proffered charms must rest on his affection for her stepdaughter. He was quite satisfied to have her think the truth, and he was grateful that she had chosen to be so good-humoured about the matter. He needed her good will.

"Amelia must leave town, my lady," he said. "I can tell that the gossip is wearing her down. She is innocent of any wrongdoing, of course, but still she must remove herself from Society for a time. She needs the kind of rest that only a sojourn out of town could give her. And I know that, if she stays in London, she'll simply find herself another post now that her charge, Miss Crane, is suitably betrothed. She shouldn't go right into another position of employment. Yet you and I are both acquainted with her independent notions. Left to herself, she'll instantly find another young lady to chaperon for next Season."

Unspoken was his thought that, once Amelia had had her "rest," he might begin to court her in earnest. He also prudently left unsaid the fact that he had tried in vain to think of anyone else who might suitably invite Amelia away. He was applying to her father's wife as a last resort.

Lady Alfred fixed him with a shrewd look. "Doncastle, tell me, if your wish is to remove Amelia from the jaws of the tattlemongers, why not simply marry her and take her wherever she may like to go? That would be much pleasanter for the girl, I'll wager, than travelling with my husband. Though it is true I can bring him round my thumb quite easily and talk him into such a journey, I don't call him the easiest man in the world to live with. And he and his daughter ain't on good terms.''

''I know that,'' said Doncastle. ''And as to marriage, my lady, I will confess to you that I have hopes. But until I can court her properly, I can't say any of this to Amelia. She deserves a leisurely wooing. I have a feeling she might be frightened, you see, because of her first marriage.''

The lady nodded. ''You may be right. She is a timid soul when it comes to the men. I've noticed that many of the most delightful gentlemen are ready to throw themselves at her feet, and she'll have none of them.''

Doncastle was tempted to make a satirical remark about the sort of men who tried to gallant Amelia; then he thought better of it. Lady Alfred Montresor was likely oblivious to the little social niceties which put all those rakes beyond the pale.

He was doubly glad that he'd made no slighting comment when Lady Alfred added, in a confiding manner, ''I've even managed to steal away one of Amelia's beaus. A charming man, and precisely the romantical sort I'd nearly despaired of meeting. Perhaps you know him, sir? Count Riccoli.''

Doncastle held back a laugh just in time. So Lady Alfred's project of playing her husband false was progressing apace. He confessed to a nodding acquaintance with the count, and Lady Alfred dimpled and preened, obviously elated with her exotic foreign conquest.

"Well, my lady," he then said, returning to the subject uppermost in his mind, "may I count upon you to invite Amelia to go away?" He paused, then added, "You see, I mean to follow you to whatever spa or country place you hit upon and begin my formal pursuit of your stepdaughter."

"Oh, how charming," said Lady Alfred with a wink. "As it happens, sir, Lord Alfred and I have been talking for some time of a stay at Bath. For his gout, you know, and then I have never been to Bath. We are off next month, and I'll invite her as soon as ever I talk him round to it. I quite agree with you that Amelia must leave town. Not only for her own peace, but for—another reason."

Doncastle started at the sudden seriousness of her voice. "Another reason?"

"She is in danger of some sort, Doncastle, from her brother-in-law, Jeffries-Hodge," said Lady Alfred earnestly. "Heaven knows why he confided it to me, but I believe it is because he thinks I dislike her. He noticed how I invited her to come after dinner that evening, which Lord Alfred insisted upon. I knew it to be an insult, but she was so sweet as to overlook the slight."

"And what does that troublesome cad mean to do?" asked Doncastle. Suddenly he was in a near-rage at the thought of the despicable Jeffries-Hodge, who had already made his sister-in-law's name a byword, causing further trouble to Amelia.

Lady Alfred's eyes opened wide at his angry tone. "Do recall that I am not the one wishing her harm, my lord."

"Your pardon. What does he intend to do?"

She shrugged. "He would say no more, merely that he planned to serve Lady Jeffries-Hodge—the dowager, as he calls her in that vulgar way he has—an ill turn for her impertinence."

"Her impertinence! And what is she supposed to have done?"

Lady Alfred examined a huge yellow diamond which she wore upon the little finger of her right hand. "I would wager he's made improper advances, and she has refused him."

"I have the same impression, my lady." Doncastle sighed and shook his head. "He's already hurting her by his vile slander. Does he stick to that inane story that she killed her husband?"

To his surprise, the lady laughed merrily. "Oh, he cannot say such things to *me*, dear sir." She winked. "You see, I'm the one person in the world who would never believe it."

"Really?" Doncastle sensed that a diverting and informative story was about to unfold. Lady Alfred leaned nearer while she told it.

MEANWHILE, AMELIA HERSELF was busy arranging for her leave-taking. One day, shortly after Calliope announced her engagement, Amelia sat down in her bedroom to write a letter to the mistress of her old seminary. The new advertisement she had placed in the *Gazette* had been running for a full two weeks, without success. She was beginning to fear that she was too notorious to be hired through ordinary channels; but Miss Towers might have word of a chaperon's situation and be able to recommend her former pupil. Or—Amelia's pen hovered over the paper as she considered whether to write down the dreadful words that she would consider a position as a governess. Had she sunk that low?

She looked up, astonished, when the door opened. Mrs. Winkle entered the room. The woman had never before invaded Amelia's sanctum.

"My dear, I was so excited that I had to come to you at once," stated Mrs. Winkle with a broad smile.

"Were you?" said Amelia, hoping the coolness her voice betrayed would not cause Mrs. Winkle to fly up into the boughs.

The elder lady fished from her bosom a letter, which she passed to Amelia with an air of triumph. "There! As you may read, my dearest friend Mrs. Childers has a most pressing need of a sponsor for her daughter. Young Zenaida is to come out this summer, at Brighton, as Minerva says there, and the family is confident that you could introduce them to the sort of society they most wish for their daughter."

"You wrote to a friend about me?" Amelia asked in disbelief.

Mrs. Winkle looked even more pleased with herself. "Of course. I knew that you would be needing a place to go as soon as Calliope was married off, my lady, and seeing the way the wind was lying with the Guildford boy, I determined to do you a service by writing those of my friends with daughters coming out of the schoolroom."

"How very obliging of you," said Amelia in distraction. In reality, Mrs. Winkle's meddling was insufferable, but, as Amelia scanned the letter from Mrs. Childers, she had to admit that the place looked like a real possibility. Mrs. Childers, if she was a friend of Mrs. Winkle's, would likely be a woman on the vulgar side. The misspellings of her note seemed to bear this out. She would be the sort of woman Amelia had thought to encounter on her first foray into the world of employment: one who knew nothing of really good society and would be enchanted to employ someone with "Lady" attached to her name, no matter if that name were a little tainted.

"As you may read, my lady, the Childers family will reimburse you for your journey down to them by post," said Mrs. Winkle. "I would go almost at once if I was you. No telling who else they might find if you delay."

"Curious," said Amelia. "She wishes me to join them at their estate in Sussex. One would have thought it would be more practical simply to meet them in Brighton."

"They must wish to become acquainted with you before bursting upon the social scene," suggested Mrs. Winkle, and this seemed a reasonable enough motive to Amelia.

She was wild to leave London. Doncastle might try to mend her reputation with drives in the Park and other little kindnesses, but she was still a scandalous woman in the eyes of the ton. Lady Manville had cut her in Piccadilly that very morning.

As for Jeremy! He was kinder now, much kinder, but it was evident from his cool, detached manner that no rekindling of their love was in his plans. And Amelia did not wish to stay in his proximity without the hope of future happiness.

Her salary from Sir Ethelred, though generous, would not support her own establishment for long. But a few more Seasons of chaperoning would indeed line her pockets enough to feed and clothe her and her servants—possibly only Higgins, for Lewes was so infatuated with Green that she might wish for a post in the Cranes' household. If that happened, Amelia intended to recommend Lewes as Lady Margot's dresser. Heaven knew her friend needed a skilled abigail.

"You have been most kind, Mrs. Winkle," said Amelia in decision.

Before the older woman left the room she had the satisfaction of seeing Lady Jeffries-Hodge dip her pen in ink, all ready to compose a letter of acceptance to the obliging Minerva Childers.

"OH, NO, AMELIA," SAID Calliope when she heard the news. "You can't leave before my wedding. And what about Papa's? You will wish to see Lady Margot married."

Amelia smiled, flattered that the girl she had come to love so well would miss her. "I have that all thought out, my dear. Your Papa is going to be married privately, in a small ceremony. Only you and Margot's father will attend. And as for your wedding, I will simply tease you to invite the Childers family to the breakfast. If they're the sort of people I assume they are, an invitation from anyone in the ton will send them into raptures. They ought to be well able to afford a trip into London, judging from the salary they have offered. And I'll be with you when you marry Sam."

"That does help lessen the blow," said Calliope, frowning, "but I still wish you would simply stay and help me prepare. I won't have any idea what to order for wedding clothes," she added slyly, knowing well Amelia's weak points.

For once Amelia was not to be cajoled. "No use pressing me, my dear, you no longer really need me. From now on my attentions must be for Miss Zenaida Childers. I wish Sam had a brother."

Calliope laughed at this, and the light joke provided the termination Amelia wanted to the dangerous subject of her leave-taking. Amelia did not notice that Calliope's small jaw was set as determinedly as her own. Nor did she remark the tell-tale way in which the girl pushed her spectacles up her nose, a habit indicative of deep thought.

LEAVING AMELIA AT HER work in the morning-room, Calliope marched down the corridor without further ado and entered her father's study.

Sir Ethelred, seated at his desk, was transferring a liquid from one beaker to another. He jumped in surprise on seeing his daughter, and the resulting rain of chemicals upon his papers busied him and Calliope for some time.

"What do you mean by coming here, daughter?" said the baronet with as much severity as he could muster; which, given his own idyllic romance and his happiness at Calliope's choice of a scholar for her mate, was very slight.

"It's Amelia, Papa." Calliope sat down in a stained leather armchair and sighed deeply. "She has found a position somewhere out in the country, and she's leaving us."

Sir Ethelred stared. "You don't mean it."

"I certainly do. Cousin Dorinda helped her, it seems, and Amelia is to leave this very Friday. We can't let her go."

"I agree that we'll miss the lady very much, and she would do much better to stay on as our guest for as long as she likes, but how are we to prevent her departure? She's determined to earn her own living. Enormous pluck for such a small woman. Courage, I call it."

Calliope sighed. "Papa, you can't even see what's in front of your face. Did it never occur to you that the man Amelia loves might not want her to disappear into another place of employment? A place buried in the depths of Sussex?"

"The man she loves?" At this Sir Ethelred evinced some interest.

"Lord Doncastle," said Calliope.

Sir Ethelred's eyes bulged behind his spectacles. After staring blankly for a moment, he smiled.

Calliope went on, "It's plain as a pikestaff that he loves her, and she loves him, and he is being absurdly slow about coming to the point. If she leaves town before he has the chance—"

"Don't worry, my dear," said Sir Ethelred, that smile still bedecking his face. "He's always hanging about the house these days—so that's why! And when he finds out she's planning to leave us, ten to one he'll pop the question with no further ado. And should he not have done so by the day of her departure, I'll make certain Doncastle is on hand when Lady Jeffries-Hodge takes her leave. We'll contrive to get them alone somehow, and the question will ask itself."

"Why, Papa," said Calliope in pleasure, "you're becoming quite a romantic."

"Thanks to our friend Lady Jeffries-Hodge," said Sir Ethelred. "And you may be sure I intend to help along her courtship as she helped mine."

The conversation digressed into a discussion of the many virtues of Lady Margot Jamieson. Calliope and her father were confident that their machinations, if not the very fact of Amelia's departure, would bring Lord Doncastle to the point.

They reckoned without Doncastle's determination to give Amelia time to become accustomed to the idea of his attentions.

DONCASTLE WAS SURPRISED that Mrs. Winkle, of all people, had provided the solution to Amelia's immediate problem, and that his lady had a post at her command before Lady Alfred could put together any plans for an out-of-town visit.

One morning he made a grave and proper call on Lady Jeffries-Hodge, as the next step in his campaign to win her back. She happened to be alone. Calliope and Sir Ethelred would have stared to see what a mull Doncastle made of the resultant opportunity to tell Amelia what was in his heart. Rather than going down upon one knee, or clasping the lady to his bosom and declaring she must never leave him, Doncastle simply nodded soberly at news of the new position.

Another post as a chaperon was the last thing he would have wished for Amelia, but he supposed that, for now, it would be better than nothing. She would not spend long in the household of the Childers family, so it would not really matter whether the position was pleasant or not. And Doncastle could as well pass the summer in Brighton as anywhere else while he brought Amelia to the point of trusting him enough that she would accept his hand and heart.

Amelia was by now getting used to Doncastle's company. She chose to treat him as she would any close friend, much though the outward similarity of this new friendship to their former intimacy tore at her heart. "I think it a little singular that this family wishes me to visit them in the country before taking up my post, but it's a very kind notion. Bodes well for the Childers's reception of me. I have a horror of being treated like an upper servant, though that's probably silly. A paid chaperon is hardly more."

"A titled dowager must always be more," Doncastle said. "I know you have two personal servants. Are they to go with you?"

"Yes, Mrs. Childers made a special point of mentioning them. Mrs. Winkle really thought of everything."

"And will this be your first visit to Brighton?" Doncastle struggled to keep his voice even, uninvolved. A most difficult task, when he was longing instead to crush this lovely lady in his arms and make her his own with no further ado. He must wait, though, for she would doubtless need time to get used to the idea of a man's ardour.

"I haven't been anywhere in Sussex," Amelia was saying in a confiding manner. "My—my husband owned a property there, but he visited it alone, and I knew nothing about it. I suppose my brother-in-law owns it now. I'm quite anxious to see that part of the country. The downs especially sound delightfully different to someone who is used to Hampshire."

"The Sussex downs are a fine sight," agreed Doncastle, and he conversed with her for some time on the subject before he took his leave, decorous and mild as always.

THE DAY of Amelia's departure came quicker than she could have imagined. Sir Ethelred and Calliope had brought forth all their most logical arguments to entice her to stay, but in vain. Sir Ethelred did insist on sending her by his own coach, with his own horses for the first stage of the journey.

The leave-taking was abominably slow, for everyone with the exception of Mrs. Winkle wished Amelia would stay, and nobody but that forbidding dame was concerned when one of Amelia's trunks fell open on the stairs and had to be repacked, or when she couldn't find her umbrella at the last minute. Then the coachman spent an unconscionable amount of time securing the baggage to the vehicle, and, to Amelia's distress, a trunk fell open again as she was about to step up into the coach. Had

Amelia been looking, she might have noted that the Cranes did not appear as distressed as they ought at this new tragedy. They simply watched, with vacuous smiles, as a couple of the maids folded her ladyship's clothing back into the trunk and slammed it shut.

Despite all these delaying tactics, Amelia was still ready to go by the time she had planned.

Calliope and her father exchanged worried glances. They had told Doncastle that Amelia would be leaving at eleven. It was a little before that hour now, and she was about to climb into the carriage.

"Oh, Amelia," said Calliope with a sigh. "won't you change your mind?"

Her friend shook her head and smiled sadly. The little group of people who had gathered to bid Amelia good-bye moved down the steps of the house and gathered round the carriage.

"I know I leave Calliope in good hands," said Amelia to Sam Guildford, who was there for the purpose of bidding her farewell.

"Don't be silly, Amelia. I am in my own hands, as always," said Calliope with a merry glance at her betrothed.

Lady Margot was also present, and she embraced Amelia fervently, whispering a thank-you into her friend's ear.

"You, my dear Lady Jeffries-Hodge, have saved my household from itself," proclaimed Sir Ethelred, and he embraced Amelia, too. "Certain we can't entice you to stay?"

Seeing Sir Ethelred's arm about Margot's shoulders, Amelia was content, for she knew that this was one piece of matchmaking that would last a lifetime. She shook her head as she rejected the baronet's last effort to keep her among the household. "I'll miss you all," she said as she stepped into the coach.

Sir Ethelred stepped up to the vehicle to give last directions to Miles the coachman as Amelia settled herself, fighting back a fit of the dismals.

"Oh, my lady," cried Lewes. She burst into tears. She had indeed decided to stay with the Cranes and even now stood a few paces behind Lady Margot, as a good lady's maid should.

"Now, Lewes, don't start," called back Amelia from inside the carriage. Having to be cheerful for another's sake temporarily held in check her own blackening mood. "I'll be back shortly for Miss Crane's wedding."

"But it won't ever be the same, ma'am," said Lewes, sniffing.

"Indeed it won't," added Higgins in an undertone. He was to go with Amelia, and he took up the steps, shut the chaise door, and got into his position at the back of the vehicle. He had a special smile for Lewes, and a little wave of regret. They had been fast friends for a very long time.

Amelia struggled to maintain her smiling calm in the face of all this emotion. She waved her handkerchief as gaily as she could as Sir Ethelred's post-chaise bowled out of Portman Square.

"Well, Papa," said Calliope, wiping a tear from her eye, "we failed. She's gone, and Lord Doncastle didn't even get a chance to—"

"What's this about Doncastle?" queried Sam with interest.

Calliope quickly explained that they had invited the viscount to bid Amelia farewell, knowing that the pain of leave-taking must provoke him to a declaration. His lordship had unfortunately chosen to be late. Sam seemed startled at the new idea that Doncastle and Amelia might make a match of it. Lady Margot merely looked wise.

The servants had gone back downstairs, Mrs. Winkle had disappeared to the upper reaches of the house on some private errand, and the two engaged couples were just moving into the drawing-room when the front door burst open and Doncastle arrived at last.

"She's gone!" He looked around at everyone; their serious expressions confirmed the unwelcome news. "I was detained by business, you see, for I've found out something of the most shocking nature—how long has she been gone? Could I catch her up, do you think?"

Sir Ethelred smiled. "I see no reason why not, Doncastle. I knew you would wish to speak with her before she left town, so I took the liberty of telling my man just now to drive through Hyde Park as a small delaying tactic. My first attempt at military subterfuge—don't you think it a good one? You'll find her there."

"Really, Papa," spoke up Calliope. "That was not well done. I could have told you that Amelia dislikes the Park. She hates to be cut, and she detests those rakes who will persist in gathering round her. The Park is the last place you should have sent her."

"Indeed, that was ill-considered," Lady Margot added, a frown creasing her smooth brow. "You might better have sent them down Oxford Street, where the shopping traffic would delay the coach...."

Lord Doncastle heard nothing of this. He was already out the door.

"He was in a hurry, wasn't he?" said Sir Ethelred cheerfully. He winked at Sam. "He must indeed wish to marry her. And, ladies, whatever our friend's objections to the Park, you will see that she'll find it a pleasant place today. Thanks to my word in Coachman's ear, Lord

Doncastle will be able to speak to his lady. Everything will turn out well, mark my words. He'll bring her back here within the hour, and we'll have three weddings in the family instead of two.''

The ladies still worried for Amelia's feelings, but they were somewhat comforted by Sir Ethelred's sunny view of the situation.

Indeed, Amelia might not even notice that she was in the hateful Park when the man she loved was proposing to her.

CHAPTER FIFTEEN

AMELIA INDULGED HERSELF in a few regretful tears while the coach wound its way through the orderly streets of Mayfair to the Brighton Road. How very much she would miss the Cranes, and Lady Margot, and...

And why had Jeremy not arrived to bid her goodbye? Everyone had expected him to do so. He must have been detained by business. Or was the matter of her departure merely so trivial to him that he could say farewell or not, depending upon his mood?

What if he had simply forgotten?

Amelia wiped her eyes and glanced out the window. She looked again and gasped. The coach was turning into Hyde Park!

Immediately she pulled the checkstring. The carriage halted, and Higgins appeared at the door. "My lady?"

"We're in the Park, Higgins, where I least wish to be." Amelia made her voice severe.

The footman nodded, and Amelia noticed he was looking white and worried. "I understand, madam, you have much reason to dislike the Park. Don't know why the rascal—I mean to say, why Miles had to drive in here. Can't be the way to Brighton, can it?"

"For me, the Park is the way to nothing but disaster. Have him drive on and get us on the road at once," Amelia stated, thanking the stars that at least she was in a closed carriage. She wouldn't attract notice this way, and, more importantly, she could have her privacy. Resolutely she drew all the curtains shut as the coach began to move forward again—at an infernally slow pace.

She heard some sort of a commotion outside, strong masculine voices she couldn't quite identify, and then, to her distress, she felt the coach grind to a halt again. Had some would-be seducer recognized the Crane carriage and assumed Lady Jeffries-Hodge to be within? Amelia swore that, no matter what, she would not open the windows to find out.

Not a moment after she had formed this thought, a rapping came at the glass. Amelia folded her arms in stubbornness and commenced a slow, silent count in French, her usual tactic when she was obliged to wait out some tedious circumstances. She must hope that the horrid man, whichever of her gallants it was, would take a hint.

"Lady Jeffries-Hodge!" cried a familiar voice. "Please open the window."

Amelia recognised Jeremy's deep tones. With a shaky hand, she brushed back the window curtain and lowered the glass.

She found herself staring directly into his face. He was mounted upon his Arabian, and he smiled at her with such warmth that she held her breath.

"I'm so glad I've caught you," he said. "I had to speak to you before you left town."

"Did you?" Amelia noticed that she was still staring, bemused, into his dark eyes, and she dropped her lashes in a sudden fit of shyness. So he had wished to bid her goodbye. A wave of relief washed over her.

"Yes, my lady, for I've found out something most shocking. I don't know how to break this news to you, but one thing is clear. You must not go to Sussex."

"I must not?" Amelia echoed, dismayed by the note of desperation in his voice and the odd reference to breaking some news. This didn't sound like an impassioned declaration, which she had fleetingly imagined might have sent him running to her side. "Why must I not?"

"Because, Amelia—my lady—you will find yourself in danger if you persist in making this journey," he said. He swung down from his horse and approached the window, now looking up into Amelia's eyes.

"Danger." Amelia again found herself repeating what he had said. And she was quite unable to look away from him; it was as though some spell were locking their gazes together.

"Doncastle," bellowed a feminine voice at this juncture, "what do you mean by holding up that chaise? This is Rotten Row, not Hounslow Heath at midnight!"

The robust tones of Lady Manville jolted Amelia back into reality. Amelia glanced back; that dragonish lady's open landau was the vehicle directly behind the Crane chaise. Worse, none other than the haughty Mrs. Drummond-Burrell was seated beside Lady Manville.

Doubly glad to be heading out of London, Amelia told herself that she need not fear for the tongues of those two ladies nor care for their disapprobation. She caught Lady Manville's eye but chose to cut her, as she herself had been cut so often in recent weeks by that rotund star in Society's firmament.

Newly aware of her surroundings, Amelia noted that Doncastle's halting of the chaise had been observed by several gentlemen, who were even now nearing her vehicle, either mounted or on foot, and that these gentlemen were none other than several members of her ordinary court of rakish admirers. A closed carriage had not saved her privacy, then. Her heart sank.

"How d'ye do, my charming lady," called the notorious Lord Clayville from the seat of his high-perch phaeton. Immediately Amelia sat back against the squabs, but she could see that his lordship was playing his common trick of stationing his vehicle directly in front of her own, thus cutting off any immediate hope of flight.

Setting her teeth, Amelia gave a tight nod to Lord Clayville as he descended from his phaeton, throwing the ribbons to his tiger.

Lady Manville chose this instant to summon Amelia's only protector with a peremptory, "Doncastle, we request your presence here, and an explanation of why you choose to stop closed carriages which would be much better on their way out of the Park. Attend me, Doncastle. Now!"

"A moment only," Jeremy whispered to Amelia before strolling away to do his duty by the powerful arbitresses of ton.

Amelia sighed deeply and risked a glare at Lady Manville.

Captain Dawber, Mr. Johnstone, and Mr. Halliford claimed Lady Jeffries-Hodge's notice once Doncastle moved from beside her window. They bounded up to the carriage like hungry dogs, and Amelia spent several bleak moments in bestowing an icy greeting upon each man in turn. "Gentlemen, if you please, I must be on my way," she then said loudly.

This did no good, of course; a statement of her wishes never seemed to move these gentlemen. She considered her next move and was about to call to Higgins to assist her down—and out of the Park—when she saw a new contender for her attention draw near: her brother-in-law.

Jeffries-Hodge advanced, smiling at Amelia as though they were the best of friends. Their last interview, in Lady Alfred's drawing-room, had hardly been cordial, and Amelia had never expected to speak to him again. She immediately put up her guard.

"Brother Darwin." She greeted him with an offhand familiarity, her tone as unfriendly as she could make it.

He didn't seem to mind. His face, which was enough like his late brother's to make Amelia shiver, still registered only the most vapid of pleasant expressions. "My dear Lady Jeffries-Hodge," he said, "or ought I to follow your example and say sister Amelia? Though it discomfits me to think such beauty should be wasted on a mere sister."

"Sister-in-law," said Amelia. Extraordinary that she should be forced by circumstances to come face to face with the man she dreaded most. This was no place for the cut direct. Forced into a semblance of civility, she did not enjoy the fact that the other men were avidly observing this encounter, nor that Mrs. Drummond-Burrell was fairly leaning around Lord Doncastle's broad figure to hear it, also.

"I would have expected to see you well on your way to Sussex," said Jeffries-Hodge with a quizzical look at the laden carriage. "All set for travelling, I perceive."

"How did you know I was going to Sussex?" asked Amelia. She had not spread the word, hoping to dissuade her insistent admirers from following her to Brighton, and she was not best pleased to have her destination bruited about before the sharp ears of those same men.

Jeffries-Hodge shrugged a pair of well-padded shoulders. "Heard it in the clubs, I expect. Aren't you going to Sussex?"

Amelia had to admit that such was her plan, and the other gentlemen took it upon themselves to protest.

"You can't leave us lovelorn, ma'am," said Captain Dawber with a smile which was hardly visible beneath his flourishing military mustachios.

"'Pon rep', madam, the captain is right," said Mr. Johnstone. "You would throw half London into mourning."

"Unfortunate but necessary," said Amelia with a small smile. "Now, as Lord Jeffries-Hodge observes, I ought to be off. If some of you gentlemen could assist me on my way?" She looked right at Lord Clayville as she spoke, for that inveterate petticoat-chaser was the one whose phaeton now blocked her carriage.

The peer gave Amelia a raking glance and bowed languidly. He gave no orders to his tiger.

Amelia clenched her fists in frustration. Then she brightened as she saw Jeremy turning, at long last, from his enforced conversation with Lady Manville and Mrs. Drummond-Burrell.

The viscount elbowed his way through the men surrounding Amelia's carriage. "Lady Jeffries-Hodge, did I hear you talk of leaving? Don't you recall that I was warning you that you must not go to Sussex?"

"Warning me, my lord," said Amelia, recollecting. "You were telling me of some danger."

"I was," said Doncastle. He turned to Jeffries-Hodge. "Don't you agree, sir, that her ladyship's safety would be seriously jeopardized were she to go to that estate in Sussex? The one where a respectable family is waiting to meet her?"

"Lord Doncastle, what can you possibly mean by my safety?" Amelia, totally confused, looked earnestly at Jeremy.

"He means nothing," said Jeffries-Hodge. "You and I have buried our old differences, madam, and he no doubt sees in me a sort of rival. Though how I, a married man, could be a rival, is beyond me."

It was at least beyond his social sense of rectitude to admit he had offered Amelia a *carte blanche*. Amelia nearly rolled her eyes. Half of the men who had been pursuing her were married, and all of Society must know Jeffries-Hodge's virtuous posturing to be ridiculous.

"We have not buried our differences. At least I haven't heard that we have done so," Amelia told her brother-in-law, enjoying the look of raw anger on his face almost as much as she did Jeremy's pleased expression at her rudeness. "Now do tell me, Lord Doncastle." She turned to him eagerly. "Why do you fear for my safety in Sussex?"

"For the simplest of reasons, my lady," he said. "You're being drawn there by a ruse. A common sort of scheme, thought up by a small mind. Tell me, what is the name of the property you are to visit?"

"Down Priory," said Amelia at once, puzzled by his words. "And what do you mean by a ruse, sir? I've been hired by a family in the most ordinary way possible. Sir Ethelred's cousin arranged the matter."

Doncastle smiled in triumph and turned to Lord Jeffries-Hodge. "Perhaps you can tell me, my lord, why your own property in Sussex bears the name of the place Amelia—Lady Jeffries-Hodge—is heading. I suspect she would meet no one at Down Priory but your lecherous self, and that the family is a fiction. Perhaps you can also explain how you drew that detestable Mrs. Winkle into your schemes. I would wager she was more than glad to get Lady Jeffries-Hodge out of her cousin's house, for she has always been jealous of the favour this lady enjoys in the family circle.''

Doncastle was speaking in a loud voice, as though to draw as many witnesses as possible to this extraordinary accusation. He ought not to have feared that the select group of spectators would lose interest. At this point in his disclosure Lady Manville called out, ''Dorinda Winkle is a wrong 'un, Doncastle, you've got that. She talked against this woman from the day her ladyship stepped foot into the Crane house.''

''As did you, I believe, Lady Manville,'' said Doncastle with a bow.

''Deuce take it, I wish I'd thought up such a scheme,'' Captain Dawber was exclaiming. ''Good thinking, Jeffries-Hodge. A little country seduction, what? Bound to turn the trick.''

Amelia felt ready to sink. Worse even than the shocking thought that Darwin had been drawing her away to a secluded place, no doubt bent upon seduction and retribution, were the circumstances of the disclosure. Luckily, the present altercation was not drawing a crowd; even so, everyone in London would be talking about this by nightfall, and now Amelia had nowhere to go to escape the town!

Jeffries-Hodge, with a brittle laugh, was busily denying the whole thing. ''You've mistaken the name of my property, Doncastle, in your zeal to make me out a villain. It's—Hodge Priory.''

''Can't have been changed since I was there with a party two years ago, before you inherited,'' put in Lord Clayville. The elegant voluptuary looked to be enjoying the scene immensely. ''Down Priory it was, and had been forever. A delightful party. Your brother and a dozen of us, plus some of the sweetest little high-flyers in the district. We talked of forming a cousin to the famous Hell-Fire Club...."

"Lord Clayville! Remember you are in the presence of at least *some* ladies," called out Lady Manville from her landau.

Doncastle nodded his appreciation at Clayville, a man he ordinarily wouldn't recognize, and returned his attention to Jeffries-Hodge. "Don't bother with your excuses, my good man. I'm quite willing to call you a liar. And you may be wanting to name your seconds."

"You mustn't fight!" gasped Amelia, horror-struck.

"I wouldn't fight over this trollop if you knocked me down and trod on me," snapped Jeffries-Hodge. "Not only is your story pure fabrication, I have no reason to care for the honour of the woman who killed my brother."

Amelia put a trembling hand over her face. It had been virtually nothing to hear Lord Clayville confirm for the ears of the ton her late husband's predilections. But this!

Doncastle grabbed the baron by the cravat and said, in a dangerously calm voice. "You'll regret those words and you'll fight because I call you a liar and a philanderer." Having thus spoken, he tossed his adversary down and sent him reeling.

Jeffries-Hodge was caught by Captain Dawber and Mr. Johnstone, and as soon as he was upright again he shouted, "That strumpet killed my brother, and I have proof!"

"How singular. I have proof that your late brother died of his own vices. He was carried off by a fit of apoplexy or some such, while in the company of a female not his wife. I can produce the lady if need be."

"You can produce the lady?" said Mrs. Drummond-Burrell in excitement.

"Yes, ma'am, but I hope I won't have to. Her privacy must be considered," said Doncastle. He directed his next words to Jeffries-Hodge. "If need be, though, I'll drag your name through the lords for your vile rumour-mongering, produce the many people who were at hand when your brother died, and also the wife of the local vicar, whom Lady Jeffries-Hodge was visiting at the very hour the unfortunate demise occurred."

Jeffries-Hodge had some retort to make, but Amelia didn't hear it. Her cheeks were scarlet, and she had been leaning back, away from the carriage window, in dreadful anticipation of each new disclosure. Now, unnoticed by anyone, she looked out of the opposite window from the one Jeffries-Hodge, Doncastle, and the rest of the small circle of spectators still stood beside. "Higgins!" she hissed.

The familiar long face leaned around. "Madam?"

He looked sorry for her, Amelia saw, and she was more embarrassed by the situation than ever. Higgins knew, if anyone did, how she had hoped that word of her husband's conduct would not become meat for gossip. Her dignity had been all she could cling to in her marriage.

The quarrel was growing ever louder as Doncastle tried every insult at his command to force Jeffries-Hodge to a duel. Amelia prayed he would not succeed. She suspected her brother-in-law would be too cowardly to fight, and she was grateful for his lack of character.

"Escort me out of the Park and back to Portman Square," she commanded Higgins quickly. "I have nowhere else to go, and I must get out of here. There must be room to turn the coach about. See to it. At once."

"Right away, madam." Higgin's concerned face disappeared, and Amelia immediately closed the windows and curtains which had exposed her to the public. Protests sounded from all of the men, including Doncastle; audible grumbling came from the coachman, as well as a few curses exchanged with Lord Clayville's tiger and Lady Manville's driver.

Amelia did not care. Secure within her movable sanctuary, she waited patiently and at last was rewarded as the coach began to move, with a jolt, out of the Park and back to Portman Square.

The last words she could make out were from Doncastle. ''No, Jeffries-Hodge, I will not let go your arm. Here we stand until you agree to give me satisfaction!''

A chorus of cheers from the rakes and a few interested strollers followed this exclamation. Amelia shuddered.

IN PORTMAN SQUARE, GREEN let Amelia in and listened to Higgins's whispered explanations. Lady Jeffries-Hodge was looking pale as death, and the butler suggested that her ladyship go immediately to her room if she would rather not join the family in the drawing-room.

Amelia shrank from the mere thought of facing the kind Cranes when she felt ready to cry. Nodding her head in answer to Green, she ran up the stairs as fast as she could, wild to reach the shelter of the room she had come to know well. There was no other place she could even begin to think of as home.

Coming to a halt right inside the door of her former chamber, she stared in surprise. Mrs. Winkle, with folded arms, was supervising two harried-looking maids in the stripping of the bed linen.

''Lady Jeffries-Hodge!'' cried out the woman. ''You should be in Sussex by now.''

''Yes, in Sussex, in the repulsive company of your co-conspirator,'' said Amelia with snapping eyes. ''Please leave this room, Mrs. Winkle. I intend to inform Sir Ethelred of your treachery."

Mrs. Winkle let a telling flash of understanding cross her plump face before she said in a huff, "I have no authority to let you back into the house, Lady Jeffries-Hodge. Here I stand until my cousin tells me you are welcome."

Amelia was tempted to break down into tears, but she held herself erect, dignified. "Ma'am, you are a jealous and—and ugly old harridan. Will you leave, or shall I have my footman carry you out?"

Higgins, who had followed Amelia and was standing behind her shoulder, let out a gasp of alarm.

"No need to bother, Higgins." A voice was heard in the corridor, and Lord Doncastle strolled into the room. He eyed Mrs. Winkle in distaste. "I'm perfectly capable of removing this woman. Shall I hoist you over my shoulder, madam?"

"Well!" Mrs. Winkle's little dark eyes nearly popped, but she left tamely enough. The maids shuffled after her.

Higgins closed the door behind the procession, shutting himself out with the others. Amelia and Doncastle were alone.

They stood facing each other, silently looking into each other's eyes. Then Amelia spoke, words tumbling over one another in her agitation.

"I can't begin to tell you how grateful I am to you. I ought to be angry that your disclosures came so publicly, but I know you couldn't help it. You had to warn me. The important thing is that I didn't go to Sussex. When I think what might have happened—"

Jeremy interrupted her. "As you might suppose, Jeffries-Hodge has refused to fight, so my satisfaction for that dastard's behaviour must lie in the fact that some loose-tongued individuals saw and heard him prove himself a coward.'' He tossed off the words gruffly, but his expression was very tender.

"They also heard all about my husband's way of life—the way he treated me," said Amelia with a sigh. "I can never show my face in town again."

"Perhaps the dowager Lady Jeffries-Hodge had better not," said Jeremy. "But nothing could be easier to alter. With a wave of your hand you might see to it that Lady Jeffries-Hodge never has to appear again. It would seem to me, my lady, that marriage and a long honeymoon out of town would be the most practical solution to your problem. The talk could die down, and if you made a respectable match that would be the best answer to anyone who persists in sullying your name." He paused. "And if you married me, that would be the most practical solution to *my* problem."

Amelia was gazing at him in disbelief. "Your problem?"

He stepped forward and grasped her hands. "That of loving you to distraction. My dearest Amelia, I had sworn to go slowly in this matter, but decorous courtships be hanged, I'm going to take my chance now. I'm quite shameless, my dear. You need me now, and I mean to tempt you to make use of me if I can't entice you into loving me."

With a shaky hand, Amelia groped for a chair and sank into it. Doncastle went down upon one knee before her.

"Can I make you love me again, my dear?" he asked.

He looked quite humble, nothing like the proud Lord Doncastle, more like the Jeremy Searle of seven years ago—so endearing, in fact, that Amelia was moved to put out one hand to touch his cheek.

He clasped the hand and kissed it.

"I'm so touched, dear Jeremy," said Amelia. "So deeply touched."

"But you're not answering my question."

"How can I?" she whispered. "Do you suppose I ever stopped loving you? Do you really think my feelings changed?"

His eyes were so full of joy that Amelia had to look away. "My dearest, what's to stop us, then? I've long since discovered how mistaken I was in you, that you have never been mercenary, or heartless, or anything I thought you. You were only a victim of circumstances— of the dreadful circumstances which led to your marriage. When I think how that villain attacked you—if I could only get my hands on him—"

"You know?" gasped Amelia. She turned bright red and began to tremble.

Jeremy rose and pulled her to her feet to clasp her tightly against his chest. Her quaking ceased little by little as she clung to him. "I know," he whispered into her ear. "I couldn't understand, when first I learned your secret, why you didn't come to me all those years ago. I wouldn't have held his violence against you."

"How could I ask you to love me still, when I'd been ruined?" said Amelia. "I had such dreams of coming to you a happy bride, and they had all been crushed. And then there was my father, insisting that I marry Jeffries-Hodge—"

Jeremy sighed. "Yes, I can accept that you would have thought yourself ruined and let yourself be bullied by Lord Alfred. You were a very young girl, and I forgive you. Not for jilting me, you couldn't help that, but for not trusting me."

"I'm so glad you forgive me," said Amelia, gently disengaging herself from his arms. She moved back a step. "I can't marry you, you know. I'll need your good will if you're to forgive me once again."

"Why can't you marry me?" His voice, which had been so tender, turned almost harsh as he looked at her in disbelief.

"Because—" Amelia took a deep breath. "Because I vowed upon my husband's grave that I would never again put myself into any man's power. I can't—"

"Can't what? Is it that you can't trust me?"

"No, it isn't that," she said. She searched for words to explain the stand she must take. The story of the vow was true enough, but there was another reason she could not quite bring herself to relate. She stood helplessly, looking at Jeremy with eyes full of sadness.

He was throwing out anything he could think of as a logical explanation. "Do you suppose I would change into the kind of monster you were married to before?"

"No," said Amelia. "If there was one thing my marriage taught me, it's that people don't change. Jeffries-Hodge started out in the vilest way possible, by forcing himself upon me; I could hardly be surprised at anything else he might do." She managed a small smile.

"What is it, then, my love?"

Amelia shrugged and was silent once more. She was still determined, for his sake, not to give in to his demands no matter how he might press her.

Jeremy took a deep breath. "I believe that you're forgetting, my dear, that you gave yourself into my keeping already, seven years ago. Are you meaning to renege on that promise?" He kissed her hands. "There. I've played my last card."

It was a compelling one. Amelia stood still as a statue, seeming to be watching herself as if from a distance as Jeremy gently caressed her hands.

She had never paused to consider it, but she felt in her bones now, realized that she had always felt, that her long-ago promise to Jeremy did still bind her. If she had ever felt married in her life, she had felt married to him. "Why, of course," she whispered. "I did give you that promise, but I can't honour it, my dear Jeremy. Don't you see? I couldn't possibly let you marry a penniless, scandal-bound woman. The talk—"

He stared. "You'd refuse me because some idle-brained tattlemongers may talk?"

"Gossip and the ton's ill treatment are forces I've battled ever since my marriage," said Amelia. "I lost the battle today. I can't see you dragged down with me."

"You're forgetting, my love, that I'm not an unprotected widow, and neither will you be in a few days' time. Mark my words, what little gossip there is will be a nine days' wonder, and we won't be in town to hear it. And as for when we return: can you honestly picture anyone refusing to receive us? The curiosity alone should assure our reception at the greatest houses in the land, if you've a mind to mingle with the gabblers."

Amelia had to smile. She had little or no desire to see anyone in Society ever again, aside from her particular friends, but she was willing to accept that, far in the future, she might feel differently. And she had to admit that Jeremy's arguments had logic to back them up.

"Now about that promise you made me." Jeremy stepped forward, encouraged by her smile. "You said once that you'd be my wife. Were you telling the truth?"

Amelia had no more excuses to give. Her future was before her, and she had no choice but to meet it with courage. "I did give you that promise, and I'll honour it. I do trust you, and I want to marry you more than anything. If you're certain that you don't care for the scandal."

"The scandal can go hang. There's nothing to stop us," he answered with a broad smile.

"Well, there is one other small matter, something I must know," she said in so soft a voice that he had to bend down to hear her. "Could you bear to be married to a woman whom you couldn't stand to look at—unclothed?"

He stared. "What in heaven's name—"

"I—" Amelia blushed. "I was beaten, as many wives are. Did you learn that also?" At his nod, she continued. "There are scars. I wouldn't wish you to be unpleasantly surprised, after we are married—"

"Oh, my dear," he said in a truly anguished tone. "How could you think such a thing could make a difference to me?" He took her in his arms and held her tightly. "That devil! To think of him touching you at all, let alone in anger! I love you, Amelia. You're safe with me."

"I know that," Amelia whispered into his coat-front. Tears were glinting in her eyes.

Their lips met for the first time in seven years. It was a kiss of longing, of sadness, and of hope.

"I was afraid that, after what you'd been through, you couldn't stand to be touched," he said, stroking her black curls. "I resolved to go ever so slowly in our new courtship to avoid distressing you."

"So that was it," said Amelia. "You seemed kinder all of a sudden, but not at all like a man who admired me. I thought you had merely forgiven me, for heaven knows what reason, and meant to forget me in future.''

"I had spoken to your servants, if you want the truth. They told me your secret, and finding out that your first time with a man had been an assault made me assume you wouldn't like a show of ardour.''

"The servants! I might have known. Well, if you want the truth from me, I've been wishing for nothing so much as a show of ardour from you since the first time I saw you on the stairs, my dearest,'' said Amelia. She lowered her lashes. "I did go through a time when the very thought of a man's touch repelled me. I used to jump when the vicar shook my hand. But I got over that long ago.'' Boldly, she embraced him round the neck. "I've been trembling at your touch for what I assume are the usual reasons.''

Jeremy caught his breath. One arm tightened about her as he reached for the bell-pull. "You try my patience sorely, my love. We mustn't be alone much longer. Let's ring for Higgins and Lewes. We'll want to thank them together.''

"I do want to thank my dear friends.'' Amelia caressed her beloved's cheek. Seven years would not be made up for in one day, but they must do their best to mend the loss of precious time. "But couldn't we thank them later? We have so much to catch up on.''

"We do indeed, my lovely Amelia,'' Jeremy answered with a shrug and a crooked smile. He bent to kiss her again, a loving, absolutely satisfying promise for the future. "What a shame it is that I've already rung the bell.''

H·I·S·T·O·R·I·C·A·L
Christmas
S·T·O·R·I·E·S 1·9·9·0

Once again Harlequin, the experts in romance, bring you the magic of Christmas —as celebrated in America's past.

These enchanting love stories celebrate Christmas made extra-special by the wonder of people in love....

Nora Roberts	**In From the Cold**
Patricia Potter	**Miracle of the Heart**
Ruth Langan	**Christmas at Bitter Creek**

Look for this Christmas title next month wherever Harlequin® books are sold.

"Makes a great stocking stuffer."

HX90-1

HARLEQUIN
American Romance®

November brings you...

SENTIMENTAL JOURNEY

BARBARA BRETTON

Jitterbugging at the Stage Door Canteen, singing along with the Andrews Sisters, planting your Victory Garden—this was life on the home front during World War II.

Barbara Bretton captures all the glorious memories of America in the 1940's in SENTIMENTAL JOURNEY—a nostalgic Century of American Romance book and a Harlequin Award of Excellence title.

Available wherever Harlequin® books are sold.

ARSENT-1

Take 4 bestselling love stories FREE

Plus get a FREE surprise gift!

PASSPORT TO ROMANCE
SWEEPSTAKES RULES

1. **HOW TO ENTER:** To enter, you must be the age of majority and complete the official entry form, or print your name, address, telephone number and age on a plain piece of paper and mail to: Passport to Romance, P.O. Box 9056, Buffalo, NY 14269-9056. No mechanically reproduced entries accepted.

2. All entries must be received by the CONTEST CLOSING DATE, DECEMBER 31, 1990 TO BE ELIGIBLE.

3. **THE PRIZES:** There will be ten (10) Grand Prizes awarded, each consisting of a choice of a trip for two people from the following list:
   - i)   London, England (approximate retail value $5,050 U.S.)
   - ii)   England, Wales and Scotland (approximate retail value $6,400 U.S.)
   - iii) Carribean Cruise (approximate retail value $7,300 U.S.)
   - iv)   Hawaii (approximate retail value $9,550 U.S.)
   - v)   Greek Island Cruise in the Mediterranean (approximate retail value $12,250 U.S.)
   - vi)   France (approximate retail value $7,300 U.S.)

4. Any winner may choose to receive any trip or a cash alternative prize of $5,000.00 U.S. in lieu of the trip.

5. **GENERAL RULES:** Odds of winning depend on number of entries received.

6. A random draw will be made by Nielsen Promotion Services, an independent judging organization, on January 29, 1991, in Buffalo, NY, at 11:30 a.m. from all eligible entries received on or before the Contest Closing Date.

7. Any Canadian entrants who are selected must correctly answer a time-limited, mathematical skill-testing question in order to win.

8. Full contest rules may be obtained by sending a stamped, self-addressed envelope to: "Passport to Romance Rules Request", P.O. Box 9998, Saint John, New Brunswick, Canada E2L 4N4.

9. Quebec residents may submit any litigation respecting the conduct and awarding of a prize in this contest to the Régie des loteries et courses du Québec.

10. Payment of taxes other than air and hotel taxes is the sole responsibility of the winner.

11. Void where prohibited by law.

COUPON BOOKLET OFFER TERMS

To receive your Free travel-savings coupon booklets, complete the mail-in Offer Certificate on the preceeding page, including the necessary number of proofs-of-purchase, and mail to: Passport to Romance, P.O. Box 9057, Buffalo, NY 14269-9057. The coupon booklets include savings on travel-related products such as car rentals, hotels, cruises, flowers and restaurants. Some restrictions apply. The offer is available in the United States and Canada. Requests must be postmarked by January 25, 1991. Only proofs-of-purchase from specially marked "Passport to Romance" Harlequin® or Silhouette® books will be accepted. The offer certificate must accompany your request and may not be reproduced in any manner. Offer void where prohibited or restricted by law. LIMIT FOUR COUPON BOOKLETS PER NAME, FAMILY, GROUP, ORGANIZATION OR ADDRESS Please allow up to 8 weeks after receipt of order for shipment. Enter quickly as quantities are limited. Unfulfilled mail-in offer requests will receive free Harlequin® or Silhouette® books (not previously available in retail stores), in quantities equal to the number of proofs-of-purchase required for Levels One to Four, as applicable.

PR-SWPS

OFFICIAL SWEEPSTAKES
ENTRY FORM

Complete and return this Entry Form immediately—the more Entry Forms you submit, the better your chances of winning!
- Entry Forms must be received by **December 31, 1990**
- A random draw will take place on **January 29, 1991**
- Trip must be taken by **December 31, 1991**

3-HRG-2-SW

YES, I want to win a PASSPORT TO ROMANCE vacation for two! I understand the prize includes round-trip air fare, accommodation and a daily spending allowance.

Name_____

Address_____

City_____ State_____ Zip_____

Telephone Number_____ Age_____

Return entries to: **PASSPORT TO ROMANCE**, P.O. Box 9056, Buffalo, NY 14269-9056

© 1990 Harlequin Enterprises Limited

COUPON BOOKLET/OFFER CERTIFICATE

	LEVEL ONE Booklet	LEVEL TWO Booklet	LEVEL THREE Booklet	LEVEL FOUR Booklet
Item	1	1 & 2	1, 2 & 3	1, 2, 3 & 4
Booklet 1 = $100+	$100+	$100+	$100+	$100+
Booklet 2 = $200+		$200+	$200+	$200+
Booklet 3 = $300+			$300+	$300+
Booklet 4 = $400+	___	___	___	$400+
Approximate Total Value of Savings	$100+	$300+	$600+	$1,000+
# of Proofs of Purchase Required	4	6	12	18
Check One	___	___	___	___

Name_____

Address_____

City_____ State_____ Zip_____

Return Offer Certificates to: **PASSPORT TO ROMANCE**, P.O. Box 9057, Buffalo, NY 14269-9057

Requests must be postmarked by **January 25, 1991**

✂- -

 ONE PROOF OF PURCHASE   3-HRG-2

To collect your free coupon booklet you must include the necessary number of proofs-of-purchase with a properly completed Offer Certificate   © 1990 Harlequin Enterprises Limited

See previous page for details